FOREIGN
AFFAIRS

Also by Patricia Scanlan

City Lives
City Girl
City Woman
Apartment 3B
Finishing Touches
Promises Promises
Mirror Mirror
Francesca's Party

Published by Poolbeg

FOREIGN AFFAIRS

PATRICIA SCANLAN

POOLBEG

Published 1994
by Poolbeg Press Ltd.
123 Grange Hill, Baldoyle,
Dublin 13, Ireland
Email: poolbeg@poolbeg.com

3 5 7 9 10 8 6 4

A catalogue record for this book is available from the British Library.

ISBN 1-85371-446-1

Printed by Litografia Rosés, S.A, Spain

www.poolbeg.com

Acknowledgements

Give thanks to the Lord for he is good
I give the Lord my thanks.

My thanks to all in Poolbeg: to Brenda and Nicole for a wonderful cover. To the other Nicole for all the help with the ms. To Maeve who is invaluable. To Terry and Niall, my heroes. To Bernadette, Michael, Ivan, Deirdre, Zoë, Gerard and Karen thanks for everything.

To Francesca, Tony, Garry, Larry, Jenny, and Mark, my Bantam family who've made me feel so welcome.

To Sarah Lutyens and Felicity Rubinstein – who've become like sisters to me.

To Feile and Cliona Morris, Ger Conlon, Helen McCartney and Alil O'Shaughnessy. Thanks for all the info.

To Kieran Connolly – a man in a million. Thanks for putting up with all the phone calls and listening to all the moans. May you get the Harley of your dreams!

To Chris Green – for all the larks . . . and the ones to come.

To Anne Schulman – who knows what it's like.

To Sally and the gang in O'Connell Street and to Ruth, Paula, Gary and the gang in 'The Green' for all the kindness and support.

To Audrey, Brenda and Olive in Mac's Gym – the nicest sadists I know.

And to my godmother, Maureen Halligan who provided a wonderful haven when I needed it most. Thanks for that great week in April.

Dedication

I dedicate this book to the very special people who have supported and encouraged and gone out of their way to help me in the writing of this and my other books.

To my lovely supportive family and especially to Ma, Da, Mary, Henry, and Yvonne who looked after me when I was really under pressure.

To my editor, Kate Cruise O'Brien – whose loyalty, integrity, good-humoured support, jolly lunches and daily phone calls have made this a unique writing experience for me.

To Breda Purdue, deputy MD and Sales & Marketing director of Poolbeg, who combines motherhood, wifehood, and career superbly and still has time to be a great friend. I admire her enormously. Thanks Breda for being there from the start, it wouldn't be half as much fun without you.

To Margaret Daly, whose wisdom and friendship I greatly cherish.

To Philip MacDermott and Kieran Devlin whose support and advice is constant and unstinting.

And finally and especially I dedicate this book to Deirdre Purcell – a truly kind and caring friend who in an act of unselfish generosity set in motion a chain of wonderful events that can only enhance my writing career. Thank you, Deirdre, I owe you one.

Oh, the gladness of a woman when she's glad!
Oh, the sadness of a woman when she's sad!
But the gladness of her gladness
And the sadness of her sadness
Are as nothing to her badness, when she's bad.

Anon

Prologue

'Flight 507 will depart at twenty-three hundred hours. We are sorry for any inconvenience caused by the delay.' The calm voice of the announcer floated over the Tannoy system. A collective groan came from the passengers assembled at gate twenty.

'For heaven's sake!' Brenda Hanley fumed. 'You'd think TransCon Travel would use a *reliable* airline.'

Paula Matthews shot her a daggers look. It went against the grain to hear anyone, let alone Brenda Hanley criticizing the travel company she worked for.

'Give it a rest, Brenda,' Jennifer Myles said evenly. She was Brenda's sister and she was heartily sick of her moans.

'I don't mind at all.' Rachel Stapleton giggled. It was her first foreign holiday, she was tipsy, and she hadn't a care in the world.

The four women sat in silence, lost in their own thoughts.

She never felt less like going on holiday in her life, Paula reflected as she stared out onto the concourse and watched their jet refuelling. She and Jenny had been away together and had worked abroad for several years. Paula had always loved the excitement of packing and going to the airport and treating herself in the duty-free. But not this time, she thought unhappily. Her life was a shambles. Not professionally. She was an extremely successful career woman. But she had made such a mess of her private life. Whoever said 'love hurts' didn't know the half of it.

She could hear Brenda grumbling away and she felt a surge of irritation bubble. The thought of being in

Brenda's company for the next ten days did not make Paula ecstatically happy. She had known Brenda and Jenny a long time now and it still amazed her that the two sisters could be so totally different. If she managed to get through this holiday without flying off the handle at Brenda, it would be a miracle, Paula thought glumly. She was suffering from a broken heart but Brenda would be suffering from a broken neck if she didn't shut up. Paula scowled, opened her copy of *Vanity Fair* and tried to concentrate.

Brenda sat silently raging. She'd seen the filthy look Madame Matthews had thrown her, just because Brenda had criticized her precious TransCon. Paula thought she was the absolute bee's knees in her Lacoste sweater and her dark dramatic Ray-Bans. And so she might look like a film star, *she* didn't have three kids and a husband dragging out of her like Brenda had.

Well Paula or no Paula, she was going to enjoy this holiday. Ten days of no cooking, washing, cleaning, ironing and all the thousand and one things a busy housewife had to do, were not going to be spoiled by the Prima Donna on her right. What Jenny saw in the girl, Brenda could not fathom. But Paula and Jenny were more than best friends. They were as close as sisters. Closer than she and Jenny. The familiar flame of jealousy flared. Why couldn't Jenny and she have that closeness? Paula Matthews was just a user and the sooner her sister realized it, the better.

Brenda took out her nail file and began to shape her nails. She hadn't had a chance to beautify herself, she'd been so busy getting the kids organized. She cast a surreptitious glance at Paula's perfectly manicured varnished nails. Easy knowing she never did a tap of housework, Brenda sniffed as she filed with a vengeance.

Maybe she might go and phone home, Jennifer thought. Just to see if he was all right. But then, maybe he wasn't home yet. She sighed. She was missing her husband like crazy already and she'd only kissed him goodbye an hour ago. This delay was a drag. Jennifer glanced at Brenda who was filing her nails as if her life depended on it. She had a face on her that would stop a clock. Paula had her head stuck in a magazine. Keeping the pair of them from having an all-out humdinger of a row was going to be hard work. Keeping *herself* from having a humdinger of a row with Brenda wasn't going to be easy either if her sister kept up her nonsense.

She and Brenda had never been on holidays together before. Although they'd grown up together and shared a bedroom for years, Jennifer had to admit that Brenda was not an easy person to get on with. The trouble with Brenda was she couldn't be thankful for what she had. She didn't know how lucky she was, Jennifer thought sadly, as pain darkened her eyes.

Don't think about it now! She banished the memory and bit her lip to stop it from trembling. She had to think positive and get on with life. This holiday was a positive step, there was no looking back.

Rachel had never been so excited in her life. This was all totally new to her. She was fascinated watching the huge jets landing and taking off. Soon she'd be on one of them. It gave her butterflies to think of it. Rachel didn't mind a bit being delayed, it added to the sense of anticipation. She was having a ball! She'd spent a fortune in the duty-free, spurred on by the others, and she'd treated herself to three blockbuster novels.

Rachel lifted her wrist to her nose and inhaled the fragrant scent of *White Linen*. It was a beautiful perfume. It was the first expensive perfume she'd ever bought herself. Normally she just used Limara body sprays. Well not any more, Rachel thought happily as she took out the bottle of perfume she'd bought only twenty minutes ago and sprayed another little bit on her neck. She was a new woman with a new image and this was only the beginning. She was going to live life to the full from now on. She caught sight of the packet of condoms nestling in the small side pocket of her bag. Even now, Rachel was surprised by her own daring. Her father would call her a lost soul if he knew, but let him, she didn't care any more, Rachel thought defiantly. She was being sensible. If there was the slightest chance of her having a foreign affair at least she'd taken care of her own protection. That was a very Nineties thing to do, Rachel thought approvingly. For the first time in her life, she was standing on her own two feet, making her own decisions. It was a heady experience.

She was dying to get to Corfu. The thought of blue skies, sparkling seas and golden beaches was heaven after the winter of gales and rain they'd endured. Rachel gave a little giggle. She was a bit tiddly. It was a nice feeling. She stood up and addressed her three companions.

'I don't know about you lot, but I'm going to have another brandy,' Rachel announced happily. 'To celebrate the start of the holiday of a lifetime.' She giggled again and headed for the bar, much to the amusement of Paula, Brenda and Jennifer.

Book One

Chapter One

'I'm afraid, Mr Stapleton, your wife has had a very difficult labour and it was touch and go for a while at the birth. However she has been safely delivered of a baby girl and both will survive. There can be no more children.' Doctor Ward was quietly emphatic.

William Stapleton drew a deep breath, the nostrils of his aquiline nose turning white. 'I see,' he said stiffly.

'Her heart won't take it and I've told her of the danger. You understand?' Doctor Ward's piercing blue eyes, not dimmed by age, stared into the eyes of the younger man. It was a hard thing to do, to tell a young man of thirty-three that his sex life was to be curtailed and two children was his limit. Normally he would have felt pity for any unfortunate in that position. But Doctor Ward just couldn't take to William Stapleton. He had a way of looking at you as if he thought he was far above you and he treated his young wife like one of his pupils from the village school. The doctor gave William a stern look. There was no doubt in his mind that another child would kill Theresa, it was up to William to see that that never happened.

'I don't want to see Theresa in my surgery telling me she thinks she's pregnant. I've told this to Theresa and I'm telling you now. Another child would kill her. And I won't have that on my conscience. Now I've done my duty you must do yours,' the doctor said gruffly. What that lovely young girl had married that dry old stick for, he could not imagine.

Theresa Stapleton was a quiet, gentle, shy young woman, ten years younger than her husband. Thoroughly dominated by him, and unable to assert herself, she was

19

smothered by her husband's authoritarianism and felt herself inferior to him in every way. Her husband encouraged this belief. Doctor Ward, who was a shrewd judge of character, was quite aware of this. 'You understand, Mr Stapleton?' he repeated sternly.

'Yes, Doctor, I do,' William said coldly. 'Thank you for all your help.'

'I'll be back tomorrow and every day for the rest of the week. Your wife is in a very weakened condition, she must have complete bed rest for at least a fortnight. You have someone to look after the little lad?'

'My mother,' William replied. God help us all, thought Doctor Ward as he slipped into his tweed overcoat. Bertha Stapleton was as bad, if not worse than, her son. God help that poor unfortunate up in the bed, with the pair of them.

'Goodnight then.'

'Goodnight, Doctor.' William closed the door, not even waiting for Doctor Ward to get into his ancient Morris Minor. Stupid old codger, he thought sourly. What would he know, he was only an old country quack. Millions of women had children like peas popping from a pod, why did he have to marry a woman who made a production out of it?

Slowly he walked up the stairs of the fine two-storey house he had installed his wife in when he married her three years ago. She had done well for herself, had Theresa Nolan. Married the schoolmaster. Lived in a house half the women in the village would give their eye-teeth for. Lacked for nothing. Had a fine healthy one-year-old son, and now a daughter. And what did he have? William thought irritably. Just responsibilities and burdens and now not even the comfort of the marriage bed to look forward to. He might as well be bloody single, he reflected as he opened the door to their bedroom. Still, he was not a man to shirk his duty. And his duty was to provide for his wife. She would not find reproach in his eyes when he looked at her.

Theresa lay in the wide brass bed, her face the colour of faded yellow parchment. Two big bruised brown eyes turned in his direction as he entered the room. Curls of chestnut hair lay damply against her forehead and he could see the sheen of perspiration on her upper lip. In her arms she held a small swaddled bundle.

'I'll just go and make you a cup of tea, pet, while you show your husband the little dote.' Nancy McDonnell, the village midwife, smiled as she gathered together her bits and pieces.

'Thanks, Mrs McDonnell,' Theresa murmured weakly, staring at her husband.

'Rest yourself now, Theresa, like a good girl. Don't talk too much. Your husband won't mind, he'll be too busy looking at his little beauty.' Nancy beamed as she fluffed up the pillows before leaving them alone.

'How are you feeling?' William said gruffly.

'Tired, sore.' She hesitated. 'Did you talk to the doctor?'

'I did.'

'What are we going to do?'

'I'll move into the spare room,' William said coldly. 'I'll not be accused of being irresponsible by Doctor Ward or any other.'

'I'm sorry, William,' Theresa said quietly. Although if she was completely honest, she felt a great relief at his words. Theresa was a dutiful wife but she did not love her husband. She had only married him to obey her parents' wishes. Marrying the schoolmaster was considered almost as good as marrying a doctor or the like. Theresa's mother had been terrified that her daughter would end up on the shelf and she had encouraged the match strongly. Marriage was not for pleasure, her mother had told her often enough. Marriage was a duty and Theresa had been brought up to be a good attentive wife. Able to run a house and when the time came, have and take care of the children God would bless her with. She was lucky, her mother informed her over and over again, that a man of William Stapleton's calibre was taking an interest in her. The day of her wedding had been one of the happiest days of her mother's life. Theresa had felt utterly and completely trapped.

Only today, when Doctor Ward had told her no more children and William had informed her that he was moving into the spare room, had she felt the slightest glimmer of hope. A little fluttering of freedom. She would make this bedroom a haven, a peaceful place, Theresa decided. Here she would read and sew and look out at the hustle and bustle of village life. It would be her refuge from her husband. Happiness flickered briefly.

'What will we call her?' Theresa asked her stern-looking husband as she tucked the shawl closer around her baby.

'Call her what you like,' William answered with hardly a glance at his new-born child.

Theresa's hold tightened on the sleeping baby in her arms. So that was going to be the way of it, she thought. God help the poor child, William would hold this against her. Well she would do her best to make her feel happy and loved, after all, her arrival had given Theresa a freedom of sorts and for that she would always be in her daughter's debt. Almost to herself she murmured, 'Rachel, that's what I want to call her. I'm going to call her Rachel.'

Chapter Two

Rachel Stapleton wished with all her might that the school bell would ring. They were starting their summer holidays today and she could hardly wait. They were supposed to be having a little party but Miss O'Connor was out sick and her father had set them a whole blackboard of sums to keep them quiet, while he took care of his own class. Everybody was giving out about it and some of her classmates were even glaring at her as if it was all her fault. It was very difficult being the headmaster's daughter.

The sun shone in through the high windows of the classroom. She could see the sky outside, so blue and clear, it was like a picture postcard. Rachel wished she was down playing by the stream. It was her favourite place. She liked throwing in leaves and bits of sticks or paper and watching them swirl away out of sight. Were they going to the sea, what foreign shores would they land on? Rachel loved imagining their journeys. Sometimes her brother Ronan let her play with him. Ronan, at nine, was a year older than her and very brave. He wasn't afraid to swing across from the old oak tree to the other side of the stream. He was a special agent for UNCLE, Napoleon Solo and Illya Kuryakin depended on him. She knew he was only pretending but sometimes it got very exciting, especially when they had to crawl through Murphy's hedge and run through the field where the bull was.

Rachel was terrified of the bull, but Ronan wasn't a bit scared. He wasn't scared of anything. Not even of their father. A little frown creased Rachel's forehead. She was scared of her father. He was very cross sometimes, especially if she made a mistake in her homework. He always checked it for her and woe betide her if there was a mistake in it.

'Do you want Miss O'Connor to think we've a dunce in the family?' he'd say. 'It would match you better, Miss, if you'd learn your spellings instead of playing with those dolls of yours. Dolls will be no use to you when you're doing your Leaving Cert.' The thing was, she knew her spellings but when her father made her stand in front of him while he stood with his hands behind his back, waiting for her to rattle them off, butterflies would start dancing up and down her stomach and she'd get nervous and make mistakes.

Why, she often wondered longingly, couldn't she have had a farmer for a father, like Martina Brown. Martina and her brothers and sisters were allowed to stay up really late in the summer to help get the hay in. They were allowed to play in the haystacks and in the barns and camp in the paddock behind their house, and their father *never* made them say their spellings to him at night.

Even better was to have a shopkeeper for a father. Mr Morrissey owned the sweet shop and newsagents in the village and it was open until ten o'clock at night. Hilda Morrissey was allowed to stay up late during the summer to help her father in the shop and she was even allowed to work the cash-register. How Rachel would have loved a cash-register. When she grew up and had loads of money she was going to buy a real one. Santa had brought her one last Christmas and although she had great fun playing shop she would still give anything to have a go of Morrissey's real one.

Her thoughts were interrupted by a stinging sensation to her ear. A marble rolled down the front of her jumper. Rachel's stomach twisted into knots. Patrick McKeown was flicking marbles at her again. Her ear hurt so much she wanted to cry, but they'd all call her a cry-baby. Patrick McKeown was the meanest, slyest, biggest bully in the class. He was always picking on her because he knew she'd never ever tell her father. If she told her father, the whole class would call her a tattle-tale and to be a tattle-tale was the worst thing. She pretended nothing had happened and kept her head down, staring at her copy book. Another missile reached its mark. This time on the back of her neck. A few of the other children sniggered. Rachel swallowed hard and bit her lip. She mustn't cry in front of them. Why did Miss O'Connor have to be out today of all days? Rachel was petrified her father would come in and catch Patrick McKeown flicking marbles at her. Then he'd be punished and she'd really be in for it. He would wait for his chance, some day when she was on her own, and stuff worms or slugs down her dress. That was his favourite punishment. Rachel never knew when it was going to happen and consequently she always had to be on the look-out. She couldn't tell anybody about what was going on because if she did, Patrick swore that he would murder her and bury her body in Doyle's woods and no-one would ever find her. She woke up in bed at night her heart thumping in terror at the thought of it.

'Have you got the answers to those sums, Swotty Stapleton?' Patrick McKeown demanded, one eye on her, and one eye on the door. Rachel's fingers shook as she passed back her copy book. Patrick grabbed it and swiftly copied down her answers. Then, slowly, deliberately, he ripped the page out of her copy book and scrunched it up in a tight hard little ball, flicking it at her with his ruler. 'Do them neater,' the hated bullying voice ordered. The rest of the class looked on approvingly as he threw her copy book back up towards her. Getting at Rachel Stapleton was almost as good as getting at the Master. With the eyes of the class upon her and to jeers of 'Swotty' from Patrick McKeown, Rachel stood up and walked down the passageway to retrieve her copy. Just at that moment her father walked through the door.

'What are you doing out of your seat, Rachel Stapleton?' He always called her by her full name at school.

'Nnn . . . nothing, Sir,' she stammered. Rachel had to call her father Sir at school.

'Why is your copybook lying in the middle of the floor?' the Master demanded. There was a collective intake of breath. Out of the corner of her eye, Rachel could see Patrick slowly drawing his finger from one side of his throat to the other in a slitting gesture and making horrible faces. Her heart began to pound. Her father glaring at her and demanding an explanation and Patrick McKeown prepared to slit her throat and God knows what else.

'I'm waiting, Miss,' the Master said sternly, his blue eyes like flints.

'I . . . I let it fall.' Her voice was no more than a whisper.

'I can't hear you.' Her father folded his arms as the rest of the class waited in delicious trepidation. Would he give her the stick? Would he make her stand in the corner? And if he did, would she tell on Patrick McKeown? There'd be wigs on the green then. They sat enjoying every minute of the drama.

'I said I let it fall, Sir.' Rachel's voice had a wobble in it and to her horror she could feel tears at the back of her eyes.

'Stand in the corner for being out of your chair, Rachel Stapleton, and the rest of you get ready to give me the answers to your sums,' the Master instructed, glaring at Rachel as she went over to the corner by the door. He was very annoyed with her, she knew, and he would not speak to her for the rest of the day. He would go home and tell her mother that their daughter was a disobedient child and how could he expect the rest of the school to obey him if his own daughter wouldn't?

Plop . . . plop plop plop. Big tears fell on to her shiny patent shoes as she stood with her back to the rest of the class and heard them calling out the answers to their sums, Patrick McKeown's voice the loudest of them all. She had been so looking forward to today. To the party. To the bell going early because they were having a half-day. To running home to her mother with the news that they were off school until the first of September.

26

It was going to be one of her happy days and now it was ruined.

She heard her father say, 'Very good, Room 4, now tidy up your bags, I'm letting you off twenty minutes early because Miss O'Connor is not in. Walk quietly, now,' he warned, 'or I'll change my mind. Rachel Stapleton, stay in the corner please until you hear the bell go.' There was silence until he left the room and then a frantic scrabbling as bags were packed at speed, the sooner to get out of the schoolhouse. Rachel stood with her back to them. At least the ordeal would soon be over and she didn't mind waiting in the corner on her own. Patrick McKeown and his pals would be gone by the time she got out of school.

A sharp stabbing pain in her bottom made Rachel yelp in pain.

'Shut up, ya stupid cow, that's just so ya don't forget me,' Patrick McKeown hissed as he brandished his compass at her. Just for good measure he stabbed her with it once more and then he was gone, followed by the rest of them, leaving her crying, in the hollow emptiness of the big classroom. Rachel hated Patrick McKeown with all her might and many was the night she went to bed and planned delicious revenge upon him. But much as Rachel hated her vicious classmate, she hated her father far more.

Theresa Stapleton shook the flour off her hands and placed the apple crumble in the oven. She smiled to herself. Apple crumble was Ronan and Rachel's favourite dessert and they'd relish it. She put the kettle on to boil, made herself a cup of tea and drank it standing at the sink looking out into the garden. It really was a beautiful day, she thought. One of the best so far this summer. A perfect day to be starting your school holidays. Maybe she'd pack up a picnic for tea and the three of them would go off down a country lane and find a nice field with a shady tree to sit under. She wouldn't even bother to bring the paper, Theresa decided as she glanced at the headlines.

She wanted to forget about the troubles of the world. Although it was good to see that Preside t Johnson had signed a Civil Rights Act, containing the most sweeping civil rights law in the history of the US. Her eyes slid down the columns. There was trouble in Algeria, an army leader rebelling against Ben Bella's rule.

Enough! she decided. She didn't want to read bad news today. She wasn't in the humour for it. Usually Theresa was an avid reader of her husband's *Irish Times*, mentally doing the Crosaire while he was at school. She wouldn't dream of putting down the answers. William would have a fit. It was his habit to sit with his crossword in the evening after the Rosary and spend a pleasant hour or so stimulating his brain. He needed it, he often told her, after putting in six hours with the young hooligans he had to teach. This amused his wife although she never let on. The children of the village of Rathbarry and its surrounding areas could in no way be considered hooligans. If he had to teach in some of the tough schools up in Dublin he might have something to moan about. He had a cushy number as headmaster of the village school, a promotion he'd got three years ago.

You'd think from the way he carried on that he was teaching in the Bronx, Theresa reflected, sipping her tea. William loved to make out that he had a hard life instead of counting his blessings and enjoying all the free time he had. But William was not one to enjoy himself, she thought glumly. He was very strict with the children and authoritarian towards her. He wore his title of headmaster with great pride and dignity and was very much a 'presence' in the village. Unfortunately, like the Queen, who is royal twenty-four hours a day, so too was William a headmaster twenty-four hours a day, seven days a week. It was extremely wearing. Although Theresa was looking forward to having her children off school for the summer holidays, she couldn't say the prospect of having William under her feet all day made her dizzy with delight. Well she didn't care. This summer was going to be the best ever for Ronan and Rachel. They were good kids, they deserved a bit of fun out of life. So today she was going to get things off to a good start with a picnic. She was going to take them to Bray a couple of times to go to the amusement arcades and to hell with William if he didn't approve. Just because his mother had been very strict and he had no fun growing up as a child was no reason why his children should suffer the same fate.

William Stapleton watched through the grimy windows of Room 6, as his daughter trudged across the school yard, head down, hands stuffed into her pockets. He shook his head and gave an annoyed 'tsk.' What kind of a way was that to walk? He'd have to tell Theresa to get on to Rachel about her posture. You couldn't slouch your way through life. It didn't make a good impression. He was sorry he'd had to be strict with her earlier on but he couldn't let her away with disobedience.

He had specifically told Room 4 they were not to leave their seats and what did he find upon walking in to check up on them but his own daughter out of her seat. He *had* to punish her. He couldn't be seen to make a favourite out of his own child. Her classmates would be very resentful if he did. It was very difficult being a parent and headmaster to two children in the school. His son Ronan had once accused him of *picking* on him if you don't mind. He'd got a clip in his ear for his impudence and Theresa hadn't spoken to William for a week, accusing him of being too harsh.

Theresa was far too soft on the children, he mused as he closed the window with a resounding bang. She would have them destroyed if he let her do half the things she wanted to do for them. Children had to be ruled with a firm hand. Some of the brats he had to teach were brats because they were allowed to do what they liked and go where they wanted. Well Rachel and Ronan would thank him in years to come. They might not appreciate the discipline now but when they were married with children of their own, they'd see that it was no easy task to rear a child.

This summer they could both put in a bit of extra study, especially Rachel. That Miss O'Connor wasn't the world's greatest teacher as far as he could see, far too fond of letting her class do drawings and act out little plays. Too much nature study and not enough arithmetic and grammar and Gaeilge. A few hours' tuition by him would benefit his daughter enormously and Master Ronan could sit in for it as well, he was much too casual in his approach to his studies.

Well this summer there'd be plenty of chores and some extra studying and at least they wouldn't come out with that dreadful whinge, 'I'm bored.' There was no place in *his* house for that sort of thing. William wiped off the blackboard with vigour and a sense of great self-satisfaction.

'What's wrong, love? You seem terribly down in the dumps and imagine being down in the dumps on the first day of the holidays,' Rachel heard her mother say as she let herself in through the back door. There was a lovely smell coming from the oven and she began to feel a little better now that she was safe at home in her own kitchen with her mother smiling at her.

'It's just a bit warm,' Rachel fibbed, wanting and yet not wanting to burden her mother with her woes.

'Well take off that old pinafore now, you won't have to wear it for eight whole weeks!' Her mother smiled, ruffling Rachel's fair curly hair. 'I have your shorts and a T-shirt for you up on the bed so go and get washed and put your other stuff in the dirty clothes basket for me. Then after lunch I was thinking that you and me and Ronan might go for a picnic. It's such a lovely day and it would be a nice start to the holliers.'

In spite of herself Rachel's spirits began to lift. A picnic with her mother and Ronan. No school for eight weeks. With any luck she mightn't even see Patrick McKeown for the rest of the summer. Maybe things weren't so bad after all. Of course her father would be home later and no doubt he'd have something to say about her bad behaviour, but at least she'd have the picnic to look forward to after it.

'Stop daydreaming, Rachel, and run up and get changed.' Her mother gave her a gentle nudge.

'I'm going, Mammy.'

Upstairs in her yellow and cream under-the-eaves bedroom, Rachel flung off her hated navy pinafore. Her mint-green shorts and a green and white striped T-shirt lay neatly on her patchwork quilt. Her Nana Nolan had made the quilt two years ago for her sixth birthday and Rachel loved it. It was full of different-coloured squares edged with navy and yellow trim and it gave the little room a homely rustic look. Rachel was sure her bedroom looked like Laura's in *Little House on the Prairie*. One of her favourite books. Rachel loved to wrap herself in her quilt when the wind was howling down the chimney in winter and pretend that she was in the little cabin on the prairie and that they were being snowed in by the blizzards. In the privacy of her bedroom, Rachel became a different person. Sometimes she was Laura, sometimes she was a Fifth Former at St Clare's, like her heroines from the Enid Blyton books that she got from the library every week and that she had to hide from her father because he didn't approve of Enid Blyton. Sometimes she was Jo out of *Little Women*. She would wrap herself in her quilt and tie string around her middle and have a gorgeous long robe just like they had in the olden days. Rachel admired Jo enormously. She was so brave and determined and kind to a fault. Rachel envied her the love of her father. She had felt a huge lump in her throat when she read about her heroine cutting off her hair and selling it to make some money for her poor sick father. Rachel would *never* cut off her hair to make money for *her* father. He could die for all she cared. Sometimes she wrapped herself in her quilt robe and put one of her father's big white handkerchiefs on her head and pretended she was the Blessed

Virgin Mary appearing at Fatima. Her dolls were a rapt audience, sitting in a row at the end of the bed, and the Blessed Virgin always had a special message for Patrick McKeown. 'You must tell him to mend his ways or the fires of hell will consume his immortal soul.' The thought of Patrick McKeown and his soul being consumed by the fires of hell cheered Rachel up enormously.

Mary Foley, the girl from down the road who sometimes played with her and who sat three rows behind her at school, thought Rachel's bedroom was the nicest bedroom she had ever been in and envied her hugely. Mary had to share a bedroom with two sisters and a baby brother. There wasn't any room to play the great games that Rachel could play. It was a nice room, Rachel decided as she untied the straps of her shoes and took off her socks. As well as her quilt-covered bed, she had a small oak wardrobe and a dressing-table. It had three mirrors that you could move backwards and forwards and, although parts of it were chipped and stained, Rachel was able to view herself from any angle. Which was very satisfying when you were dressing up.

When she was sick enough for her father to think she could stay home from school, her mother would light a fire if it was winter. Rachel would watch the flames crackling and flickering, casting great dancing shadows on the walls, and feel very safe and sound. Patrick McKeown and his cronies couldn't get at her in her little haven. She sometimes longed to develop some dreadful illness that would keep her bedridden until her schooldays were over. It was something she prayed to God for when things were very bad. So far, He had not obliged.

It was just as well she hadn't any serious illness today though, she decided as she stuck her head out the window, otherwise she wouldn't be able to go on the picnic. And anyway it wouldn't be very nice to have to spend the summer holidays in bed. It was beautiful outside. The main street was bathed in sunlight. She could see a heat haze shimmering around the church spire at the end of the street. Flynn's grocery shop, across the road, had a big canopy over the entrance to protect from the heat. Martin Ryan, the butcher, had one too, with a big red stripe that could be seen a mile away from the top of Barry's Hill. Beside them was Morrissey's newsagents and sweet shop, where Hilda, her classmate, was allowed to use the cash-register. In the summer, Mr Morrissey opened up the little lean-to beside the shop. In it he stocked souvenirs of every kind, for any tourists who might pass through the village. Leprechauns, mugs with shamrocks, tea towels with *A Taste of Ireland* written on them. There was all sorts there and it gave the village an air of excitement when the lean-to was opened.

'The tourist season is on us again,' people would say. Windows would be washed, doorknockers polished and Powells and O'Hanlons would put out their B&B signs. There was fierce rivalry between the Powells and the O'Hanlons for the tourists who came to the village in summer. Last summer Bridie Powell caught Cissie O'Hanlon actually poaching a tourist who was heading up Bridie's drive. Cissie assured the elderly American that *she* ran a much better guest house at very reasonable rates and that Powell's was just a dirty old kip of a place. Bridie had been incandescent with rage. She gave a shriek that would have woken the dead up in the cemetery, flung open her front door and launched herself on Cissie, much to the dismay of the poor tourist, who took to his heels and departed the village with remarkable speed, muttering something about it being safer to live in the wild west. The fisticuffs had been the talk of the village for months. Sergeant Roach had to separate the pair and threaten to arrest them. Solicitors' letters had been exchanged and both women ended up in court and were bound over to keep the peace. It had been a delicious topic of gossip for the inhabitants of Rathbarry and great mileage had been got out of it for months after.

So far today, Rachel observed as she peered out of the window, there were no tourists in Morrissey's lean-to, none heading for Bridie's or Cissie's. It was a quiet day in the village of Rathbarry. Only Ryan's dog sprawled lazily outside the butchers, his nose twitching in annoyance as the flies buzzed around him. A delicious smell of apple crumble floated upwards. Rachel's stomach rumbled with hunger. She skipped out of her bedroom into the bathroom across the landing. She filled the sink and washed her hands and face, wincing as the face-cloth touched her ear and neck where Patrick McKeown had flicked the marbles at her. She was blowing a big soap bubble when she heard her mother's footsteps at the top of the stairs. Hastily Rachel let the water out of the sink. She'd better stop dawdling, her ma was always chiding her for daydreaming and dawdling.

'Are you ready yet, Rachel?' Theresa asked and then Rachel heard her give a little gasp. She turned around and saw that her mother had gone pale. 'Jesus, Mary and Joseph, child!' she exclaimed. 'Who did that to you?'

Chapter Three

Rachel felt the blood rush to her cheeks. 'Who did what, Mammy?' she asked lightly, but her heart was beginning to thump.

'Look at you! Look at the bruises on your neck, look at the blood on your knickers.' Her mother was down on her knees examining Rachel's bottom. Rachel peered over her shoulder and with a sense of shock saw that there were two huge bloodstains on her knickers. It must have been where Patrick stabbed her with the compass. She was mad with herself. If she hadn't dawdled her mother would never have seen her bruises. Her heart sank as Theresa, who was still kneeling, put her arms around her and stared into her eyes. 'Tell me the truth now, Rachel. I want to know who did this to you, because I'm going to kill them.' Her mother's eyes were bright with anger in the whiteness of her pale face.

Rachel wanted so badly to burst out, 'It was Patrick McKeown,' but she knew if she did, and her mother told her father, Patrick McKeown would be in serious trouble and she would be dead. With her throat slit from ear to ear. 'Mammy, it was no-one,' she said hastily.

'Rachel! I want to know what's going on. Who did this to you?' Theresa cuddled her close. 'Come on, tell me now,' she urged. Rachel's lower lip wobbled.

'Don't tell Daddy, sure you won't? Promise me you won't tell Daddy.' She sniffled.

'I have to tell Daddy, love,' Theresa declared.

'Well then I'm not telling you.' Rachel pulled away from her mother and started to cry.

'Why can't we tell Daddy?'

''Cos we can't. Promise. Promise, Mammy. Please.'
Rachel was desperate.

'All right, all right. Just tell me who did it.' Theresa
was frantic.

'It was Patrick McKeown, and Mammy if he knows I
told you he's going to slit my throat an' murder me.' It
all burst out of her. After three years of suppressing and
hiding her fear and torment, the relief of telling made her
cry even harder.

'Stop crying, pet. Stop crying, no-one's going to murder
you and no-one is ever going to do this to you again.'
Her mother hugged her so tightly Rachel could hardly
breathe, but she didn't care. Having her mother hold
her tightly made her feel safe and secure. Her mother
was the best mother in the world.

'Sure you won't tell Daddy so Patrick won't get into
trouble 'cos then I'd be called a tattle-tale at school and
everyone hates tattle-tales!' Rachel begged. Now that
her mother knew, Patrick McKeown didn't seem such
a terrifying personage.

'Oh Rachel,' her mother murmured, burying her face
in her little girl's curls. 'Don't worry, I won't tell Daddy.'
I'll handle it myself, she decided grimly. Rachel, unaware
of her mother's plans, suddenly felt quite light-hearted.
She had no school for two whole months. With luck
she wouldn't see that horrible bully for the whole summer. They were going on a picnic. And there was apple
crumble for dessert.

'You're very quiet in yourself, Theresa,' William remarked as he stirred the Ovaltine into their mugs. Now
that he was finally on his holidays he felt quite pleased
with himself and was ready to chat to his wife. When
he'd got home from school there was a note to tell
him to heat his dinner in a saucepan because Theresa
and the children had gone on a picnic. He'd felt quite
miffed actually. They could at least have asked him if
he wanted to go instead of just gadding off without him.

True, he might not have gone. He had some paperwork to do. But it would have been nice to have been asked all the same. More to the point he might very well have refused Miss Rachel permission to go after her misbehaviour. If her mother knew about it she might not have taken their daughter on a picnic.

He hadn't had the chance to tell Theresa about Rachel's misdemeanour because he'd had to go to a board of management meeting for the school at seven pm and they still weren't home from their picnic then. By the time he'd got back at nine, Rachel and Ronan were in bed fast asleep and his wife wasn't in a very chatty mood. Even now, when he told her that she was very quiet in herself, she just sat staring into the middle distance as if she hadn't heard a word he'd said.

'Are you listening to me at all? I said you're very quiet in yourself.' William handed his wife her Ovaltine and sat down in the armchair opposite her. The sun had set and dusky shadows of umber and terracotta darkened the room. William stretched up his hand and switched on the lamp above his head, arching an inquiring eyebrow at his wife.

'I'm just a bit tired, that's all,' Theresa murmured, sipping her hot drink.

'Well what can you expect going all over the country-side on a picnic? You know you're not supposed to exert yourself,' he lectured self-righteously. 'At least if you had waited until I came home I could have carried the picnic basket.'

'I didn't know what time you'd be home from school what with it being your last day and I wanted to give the children a bit of a treat to start off their holidays. They deserve it,' his wife answered.

'Indeed and Miss Rachel didn't deserve it,' William retorted. 'I had to put her standing in the corner today for disobedience.'

'You did what?' Theresa looked horrified.

'I had to put her standing in the corner for getting out

37

of her seat when she and the rest of the class were expressly told not to,' William said coldly, rather taken aback by his wife's reaction.

'Did you ask her *why* she was out of her seat?' Theresa demanded, jumping to her feet. 'She probably had a perfectly good explanation. How can you do that to your own daughter? You're always picking on her. You bully her and you always have done.' Two pink spots stained the pallor of Theresa's face as she glowered at her husband.

William was shocked. What on earth was wrong with Theresa? This was most extraordinary behaviour. Usually she was extremely placid. He felt very hurt by her accusations. Didn't she realize that he couldn't possibly treat his daughter, or son for that matter, any differently from the other pupils. 'That's a most unfair accusation, Theresa. I don't know why you're making it,' he said huffily. 'You know I can't give Rachel and Ronan special treatment at school just because I'm their father. I have to treat them like the other children.'

'That's just an excuse, William, you never miss an opportunity to put her down or correct her. And don't think I don't know why, because I do!' Theresa was beside herself with anger.

'What on earth are you talking about, woman? What's got into you?' William growled, totally mystified as to why his normally mild wife should have turned into this virago standing in front of him, with blazing eyes.

Theresa pointed an accusing finger. 'I know you've always blamed Rachel because we can't have marital relations. I know you feel it was her fault because of the hard time I had giving birth to her. You've never shown the poor little scrap any love or affection. Don't think for one minute that you've fooled me because you haven't. You hold her responsible because you've been deprived. Well I'll tell you one thing, William Stapleton, you should be ashamed of yourself. You don't deserve the children you've got and they deserve much more than what you get from you.'

The bitterness in his wife's voice left him speechless. How could Theresa accuse him of blaming Rachel because he had to abstain from relations with his wife. It was ludicrous. He had never once made any demands or reproached Theresa because of her failure as a wife in that area of their marriage. It was a point of pride with him that he could control himself and act responsibly. How could she possibly say he held it against Rachel? It wasn't true. Not in the slightest.

'I think you've said enough,' he said stiffly. 'I don't know what's got into you. Perhaps you should go and see the doctor in the morning. I'm going to bed.'

'I'll tell you what's got into me, William Stapleton. Our daughter came home from your school today covered in bruises. Bleeding from being stabbed with a compass. And what do I hear from you? That you put her standing in a corner because she was out of her chair. She was probably trying to get away from the little bastards who were bullying her. You didn't bother to find out, did you? Oh no! You just did your big headmaster act. Some headmaster! When you can't even see what's going on under your own nose.' Theresa's voice shook with emotion.

William was flabbergasted. 'Who . . . how . . . what . . .' he stuttered, stunned at what he'd just heard. Rachel being bullied at school. Surely not! No-one would have the *nerve* to bully the headmaster's daughter. 'Are you sure of this?' he demanded. 'Why didn't she tell me?'

'Tell you,' Theresa said scornfully. 'You'd probably say she shouldn't tell fibs or something. The child is afraid of her life of you.'

'Theresa, I am not an ogre,' he barked. 'That's patent rubbish. Now tell me who bullied Rachel so I can deal with it.'

'Oh no, William!' She shook her head vehemently. 'Rachel nearly had hysterics when I said you should know. She made me promise not to tell you so the little brat won't get into trouble and she'd be branded as a tattle-tale. And you know, maybe she's right.'

'Don't be preposterous, Theresa,' he interrupted his wife angrily, 'I demand to know the name of this child who's bullying Rachel. For all we know maybe he or she is bullying other children as well. It's my duty as headmaster to know about things like that.'

'Sod your duty as headmaster. What about your duty as a father?' William's eyes widened behind their spectacles at Theresa's uncharacteristic language. 'I promised Rachel that I wouldn't tell and I'm not going to break that promise. I'll deal with this myself whether you like it or not. And if that doesn't suit, well you can go to hell. And from now on you take it easy with Rachel and Ronan. I've let you away with too much in the past. I won't let them be bullied any more, William. Rachel is scared stiff of you. I want my children to grow up with a damn sight more self-confidence than I ever had. I want them to grow up happy and confident. Not two introverted little scholars, passing all sorts of exams and without a friend or a bit of joy in the world. And I'll tell you one thing.' She glared at him. 'You can forget this nonsense about you giving them extra tuition for the holidays because that's out. Those children are going to have a happy carefree summer for once in their lives and if you don't like it you can lump it.' Theresa marched out the door, giving it a hard slam for good measure.

Never in all the years of their marriage had Theresa spoken to him like that. With such disrespect. He couldn't understand it. Naturally she was upset because Rachel had been bullied. Who wouldn't be? He was upset himself and he was going to get to the bottom of it. But it was almost as if she blamed him for it. And she'd called *him* a bully. That was no way for a wife to behave. He felt extremely hurt. What was wrong with Theresa? He was a bloody good husband, better than a lot he knew. She never wanted for anything. There was always plenty of food. He didn't skimp on coal. Whatever she needed she only had to ask. And whatever she said, he was a good responsible father who wanted the best for his children. There was nothing wrong with wanting them to do well at school. That was the only way to get on. It was all very well having carefree summers. Fun and games didn't get you through exams and without exams they wouldn't get proper jobs. It was a hard world out there. Theresa, cushioned by the comfortable sheltered life she led, didn't realize that.

Whatever was wrong with her, he hoped it wouldn't last for long. This kind of behaviour was most unsettling. Maybe she was starting the change or something. Women went a bit peculiar around that time of life, or so he heard. With a heavy heart, William switched off the lamp and went to his bed.

Theresa lay in bed, her heart racing. She couldn't believe that she had stood up to William and let fly at him the way she had. But she had felt outraged and angry when he'd told her about putting Rachel in the corner at school. Again the images of the bruises and bloodstains on Rachel's poor little body came to mind and tears sprang to her eyes. It was awful to think that you couldn't protect your child from bullies like Patrick McKeown and from all the hurt and trauma that was out there in the world.

She felt a surge of hatred for her husband. He *was* a bully. He enjoyed the power he held over her and Rachel and Ronan. It wasn't physical bullying but an insidious intimidation that he constantly practised on them. He made his children feel inferior and he did much the same to her. Well tonight her anger and her desire to protect her daughter had freed her from his authority. For once in her life she was going to put her foot down. And from now on, she was going to keep it down. If Rachel and Ronan were to have any bit of fun and happiness it was going to be up to her to see that they got it. Imagine wanting to give them lessons during their holidays! She grimaced in the dark, wiping the tears from her cheeks. It wasn't as if they were backward or anything. They were bright intelligent children, they didn't need extra tuition.

Tomorrow she was going to get that little bastard Patrick McKeown and put the fear of God into him and then she was going to take the children into Bray for the afternoon and bring them to the amusement arcade and let them do whatever they wanted. Slipping out of bed she padded softly across the landing and into Rachel's room.

Her daughter lay with one arm under her cheek, fast asleep, untroubled by her previous upsets and worries. In the moonlight, Theresa could see the bruises on her neck and ear from the assault with the marbles. Gently she leaned down and lightly brushed her lips against the vile marks. A ferocious need to protect her precious daughter rushed through her. Rachel was so timid. Life was going to be hard for her. Ronan had much more spirit and was less daunted by his father. He bounced back after every chastisement. She would never have to worry as much about her son as she would about her daughter. Ronan's lively personality would ease his way through life. He had the sort of personality that not even William could dim. But Rachel was so like her mother, she would always be easily cowed and overshadowed by more forceful egos. Well she was going to do her utmost to make sure Rachel didn't end up like she had. A doormat to an autocratic husband. A woman who had never achieved anything by herself. She was going to instil confidence in her daughter and praise every little achievement to the heavens and if William *dared* to suggest that Theresa was spoiling Rachel or making her big-headed, she'd go for him just as she had tonight.

It had actually felt good to let her husband know exactly what she thought of him. He'd been shocked when she spoke to him in such a fashion. Theresa smiled in the moonlight. It had given her a feeling of power to be able to render her husband almost speechless. He had stuttered and blustered and not been his usual lordly self. It suddenly dawned on her that by standing her ground with her husband earlier she had, for the first time in their marriage, refused to let him make a decision for her, refused to accept his authority. For once she had acted as a person in her own right. By confronting his bullying she had rendered him powerless over her. Theresa stood at her daughter's bedside and realized it had been the single most liberating moment of her life. The chance to be her own woman was, as it always had been, within her. But until now she had been too fearful and intimidated, content to have first her parents and then her husband make all her decisions for her. It was up to her and her alone to make something of her life and, by taking back her right to assert herself, she was going to help not only herself but also her children. Theresa felt an exhilarating sense of freedom surge through her.

'Sleep well, darling, Mammy's going to take care of everything,' she whispered. It was a long time before sleep came to her that night, so full of plans was she for the future.

Patrick McKeown scoffed his breakfast as quickly as he could, cramming brown bread and marmalade into his mouth and whipping the last slice of toast off the plate just as his younger brother reached out to get it. He was in a hurry. The gang had arranged to meet up at the cemetery to have a few smokes and make their plans for the summer. As soon as his mother's back was turned he was going to leg it out the door. He didn't intend getting caught for the breakfast washing-up. He bided his time until his mother went out to the front door to bring in the post and then he nipped out the back door and down the lane at the back of their small terraced cottage. The dog from next door ran growling out from the back yard and Patrick turned and kicked hard. 'Gotcha,' he exulted as the dog yelped in pain. He hated that dog and was always planning ways of making him die a horrible death. Knowing that he had managed to land a kick that hurt put Patrick in extra good humour and he swaggered down the fuchsia-flowered lane full of anticipation for the meeting ahead.

It was a beautiful summer's morning. The sky was blue as could be, with not a cloud in sight. It was going to be a scorcher. Maybe they would go swimming in the river. He turned out of the lane on to the main street where all the poshies lived. The doctor, the sergeant, the headmaster, the Powells and the O'Hanlons. All in their big houses with front gardens nicely tended not like his own shabby cottage with the postage-stamp lawn that grew like a jungle because his da wouldn't cut it. He was too busy playing darts in Doyle's pub. His ma was always screeching at him to get the grass cut but his da just told her to fuck off and not be annoying him.

He passed Rachel Stapleton's house and felt immense satisfaction as he remembered the show he had made of her at school yesterday. Imagine her being made to stand in the corner. It had been brilliant, all his mates had told him he was the greatest. He'd got a fair stab at her with his compass too. It was nearly as good as stabbing old big-nose Stapleton himself. He farted loudly as he passed by. Old Stapleton couldn't do anything to him for two full months. He hoped he heard the fart. There was a fine pong off it too, pity it couldn't poison the whole lot of them. Unfortunately there wasn't a sinner around this morning to be poisoned or otherwise.

Patrick whistled jauntily and felt the five Sweet Afton in the pocket of his jeans. He had nicked them out of his father's cigarette packet that lay in the pocket of the tweed jacket that was flung on the armchair from last night. He was going to have a right smoking session today and that would deeply impress the rest of the gang, who looked up to him as their leader. He was nearing the end of the street where the church and the priest's house were when he felt a firm grip on his shoulder. Shocked by the unexpectedness of it, he turned around to find Mrs Stapleton staring down at him.

'I want to talk to you, Patrick McKeown,' she said and he felt a flutter of panic. He tried to wriggle free from her grasp but the next minute she had his earlobe between her thumb and forefinger and she was hustling him down the lane that led to Lynch's farm out of sight of anyone who might be passing on the main street.

'Ouch, that hurts!' he protested.

'Good. It's meant to,' she said unsympathetically as she increased the pressure.

'I'll tell the sergeant you've kidnapped me,' Patrick blustered, kicking out, but she squeezed his ear so hard the tears came to his eyes.

'Jasus, I'll tell me da on ya!' he yelled. For such a small woman she was very strong. She was taking something out of her pocket and with horror Patrick realized it was a compass. That little bitch! She must have ratted on him. Boy, was Rachel Stapleton for it when he got his hands on her.

Mrs Stapleton said very calmly, 'You listen to me, you little brat. If I *ever* hear of you touching Rachel again, by God but you'll wish you were dead. Do you know what will happen to you if you ever lay a finger on or threaten my daughter again?'

'I did nuttin' to her,' Patrick sneered.

'Don't tell lies, Patrick McKeown. Do you know the Reform School a couple of miles up the road?' Patrick's insides gave a lurch of fear. Everyone knew the Reform School where bad boys were sent and beaten and starved. Living only on bread and gruel and water. What had the Reform School to do with him? What was this mad mother of Rachel Stapleton's rabbiting on about?

'Let me go.' He struggled and felt his ear being tugged again.

'If I tell the headmaster what you did to Rachel he'll have you put in the Reform School so fast you won't know it,' Mrs Stapleton said. 'I won't tell him this time. I'll give you one last chance but if I hear of you bullying Rachel or anyone else in the school you're for it. Do you hear me?' He said nothing. His ear was tweaked again.

'Do you hear me, Patrick McKeown?'

'Yeah,' he said sullenly.

'Oh and before you go . . .' Before he knew what was happening Mrs Stapleton had turned him around and stuck the compass hard into his arse.

'Yeouch. Aarrgh ow . . . that hurt!' he screeched.

'Now you know what it's like!' the mad woman said. 'I'll be keeping a strict eye on you, Patrick McKeown. And remember . . . any more bullying and it's the Reform School for you. Now get out of here.'

'I'll tell me da on you what you done,' he yelled as he took to his heels.

'And I'll tell on you and it will be the Reform for you so watch it,' she called back. Shaken beyond belief Patrick ran back down the lane and in around behind the church. He couldn't believe that a lady would stick a compass in him. Adults didn't do that. His arse was stinging him something awful. He was going to go home and show his da and get Mrs Stapleton arrested by Sergeant Roach. That's what he'd do. He turned around to retrace his footsteps in the direction of home. Mad bitch, she wasn't going to get away with sticking a compass in him. He started to walk down Main Street. Ahead of him he could see Mrs Stapleton pause outside the sergeant's house to stop and say hello to Mrs Roach. Then the sergeant appeared and stopped to talk to her. Patrick halted in his tracks. No-one would believe him if he told them what had just happened. He could hardly believe it himself. If she was so friendly with the sergeant maybe she would be able to get him sent to the Reform.

Slowly Patrick McKeown turned on his heel and slunk away.

Theresa dug her hands firmly in the pockets of her full floral skirt to try and steady them. Her right hand curled around the compass with which she had just stabbed Patrick McKeown. She couldn't believe that she had actually stabbed a child with a compass. She felt slightly sick, but triumphant at the same time. Sauce for the goose was sauce for the gander and he might think twice about stabbing someone with a compass again. The memory of her daughter's bruises had been just what she needed and she'd wanted to more than stab the little savage with a compass. She'd wanted to tear him limb from limb. Maybe she was a savage too but she didn't care. He'd never lay a finger on her child again. He'd nearly died when she'd said about the Reform School. She'd seen the fear in his beady little eyes. That had been a brainwave on her part. That had got to him. She could have gone to his parents, but she knew Jimmy McKeown, he'd only curse her out of the house, and his wife, Ella, couldn't control Patrick anyway so she wouldn't be much use. No, the best thing had been to confront Master McKeown himself. Hopefully that would be the end of the bullying but she'd be keeping a very watchful eye on her daughter from now on.

She walked briskly down the lane and back on to Main Street. She had left Rachel and Ronan eating their breakfast. William had his earlier and had gone to the school to organize his office for September. It was the luck of God that she had glanced out the window and seen that little brat walking past the house. It was a God-given opportunity to settle his hash for him.

William once again demanded that she give him the name of the culprit and she once again refused, stating that she would handle it herself. He was fit to be tied but she left him sulking over his breakfast. She ignored him, which didn't go down well. When she had informed him that she was taking the children to Bray for the afternoon to go on the amusements, he was furious.

'You're spoiling them.'

'And about time too,' she'd retorted, much to his chagrin. Let him sulk and he could go and get fish and chips for his dinner, she wasn't even going to make a meal at midday. No! she decided. To hell with it, she'd bring the children to a restaurant and have a treat for herself as well. She was fed up slaving over a hot stove and getting no thanks for it, she was entitled to a day off now and again. She'd go home this minute and organize the children to be ready for the eleven o'clock bus to Bray. They might as well make a day of it. Theresa was almost giddy with anticipation. It was a great feeling, making decisions on her own. It made her feel much more in control. And it must be psychological but even the breathlessness that affected her didn't seem so bad. She certainly didn't feel as weary and washed out as she sometimes did. She felt full of beans actually. Wait until she told the children of her plans. They'd be delighted. She might use the opportunity of being in Bray to buy them all some new summer clothes as well and let William put that in his pipe and smoke it.

'Good morning, Mrs Roach,' Theresa greeted the sergeant's wife light-heartedly. 'Isn't it a beautiful day?'

It was the best summer Rachel could ever remember. They went on picnics. They went to Bray once a week. They even went in to Dublin on the train. That was the most exciting thing of all. Getting into Dublin early in the morning. Walking from Amiens Street Station up Talbot Street and North Earl Street. Inhaling the lovely smells from the Kylemore cake shop. Then into Boyers and Clerys and after that, crossing the enormous width of O'Connell Street and on to Henry Street, where Dunnes and Roches were. And best of all there was Woolworths, where she and Ronan had been given a ten-shilling note each by their mother and told to buy what they liked.

That had been a magical day. And her daddy had been very pleased when Rachel had presented him with the plug of tobacco and the handkerchief she bought as a present for him. He told her she was a kind daughter and she hugged those words to herself that night as she lay in bed feeling very happy. Her mother even persuaded William to bring them to Brittas Bay a few times and he read his paper sitting in a deckchair with a white handkerchief over his head to protect his bald spot from the sun.

There had been no mention during the holidays of the extra lessons her father had been talking about although she had heard her parents arguing about it one day. Her mother had been very cross with her father, which was most unusual for her, and Rachel heard her say, 'William, they're not even in secondary school yet. They're only children. Let them enjoy their childhood.' Her father muttered something about fun and games not helping anyone to get their Inter and Leaving Certs but Theresa had been uncharacteristically firm and Rachel heard her tell her father, 'William. No lessons. I'm putting my foot down for once in my life.' Her father had gone off in a huff but it had worn off eventually when he realized that no-one was taking any notice of him because they were having too much fun. And after that lessons hadn't been mentioned again and William had even taken them out a few times in his shiny red Morris Minor, of which he was very proud.

She only saw Patrick McKeown twice during the whole summer because he went to stay with his cousins in Tramore. She saw him once at Mass, and he stuck his tongue out at her after making sure her mother and father were deep in prayer. But she didn't really care. Her parents were with her and she felt protected. The second time she was on her own, skipping down the path towards the Ball Alley, where she'd been sent to call Ronan for his tea. Patrick had been coming in the opposite direction and her heart started pounding as she saw her tormentor approaching her.

'You've got a mad mother, ya stupid cow,' he muttered as he came abreast of her and then, to her amazement, he walked past without pulling her hair, or kicking her on the shins, or even digging her in the ribs or spitting on her, as was his wont if he came upon her alone. Relieved beyond measure at her easy escape, Rachel ran towards the Ball Alley without a backward glance, in case he should change his mind and follow her. But he didn't and she had her brother for company on the journey home.

Rachel lay in bed that night, and wished the summer could go on for ever and that she could always be as happy as she was right at that moment. The dusky rays of the setting sun bathed her little bedroom in a golden light and up in Doyle's wood, the wood-pigeons cooed and the unique song of the cuckoo could be heard for miles around.

Chapter Four

Rachel shivered and pulled up the collar of her coat as she stood outside St Angela's trying to decide whether to go down the town and buy some Valentine cards or not. Hordes of schoolgirls were erupting out of the majestic portals of St Angela's, the secondary school she had been attending for the last five years.

Spots of rain blurred her glasses and she sighed in irritation. Glasses were such a blooming nuisance. She hated wearing them, they made her look like a right swot. If only she could look like Michelle Butler, Rachel thought enviously as she watched her classmate emerge through the brown front doors of the school. Despite the fact that Michelle was wearing exactly the same uniform as Rachel, the other girl looked like a model. On Michelle, the bottle-green skirt and jumper looked decidedly chic. Of course she wore the skirt a few inches shorter than it was supposed to be worn, and it was immaculately pressed, unlike Rachel's, which always got wrinkled and hung on her skinny hips like a sack. Michelle Butler was blessed with curves in all the right places. Her bosom was the envy of 6S. Indeed Michelle herself was the envy of the entire class. She had more boyfriends than she knew what to do with. She was the captain of the basketball team, the best actress in the drama society, and despite a hectic social life, managed to get good marks. Michelle was Rachel's ideal. If she could have been born with Michelle Butler's looks and personality she would have been deliriously happy. Of that, she was certain. No doubt the postman would stagger up Michelle's path weighed down under the load of Valentine cards.

'Hi Rachel.' Michelle smiled as she went past and Rachel smiled back. Michelle was a very nice person, she always said hello and made an effort to be friendly with Rachel. Most of the others in the class didn't bother. Of course it was her own fault for being so shy, but even after five years she could still feel awkward and tongue-tied during a class discussion or debate.

She couldn't say she had been unhappy exactly at her secondary school, she enjoyed the classes. Some of the teachers had been very stimulating. But she never clicked with a crowd. She always found herself floating on the fringes with the other outcasts, as she privately termed them. Girls like Mary Kelly, whose father was an alcoholic and who caused such rows at night that poor Mary never got a decent night's sleep. She often nodded off in class, much to the amusement of the rest, who would nudge each other and whisper, 'Dozy Dora's off again.' Or Sandra Moran, who had terrible BO and bad breath and who looked as if she had slept in a haystack and who hadn't much of a clue about her studies. They called her 'Smelly Nellie.'

Rachel knew her own nickname was Specky-Four-Eyes. She'd heard Eileen Dunphy call her that one day in third year, when she was playing basketball and missed a shot. Eileen turned to Vivienne Riordan and said scathingly, 'Why on earth does Michelle pick Specky-Four-Eyes Stapleton for her team? The moron hasn't got a clue!' This only served to make Rachel feel even more awkward and clumsy and twice she fumbled the ball as she dribbled it, allowing the opposing team to take possession. After that humiliating débâcle she stopped playing basketball, and retired instead to the library at lunch-time, or went for a solitary walk along the prom.

She had been full of hope when she started secondary school. Away from the stern eye of her father, Rachel decided that she was going to turn over a new leaf. After all, she was thirteen, a teenager, and she had been eagerly devouring the pages of *Jackie*. She had learned all about how to be self-confident. She knew she had to make an effort to talk to other people and to remember that they might be just as nervous as she was. She was to look people in the eye and be very interested in what they had to say and that way she would forget her own shyness and she'd be fine. Her father didn't know that she read *Jackie*. He certainly wouldn't approve, he preferred for her to read *The Pioneer* and *The Messenger*. The trouble was, her father was terribly old-fashioned. He wouldn't even let her wear nail varnish. God knows how she was ever going to manage to go with a fella. That is if she was lucky enough to be asked to go with a fella.

At the moment she was madly in love with Harry Armstrong. He was a friend of Ronan's and he was just *gorgeous*. He had the most amazing brown eyes and jet-black hair and he was always teasing her in a nice way. He'd make jokes about what a pest of a younger sister she was. Even worse than Becky, his own pest of a sister. Rachel loved it when he slagged her like that. But what made Harry a god in her eyes was that he had given Patrick McKeown a black eye and a bloody nose on her behalf. No wonder she fell in love with him. For that alone she would love him forever.

She'd been walking home from school one winter's evening when she was in fifth class. It was snowing heavily and she was slipping and sliding on the slushy ice-covered ground. She was on her own, as usual, pretending that she was Laura in *Little House on the Prairie* in a howling blizzard that was getting worse by the second. She was jerked out of her reverie by the hard cold smack of a snowball against her cheek. Then another and another. A barrage of white missiles assaulted her, blinding her, causing her to slip on the ice. As suddenly as it started, the onslaught ceased and she heard shouting and roaring. Rubbing her eyes, she turned to see Ronan's friend, Harry Armstrong, dragging Patrick McKeown out from behind a wall, as the rest of his cronies ran away. Harry grabbed a handful of snow and shoved it down Patrick's neck as the other boy

53

yelled blue murder. Patrick swung out with his left hand, Harry ducked and the next minute, with two neat blows, had bloodied Patrick's nose and given him a black eye.

'Now get out of here, you little toad, and don't try that trick on a girl again or you'll have me to deal with if I hear of it,' Rachel heard her Sir Galahad say as he gave her assailant a kick in the arse for good measure. Patrick staggered off down the road stunned and Harry crossed over to where Rachel was sitting. He held out his hand and pulled her upright. 'Are you all right, Rachel?' he asked kindly.

Mute, she nodded.

'Come on, I'll walk home with you, it's very slippy out, and if ever that little rat annoys you again just tell Ronan or me and we'll sort him out,' her hero assured her. Though her teeth were chattering and her coat was soaking, Rachel didn't notice. All she knew was that Harry Armstrong had saved her in her hour of need and now he was walking home with her.

That night as she lay in bed sniffling and coughing Rachel decided that it was worth getting snowball-attacked by Patrick McKeown to be rescued by Harry. It was rather romantic, she thought happily, inhaling her Vick-covered handkerchief and giving a mighty sneeze. And he had assured her that if Patrick McKeown troubled her in the future, he would take care of him. To have a pro-tector like Harry Armstrong was any maiden's dream.

Harry was the deputy chief altar boy and Rachel spent Sunday Mass when he was serving watching every move he made. She enjoyed the way his cassock flowed around him as he walked from one side of the altar to the other, performing his duties with an air of solemn authority. Not one prayer did she say on the Sundays when Harry Armstrong was serving at Mass. It was a joy just to sit watching her hero.

Harry remained her hero throughout her secondary schooling. Although he never had cause to rescue her from Patrick McKeown or anyone else for that matter, she still worshipped from afar. Harry treated her like a younger sister, much to her dismay. How she would have loved to be a real girlfriend to him. How she would have loved to parade down the prom in Bray holding his hand as the rest of her classmates did with their boyfriends. It was her greatest dream that he would suddenly take a second look at her and realize that she wasn't just Ronan's younger sister, but a scintillating, athletic, confident young woman (just like Michelle) who would make a wonderful girl-friend. Each night Rachel said a special prayer to St Jude, the patron saint of hopeless cases, beseeching him to open Harry's eyes. Ever hopeful, she patiently waited for the moment when the scales would fall from his eyes and he would realize just what was missing from his life.

Then she heard that Harry had started going with Ciara Farrell. She lost all faith in St Jude and herself. Rachel was deeply depressed because she was sure that she would be manless forever. It caused her such trauma at school. At least half the class were dating boys. And the other half were made to feel complete failures because of their lack of success with the opposite sex.

There was one particular girl whom Rachel hated with a vengeance. Her name was Glenda Mower and she made Rachel's life a misery. Glenda was a skinny gangly girl who seemed to have taken a dislike to Rachel the first time she met her. She had big brown eyes and straight lank brown hair cut in a bob and she thought she was the greatest thing since fried bread. She had oodles of self-confidence. Glenda took the lead in class debates and discussions and she loved the sound of her own voice. She wanted to be the most popular girl in the class. She was very sweet to everybody, batting her eyelashes, her cocker spaniel eyes as innocent as could be.

'Hi Rachel, you've got a hole in your tights,' she'd say ever so helpfully in her loud penetrating voice. 'You should rub soap on it to stop it running.' Rachel would be highly embarrassed as all eyes turned to look. Once when the lunch-time discussions turned to talk of boyfriends,

Glenda said sweetly, 'Rachel, have you ever had a boy-friend? Why don't you bring him to the disco on Thursday nights?' Rachel, of course, nearly died and turned scarlet as her classmates waited for her answer. She wanted to curl up in mortification. Even if she had a boyfriend, her father would never allow her to go to a disco in Bray.

'I don't have a boyfriend,' she muttered, inwardly cringing.

'Oh dear,' Glenda sympathized with honeyed insin-cerity. 'Well maybe there aren't many eligibles in your little village but now that you're here in school in Bray you'll have no problem finding one. Isn't that right, girls?' she addressed the others, grinning. Some of them tittered and then Michelle Butler said with a cold glare in Glenda's direction, 'Let's hope Rachel will have more luck than you had with Robert Tobin, he was going with Rita Clarke at the same time as he was going with you, wasn't he? And neither of you knew for ages he was two-timing.'

It was Glenda's turn to redden.

'Well I'm not going with him any more, Michelle. I'm going with Marty Campbell now and he's real nice.'

'Hmm,' Michelle said sceptically, and as she turned to walk away she winked at Rachel. After that, Glenda never gave Rachel a minute's peace and she would have faced Patrick McKeown's physical bullying a million times over rather than have to suffer her classmate's sly barbs.

Even now, some three years after that episode, Rachel felt a total failure. She was still without a boyfriend, much to Glenda's satisfaction. When she turned sixteen her mother insisted that her father let her go to the disco in Bray, but he always ruined it by coming to collect her promptly at eleven, to her great embarrassment. Now she was in for an interrogation from Glenda as to whether she'd got any Valentine cards or not. Rachel hated Valentine's Day. It always emphasized her sense of failure and inadequacy. Watching the other girls passing around their cards and giggling over the messages in them made her feel utterly lonely. Maybe this time next year it might be different, she would comfort herself. But now in her last year in secondary school she was still on her own. Had never been the recipient of a much-longed-for Valentine card and still harboured an unrequited passion for Harry Armstrong. She could see herself at ninety, still manless, she thought forlornly as she turned right and headed in the direction of the town centre.

'Hi Rachel, are you going for the bus? We could do our maths homework together.' She turned to find Mary Foley walking along beside her.

'Hi,' she echoed grumpily. Mary Foley was not exactly her favourite person. Mary and she had played together in primary school and had started secondary at the same time and ended up sitting together in the same class. Rachel had been delighted to see a familiar face. Mary and she had great discussions on the bus going to and from school about their exciting new world. It was so different from the schoolhouse in Rathbarry. Gradually Mary made friends with other girls in the class and soon dropped Rachel like a hot potato. At the beginning of their next term she sat beside Susan Shannon and left Rachel to sit alone.

Mary's rejection cut Rachel to the quick and erased the faint sense of self-confidence that she had begun to develop in her new school. Mary, longing to be part of the gang, often giggled at Glenda's smart remarks about her former friend. Many nights in the privacy of her bedroom Rachel cried her eyes out because of them. When Mary was on her own and wanted company on the bus she was perfectly friendly with Rachel, but in class or if she was with the others, she ignored her.

Well today, Rachel decided, Mary Foley could just go take a running jump. If she thought she was going to pick Rachel's brains for her geometry she could think again. There and then, Rachel decided she was not going home on the first bus. She would wait until the later one and go and look at Valentine cards and treat herself to *Jackie*, a cup of tea and a cream slice.

'No, I'm not going home, Mary. See you,' she said coolly, quickening her pace and leaving her erstwhile friend with her mouth open looking after her.

Shook you, Mary Foley! Rachel thought with satisfaction, feeling marginally better. She hadn't acted like a doormat. She decided to buy a Valentine card for Harry. She would disguise her writing very thoroughly and maybe she just might buy a Valentine card and send it to herself and bring it in to school and wave it around triumphantly.

She spent a happy hour browsing through cards and bought the most romantic one she could find for Harry. She chickened out of buying the one for herself. It would be much too obvious. Everyone would know that she had been reduced to that pathetic deception. Next year, she comforted herself as she ate her cream slice and sipped her tea, next year she wouldn't have to undergo this ordeal. She would be finished school, she'd be a free woman. And maybe, just maybe, with St Jude's help, she'd have a boyfriend. Preferably, if he could really see his way to answering her prayers . . . Harry.

Chapter Five

'Honest to God, wouldn't you think you'd have more sense at your age, and your sixth at that!' Helen Larkin scolded her sister Maura as she divested herself of her fur coat and plonked a bag of fruit and a bottle of Lucozade on the dressing-table.

'It's nice to see you too,' Maura murmured dryly, pulling herself up into a sitting position and wincing at the dart of pain that ran through her. Helen pulled up the comfy but shabby old rocking-chair and cast an affectionate glance at her older sister.

'Well it *is* nice to see you, you know that! It's just you'd think you'd have had enough of this carry-on by now.' She waved a hand in the direction of the Moses basket at the other side of the bed.

'Well it was a bit of a shock, but sure she's here now and we're delighted to have her, God love the angel.' Maura was not a bit fazed by her sister's outburst. She'd been expecting it. It had been the same the last time she got pregnant two years ago.

'Do you not take any precautions?' Helen said in exasperation.

'We were practising the safe period.' Maura couldn't keep her face straight. She was a terrible giggler, a habit that had stayed with her since childhood, and the sight of her sister's face was enough to start her off. 'And anyway,' she chortled, 'we had great fun for the whole nine months. I was as randy as hell and Pete thought he'd died and gone to heaven.'

'Oh for heaven's sake, Maura! You haven't an ounce of wit.' Helen started to chuckle herself. Maura was one

59

of the happiest people she knew. Happy and earthy. She and Pete had a very good marriage.

She was happy with Anthony, Helen mused as she gently started to rock in the old chair that had belonged to their mother. Anthony was a kind and considerate husband. But they just didn't have the *fun* that Maura and Pete had. Maybe if they'd had children of their own it would be different. The old familiar heart-scald seared her chest. Here was Maura with six and she wasn't able to have one of her own. God could be so cruel. There were so many people in the world who didn't deserve children. People who beat them, starved them, and committed unspeakable atrocities against them. And here was she who would give up her fine house in Dublin, her furs, her jewels, just to hold a child of her own in her arms. The doctors had told her they could find no reason for her infertility. She'd even gone to a specialist in London. He had told her to go home and stop worrying about it – it would happen eventually. Time passed and still the arrival of her monthly period was a day of frustration, bitterness and sadness. It was a great grief in her life and though she loved her sister dearly, Helen had cried her eyes out when she'd heard of the latest pregnancy.

'You're very good to come down.' Maura interrupted her musings. Helen's face softened.

'Of course I'd come down, haven't I come down for them all?' she retorted.

'I know you have, Helen, and I know it's terribly hard for you.' Maura squeezed her sister's hand tightly. A lump the size of a golf ball lodged in Helen's throat.

'Do you know how lucky you are, Maura? God, I wish you lived near me in Dublin so I could see the children. St Margaret's Bay is in the back of beyonds.'

'Don't say that about your birthplace,' Maura chided gently.

'Well it is!' Helen declared with a sniff. 'All those nosy old biddy-bodies. I was glad to get out of the place.'

'Oh you've gone very grand since you've gone to the big smoke, at least the people here will pass the time of day with you. Mind,' Maura gave one of her giggles, 'I don't know if Lancy Delaney will ever speak to me again. I drowned him with me waters at Mass yesterday.'

'You're not serious, Maura!' Helen's face was a study. 'Lancy Delaney, did he ever get married? God, he was the bane of my life. He must be fifty-five if he's a day. Do you remember he told Ma he had twenty acres and a bull and I'd never be sorry if I married him, and he old enough to be my father.' The two sisters erupted into guffaws.

'You broke his heart all right.' Maura wiped the tears from her eyes. 'He always asks after you. That's why he was sitting beside me at Mass.'

'Oh God Almighty, I'll be looking over my shoulder the whole time I'm down here.' Helen groaned. 'In the name of God what were you doing at Mass and you so near your time?'

'Sure didn't she come two weeks early. I wasn't expecting it to happen for at least a fortnight,' Maura protested.

'How did you drown Lancy?' Helen grinned. Maura threw her eyes up to heaven. 'Oh wasn't I running late trying to get the five of them ready and I didn't want to traipse up to the top of the church. And anyway Thomas is always tormenting me to go up on the gallery. They all are. We were the same when we were kids.'

'Don't I remember,' Helen agreed. 'It was such a treat to go up on the gallery. Everything seemed much more interesting and I always loved clattering down the wooden stairs to Communion.'

'And you could clatter better than anyone,' Maura said.

'I always liked to cause a stir,' Helen laughed. 'Anyway get back to the story.' Maura shifted more comfortably in the bed.

'Well I was coming down the stairs behind Lancy after Mass and the waters just went with a whoosh. It was a bit like a tidal wave actually.' She started laughing. 'Poor Lancy got the brunt of it in his socks and shoes and you know, I think he thinks I wet myself. I nearly did, I laughed so much. It was so funny, Helen. You should have seen the face of the poor old eejit.' Tears of mirth were streaming down Maura's face and Helen laughed with her.

'Maura Matthews, but you are incorrigible and there's no doubt about it.'

'I was lucky I didn't have her there and then. I was only in labour an hour and a half. That's the best ever,' her sister declared proudly.

'I hope it's the last time ever,' Helen said firmly. 'That safe period is a dead loss at your age.'

'I suppose you're right.' Maura yawned. Dusk had fallen and the rhythmic beam from the lighthouse illuminated the small bedroom. A log in the fireplace collapsed into a heap of ash scattering sparks up the chimney and the coals glowed deep orange. A whimper from the Moses basket caused two pairs of eyes to turn in that direction. 'Aren't you going to have a look at her?' Maura urged softly.

Helen gave a deep sigh, she had been delaying this moment for as long as she could. Slowly she walked over to the old well-worn but spotless basket. Peeping in she saw a pair of tiny hands waving impatiently. Gently she leaned in and picked up the tiny bundle. The old familiar ache ripped through her. She held the child close and felt it nuzzle at her face. 'She's beautiful, Maura, she's so tiny.'

'She's small all right, she was only five pounds. She's going to be petite, like Mam. I know you're Louise's godmother, and say no if you want, but I'd really love if you'd be godmother to this one too.'

Helen stared down at the tiny little being in her arms, her heart bursting with love for her already.

'I'd love to, Maura, what are you going to call her?' Maura smiled contentedly.

'We're going to call her Paula.'

Chapter Six

Paula Matthews was so excited she had knots in her stomach. Anxiously she peered out of the sitting-room window into the gloom. Her eyes scanned the darkening sky where the first stars were beginning to twinkle. No sign of anything yet. She knew that soon Santa would be leaving the North Pole and he had to cross Greenland and Iceland before getting to Scotland, England and then Ireland. Her daddy had told her that. Paula studied the skies carefully. Santa's fairies were still about, checking that there were no little children being bold.

'Hello my darling, what are you doing?' Auntie Helen lifted her out of the window-seat and sat down on it herself and gave Paula a great big cuddle. She had arrived from Dublin laden down with parcels. Of course she oohed and aahed when she saw Paula and exclaimed how big she'd got and how golden her curls were. She told a proud Maura that Paula was a beautiful child. It just confirmed everything that Paula knew about herself. She was perfectly happy to spend the rest of the afternoon admiring her golden curls and telling herself how beautiful she was.

Paula loved her Auntie Helen. She loved the scent of perfume that always seemed to waft from her. She loved the softness of the clothes she wore. She loved the jangly charm bracelet and the glittering earrings that adorned her aunt's wrist and ears. Most of all Paula loved the way her aunt always made a huge fuss of her. If there was one thing that Paula enjoyed it was being the centre of attention.

She was the pet of the family, her older brothers and

sisters took good care of her and always let her win at games. She had five brothers and sisters. The twins, Thomas and Louise, were the eldest. They were eleven. Then there was Rebecca, who was nine and a bit bossy, Joseph, who was eight, and John, who was seven. Paula had been five on her last birthday and had started school that September. She felt very grown-up setting off to school each day with John. John was her best friend. They had the greatest adventures together. Searching for buried treasure on the beach. Picking periwinkles on the rocks. Catching crabs and chasing each other with the claws. John was as excited as she was about Santa's impending arrival. He had asked for a rescue helicopter and a surprise and Paula could hear him anxiously asking their mother, 'Do you think he'll remember it's me that asked for the helicopter an' not Joseph or Thomas?'

'Stop worrying, John,' Paula heard her mother say. 'You've sent so many letters up that chimney he couldn't possibly make a mistake.' They had all had their baths and the youngest ones were getting their hair washed in a big basin in front of the fire in the kitchen. It would be her turn soon. Paula hated getting her hair washed. It always got tangled and she would screech when her mother brushed the tangles out for her.

'Are you excited?' Auntie Helen asked as they gazed out at the lighthouse in the middle of the sea. The wide golden beam lit up the steel-grey waters and darkening sky every sixty seconds. Surely if Paula kept looking at it she might see Santa and his sleigh. She gave a little shiver of anticipation.

'I wish it was Christmas Eve every night. I really hope I get my nurse's set. I wonder what surprise will I get?' Paula felt a wave of impatience. She wished she could just shut her eyes and open them and it would be Christmas morning.

'I bet your surprise will be lovely,' her aunt assured her, 'and wait until you see what I have for you under the tree.'

'Tell me! Tell me! Pleeezze, Auntie Helen, Please please please.' Paula felt like bursting with exhilaration.

'Then it wouldn't be a surprise,' Auntie Helen laughed. 'Come on, I'll ask Maura if I can wash your hair while she's drying John's.' They walked hand in hand into the snug aroma-filled kitchen. On the big table opposite the fire lay the huge turkey all plucked and cleaned and ready to be stuffed. Beside it lay a big platter of chopped onions, herbs and parsley, mashed potatoes and sausage meat. A big bowl of breadcrumbs waited to be mixed into stuffing.

They had all sat around the big table earlier rubbing chunks of bread together and crumbling them into the smallest crumbs. Only Louise, the eldest, was allowed to use the grater. It was her job to grate the crusts when the rest of them had finished crumbling. Paula longed with all her might to be allowed to use the grater. It was an important job. It wasn't fair that Louise was the only one allowed to do it.

When her older sister's back was turned, she stretched out and grabbed the grater and started grating her own crusts, much to Rebecca's chagrin. Rebecca too felt that she should be allowed to use it.

'Mammy, Paula's using the grater.' Rebecca snatched the offending article from her younger sister, causing Paula to graze her thumb. Blood stained the soft white pile of crumbs in front of her. Paula yelled blue murder.

'Look what she did, Mammy! Look what she did! Santa Claus won't come to you, Miss Rebecca Matthews.'

'For heaven's sake,' Maura exploded, wiping Paula's thumb and giving Rebecca a clip on the arm at the same time. 'Santa won't be coming to anyone in this house. If you all don't behave yourselves, I'm going to send the lot of you to bed and give the turkey to the poor.'

'We didn't do anything,' Joseph exclaimed indignantly.

'We're on our best behaviour, not like them two,' John said sanctimoniously.

'That's enough. I don't want to hear another word out

of anyone,' Maura warned and peace reigned for another while although there were a few protests during the hair washes. But that was nothing new.

When her hair had been washed and brushed it looked even more shiny and golden and Paula sat with her aunt's hand-mirror and brushed it over and over again. She looked a bit like the fairy princess in the lovely book of the *Sleeping Beauty* which Auntie Helen had given her for her last birthday.

Then her daddy arrived home with the Christmas tree. Paula stared in awe at the huge deep green pine that he was arranging in a bucket in the sitting-room. 'A few more rocks, lads, to keep it steady and we're away on a hack,' he told the boys, who were bringing in stones and rocks from the garden. When the base was covered with soil and rocks and the tree was centred just to her father's satisfaction he turned around and smiled at them all.

'I think it's time to try out the lights.'

'Yippee!'

'Great!'

'Massive!'

'Can I help, Daddy?'

'Santa Claus is coming to town.'(This was Joseph singing off-key.)

Paula was too excited to speak.

They watched as their big strong father climbed up the stepladder and hoisted himself into the attic and then the glory of glories started appearing. The big box with the crib in it was handed to Thomas, who was now, importantly, atop the ladder. Thomas passed it tenderly to Louise, who was waiting at the bottom. Next came the box with all the paper decorations. Then the box with the tinsel. Paula could see a piece of glittering red hanging down the side of the brown cardboard. She touched it reverently. How beautiful it was. How soft and lustrous.

'Be careful of the shiny balls now,' her father's disembodied voice came from the attic. His face suddenly appeared again as he handed down his precious cargo.

Then, most thrilling of all, came the lights. Through the plastic top Paula could see the face of a little fat Santa with a red hat and red cheeks and she wanted to do a little dance of happiness. This was *really* exciting. The time was getting nearer and nearer to Christmas Day. Her father handed down another box, this time multi-coloured carriage lights. Last came the box of Christmas candles.

Paula watched, a little scared, her father's legs dangling from the attic as he sought the top step of the stepladder. It was with great relief that she saw him pull across the trapdoor and descend the ladder.

'Right then, let's hope they're all working.' He gave the thumbs-up as they all trooped into the sitting-room after him carrying their treasures. Pete positioned himself by the tree and uncoiled the leads from the boxes. Placing the plugs into the adaptor, he crossed his fingers and smiled at the six anxious faces staring around in a semicircle. 'Switch off the light!' Thomas crossed the sitting-room and switched it off. Only the glow of the fire lit the room, the flames casting weird dancing shadows on the walls.

'Ready?' their father inquired as he plunged the plug into the socket.

'OOOHHH!!!!!' A symphony of delight echoed round the room as the Christmas lights illuminated the place with a magical radiance.

'Boys oh boys!' exclaimed their father. 'Quick, lads, get your mother. We have to show her this.' Maura and Helen were ushered in from the kitchen and Paula saw her mother smile at her daddy for long seconds, a special smile that excluded her and all the others in the room, and then it was gone and Maura laughed and said, 'Pete, it's going to be the best tree ever.'

Paula thought Auntie Helen looked strangely sad so she slipped her hand into her aunt's and whispered, 'I've got a present for you too. It's going to be under the tree tomorrow.' Helen swept her up in her arms and hugged her tightly.

'Have you, my darling? You're my pet, aren't you?'

'Yes I am,' she agreed happily, snuggling into her aunt's embrace.

Then the lights went out.

'Oh no!' came a communal moan, consternation replacing delight on all their faces.

'It's only a fuse,' reassured her daddy. 'I'll fix it in a jiffy.'

After the testing of the lights came the arranging of the crib. The six of them, under Auntie Helen's instructions, positioned the crib on top of the bookcase, beside the wireless. Auntie Helen was very artistic and she laid a pile of books behind the crib and covered it with black papier-mâché so that it looked like cliffs and mountains. They got the ivy and greenery which they had all helped collect earlier in the day and draped it around the top of the crib and down the mountainside before placing the figures in the crib. After that it was tea-time.

The smell of rashers and sausages sizzling on the pan made Paula's mouth water. The turkey had been stuffed and now reposed on top of the cooker in its big roasting dish. Its bluey-veined white breasts were covered with neatly arranged streaky rashers. As a treat, they were given fried bread and mushrooms as well, but after a few mouthfuls Paula could eat no more, she was in such a tizzy of excitement. On the big black mantelpiece over the crackling flaming fire, she could see six long grey stockings waiting to be collected on the way to bed. She knew what would be in those stockings in the morning, if Santa came. Shiny red pennies. Sweets. Balloons. Little round oranges and a juicy red apple.

'Has he left yet, Daddy?' she inquired anxiously.

'Good gracious, what time is it?' exclaimed Maura, looking at the clock on the mantel. 'Time to listen to Santa on the wireless.' She got up from the table and went into the sitting-room and switched on the wireless. Up on the dresser, beside the delph, was a speaker, and the spellbound children heard a whistling howling gale as Santa asked his helper Aidan to give the reindeers more hay. Paula's eyes grew wider and wider as she listened to Santa reading out letters from girls and boys.

'Don't forget my nurse's outfit and my surprise!' she burst out.

'And my helicopter,' John exclaimed.

'And my Cowboys and Indians set.' Joseph was not to be left out.

'He won't forget,' Maura reassured them. 'Listen now, Santa's getting ready to leave the North Pole.' They sat listening as Santa mounted his sleigh and straightened the reins. Then they heard the jingling of bells and Santa was on his way.

It was time to get their faces and hands washed and to take their stockings, which Maura solemnly handed out to each of them. This was the moment for the last ceremony of the evening. In silence they watched as Maura lit the big red candle that stood in a terracotta plant pot which was covered in tinfoil and decorated with holly and ivy. Placing it in the centre of the sitting-room window, Maura said softly, 'Let this light welcome your arrival this Holy Night, Sweet Jesus.'

'Amen,' they all responded.

'And let it help Santa Claus find his way to us too,' Joseph remarked firmly.

'Let me look out, Daddy,' Paula commanded. Her father lifted her up in his strong arms and she nestled close against him, loving the bristly feeling of his chin against her skin. 'Where is he now, Daddy?' she whispered.

'Heading for Iceland now, I'd say,' Pete said reflectively.

Outside in the wintry dark Paula could see the beam of the lighthouse. She could hear the crash of the waves against the pier and the whistling of the wind as it blew around the gables and down the chimney. Along the village she could see the flickering glow of candles in the windows of the other houses. Some houses even had their Christmas Trees up and their twinkling sparkling lights were like stars in the windows. Her daddy was

69

going to decorate the tree when they were in bed. In the morning the whole house would be transformed into a magical wonderland and it would be Christmas Day. Santa would have come and then they would go to early Mass while it was still dark and she would see baby Jesus in his crib and feel so tender towards the smiling child as she listened to the story of His birth. Like her, Jesus was a special child. How *she* would love to have been born in a stable and laid on a bed of straw in a manger, with all those kings from foreign countries coming to worship her with their gifts of gold, frankincense and myrrh.

'I think it's time for bed, Missy,' her father interrupted her reverie. 'Have you got your stocking?' Paula waved the precious sock at him. Soon it would be filled to the brim with goodies.

Auntie Helen helped her to tie her stocking onto the end of her bed and then her mammy and daddy came in to kiss them and tuck them up and tell them to hurry on and go to sleep. Auntie Helen gave her one last hug and the light was put out and only the rhythmic beam of the lighthouse illuminated the room. Paula lay cosy and warm in her flannelette sheets and squeezed her eyes tightly shut. Out there amid the whistling wind and the roar of the sea she was certain she had heard the faint tinkling of sleigh bells. Santa was on his way for sure.

'Now what have I got left to do?' Maura murmured to herself as she dried up the dishes after the tea. 'Steep the peas. Parboil the potatoes. Peel the sprouts and make the brandy butter.' It had been go, go, go, for the past two weeks. Getting the house spick and span. Washing windows and curtains. Doing the Christmas shopping.

That was no joke, she smiled to herself. John had changed his mind three times before finally settling on that rescue helicopter. And Louise! Maura was sure she knew there was no Santa. She couldn't decide whether she wanted the shiny long boots or a fashion doll with all the accessories. In the end, Maura asked Helen's advice, and bought the boots for Louise. Helen had bought her a doll for under the tree. The excitement that had been building in this house for the past month had more energy and power than several atomic bombs, she reflected with a smile.

They had been rowing and squabbling until she was nearly driven mad. But it was always the same coming up to Christmas, and of course with Pete working all the hours that God sent, it was she who bore the brunt of it. Still, it would be worth it all in the morning to see their faces, Maura thought happily as she poured a kettle of boiling water over the marrowfats and watched it turn cloudy.

It was a real bonus having Helen to stay as well. Poor Helen, unable to bear a child, and she blessed with six of them. God, the huge eyes of Paula as she watched the candle being lit. Those moments were so precious. And Helen would never have them. No wonder she spoilt Paula rotten. Maura should put her foot down, but Paula was the nearest Helen would have to a child of her own and there was a strong bond between them. Her sister was an exceptionally kind and good aunt to the other five but Paula was her pet, there was no denying it. If it gave her sister happiness, Maura wouldn't interfere.

'How's it going?' Pete came in to the kitchen and slipped his arms around her. Maura nuzzled in against him contentedly.

'Not too bad, I just have to do the spuds and sprouts and the brandy butter and then I'm more or less organized.'

'Did you see the faces of them? I thought Joseph was going to burst when he hung up his stocking, he was being ever so particular about the angle of it,' Pete laughed.

'Wait until Thomas sees the train set,' Maura grinned. 'And can you imagine the faces of Rebecca and Paula when they see their Cinderella high-heeled slippers. I love Christmas.'

'And I love you. Wasn't I the lucky man the day I married you?' Pete turned her round to face him and lowered his head and kissed her. Maura returned his kiss ardently. She loved her husband passionately. He was a kind hard-working man who wanted only the best for his wife and family and even after all these years of marriage and six children, he could still make her tingle with pleasure when he touched her and kissed her.

'Stop it, Pete.' She giggled as she felt him respond to her. 'The turkey's looking.'

'Let him look, I bet he wishes he was me.' Her husband grinned down at her.

'Get in there and fix that Christmas Tree and Santa might come to you tonight if you're good.' Maura's eyes sparkled with fun and the promise of pleasures to come.

'Oh!' Helen came into the kitchen and stopped suddenly at the sight of them. 'You pair! Do you want a cup of tea to cool your ardour?'

'Spoilsport! Your sister was trying to seduce me in front of the turkey. She gets her kicks in strange ways. I'm worn out with her. Look at the pathetic wreck of a man I am compared to when I got married.'

'You're not looking too bad,' Helen said fondly as she filled the kettle.

'I'd better go and start decorating, I suppose.'

'You'd better!' his wife grinned. 'We'll bring you in a cup of tea.'

'What will I do for you?' Helen plonked herself on the little red cushioned seat beside the fire. Maura sat herself on the opposite one and they toasted their hands against the blaze.

'Would you do the sprouts?'

'Sure I will,' Helen smiled. The flames lit the creamy skin on her face, and highlighted the burnished glints in her chestnut hair. Maura felt dull and dowdy beside her. Helen was so elegant and *soignée*, never a hair out of place. Her nails were always perfectly shaped and varnished, her eyebrows plucked so that not a stray hair showed. Maura had meant to do her own, and she'd meant to get to the hairdresser today as well, but she just hadn't managed it.

'I wanted to get my hair done today.' She ran her hand through brown curls that were beginning to show faint traces of grey.

'Wash it when you're ready and I'll set it for you,' Helen offered.

Maura brightened. 'Thanks, Helen, sure that's as good as going to the hairdresser. I'm really glad you're able to spend Christmas with us. It's a big treat for us and Paula's in the seventh heaven because her favourite aunt is here.'

'It's a real treat for me too, Maura. A real treat and thanks for having me. You and Pete. I'm lucky to have you.' Helen got up from her little seat and leaned across and hugged her sister.

Maura hugged her back tightly. Helen and she had always been close. It was a closeness that had sustained her all her life. 'You're a great sister, Helen.' She smiled, giving Helen a squeeze. 'You're so good to my children and they all adore you. I hope this will be one of your best Christmases ever.'

Helen lay wide-eyed, watching the magnificence of Pete's Christmas Tree with pleasure. In a minute she would hop out of bed and switch off the lights. But it was so delightful to lie in her comfortably made up bed toasting her feet against the hot-water bottle that Maura had filled for her. It reminded her of childhood Christmases, being in this room with the garlands lacing the ceiling and the rich red and green holly adorning the pictures on the walls. Maura's shining old-fashioned candlesticks held two red candles on the mantelpiece and between them Christmas cards lay along the top, giving it a most festive air.

Helen sighed. She hadn't bothered to decorate her home in Dublin this year. It just hadn't seemed worth it. Anthony was going to his mother for Christmas and she had made the spur-of-the-moment decision to go to Maura and Pete's. To hell with it, she'd thought. After spending Christmas with the Matthews, it would only be an anticlimax coming home to her silent elegant house.

She wondered how her husband was getting on. Poor Anthony, he'd felt so bad about spending Christmas with his mother and leaving her. But there was no point in her going with him. Stephanie Larkin couldn't stand Helen and had never given an inch from the moment she had married her son. In her eyes Helen was not of the same social class as the affluent Larkins, and never would be. She was an intruder who had wormed her way in. Stephanie always referred to her, in the most disparaging of tones, as 'the country girl.'

Helen had made a tremendous effort for her husband's sake, enduring the snubs and rebuffs and downright rudeness of her mother-in-law.

Anthony had rebuked his mother sternly, several times, because of her treatment of Helen but this had only increased her antipathy towards her only son's wife. In the end Helen had called a halt and told her husband that she was no longer going to visit Stephanie and that he could go alone. He had to agree that it was the best solution. Mrs Larkin was delighted to have her son to herself and told the rest of the family that 'that awful country girl couldn't even be bothered to visit her mother-in-law.'

Stephanie lived with a housekeeper in a big house in Dalkey and Anthony visited her twice a week, on Wednesday evenings and Sunday mornings. About two weeks before Christmas she got a bad dose of flu and convinced herself and everyone else that she was dying. She pleaded with Anthony to come and spend Christmas with her, just this once, as she was sure it was to be her last. When he suggested that she come and spend it with him and Helen, she recoiled as though he had struck her.

'I'll not go where I'm not wanted and that wife of yours doesn't want me in your house. I'll stay here with Vera where I'm not a nuisance to anyone. Thank you very much!' Anthony was fit to be tied.

'I don't mind having her, honestly, Anthony,' Helen assured her husband, lying through her teeth.

'I know you don't, darling, and I really appreciate it. But you know my mother.'

Only too well, Helen thought grimly. In the end, seeing how troubled he was and knowing the pressure Stephanie was bringing to bear, she told him to go to his mother's for Christmas. That way neither of them could ever reproach themselves in the unlikely event of Stephanie's sudden demise.

'I can't leave you on your own for Christmas,' Anthony announced but she felt it was only for form's sake. Anything for a quiet life was Anthony's motto. Her husband was not a man to wear his heart on his sleeve or be overly demonstrative. He loved her in his own quiet way. And she supposed she loved him too. Although there were times she cast an envious eye on Maura and Pete's marriage, envying them their spontaneity and fun and earthy lust for each other.

She was nineteen when she met Anthony. She had been staying with a schoolfriend who was living in Dublin and they had gone to a dance in the local tennis club. Because it was all so new and exciting and sophisticated, Helen had a ball. She was exceptionally pretty and vivacious and she did not lack for partners. A tall dark-haired man smiled in her direction and she smiled back. He was a good deal older than she was. In his late twenties at least.

'Who is he?' she nudged her friend Breda.

'That's Anthony Larkin, isn't he gorgeous? People say he's stuck-up but I think he's just shy. He's a stockbroker.'

'Is he going with anyone?'

Breda giggled. 'I don't think so. Do you fancy him?'

'Of course not. I don't know him. He just smiled at me, that's all. It's probably because I'm a new face in the crowd.'

'It would be just typical of you to come up to Dublin and swipe the most eligible bachelor in the club right from under our noses.' Breda grinned.

'Fat chance,' laughed Helen.

But he did ask her to dance. The last dance. And

he asked to see her home. Breda's eyes were out on stalks. 'Told you,' she whispered as they queued for the ladies just before leaving.

'Give over, Breda, do I look all right?' Now that he had asked her she was beginning to feel a bit nervous. What on earth would she talk to a stockbroker about?

Helen smiled to herself in the half-dark remembering that first date. Anthony had been more nervous than she was and it was she who did most of the talking, telling him about her family and her job as a clerk in a shipping office in Waterford. For the rest of her holiday he squired her around Dublin. And brought her to concerts and the theatre and art galleries and restaurants. Going back to St Margaret's Bay a week later, Helen knew she would never settle there again. She wanted to live in Dublin. Wanted to be part of the buzz and excitement of the capital. She began to apply for positions advertised in the national papers and, after several interviews, landed a job in a big insurance company.

Her parents had not been too happy when she told them she was moving up to Dublin. Her father went so far as to forbid it but she went, too restless and bored to stay in her home village any longer. Her father got over his daughter's defiance of him, eventually, and she was glad of that because they were a close family and it wasn't nice having bad feelings between them.

Helen took to life in the city with gusto. Before long she met Anthony again at another tennis club dance which she went to with Breda, with whom she was now sharing a flat. He had been so pleased to see her, much to her delight and surprise. She never expected someone as cosmopolitan and urbane as Anthony to be interested in someone as unsophisticated as she was. But he *was* interested. He found her very easy to relate to. Less than a year later they were married, much to his mother's chagrin.

Helen stretched out her limbs in the bed and gave a deep sigh. She supposed as marriages went they were happy. It was always the same, though, when she came back to St Margaret's Bay and saw how close Maura and Pete were, the fun they had, and the joy they got from their young family. These visits always left her feeling vaguely dissatisfied.

She had a very good life in Dublin. She had plenty of friends. She did a lot of entertaining and was in turn entertained. They travelled regularly. Went skiing every February. She had a husband who appreciated her, a beautiful home. Everything . . . except a child of her own. It was her greatest grief. The doctors had told her they could find nothing wrong with her and so she had tentatively suggested her husband go for tests. He freaked out and told her angrily that there was absolutely nothing wrong with him, going for tests was out of the question. She begged him over and over to go to be tested and he always stubbornly refused. He wouldn't consider adoption either and it was causing enormous tension between them. He was like a bloody ostrich with his head in the sand, refusing to face the fact that their childlessness might be his fault. There were times when Helen felt that she hated her husband for putting her through this misery and expecting her to take the blame for it in the eyes of their families and friends.

When Anthony said he couldn't leave her alone for Christmas, she instantly thought of Maura and her family. She actually felt glad that he had given her an excuse to get away. What a joy it would be to share her darling Paula's excitement. How she loved that child. The exquisite perfection of her. Those beautiful big blue eyes, that soft golden hair. From the moment she had picked her up out of that wicker basket when she was only a day old, Helen felt for that baby as deeply as she would feel for a child of her own. That feeling had grown stronger over the years. Her biggest joy was to have her precious niece stay for a few days with her in Dublin. It wasn't that she didn't love the others. She did, of course. How could she not? But Paula was precious, her little darling.

Maura had let her fill her stocking tonight. She couldn't

77

describe the happiness she felt as she watched her beautiful niece fast asleep, one hand tucked under her face, her little cheeks rosy in the torchlight. She'd filled that stocking with all the goodies Maura handed her and vowed to herself that as long as she was alive Paula would have everything her dear little heart desired.

Drowsily, Helen remembered the Christmas Tree lights and slid reluctantly out of bed to switch them off. She was tired, but very happy. Maura had said she hoped it would be one of her best Christmases ever. Well it looked as if it was going to be just that.

Chapter Seven

Paula lay very still in the dark. Her heart was thumping so loudly she could hear the rush of blood in her ears. Slowly, cautiously, she stretched down her left foot. Yes! Yes! there was something there all right. Something hard and deliciously heavy on top of her toes. Something that felt like a box or a parcel. Her eyes widened. She could hear Joseph shouting something in the other room. Something about Santa. She wriggled her toes again. After all the waiting and wondering, the morning had finally arrived. Santa Claus had left something for her on the end of her bed. Paula savoured the moment, knowing that it would be another three hundred and sixty-five days before it could happen again. She felt Rebecca stir beside her in the double bed.

'Santa's come,' she whispered, still too scared to get up and find out what he had brought her. He could still be in the house for all she knew. Paula was sure she could hear the reindeer's bells tinkling on the roof. Rebecca shot up in the bed, and in the white beam of the lighthouse, Paula thought she looked like a scarecrow with all her hair sticking up on her head.

Then Joseph and John exploded through the door, waving their bulging stockings and yelling, 'What did you get?'

'Did he come to everyone?'

'Ya should see Thomas's train set. Daddy is getting up to play with it. He's coming to see what ya got. Wake up, wake up.' Joseph was hopping up and down, his cow's-lick sticking out even more than usual, as he delved into his stocking and pulled out three bright shiny pennies. 'I'm going to buy trillions of sweets,' he declared. 'See did you get some, Paula. Quick, look.' John tried to say something but his cheeks were bulging with toffees and he couldn't speak.

Rebecca leaned down the bed, yanked up her stocking and pulled up the big box that lay against her side. Paula reached down tentatively and poked the box which was lying on her toes. It felt very mysterious. Slowly she got out of bed and walked down to the bedpost where her stocking was. Last night when she had hung it up, it had been limp and empty. Now it was full to the brim. Her little hands traced the outline. Down in the toe there was something round. Along the middle something rustling. Something soft up near the top. Her blue eyes wide with wonder and excitement, she pulled out a shiny tin with ladies in long dresses on the lid. She opened it and saw that it was full of toffees, all wrapped in papers of different colours. A tin of sweets! All for herself. What luxury. Two red and white balloons fell out. Her daddy would blow them up for her. A white lacy handkerchief came next and then a packet of crayons and a colouring book. Another book fell out and Paula gave a squeal of pleasure. It was a cut-out doll book with different outfits. Emily Leahy had one and would never share it. Paula could only sit and watch her playing at dressing up her dolls. Now she had one for herself.

She delved deeper and pulled out an apple, and right down in the toe, a little orange, and then she heard the clink of coins and triumphantly curled her fingers around her shiny pennies.

'What else did he bring?' Paula heard her daddy ask. He was standing at the door with her mother and they were smiling in at the scenes of delighted discovery. In her excitement Paula had forgotten her big box. Rebecca and Louise had already opened theirs and Louise was parading around with her shiny boots on her bare feet under her nightdress. She had got a matching shoulder bag as well and she thought she was the bee's knees.

Rebecca was entranced with her easel and painting-by-numbers kit and couldn't wait to get started on a picture.

'Open up your present, Paula,' she heard her mother say and, suddenly brave, she tore at the wrappings on the rectangular box. Eyes wide, she discovered a white apron with a red cross on the front of it, a navy cloak, white armbands and a white nurse's hat. In a separate section there was a stethoscope, thermometer, nurse's watch and a notebook and pen. Paula was ecstatic. She loved nurses and what fun she was going to have pretending to be one.

'Look.' Her daddy pointed to another smaller box which she hadn't even noticed. Paula couldn't believe her luck. Another gift as well as her nurse's outfit. Santa must have thought she was a very special girl indeed. Her heart almost burst with happiness when she saw the pair of gold high-heeled Cinderella slippers which nestled in white tissue. High heels! How grown-up. She couldn't wait to get into them.

Paula was not allowed to wear her magnificent new shoes to Mass and so she threw a mighty tantrum. She knew she was quite safe in misbehaving as Santa had come, and there was no danger that she would be the recipient of a sack of ashes.

She wanted so badly to show off her new Cinderella shoes. She wanted everyone at Mass to look at her and admire her golden curls and glorious high-heeled slippers. Emily Leahy would be *so* jealous of her.

'They're not for wearing outside. They're not real shoes, pet. You couldn't walk to Mass in them. You can wear them when you get home,' her mother explained patiently as she pulled the velvet dress that Auntie Helen had bought her over Paula's head.

'But I *want* to wear them.' Paula was outraged that her mother would not give in to her wishes.

'Paula, don't be a bold girl now on baby Jesus's birthday, after Santa was so good to you.' Maura began brushing her daughter's hair.

Paula pulled her head away and said petulantly, 'Don't want you to brush my hair. Want Auntie Helen to do it. She's my *kind* auntie.'

Maura gave a sigh of exasperation. 'Suit yourself.' She handed her daughter the brush. Paula was one of the most stubborn little characters she knew. She'd have a face on her for hours because she wasn't allowed to wear her Cinderella slippers to Mass. Well let her, Miss Paula had to learn that she couldn't always have her own way. The trouble with her was she got her own way far too often.

Helen pulled her cashmere scarf tighter around her neck. It was a crisp cold morning and frost-wrapped leaves crunched underfoot as they all made their way to the Star of the Sea Church for the first Mass of Christmas.

It was still pitch-dark and Helen took great pleasure in gazing at the sky. You'd never get a sky like this in the city, she mused. It looked as if someone had flung a scattering of sparkling diamonds into a sea of black velvet. The stars were so bright and so near, it added to the sense of wonder and magic. All around, people were making their way to church, calling out Christmas greetings to their neighbours. Everyone was dressed in their best finery and Helen smiled to herself as she saw Florence Crosbie wearing a frothy veiled creation in rich emerald green. Florence was noted for her hats and always had something new for Easter and Christmas. Her hats were almost a village tradition. Children danced up and down, calling out to their friends what Santa had brought them for Christmas.

She'd forgotten the closeness and community spirit of village life, especially around Christmas time. Living in an affluent suburb in Dublin, going to Mass on Christmas Morning in that big cold Corpus Christi Church which was their parish church, couldn't compare with this joyful morning in Star of the Sea. Maybe if she had children of her own it would have been different up in Dublin.

Now, as she entered the sturdy wooden doors of the church, Helen felt almost like a child again. Some things never changed. The wooden posts along the nave were entwined with holly and ivy. The altar was a picture in green and red-berried glory. To the right, behind the altar rails under the big statue of Our Lady, an enormous crib with large realistic figures of the Nativity was the focus of wide-eyed wonder as children crowded two and three deep to look.

Passing under the gallery, Helen could hear Nancy Farrell, the organist, tuning up as the choir shuffled their music and cleared their throats. Helen knew they were in for a treat. The choir was the pride of the county and they had been practising for weeks. She saw the Todd sisters and their niece Maureen heading up to the gallery at speed. They were the stalwarts of the choir and had the sweetest voices. It was something she really looked forward to, coming back and hearing St Margaret's Bay Choir sing the hymns of her childhood. How she wished Anthony was with her to share it. He would enjoy the carols, they were the part of Christmas that he liked most. Helen felt a surge of resentment. If it wasn't for that old bitch Stephanie and her carry-on, they would have been together.

She had called him last night from the phone opposite Mooney's bar, because Maura and Pete didn't have a phone. Stephanie answered the phone, full of beans, and not at all like someone as near to death's door as she was supposed to have been.

'Oh Helen, it's yourself!' Knowing that her daughter-in-law was more than a hundred miles away and in no danger of taking her darling son away from her this Christmas, Stephanie could afford to inject a note of artificial warmth into her voice. 'I'm feeling much better, you know. It's such a tonic having Anthony with me. He's a wonderful son. It's going to be a splendid Christmas. He's taking me to Midnight Mass in the Pro-Cathedral. I haven't been for *years* and I'm so looking forward to it. Then the entire family are coming over tomorrow evening for mulled wine and mince-pies. Such a shame

83

you're down there in . . . where is it . . . St Mary's?
You'll miss it all.' The honeyed falseness of her mother-
in-law made Helen's fingers curl in her palms. Oh what a
two-faced bitch that woman was. There had been nothing
wrong with her at all. It had all been a great big act to
have Anthony to herself for Christmas. And he, the fool,
couldn't see that. He had swallowed the act, hook, line and
sinker, and because of it he was up in Dublin and she was
here feeling furious and resentful. Why couldn't he stand
up to his mother when it really mattered? Sometimes
Helen wondered if her husband felt, deep down, that
he had married beneath him. God knows Stephanie had
indoctrinated him enough. It was far from mulled wine
Helen had been reared on, certainly, but she could carry
herself anywhere and had always known how to behave.
Her parents might have been from a small country village,
and not have been very well off, but they had taught all
their children manners and how to treat other people with
respect. Stephanie would think that St Margaret's was so
parochial. Anyone outside the Pale was a peasant as far
as she was concerned. For all her airs and graces and
so-called breeding, the woman was pig-ignorant.

Anthony sounded mightily pissed off when he came to
the phone.

'I miss you, darling,' he sighed.

'I miss you too,' Helen said with forced cheeriness.
'But I'm having a ball here with Maura and the kids.
It's all such fun.'

'Oh . . . ' Anthony sounded a little surprised that she
seemed to be enjoying herself. Well tough luck, if he was
stuck with Stephanie, that was his choice. Not hers. Let
him be miserable on his own. She wasn't going to play
the role of martyr, she thought crossly.

'Well enjoy yourself,' her husband said.

'Oh I will, Anthony, and you too. God bless, love,'
Helen said firmly. Let Anthony feel sorry for himself, she
was going to enjoy her Christmas. But the phone call had
upset her. The spite of her mother-in-law in setting up

84

the whole thing and her husband's failure to see through her really annoyed Helen. It meant he was putting Helen second in his life. That depressed her, especially when she saw the closeness of Maura and Pete in comparison.

'Can I sit on your knee 'cos I can't see anything?' A much-loved voice interrupted her musings. Helen looked down to see Paula, looking adorable in a little red hat and muffler, gazing up at her.

'Certainly you can, my darling,' she beamed, leaning down and lifting her niece in her arms. Of course, if it wasn't for Stephanie she wouldn't be spending Christmas with her precious dote. She followed Maura, who led the way into a seat near the front of the church, and had to smile when the rest of the gang trooped in after her. Maura, Pete and their offspring took up a whole pew.

The bell rang. The organ played forth and the glorious sound of sopranos, contraltos and baritones complementing each other in harmony as the choir raised the rafters with their first offering, *The First Noel*, brought a lump to Helen's throat. This I am going to enjoy, she decided firmly. And to hell with the Larkins and their mulled wine and mince-pies!

It was a scrumptious dinner, the stuffing – her favourite – tasted divine but now the washing-up was all done and the next exciting event was about to take place. Paula felt a tingle of anticipation. There was an enormous pile of presents awaiting her under the Christmas tree. Presents from their nanas and grandads and aunts and uncles. There had been loads of visitors after Mass and the house had been bursting at the seams. She was in her element having finally got to wear her high heels and nurse's uniform. Everyone oohed and aahed at her and told her she was cute and gorgeous. Her earlier bad humour evaporated and she swanned around feeling terrifically important.

But now Paula was glad all the hustle and bustle was over and it was finally time to settle down to the opening of the presents. Her mother was ensconced in the arm-chair beside the twinkling Christmas Tree. Her father put more coal on the blazing fire and the rest of them sat on the floor, waiting patiently for the ceremony to begin.

'Come and sit on my knee.' Auntie Helen held out her arms, but Paula shook her head. She wanted to be right beside her mother, to be first to get the presents. She didn't see the brief expression of hurt that flashed across her aunt's face. All she was concerned about was her presents.

Maura reached down and pulled out an intriguing-looking parcel wrapped in bright paper. 'To Paula from Nana and Grandad Matthews.'

Paula beamed around at her brothers and sisters. She'd got the first present, she felt like the cat that had got the cream.

This was the part of Christmas Day that she liked best, Maura decided as she settled in her armchair and pre-pared to snooze. The fire was blazing up the chimney, bathing the room in a yellow-orange glow. In the corner, the magnificent tree, with its twinkling fairy lights, shone with a soft magical incandescence that was beautiful to behold. It was just getting dark. Soon she would have to pull the curtains and switch on the lamps, but this was her favourite time, when peace descended on the household after the hectic gaiety that had gone before. Pete was already asleep in his chair, and she could see Helen strug-gling to keep her eyes open as she read the Agatha Christie novel that had been part of the children's present to her.

Maura smiled happily to herself. There wasn't a peep out of her offspring as they sat in various poses, on the floor, or on the sofa, deeply engrossed in the annuals which had been the presents from Mammy and Daddy under the tree. Rebecca was swapping her *Bunty* for Louise's *Judy*, and John, Joseph and Thomas were up to their ears in *The Beano*, *The Dandy* and *Boy's Own*, jaws chomping on their toffees. Paula, her nurse's hat awry, her beloved slippers half off her feet, had her arms curled around her Teddy and was fast asleep. The face of her that morning when she trailed down the stairs in her bare feet with her presents under her arm and walked into the sitting-room and saw the tree and all the decorations. It had been such a precious moment for herself and Pete to see the awe and delight on their children's faces. It had been worth all the hard work and lack of sleep.

They grew up so quickly. Louise had confided that she didn't believe in Santa and Maura felt like crying. She wished she could freeze this moment for ever, that things would never change, that her children would always stay as they were. But that was wishful thinking. It seemed like only yesterday that Paula was a baby. One day she'd want to go shopping for real high heels. Today would be just a memory. A very treasured memory.

Chapter Eight

A long appreciative wolf-whistle brought a smile to Paula Matthews's lips as she made her way past the building site where the new Credit Union premises was being built. It was early, only seven-fifteen, but the builders were there already, shinnying up and down their scaffolding with lithe agility. Paula loved walking past the site. She enjoyed covertly eyeing up the bronze bare-chested men with their rippling muscles. They were ever so sexy. Now that she was fifteen, a teenager at last, she was almost grown-up. She had a boyfriend, Conor Harrison, Doctor Harrison's son. He was quite a catch and three years older than her. Conor had just finished his Leaving Cert and, if he got enough honours, was going to UCD in September to study medicine. Much as she liked Conor, Paula was enough of a realist to know that once her boyfriend went up to the big smoke, he wouldn't be thinking of the girl he'd left behind. Not unless she gave him something to think about . . . She smiled to herself as she walked past the whistling workmen. There was one whom she particularly liked. He was in his early twenties, fair-haired, about six foot, with a body that would tempt any virgin. He was a good bit older than her, of course, but then she was attracted to older men. They were so much more sophisticated, not like the spotty gawky youths of her own age. God, she wouldn't give them a second glance. Jim Carr and Cormac Walsh were always mooning after her, pretending to be two real hard chaws, smoking and boasting and swaggering around in two awful moth-eaten leather jackets.

Did they actually think that she was the slightest bit

interested? Pathetic geeks like them with their spotty acne and greasy hair. At least Conor had a bit of class and sophistication. His father, of course, being a doctor, was loaded and Conor always had plenty of money to treat her like a lady. He had bought her heated rollers and a curling tongs last Christmas and her friends, not to mention her sisters, were pea-green with envy. Rebecca's fella had given her one of those soap and talc sets and she'd been furious. And would you blame her? If any fella ever gave *her* one of those cheapie sets he'd have his walking papers before he knew it. Anyway, Rebecca was only going out with Niall Cronin because she was desperate to have a bloke. Niall Cronin was a lazy good-for-nothing who didn't even wash himself half the time. The smell off him sometimes. Paula wrinkled her pert nose as she walked past Mooney's bar. If she'd been Rebecca, she'd have given him back his soap and talc set and told him to use it on himself. How her sister could let that smelly oaf near her, Paula could not fathom.

He was such a shit too, he'd actually made a pass at her. Now Paula knew that men in general found her attractive. She was rather pretty, she had to admit, she mused, as she walked past the Star of the Sea and saw Father Doyle going in to prepare for eight o'clock Mass. Probably Father Doyle secretly fancied her as well, for all she knew. She giggled happily to herself. It was nice that men fancied her. Conor was always telling her how beautiful she was and no doubt Niall just got carried away and couldn't help himself. But to seriously think that she would be interested in him with his BO and he her sister's boyfriend. She didn't know which she had found the more insulting. The trouble with Niall was that he thought he was such a cool dude, well there was nothing cool dudey about Niall BO Cronin and she had told him so in no uncertain terms. He had been most upset when she called him a cretin and suggested he treat himself to a bath. She hadn't told Conor about Niall's pass. He'd go mad and probably sock him on the jaw. He was always very possessive of her. Maybe she just might let it slip and see what happened. Somehow the idea of men fighting over her was rather appealing.

Paula walked briskly through the village, her long blond hair blowing behind her in the warm breeze. She was really looking forward to today and what a beautiful day it was. It was a scorcher, just the way she liked them. If there was one thing Paula loved it was lying in the sun. A tan always looked really well on her and accentuated the deep blue of her eyes and highlighted the blond of her hair. Today, she was going to look very well as she already had a light bronzed glow. Today she was going to be a bridesmaid at her sister Louise's wedding. Today was her last day in her summer job. Today was the Day of Days and tomorrow . . . she felt like doing a little twirl of happiness. Tomorrow she would be in Dublin with Helen for the last few days in July and the whole month of August. What joy! What bliss! Helen's house was pure luxury and Paula had a gorgeous room all to herself. A delightful room where the curtains matched the bedspread, there was even a matching lampshade and waste basket.

Paula loved that room. She loved it much more than her grotty old bedroom at home. God, what a mess that was! Sharing with two other sisters was such a drag. Sleeping with Rebecca was an even bigger drag. They were always fighting. Rebecca was the noisiest person to sleep with, she was always cucking. Paula would lie in bed fuming while her sister gave a little snore and then a cuck, and then a snore and then a cuck. It was enough to drive anyone batty. When she couldn't take it any longer she would give her an elbow in the ribs and tell her to keep her mouth shut and stop snoring. Then Rebecca would get mad and curse at her and there'd be a row. At least now that Louise was going they'd have a bed each. That was one of the joys of going to Helen's for her holidays. Not only had she a bed to herself, she had a *room* to herself with an entire wardrobe for her clothes and a dressing-table full of fabulous creams and perfumes and talcs and exquisite nail varnishes. Going to heaven was surely only half as nice as going to her aunt's house on holidays.

And how glorious it would be to get out of boring St Margaret's Bay. It was so dull, it drove her nuts. Paula cast a jaundiced eye around the neat little village overlooking the Irish Sea. A row of cottages, with the odd two-storey or dormer bungalow. Then Mooney's Bar & Lounge. Beside it, Connolly's supermarket and post office. Beside that, the Star of the Sea Church. Then there was the new Credit Union building that was under way. The poshy houses, where the priest and doctor and old Colonel Rogers and his alcoholic wife lived, bordered the site. The gardens were large and shrub-filled and all immaculately kept, in stark contrast to Walter Kelly's ramshackle plot and tumbledown cottage which adjoined the colonel's, much to his immense dissatisfaction.

'You're not in the army now, matey, so don't be giving me any of yer lip,' Walter would snort when the colonel periodically took him to task about the state of his property. When Walter went on one of his renowned benders he would stand outside the colonel's house and holler drunken abuse until the sergeant came along with his uniform on over his pyjamas, and dragged him home, promising him that if he carried on like this again he'd find himself up in Mountjoy Prison. He had been promising Walter this for the last ten years.

That was about the height of excitement of life in St Margaret's Bay, Paula thought glumly as she walked past Walter's neglected house and garden. If she thought she had to spend the rest of her life here she'd go mental, she assured herself.

When she left secondary school in Waterford she was going to Dublin to live life to the full. Dublin was like an unbelievable dream to her. An Aladdin's cave of delight. All the shops and hotels. The cinemas, the theatres and art galleries and restaurants. How wonderful it would be to be able to hop on a bus and be in the city centre in ten minutes. If you wanted to get to Waterford from this Godforsaken back of beyonds you had to hitch. Except for going to school, of course. There was a school bus for that. Louise was going to live in Waterford with her new husband, but Waterford was really only a town, not a city, not like Dublin, and Dublin was her Mecca, living there her ultimate goal.

There was no way she'd miss Maggie's Bay, that was for sure, she assured herself as she stopped to look across at the pier where Lancy Delaney was chatting to Mattie Fortune as Mattie sat mending some fishing nets. Lancy Delaney, according to her mother, carried a torch for Helen. Imagine! An ould eejit like that with wellington boots covered in cow-shit and a jumper nearly down to his knees it was so stretched. Paula grimaced at the thought of him and her precious Helen, who was the height of elegance and Paula's ideal.

Gulls circled above screeching and diving as one of the trawlers disgorged its haul from a night's fishing. The sun cast prisms of sparkling light on a tranquil sea that glittered more brightly than the most expensive chandelier ever could. Along the curve of the coast, green and gold fields were fringed by miles of clean white sand lapped by gently surging waves. The melody of birdsong echoed from tree to tree and shrub to shrub. The air was so fresh and sea-scented it invigorated mind and body. Yet Paula appreciated none of it. She had grown up with the view and the fresh unpolluted air and took it totally for granted. Dublin with its fume-filled streets and noisy traffic was a far more attractive proposition in her eyes.

She couldn't understand how tourists would prefer to come to somewhere as quiet as St Margaret's Bay in preference to a place where they could shop in huge department stores and visit places of interest such as Trinity College to see the Book of Kells, or the Zoo and the Phoenix Park, or hundreds of other fascinating places. They could eat in the fanciest of restaurants and then go dancing in the night-clubs in Leeson Street.

Or *The Strip* as it was known, according to Monica Boyle, who boasted of having been there.

Paula grimaced as she turned into the manicured, landscaped lawns of the Sea View Hotel, where she had been employed for the past six weeks as a chambermaid, or house assistant as they were called in the hotel. The Sea View was only in its second season, having been purpose-built by Gerry Murphy, who owned the site. It had been left to him by his uncle. Gerry Murphy was a young man in a hurry. He had plans for St Margaret's Bay. Big plans. Hotels, resort centres and leisure activities. Gerry wanted a big slice of the tourist action and he was determined to get it. The Sea View had been built in record time and nothing but the best had gone into it. With sixty bedrooms, a swimming-pool, hairdressers and a crèche, it seemed like the *crème de la crème* of hotels to Paula's innocent way of thinking.

She loved working there, not particularly as a house assistant . . . reception was where she aspired to be. But the air of hustle and bustle and glamour and elegance were like an injection of adrenalin into her veins. She loved watching the guests. Their clothes, their expensive luggage all fascinated her. Some day, she too was going to be able to swan into a hotel and order drinks or room service at the snap of her fingers. Out of the corner of her eye she saw Monica Boyle heading up the path on the other side of the large dividing lawn where Tony, one of the porters, was laying out loungers and umbrellas.

Paula quickened her step, she wanted to get in before Monica. Monica Boyle was a prize cow and Paula hated her guts. It hadn't been her fault that Monica's boyfriend, Peter, had developed a crush on Paula and kept pestering her to dance every Thursday night at the local disco. Did Monica honestly think that she would look twice at Peter when she was going with a catch like Conor Harrison? Was the girl deluded? Whatever had got into her head, she accused Paula of deliberately flirting with Peter and trying to break them up. Nothing that Paula could say to her would convince her otherwise. Since then she'd been a real wagon and unfortunately was also working as a house assistant in the Sea View for the summer holidays. Her snide comments and sneaky little ways had been very difficult to put up with. But who cared any more, thought Paula happily, today was her last day there.

Monica Boyle gave a great sigh of exasperation when she saw Paula Matthews striding briskly towards the hotel's entrance. How she detested that stuck-up little bitch . . . and how she envied her. Monica knew that when the Lord had been handing out good looks, He had skimped on her. God's gift to men she wasn't, especially when compared to Princess Matthews. Monica, at five foot seven, overweight and spotty, always felt like a lumbering elephant beside the petite but perfectly rounded blonde. As hard as she might try and find a flaw . . . and she *had* tried, Monica had to admit that when God created Paula Matthews He had given her it all. Big blue eyes, framed by perfect dark wing-tipped eyebrows. A delightful little button nose (not like her own beak). Shiny blonde hair, skin so creamy and peachy and completely unmarred by spots it would make you weep. A body that was slim and lithe with curves where curves were meant to be, not wobbly flabby bulges like her own. If that wasn't enough, Little Miss Perfect oozed self-confidence and had a bright bubbly personality that made her one of the most popular girls in the school. Whether Monica liked it or not, Miss Paula Matthews was perfection on legs. Some people just had all the luck. Still, that didn't give her the right to swipe other girls' fellas.

Monica gave a snort as she quickened her pace. She had been dating Peter Reilly for six months and had practically let him go all the way, the shit, when the Princess fluttered her eyelashes at him one night in the parish disco. Paula had been there on her own because that Conor Harrison, her boyfriend, was up in Dublin. Blatantly. Deliberately. Right under Monica's nose, she flirted with him. And Peter had gone running, as quick as his bandy legs could carry him, asking her to dance and making a right prat of himself.

Humiliation seared her heart at the memory. Her cheeks burned as she recalled the sly nudges of her classmates, who tittered and giggled as Peter made an ass of himself, buying Paula drinks, flattering her, saying she was the most beautiful girl in the world . . . no . . . not the world . . . the universe. Of course he'd been as pissed as a newt. He'd drunk half a flagon of cider before going to the dance. But Princess Paula lapped it all up and enjoyed the adoration. Needless to say, the following week, when Mister Conor was back, the two-faced wagon hadn't deigned to give Peter a look, despite all his efforts. Then of course he'd come crawling back to her.

It had been a hard decision to make, whether to take him back or not. But a faithless, fickle boyfriend was better than no boyfriend. Beggars couldn't be choosers, she decided after a turbulent wrestle with her hurt pride. So she took him back, but she was being very grudging with her favours. Much to Peter's dismay.

Well, thought Monica grimly, putting on a spurt as she saw her hated rival come parallel to her on the opposite path, Paula Matthews had better watch her step because if she could do her a bad turn ever, she would . . .

'Good morning, Miss Kelly.' Paula greeted the head housekeeper cheerfully as she signed her name in the attendance book. Behind her, she could hear Monica Boyle thundering along the corridor. Paula gave a little smile of satisfaction. She had made it to Miss Kelly's office before her antagonist. That would give Miss Boyle the needle for the day. Now she was in the best position to get the job of cleaning the manager's office. There was always fierce rivalry over the job of cleaning Mr Gorman's office. Cleaning the manager's office was the one way of getting noticed by him and getting noticed by the hotel manager was of paramount importance if one wanted to go further . . . to reception, for instance. Meeting people at the front desk. Being in the thick of it. It would give her great experience for when she finally went looking for a job in Dublin, after she'd finished school. Besides which, cleaning Mr Gorman's office was a doddle compared to cleaning the public areas, like the foyer and toilets, which were always done before breakfast. The hotel manager was a neat and tidy person, and so was his office.

'What do you want me to do this morning, Miss Kelly?' Paula asked politely just as Monica barged past her to sign on. Sheila Kelly tapped the duty roster with her pen.

'Today's your last day, Paula, and you've a family wedding, haven't you, later this afternoon so you wanted to go a bit early?'

'That's right, Miss Kelly.' Paula gave her boss a smile. Miss Kelly smiled back thinking it was a pity all her house assistants weren't as hard-working and dependable and as cheerful as the young teenager in front of her. She had been a bit dubious about taking her on, and Monica Boyle too, for that matter. They were both only fifteen. But Mr Gorman was all for employing staff from the locality and once there was a letter of permission from the parents all was in order. Paula Matthews had proved to be an excellent worker despite the housekeeper's misgivings and she was only sorry she was leaving so early in the season.

Miss Boyle was another kettle of fish and could do with pulling her socks up a bit. She was far too fond of nipping into the staff hall for a cigarette, and flirting and gossiping with the housemen and porters. And she was just a bit too lax about her work. Only last week her duties had included cleaning the manager's office and she had forgotten to empty the wastepaper basket. Mr Gorman was decidedly unimpressed and, as Monica was on the housekeeping staff, this reflected badly on the head housekeeper's training of her assistants. Sheila was furious and ordered one of her assistant housekeepers to keep a very watchful eye on Madame Boyle's work.

Paula did her share of flirting and gossiping, to be sure.

She was extremely popular with the male staff but her work was always done properly and that was all Sheila cared about. Paula Matthews's bedrooms were a credit to her. They were always finished by the end of her shift. She wasn't like that lazy lump Mrs Gunne, who invariably left two or three rooms unfinished which the rest of the assistants had to help her with. The housekeeper didn't mind someone not being finished before the end of shift. Sometimes it was unavoidable. Guests often liked to linger in their rooms and that tended to delay the process. But Mrs Gunne was far too cute, and used that excuse at every opportunity. If she thought that the housekeeper wasn't wise to her tricks, she had another think coming. Sheila Kelly had worked her way up from the bottom to her present position. She knew all the tricks of the trade, and young and all as Paula was she was worth three Josie Gunnes any day. She had actually caught the woman sitting on a bed in one of the rooms eating fruit from the complimentary basket. Josie hadn't even the grace to look ashamed. What a pity Paula was leaving, a good worker was worth her weight in gold in the housekeeping section.

Paula waited patiently as the housekeeper flicked through the duty lists until she found hers.

'Ah yes, here we are, Paula. I've given you the manager's office, my office, and five overnights on the top floor. The room numbers are on your sheet. Then you can just relieve Maddy Carroll in the linen room for an early lunch at twelve and you'll be free to go at twelve-thirty.'

'Thanks very much, Miss Kelly.' Paula was secretly chuffed. This was the third morning in a row that she'd been given the manager's office and only overnights. That was brilliant, most of the overnights left after breakfast so she wouldn't have to hang around waiting for her rooms to be vacated. And Miss Kelly had only given her five rooms to do. Usually she had twelve. Miss Kelly liked her, she knew that. The housekeeper had told her several times that she was an excellent worker. God knows her mother had trained her well. There was always plenty of hoovering and polishing and bed-making to be done at home and, whether she liked it or not, she had to do it. Getting paid to do it made it much more palatable. Paula knew if she was going to get on, her work would have to be up to scratch. Any fool knew that. And it paid off. Look at today when she'd only five bedrooms to do before getting off early. In the background she could hear Monica's sharp intake of breath as she read her duty list. The assistant housekeepers were always on Monica's trail, checking out her work. It was her own fault, of course, because she was so slapdash. If she wasn't careful she'd get the boot. Monica had once called Paula a lick-arse after Miss Kelly complimented her on her work. If Monica expected Paula to be annoyed she'd made a big mistake.

'Monica, the fact that you can't differentiate between lick-arsery and ambition is the reason you'll never amount to anything and I will.' The other girl was horsing mad and had called her a stuck-up fuckin' bitch.

'Charming,' Paula drawled, not in the slightest put out. She didn't give a hoot what Monica Boyle thought about her one way or the other.

'Oh and Monica, I want you and Esther to divide up Paula's remaining rooms between you as she's leaving early today,' the housekeeper instructed her thoroughly disgruntled colleague as Monica went to replenish her work-basket with clean dusters and polish and bathroom cleaner.

She had cleaned the two offices before it was time for breakfast in the staff hall and at eight-thirty was tucking into bacon and egg. Monica arrived five minutes later, full of glowers and muttered comments about people skiving off expecting other people to do their work. She was just about to fill her plate when one of the assistant housekeepers came and demanded that Monica finish hoovering the foyer before she started breakfast. She told her that she should know better than to leave one of the public areas half done before breakfast.

Thank God I won't have to sit looking at her mush for breakfast, Paula thought gratefully. And then I won't have to see her until September. The thought cheered her up immensely and she enjoyed her breakfast, joining in the lively chit-chat and banter that went on around her. She was just finishing her coffee when Esther Walsh arrived in beetroot red and giggling uproariously.

'Oh lads, ye'll never guess. Amn't I just after barging in on top of the hunk in 301 and there he was standing in all his glory with a willie on him that would put a randy elephant to shame. I'm not the better of it.' She collapsed in a chair all afluster.

'Arrah you have all the luck, Esther Walsh, he's a fine thing, why didn't you give his stalk a pull, you might have got a big tip when he was leaving?' Josie Gunne gave a lewd chuckle.

'Oh you're a filthy-minded slut, you never think of anything else,' giggled Esther.

'That's 'cos I never get any, my fella's got a permanent brewer's droop,' Josie snorted.

That's what you think, Paula said to herself. Charlie Gunne was a notorious lecher always making crude comments to the young girls of the village. It was well known, except to Josie, that he was having an affair with Angela Brennan, the local hairdresser. And hard up she must be to let a creep like Charlie Gunne near her, Paula considered as she finished her coffee and headed off to make up the bedrooms.

Number 208 was vacant so she drew the curtains, opened the windows wide, put the breakfast tray outside the door and then began to strip the bed. The guest who had stayed the previous night had left the room in good condition. Sometimes people left them in a shambles, she reflected, as she put on fresh pillowcases and spread freshly laundered crisp white sheets on the mattress.

She didn't get away so lightly with her second room. There were red wine stains on the bedspread so she had to go and get a clean one from the linen press. There was a big cigarette burn on the bedside locker that necessitated a call to maintenance, and there were two shitty disposable nappies in a corner of the bathroom and a scummy ring around the bath which made her heart sink.

When she knocked on the door of her third bedroom, the door was opened by a woman in her mid-twenties. She was wearing a pristine terry-towelling robe and had obviously just showered and washed her hair. She was tanned and glamorous-looking and Paula felt a familiar twinge of envy. How she would love to be on the other side of that door. It must be wonderful to be a guest in a hotel. To have room service breakfast and not have to wash up after it. To be able to get out of bed and not have to turn around and make it. To be able to linger in a bath with water that came up to your shoulders and not have to worry about how much hot water you were using. What luxury.

'I'll be checking out in about twenty minutes,' the woman assured her, and in the background Paula could see a smart suit laid on the bed and a slim leather briefcase open on the floor. A businesswoman! Paula was deeply impressed. Businessmen occasionally stayed at the hotel but this was the first time she had seen a smart sophisticated businesswoman. She wondered what line of business she was in. It didn't matter. It was clear she had it made whatever she was. Paula closed the door with a smile. She could do up the room next door. She knew it was vacant because she'd seen the couple who'd occupied it walking down the corridor with their luggage. She'd made up the bed and was standing at the big trolley in the corridor getting soaps, shower caps and shampoo for the bathroom when the woman walked out of the bedroom. She smiled at Paula and strode briskly down the corridor. Paula watched with huge admiration. The woman looked so classy and in control in her superbly tailored grey suit with a scarlet silk scarf around her neck and a matching red silk triangle in her breast pocket. In her right hand she carried her briefcase, and over her right shoulder a smart shoulder bag. In her left hand she carried an elegant overnight bag. She oozed confidence and Paula felt uplifted looking at her. There was nothing to stop her from being like that woman. Nothing at all. One day people would look at her and be as impressed as Paula was right now. With renewed vim and vigour she turned back to her trolley. Somehow she knew she was going to get out of St Margaret's Bay and go on to greater things.

A door across the corridor opened and she saw Brian Whelan, one of the barmen, emerge with his arm around Kim Bennett, one of the waitresses. He winked when he saw Paula. Kim, who was only six months married to a local fisherman, laughed as brazen as you like. Helen maintained that St Margaret's Bay was a den of iniquity. Sin City she called it. Her aunt was always amazed to hear of the various affairs and carry-ons. Dublin was only trotting after them, she maintained.

Paula was dying to see Helen. They were going to have so much fun in the next few weeks. She had been living for her trip to the capital and now it was almost upon her. Paula hummed a cheerful ditty to herself, knowing that in a couple of hours she would be as free as a bird for the rest of the summer.

'Are you sure you don't want me to come to this wedding with you, Helen?' Anthony Larkin inquired grimly.

'No, thank you,' his wife responded curtly with icy politeness.

'You can't go down there on your own. What are people going to say?' Anthony paced up and down the kitchen.

Helen glared at her husband as she paused momentarily from wrapping Louise's wedding present.

'Frankly, Anthony, I couldn't care less what people say. If you think for one minute I'm going down to St Margaret's with you in tow playing lovey-dovey couples just to keep other people happy you've got another think coming. A hypocrite I am not and never have been. I don't go around being two-faced about things. I leave that to you,' she said bitterly.

'There's no need for that,' he retorted. 'No need for that at all. I think you're being totally unreasonable. I'm only thinking of you.' Helen ignored him. How dare he! Just how bloody dare he arrive in at that hour of the morning as if nothing was wrong, all prepared to go to Louise's wedding. And the galling thing was he expected her to fall at his feet and thank him for his magnanimity. Well stuff him!

'Look, Helen, there's no need for this kind of behaviour. We should discuss it. We are adults, after all—'

'Listen, Anthony, don't you dare come and lecture *me* on how to behave. What a nerve. I have nothing to discuss with you. Absolutely nothing. Now or ever. You don't have to worry about me. It's a bit late for that now. You made your choice, now I'm making mine. So if you'll excuse me I'm leaving to go to Louise's wedding. On my own . . .'

Paula breezed into the linen room all ready to relieve Maddy Carroll, who went eagerly to her lunch. It was hot and very stuffy and there was a constant noisy drone from the big washing-machines and dryers. Paula was glad she didn't work in here all the time. It was very hard work. She had just filled one of the huge washing-machines with sheets when a call came on the internal phone to tell her she was wanted at reception by one of the American guests who was checking out. She left what she was doing and walked swiftly down the corridor and along by the offices.

'Paula,' Miss Kelly called her as she passed the head housekeeper's office.

'Yes, Miss Kelly?'

'Aren't you supposed to be in the linen room?'

'Yes, Miss Kelly, but a guest is asking for me at reception,' Paula explained. The housekeeper smiled. 'That will be Mr Munroe. He was asking me about you earlier.

It seems he was very impressed by your courtesy and helpfulness and he wants to say thank you personally. Congratulations. That's the kind of thing we like to hear. It gives the hotel a good name.'

'Thank you, Miss Kelly,' Paula murmured. Mr Munroe was an old dote. She had given him extra pillows and blankets and flirted away with him. After all, he was harmless, he was nearly eighty.

'Go up and say goodbye to Mr Munroe then, he's waiting,' her boss instructed.

Where was Paula Matthews sneaking off to, Monica wondered as she saw the petite blonde marching down the corridor looking as if she owned the place. She peered into the linen room. It was empty. She might as well have a quick fag, she decided. She was starving but she was on late lunch, she had a bar of chocolate in her pocket so she could scoff that to keep her going. She munched away happily and lit up a cigarette. Still no sign of Princess Matthews. Monica's gaze alighted on the only silent washing-machine in the room. The door was still open and a pile of dirty sheets were waiting to be washed. A devilish thought made her eyes gleam and she peered around looking for the starch. She found it among the huge containers of washing powders and set to work with great haste. When she had finished that little task she set the dials to the hottest boil wash and started to laugh.

Ha ha, ya little Queen of Tarts, she thought happily. Let's see the smug smirk wiped off your face when this lot comes out of the wash.

'Ah, Monica,' she heard a familiar voice say. 'It's nice to see someone happy in their work. I've just come to attend to that last wash. Paula told me she hadn't done it, but I see you've done the job for me. I let her go early. I'll stay here for the next twenty minutes until Maddy comes back so you can get back to your rooms. I'm sure you've a few to finish yet?'

Monica swallowed hard . . . twice.

'Mmm . . . aah . . . yyy . . . yes, Miss Kelly,' she muttered, raising a mental fist to the Almighty. Couldn't He have let her away with it just *once*?

Like Eliza Dolittle, she could have danced all night, Paula thought happily as Conor whirled her around the dance floor. It had been a wonderful wedding. After the Mass in the Star of the Sea, they had all driven in convoy to the hotel in Waterford where the reception was being held. Paula was the Belle of the Ball in her aquamarine off-the-shoulder bridesmaid's dress. There was no denying it. She was having a great time. There was as much fuss being made of her by the friends and relations as there was of Louise, who was a vision in white satin and tulle.

Conor could hardly keep his hands off her and when they danced the slow sets he got a huge erection. Paula smiled at Helen, who was dancing with Pete. Helen smiled back but her heart wasn't in it. Her aunt looked awfully strained and tired, Paula reflected. She definitely wasn't her usual bubbly self. Anthony had to go on an unexpected trip so he'd missed the wedding and Helen drove all the way from Dublin after leaving at eight am. Maybe she was just tired. Thoughts of her aunt were instantly banished as Conor nuzzled her ear. Paula smiled to herself. She had great plans for them later on. She pressed herself against him and heard his breathing quicken.

'Oh Paula! Oooh Paula Paula,' Conor groaned, rubbing himself frantically against her thigh as he shoved her petticoats and voluminous dress up around her waist in his desperate search for her panties. Gasping for breath he struggled to move them down Paula's lissom legs.

'Don't be in such a rush,' she murmured. His frenzy excited her enormously. Louise wasn't the only one who'd be losing her virginity tonight, she thought with satisfaction as Conor panted noisily.

'Calm down.' She smiled into glazed eyes. 'We have all night.'

'I can't. I can't! Oh I love you I love you I love you!' He moaned and then, before she knew it, he entered her, gave two hasty thrusts and collapsed in a heap on top of her.

Paula's eyes opened wide in dismay and her jaw dropped. Was that it? Was that what all the fuss was about? What a swizz. What an absolute and utter swizz. She was so annoyed she felt like shaking Conor off her and going home.

'*That* was awesome,' her lover breathed, using his current favourite Americanism.

Paula did not share his enthusiasm. He had let her down . . . badly. According to himself he had had more women than hot dinners. What a spoofer. He'd been just as much a virgin as she had. She'd stake her holiday savings on it. And she'd been so looking forward to tonight. Well Mister Conor Harrison was not going to practise on her. She wanted a real man who knew what he was doing. Tomorrow she'd be going to Dublin and Mr Magnificent was going to be dropped like a hot potato. The cheek of him, letting on he was a man of the world. She was mad with herself for having fallen for it.

'Bring me home,' she snapped, hoping that Louise was faring better than she had.

Conor couldn't believe his ears.

'But I've a free house! The folks are in Provence and Amy's gone to Cork for the weekend.'

'I have to pack to go to Dublin.' Paula wriggled out from underneath him and adjusted her clothing.

'Ah Paula!' he wailed, 'you said we had all night.'

'I changed my mind,' she retorted, hauling her hoop up under her petticoats.

'All right,' he said sullenly, reluctantly pulling up his trousers and underpants, which were at half mast around his calves.

If he'd told her to get lost and go home by herself she'd have had more respect for him, she thought glumly as they walked down the street to her house in silence. But no, he'd let her walk all over him and acted the wimp. Now that he'd fallen off his pedestal she was going right off him . . . even if he did love her. Hearing him say it hadn't been half as gratifying as she'd anticipated. The night was a complete fiasco as far as she was concerned.

'Goodnight, Conor.' She gave him a swift peck on the cheek and, before he could protest, she was inside her house and the door was shut firmly in his face. Paula paused for a moment to compose herself and an unaccustomed sound made her frown. It was the sound of crying. Something was wrong. What was it? She opened the door of the sitting-room and saw Helen cradled in Maura's arms sobbing her heart out. Her father looked grim-faced.

'What's wrong? What is it?' she asked in alarm.

'It's Anthony. He's having an affair and he's left Helen. The bastard.' Maura swore.

'My God!' Paula was dumbfounded.

'Go to bed, Paula,' her father said quietly. 'Helen will be up in a while.' Silently she did as she was bid, too shocked by what she had heard to say anything. It was totally incredible. Anthony was the last person in the world she would ever have thought would have an affair. He was mad about Helen. He was always buying her treats and bringing her out to dinner, not to talk about the expensive holidays. How on earth could he prefer another woman to her glamorous, gorgeous-looking aunt? She just couldn't fathom it. She tossed and turned waiting patiently for Helen to come to bed. There was no need for the couch tonight. Rebecca was staying with a friend in Waterford and Helen was sleeping in Louise's bed. Her own little drama was almost forgotten as she tried to imagine the reasons for her uncle's affair.

Dawn was breaking before her aunt slipped into the room, red-eyed and exhausted-looking. Paula sat up in bed and held out her arms to her. 'I'll tell you all about it on the way home tomorrow, my darling,' Helen whispered. 'I'm too tired now.'

'Helen, I've been lying here thinking. You'll probably need company and someone to help you through this,' she said breathlessly, her eyes shining. 'Why don't I come and live with you in Dublin?'

Chapter Nine

'I'm scared, Jim,' Kit Myles said in the taxi that was taking her to the Rotunda Hospital. She was having labour pains, it was her first baby and she was absolutely petrified.

'Don't be, you'll be fine. The doctor said there was nothing to worry about,' her husband sought to reassure her. She gripped his hand even more tightly and he tried not to grimace. Her nails were digging into the palm of his hand.

It was all right for him to tell her not to worry, he wasn't going to have to face what she was, she thought miserably. Pain and lots of it, as well as being shaved and having an enema. After that it was the great unknown.

Last week she'd been coming home from town on the bus and a woman sat beside her. Seeing Kit so obviously pregnant she'd settled down and proceeded to regale the horrified Kit with every gory detail of her five confinements. Each birth was considerably worse than the last, she assured her with relish. Kit got off the bus pale-faced and cried for hours afterwards. She'd never ever do that to someone, especially someone expecting their first baby. It was too cruel for words.

'Nearly there,' Jim said comfortingly. This had the effect of doubling her heart rate and making beads of perspiration stand out on her forehead. She thought she was going to be sick she was so nervous. It was a Sunday afternoon and people walked through town, carefree and happy. She saw couples going into the Gresham Hotel and envied them so much. What she would give to be strolling down O'Connell Street hand in hand with Jim.

Without a care in the world. Kit walked through the portals of the Rotunda Hospital as if she was going to her doom.

'We'll take care of your wife now, Mr Myles,' a nurse said reassuringly. 'You can wait in the fathers' waiting-room.' Jim kissed her and gave her an encouraging hug. As she watched her husband disappear down the corridor, Kit had never felt so alone and scared in her life.

'Don't worry, Mrs Myles, you'll be fine,' the nurse comforted her. 'Just relax and do what we tell you and you'll have no trouble at all.'

'I bet you say that to everyone.' Kit gave a shaky smile. But to her surprise she started to feel less nervous.

'Of course I do,' laughed the nurse. 'Just think, this time tomorrow it will be over and you'll have a little girl or boy in your arms. You'll have forgotten all about this. Just keep thinking like that and you'll be grand.'

This time tomorrow it will be all over, Kit told herself as she was shaved.

I'm never having another child, she promised herself as she endured her first enema.

I'm never speaking to Jim Myles again, she vowed fiercely, trying not to yell as the pains gripped her. There was hardly any respite between them. The woman next door had no compunction about yelling. The screeches out of her as she called her husband all the names she could think of would have been funny at any other time. Right now, Kit was incapable of finding it funny. She didn't want to make a fuss, but she was very much afraid that if the pains got worse she was going to end up screeching too and she knew the names she'd be calling Jim. If he thought for one minute that he was ever going to have sex with her again, he was very much mistaken. Their sex life was well and truly over and that was for sure.

She was never ever going to go through an ordeal like this again. And the only way to ensure that she never got pregnant again was by never having sex again. The nurse laughed when Kit told her of her decision through gritted teeth.

'If I had a pound for every time I heard that, I'd be a rich woman. You'll be here again, Mrs Myles, don't even doubt it.'

'Oh no I won't.' Kit groaned as she gave her final push and heard a baby's cry.

'It's a girl, Mrs Myles. Congratulations, you were great!' the nurse praised her as Kit burst into tears.

Later, the nurse handed Kit her baby. 'Now! Wasn't it all worthwhile?' Kit looked at the downy little black head nestling against her breast.

'Yes,' she smiled tearfully. 'She was. Tell Jim, won't you? I hope he won't be disappointed, he was hoping for a boy. We were going to call him Brendan.'

'He'll be thrilled,' the nurse assured her. 'You'll be able to call her Brenda now.'

'Yeah.' Kit smiled happily as she forgot all about her ordeal and enjoyed the truly special pleasure of holding her first-born child.

'Brenda suits her down to the ground.'

Chapter Ten

'I want to wear my pink dress, Daddy. Mammy always lets me.' Four-year-old Brenda Myles stamped her little foot as her father looked on helplessly. It was three days after the birth of his second daughter and he was bringing their first-born to the hospital to see her mammy and new baby sister.

'It's not ironed, Brenda, and we don't have time. Now put on this gorgeous white dress and come on, Mammy's dying to see you and wait until you see the baby.'

'Don't want to see the baby,' Brenda said sulkily. Baby! Baby! Baby! that's all everyone was talking about these days. She was just getting fed up with it, she thought as she put her arms up for her daddy to put the hated white dress on. She didn't like all this carry-on. She wanted her mammy to be at home and not in that place they were going to this afternoon. Everybody kept asking her if she was excited about the new baby. Everything was going to change, she just knew it was. Mammy and Daddy kept talking about this new baby who was coming to live in their house. Brenda didn't want anyone else living in her house. Just Mammy, Daddy and herself. They could give this new baby to Auntie Ellen. That's what she'd tell Mammy. Why didn't she think of it before? 'Am I beautiful, Daddy?' Brenda did a happy twirl.

'Beautiful, like a princess,' her father assured her, lifting her up and swinging her till she screamed with delight.

Brenda felt very pleased walking beside her daddy up the stairs of the big place where her mammy was. Her mammy would be home soon and the new baby was going to go to Auntie Ellen's.

'Look, there's Mammy and the new baby.' Daddy pointed a finger into a room with a lot of beds in it. She could see her mother in the middle of the room, sitting in a big chair beside her bed. Brenda ran across the floor, her shoes making a loud noise on the wooden floorboards. 'Mammy, Mammy, Mammy.' She held out her arms and was enfolded in a hug that she didn't want to end. Brenda buried her face in her mother's neck. 'Will you come home today and you can give the baby to Auntie Ellen 'cos she's no babies?'

'Oh Brenda,' she heard her mother laugh. 'Holy God gave me the baby for you.'

'Tell him it's all right, we don't need one,' Brenda said in desperation. Somehow she knew the Auntie Ellen plan wasn't going to work. Her heart sank and she wanted to cry. It wasn't fair. It just wasn't fair and why did Holy God want to go interfering sending down a new baby to her when she'd much prefer to have had a new doll or even better, and what she really longed for . . . a puppy.

'Look, Brenda,' she heard her mother say. 'Say hello. Say hello to your new sister, Jennifer.'

Chapter Eleven

'But it's my birthday, Mammy. What about my party? You said I could have a party. I don't want to go into the hospital to see Jennifer. Why does she always have to be sick and ruin things? It's just not fair.' Brenda flung herself down on the sofa and started snivelling.

'Oh for heaven's sake, Brenda,' her mother said impatiently. 'We'll be having your party after we've gone in to visit Jennifer. Stop being selfish.'

'I'm not being selfish,' Brenda screeched. 'Nobody cares about me anyway. It's always the same. Everyone always makes a fuss of Jennifer and the boys. I just hate being the eldest.' She was feeling ever so sorry for herself. She'd been really looking forward to her party for ages and ages. All her friends on the street, and some of her friends from school, had been invited. Then Miss Jennifer had gone and got sick yet again and all the attention was on her. She did it on purpose, Brenda knew she did.

Her mother sat down beside her. 'Come on now, lovie, don't be like that. I know you're looking forward to your party and we'll have one. It's just unfortunate that poor old Jenny had to go into hospital again. And if you were in hospital, wouldn't you like the family to come in and see you?' Kit Myles tried to keep the irritation out of her voice.

'I suppose so,' Brenda said sulkily, feeling very hard done by. She wanted to make her mother feel guilty for upsetting her party by insisting on going into Temple Street in the afternoon.

'Run up and put on your new dress and brush your

hair and give Sean's hair a brush while I change the baby's nappy.'

'Ah Mammy, do I have to brush his hair, he always yells?' Brenda pouted. 'And anyway it's my birthday. No-one has to do anything on their birthday. That's the rule.'

'Oh go on,' her mother sighed. 'I'll do it myself.'

Brenda gave a martyred sniff. Now she was being made feel guilty. It was always the same, she fumed as she headed up to the bedroom she shared with Jennifer. It was such a nuisance being the oldest. She always had to help out with the baby, and Sean, and of course Jennifer. Jennifer who was always sick with that kidney thing and ended up in hospital getting loads of fuss made of her. Brenda plonked herself down on the bed and gave a deep sigh. She longed to break an arm or a leg or an ankle or a wrist, just so she could land herself in hospital and get tons of sympathy. She'd never been in hospital in her life. Except when she was born, of course, and that didn't count because she couldn't remember it. Her friend Kathy was in the same boat. She was the eldest too and had to look after her younger brothers and sisters too. She was even worse off than Brenda. There were five younger than Kathy in her family.

She gave another deep sigh. She'd been really looking forward to her eighth birthday for ages. After much pleading and promises that she'd never ask for anything else again as long as she lived, her mother had finally agreed to have a party. Brenda had been thrilled skinny. She'd told everybody on the street about the forthcoming party weeks in advance. In a way she was sorry she was on her school holidays. She would have liked the whole class to know that she was having a party. Some of her friends on the street were in her class but she would have liked Cora Delahunty, who was a real snooty show-off, to know. Cora went to acting and dancing classes and could recite the entire alphabet without drawing a breath. She really thought she was *IT* and she pranced around in skirts so short that you could see her knickers. Of course, Cora didn't wear navy or plain white cotton knickers like everyone else. Oh no, hers were pink or blue frilly things. She was always dressed to the nines.

Cora Delahunty was really sly too. Brenda frowned thinking of her classmate's slyness. The great craze this year at school had been collecting beads. Practically every girl, from first class to sixth class, had a collection of beads and the thing was to swap for a particular bead you might fancy. Well of course Madame Delahunty had *the* collection but Brenda had a beautiful set of amber glass beads that her gran had given her and Cora asked her would she like to swap one for one of Cora's. Brenda said no at first but Cora was not one to give up easily and she was ever so attentive to Brenda that week in school. Playing with her, flattering her, linking her in the playground. Finally Brenda succumbed and agreed to swap for a pretty mother-of-pearl bead. Cora was overjoyed that she'd at last got the bead she wanted. Beaming, she dropped her own bead into Brenda's box. It was only later that Brenda noticed a dirty off-white plastic bead in her collection. She just couldn't believe that Cora had played such a dirty trick on her. But she had. No mother-of-pearl type bead reposed in Brenda's box. Of course, Cora denied outright that she hadn't given the mother-of-pearl bead to her classmate and accused Brenda of losing it. After that, there was no more flattery, no more linking in the yard. In fact Cora dropped Brenda like a hot potato. Secretly Brenda was devastated. She had very much enjoyed being part of Cora's much-envied entourage. She'd even gone to tea at Cora's, which was a treat reserved for only the chosen few. Kathy and the others who sat in Brenda's row at school had been deeply envious. Now Cora was ignoring her as if she didn't exist. It was extremely galling.

If she'd been at school, Cora would have heard all about the party and, being Cora, would be mad to go to it so she could do her fancy dancing and recitations and impress everybody. Brenda would've had the pleasure of keeping her on tenterhooks as to whether or not she was going to get an invitation. That revenge would have been sweet. But, Brenda reflected, the way things were going, maybe it was just as well Cora didn't know about the party. Having to delay it while they all went into Temple Street was nothing to boast about. With another sigh, Brenda went to put her party dress on.

'Ah Gerard!' Kit exclaimed in exasperation as she heard her one-year-old son performing in the clean nappy she had just put on him. If she didn't get a move on, they'd miss the two o'clock bus from the terminus, and it would be all hours before they got into the hospital. God knows she could do without Brenda's party today, she mused as she unfastened her son's nappy and wiped his dirty bum. It was unfortunate that poor Jennifer's kidney infection had been such a bad one. The poor child was as sick as a dog and they'd decided to keep her in until her temperature was normal. It had been a good while since she'd had that old infection, the doctors had told Kit that she would grow out of them.

The sooner the better, Kit thought tiredly as she put her squalling infant back in his pram and went in search of Sean, his three-year-old brother. Sean, as usual, did not want his hair brushed and a yelling match ensued. By the time she had him cleaned up she was fit to be tied. She was just coming up to her period and she was like a demon. She had one of those awful hormony headaches that made her feel as if her brains were going to explode out of her head. Her stomach was horribly bloated, she felt queasy and she wanted to scream at the children. It was such an effort to keep her temper under control. More than anything, Kit would have loved to go up to bed, pull the curtains, and lie in the soothing darkness and shut out the world for an hour even. Well at least she wasn't pregnant, she thought wryly as she ran a comb through her hair and traced a coral lipstick across her lips.

Her mother-in-law was ailing too. Kit usually called in to do a bit of cleaning for her, or make the tea. Today, with the party and everything, she'd have to skip it. Mrs Myles wouldn't mind but no doubt that old rip of a husband of hers, Dan, would have a face on him because his tea wasn't on the table.

Kit's mouth tightened at the thought of her father-in-law. She couldn't stand him. He was a right old bully. His word was law, as far as he was concerned. He even had the nerve to try and tell her what to do and she a grown woman with four children. Jim allowed his father to treat him as if he was a child. It infuriated Kit and they often rowed about it. His own daughter would have nothing to do with him and Kit couldn't really blame her. He had ordered her not to marry her boyfriend or, if she did, never to darken his door again. The poor girl had been in bits. Kit had had a terrible time trying to persuade her to marry John, who was a lovely chap. He was an artist. In Dan's eyes this was most definitely not a proper job. No daughter of his was going to marry a layabout who couldn't afford to keep her, he ranted and raved. In the end, there'd been a huge row. Ellen left home and went to live with Kit and Jim. It was from their house she had finally married her artist. Jim gave her away. Kit was her matron-of-honour and the only other guests were John's family. Mrs Myles was heartbroken not to be at the wedding of her only daughter, and never got over it. Her husband's hold on her was strong and he'd issued an edict that she was never to see or speak to her daughter again.

'Nonsense,' Kit fumed. 'Just let me know when you're dropping in for a cup of tea and a chat and I'll arrange for Ellen to be here. He'll never know,' Kit instructed her mother-in-law. The first time Mrs Myles met her daughter at Kit's she'd been a nervous wreck, even though her husband had been at work in the factory where he was a foreman, on the other side of the city. Gradually, over the weeks and months, she'd begun to relax until she got to the stage where she really enjoyed the illicit meetings.

She liked getting the better of her husband for the first time in years of marriage, she confided one day as she and Kit washed up after their very enjoyable afternoon tea. Kit loved to see that sparkle of excitement in her mother-in-law's eyes when she arrived on her weekly visit. She was very fond of Mrs Myles and she couldn't fathom how she'd lived with Dan and his overbearing ways all these years. Dan, who couldn't conceive of the notion of his wife flouting his authority, never discovered the secret meetings. They went on over the years, and Mrs Myles had the joy of holding Ellen's babies in her arms and watching them grow into two happy-go-lucky children.

Then she'd got sick and, as her illness took hold, her visits became less frequent until finally she became too sick to leave her own house. Ellen went home a few times during the afternoons when her father was sure to be at work but Mrs Myles had been so edgy and nervous about it she stopped going. Looking at her mother-in-law, who was visibly failing, Kit knew she wasn't going to last much longer. Well by God, when she died, that was the last Dan Myles would see of her. She'd never set foot in his house again. Jim could go and see his father if he wished. That was up to him. But she wanted to have nothing to do with him. The mean old bastard. He would have let his wife die without seeing her daughter and grandchildren. Kit hoped he'd rot in hell.

Somehow or another she'd get a chance to pop round and visit her mother-in-law, she decided as she finally got her offspring out the front door. Rounding the corner at the end of the street, Kit almost wept with frustration as she saw the No. 13 bus disappear down St Pappin's Road.

Brenda was having a splendid time. Auntie Ellen and Mammy had made loads of lovely sandwiches. There were egg ones, her favourite. And banana, and chicken and ham roll. There was lovely ice cream and jelly and Perri crisps and jelly babies and lemonade. It was a *brilliant* party. Everybody was saying so. Her cousins

Pamela and Susan were there and all her friends on the street and they were having a picnic in the back garden. She'd got some lovely presents too. Even Jennifer had drawn her a card and sung *Happy Birthday* to her in the hospital. Then she'd started bawling crying when they were leaving. Brenda had seen her mother crying too as they walked down the stairs of the hospital, with Jennifer's wails following them. It had given Brenda an awful shock to see her mother with tears sliding down her cheeks as they left Temple Street. She'd felt a bit lonely and scared. She'd never seen her mammy crying before. She was crying because she was sad leaving Jennifer. Jennifer was her pet, Brenda just knew it and it made her feel most unhappy.

She'd only stopped feeling unhappy when they'd finally got home and the party guests had started arriving. Then she'd started to feel special again. And when her mammy brought them all inside and lit the eight candles on the cake and everybody had sung *Happy Birthday* and *For She's a Jolly Good Fellow*, she felt so excited and happy. She blew out the candles and everybody cheered and her mother put her arms around her and hugged her and told her she was very proud of her. Then her daddy came in from work and made them light the candles again so he could sing *Happy Birthday* to her and she felt like bursting with pride. Then they all played blind man's buff and while they were in the middle of it, there was a knock at the front door. Brenda was the nearest so she opened it. Standing on the step, wearing the frilliest dress Brenda had ever seen, was Cora Delahunty. Standing two paces behind her was Cora's best friend, Claire Regan. She too was wearing a posh dress, although it wasn't quite as frilly as Cora's.

'Hello Brenda,' Cora said, giving her sweetest smile.

'Hello,' Brenda responded guardedly. What was Miss Cora up to? Then it dawned on her. Of course. Cora had found out about the party and had decided it was time to be friends so she could get in.

'Would you like to swap some beads?' Cora held out her box. 'You can have whatever one you like.' She smiled ingratiatingly.

Intense happiness flooded through Brenda as she stood at her front door watching Cora demean herself. Suddenly all the hurt and frustration of being dropped like a hot potato was worth it. Just for this moment.

'No thank you, Cora,' she said cordially as the noise from the sitting-room reached a climax because her father had been caught and a crowd of cheering guests had launched themselves upon him.

'I can't stop to swap beads now,' she explained ever so politely. 'It's my birthday, you see, and I'm having a party.' Then Brenda closed the door, leaving Cora and her attendant in tears of rage. It was the best birthday party of her entire life, she thought, admiring herself in the mirror before rejoining her guests. She felt very grown-up. When she went to secondary school she'd be able to have boys at her party. *That* was something to look forward to.

Chapter Twelve

'Will you come on, we're going to be late,' Jennifer heard her sister yell up the stairs. She threw her eyes up to heaven. That Brenda, she was always making a fuss about something.

'It's fine, Mammy,' she said hastily to her mother, who was arranging her Holy Communion veil on her head.

'Brenda can wait a minute or two, you've loads of time,' Kit said calmly.

'Ooh Mammy, you know her,' Jennifer groaned. 'She always likes to be early.'

'Go on, go on, here, don't forget your basket.' Kit handed her the basket filled to the brim with rose petals and apple blossom. Jennifer was a flower girl in the Corpus Christi procession and Brenda and Kathy, who were prefects in the sodality, were in charge of the flower girls.

Jennifer raced down the stairs trying not to let any of the precious petals escape from the basket. It was a great honour to be a flower girl. All the Holy Communion class and several girls out of each of the other classes had been chosen specially. Beth and herself and Norma Murray and Suzy Doherty were the girls picked out of her class.

'It's about bloomin' time,' Brenda snapped. 'You're always the same.'

'Would you get lost, you didn't have to wait. Beth and I can go by ourselves.'

'Mammy said you were to come with Kathy and me. You're only a *child*.'

'I am not,' Jennifer exploded. 'I'm nearly nine.'

'And I'm a teenager,' her sister said with disdain.

'Not yet, you're not,' Jennifer fumed. 'Not for two months.'

'Oh shut up and come on,' Brenda said impatiently.

'Bossy boots.' Jennifer scowled.

'For heaven's sake the two of you, would you stop fighting!' Kit appeared at the top of the stairs. 'A fine pair to be going on a procession. Heavens above, wouldn't you think you'd make an effort to get on. I wish I had a sister to share my trials and tribulations with and God knows I've enough trials and tribulations with you two.' She glared at them. 'Don't make a holy show of me arguing on the street, I'm warning you. Now off you go and behave yourselves. I'll be keeping an eye on you so be told.'

In sullen silence the two girls walked out the front door and headed for Kathy and Beth's house. Jennifer was raging. Brenda had gone and got her into trouble with her mother for nothing and she'd wanted to ask her if she could stay with her cousin Pamela for the night. If there was one thing Jennifer really enjoyed it was sleeping over at her cousin's. Pamela's house was a bit posh. She had her own room and Susie, her other cousin, had hers. Pamela had a record player in her room and a collection of Beatles records. Jennifer adored the Beatles but her absolute favourite was Elvis. Pamela let her play *Wooden Heart* as many times as she liked when she stayed over. Pamela also had a collection of make-up filched from her mother's dressing-table. Used lipsticks and foundation and eyeshadows. They had the greatest fun experimenting in the privacy of Pamela's room.

Then, of course, there were the suppers. Jennifer never had supper at home. Once tea was over, that was it in the Myles household. But Auntie Ellen and Uncle John always had supper and so did Susie and Pamela. Pamela was allowed to make her own. She always had cocoa with loads of sugar in it. And cream crackers and cheese. Or cheese on toast, which was Jennifer's favourite. After which they'd have biscuits. And not just plain Marietta or Arrowroot either. After an evening playing 'Office' Jennifer was more than ready for a hearty supper.

'Office' was a game of her own invention and they had such fun playing it. They had two cases of 'documents' collected from all kinds of places. The local supermarkets were excellent sources. She and Pamela would collect as many promotional and competition leaflets as they could. They had loads of invoices from Findlaters, who delivered Kit's weekly groceries, and Pamela's father brought home great stuff from work. They would spend hours filing and refiling and ticking off with red biro. They pretended to talk to customers using two imitation phones that Pamela owned. It kept them entertained for hours and they felt so grown-up, wearing lipstick and smoking sweet 'cigarettes' for added effect.

Pamela was allowed to read until late. Jennifer and Brenda had to have their lights out by nine o'clock. Pamela had a *huge* collection of Enid Blyton books. The mystery books were brilliant. How Jennifer longed to be part of a gang like *The Secret Seven* or *The Famous Five*. What mysteries she would solve. She and Pamela were sure that Miriam Kelly's father was in a sinister conspiracy of some sort. He looked a bit like a spy. He was always going abroad and Miriam mentioned once that he regularly had meetings with men who spoke foreign languages.

Pamela, Beth and Jennifer had followed him one day. Trailed him, just like Fatty and Co in the *Five Find-Outers*. It had been a bit of a disappointment as he'd just gone down to Dignan's and bought himself a plug of tobacco. They'd watched intently as he'd handed over his money, just in case he was passing a secret message. They hadn't caught him, but they knew he was up to no good and they would stay on his trail until they caught him in the act, they vowed.

123

Well sinister Mr Kelly could be meeting a Russian spy tonight and she wouldn't be able to do anything about it, because she'd be stuck at home thanks to Miss Brenda, Jennifer thought glumly as they reached their friends' house. Brenda, ignoring her with haughty disdain, knocked on the front door and turned her back on her. There were times, Jennifer thought angrily, that she almost hated her sister. Brenda would have a face on her now for ages and life would be most uncomfortable. Especially in the bedroom. If she even dared to put anything on Brenda's half of the dressing-table by mistake, there'd be war. If Brenda caught her reading her *Bunty* she'd be thumped. And she had a brand-new one that she'd only got yesterday and Jennifer was dying to read *The Four Marys*.

'Sorry for delaying you. I suppose you're not going to talk to me now,' she ventured, as usual being the first one to hold out the olive branch. A contemptuous silence greeted Jennifer's overture. 'Well I think you're very mean,' she burst out as Beth opened the door.

'What's wrong with Brenda?' her friend inquired as they walked behind their respective older sisters *en route* to the procession.

'Oh she's in a huff as usual,' Jennifer sighed.

'What's new?' Beth retorted. 'I know Kathy's moody but Brenda's ten times worse. When she's having a row with you, she ignores me, as if I did anything on her,' she added plaintively.

'Don't mind her.' Jennifer snorted. 'Wait until you see the two of them showing off just because they're prefects.'

'They just think they're it. Thank God they're going to secondary school after the holidays. At least they'll be out of our hair.' Beth scowled.

A big crowd had gathered at the starting point of the procession. The army and police were there to escort the priests carrying the monstrance under the big canopy. The St John's ambulance brigade, the Order of Malta, the girl guides and boy scouts in their uniforms all stood to attention waiting to move off. A priest gave instructions about the route from a car with a loudspeaker. And in front of all of this were the flower girls, ready to strew their petals on the ground in honour of Christ.

Jennifer felt a tingle of excitement. She could see the road ahead lined on each side with people who were not walking in the procession. Many of the houses displayed colourful bunting flying decoratively in the breeze. Some had little altars in their windows with a picture or statue of the Sacred Heart surrounded by fresh flowers.

'Get into your place quickly,' Brenda ordered officiously. She had a little notebook in her hand and was ticking off the names of the arrivals.

'Show-off,' muttered Jennifer as she stepped into line. One of the teachers arrived and issued them with their instructions. They were to follow the teachers at the front, who would be following the car with the loudspeaker. The prefects would walk at the end of each line. There was to be no talking or laughing of any sort. They were to throw their petals on the ground in front of them and try and make them last until they got to St Pappin's Church. The entire Holy Communion class were first, followed by the representatives of second, third, fourth, fifth and sixth classes. Turning around, Jennifer could see the famous Cora Delahunty behind her, dressed all in white with a veil so long it was almost tripping her up.

'Look at Cora Delahunty,' she whispered to Beth. 'Does she think she's getting married or what?' It was ridiculous. Only the Holy Communion girls wore white dresses with their veils. Beth and Jennifer were both wearing their Sunday best topped off by their Holy Communion veils but of course Cora, being Cora, had to go the whole hog. Jennifer and Beth were fascinated by Cora, having heard great tales about her from Brenda and Kathy. She was definitely the most glamorous person in the school.

'What are you gawking at?' the most glamorous person in the school drawled.

'Nothing much, it hasn't got a label on it,' Jennifer retorted, annoyed with herself for having been caught staring.

'You're Brenda Myles's sister, aren't you? She's dead common too,' Cora sneered.

'It takes one to know one,' Jennifer riposted, turning her back on the vision in white.

'Sarky cow. She thinks she's somebody, doesn't she? You gave her her answer.' Beth grinned. The next minute the pair of them nearly jumped out of their skins as the voice in the car with the loudspeaker boomed out the first line of the hymn *Sweet Sacrament Divine*. The procession began to move off down Ballymun Avenue and the voices of the people as they joined in the hymn could be heard in homes a mile away.

Slowly, rhythmically, the girls began strewing their petals on the ground as they walked proudly at the head of the procession. After the first hymn, there was a decade of the Rosary. Jennifer much preferred the hymns, she decided as she sprinkled a handful of rose petals on the ground. They were beautiful petals. Soft, scented petals of every hue and colour. She and Beth had gone to all their neighbours asking for contributions to the petal basket. They'd gone down to the Rose Garden in the Botanic Gardens and asked the gardener if they could have any petals on the ground. They'd told him what it was for and he'd been more than agreeable. They'd got loads of petals. Her dad had taken them for a spin in the country and they'd gathered lovely scented apple blossom petals as well. Their teacher was very pleased with their hard work and had commended them in front of the whole class.

After two hymns and three decades of the Rosary they left the houses and were on the winding road up to St Pappin's. It was a while since she'd been along this road. Jennifer reflected, as she heard a cow lowing in one of the fields. None of them went to St Pappin's School any more. They no longer had to get the Lea's Cross bus to the little country school. A brand-new school had been built for them at the end of Ballymun Avenue, called Our Lady of Victories. It had big bright classrooms with huge blackboards. And venetian blinds on the windows. It was Jennifer's job to open the blinds in the morning and she relished it. She loved twirling the little baton around to open and close them. At midday when the sun streamed right in on top of them, it was her job to close them. It was Beth's job to clean the blackboard. They no longer sat at wooden desks, they had tables. Jennifer missed the wooden desks with their little inkwells in the middle and the groove that ran along the top for them to put their pens in. They didn't use pens with nibs on them any more either. She'd always liked dipping her pen into the inkwell and making large neat letters in her copy with the red and blue lines when they had been learning how to write. Now they just had ordinary copies.

Walking along the country road brought back memories. Her favourite time had been picking blackberries in the autumn or having snow fights in the winter when the snow was crisp and deep on the roads and footpaths. Now it only took her ten minutes to get to school. She didn't have to get a bus any more and couldn't save a ha'penny on her bus fare by racing to the stop at the end of Ballymun Avenue, instead of the stop up by the shops.

A hysterical screech jerked her out of her daydream. She turned to look in the direction of the commotion. Cora, lepping around like a mad woman, was being chased by a bee. Of course, in an effort to outdo everybody else, she had, at the start of the procession, sprinkled her basket of petals (a basket twice as large as everybody else's) with lavender water perfume. Now she was paying the price for the sickly sweet scent.

'Get it away from me! Get it away from me!' she squealed, barging through the girls in front in an effort to shake off her pursuer.

'Be quiet! Be quiet, you silly girl,' one of the teachers thundered, grabbing the yelling Cora by the arm.

'I'm being attacked by a swarm of bees,' Cora bawled. This was a slight exaggeration. Another bee had indeed joined his comrade, attracted by the heavenly scent of lavender, but a swarm was a bit of an overstatement.

'I've been stung,' she yelled as a bee landed on her arm. She tore herself from the teacher's grasp and made another run for it.

This naturally caused consternation in the ranks and white-veiled girls hopped and screeched with abandon, much to the fury of their teachers.

'Stop that nonsense this minute, Cora Delahunty, and the rest of you. Making a disgrace of the school. Have some reverence,' commanded the teacher. Cora was oblivious to her. In her blind panic, she tripped over her veil and sprawled in their midst, her petals scattering to the four winds.

Sobbing dramatically, she was led from the procession, her white dress covered in dust. Snorting and sniggering, the rest of them regrouped and began to walk again, to the great relief of the holders of the canopy, who at this stage were almost on top of the leading group. They were having a hard job keeping straight faces. Jennifer caught Beth's eye and, in spite of themselves, they burst into giggles. Their teacher cast them a look that would have intimidated the Pope and Brenda hissed, 'Shut up, you two.' It was with considerable difficulty that they composed themselves. Every so often they'd remember Cora's spectacular retirement from the procession and they'd start tittering again.

'Making a show of us, Mammy, she was,' complained Brenda to her mother later that evening. 'The teacher told her to stop laughing three times. I was mortified.'

'I couldn't help it, Brenda. Every time I thought about it, it was funny. And you're just an old tattle-tale anyway,' she burst out, hurt by her sister's disloyalty.

'Stop that, Jennifer,' her mother ordered. 'You shouldn't have been tittering and giggling when you were leading the procession. It's just as well I didn't see you or you'd have got a right telling-off from me.'

'It's not fair, Mammy. I wasn't laughing on purpose and she's always telling on me and I never tell on her!' Jennifer was outraged at her mother's rebuke.

'That's because there's nothing to tell,' Brenda retorted smugly.

'There is so! There's loads to tell!' Jennifer yelled petulantly. Brenda paled slightly. 'Beth caught you and Kathy taking a sip out of her granny's sherry bottle, Miss Brenda Myles, so there, and I never told on you,' she shot back furiously. Their mother nearly had a seizure.

'Brenda Myles, is this the truth?' She was horrified.

'Don't mind her, she's telling lies,' Brenda exclaimed.

'I am not,' Jennifer said sourly. She knew she'd really done it now. There'd be ructions.

'Have you broken your Confirmation pledge, Miss?'

Brenda stayed mute, casting daggers looks at her sister. Jennifer began to feel very sorry that she'd opened her mouth. That was a serious tale that she had tattled but it just burst out of her, she'd been so annoyed by her elder sister's ratting on her about laughing in the procession. It wasn't as if she had laughed deliberately. Everyone else was laughing too, she thought miserably. But breaking the Confirmation pledge not to drink until you were twenty-one, that was serious. Her sister was in deep trouble.

'Brenda, I'm speaking to you,' her mother said angrily.

'We were just having a sniff of it,' she argued.

'Yes, they were just having a sniff, I think,' Jennifer echoed quickly, anxious to undo the damage.

'Don't tell me fibs, the pair of you. I'm going straight down to Mrs Cleary immediately to get to the bottom of this.' Kit was hopping mad. 'Stay here both of you until I get back and don't budge.'

'Now see what you've done, you little wagon. Kathy will never speak to me again for getting her into trouble. And Da will murder me if he finds out,' Brenda shrieked.

'Well I didn't mean to. It was all your fault anyway. You had to open your big mouth about me laughing at the procession. Didn't you?' Jennifer yelled back. 'You're always the same. Always trying to get me into trouble. I wish I didn't have you for an older sister. Kathy Cleary is much nicer to Beth than you are to me. She always shares her clothes and her comics with her. You never do.' Jennifer was distraught.

'If I get into serious trouble over this I'll never speak to you again.' Brenda burst into tears, marched upstairs and slammed the door of the bedroom. Jennifer burst into tears herself. She hadn't meant to get Brenda and Kathy into trouble. But it looked as if they were for it.

Kit came back ten minutes later looking grim. 'Tell your sister I want her,' she instructed Jennifer.

Jennifer raced up the stairs. Her heart was pounding. If Kit decided to tell their father there would be a dreadful row. Why, oh why, had she opened her big mouth? She'd just have to learn to control that temper of hers. 'You're wanted,' she said breathlessly. Brenda cast her a filthy look and followed her out of the room.

'I'll say nothing to your father this time, Brenda, but if I ever hear of anything like this again you are in serious trouble, madam. You are not to touch alcohol. Do you hear me? You make sure you tell this in Confession and go and take the pledge again. Now get to bed, the pair of you.' Their mother was highly annoyed.

'Sorry,' murmured Jennifer as she undressed for bed. Her apology was ignored. Jennifer, in all honesty, could not blame Brenda. It had been a terrible thing to rat about. There'd be a mega-huff for the next few days, but it would all blow over, she hoped. Her father hadn't been told and that was good.

Jennifer lay in bed casting her mind back over the events of the day. One thing though, she smiled to herself under the covers remembering Cora, it had certainly been the best procession ever.

Chapter Thirteen

It was great going back to secondary school, Brenda reflected as she stood at the No. 13 bus terminus with Kathy. There were loads of students at the bus stop gabbing nineteen to the dozen. There were girls from the Holy Faith in their navy uniforms, girls from Eccles Street in their maroon and cream, and girls from St Theresa's, her own school, in their green and white. There were fellas from Vincent's and Belvedere and there was a lot of good-natured jeering and slagging between them all. Brenda loved being in the thick of it.

She had been so bored at home that summer. All she seemed to do was housework, or read, or watch TV. At night she and Kathy went over to the big green to meet up with the rest of the gang and sneak the odd fag and have a laugh with the fellas. But she always had to be in by nine-thirty. Her father was very strict like that. It was embarrassing having to slip away from the crowd. Even Kathy was allowed to stay out until ten. Which seemed much more grown-up.

Brenda and her da were constantly fighting about it. Sometimes she just hated him. Even her mother thought he was being too strict and once there'd been a huge row when Kit accused her husband of being as bad as his father. Her da hadn't spoken to Brenda for weeks after it. Blaming it all on her. Having a strict father was the worst thing in the world. How was she ever going to be allowed to go to dances when she was older? Brenda could see stormy times ahead, that was for sure.

She saw Eddie Fagan smiling at her. Brenda smiled back. She liked Eddie and she knew he liked her too.

He often gave her a cigarette when they were all together on The Green. He was talking to his mates but he kept looking over at her and smiling at her every so often. She could feel herself going scarlet.

'He fancies you, Bren, I'm telling you,' Kathy giggled. She was conducting a flirtation with Kenny Lyons, who was Eddie's mate.

'I'd love to get off with him, I really fancy him too,' Brenda sighed as the object of her affections said hello to one of the girls from Eccles Street and started chatting her up. Brenda's heart sank to her boots. She knew the girl by sight and she was very pretty. There was no way Eddie would give her a second glance now.

She saw Marty Hayes arrive on the scene and caught his eye and waved. Marty arrived over, and Brenda immediately engaged him in vivacious conversation, keeping half an eye on Eddie all the while. The bus arrived and there was a mad scramble upstairs to get the front seats.

To her great dismay Eddie and the pretty girl went down to the back and so she and Kathy sat up in the front. They wouldn't turn around because that would be far too obvious. Fortunately Marty came and plonked himself in the seat behind them so Brenda had an excuse to turn and talk to him and was able to observe the pair at the back. It looked as if they were getting on like a house on fire. Completely disheartened, she left Kathy to chat with Marty and stared out the window with mounting gloom.

It was a lovely warm sunny September day. The Green, empty of people, looked like a huge emerald carpet right in the middle of the square of houses. At the opposite end of The Green, with the Dublin mountains behind them in the distance, were the maisonettes. On two sides of the big wide grassy rectangle ran streets of terraced houses. They were nice houses, Brenda mused, catching sight of her own yellow front door as the bus curved around the terminus end of The Green and on to St Pappin's Road. The painters had just painted their front door two days previously and they were working on some of the others. She could see one of them, in his bright white overalls, kneeling down at Kathy's door, which was two doors away from hers.

She saw her own brother Sean out on the footpath playing hopscotch with Gerard. They didn't have to go to school for another three-quarters of an hour and their school, the Sacred Heart, was only five minutes across The Green. No doubt her mother would be washing up after the breakfast before going upstairs to make the beds. She wouldn't have Brenda to help her today. Making the beds was a chore she hated. There were five beds to be made in the Myles household. Her parents' double bed, her and Jennifer's divans and the boys' bunks. Still, that wasn't bad compared to Kathy's. There were six children, two parents and a granny living in her best friend's house. They had had to turn their dining-room into a bedroom for their granny. Before she'd come to live with them, Kathy and Brenda usually went into the dining-room when they wanted a bit of privacy. But now there was nowhere private in her friend's house. Kathy came down to Brenda's house now. Mind, there wasn't always privacy there either. Jennifer was usually playing one of her ridiculous games such as 'Office' or 'Emergency Ward 10.' She'd have a face on her then and there'd often be a row. Kit would get narky and start yelling and it could be a bit mortifying in front of Kathy. Honestly, it was extremely irritating having a nuisance of a younger sister who was only ten. You'd think Jenny would have a bit of respect for her older sister. After all, Brenda was a teenager, fourteen, and a third year student at that!

It was great to be a third year, she mused as the bus swung right onto the Ballymun Road. She wasn't a junior any more. All the new intake would be feeling nervous and apprehensive, just as she'd been on her first day in St Theresa's this time last year. She'd even worn her beret. Imagine! She'd felt a right prat. When she saw that no-one else was wearing theirs, she'd whipped it off her head and rolled it up in her bag, where it had stayed for the rest of term.

The mountains were really clear, she noted as the bus stopped to take on more passengers. You could see all the different colours. The greens and golds and purples and browns. From her eyrie on the top deck of the No. 13 she could see the rooftops of the city below her in the distance. It was a view that always gave Brenda a buzz. She loved the city. The nearer the bus got to the city centre the more she liked it. She and Kathy often went into town at lunch-time. Brenda loved window-shopping and browsing. She'd spend all day in town if she could. She loved the crowds, and the air of hustle and bustle and the sense of excitement that was part and parcel of city life.

'Hi Cora,' she heard someone call out and Brenda turned to see Cora Delahunty swanning down the aisle. She gave a mental snort at the sight of her. Cora Delahunty was still the consequence she'd been in primary school. *She* was going to a private secondary school and didn't have to wear a school uniform. She still wore her skirts as short as ever, Brenda noted sourly. And she was made up to the nines. She wore a gorgeous suede fringed jacket over a matching suede mini, and suede boots. She'd a load of hippie beads around her neck and big jangly earrings and she looked really hip. Brenda admired them enviously. She was deeply impressed when Cora took out a cigarette and lit up, inhaling slowly before exhaling the smoke in a long thin stream. She looked the height of sophistication, and seeing her, Brenda felt a right frump in her green sack tied at the middle with a sash. Not to mention her white blouse and yukky red tie. Cora had her nerve, Brenda thought grudgingly. Smoking like that in public. She and Kathy wouldn't dare. Half the neighbours were on the bus and if her da ever heard she was smoking there'd be war. Cora was doing a strong line too, with a barman. The rest of them were dead jealous. Cora acted as if she was grown-up even though she was the same age as the rest of them. There were strong rumours going around too, that she had gone all the way with her boyfriend. Brenda saw them kissing once. Really passionate like in the pictures and the barman had his hands on Cora's breasts. She and Kathy were gobsmacked . . . and not a little shocked. Well to be honest, very shocked.

'I'd never let a fella touch me there. Not unless I was married,' Kathy whispered as they hurried on past the lane where the steamy encounter was taking place.

'Me neither,' Brenda agreed whole-heartedly.

'I bet he doesn't respect her,' Kathy sniffed. 'Ted Conway touched me there once and I walloped him one in the chops.'

'Did he?' Brenda was agog. 'You never told me.'

'I was a bit embarrassed actually,' Kathy confessed, blushing.

'What did it feel like? Did your nipples go hard like Angelique's?' Brenda asked with great interest, referring to the heroine of the best-selling novel.

'Nooooo,' Kathy scoffed. 'Not with that geek. Are you mad! It would probably take Paul Newman to do that.' Paul Newman was their idol.

Thinking of *Angelique* reminded Brenda of something and she turned back from observing the decadent Cora and gave Kathy a nudge. 'Mrs Allen wants me to baby-sit tonight. Can you come down?'

'Oh great!' Kathy's eyes brightened. 'She always does lovely cream sponges.'

'Mmmm, and her currant bread is scrumptious.' Brenda felt a mite more cheerful. She enjoyed baby-sitting. It was a good way of earning a few bob and Mrs Allen was always very generous. She also had brilliant books. Kathy and she nearly went blind going through the pages of the *Angelique* and *Forever Amber* books, looking for the juicy bits. They were learning all about love-making from them.

Brenda often pretended that she was Angelique or Amber and that she'd been kidnapped by Paul Newman, who was a pirate. She would rebuff his advances and be magnificently haughty with him until he could control his lust no longer. Then he would imprison her in his strong arms after a fierce struggle, and finally he would kiss her passionately and rip her bodice off her. Then he would have his wicked way with her, despite her pleading.

What his wicked way was, exactly, Brenda was not too sure. Kathy was none the wiser either. They knew it was something to do with a fella's mickey and going the whole way. But the details of what precisely it was eluded them. Some of the girls in their class seemed to know the ins and outs of the matter. But Brenda and Kathy never let on they were still in the dark. They didn't want to appear unsophisticated. That was why they were avid readers of Mrs Allen's paperbacks. Surely one of them would have all the details and they'd find the answer to the great mystery.

'See ya, Kathy. See ya, Brenda.' With a start, Brenda realized that they were at the stop for St Vincent's. The lads were getting off. She turned to see Eddie and Kenny grinning at them. 'See ya on the way home.' They waved.

Huh! I'm hugely impressed, Brenda sniffed. Did Eddie Fagan think it made the slightest bit of difference to her whether he was on the bus home or not? But she didn't let him see how disgruntled she was that he'd sat beside the other girl. He was big-headed enough, she thought glumly.

'See you, Kenny. See you, Eddie,' she replied cheerfully, making sure to mention Kenny first. 'Enjoy being back.'

'Urgh!' Eddie made a horrible face and disappeared down the stairs, followed by Kenny and Marty. Well at least he'd said goodbye, Brenda comforted herself as she settled back in her seat feeling a little happier as the bus took a sharp turn left down Whitworth Road. The waters of the canal sparkled in the sun and a swan glided serenely past causing just the merest ripple. She could see the grim forbidding walls of Mountjoy Prison and behind them the grey-stoned prison itself. The steel bars on all the windows gave her the shivers and she wondered if anyone was looking out on the canal from behind them. She picked up her bag and nudged Kathy. 'Our stop.' They got off near the end of Whitworth Road, walked briskly along, turned left towards Drumcondra and headed up in the direction of the Bishop's Palace, which was beside the school.

Ten minutes later, all thoughts of Eddie Fagan and Mountjoy Prison were banished from her mind as she and Kathy ran up the marble steps to St Theresa's and amidst the mêlée of petrified new girls, sophisticated seniors, nuns in dark veils and harassed teachers, managed to rendezvous with various classmates. Eventually, they located their allotted classroom, adjacent to the head nun's office, which caused much gloom and doom, but didn't quite diminish their high-spirited enthusiasm at being together again. After all the excitement of being back at school, working out time-tables, arranging basketball matches, drama and debating society sessions, Brenda's brain was frazzled and she completely forgot about Eddie until the bus home passed St Vincent's School. She patted her hair, removed her tie and caught Kathy doing the same. They grinned at each other companionably.

'You'd never know who'd get on,' Kathy remarked. This time they were sitting at the back of the bus and had a bird's eye view of the stairs and who came up it. Mind, every seat on the upper deck was full, so the fellas would have to stay downstairs, as standing was not allowed upstairs. They waited expectantly as the bus drew abreast of the stop. They could see Eddie, Kenny and Marty among the hordes waiting to get on. To their immense dismay, the bus didn't stop but carried on past the howling mob of furious schoolboys.

'Well blast it anyway.'

'Aw shag it.'

The girls were disgusted as the bus raced towards Botanic Road. Weren't they ever going to have a bit of luck with men?

That night the pair set off for Mrs Allen's house in low spirits. Brenda was particularly glum. Her grandfather had been in hospital after having an accident and it looked as if he was going to be permanently disabled. Her da was up the walls, and Kit, who out of the goodness of her heart had visited him several times, was declaring that she was going visiting no more because he was so bloody rude. Brenda was glad to get away from the arguing and bad moods.

They waved Mr and Mrs Allen off. They'd only be gone for a couple of hours, Mrs Allen assured Brenda. They were just going as far as the Bon Secours Hospital to visit an aunt, and were just going to pop into the Addison for a drink afterwards. The baby was asleep, for which the girls were very grateful, because he was a cranky little bugger when he was awake. The first thing they did, as always, was to see what was in the fridge.

'Oh goody! Pickled onions.' Kathy had a passion for pickled onions. She unscrewed the lid and popped one in her mouth. Brenda was more interested in a dish of macaroni cheese, and she ate a few spoonfuls with relish. Mrs Allen had made chicken and ham roll sandwiches for them and left the cream sponge as usual, but they always had a little raid on the fridge anyway.

Then they took a couple of swigs out of the gripe-water bottle. They loved the taste of gripe-water. 'No doubt because of the 2% alcohol,' giggled Brenda as she replaced the bottle in the baby's holdall.

Next stop was the bookcase. They were deeply engrossed in *The Adventures of a Spanish Lady* who was about to be ravished by a hot-eyed, broad-shouldered, hairy-chested Duke, when the baby started screeching and Brenda's nose led her to conclude that he had a dirty nappy. 'This is where you really earn your money,' she muttered to Kathy as she did the necessary.

Fortunately, after taking six ounces of his bottle, he fell fast asleep again and the girls were able to return to the Spanish Lady and her throbbing, panting Duke.

They spent a very pleasant few hours, reading and chatting and eating their supper. Compared to their own homes, Allen's was an oasis of peace and quiet.

'I'd nearly baby-sit for nothing here,' Brenda confessed as she heard the key in the door.

'Come on, girls, I'll walk you home.' Mr Allen, who was a real gentleman, offered, after his wife had paid them generously for their endeavours.

'Not at all, Mr Allen. We'll be fine. It's just across The Green,' Brenda replied politely.

'Are you sure now?' he queried.

'Certainly,' they chorused. Besides, it was only gone ten and there was no telling who they might meet crossing The Green and they didn't want anyone to think they weren't capable of walking home in the dark. They'd look like two right prats if any of the blokes saw Mr Allen walking them home.

'He's very nice, isn't he?' Kathy remarked. 'You know the Tays?'

'Who doesn't? Isn't Mister a fine thing?' grinned Brenda.

'Wait until I tell you. That's what you think. That's what I thought too,' Kathy continued as they dawdled across The Green. 'I was baby-sitting for them last weekend and he walked me home. When he got to my house he slipped two coins into my coat pocket. I thought they were two half-crowns, of course, but you know what they were, the mean old scrooge? Two thruppenny bits. God, I was hopping mad. I was there from seven in the evening until after one in the morning. How mean can you get? Six hours for sixpence. A penny an hour. I'm telling everyone who baby-sits not to go to them. So make sure you don't either.'

'Oh I won't,' Brenda retorted. 'He might be a fine thing but after hearing that I've gone right off him. And to think we fancied him. I'm disgusted.'

'Me too,' Kathy agreed. 'What a disappointment.'

'Another hero bites the dust,' Brenda sighed as they stepped off The Green onto the road.

'Hiya girls.' Eddie and Kenny emerged from under a light where they were having a cigarette. Brenda's heart skipped a beat. She'd been hoping something like this might happen. None of the rest of the gang was around either, just Eddie and Kenny on their own.

'Where've you been?' Eddie asked.

'Baby-sitting,' Brenda answered nonchalantly. It would never do to let him know that she was thrilled to see him.

'For who?' Eddie held out his cigarette packet to the girls. They glanced at each other, nodded almost imperceptibly and took one each.

'The Allens,' Kathy said, inclining her head towards Kenny, who'd struck a match for her. Eddie took Brenda's cigarette from her, put it to his lips and lit it from his own before handing it back to her. She nearly had a palpitation at the intimacy and romance of it.

'Missed the bus home today, it never stopped,' Eddie remarked.

'It was pretty packed,' Brenda informed him, taking a long slow deep sophisticated drag (just like Cora) from her cigarette. The cigarette that had been touched by her idol's lips. Unfortunately she was not as used to smoking as the sophisticate in suede and she inhaled too deeply. Her eyes began to water, and she started spluttering and coughing, making a holy show of herself. Eddie had to thump her on the back and she was puce from lack of breath, not to talk about mortification. Kathy was looking at her in sympathetic horror.

'Sorry,' Brenda wheezed, wishing the ground would open up and swallow her whole. She'd never been so embarrassed in her entire life.

'Are you OK?' Eddie asked, concerned. Kenny gave a snort of suppressed laughter.

'Stop it, you,' Brenda heard Kathy hiss and she was pathetically grateful for her friend's loyalty. Now that she had so spectacularly blown her chances of getting off with Eddie she was going to need a friend's shoulder to cry on.

Eddie still had his arm around her but all she wanted to do was to get away and burst into tears in private. 'God, Brenda, you gave us a fright, just as well I don't smoke Sweet Afton or we'd probably be calling an ambulance,' he teased.

'Or even an undertaker,' quipped the irrepressible Kenny. In spite of herself, Brenda managed a weak smile.

'We'd better get home,' murmured Kathy helpfully, seeking to ease her friend's discomfiture.

'We'll walk you,' Eddie said matter-of-factly, much to Brenda's amazement. She couldn't figure it out. She'd have thought, after the pitiful spectacle she'd just made of herself, he'd want to beat it fast. But no, he was walking down the street talking away to her as if nothing had happened, pretending not to notice how flustered she was.

Gradually a little poise returned and she managed to give an impression of normality.

'So listen, Brenda,' Eddie said. 'Kenny and I usually hit the Dandelion Market on Saturday afternoons, would you and Kathy like to come with us this Saturday? We could go and have coffee in Bewley's afterwards.' Brenda was stunned. Eddie Fagan was asking her to go to the Dandelion Market, the place to be, on Saturday afternoon. She couldn't believe it.

'Well what d'ya think?'

'Yeah, sure, I'd better check with Kathy to see if she's available.' Brenda's voice sounded normal despite her galloping heartbeat.

'Hey Kathy, d'ya fancy coming to the Dandelion on Saturday afternoon with Kenny, Brenda and me?' Eddie called back to where the pair were walking along laughing and chatting.

'You bet,' Kathy agreed enthusiastically.

'It's a date then,' Eddie declared as they reached Brenda's front gate.

'It's a date,' she echoed, almost in a dream.

''Night, Brenda.' Kathy gave a small wink as she went on to her own house. Eddie waved at Brenda and she waved back and then she let herself in, her heart bursting with happiness.

That night she lay in bed, blissfully happy, whispering, 'It's a date! It's a date,' while Jennifer lay slumbering peacefully in the other bed, quite unaware of the hugely important event that had just taken place in her older sister's life.

Chapter Fourteen

Brenda was up with the lark, which was most unusual for her, on a Saturday morning. But she wanted to get her chores done and be ready for what she knew was going to be a wonderful afternoon. She was still dancing on air and had been all week, since that magical evening when Eddie had suggested 'The Date.' These days really were worth living, she thought happily, humming a gay little tune as she stripped her bed and got clean sheets from the hot press. She loved getting into a bed with clean sheets and pillowcases. They were sent to the Swastika laundry every week and delivered back crisp and starched with little yellow and white tags on them which had to be peeled off. Tonight when she got into her freshly changed bed she would have been on her date. She would be able to replay every precious second in her mind in the darkness.

'Come on, Jenny, get out of bed and take the sheets off,' Brenda instructed her younger sister, who was engrossed in her comic.

'Aw, Bren, it's real early, Mammy and Daddy aren't even up yet,' Jennifer protested.

'Come on, Jenny, I want to get the beds changed,' Brenda snapped. The last thing she needed was Jennifer acting up.

'There's no school today. I don't have to get up early,' Jennifer declared.

Brenda decided the best tack was bribery. 'Pleeaasse, Jenny,' she wheedled. 'I'll give you thruppence if you get up and give me a hand with the beds and the brasses.'

'OK,' her sister said brightly, hopping out of bed with alacrity and starting to pull off her sheets with vigour.

143

Great, thought Brenda, it was wonderful what a bribe could do. With Jenny's help she'd have her chores done in no time.

' "It's been a hard day's night—" '

' "And I've been working like a dog," ' finished her sister enthusiastically as they tucked in the bottom sheet on Brenda's bed.

'What's rare is wonderful.' Their mother poked her head around the door and smiled at them. 'Singing together, making the beds, no arguments, maybe I'm still asleep and having a dream.' Brenda beamed at her. She hadn't yet mentioned that she was going into town for the afternoon. Well not even town . . . the Dandelion Market. Brenda wasn't too sure how her parents would react to that. It was only in the last year, since she'd started secondary school, that she was allowed to go into town on her own with Kathy. Still, if she had all her jobs done, and there were no rows, that might help persuade her mother to let her go. She wasn't going to fib exactly. She'd just say she was going shopping with Kathy and the gang. This was not a lie, Brenda rationalized. She was going shopping . . . in the Dandelion Market and Eddie and Kenny were part of the gang.

'You won't forget to go to Confession today and take Sean and Jenny with you,' her mother reminded her.

Drat! thought Brenda to herself. She'd forgotten all about going to Confession. They went to Confession every second Saturday morning. Still, if she had all her work finished, lunch would be nearly ready by the time they got home. Because she did the brasses and changed the beds on Saturdays, Sean and Jenny had to do the washing-up, so she'd be free to go. She'd done all her homework. She'd made sure to do it last night so there'd be no obstacles in her path.

'I suppose I'd better bring you in to see Grandpa Myles,' Kit mused as she flung open the bedroom window. Brenda felt as if her heart had actually stopped beating. If Kit decided to go visiting Grandpa Myles in the Mater Hospital, she'd have to go. Her father would insist and she could say goodnight to her trip to the market.

Please don't do this to me, Holy God. St Anthony, St Theresa, please let me go to the Dandelion, she babbled to herself.

'Maybe we'll go tomorrow. Sean has a match this afternoon, so Daddy will be going to that, and anyway I want to go and see your Auntie Ellen. We'll go tomorrow then, girls,' their mother pronounced as she went downstairs to get the breakfast.

'Thanks, thanks, thanks,' Brenda breathed to the Almighty and His saints for their merciful intercession.

'Thanks for what? Who are you thanking?' Jenny was curious.

'No-one, mind your nose!' Brenda certainly wasn't going to inform her younger sister of her plans.

After the breakfast dishes were washed up and the kitchen tidied, Brenda spread some newspaper on the big wooden table and took out the Brasso from the bottom of the Welsh dresser. She hated with a vengeance doing the brasses. The pong of the stuff and the mess it made of her hands annoyed her. Nevertheless, she began polishing her mother's best brass candlesticks diligently. Sean was cleaning out the shed in the back, Jenny was dusting while her mother hoovered, Gerard was shelling peas and their father was mowing the grass. The house was a hive of activity as it usually was on a Saturday morning. Brenda didn't really like Saturday mornings at all. There was too much to be done. Cora Delahunty's mother had a woman who came in on Saturdays to clean her house. Cora was always talking about the maid.

Imagine never, ever having to polish, hoover or do the ironing. If she ever got married to Eddie, as was her greatest desire, she certainly wouldn't spend Saturday mornings doing housework. No! They'd spend all day in town, she thought happily as she finished the candlesticks and started on the ornaments.

At twelve o'clock, she had finished her jobs and Kit told her she'd done great work. Anxious to stay in her mother's good books, she brushed Gerard's hair despite his protestations and washed his face. 'He can come with us to Confession so he won't be whingeing when the rest of us are gone,' Brenda offered.

The four of them set off across The Green and Brenda sniffed the air appreciatively. What a relief it was to have all her jobs *and* her homework done. She felt like dancing. It was a beautiful Indian summer's day. The sky was blue and little fluffs of clouds drifted towards the Dublin Mountains. The breeze was balmy, all she was wearing was a light cotton summer dress and she was barelegged in sandals. This afternoon she was going to wear her new Indian fringed skirt and a T-shirt. After all, the Dandelion was where all the hippies hung out, she didn't want to look out of place. She wished mightily that she had some beads like Cora's. Maybe she'd treat herself to some today, Brenda decided. She had quite a bit of baby-sitting money saved.

The blue and silver of the galvanized iron of Our Mother of Divine Grace church, shimmered in the heat haze. Silently, they entered through the side door. Gerard insisted on getting some Holy Water for himself when he saw the rest of them dipping their fingers into the font and blessing themselves. Of course he drenched himself, and Brenda gave out stink to him and told him to behave himself or she'd lock him in the Confession box in the dark. After that, there wasn't a peep out of him.

Then Sean and Jenny started arguing about who was going first and she had to haul them back as they galloped down the aisle to the Confession box. There were two rows of people already waiting outside Father Collins's box. Her heart sank. They'd be here for ages, she groaned to herself. Just as she was about to lead the trio into the queue, she noticed a small elderly priest walking up the side of the church. Great, she thought, sometimes visiting priests heard Confession.

'Quick, quick,' she hissed, dragging the hapless Gerard behind her in her haste to get over to the other side of the church. They were first, they'd be out in a jiffy. Or so she thought. There was some shuffling and coughing as the old priest pulled the curtains behind him and arranged himself and his missals and rosary beads to his satisfaction. She motioned to Sean to go first. He grinned victoriously at Jenny and marched confidently through the Confessional door only to emerge what seemed like an eternity later, beet-red in the face.

Brenda motioned Jennifer to go next, and she seemed to be in there for ages too. Finally it was her turn and she stepped into the dark solitude.

The shutter was pulled across none too gently. 'Begin your Confession,' a crusty voice barked.

'Bless me, Father—'

'Speak up, I can't hear you,' the priest ordered. Brenda scowled in the dark, she didn't want half the church to know her sins. It wasn't her fault if he was deaf. She began again. 'Bless me, Father, for I have sinned it's two weeks since my last Confession, Father. I took the Holy Name, Father. I was inattentive at Mass, Father. I used bad language, Father,' she gabbled her usual litany. 'I had bad thoughts, Father.' She always slipped that one in in the middle hoping that it wouldn't be noticed. 'I told lies, Father. And I smoked a cigarette, Father.' She had decided to confess her smoking as otherwise she could be deemed not to have made a full Confession.

'I see,' came the ominous voice after she had paused. 'What age are you?'

'Thirteen, Father . . . no, fourteen . . . ' she whispered, flustered.

'I can't hear.'

God Almighty, Brenda thought, longing for the ordeal to be over. She vowed she'd never go to a strange priest again, no matter how long the queue for the other Confessional. 'Fourteen, Father,' she repeated.

'These are serious sins, daughter. How often have you had these impure thoughts?'

Brenda was flummoxed. She and Paul Newman had wonderful adventures every night. Last night he'd rescued her from a horde of rampaging infidels.

'Eight times,' she muttered, saying the first figure that came to mind. Trust him to latch onto that one.

There was a distinct 'tsk' from the other side of the grille.

'You must have respect for yourself, daughter. Your body is a vessel for the Holy Spirit. God cannot abide in an unclean soul. Think of Our Lady when these thoughts come into your head. Ask her to help you. Ask her to help you to be attentive at Mass also. It is a grave affront to God not to give him his due respect and attention at the Holy Sacrifice of the Mass and an insult to use His Holy Name in vain. Give up the smoking, my child, you deceive your parents which breaks the fourth and eighth commandments. Foul language is most off-putting and unladylike. You must guard your tongue, my child, and model yourself on Our Blessed Mother.'

I bet she never had to listen to someone like you blathering on, Brenda thought irreverently, hoping fervently that nobody outside could hear what was being said.

'For your penance, say the Rosary and two Our Fathers and now make a good Act of Contrition, my child,' she heard the elderly priest say. Brenda was horrified. A *whole* Rosary! *And* two Our Fathers. Usually she got five Hail Marys.

She staggered out the door of the Confessional, laden down with her penance. A whole Rosary to say, she'd be here all day.

'What did you get? I got ten Our Fathers, that's the worst I've ever got.' Sean was raging.

'The Rosary,' Brenda muttered. Her brother's eyes widened in amazement, and some admiration.

'They must have been real mortalers.' His tone was

respectful. Side by side the sinners knelt, doing their penance. It was the fastest Rosary she'd ever said.

Rushing back home across The Green, she hoped that lunch was ready. It wasn't. Her mother had decided to clean out the presses in the kitchen and there were jars and packets and tins and the like all over the table. Brenda was in a frenzy of impatience. She was meeting Kathy at two-fifteen and they were meeting the boys at the terminus for the half two bus into town. It was already gone one.

'I'll help,' she offered, trying to hide her frustration.

'Good girl,' her mother said gratefully. 'Did you ever start something and were sorry you started it?' Between them they got the presses cleaned and it was with immense relief that she heard her mother say, 'I think I'll ask Jim to go down to Cowser's and get us fish and chips for the lunch seeing as it's so late, and the lads are going to the match.'

'Yippee,' Sean approved. Fish and chips from the chipper was a rare treat in the Myles household. Thank you, God, Brenda sent up a private prayer. If her dad went for fish and chips, it would only take ten minutes.

By one-thirty the Myles family were sitting down relishing their takeaway meal. Brenda bit into crisp crunchy golden batter and savoured every mouthful. All she had to do now was to mention casually that she was going into town with Kathy and the gang and that was that. She was free to go.

'I'm going into town with Kathy and the gang,' she remarked lightly, licking her fingers. 'Do you want anything from the Kylemore?'

'Would you get me an almond ring?' Her mother delved into her apron pocket and handed her a half-crown.

'You're lucky,' Jennifer sighed, 'going into town. Daddy is taking Sean and Gerard to a match and I've nothing to do.'

'When you're in secondary you'll be able to go into

149

town with your friends,' Brenda said with the superiority of age, as she got up from the table.

'It wouldn't kill you to take her in with you for once,' Kit remarked. 'Actually it would be doing me a great favour if you took Jennifer with you because I want to go and talk to Auntie Ellen about Grandpa Myles.'

Brenda nearly fainted. Imagine bringing your sister on a *date*. How utterly unsophisticated. Imagine the faces on Eddie and Kenny when they saw Jennifer tagging along.

'Mammy, I can't do that,' she pleaded. 'None of the others bring their younger sisters.'

'It's just for once, for heaven's sake, Brenda. Poor old Jenny never gets a look-in with you. She is your sister, after all.'

'I'll bring her another Saturday,' Brenda promised desperately.

'Brenda.' Her father arched an eyebrow. 'Bring Jenny with you today to help your mother out, it's the least you could do.'

'But she has to do the washing-up and I'll be late,' wailed Brenda, frantically.

'Go on and get ready, the pair of you, I'll do it,' Kit declared. 'And here.' She reached into her pocket again. 'There's a ten-shilling note, give me back the half-crown and get the almond ring out of this and you can treat yourselves with the rest. You did great work today, both of you, you deserve a treat.'

Normally, Brenda would have been thrilled to bits to be handed all that money. Her pocket money was two shillings a week. To be given extra was a real bonus. But even if it had been a twenty-pound note, it would not have cheered her up. She was going to be a laughing-stock, having to bring her younger sister on a date. And what if her father found out she was going to the Dandelion Market? He wouldn't be a bit impressed. God, she was in such a dilemma. She couldn't turn around and say she wasn't going because her parents wouldn't stand for it. What if Eddie and Kenny said no way were they going to have a *child* traipsing after them? Kathy would probably go with them and she'd be left to bring Jenny into town on her own. What a drag.

In silence she marched up to the bedroom with a delighted Jennifer trotting behind her. She flung her dress off her and took the new Indian skirt from the wardrobe.

'What will I wear?' Jennifer asked eagerly.

'You can stay as you are, Miss. It's just not fair, I can't even go into town by myself with my friends without you making a fuss.' Brenda was almost in tears.

'Oh!' responded Jennifer, deflated.

Brenda flounced out of the bedroom and went into the bathroom. Slamming the door behind her she let out a string of curses that would probably have earned her a dozen Rosaries had she confessed them. She didn't care. God had not played fair. Tears slid down her cheeks. She had been so looking forward to this afternoon. It would have been her big chance to get off with Eddie and now it was most certainly ruined.

Fifteen minutes later she was knocking on Kathy's door.

'Hiya,' Kathy opened the door looking very fetching in a pair of psychedelic trousers and an orange blouse. She saw Jennifer and assumed she had come calling for Beth, her younger sister. 'Beth's out the back.'

'She's coming with us,' Brenda informed her mournfully. Kathy's jaw dropped.

'But . . . But . . . she can't! What about . . . Well you know . . .' Kathy was aghast.

'I know, Kathy, there's nothing I can do about it. I have to bring her with me and that's it.'

'Can't we leave her here with Beth?'

Brenda wavered. What a brainwave. She looked hopefully at Jennifer.

'OK,' said her sister dolefully, recognizing defeat.

'Now you're to wait here until me and Kathy get back from town. You can't go home 'cos there won't be anyone there. I'll buy you something nice in town.'

Jennifer looked very fed up and went out the back to play with Beth. Kit, who was hanging out clothes two gardens away, spotted her. 'I thought you were going into town with Brenda,' she called over.

'I'm playing with Beth,' Jennifer explained. Unwilling to rat.

'Are Brenda and Kathy gone yet?' Jennifer shook her head. 'Tell Brenda I want her,' Kit said crossly.

Jennifer went back into the house and called up the stairs to Brenda, who was putting lipstick on in Kathy's bedroom. Kathy's mother didn't mind her wearing make-up, but Mrs Myles would not allow Brenda to use it until she was older.

'Brenda, Mammy wants you,' Jennifer called.

Brenda nearly had a fit. 'Christ Almighty! What did you say to her?' she thundered.

'I never said anything. She was hanging out clothes in the back and she saw me an' Beth playing and she asked me if you were still here,' Jennifer explained.

'You should have ducked when you saw her, or stayed inside until she was gone to Auntie Ellen's.' Brenda wiped off her lipstick angrily, throwing her eyes up to heaven. 'I'll be back in a second,' she said to Kathy.

'I hope you weren't intending leaving Jenny in Kathy's for the afternoon. Her mother has enough children of her own without having to look after one of mine.'

'I wasn't going to,' Brenda fibbed sulkily. So far, she had used the Holy Name, cursed and fibbed, and it was only a few hours since her Confession.

'Good,' said her mother. 'Enjoy yourself.'

Kit watched her daughter's retreating back with a frown. Honestly, you'd think she'd been asked to do something dreadful instead of bringing her sister to town. Jenny hero-worshipped her older sister but Brenda treated her like the greatest nuisance and wouldn't give her the time of day, the poor little mutton.

Kit sighed. It wasn't as if she wanted to get rid of Jenny this afternoon. Normally she wouldn't mind any of them coming to Ellen's with her. But today was different. Today she wanted to get things settled about Mr Myles. After all, Ellen was his daughter. All right, there was bad blood between them, but that would have to be forgotten and put aside. The man was disabled after his accident at work. He was having a lot of difficulty walking. He just couldn't fend for himself.

Ellen only had two children to look after. Kit had four. Ellen also had more room than she had. They had bought a bigger house on Canice's Road when John got that great job in an advertising agency. In all honesty, Kit reasoned with herself, as she slipped a linen jacket on and applied a bit of lipstick, Ellen and John were in a much better position to take care of Mr Myles than she and Jim were.

'I'm sorry, Kit,' her sister-in-law declared emphatically when Kit put it to her. 'In this case blood is not thicker than water. I don't care if the bastard rots in a poorhouse. I'm having nothing to do with him and that's final. And if you've any sense, you'll put your foot down and have nothing to do with him either. He'll take over your household. He'll make the kids' life a misery. Well he's not going to do that to mine and I mean it, Kit, even if we have to fall out over it.' Ellen was shaking with emotion.

She supposed she couldn't blame her sister-in-law, Kit reflected as she walked slowly up the Ballymun Road. She was taking the long way home. She needed time to think. And she needed to gear up for the arguments that faced her. Ellen was right. She'd have to put her foot down if she wasn't going to get lumbered with her father-in-law. And why should she be stuck with him? she thought fiercely. He wasn't her responsibility. But he *is* Jim's, she thought glumly. And Ellen's too. Fair was fair, after all. Why should she have to shoulder the burden? For two pins, she'd go into the Slipper and get pissed, she thought furiously as she passed the pub. And to hell with the whole bloody lot of them. Kit gave a wry laugh. She wouldn't have the nerve to go into a pub on her own in the middle of the afternoon. The trouble with her, she decided, was that she let people walk all over her. Well no more. With a determined tread, Kit turned up St Pappin's Road towards home, rehearsing in her mind what she was going to say to her husband.

'Huh!' snorted Brenda as she raced back to Kathy's after her encounter with her mother. 'Enjoy yourself. What a laugh! Fat chance.' Hastily she reapplied her lipstick and pointed a warning finger at Jennifer. 'Don't you dare say one word.'

'I won't,' her young sister said solemnly. 'Can I have some lipstick?'

'No, you can't. Come on.' Brenda's heart felt like lead as they crossed The Green and headed for the terminus. Eddie and Kenny were already there and they greeted the girls enthusiastically.

'I have to bring her,' Brenda muttered shamefacedly, glowering at Jennifer.

Eddie shrugged his shoulders. 'No big deal. Hi.' He smiled at Jennifer.

Jennifer smiled back.

'Hello,' she said shyly.

Brenda was gobsmacked. He didn't mind. After all her worry and stress, Eddie didn't seem to mind that Jennifer was coming along as well. A distressing thought struck her. Maybe he didn't consider this a real date. Maybe it meant nothing to him and that was why he didn't mind about Jenny being with her. Her heart sank to her toes. She felt like crying.

'Cheer up,' Eddie instructed. 'You've a face on you that would curdle milk. We're going to have a bit of a laugh.' Brenda did her best to cheer up but her heart was heavy. Nevertheless, when they got off the bus at the end of O'Connell Street, her spirits lifted. Town was buzzing. Buskers on O'Connell Bridge played a jaunty tune. A street artist was drawing a picture of the Ha'penny Bridge and they stopped to look, impressed by his talent. They strolled on towards Grafton Street laughing and chatting. Jennifer walked quietly behind, eyes wide as she watched all that was going on around her. Soon, Brenda almost forgot that she was there. They walked the winding length of Dublin's poshest street. Peered in through shop windows, commenting on this and that. The gorgeous fashions greatly impressed the girls.

As they got nearer to the top, Brenda really started to enjoy herself. She was not used to this end of town. It seemed much more exciting than Henry Street and O'Connell Street. She could see Stephen's Green. The famous Gaiety Theatre where Maureen Potter played in her famous pantos at Christmas was nearby. They'd gone to the panto last Christmas and it had been brilliant. Suddenly, Brenda felt very grown-up sauntering along past theatres and restaurants and expensive department stores on a Saturday afternoon with two fellas. Cora Delahunty, eat your heart out, she thought happily. When they left the twisting claustrophobia of Grafton Street behind, Brenda drew a deep breath and gazed around her in pleasure. To her left she could see the stately Shelbourne Hotel, and to her right, down a lane, was the famous Dandelion Market. Hundreds of people crowded around the stalls hunting for bargains, and with a happy smile at Kathy she followed Eddie and Kenny through the traffic.

The five of them had a ball. They pored over the records. They examined the jewellery displays. They rummaged through clothes rails. They viewed the bric-à-brac with interest, she and Kathy picking out goodies they would love to have in their bedrooms. They watched an old man dancing, and enjoyed the music of the buskers. They bought ice cream and chocolate. Brenda bought her beads, Kathy bought nail varnish. Jennifer bought a second-hand Enid Blyton mystery book. Eddie bought a penknife and Kenny bought a second-hand army jacket and insisted on wearing it, although it was very warm.

After a couple of hours of absolute enjoyment, they bought crisps, cream buns and Coke and headed for Stephen's Green, where they had a lovely picnic in the late afternoon sun. Regretfully, Kathy and Brenda told the lads they'd have to go home. Kenny and Eddie were going to go to a picture in the Green Cinema later, they told the girls.

Eddie drew Brenda aside on the pretext of feeding the ducks and as they hunkered down together throwing bits of the top of her mother's almond ring to the eagerly awaiting ducks, he said offhandedly, 'There's a Céilí in school next Thursday, d'ya fancy coming with me?'

Brenda felt her heart soar with happiness. So he *was* interested.

'Yeah, I'd love to,' she mumbled. Eddie grinned and leaned over and gave her a hasty peck on the cheek.

'See you on the bus on Monday morning.'

Brenda couldn't speak, she was so happy.

'Don't you dare say one word about anything,' she warned her sister as they reached their front door an hour later.

'I won't,' Jennifer promised, eyes shining at the excitement of it all. 'Are you going with him?'

Brenda smiled happily and put her finger to her lips.

'Yes I am, but not a word, mind.'

She knocked on the door, because she'd forgotten her key, and it was opened a few minutes later by a subdued Sean. 'Somethin' awful's happened,' he blurted out. 'Mammy an' Daddy's after having an awful row an' Mammy's crying up in her bedroom an' Daddy's gone off in a temper.'

'What did they have the row about?' Brenda was horrified. Her parents rarely exchanged cross words. If her mother was crying and her father had gone off in a temper, it must have been something bad.

'Come on, Sean. Tell me,' she said worriedly.

'Well Mammy went to visit Auntie Ellen about

Grandpa Myles, an' Auntie Ellen said she was havin' nuttin' to do with him,' her brother explained breathlessly. 'An' Daddy said Grandpa Myles will just have to stay here when he comes out of hospital, until he gets better. That's if he ever gets better,' he added glumly.

Brenda felt her cloud of happiness evaporate into thin air.

Chapter Fifteen

'Jennifer, I want you,' she heard her grandfather call. God Almighty, I'll be dead late, she thought in exasperation. Why is he always annoying me? She was up to ninety. It was her first day in secondary school. She'd had a row with her mother, who wanted her to wear Brenda's blazer, which even she had only worn once or twice. And Jennifer couldn't blame her. Blazers were ultrahickey. Beth was waiting for her at the gate and now here was her grandfather bellowing at her from what used to be their dining-room, but which was now his bedroom. Swallowing her frustration she popped her head around the door. The fug of tobacco smoke nearly made her cough. Her grandfather smoked a pipe and the house reeked of the smell of it. It drove Kit mad.

'Good morning, Grandpa,' she said politely, feigning cheeriness.

'Come in here until I have a look at you,' he ordered, his grey bushy eyebrows drawing together as he scrutinized her. She looked at the elderly bald man sitting in his bed. Although he was disabled and was only a small wiry man, he had a very commanding air about him. Ever since he'd moved into their home three years ago he'd made his presence felt. Interfering in everything. Bossing them all about, even their father. He commented on everything even though Kit told him to mind his own business. Since Grandpa Myles had come to live with them, there wasn't a bit of peace in the house. Her mother was always narky. Her father was much stricter with them than he used to be and the pair of them were always arguing. Jennifer sometimes had the horrible thought that it was a pity the accident that disabled him hadn't killed him and saved them all from a life of hassle. Her cousins Susie and Pamela couldn't call any more because of the feud with Auntie Ellen. And Kit wasn't too keen on Jennifer going to stay the night with Pamela any more because she was a bit annoyed with Auntie Ellen for lumbering them with Grandpa. There was a coolness that had never been there before and it was all because of the grumpy old man in the bed.

'You look very smart, Jennifer, although it's a pity you don't do something about that fringe of yours. It's bad for your eyesight hanging down over your eyes like that. Your mother should know that.'

'I have to go, Grandpa, I'll be late,' Jennifer said politely, although she was furious at the way he criticized her mother.

'Oh always in a hurry. Never a minute to spend with your poor ailing grandfather,' he moaned. 'All of you, you're all the same. If only God had spared your poor grandmother to look after me.'

Oh no! Not the poor grandmother bit, Jennifer thought in desperation. This speech she had heard a thousand times.

'Grandpa, I really have to go now. I'll miss the bus.'

'Go on with you, and here.' He held out sixpence to her. 'Here's a tanner for your first day at your new school. I'll be waiting for you to tell me all about it when you get home,' he said brusquely. Jennifer felt like a heel. Here she was thinking all these dire thoughts about him and he'd gone and given her sixpence to spend because it was her first day at her new school. Brenda was always jeering her and saying that she was his pet, and maybe she was. Brenda hardly ever spoke to him. And when she did she could be a bit rude. Jennifer would like to be rude as well sometimes but she just couldn't bring herself to be.

She knew her grandfather was lonely. He loved to talk about the old days, but the boys were usually out playing football on The Green and Brenda ignored him completely so that just left her. Sometimes she felt sorry for him so she would sit and listen to his tales and actually enjoy them now and again.

She looked at the sixpence in her hand and felt her heart soften. Impulsively she leaned over and kissed his stubby lined cheek. 'Thanks, Grandpa.' Although he didn't let on, Jennifer knew he was pleased.

'G'wan out of that now, all the same you've a bit more feeling for me than the rest of that lot put together. I know I'm a great thorn in their sides. And that Brenda lassie is an ignorant young madam.' He waved a knobbly forefinger in the direction of the hall to indicate Brenda and the rest of the family.

'I'll see you later, Grandpa,' Jennifer said wearily, resentment surging again at the criticism of her family.

'What did he want?' her mother inquired, her voice a trifle cool after the contretemps over the blazer.

'He gave me sixpence because I was starting in secondary,' Jennifer explained. She was in a frenzy to be off but she wanted to try and make up for their previous argument.

'Huh!' Kit snorted. 'Aren't you the lucky one? All I get from him day in, day out, is impudence. I wish I was able to go to secondary school and get out of here for a while. I wouldn't mind having to wear a blazer if I could get some peace from that fella.' Jennifer sighed deeply, it was obvious her mother was still in a bad humour.

Kit, noting the sigh, looked at her and threw her eyes up to heaven. 'Don't mind me,' she said, in a softer tone. 'I'm getting my period and I'm like a demon. I shouldn't be taking it out on you. I'm sorry, Jenny. Off you go and have a lovely first day in secondary school. You look smashing in the uniform. I hope you and Beth will be in the same class. I'll be dying to hear all about it when you get home.' She held out her arms and Jennifer moved close for her embrace. Kit hugged her tightly and kissed the top of her head. 'Bye lovey.'

'Bye Mam, I'll see you later and tell you all about it,' Jennifer promised. She felt sorry for her mother. It was bad enough having to put up with her grandfather but she was getting her period as well. That was the pits. Jennifer had got her first period several months ago, and their subsequent appearances had not changed her attitude to them. She was not the slightest bit impressed by them and thought the whole palaver a dreadful messy nuisance. 'If you like I'll go for a walk with you this evening,' she offered generously, knowing that her mother enjoyed a walk but not on her own because she was afraid of dogs.

'Thanks, pet.' Her mother stood at the door and waved as she and Beth set off on their great new adventure.

As she watched Jenny and Beth march up the street in their new uniforms, a lump came to Kit's throat. It seemed like yesterday when she'd brought the pair of them to St Pappin's for their first day at school. Where had the time gone? And look at the way their lives had changed. And not for the better, she thought miserably as a tear rolled down her cheek. She'd been a bitch to her daughter this morning over that blazer. Poor Jenny had enough on her mind. Naturally she was a bit nervous starting a new school. Kit had been looking for someone to vent her frustration and temper on and she had taken it out on Jenny. Poor kind soft Jenny who was the most obliging of her children and the one she had the least trouble with.

The single tear was followed by a torrent and Kit, fearful that the father-in-law would catch her, stifled her sobs in her apron and hurried up the stairs to the relative sanctuary of her own bedroom. Not that it was much of a sanctuary any more, she thought dolefully, and the torrent turned into a waterfall. More often than not she lay awake seething at Jim, angry about his immense disloyalty to her. When it came to his father, there was no discussion. He just didn't want to hear. Kit felt frustrated and shut out. Having his father come to live with them had driven a wedge between them. The longer he stayed, the wider the chasm dividing them.

As the years passed and her misery deepened, Kit became even more depressed. She felt that it had come down to a choice between her and his father and Jim had chosen his father. Hurt, anger and resentment were eating away at her. She was taking it out on her children, snapping at them. Arguing with them over trivial things as she'd argued with poor old Jenny this morning. She was trying her best not to let her children see the antipathy she felt towards their grandfather. It was important that they treated him with respect. He was, after all, an elderly man. She wasn't going to have him saying that his grand-children weren't being brought up to respect their elders.

If only her father-in-law appreciated the care she gave him, she could have coped. But he was a rude garrulous cranky old man who loved the sound of his own voice and who firmly believed it was his right to dictate how the entire family should live and behave.

She'd lost her dining-room, which was turned into a bedroom for Dan. She had to endure him in the kitchen under her feet and in the sitting-room at night when she was trying to relax. Day in, day out. It was so wearing on the nerves that she felt her health was being affected. She'd spoken to her doctor about the tension headaches, the insomnia and the dreadful feeling of being wound up all the time but he just murmured something about her starting the change and offered her sleeping pills for the insomnia. Kit wondered sometimes if she was starting to have a nervous breakdown. It frightened her.

She was angry with Ellen. It took a huge effort to be civil to her. Their relationship had become strained and frosty. Of course, Ellen had stopped visiting when Dan had come to stay. Deep down, Kit understood her sister-in-law's enormous animosity towards her father, but dammit he was *her* father and not Kit's. Why didn't she take the responsibility for him and put him in a nursing home or something? Whenever Kit said that to Jim he would go spare. He'd say how would she like it if he'd suggested anything like that when her parents were alive.

'My parents weren't destroying my marriage,' she'd exploded bitterly after one particularly vicious row. She'd accused him of not loving her any more. Because if he did, he'd never allow his father to treat her as he did. Jim was so angry he'd gone downstairs and slept on the sofa. For the first time.

The memory of that made her cry even harder and she buried her face in the pillows and cried her eyes out. It was hopeless. Her life stretched out ahead of her, a life of rows and misery and repressed anger and all because of that awful little man downstairs who had ruined her happy family. And who looked as though he was going to live forever.

'Any chance of a cup of tea and a bit of brown bread or does a disabled man have to go and get his own breakfast?' she heard him call.

'If I get my hands on you, you little bastard, I'll disable you. Don't you worry, you horrible little weasel,' she swore, sitting up and rubbing her eyes. Kit got off the bed and went to brush her hair. It was liberally streaked with grey now, she thought despondently. Much of it put there by the Antichrist downstairs. A sudden determination gripped her and with swift economical movements she dressed and applied a light make-up. The boys called goodbye and she stood at the landing window and waved them off.

'Have I to go and get my own breakfast or what?' Dan appeared at his bedroom door, dressed in a worn grey dressing-gown and down-at-heel slippers.

'Yes Grandpa, I'm afraid you have. I've an appointment in town. And you'll have to get your own lunch too. I won't be back until this afternoon,' Kit informed him briskly. 'You can leave the washing-up and I'll do it.' Without a backward glance she marched out the front door, leaving her father-in-law staring after her in dismay.

Chapter Sixteen

'Well Mrs Myles, and what do you think of it?' The young man who had just cut and coloured her hair stood proudly behind her chair surveying his handiwork.

Kit studied her reflection in the mirror and felt exhilarated and a bit shocked at the same time. She'd never done anything so drastic in her life. Instead of grey straight hair she had strawberry blonde tresses that were cut in a neat geometrical bob to frame her face. 'Vidal Sassoon, eat your heart out,' grinned the young man. He was wearing too-tight jeans and a black shirt opened to reveal a tanned hairy chest which was adorned with gold medallions.

'It's very nice,' she murmured.

'Nice! It's fab, way out, it takes ten years off you, baby,' the young man exclaimed enthusiastically, running his fingers through his own permed and highlighted locks.

'Come back to me in six weeks. I'll trim your fringe if you need it. OK?'

'OK,' Kit agreed, wondering what had possessed her to go in to the unisex hair salon and make such a dramatic change in her hairstyle and colour.

You did it because you were letting yourself go. You were getting old before your time. You're not Methuselah yet, she thought wryly. Nevertheless. The exercise had had the desired effect. There was a spring in her step as she marched down Abbey Street and crossed O'Connell Street and went into Easons.

Kit was really starting to enjoy her unscheduled little jaunt. Something inside her had snapped that morning. When she saw the haggard face with the greying hair reflected in the mirror she'd decided she wasn't going to give in without a struggle. She wasn't going to let her life be spoiled by a crabby old man who needed a good kick up the arse. If her husband wanted to look after him, let him, Kit decided firmly. Enough was enough. She was going to start living again instead of existing in dreary drudgery for which she got no thanks.

A rare light-heartedness enveloped her as she caught sight of her glamorous new image in a mirror. Her haircut totally changed her looks. The hairdresser was right, it did take years off her age. Even her eyes seemed to have a bit of extra sparkle. She resolved there and then to treat herself to some new make-up and a new outfit. But first things first, she decided as she scanned the huge display rack of magazines until she found *Woman's Way*. Yes, first she was going to treat herself to lunch in Woolworth's café, have a read of her magazine and enjoy a cigarette in peace and quiet with no whining father-in-law to annoy her.

Kit relished every mouthful of her little treat. It was nice to sit back sipping her coffee and watch people bustling about. She didn't have to hurry anywhere. Afterwards, she spent ages testing and trying out new make-up. Then she went to Roches where she bought herself a navy tank top and flowery blouse and a flowing patterned skirt. A rush of adrenalin surged through her as she paid for her purchases. This was better than sex any day, she thought giddily. Jim had better not open his mouth about how much she'd spent or she'd let him have it. Though to give him his due, he was not a mean man. He'd been a very considerate husband until his father arrived.

It was amazing, Kit reflected, as she stood waiting for the 13 bus, how a trip to the hairdressers and lunch and a spree in town could lift the spirits so dramatically. She couldn't believe she was the same woman who'd been so weepy and depressed this morning. She felt rejuvenated. Don't lose this feeling, Kit warned herself as she sat, surrounded by her parcels, on the back seat of the almost empty bus. She knew it would be all too easy to slip back into her negative mood if she let herself. Well she wasn't going to let herself. She was going to fight back and reclaim what she could of her life, because otherwise she could see herself ending up on Valium. She'd seen the signs of it in the mirror that morning and it had shaken her. The only one who could do anything about it was herself and she'd taken the first step with her impulsive trip to town.

I'm proud of you, Kit, she congratulated herself, trying to give herself courage as she walked across The Green. She wondered what kind of a reception she'd get when she got home.

'Mam, it's fantastic. You look brill,' Jennifer enthused as she came out to the hall to welcome her mother home. She'd been worried about her, and here she was looking a million dollars with a new haircut and a lovely colour in her hair. She'd had her face made up too and she looked really well. Better than Jennifer had seen her looking in months.

'Do you like it?' Kit gave a sheepish smile. 'It's a bit drastic, isn't it?'

'It's just what you needed,' Jennifer insisted. 'What did you buy?'

They went through her purchases, holding them up against Kit for effect.

'Did you get home early? The boys aren't home yet, are they?' Kit inquired as she folded her new clothes neatly and put them back in the bags.

'I got off early because it was our first day,' Jennifer told her. 'Come on, let's have a cup of tea and I'll tell you all about it.'

'Where's himself?' Her mother grimaced.

'Sitting out the back smoking his pipe and reading his paper. He's in a huff because he had to get his own breakfast and lunch.'

'Isn't it a pity about him? He's lucky he's still alive to

be in a huff, and that I didn't murder him this morning,' Kit retorted sarcastically. 'I'd better go and make the beds before I sit down for a cup of tea. You go and put the kettle on.'

'The beds are made and the table is set for the dinner,' Jennifer declared, taking her mother firmly by the arm and leading her into the kitchen.

'You're a dote and I'd be lost without you.' Kit hugged her warmly and Jennifer hugged her back, glad that her mother seemed much more cheerful in herself.

They sat at the kitchen table, drinking their tea and gossiping about their respective days. The afternoon sun streamed through the small window in the front, shining on her mother's newly coiffed and coloured hair. Jennifer was extremely impressed with the style and cut of it. Before, her mother's hair had hung just to the top of her shoulders and had been well streaked with grey. It was now a lovely reddish blond and the cut was sharp and short, emphasizing her mother's fine cheekbones and lovely grey eyes. It was a complete transformation.

They were peeling the potatoes for the dinner when her grandfather walked in through the back door.

'Where've you been? The bread-man came and I didn't know what to get and those Imco cleaners came and I didn't know if you were sending anything to be cleaned. It's a bloody nuisance answering the door all day when you don't know what to be saying to people,' he grouched. He couldn't see Kit clearly because the sun was shining directly in his eyes. He moved out of the glare just as she turned around to answer him.

'Holy Hand a the Livin' God! What have you done to yourself, woman?' he expostulated. Jennifer turned away to hide her grin.

'I went to the hairdressers,' Kit retorted, 'is that a crime?'

'It is when you spend good money and come out looking like that,' the old man snorted as he limped through the kitchen and gave the door a ferocious slam.

Jennifer and Kit looked at each other, open-mouthed at his rudeness.

'Could you beat that?' Kit scowled. Jennifer couldn't help it, she burst into giggles.

'But did you see the face of him? It was priceless,' she chuckled. Her mother saw the funny side of it and started to laugh herself. The boys arrived home about ten minutes later and, after the initial shock of their mother's changed appearance, forgot all about it and went off to play football.

Jennifer was pouring milk into the jug when she heard her father's key in the door. She heard her grandfather emerge from his bedroom, where he'd been sulking, to go and greet his son.

After he'd said hello, Jim asked him how he was. 'And how would you expect me to be and I left here to my own devices all day? Had to get my own breakfast and lunch and answer the door to every Tom, Dick and Harry that called. That wife of yours has lost the run of herself. She went off into town and got a new-fangled hairdo. And I could have starved for all she cared.' Jennifer was furious. The nerve of him. The first time in ages that Kit had a day to herself and he was making a fuss about it. She was sorely tempted to go out and give him a piece of her mind, but her father wouldn't take too kindly to it. He never let them cheek their grandfather.

Jim walked into the kitchen looking tired. 'Hi Dad.' She gave him a kiss.

'Hi Jenny, how did your first day go?' Her father smiled at her as he walked over to the sink to wash his hands.

'It was great. Beth and I are in the same class. We're sitting together and we've got a lovely form teacher, Sister Agnes. She's really young and quite modern,' Jennifer assured him.

'That's good.' His lips twitched in amusement at the 'quite modern' bit. He turned to face her. 'Where's Brenda? Is she not home from school yet?'

· 'She's in Kathy's, they're doing their homework

together. Mam's leaving her dinner in the pot,' she explained.

'Where's your mother? I believe she's got a new hairdo?'

'Oh Daddy, it's lovely,' Jennifer said eagerly. 'And tell her that when she comes in. She's hanging out some tea towels.' Kit arrived in a minute later and stopped short when she saw her husband.

'Good Lord!' Jim stared at his wife. Jennifer watched him warily. She hoped he wouldn't say anything uncomplimentary as Grumps had done.

'I needed a change, I was getting in a rut,' Kit explained defensively.

'It's very nice, it's a bit different but it's very nice, Kit,' her husband approved. 'I like the colour.' They smiled at each other. Jennifer felt a huge wave of relief wash over her. Slowly she exhaled the breath she'd been holding. Sometimes things were a little tense between her parents. Anything could start a row. After Grandpa's ear-bashing and complaints a minute ago, Jennifer had been anxious about how Jim would react. He seemed to like it and that was the main thing.

They were sitting down having a cup of tea after their dessert when the subject came around to Kit's hairdo. Jim asked about the price, but before his wife had a chance to tell him, Grandpa Myles, who hadn't said a word all through the meal, butted in truculently, 'Waste of bloody money if you ask me. A woman of your age trying to look like a young wan. It's ridiculous. If you're grey you're grey, that's the way the good Lord meant it to be.'

'Nobody asked you,' Kit said hotly. 'It's got nothing to do with you. Nothing at all. So mind your own business.'

'Oh yes it has. It's got plenty to do with me,' he argued triumphantly. 'It is my business when I'm left here to look after myself and me a cripple and people knocking at the door and I not knowing what to say to them. It's got plenty to do with me, when you're out spending good money that my poor son has had to work himself to the bone for and you're frittering it away on nonsense,' he blustered.

Jennifer saw her mother's face go pale. In an instant she jumped from her chair, lifted the jug of milk off the table and flung it at her father-in-law, drenching him. 'I'm sick to death of you,' she shouted. 'I'm fed up to the back teeth listening to you criticizing me and my children. I don't want you here, you ignoramus, but I've got to put up with you because your own daughter won't have you in her house. I'm not taking any more nonsense from you, Dan Myles, so shut your goddamn mouth.'

'Kit, that's enough!' Jim shot up, grabbed a tea towel and started wiping his stunned father's shirt.

'Don't you DARE tell me that's enough, Jim Myles! Don't you bloody dare! You stand up for him. You've never once stood up for me against him and I'm supposed to be your wife. Ha!' she snorted. 'Well from now on he's your responsibility. If I feel like a day out I'm going to have a day out. Because I've had enough of the pair of you.' Face contorted with anger, she walked out the door and slammed it so hard it shook the picture of the Holy Family on the wall.

There was silence at the table. Jennifer felt sick.

'That woman is going off her head, and what kind of a way is that for any wife to talk to her husband? You'd want to give her a proper telling-off, Jim. I wouldn't have stood for that impudence from your mother,' her grandfather declared.

Fury welled up in her.

'You leave my mother alone, she's very good to you and all you do is upset her,' she burst out. 'You're a mean pig.'

'Jennifer!' her father roared. 'Apologize to your grandfather immediately.'

'I will not because that's what he is,' she yelled. 'And you never stand up for Mammy. It's always him.'

'Be quiet,' her father shouted. 'And don't give me back cheek or I'll let you know about it. Don't think because you're in secondary school now you're going to start getting notions about yourself. Leave the table and go to your room and don't let me hear another word. And you,' he glared at his father, 'be quiet.'

Jennifer burst into tears. Her father was pointing his finger right in her face. She wanted to thump him and to tell him to stop picking on her, which he always did when he was angry. It wasn't her and her mother he should be shouting at, it was his trouble-maker of a father who had caused all the fuss in the first place.

Crying, she rushed out of the kitchen and ran upstairs to her bedroom. I'm never ever getting married, she vowed bitterly, and when I grow up I'm never going to let any man boss me around the way my dad does. I just hate him, she sobbed to herself. She could hear her mother weeping in the adjoining bedroom. All of a sudden she felt very scared. Her parents were not getting on well any more. Was it always going to be like this? Jennifer felt as if the weight of the world was on her shoulders as she went to comfort her mother.

Chapter Seventeen

'Jenny, will you go to the shop for me?' Brenda asked.

'Ah Bren, I'm tired,' she raised her head from the brilliant Georgette Heyer book she was reading and gazed over at her sister, who was sprawled across her bed gazing at a photo of Mick Jagger.

If Jennifer heard *Satisfaction* just once more she'd freak. Brenda played it night and day.

It was a Sunday afternoon and the house was peaceful. Her mother was off visiting an arts and crafts exhibition at her ladies' club. Her father was at a football match with her brothers. And from the rumbles downstairs, Jennifer deduced that her grandfather was snoring his head off enjoying an after-dinner nap. To tell the truth she felt like going for a nap herself. She'd been working all summer, in a jam-making factory. Yesterday had been her last day and she'd got overtime as well but she was absolutely whacked. It was her turn to make the Sunday dinner so she couldn't even have a lie-in this morning. The last thing she wanted to do was to go traipsing off to the shops. Besides, it had started to bucket rain. So much for summer, she thought dispiritedly. In two days' time, her mother, the boys and herself were heading down to a caravan site at Carne beach for ten days' holiday. Beth was coming too and Jennifer was living for it. Beth had been working in a café in town and she was even more exhausted than Jennifer was because she'd had to work shift hours. All they were going to do was sleep and eat, they promised themselves. They weren't looking forward to going back to school this year either. It was their Inter Cert year and they were going to have to knuckle under and get some serious study done.

'Please, Jenny, I'm dying for some chocolate,' Brenda interrupted her musings. 'I'll treat you as well.'

Jennifer sighed. She knew Brenda would nag and nag and the afternoon would be ruined if she didn't go and get the bloomin' chocolate. She could, of course, refuse outright and then her sister would have a face on her and go into one of her huffs. It was such a pain in the neck. All Jennifer wanted to do was snuggle under her quilt with her book and drop off into a nice doze when her eyes got heavy. The rain was beating against the window. In the distance, over the mountains, she could hear the rumble of thunder. It was a perfect afternoon to be lazing in bed. Why couldn't Brenda just piss off and leave her alone?

'Come on, let's have a binge. Just think, crisps and chocolate and lemonade, you can have what you like,' her sister wheedled.

'Oh give me the money!' Jennifer barked, throwing back her quilt and getting off the bed. There was no point in sitting listening to that carry-on for the afternoon. She might as well get it over with so she could finally relax.

Brenda threw her a pound note. 'Just spend the lot of it, I don't care,' she instructed. 'Get me two packets of crisps, some chocolate and whatever else you like.'

'You're going to hate yourself after. You'll be moaning about putting on weight,' Jennifer warned, hoping against hope that Brenda might reconsider.

'Who cares? I don't. I just want some chocolate,' Brenda declared glumly, staring at her favourite picture of herself and Eddie. They'd had a tiff.

'Look, you're going to be huge if you keep having feasts like this,' Jennifer cautioned.

'I'll start my diet tomorrow,' Brenda promised. 'Would you get me a fruit slice, if they have one, as well?'

It was hard living with someone who was in love, Jennifer reflected as she stepped over a huge puddle and tried to keep her umbrella from blowing inside out. It was more like the middle of winter than summer.

It would be such a relief to get away for a few days, she thought as she battled her way home, ten minutes later, with a bag of goodies under her arm.

An ambulance went roaring past, its siren wailing, its lights flashing, and she said a quick prayer for the occupant. She hadn't seen which direction it had come from, she'd been so busy keeping her head down against the sheets of rain that were blowing into her face. She arrived home, dripping wet, cold and miserable but with the prospect of her book and bed and some chocolate to cheer her up. Brenda met her at the foot of the stairs. She looked concerned about something.

'Jenny, Beth's had a terrible accident. She's just been taken to hospital in the ambulance. Kathy ran in to tell me. It's very serious,' she heard her sister say. Jennifer felt tears spring to her eyes. That was the end of Beth coming on holiday and she had been so looking forward to it.

'What happened?' she asked, shocked.

'She was standing on a ladder while her brother was passing her down a case from the attic and the ladder moved and she slipped and lost her footing and fell over the banisters on her head.'

'Oh God, it's all my fault. If I hadn't asked her to go on holidays she wouldn't have been getting a case from the attic.'

'Don't be daft, Jenny, these things happen. You can't blame yourself. It was the hand of God,' Brenda declared. 'Did you get my chocolate?'

Mutely, Jennifer handed over the bag. Brenda was so self-centred. Imagine asking if Jennifer had bought her chocolate at a time like this, she thought in disgust. All Jennifer wanted to do was to go into the hospital and see how Beth was. The prospect of going on holidays without her was most unappealing. Nothing ever turned out the way you wanted it to, she thought forlornly, refusing Brenda's offer of a bar of whole-nut. Her stomach was

174

tied up in knots. Beth was seriously ill. Just how serious was serious? Was it broken limbs or was it much worse? Please God, let Beth be OK, she prayed silently, wondering should she call down to Clearys but not wishing to intrude. The ambulance had only passed her a few minutes ago. There wouldn't be any news yet.

The news, when it came, was not good. Beth was unconscious with a broken neck. They didn't know the extent of the injuries. Beyond that they could not say. Jennifer was devastated. Only family were allowed to visit and Mrs Cleary insisted that Jennifer go on holidays with her mother and brothers as planned. 'There's nothing you can do by staying at home, pet,' she insisted. 'They won't let you in to see her so you might as well go. You can phone me every night and I'll tell you what's happening.'

Jennifer went to the mobile home with her mother and brothers, but it was the most miserable holiday of her life. First of all, she was plagued by guilt. Guilt at being on holidays when her friend was seriously ill in hospital and guilt at feeling responsible for the accident. It didn't help that it rained for eight of the ten days and all she could do was sit staring out at the grey gloom trying to figure out where the sky merged with the angry leaden sea. Reading offered her no solace. Her thoughts constantly strayed towards home and Beth. Each night she phoned Mrs Cleary to be told the same news. Beth was in a coma and her condition had not improved. Trapped in the claustrophobic confines of the holiday home, listening to her mother moaning about having to put up with her father-in-law in the house, listening to her brothers arguing the toss out of boredom, Jennifer felt like screaming.

'Oh for God's sake, can't you talk about something else?' she snapped one evening after listening to Kit giving out yet again about Dan. He'd answered the phone when Kit called to speak to Jim and informed his daughter-in-law that there was great peace and quiet in the house.

He more or less implied that she wasn't missed in the slightest.

Kit was disconcerted by her daughter's rebuke and silently she wrapped herself in her anorak and marched out the door of the mobile home. She gave it a good slam as she went. Jennifer watched her go and felt that she couldn't take much more.

Kit walked along the beach, head down into the wind. Salty rain stung her cheeks and lips. Damp sand clung to her runners as her feet sank into the cloying softness beneath them. Small fishing boats bobbed up and down alongside the pier and the frothy white spume of the waves crashed over their bows.

Jennifer had been *rude* . . . There was no need for such bad manners. Kit had a lot to put up with. That old scourge up in Dublin was enough to drive anyone barmy. Kit gave a tight smile. Ever since she'd thrown the milk jug at him though, he'd tread a bit more warily. He didn't give her as much impudence as before and he was now well used to getting his own breakfast and lunch when the need arose. As it often did, she thought with satisfaction. Since that day when she'd gone into town and had her hair cut and coloured, Kit had clawed back a life for herself. She'd joined the local ladies' club. She'd taken up embroidery and patchwork. She went swimming three times a week, as well as joining an exercise class. She enjoyed all of her activities, especially the physical ones. They helped to keep her sane. More importantly, they helped her feel she had taken back some control of her life. Because she could work off her frustrations and resentments in exercise, she wasn't so touchy and wound up at home. Much to her husband's relief. Between them, there was an unspoken if somewhat fragile truce. Jim had been terribly shocked at her outburst that evening and had told her that if it was what she really wanted, he would put his father in a home. It was such a glorious proposal that she'd agreed immediately. But after several hours of reflection, she knew she couldn't let Jim go through with it. Nevertheless, it was a night that marked a turning point in her life. She felt now that, if really pushed, her husband would make the choice between her and his father and she would be his choice. Kit gained back a measure of self-esteem which helped her through the rough patches when Dan was driving her nuts.

Kit sighed and turned her face towards the sea. One of the ferries was ploughing through the waves past the slender white column of the Tuskar Rock lighthouse. She watched until it disappeared around the curve of the bay and headed towards the safety of Rosslare Harbour. Maybe she had been moaning a bit to Jenny. After all, the poor girl was in an awful state about Beth. But she always felt she could pour out her woes to Jenny. Much more so than to Brenda, who was totally wrapped up in herself. If Kit thought she had woes, her eldest daughter could out-woe her anytime. She'd been unfair to Jenny, she decided. It was something she must guard against. Turning towards home, Kit prepared her words of apology.

It was strange to be sitting on her own at school, Jennifer thought sadly. If only Beth was with her on the first day back. At least she was out of her coma and that was the best news that could have greeted Jennifer on her return home to the city after her disastrous holiday. She was not allowed to visit as Beth was still seriously ill. But the doctors were optimistic that in time her best friend would make a satisfactory recovery. It would take months, but it was good news. The headmistress had asked the whole school to pray for Beth at assembly that morning and Jennifer was sure that so many heartfelt prayers would not go unanswered.

She was delving deep into her schoolbag when she heard Sister Imelda's voice above her. 'Jennifer, this is a new girl. I'm sure you won't mind if she sits beside you until Beth returns to us.'

Oh no, thought Jennifer to herself. The last thing she needed was polite small talk with a stranger. She felt quite resentful that someone else would be sitting in Beth's seat. She looked up to find a very pretty petite blond-haired girl smiling at her.

'Hello,' the stranger held out her hand. 'It's nice to meet you, my name is Paula Matthews.'

Book Two

Chapter Eighteen

Rachel felt sick with nerves. The supervisor handed out the Honours English papers. There was a last-minute shuffling and coughing and fidgeting as the sixth years of St Angela's prepared to do their Leaving Certificate exam. It was very important that Rachel do well in English, Irish and Maths. Good results in these subjects would make all the difference to her application to St Patrick's Teacher Training College in Drumcondra.

Rachel didn't particularly want to be a teacher. She dreamed of being an air hostess. She could wear contact lenses and look very glamorous and fly around the world.

'Indeed and you won't be an air hostess, Miss,' her father pronounced when he heard this sensational piece of news. 'I'm not having any daughter of mine working as a glorified waitress and wasting her good education.' In vain had Rachel pointed out that an air hostess needed to have foreign languages, and had to be capable of giving first-aid treatment in an emergency. Serving food was only a small part of the job. Her father was not impressed.

'Nonsense, Rachel, you don't know what you're talking about.' Her father's constant put-down for as long as she could remember. It enraged her. She never answered him back. One didn't with William Stapleton. Even her mother didn't often argue with him. He was too much of an autocrat.

Rachel gave vent to her fury only in the privacy of her bedroom. She'd make scathing retorts to the photograph of him she kept for that purpose. 'You stupid, ridiculous, horrible man. You old-fashioned idiotic clod of a schoolteacher. What would you know about it? What would you know about anything in the modern world? You fossil, you. You bald-headed bastard. Someday . . . Mister. Someday I'm going to tell you exactly what I think of you.' This thought kept her going and made life bearable. Someday she would certainly turn on her father and tell him to get stuffed. And that she was leaving Rathbarry for good. Just when she was going to do this, Rachel hadn't decided. She'd have to wait until she got a job. Now that her father had insisted she become a teacher, she was going to be beholden to him for the next three years of her teacher training. What a pain in the neck, she thought glumly as the supervisor placed the exam paper face down on her desk.

Rachel loosened her tie. It was warm. They were taking the exam in the school library. How ironic, reflected Rachel as she gazed around at the book-filled wooden shelves that lined the walls of the bright, airy, rectangular library, that the place that had been her greatest haven at school should now be the scene of this ordeal. She'd been dreading her Leaving Certificate exam for months. Her father never lost an opportunity of pointing out that it was the most important exam in a student's life. The gateway to life itself, he was fond of saying.

Her father warned her that if she didn't do well in the exam, she was going to have to repeat sixth year. If she did do well, she'd be off to St Pat's for another three years of swotting. It was a no-win situation. Or maybe not, she mused. If she went to St Pat's, she'd live in college and that could be good fun. It would be marvellous not to have her father constantly telling her what to do. She'd have her own room. The rules of the college could hardly be any stricter than the rules of William Stapleton. There'd be discos and societies to join and a chance to meet men and even go on dates. Maybe teacher training college wasn't the worst thing in the world. It would be very exciting living in Dublin after the languid pace of life in Rathbarry. Ronan loved Dublin. But then Ronan was much braver than she was. Her brother never allowed their father to boss him around. She should take a leaf out of Ronan's book, she decided firmly. That was if she did OK in her exams. She was beginning to feel very apprehensive.

'You may turn over your papers and begin, girls,' the supervisor said. Then she discreetly took a Mary Stewart thriller out of her bag and settled down to a peaceful morning's reading.

Rachel's heart thumped as she turned over the paper and began to read through it. At first everything was a blur. Words jumped out at her. The *Portrait of a Lady* question looked poxy. So did the one on *Coriolanus*. Oh God! This was a disaster. Calm down, she thought frantically. Take deep breaths. In front of her, Glenda Mower was already beginning to write. So was Eileen Dunphy. This panicked Rachel even more. Maybe it was just she who found the paper difficult. Her palms began to sweat. She felt dizzy. Her stomach cramped and she felt a bit pukey. Why did her period have to arrive this morning? It was the last thing she needed. She'd been horrified when she woke up to find it had come. When she had her period she sometimes felt a bit woozy in her thinking. As if her thoughts were smothered by cotton wool. She needed to have her wits about her today. Her brain had to be sharp and functioning. Oh God, what am I going to do? she thought desperately. Across the aisle, Michelle Butler was chewing the top of her pen pensively. She hadn't started to write yet. And Michelle was one of the brainiest in the class. Michelle smiled at her and threw her eyes up to heaven. Relief flooded through Rachel, Michelle wasn't too enamoured of the paper either.

She slipped a Polo Mint into her mouth, Polo Mints always helped her feel less queasy when she had her period. Her panic lessened. She began to read her paper again. The question on *Coriolanus* wasn't as awful as she'd thought, she decided. Rachel took the top off her pen and began to write, a little shakily at first until she got into her stride. She couldn't believe it when the supervisor called for their papers two and a half hours later. It had only seemed like twenty minutes. It hadn't been half as bad as she'd thought it was. Rachel was quite light-hearted as she listened to the post-mortem afterwards and felt that she had answered her questions reasonably well.

'O Sacred Heart of Jesus, I place all my trust in thee,' Theresa prayed with heartfelt urgency as she glanced at the clock on the mantelpiece in the kitchen and saw that it was after twelve-thirty. The exam should be over by now. God grant that Rachel had done well. The poor child had been so nervous going in to school this morning and she'd got her period unexpectedly as well. The things women have to put up with. Theresa sighed.

She was going through the change herself. It was a nightmare. The sweats and hot flushes were most distressing. She'd been sitting listening to the sermon at Mass last Sunday when she'd been struck by a hot flush. She could feel her face boiling. Perspiration trickled down the collar of her good white blouse. She'd felt terribly hot and agitated. It would have been a relief to slip out of the church but they were in the front pew. William would never consider sitting anywhere else. As headmaster, he had to set a good example. Theresa hated sitting in the front row. She'd much prefer to sit in the seats near the side door, which was where she sat when she went to Mass by herself during the week. But on Sundays she had to sit where her husband sat, no matter how uncomfortable she felt.

It had been a long hot flush. She hadn't been able to say another prayer. All she'd wanted to do was to get away by herself. Theresa felt she couldn't go out. She'd have to disturb the other people in the seat and there'd be the long walk down the aisle of the church with everyone looking at her. William would not be impressed. It was too awful to contemplate. She'd lasted until the end of Mass, but it had been extremely stressful. The thought of going to Sunday Mass was now a big worry. What if the same thing happened again? She'd offer it up, she decided, so that Rachel would do well in her Leaving Certificate. Her daughter would have a bit of freedom if she went to Dublin to do teacher training. Like Ronan, who was studying electronics in Bolton Street Tech.

Theresa smiled as she thought of her son. Ronan didn't let his father browbeat him. There'd been a fierce argument when William insisted that his son must go to university to get a degree and Ronan had insisted on going to Bolton Street to study electronics.

'It's either electronics or else I'm not doing third level at all, I'll get whatever job I can get and leave home,' Ronan declared. William caved in. He couldn't take the idea of his son having no qualification in life. Theresa had been secretly delighted. It did her heart good to see her son standing up to his father. She had no fears for Ronan but she worried desperately about Rachel. Rachel would never defy William. She would always be under his thumb unless she moved away from home and stood on her own two feet. If she did teacher training, she could live in one of the halls of residence. Theresa knew her daughter didn't want to be a teacher, but it might be the making of her . . . Rachel needed to get away from her father and get a bit of self-confidence. It would be hard not having her daughter at home. Theresa missed Ronan dreadfully although he came home for weekends but knowing that he was becoming self-sufficient was enough to make up for it, Theresa mused as she stood looking out the kitchen window at William mowing the grass in the back garden.

He thought he was a great father. Concerned for their welfare and education. He would have been truly horrified if he'd realized that he was viewed as a tyrant by his wife and children. Theresa knew this. She'd tried to make him see that constantly exerting authority was not necessary. William was convinced that his children were his own personal property to do with what he would. The idea that they were people in their own right was totally alien to him. He knew what was best for them.

That was what a father was for, to guide, to instruct and to be obeyed, he told Theresa over and over when she tried to argue that Ronan and Rachel were entitled to make their own decisions about their futures. The trouble with William was that he had to be in control . . . of everything. Theresa sighed, as she started to make the gravy from the juice of the stuffed lamb cutlets that were sizzling away in the tinfoil.

William mowed the grass with vigour and precision. His lines were straight, giving a neat manicured effect to the lawn. He wondered how Rachel was doing in her Honours English. It should prove to be relatively easy, after all, he had given her extra coaching after school. At least his daughter would let herself be advised by him, not like that scut Ronan, who was becoming far too obstreperous for William's liking.

It wasn't William's doing that Master Ronan was living in digs in Phibsboro. No indeed. That was all due to Theresa. William wanted his son to commute to the city daily and return home to his own bed at night. But Ronan had started to moan. He maintained that time spent on buses would be better spent studying in the college library. Ronan announced he wanted to do extracurricular classes in computer studies in the evenings. In the end, and much against his better judgement, William had given way and agreed to let his son live in digs in Dublin, on condition that he come home at weekends. It was the thin end of the wedge, there were weekends now when Ronan only made a brief appearance. He'd come home on Sunday mornings, with the excuse that he'd been studying on Saturday. William suspected that his son was out carousing!

Rachel certainly wouldn't be living in Dublin for the duration of her teacher training. William was unequivocal about that. Rachel would commute and there'd be no arguments about it. The trouble with this family was that nobody listened to him. Theresa let the children away with murder. This time he was going to put his foot down. He couldn't allow his daughter to live in Dublin on her own. It was unthinkable. There was so much crime these days. Young women weren't safe on the streets. Rachel was a timid soul. She wouldn't manage on her own in the city. Even in a hall of residence. Theresa had better not start any arguments to the contrary. She had no concept of parental responsibility. Giving in to children might be kindly meant but it was much harder to be firm. In some ways firmness showed a much greater love. His wife couldn't see that. She had always accused him of being too strict. That was an unfair accusation, he thought self-righteously.

This time he wouldn't budge, William vowed as he pushed his lawnmower and beheaded several dandelions that had no business being in his lawn.

Chapter Nineteen

Rachel couldn't believe that the Leaving Cert was finally over. The relief of it. It was as if a great weight had been lifted from her. She felt quite buoyant as she left the library for the last time, having handed up her last exam paper. She hadn't done too badly once she'd got over her nerves. She would surely get enough marks to go to college in Dublin.

Mary Foley and Eileen Dunphy and some of the others were discussing the exam in the middle of the Blue Corridor.

'It was a disaster,' wailed Mary. 'I know I've failed.'

Rachel couldn't help feeling a bit smug. She'd had no difficulties with the paper. If Michelle Butler had felt she'd done badly, Rachel would have been sorry for her. But it was good enough for Mary Foley. Rachel still felt bitter about the way Mary had dropped her like a hot potato once they'd started school and she'd made new friends. Mary Foley was as two-faced as they come. Rachel wasn't going to waste any sympathy on her.

'Forget about it,' Eileen urged. 'We're free at last, let's think about the joy of leaving this dump forever. There are much more important things to discuss than a bloody exam. The Debs, for instance,' she said briskly. Rachel's heart sank. In the hectic worry-filled days coming up to the exams, she'd almost forgotten about the next big ordeal. The Debutantes' Ball. The Debs Ball was a big occasion. All the sixth years were invited to attend. Gowns had to be bought or made. The girls would call in to the nuns to show off their finery on that special night, before setting out for the hotel. But you had to have a fella if you wanted to go to the Debs Ball.

Rachel sighed as she heard Mary say excitedly, 'Oh yeah, I forgot about that. I can't wait. Gerry's going to come with me.' There was a babble of excited chatter from the rest of them.

'I'm on the organizing committee. And I want to get cracking. I'd better start asking who's coming so I can begin arranging the tickets,' Eileen said crisply, rooting in her satchel for a notebook.

Oh God Almighty, Rachel thought in panic. She quickened her pace. Why had Eileen Dunphy picked the moment she was walking down the corridor to start organizing the blasted Debs Ball? To say you weren't going to the Debs because you hadn't got a fella to take you was an admission of complete and utter failure. If it had been two minutes later Rachel would have been out the door. And she'd never have to see Eileen Dunphy again. She'd only have to put up with Mary Foley as she also lived in Rathbarry.

Trying to make herself as inconspicuous as possible, Rachel edged her way along the corridor past the knot of girls standing in the middle of it. The stairs leading to the main front door were in sight. She didn't have to collect anything from the cloakrooms, she would just slip out as quickly as she could. Rachel walked faster, feeling a faint sense of relief that she'd almost made it.

'Rachel! Rachel Stapleton!' Rachel's heart plummeted as the imperious tones of Eileen Dunphy echoed down the corridor after her. She turned reluctantly. They were all looking at her. Grinning. Rachel could see the smug, superior expression on Eileen's face.

Eileen Dunphy was small, wiry, with bushy curly hair. What she lacked in stature, she made up for in loquacious-ness. Eileen had an opinion on everything. If you said something was black, Eileen would say it was white. She couldn't argue a topic quietly. Eileen liked confrontation, the more heated the debate the better. Rachel always kept out of her way.

'Come here,' Eileen ordered. Rachel was furious. Who did Eileen Dunphy think she was, talking to her like that? She badly wanted to stay where she was and make Eileen walk to her, but timidity got the better of her as usual. With leaden feet she retraced her steps.

'I'm in a bit of a hurry, Eileen,' she muttered, feeling like someone who was being led to the gallows.

'This won't take long,' Eileen retorted. 'I'm just making a list of people going to the Debs.' Some of the others tittered. 'Will you be coming?' Eileen stood, pen poised over a notebook. Rachel's cheeks flamed. She could see Mary Foley and her cronies grinning. Enjoying Rachel's discomfiture. Rachel cringed inwardly. The cruel bitches. How she hated them. How she longed to turn on them and tell them exactly what she thought of them. Why couldn't she be as fluent and articulate as she was when she was in the privacy of her bedroom? There, she would make smart cutting answers to the mirror, and pretend she was talking to them. Why couldn't she think up a smart answer right now? When she was sitting by herself on the bus home to Rathbarry she'd have no trouble thinking of a crushing retort.

She took a deep breath and stared at Eileen. A madness seized her and Rachel threw caution to the winds. 'Of course I'll be going to the Debs. Put me down for two tickets,' she said offhandedly as if it was no big deal. Several jaws, including Mary Foley's, dropped. Much to Rachel's satisfaction. 'I have to go, I'm in a rush. See you,' she said hastily to the now silent group. Rachel marched down the corridor with her head held high. Fuck them, she thought defiantly. She could always pull out of it later. *If* she couldn't get anyone to go with her. Harry, Ronan's best friend, would be home at the weekend. Her Sir Galahad from that snowy day long ago. She fancied Harry like mad and as far as she knew it was all off with Ciara Farrell. Maybe she'd pluck up the courage to do something brave just this once and ask Harry to be her partner at the Debs. If she appeared on the night, escorted by Harry Armstrong, that would knock the smirks off their faces.

But would she have the nerve to ask Harry? And would he agree, or would he say no and be embarrassed that she'd asked him? The heavy weight was back on her shoulders. Another ordeal to endure, she thought despondently as she waited at the bus stop. Rachel decided to start praying even harder to St Jude.

Chapter Twenty

Rachel lightly rubbed margarine and flour between her fingers. She was making a tart for tea. She already had made two dozen fairy cakes and a dozen scones. It was a Sunday afternoon, about a month after the fateful encounter with Eileen Dunphy. In that month she had not had sight nor sound of Harry Armstrong. He hadn't come home the weekend he'd been expected. He was working as a barman in Dublin for the holidays, according to Ronan. He needed the money to help put him through law school.

Rachel wished that she could ask him about the Debs and get it over with. At least if he said no, she'd know that was the end of that, she was going to lose face in front of the others. It was the not knowing that was the unsettling thing. Mary Foley had accosted her on the street the other day to tell her that Eileen was looking for a booking deposit.

Bully for her, Rachel felt like saying but she just made some non-committal reply and rushed on. Was there to be no peace from them, ever?

She'd hurried along to Healy's Tea Rooms, where she was working for the summer holidays. Rachel liked working for the Misses Healy. The Tea Rooms opened for the summer and Rachel had been working as a waitress there for the last two years. They opened at ten in the morning to catch the daily Mass-goers. Sometimes Theresa came in to have a scone and a cup of coffee with Sergeant Roach's wife. Tourists dropped in to enjoy the delicious pastries that the two sisters baked. But their main customers were the seasonal workers from Doherty's fruit and veg farm, where Ronan was working for the summer. They came for the freshly made soups and sandwiches and rolls that the Misses Healy served for lunch. Rachel was usually run off her feet at lunch-time. But she liked it busy, the day passed much more quickly that way and she always made much more in tips.

She would have preferred to go to work in one of the hotels or guest houses in Bray, but her father wanted her to stay near home. He thought it was ideal that she had a job down the road.

Of course he would, Rachel thought sourly as she slapped the dough out on to a floured board and began to knead it. William Stapleton had to be the most unadventurous soul in the world. He was sitting in a deck-chair in the back garden listening to a hurling match on the radio and reading the Sunday newspaper. His usual and unvarying Sunday routine. Her mother was in bed, not feeling the best. Rachel had made the dinner and cleaned up after it and decided to do some baking so her mother wouldn't have to do it the next day. When she was finished she was going to take her book down to the riverbank and relax in the sun. It was a warm sunny day. She was looking forward to getting out in the fresh air.

She was just taking the cooked tart out of the oven when Ronan poked his head around the back door.

'Hi Rach, that smells fabbo, any chance of a slice? And look what the wind's blown in,' he announced, giving her a little wink. Rachel looked out from behind her steamed-up glasses to see Harry walking in behind her brother.

Oh hell! she thought in dismay. How typical. Here she was, with her cheeks roaring red from the heat of the kitchen, her glasses fogged up, her hair all over the place and not a screed of lipstick or mascara on. Could you have luck?

'Hi Harry,' she said shyly. 'Excuse the mess, I was just doing a bit of baking for Mam.'

'That's what I call good timing,' Harry said cheerfully, eyeing the plate of fairy cakes. 'Can I have one?'

'Sure, go ahead.' Rachel laughed. Ronan was already putting on the kettle for a cup of tea. Harry scoffed the little cake in seconds.

'Have another one,' she invited.

'Don't mind if I do.' Harry grinned at her and devoured a second cake. 'You're a lucky sod having a sister who can cook,' he commented to Ronan, who was making fast work of a scone. 'My sisters couldn't cook a tart to save their lives. Speaking of tarts,' he teased, 'do you want me to sample a bit of that one?' He indicated the golden tart that was cooling on a baking tray.

'If you want to.' Rachel was delighted her baking was such a hit. 'I'll just whip up a bit of cream for it.' She whisked up the cream while Ronan made a pot of tea.

'Will I see if Mam would like a cup?' Ronan said. 'Here, I'll bring her up one and a cake as well, she didn't eat much dinner, she might be peckish.' Rachel felt her insides flutter. She knew Ronan was leaving her alone so she could ask Harry about the Debs. She had confided in her brother that she needed someone to go to the Debs with her. She'd asked him if he thought Harry might oblige her.

'All you can do is ask,' Ronan declared firmly. 'He who dares . . . wins. Ask and you shall receive,' he teased. It was all right for Ronan to say 'ask.' Asking took courage and she was a notorious coward.

Ronan left the kitchen to go on his errand of mercy and Rachel felt her hands go sweaty as she held the whisk. In her agitation, she whisked even more energetically than before and splattered cream all over the place. Harry came and stood beside her and dabbed his finger in a big blob of cream on the worktop and licked it. 'Ronan says you're happy enough with the Leaving,' he said.

'It wasn't too bad,' she responded shyly, wishing she didn't feel so tongue-tied. All the wonderful sparkling witty conversations she'd imagined with Harry and now, of course, she couldn't think of a word to say to him.

'When you come up to Dublin the three of us must

meet for a drink now and again,' he said as she cut a generous slice of apple tart and put a huge dollop of cream on it.

'That'll be great,' she enthused, handing him the plate. 'I hadn't thought of that. St Pat's isn't all that far from where Ronan's living.'

'I don't live too far from Ronan either, I'm on the North Circular Road. I'm in a flat. I asked Ro would he come and share but your dad wasn't too happy with the idea. Actually he put his foot down and said no,' Harry said between mouthfuls of tart.

'That's no surprise,' Rachel murmured.

'It'll be nice for you having a bit of freedom at college,' Harry said diplomatically.

'I know, I can't wait.' Rachel smiled as she poured herself a cup of tea. Do it! she kept telling herself. Do it now!

'More tea?' she inquired, chickening out.

'No thanks,' Harry replied.

'Mmm . . . I was just wondering, Harry?'

'Yes, Rachel?' he said helpfully.

'Aaah . . . aa . . . would you like a scone?'

'Maybe I will,' he agreed. 'I don't get treats like this when I'm cooking for myself.'

'Mmm . . . Harry . . .' she began again, her voice almost quivering. Ronan arrived back into the kitchen. He cast her a look of inquiry. Rachel gave a little shake of her head and he threw his eyes up to heaven behind Harry's back.

'I'll just bring Dad out a cup of tea, he might enjoy it,' he said. 'Although he hasn't asked . . . he shall receive,' her brother said pointedly as he poured the tea and placed a fairy cake on the saucer. He went out into the garden to their father and Rachel took another deep breath. Before she had time to think about it, she just plunged in.

'Harry, it's my Debs in September and I need someone to go with and I was . . . I mean . . . I was wondering if you'd like to come?'

Chapter Twenty-One

'I'd be delighted to go with you.' Harry smiled. Rachel stared at him. 'Just let me know the exact date.'

'I . . . I don't know the exact date yet,' she stammered.

'As soon as you find out, let me know,' Harry said cheerfully. Rachel couldn't believe it. Harry Armstrong was going to come to the Debs Ball with her. He hadn't turned her down. He'd said yes, just like that. It was amazing.

'Have you any word about your interview for St Pat's yet?' Harry asked matter-of-factly. Rachel shook her head as her heartbeat began to return to normal.

'I have to wait for my results first.'

'That's a bit of a pain.' Harry sat back in his chair and drank his tea.

'Yeah, it is,' Rachel agreed happily. She was on cloud nine. Just wait until Glenda and Eileen and Mary got an eyeful of Harry. They'd be pea-green with envy. Harry was an out-and-out hunk. There was no denying it. He had lovely black curly hair. Brown eyes. A very sexy smile, and a six-foot body that she could spend hours admiring. Harry played a lot of football. He was very fit and muscular, not like Mary Foley's Gerry, who was rather on the podgy side and no athlete.

'I'd better go out and say hello to your da.' Harry uncoiled his long length from the chair. 'As soon as you hear anything about the date, give me a shout.'

'I will,' Rachel promised shyly. 'Thanks for coming.'

'Thanks for asking me.' Harry smiled. She watched him go out to join Ronan and her father and her heart soared with happiness. 'Thanks, St Jude. Thanks a million,' she murmured as she rinsed his cup and plate and caught sight of her reflection in the strip across the top of the cooker. She had a big smudge of flour on her right cheek. So much for her notion of looking glamorous and sophisticated for him. If he could agree to accompany her to her Debs when she looked like this she'd make damn sure she looked her best in September. Harry would be proud of her, she thought happily as she raced upstairs to tell her mother.

Theresa was lying against the pillows, her big brown eyes enormous in the thin pallor of her face. She looked tired. Rachel was too overjoyed to notice. 'Mam! Mam! Wait until I tell you my great news,' she exclaimed excitedly.

'What's that, pet?' Her mother smiled.

'Harry's going to come to the Debs with me.' Rachel sat on the side of the bed and took her mother's hand in hers. 'Oh Mam, will you make my dress for me? And can I have something very glamorous? I want to look my very best that night. I'm not even going to wear my glasses.'

'Rachel, that's great news. I'm delighted for you, love. And of course I'll make you a glamorous dress. We'll go to Dublin next Saturday. Tell the Healys you need a half-day off. We'll get a pattern and the material and we'll treat ourselves to lunch. How about that?'

'Oh Mam, it sounds great.' Rachel leaned over and kissed her mother's cheek.

'You're the best mother in the world,' she exclaimed.

'And you're the best daughter.' Theresa smiled, holding her tight.

'This has been one of my really happy days,' Rachel declared. 'I think Harry's lovely.'

'He's only agreed to go to the Debs with you, mind. I'm sure he's got a lot of girlfriends at university. Don't start getting a crush on him,' her mother warned gently.

'I know.' Rachel smiled. 'I won't get a crush on him.' Because I have one on him already, she thought happily. Maybe when Harry saw her all dolled up to the nines, he might realize she was more than his best mate's sister. Maybe it would be the start of a great love affair.

Harry left Stapleton's house having resisted a strong urge to box his former headmaster in the jaw. That William Stapleton was something else, he fumed. The way he treated Ronan and Rachel was outrageous. Ronan had once again broached the idea of sharing a flat in September with Harry, and Mr Stapleton had the nerve to say that he certainly wouldn't allow Ronan to share with someone who was working in a bar. The way he'd said 'bar,' you'd think it was a den of iniquity that had nothing on Sodom and Gomorrah. What did he think Harry did all day, drink himself insensible? Silly old bugger. If he was Ronan, he'd have split long ago. He knew Ronan would too, if it wasn't for his mother.

Harry liked Mrs Stapleton. She was what his own mother would call 'a real lady.' She was a gentle sort. Much too soft to argue with old Willy, although Ronan had told him she could be stubborn enough if she got an idea into her head.

As for Rachel, Harry shook his head as he walked past the Tea Rooms where she worked. It was just as well she was going to St Pat's. It was her big chance to get out from under her father's thumb, and God knows she needed to. She was so shy and timid. The state of her when she'd asked him to go to the Debs with her. Just as well Ronan had put him in the picture beforehand. Ronan had been a bit embarrassed when he'd mentioned that Rachel needed an escort to her Debs and that she was going to ask him.

'She's so shy, Harry, I know she has a hard time of it at school with those wagons, Mary Foley and Glenda Mower. If you could just take her to this Debs thing so she won't feel like a social outcast, I'd be dead grateful,' Ronan said.

'Sure I will,' Harry'd assured him. If you couldn't do a mate a favour, you weren't much of a mate yourself was

Harry's motto. Anyway, she looked so pleased when he agreed, it was nearly worth it. Poor old Rach, he thought sympathetically, remembering her flustered air and the trusting way she gazed at him with those big blue eyes of hers. She'd a tough old life with that da of hers. No wonder she had no confidence in herself. She was a hell of a good cook though, Harry reflected as he turned left at the church towards home. And behind those awful glasses, her eyes were as blue as cornflowers.

Theresa smiled at the sound of her daughter humming in the bedroom next door. If she could get her hands on Harry Armstrong she'd kiss him. He'd really made Rachel's day by agreeing to go to her Debs. Her eyes were sparkling with excitement. She'd been bubbling about the bedroom making plans. It was wonderful to watch, Theresa thought a little sadly. It grieved her to see how shy and unsure her daughter was. She had tried her best over the years to bolster Rachel's confidence. But William never gave her a chance. He was always pushing her to study more. When she tried to express an opinion he told her not to talk nonsense.

Theresa could see *exactly* what was happening. Ronan was testing the waters, spreading his wings. William knew he was losing him. Ronan was growing up to be his own man. It was a bitter blow to her husband when he realized that he no longer had total control over his son. His authority was rapidly dwindling, especially when Ronan put his foot down over not commuting. It was obvious that William was not going to relinquish his authority over Rachel. And she wasn't a strong enough character to stand up for herself the way her brother did.

No doubt William would have a say about this Debs thing. He'd probably insist on her being home by eleven. Theresa drew a weary breath. She'd need to be in the best of health for this one, she thought tiredly. She just couldn't let Rachel down. For some reason, she remembered the time she'd discovered the bruises from Patrick

McKeown's compass on Rachel's little body. Rachel had pleaded with Theresa not to tell William. She'd been eight then, ten years ago. And William was still a figure of dread to her. Please God she would get her place in college, Theresa prayed. She'd hate her daughter to leave home but Theresa knew it would be the making of her. If only she could wave a magic wand and protect her daughter from all the pitfalls ahead. It was awful sending your children off out into the world knowing you could do nothing more for them. Theresa felt very guilty about Rachel. She should have stood up to William on her daughter's behalf much more than she had, she thought as a tear slid down her cheek. It was just that she always felt so tired and lifeless. She simply hadn't the energy, especially lately, to engage her husband in battle. There were times she felt that she had let her daughter down badly.

'Five honours, not bad.' Her father read her exam results and handed them to her.

'It's wonderful, Rachel, I'm proud of you,' her mother exclaimed, flinging her arms around her. 'You worked very very hard.'

'Thanks, Mam. It should be good enough for St Pat's.' Rachel couldn't believe it herself. Five honours was a very good result no matter what her begrudging father thought. That trip to the school to get the results had been a nightmare.

Her hands were shaking when Sister Martha handed her the envelope. She couldn't believe her eyes when she saw the three Bs and two Cs. Michelle got five honours too. Mary Foley and Eileen Dunphy each got three, and Glenda Mower only got a pathetic one, although she got a C mark on a pass paper and was claiming it as an extra honour.

Rachel had been dying to get home to show her father her results. And then he came out with 'not bad.' It was good enough for St Pat's anyway if it wasn't good enough for him, she thought defiantly.

'Don't count your chickens before they're hatched. A lot depends on the type of interview you do before you get into teacher training. Five honours is no guarantee of anything,' he warned.

'Yes, Dad,' she agreed dutifully. Now that she had her exam results she was going to have to face the ordeal of an interview in St Pat's. It wasn't so much the interview she was dreading, it was the singing test. She would have to sing two songs, one in English and one in Irish, in front of an examiner. The thought of it made her mouth go dry. She was practising singing in front of her mother. But singing to your mother was one thing. Singing for a complete and utter stranger . . . was another. At least she had the Debs to look forward to.

If things went according to plan, Harry and she would meet for drinks in Dublin and who knows, maybe they'd end up dating. She had to do well in her interview if she wanted to go and live in Dublin and be near Harry. That thought would get her through her interview, Rachel told herself firmly. This was her one big chance, she wasn't going to mess it up.

Chapter Twenty-Two

'*Báidín Fheidhlime . . .*' Rachel tried again. Her voice was far too high and she got stuck on the top notes. She had sung her English song, the old reliable *Skye Boat Song*, for the examiner. Now she was attempting to sing her Irish one. It was torture. Her mouth was dry and she could hear her voice quavering as she sang. She'd never get in to St Pat's after this performance.

The examiner gave a wry smile when she'd finished. 'You'll hardly be taking up opera-singing,' he remarked as he made some notes. 'You may start the sight-reading now.' Rachel was completely drained when it was over. She would have liked to go in to town and have a cup of tea and a cream cake and have some time to get over the ordeal, but her father was waiting in the car outside. He had insisted on driving her to Dublin. He'd gone on and on for the whole journey up to the city, telling her what the interviewers would be looking for in a prospective primary school teacher. By the time they'd arrived she'd been a bundle of nerves.

'How did it go?' a friendly girl called Pauline asked. She was next in line to be interviewed.

Rachel threw her eyes up to heaven. 'I can't sing for nuts,' she murmured. 'But he's nice enough.'

'Would you like to wait for me? We could go and have a look around and maybe have coffee,' Pauline suggested.

Rachel shook her head. 'I'd love to, but I have a lift outside. Maybe if we both get places, we could go do it when we're living here?'

'Sure,' Pauline agreed. Then her name was called.

'Good luck,' said Rachel, watching the other girl take

a deep breath before entering the room. Oh please let me get a place, she begged the Almighty as she walked slowly down the corridor. She would have loved to explore the college and grounds. She liked what she'd seen so far.

The college was on the main road to the airport. On the other side of the road she'd seen a busy shopping area. A pub called the Cat & Cage was a little further up. She'd heard some of the lads who were waiting for their interviews making plans to go there later and wet their dry throats. The college itself was set in well-kept tree-lined grounds. It was surrounded by a huge brick wall that closed it off from the hustle and noise of the city. Rachel felt excited when she looked at the residential halls. Soon she might be living in one of them. Soon she might be living a life of fun and freedom. Ronan was always telling her about the things students got up to in the Tech. Boozy nights at the pub, lively debates, parties, card games and Scrabble. It sounded so different to her desperately boring existence.

No-one would know her here. No-one would know that her father was the headmaster of a village school and full of his own importance. No-one would know that she was dead shy and had never been out with a fella, let alone been kissed by one. That girl Pauline had been very easy to talk to. She'd assumed Rachel was NORMAL.

Well she would be, when she came to live here. She wouldn't let her shyness ruin her life as it had done until now. If people didn't know she was shy, they wouldn't treat her as a shy person. So Rachel would pretend that she was an absolutely normal un-shy person and perhaps she would get to the stage where she wouldn't need to pretend any more. Full of good resolutions, she walked out into the grounds.

The sight of her father sitting reading his *Irish Times* in his Cortina sent a surge of deep resentment through her. If he hadn't insisted on driving her to Dublin she would have been able to go exploring with her new friend. He pretended it was out of the kindness of his heart, but

Rachel knew it was just downright nosiness. He wanted to keep her under his thumb. Well not for long, she vowed. Soon she would be her own woman.

'How did you get on, Rachel?' he asked as soon as she got in beside him.

'All right,' she murmured.

'What kind of an answer is that?' William asked crossly. 'Tell me the questions you were asked and the answers you gave, so I can get some indication of how your interview went.'

'They asked me all the questions you said they would, and I gave them all the answers you said I should. And I've got a headache and I want to shut my eyes for a while,' she fibbed. This was the start of being a new woman, she decided with satisfaction, closing her eyes and ignoring her father's tight-lipped annoyance. They didn't speak once on the return journey. Rachel kept her eyes closed and imagined her joyful new life. She'd go to the Cat & Cage with Harry. She'd share a communal kitchen with friends in the hall of residence. They'd have long gossipy chats over coffee. It was going to be great!

William fumed. That Rachel one was getting to be an impertinent little madam. Brushing him off like that. She wasn't a bit grateful that he had given up his whole morning to take her to Dublin. And he'd given her pertinent advice for her interview. And *then*, when he asked her a civil question, a question that showed interest in her welfare, she'd not been one bit gracious about it.

She need not think she was going to get any notions about herself as her brother had. Just because he was living in Dublin. Rachel wouldn't be living in Dublin and, as long as she was under his roof, she'd treat him with respect. No daughter of his was going to behave in such an offhand manner. William sat primly behind the wheel doing a sedate forty mph and felt very hard done by indeed.

* * *

'How did it go?' Theresa was waiting to greet them. She had the lunch ready and Rachel was suddenly starving. It was steak and kidney pie, her favourite. Her mother had cooked it as a special treat. And lemon pudding for dessert. Rachel could see the golden fluffy pudding on the dresser. Yummy, she thought as her stomach gurgled.

'Oh Mam, it was OK, I think,' she said excitedly as she hugged Theresa. 'I met a very nice girl there called Pauline. She asked me to go for coffee with her but I couldn't, because of the lift.'

'Your headache seems to have disappeared.' William sniffed.

'What headache?' Theresa inquired as she began to dish up.

'She had a headache on the way home and she couldn't tell me how she did in the interview,' William said huffily.

'I told you, they asked me the questions you said they would and I gave them the answers you told me to,' Rachel said.

'That sounds fine to me,' Theresa said placatingly. 'Sit down, William, here's your dinner.'

Rachel glowered at her father behind his back. Trust him to start.

'Tell me about Pauline,' her mother encouraged as she set Rachel's steaming dinner in front of her.

Rachel forked some pastry and steak into her mouth. 'This is scrumptious,' she declared. 'Pauline Hegarty is her name and she's from Clonmel in Tipperary and she wants to be a teacher because of the long holidays.' She laughed.

Her father shot her a disapproving look. 'Obviously a totally unsuitable candidate. If she were to say that at an interview, she certainly wouldn't get a place.'

'It was a joke,' Rachel murmured. She wanted to say, Don't be such a daft eejit, of course she's not going to say that at an interview. Even if it is one of the reasons why lots of people want to be teachers. But she didn't say anything of the sort. As usual.

'When would you be starting, if you do get a place?' Theresa asked.

'It starts in October. You do two degree subjects in first year as well as your primary subjects. So I think I'll do English and geography. There are lots of societies to join as well. I think I'd like to join the geography one, definitely,' Rachel said between mouthfuls. 'You'd go on field trips to see corrie lakes and evidence of glacial erosion and things like that. It would be fascinating.'

'They didn't have any of that nonsense in my day. You went and did your studying out of textbooks. Those things are only an excuse for socializing and boozing.' Her father snorted.

'Things have changed a lot since your day, William, and probably for the better.' Theresa's tone was a rebuke. William's Adam's apple bobbed up and down in indignation and his cheeks reddened.

'You don't know what you're talking about, Theresa,' he snapped. 'When I was there this morning, I heard young lads who've just done their Leaving Cert saying they were going to the pub. I ask you? What kind of carry-on is that? Is it any wonder the country's in the state it's in? Young people don't want to work these days. They've no manners, no respect for their elders. Society is going to the dogs.' Rachel and Theresa exchanged glances. Both sighed almost simultaneously. They had heard this diatribe many times before.

'The halls of residence look very modern,' Rachel said cheerfully, hoping to side-track him. 'You have your own bedroom cum study and you share a kitchen and bathroom with the other people who live on your landing. The rooms are supposed to be very nice and you can decorate them any way you want. Can I bring my patchwork quilt with me when I'm going?'

'Of course you can, love,' Theresa agreed. 'If you like I'll even do you a new one.'

'Just a minute there,' William said sternly. 'You won't be going anywhere, Rachel, except home to your own bed at night. I don't know where the two of you got the idea that you were going to be living in a hall of residence. But it's out of the question. You, Rachel, will commute.'

Rachel and her mother stared at each other in consternation.

'But Daddy—'

'But William—'

'Enough.' William put up his hand. 'I don't want to hear another word. Rachel lives here. There are plenty of buses from Bray. I'll leave her over in the morning and pick her up at night. And that's my last word on the subject.'

Chapter Twenty-Three

Theresa stared at her husband. Anger, more violent than she had ever experienced, surged through her. 'It might be your last word on the subject, William Stapleton, but it certainly isn't mine.' Her voice shook. William, deeply offended by the venom in her tone, sat opening and closing his mouth. Rachel, shocked speechless by her father's edict and her mother's uncharacteristic wrath, thought William looked like a turkey gobbling.

'Sit down, Theresa, and don't be upsetting yourself. I don't want any arguments in this house,' William ordered.

'Don't you?' his wife fumed. 'That's your hard luck then, William, because you're going to get one from me. For once in my life I'm not going to let you dictate the law in this house. I have some say too, you know. I bore Rachel in my womb for nine months. I think that gives me far more right to make decisions about her than you'll ever have.' She glared at him, her usually gentle brown eyes like two flints.

'Have you gone completely out of your tree?' Theresa raged. 'What sense is there in dragging Rachel home every night of the week, stuck in traffic jams and the likes when she could be studying away like everyone else from the country in one of those residential halls? It's hard enough having to study without being exhausted from travelling. Think what it's going to be like in the cold winter mornings and the dark wet evenings. *You* won't have to stand waiting for buses in the rain. You know, whether you like it or not, you're going to have to face the fact that our children have grown up. Why are you trying to deprive Rachel of the chance to make new friends and stand on her own two feet? I don't understand you, William, I really don't,' she finished angrily.

'And I don't understand *you*,' William said heatedly. 'I'm trying to protect our daughter. I'm trying to save her from the wildness of the youth of today. The city's no place for a young girl on her own—'

'Rubbish!' Theresa snorted. 'Look at Jacinta Collins, gone to New York on her own and doing very well, according to her mother. Rachel's only going to Dublin *and* she's going to be living in supervised accommodation.'

'Jacinta Collins's mother *would* say that,' William said curtly. 'That argument doesn't impress me. Don't forget I'll be giving up my time to drive her to Bray to the bus or train. She won't get wet in the car,' he said scathingly. 'I'll have to leave the comfort of the house to go and pick her up in the evening. But I'm not complaining. I'll willingly do that to make life easier for Rachel. But I will not permit her to live in Dublin on her own. I let you persuade me, against my better judgement, to allow Ronan to stay in digs and look at the state of him.'

'What are you talking about?' Theresa said furiously. 'What state of him? Ronan's a very good lad. He's very attentive to his studies. He's never caused us one bit of worry. You're talking through your hat, William, and you know it.'

'I beg your pardon,' William said coldly. 'Look at the length of his hair! Look at the scruffy old army clothes and jeans he wears. He frequents public houses with that Armstrong lad. He doesn't come home half the weekends he's supposed to. There's always some excuse. Let me tell you, Theresa, I bitterly regret giving in to your pressure over our son, but by God I won't make the same mistake with Rachel.'

'But Daddy, it's not fair!' Rachel was unable to contain herself any longer.

'Be quiet and stay out of this, Rachel. It's got nothing to do with you,' her father ordered.

'That's the most stupid thing I ever heard in my life,' Rachel said savagely. 'Of course it's got something to do with me. It's my future you're talking about. I have the right to be consulted about what *I* want to do. The only reason I want to go to St Pat's is to get away from Rathbarry. You wouldn't let me apply to Aer Lingus. *You* insisted I train as a teacher. Well if I'm going to train as a teacher I'm bloody well going to live in college,' Rachel exploded, too furious to be intimidated.

'How dare you, Miss! How dare you speak to me like that, using such disgraceful language. How dare you issue ultimatums to me. Let me tell you, Rachel Stapleton, as long as I'm paying for your education, and as long as you're living under my roof, what I say goes. Such self-ishness. You'd think at least that you'd consider your poor mother. You know she isn't well and yet you're quite happy to take off to Dublin—'

'By God, William, I won't have it.' Theresa was white with rage as she sprang up from her chair. 'That is the most despicable thing I've ever heard. Don't you dare use me as an excuse to stop Rachel leading her own life. I'll never forgive you for this as long as I live.'

'I hate you, I fucking hate you,' Rachel screamed at her father. Tears streamed down her face. She wanted to fling her plate of dinner at him. She wanted to pick up her knife and stab him with it. All the years of pent-up anger, bitterness and resentment welled up and over-flowed. 'You've ruined my life, you've ruined my life. It's all your fault,' she sobbed.

William was horrified. 'Stop that! Stop that nonsense this minute, go to your room until you've composed yourself.'

'Leave me alone and stop telling me what to do! Just leave me alone!' Rachel screeched hysterically. Theresa gave a little gasp and went pale. She sank into her chair.

'What's wrong? What's the matter, Theresa?' William said sharply. 'Rachel! Rachel! Help your mother.' Rachel
.

drew a shuddering sobbing breath and ran to Theresa's side. Her mother was gasping.

'Mam, Mam! What's wrong?' she asked frantically. Her mother didn't answer. Theresa's eyes rolled in her head and she fell unconscious.

'I hope you're satisfied,' William said harshly. 'Now look what you've caused with your selfishness.' He ran out to phone the doctor.

Oh God, please don't let Mammy die, Rachel pleaded. I'll stay at home and look after her. Please don't let her die.

Chapter Twenty-Four

Theresa sat in the rocking-chair in her bedroom putting the finishing touches to Rachel's ball gown. She felt tired. Ever since her heart attack a few weeks ago, she was finding it hard to get back to normal. She took off her glasses to rest her eyes and stared out the window. It was late afternoon. The September sun was slanting westwards towards the hills. The leaves on the oak trees in Daly's garden had turned a deep red-gold. A faint breeze shook them to the ground, where they lay in crisp piles. Autumn had come early. The light filtered through her yellow and white bedroom casting warm shadows on the faded wallpaper. A sunbeam danced on the colourful patchwork quilt. She usually found peace and tranquillity sitting in her chair looking out over the goings-on in the village from her little eyrie. But not today.

Theresa felt terribly depressed. Rachel absolutely refused to leave her and go to Dublin to live. If she had not collapsed, Theresa was sure Rachel would have defied William. It was the first time Rachel had ever stood up for herself. It should have been a turning point in her daughter's life. Now she was even worse off than before. She'd never leave home as long as Theresa needed her. Theresa had become even more of her daughter's jailer than William.

Sadness overwhelmed her. She had so wanted Rachel to go to Dublin to spread her wings and enjoy her life. She wanted Rachel to do all the things she'd never done. Take the chances she'd never been offered. To go dancing and partying. To have holidays abroad. To learn to drive. Especially to learn to drive. Being able to drive gave a woman such independence. She'd asked William to teach her to drive once when the children were young. He wouldn't hear of it and asked her why she wanted to learn to drive when he could drive her wherever she wanted to go. Theresa hadn't asked again.

It was different for women now. They were buying their own houses. Driving their own cars and going to the far corners of the earth on holidays and to work. They were edging up the career ladders, and having babies and still continuing to work. The worm had turned and if Theresa couldn't reap some of the benefits, she badly wanted Rachel to. She wanted her daughter to do as much as she could and be as independent as she could. Rachel had had that chance. For one brief glorious moment it had been within her grasp. And then, her useless old mother had let her down. It was a guilt Theresa knew she'd carry with her to the grave. Theresa had begged her to reconsider but Rachel wouldn't budge. 'I'm not leaving you, Mam, I'd always be worrying. I'd much prefer to be with you. It's nothing to do with *him*,' she'd said earnestly.

'Why didn't You give her the chance You denied me?' Theresa turned angrily to the statue of the Sacred Heart on the mantelpiece. 'It wasn't such a huge thing to ask.' She was very angry with God these days. Angry and bitter. Her prayers gave her no succour any more. She was even beginning to doubt His existence. There were so many vile deeds happening in the world. So much violence. And not only in faraway places either. Every day on the news she heard of the troubles in the North, not much more than two hundred miles from where she lived. Why did He allow drugs to scourge the minds and bodies of so many young people? Why did He let young children and babies starve to death in famine-ridden countries? And even in her own little world, He caused grief. What had she done that was so dreadful that she'd been afflicted with a husband like William? True, he didn't beat her or starve her and he was a good provider. But he was a cruel man just the same, imposing his will on the family as if it was his right. And just when Rachel had needed her most, God had given her a heart attack.

Tears slid down her cheeks. 'Jesus, do what you like with me but look after Rachel, she's a good girl, she deserves a chance.' Theresa dropped the dress and folded her hands in heartfelt prayer.

'How's your mam?' Harry was home for the weekend and Rachel had just bumped into him as he came out of the shop. She was on her way home from work.

'A bit better,' Rachel said.

'How are you?' Harry gave her a concerned look.

'I'm OK,' she said glumly.

'You look awful,' he said kindly. That was all she needed to know. She knew that her hair needed a wash and her face was pale, and that she had big black circles around her eyes from lack of sleep. But to be told it, and by Harry, was the last straw. To her great horror her lower lip started to quiver. Mortified, she turned away.

'Rach, Rachel! I'm sorry! I didn't mean to upset you,' Harry exclaimed in dismay. He took her by the arm and turned her to face him.

'It's all right, it's all right.' She tried to keep her voice steady, but the tears brimmed in her eyes.

'Come on, let's get out of here. Come on down behind the Ball Alley and we'll have a fag,' Harry said briskly. He took her hand and they walked across the street and turned down towards the Ball Alley. Luckily it was deserted.

'I only meant that you looked very tired, I didn't mean that you looked . . . awful . . . if you know what I mean,' Harry tried to explain.

'I know.' Rachel sniffled, feeling like a real fool. 'Don't take any notice of me.'

'Is it dreadful at home?' Harry asked gently. The sympathy in his voice was too much for her and she started to cry again. Harry put his arms around her and hugged her tightly.

'My father blames me for Mam's heart attack,' Rachel sobbed. 'We were having a row about me going to live in college and she was standing up for me and I lost my temper and started cursing at my father and then she had the heart attack. It was all my fault.'

'It wasn't your fault, Rachel,' Harry said firmly. 'Get that idea out of your head. If it was anyone's fault it was your father's for being so unreasonable. And anyway your mother's always had a weak heart, hasn't she?'

'Yeah. Ever since I was born. So it *is* my fault.'

'Rachel. Stop that.' Harry gave her a little shake. 'Stop blaming yourself for something that's not your fault. Your mother is very lucky to have a daughter like you.'

Rachel rested her cheek against his chest. She could feel his heart beating steadily beneath the soft material of his sweater. It was very comforting being held by him. She had a lovely warm protected feeling. And she didn't mind any more that her eyes were red from crying. She no longer felt embarrassed. Harry was a friend.

'Do you want a cigarette?' Harry asked.

'Why not?' She suddenly felt reckless. They walked over to the old weather-worn wooden seat that had been there since before they were born. Harry offered her his packet of Carrolls and she took one of the tipped cigarettes. Her hand shook as she placed it between her lips. Harry cupped the match with his hand and she bent her head to light her cigarette. This was how other girls behaved with fellas. Maybe they didn't burst into tears and sob all over them, but they let them light their cigarettes and sat chatting beside ball alleys with them. She began to feel much better as she cautiously inhaled the cigarette. She and Ronan had puffed a few on the sly, but she wasn't what you'd call an experienced smoker and she didn't want to make a show of herself.

'How do you feel about getting the place in college?' he asked, after lighting his own.

Rachel shrugged. 'When I went to do the interview I was excited. I met a very nice girl called Pauline and I was looking forward to living in the halls of residence. It was a great chance to get away. Now I couldn't care less. It's just going to be three years of swotting and all that travelling. I'm not really looking forward to it.' Her tone was glum.

'Would you still not think of living at college, now that your mother's on the mend?' he asked gently.

'I couldn't do that, Harry. I couldn't leave her now. It might happen again. And besides,' she added bitterly, 'as long as my father's paying for my education I have to do as he says.'

'Don't go to college. Get a job now,' he suggested.

Rachel shook her head. 'I can't. There'd be another huge row and I don't want my mother upset. I'm stuck with teaching whether I like it or not.'

'Are you looking forward to Friday?' Harry smiled.

'Yeah,' Rachel said shyly. Next Friday was the Debs Ball.

'Now listen,' he said to her. 'Next Friday, we're going to have a great night. Ronan's going to come to the hotel with Kate Ryan and when the meal is over we can go and have a drink with them. I'm sure they'll be allowed in to dance if we say they're with us. We had it all planned to give you a surprise, but I think you need a bit of cheering up. But don't let on to Ronan that I've told you. OK?' he warned.

'OK,' Rachel agreed. She was delighted that Ronan was coming to the dance with Kate Ryan. Kate was a very jolly sort of girl. Ronan and she weren't dating, but they were great pals. They should all have a bit of a laugh. Glenda and Mary and Eileen could go and get lost. Harry was taking her to the ball, it couldn't but be a great night.

Harry walked through Rachel's front gate, scowling. He had just walked her home and had called in to see her mother. Mrs Stapleton had been delighted to see him and insisted he have a cup of tea and some cake. He'd been shocked at how thin and worn she looked. Ronan had told him all about the row and the heart attack, that was why he had been so kind to Rachel earlier.

They had their chat, and a laugh. Mrs Stapleton was a quiet sort of woman but she had a good sense of humour. Harry liked her. The headmaster hadn't been around, much to his relief, and he'd stayed a half an hour. But as Harry was walking down the path, Mr Stapleton opened the garden gate. He didn't look too pleased to see Harry.

'Hello,' he said curtly.

'Hello, Mr Stapleton,' Harry'd said politely and then the ignorant old bastard said brusquely, 'I hope you're not putting notions in my daughter's head about going to Dublin. Her mother needs her here. You've certainly tried to get Ronan to defy me by leaving his digs. Well son, I won't have it. So be warned.'

What a bastard, Harry thought as he strode down the street. Imagine having him for a father. Why Ronan hadn't clocked him one before now he couldn't fathom. He'd felt like giving him a puck in the jaw for his impudence. Who did he think he was talking to? A ten-year-old?

It was a terrible shame Mrs Stapleton had that heart attack. Harry was sure that he and Ronan could have persuaded Rachel to live in St Pat's. Her father would have given in in the end. He wanted her to be a teacher so much. To follow in his tradition. If Rachel had told him she was leaving home to get a job in the city he'd have crumbled. Just the way he had with Ronan. Harry knew it. He had the measure of William Stapleton. A bully until someone stood up to him. Except that it would have upset Rachel and her mother, Harry would have told him where to get off. But he didn't want to jeopardize Rachel's big night out. The poor girl hadn't much to look forward to.

Nevertheless, it would have been nice to excoriate William in an argument. Harry was particularly good at debate. Training to be a solicitor helped. He knew how to make his points and undermine the other person's argument. He could have wiped the floor with that old rip. Harry marched on, oblivious to everyone as he imagined how he would have floored William Stapleton.

'Harry's a very nice lad, Rachel, I must say,' Theresa said as she washed up after their cup of tea. Rachel smiled as she dried up the cups and put them on the dresser.

'I'm really looking forward to my Debs,' she confided. 'Harry told me that he and Ronan had it planned that Ronan and Kate will come to the hotel after the meal. I'm not to let on to Ronan that I know. Wasn't that nice of them?'

'You'll have a wonderful night, pet. I know you will. I have the dress just finished. You picked lovely material.' Theresa dried her hands. 'Come on, let's go and have a try-on. I only have to put on a bit of binding and I'll be finished.'

'I wished you'd been with me. I was looking forward to that day out.' Rachel gave her mother a hug.

'We'll have other days, don't worry,' her mother assured her. 'I'm feeling much better.'

'Are you?' Rachel asked eagerly. 'Is your energy coming back?'

'Oh yes,' fibbed her mother.

'That's great news, Mam. I was feeling real down in the dumps today, and then I met Harry on the way home. And now you're feeling better, so it's turning into a good day.'

'Wait until you see the dress.' Theresa laughed. 'It's gorgeous. It'll really put the icing on the cake for you. Come on, I can't wait to show it to you.'

'Here's Da,' Rachel sighed. 'I'd better make his tea for him.'

'Let him make it himself,' Theresa declared. 'It won't do him a bit of harm.' Since her heart attack, her mother didn't run around after William the way she once did, Rachel noted. As for her own relationship with her father . . . they hardly spoke. Rachel would never forgive him for the row that led to her mother's collapse. She was polite to him for her mother's sake, but when they were alone she ignored him and he did the same.

'What did that Armstrong fella want?' William inquired as he walked into the kitchen.

'I invited him in for a cup of tea,' Theresa said coldly. 'There's a tin of salmon in the dresser and tomatoes and cheese in the fridge if you want them for your tea.'

William looked at her, affronted. 'Where are you two off to? Surely Rachel could make my tea for me if you're too tired.'

'Rachel's been working all day. She made our tea and now she's going to help me to finish off her Debs dress. There's some fruit cake in the cake tin,' Theresa snapped. Rachel said nothing, but she didn't miss the glare her father gave her.

Let him glare, she thought. He wouldn't start a row now, he was as scared as she was about Theresa having another heart attack. For all his bossiness and self-importance, he was hopeless around the house and sorely missed his wife's pampering when she was laid up. Rachel hadn't put herself out for him. She'd concentrated on looking after her mother.

They left William and went upstairs to Theresa's bedroom. The dress lay on the bed, a froth of white taffeta. It was the most beautiful dress Rachel had ever seen. And the most sophisticated. She'd picked the pattern especially for its glamorous sweetheart neckline, nipped-in waist and full skirt. She'd bought a pair of long white gloves to set it off. Her mother was lending her an amethyst pendant and matching earrings.

'Slip it on,' Theresa urged. Rachel undressed rapidly. Standing in her bra and panties, she stood patiently while her mother dropped the rustling material over her head. It slid sensuously down over her shoulders and breasts and hips. She pulled on the long white satin gloves. Her mother arranged the full skirt and stood back to admire her handiwork. Her eyes lit up at the vision in front of her.

'Oh Rachel!' she said proudly. 'Pet, you look beautiful. Wait until Harry sees you.' She led Rachel to the cheval mirror in the corner of the room and stood behind her. Rachel stared at her reflection in the mirror. Even with her glasses on she looked completely different. The bodice fitted like a glove, emphasizing the slender curves of her body. She'd never really considered her figure attractive, but looking at her reflection in the mirror, she saw with a little sense of shock that she looked very womanly. A little bit sexy even, she thought with delight, admiring her discreet *décolletage*.

She felt like a million dollars. Rachel did a twirl of delight, spreading her flowing skirts, as her mother looked on with pleasure. Today, Harry'd put his arms around her. Next Friday, when he saw her in this, he might even kiss her. That night, she lay in bed practising her kissing. She covered her forearm with hot wet kisses, pretending it was Harry she was kissing. In a week's time, if all went well, it wouldn't be pretend kisses she'd be doing. If her greatest dream came true, she'd be kissing Harry.

Chapter Twenty-Five

A dab of *Apple Blossom* on her wrists, neck and cleavage and, like Cinderella, she was ready for the ball. Rachel took a critical look at her reflection . . . and was happy. She'd never looked as well in her life. It was a far cry from her usual dull, uninteresting appearance. Mind, it had taken a lot of practice. When she'd first started experimenting with make-up, she'd ended up looking like a clown. Put on less, her mother advised when Rachel asked her what she thought. At first she resisted, much preferring to slather lots of the stuff on her face, but gradually she took her mother's advice and soon she was looking more presentable.

Tonight, she wasn't wearing her glasses and she was wearing a smoky grey-blue eyeshadow to emphasize the blueness of her eyes. Rachel was pleased with the effect she'd achieved. Although she rarely used eyeshadow, she'd taken note of an article in *Woman's Way* that showed how to smudge and blend and put the darker shade on the outer part of the eyelid, to make the eyes seem bigger. She was also wearing make-up, and she marvelled at the smooth silky sheen it gave her skin. She'd used a very small amount of blusher too. Her lips glistened with *Dusky Rose* lipstick. Excitement mounted as she fastened the amethyst pendant around her neck. She had terrible butterflies in her stomach. She had blotches on her neck. Hastily she applied some make-up to cover them. They were a dead give-away that she was nervous. Tonight she wanted to appear calm and sophisticated. She wished the butterflies would do a flit elsewhere. Just say Harry didn't arrive. What would she do then?

'Stop it!' she ordered. Harry would never do something like that to her. Harry was the best.

Theresa knocked and entered the room. 'Let me see you,' she commanded.

Rachel did a twirl for her mother and was rewarded by the smile of pleasure and pride that lit up her face. The material of the dress swirled luxuriously around her.

'Let's go and show your father.' Theresa smiled.

William was sitting at the dining table, correcting essays. 'Well let me see the debutante,' he said jovially, turning to look at her. His face fell. A dull red crept up his neck. Rachel saw the familiar bobbing of his Adam's apple and felt her heart sink. That always meant trouble.

'Theresa, what can you be thinking of?' he exclaimed. 'Rachel, you can't go out in public in that dress. It's immodest. People can see . . . can see . . . it's far too revealing,' he finished lamely. The doorbell rang. Rachel nearly jumped out of her skin.

'Theresa, answer the door,' William ordered. 'She can't let that fella see her looking like this.'

'Go and bring Harry into the parlour,' her mother said quietly. William went purple with fury.

'Theresa—'

'Be quiet, William. Go on, Rachel,' Theresa said resolutely. In a complete tizzy, Rachel went to open the door. Harry stood there looking most handsome in his dress suit. He whistled when he saw her.

'Have I come to the wrong house?' he teased. 'I'm supposed to be bringing Rachel Stapleton to a Debs Ball.'

She laughed. 'Come in, I just have to get my wrap.' He handed her a beautiful orchid and a little box. 'What's this?' Rachel was surprised. The orchid was expected, but nothing else.

'Just a little something to remind you of your Debs,' Harry said smiling. Rachel tore open the wrapping paper and lifted the cover of the little black box. Inside in a bed of velvet nestled a delicate gold R on a gold chain.

'Oh Harry! Oh Harry, it's beautiful,' Rachel exclaimed.

Forgetting her shyness and inhibitions, she flung her arms around him and kissed him on the cheek. He kissed her back, laughing.

'Good heavens!' William's exclamation caused them both to turn around. Her father was framed in the doorway looking at them in shock.

'Good evening, Mr Stapleton,' Harry said politely.

'Young man, I hope your intentions towards my daughter are honourable. It is not respectful to maul her like that,' William said icily. Rachel nearly fainted. She couldn't believe her ears. Her father was making an absolute show of her. She wished the floor would swallow her up.

Harry's face grew stern. 'Mr Stapleton, I was not mauling Rachel. I have the utmost respect for Rachel. I'll take good care of her.'

'I hope so. Our daughter was brought up to behave like a lady.' William glowered. 'Make sure you have her in by a reasonable hour.'

'Harry, you and Rachel enjoy yourselves. Off you go now. I'll be looking forward to hearing all about it in the morning.' Theresa marched past her husband and kissed Rachel on the cheek. William stood stiffly to one side. He didn't say goodnight.

'Harry, I'm really sorry about that,' said Rachel mortified. She felt like crying. The evening was ruined before it began.

Harry stopped short and turned to her. 'Now listen, Rach, we had an agreement,' he said firmly. 'Tonight we're going to have fun. Forget all that. I have. Your father is your father and there's nothing you can do about him, so just don't take any notice of him. Right?'

'Right,' Rachel murmured.

'Here, let me put your R on.' He took the little box from her and fastened the chain around her neck. 'Now, this is the moment the fun starts. OK?'

'OK,' she agreed light-heartedly. This time, Harry gave her the lightest kiss on her lips. Rachel's heart soared. Her very first kiss. Not even William could ruin that. Hand in hand, they walked out to Harry's father's car which Harry had borrowed for the evening.

'That insolent young pup,' fumed William, skulking behind the curtains as he watched Rachel and Harry embracing. 'I've a good mind to go out there and forbid her to go to that dance. That reprobate is a bad influence on my children.' He made to go to the front door. His wife blocked his path.

'You'll do no such thing, William Stapleton. You're not going to ruin Rachel's night any more than you have. How could you embarrass her in front of her young man like that? How dare you ask Harry Armstrong if his intentions were honourable? You should be ashamed of yourself.'

'I don't understand you at all lately, Theresa,' William said plaintively. 'I'm only concerned for our daughter's welfare. You don't know what it's like out there. I have far more experience of the world than you do. You must be guided by me. Young girls are getting pregnant, and even worse, going to England for abortions. You don't want Rachel to end up like that, do you?' he demanded. 'That lad has no respect for her.'

'That lad has far more respect for Rachel than you have. I can tell you one thing, I'd die happy knowing that he would look after her. He'd make a better job of it than you. Now leave me in peace, William. I'm tired and I'm going to bed,' Theresa said wearily.

William sat on his own in the kitchen and felt a burning resentment towards his daughter. Ever since Theresa's heart attack, Rachel had been getting away with murder, because he was too nervous of causing a row in case Theresa took another seizure. Well Theresa had gone to bed, she'd be asleep when Rachel got in. But he wouldn't. He'd be waiting up for her and by heavens he was going to give her what for. If she thought she was going to carry on like a trollop under his roof, she had another think coming.

'Ready?' asked Harry as he tucked Rachel's arm in his and led her up the steps of St Angela's. Mother Rosario was there to greet them.

'Rachel, you look delightful. And what a handsome young man. Go up to the Parlour and meet the other sisters and have some tea and biscuits,' she said. Rachel took a deep breath. She wondered if Glenda and Mary and the rest of them were there. She had looked forward to this moment for so long. At night, in bed, she had imagined the expression on the faces of her classmates as she swanned into the Parlour, arm in arm with Harry. It would be her moment of triumph after all the hours of misery they had caused her. Let them call her Specky-Four-Eyes now! Rachel knew that none of them expected her to turn up. Even though she'd paid for the tickets. Mary Foley had met her in the street and announced that they were all dying to meet Rachel's mystery man. She'd said it with a sneer on her face, Rachel had longed to give her a good hard slap.

Now Mary would see just who the mystery man was. And Mary's jaw would drop and she'd be mad with envy, because Mary fancied Harry like mad, according to Ronan.

Now that the moment was upon her she felt nervous. Maybe they wouldn't take any notice of her at all. Maybe she had just been building it up in her own mind all along.

'Hope there's a few chocolate biscuits left,' Harry said as they walked along towards the Parlour.

'You and Ronan are the greatest pair of gannets that I've ever met,' Rachel laughed.

'I've been to a few of these Debs things. Don't get your hopes up about the meal, you never get half enough to eat. So stock up with biscuits,' he advised. 'Anyway we can always go for chips after it and eat them on the sea front.'

'I've got to be in at a reasonable hour.' She giggled.

'I might have you home before daybreak, we'll see,'

Harry teased. They were laughing as they walked into the Parlour and the first person Rachel saw was Glenda Mower. Glenda looked at her, and looked again, an expression of disbelief on her face. Glenda, who was lanky and thin as a rake, wore a very revealing gown with shoestring straps. Unfortunately, Glenda did not possess a bust. Two fried eggs was a good description of Glenda's bosom, Rachel thought smugly. Rachel didn't even bother to say hello.

Sister Bernadette and Sister Anthony made a beeline for them. 'Rachel Stapleton, I wouldn't recognize you,' Sister Anthony exclaimed. She had a rather loud voice and everybody turned to look. Out of the corner of her eye, Rachel saw Mary and Eileen staring at her.

'Who's the fine thing she's with?' Rachel heard Eileen ask.

'His name's Harry.' Mary scowled and Rachel savoured the moment of her triumph. It was almost worth everything she'd endured at her classmates' hands.

'How is your mother, dear? And who is this young man?' Sister Bernadette asked kindly.

'My mother's feeling much better, Sister, and this is Harry Armstrong, a friend of mine.' Rachel had always liked Sister Bernadette, who was a kindly soul.

'Hello Harry.' Sister Bernadette shook hands with him. 'I wish I was thirty years younger and going to a Debs. Have a good time tonight.'

'Oh we will, Sister, don't worry,' Harry said cheerfully, squeezing Rachel's hand.

'Hi Rachel, you look gorgeous.' Rachel turned to see Michelle Butler smiling at her. Michelle looked stunning. Her auburn hair was worn in a sophisticated chignon, and her white sheath dress with the mandarin collar was very chic.

'Hi, Harry.'

'Hi, Michelle.' Harry smiled. 'You look good.' Rachel's heart sank. They knew each other. No doubt Harry was one of Michelle's legion of admirers.

226

'We're cousins.' Michelle grinned. 'You take good care of Rachel, I'll be watching,' she warned. 'Do you think we could all sit together at the meal? Rachel, when we get there we'll rearrange the place-names. OK?'

'OK,' Rachel agreed happily. She'd enjoy sitting with Michelle, now that she knew she was Harry's cousin. Harry gave Michelle and Liam, her boyfriend, a lift to the hotel. They left before the others so that Michelle could rearrange the place settings.

'I was supposed to be sitting with Glenda Mower and Co. I'm glad I'm not stuck with them,' she said to Rachel, who was waiting for her outside the function room.

'I've put Eileen and Mary and Glenda together and Joanne Douglas.' Rachel giggled. Joanne and Eileen were two of a kind. Two know-alls who were highly competitive and very ambitious. They didn't like each other at all.

'That should be good,' Michelle grinned. 'I put Lizzie McCarthy and Fay Gleeson at our table. They're good fun.'

They were indeed good fun and the gales of laughter from table eight caused Mary Foley and her cohorts to cast envious glances in their direction. The roast beef was as tough as old boots, the potatoes were watery and the vegetables stringy but the four couples enjoyed themselves. To her great surprise, Rachel was having fun. She felt very relaxed with Harry and Michelle. By the time the meal was over and they'd had a drink, she was having the time of her life. It got even better when Ronan and Kate joined them and they all danced and laughed and chatted companionably.

Some time later she and Harry jived to a lively rock and roll number and when it was over Rachel was breathless. 'Are you having fun?' He put his arm around her as they made their way back to the table.

'This is the best night of my life, Harry. Thanks for bringing me,' Rachel enthused, eyes shining.

'Thanks for asking me.' He smiled. 'I'm having a great time too and you look beautiful,' he told her. Then he bent his head and kissed her and she kissed him back and they laughed and Mary Foley and Eileen Dunphy and Glenda Mower, who were seated at the table beside them, looked on in envy. Rachel caught their exchange of glances. She didn't care. Harry was the most handsome man in the room and the nicest. Glenda's fella was pissed and couldn't put two words together. Mary's Gerry looked as if he was bored out of his skull and Eileen's was a little weed of a chap with heavy-framed glasses and a studious air. Joanne's bloke had left her in the lurch and got off with someone else, they were snogging by the fire escape.

None of her classmates were having as good a time as she was now, Rachel thought with satisfaction, wondering why she had been so impressed by them at school. She'd never have to have anything to do with them again, she thought happily as she took the glass of Coke that Harry had brought her.

Later, when the dance was over, Ronan and Kate and she and Harry bought fish and chips and a couple of bottles of wine and had a little picnic on the sea front. It was a cool night but they were having such fun none of them noticed. The wine made Rachel tipsy and she chortled away to herself.

'I'd better sober you up before you get home,' Harry said in dismay, although he couldn't help laughing.

'I don't want to be sober. I'll just tell Da to piss off.' Rachel giggled.

'Come on, we'll go back to my house and have coffee,' Harry said firmly. They drove back to Rathbarry in high spirits. Harry made coffee and instructed Rachel to drink some.

'But I don't want to be sober,' she protested. 'I feel very happy and giddy. I want to stay like this.' She was on an absolute high. The evening, despite its disastrous start, had been a dream. She was full of confidence, ready for anything, even her father.

'Oh come on, have a cup of coffee or Ronan will kill me,' Harry begged.

228

'No I won't,' Ronan said cheerfully. 'If Rachel wants to go home tipsy, let her. She's not a schoolgirl any more.'

'Please Rach, have some coffee or your father will say I'm a bad influence,' Harry teased. And to please him, she drank three cups.

He walked her home and they kissed at the garden gate.

'I had a wonderful time.' She sighed against his cheek.

'It won't be long until you're in Dublin. You can let on you're going on a field trip in geography or something and you can stay for the weekend and we can have some fun,' he said. Rachel felt incredibly happy. To think that he wanted to see her again. It was unbelievable.

'You'd better go in,' he said. He could see William's shadow against a bedroom window. 'Goodnight, Rachel.'

'Goodnight, Harry,' she echoed. Her heart was bursting with happiness. She wanted to tell him that he was the nicest most wonderful person in the world. She fingered the gold R at her throat. It would always be her dearest treasure.

'Goodnight, Harry, and thanks,' she called again before slipping quietly into the house.

Harry was worried. He knew William Stapleton was waiting for Rachel. He wondered if there was going to be a row. It *was* late, he conceded. After four am. But it was her Debs night, for God's sake. He smiled, thinking of the fun they'd had. It had been a great night after all. Rachel really enjoyed herself. The face of her when he'd given her the gold chain with the R on it. You'd think it was the crown jewels. It had been an impulse, buying that. He was walking along Henry Street. One of the jewellers was having a half-price sale and he spotted it. He just knew it was right for Rachel. Why he did it, he just didn't know. There was something sad about Rachel. Something that made him want to protect her. He usually went for very self-confident articulate young women. Like the girls he was at college with. Rachel had always been Ronan's shy younger sister and he hadn't taken much notice of her. But lately he found he was thinking about her a lot. She had lovely eyes and a very good figure, even if she didn't dress to make the most of it. When she came to Dublin he was going to make sure she didn't spend all her time swotting, he decided. Life was for living and, if he had anything to do with it, Rachel Stapleton was going to start living it to the full. Father or no father. William's light had been turned off, he noted. Did that mean he'd gone back to bed or was he giving his daughter a ticking off? He'd never met anyone who aroused such animosity in him as Rachel's father. The sooner she was free of him the better, Harry thought grimly as he walked home.

Theresa heard the voices at the gate. A sliver of light under her door told her that William had heard them too and had switched on his bedside light. She heard his bed creak as he got out of it. Theresa was out of bed in a flash.

She'd been waiting for this all night. She'd listened to her husband pacing the floor downstairs until two am. She'd heard him come up and get undressed and pace the bedroom floor. She'd heard him get into bed, and now she heard him getting out of it, all ready to confront Rachel and ruin her night.

Silently, in her bare feet, she padded down the landing to his room. Ronan wasn't in yet either. He was probably giving Harry a chance to see Rachel home.

William was standing at the window, peeping through the curtains. He jumped when his wife closed the door behind her.

'It's disgraceful what they're up to outside. We'll be the talk of the neighbourhood. Wait until I go down and tell that fella never to set foot in this house again. Where's my dressing-gown?'

Theresa calmly locked the door and palmed the key.

'You're going nowhere, William,' she said.

'Get out of my way, woman,' her husband raged.

'I have the key to the door, William, you'll have to fight me for it.'

'Have you taken leave of your senses, Theresa?' William was aghast.

'No,' she said quietly. 'But I'll not have the happiest night of my daughter's life ruined, as long as I have breath in my body to prevent it.'

'But she's behaving in an immoral manner outside our front door.'

'Good! I hope she's enjoying it,' Theresa said calmly.

'Wh . . . What?' William stuttered.

'Don't be ridiculous, William, the lad is giving her a goodnight kiss. I know you didn't kiss me until we were engaged, but thankfully not all young men are as prim and proper as you were,' Theresa retorted. Her husband was speechless. He sat on the bed, shaking his head.

'It must be the medication you're on. It's affecting your mind,' he muttered.

'Well it's a pity I didn't go on it a long time ago then,' Theresa said curtly. She heard Rachel come upstairs, go into the bathroom and a few minutes later go into her own room. Only then did she put the key back in the lock and open the door.

'If you say one word to Rachel tomorrow morning, you'll be sorry,' she warned grimly before closing the door gently and slipping back to her own room. Twenty minutes later she heard Ronan come in. Theresa lay in bed, contented. She had got the better of William. He was afraid to upset her in case she had another attack. Before, he would have completely ignored her protests and gone right ahead and caused a row. For the first time in her life she had power over him. Was she going to use it!

Rachel undressed and hung her gorgeous white dress in the wardrobe. She sat at the dressing-table and cold-creamed her face. It was vital to take make-up off after a night out. All the models said that. Tonight she felt like a model. She felt pretty and sophisticated and happy. She'd gone to her Debs and made a triumphant entrance. She'd danced the night away. Drunk wine, and most importantly, been kissed by Harry. Rachel leaned her chin on her hands and remembered the moment his lips touched hers. It had been glorious. But even more glorious was the deep French kiss he'd given her at the garden gate. Feeling Harry's tongue in her mouth, gently exploring and caressing, had been a revelation. She could have stayed kissing him all night. He'd liked it when she'd hesitantly slipped her tongue into his mouth. She was shy at first but she got braver and in the end they kissed just like film stars in the pictures. She'd felt like Ali McGraw in *Love Story*. All that practising, kissing her arm, had paid off.

Rachel sighed happily. She could honestly say this was the best night of her life. It more than made up for all her misery at school. She pulled her nightdress over her head, unchained the amethyst pendant and removed her earrings. The gold R would never leave her neck, she vowed as she got into bed and pulled the sheets up around her.

She was going to spend weekends with Harry in Dublin. Even if she had to tell fibs. The gold R would give her courage, she thought, fingering it gently. Too happy to sleep, she lay going over everything that had happened, from the moment Harry put the chain around her neck to the passionate pleasure as he kissed her. Eventually, she fell asleep, smiling.

Chapter Twenty-Six

'Stay this weekend,' urged Harry. 'You won't be in Dublin for much longer once your exams are over. Tell your da you're going to study the effects of glacial erosion in Donegal or something.'

'I can't, I've used that excuse before.' Rachel sighed. She and Harry were strolling through the grounds of Trinity on their way to Bewley's for a cup of coffee before she got the bus to Bray. Harry was doing his best to try and persuade her to stay in Dublin. She wanted to stay with him. Staying with Harry was the loveliest thing.

She'd been on tenterhooks the first time she'd stayed, just before Christmas. Sure that her father was going to come knocking on the flat door. Harry spent the evening trying to pacify her. In the end he'd asked if she wanted to go home, because if she did he'd get the last bus to Bray with her. Rachel calmed down and told herself she was being schoolgirlish and silly. William wouldn't dream of doubting her word. He'd never think in a million years that she would tell a deliberate lie. Even now, months later, she could still remember how flustered she was as she mentioned in the most casual tone she could muster that she was going on a field trip with the geography class. They would be staying in hostels, she fibbed. Her face was beet-red, her palms were sweating, she was sure the word LIAR was written all over her forehead. Apart from calling it 'high-falutin' nonsense,' William hadn't put any opposition in her way. He'd read her textbooks and had to admit that teacher training had changed greatly from when he'd been a student decades ago. These new practices didn't impress him at all, he declared disdainfully. But Rachel knew he was just annoyed because he couldn't pontificate to her about what he didn't know. That made her feel superior to her father. It was a heady experience.

She was actually enjoying her studies and the looser structure of college life compared to secondary school. She'd become friendly with Pauline, the girl she'd met at the interviews. They often went to the Cat & Cage for a drink with the rest of their classmates. After her success on the night of her Debs, Rachel made herself go to some of the college social events. She found to her surprise that she quite enjoyed herself, although her shyness was still a major problem. But she had a much better social life than she'd ever had in Rathbarry, although it was always a pain having to leave to catch the last bus to Bray. It gave her secret satisfaction that her father had to drive to Bray and collect her and had to stay up past his usual bedtime of eleven pm. If he'd allowed her to live in, there would have been no need for such nonsense. Her mother would not have had the heart attack and Rachel wouldn't have felt obliged to live at home.

Theresa was very pleased that Rachel was mixing with the others in her class and enjoying her studies as well. She had been delighted to hear that Rachel was going on a field trip. Rachel felt awful about lying to her mother. But somehow she felt if Theresa knew where she was going to be, she wouldn't disapprove. Her mother was extremely fond of Harry and often gave Rachel a tea brack, a soda loaf or scones for him.

After that first lie, it had got easier. Ronan knew, of course. Now and then he stayed in Dublin too, on the pretext of studying. The three of them, and sometimes Pauline, would stay in Harry's shabby flat eating pizza, playing Scrabble and drinking wine. Rachel felt happy and carefree on these weekends. For the first time in her life she was having fun.

She was also having a very enjoyable love affair with Harry. She'd come a long way from kissing her forearm,

Rachel thought happily. Now when she stayed with Harry she slept in the big sagging double bed with him. The first few times she'd stayed he'd slept on the sofa and given her the bed. But gradually she grew to know and love and trust him. She plucked up her courage one night and said she wished he wouldn't sleep on the sofa. He got into bed and cuddled her and they'd started to make love. Harry was very gentle and patient with her and did not pressurize her when she said she didn't want to go the whole way. Rachel couldn't believe that she was so daring. She was actually sleeping in the same bed as a man . . . naked. If her father knew he would have apoplexy on the spot. And would Glenda, Mary and Eileen ever believe it, that the caterpillar who was Specky-Four-Eyes Stapleton, had become a gloriously happy butterfly.

'Come on, Rach. Stay for the weekend and we'll go out to Howth for a picnic and go to a ballad session in the village later,' Harry urged, and she wavered.

It sounded so enticing. Howth was one of their favourite spots. But her exams were very near and she had to study. Besides, she'd promised Theresa that she'd go with her to the May procession in honour of Our Lady. Her mother would be very disappointed if she rang to say she wouldn't be home for the weekend. She couldn't let her mother down. Not even for Harry.

'I can't, Harry,' she said regretfully. 'I promised Mam I'd go to the procession with her, I can't let her down.'

'No,' he agreed. 'You can't.' Harry had a soft spot for her mother. 'Come on, let's go to Bewley's and I'll go to the bus with you after we've had our coffee,' he said resignedly.

As the bus dawdled along at a snail's pace through Shankill, Rachel thought wistfully of Harry alone in the flat in Dublin. Now that her first year in college was almost over, she longed even more for the liberty living in would give her. Her mother seemed much better the past few months. Her father, though he was still as strict as ever, seemed to be getting used to the idea that she had a social life of sorts. Maybe over the summer months she might reopen the question of living in college. It would make life much easier for her. Commuting to and from Rathbarry was an awful waste of time, and very tiring. Her father might rethink his opposition to her leaving home. She had studied hard. Her exam results might sway him if they were good, she thought hopefully as Bray Head came into sight.

Her father was waiting for her, frowning with impatience. The bus was very late. 'Hurry along, Rachel, I've got a meeting with the parish priest and the board of management and I'll be late. And if there's one thing I can't abide it's being late,' he grumbled.

Good enough for you, Rachel thought unsympathetically. Nobody asked you to be my taxi-driver. I'm perfectly capable of making my own way home. She could have left her bike in St Angela's and cycled. But William was terrified she'd be knocked down on the dual carriageway. He drove at his usual sedate pace of forty mph hogging the middle of the road, oblivious to the cars behind him. Once they got onto the dual carriageway, they were passed by irate motorists, some of them giving William the two fingers. Rachel was used to it and switched off as her father launched into his usual diatribe about how speed kills.

'I'm going straight to the meeting, I've had my tea,' her father said as they drove up to the house a while later. 'Your mother's waiting to have her tea with you.'

'OK,' Rachel said, delighted at the chance to have tea and a natter on her own with her mother. Her father drove off and she stood at the gate inhaling the sweet country air. The cherry blossoms were out and her mother's garden was a riot of spring flowers. Theresa loved gardening. Rachel smiled as she walked around the back of the house to let herself in the kitchen door. She'd bought an almond ring and a Bewley's brack, her mother's favourite, for tea.

'Hi, Mam, I'm home,' she said cheerfully, as she walked in the back door. Theresa was sitting at the table with her back to her, listening to *The Archers*. She didn't answer, her head was bowed as if she'd dozed off. 'Mam, I'm home, I've got an almond ring and brack,' Rachel said gently, putting an arm around her mother's shoulders. Theresa's head lolled sideways. 'Mam! Are you all right?' Rachel said in panic, her heart pounding. Her mother's breathing was very laboured, her skin was waxen and she was unconscious.

'Jesus, Mam! Mam, wake up! It's all right, I'll call the doctor. Oh God! Oh don't do this to me, let Mammy be all right,' she begged, laying Theresa's head down on the table. With trembling fingers she opened the little leather book of phone numbers that Theresa kept on the stand by the phone. Doctor Dunne. Where was his number? She was all fingers and thumbs as she flicked through the pages, the names a blur as she tried to read them.

'Oh God, God, please help. Don't let Mam die,' she wept as she let the book fall. Conscious that every minute was vitally important she made herself calm down and picked up the book and eventually managed to dial the number.

'Hurry, hurry,' she muttered frantically. The doctor's wife answered the phone. Panic-stricken, Rachel gabbled the details to her. Seconds later the doctor came on the line. 'I'm on my way, Rachel, I'll call an ambulance,' he said and hung up.

Her mother was a dreadful colour when Rachel went back in to her. 'Mammy, Mammy, I love you, don't die. Don't leave me on my own,' she sobbed, putting her arms around her. 'Come on, Mam, wake up. It's Rachel. I've got your favourite almond ring,' she urged. 'The doctor's coming. I love you, Mam. I love you more than anyone in the world. Please wake up.' Rachel's heart was pounding so fast she thought she was going to faint. Her terror was so real she could almost taste it. Ever since her mother's attack the previous year, she'd feared this moment. It was her nightmare come true. She didn't even know enough first aid to help Theresa. Her mother gave a strong shudder and a horrible rattling noise came from her throat.

'Jesus Christ!' Rachel screamed. 'Mam, Mam,' she pleaded as her mother's body grew limp. 'Mammy, don't be dead. Mam, I love you.' She sank to her knees knowing with a deep and fearful dread that her mother was dead. The one person in the world who truly loved and protected her was gone. From now on she was on her own.

Minutes later, the doctor, the priest and William arrived. In a daze, Rachel watched the doctor test Theresa's non-existent pulse and slowly, sadly shake his head. The priest knelt beside her to whisper an Act of Contrition in her ear and give her the last rites as the doctor went to Rachel's side and helped her up from the floor. William was sitting in the armchair with his head in his hands. 'She was fine when I left,' he muttered. 'She was looking forward to having her tea with Rachel, she had the table all set and everything.'

'Sit down, Rachel, I'm going to give you a sedative. Your mother didn't suffer. It was a massive heart attack,' the doctor said kindly. He sat her down in a chair and went out to the phone and cancelled the ambulance and called the undertaker.

'There's no need for an autopsy, because of her history. I can sign the death certificate,' he explained to William. 'Rachel, take these and come and lie down,' he said, handing Rachel some tablets and a glass of water.

'I don't want to leave my mother,' she said dully.

'Rachel, there's nothing you can do for her now,' Father Walsh said compassionately. 'Her soul is gone to God.'

Rachel stood up and went over to her mother and put her arms around her. 'I'm staying with her, leave me alone,' she said fiercely. She kissed the top of her mother's head and her eyes brimmed with tears. Despite her illness and hard life, Theresa still had soft golden glints in her chestnut hair although it was liberally sprinkled with grey. She smelt of rosewater. The scent Rachel always associated with her. 'I'm here,' she whispered. 'I'm not going to leave you alone with all these strange men. I know you'd hate that. I'll mind you, don't worry,' she murmured into her mother's hair. Gently she rocked Theresa in her arms, crooning softly, whispering endearments. 'You're the best mother in the world,' she spoke very softly. 'Thank you for all the times you stood up for me against Daddy. I know it was all my fault that you had your heart attack last year. I'm sorry, I'm really sorry. I didn't mean it.' She started crying again. Heartbroken sobs wrenched her body. Her father stood up and came over to her.

'Stop that crying now, Rachel. It won't do your mother any good. Go and do what the doctor suggests.'

'You fuck off,' she said viciously. William couldn't believe his ears.

'*Rachel*,' he hissed.

'It's all right, William, it's the shock. I'll handle it,' Doctor Dunne said hastily.

'Come and lie down, Rachel,' he said firmly.

'No,' she said.

'I think perhaps it would be nice to say the Rosary,' Father Walsh suggested gently.

'Yes, Father.' Rachel nodded. 'Mam would like that.' They prayed as they waited for the undertaker to arrive. The steady monotonous tone of the priest dulled Rachel's panic. Theresa had always said the Rosary. The Rosary was familiar. Doctor Dunne saw the hearse arrive.

'Rachel,' he said kindly, 'say goodbye to your mother for a little while, you can see her again later in the funeral parlour. I want you to go upstairs and choose what you think Theresa would like to be buried in. Will you do that for me?' He stared into her eyes, his gaze firm but sympathetic.

'Yes, Doctor,' she replied, responding to the authority in his voice. She walked upstairs in a daze. Her mother was dead, she told herself. Theresa was gone. She'd never see her again. Ever. 'Oh God, I'm scared.' She shivered sitting on Theresa's bed. She picked up her mother's scarf and buried her face in it. It still smelt of her mother's perfume. Rachel could hear the sound of men's voices downstairs. She had to go back down, she couldn't leave Theresa on her own with all of them. She hurried out on the landing and saw Sergeant Roach's wife coming up the stairs.

'I have to go down to Mammy, I have to go down. I can't leave her down there with all of them. What are they going to do to her?' Her voice was high with hysteria.

'I'll be there, I'll stay with Theresa until they're finished,' Mrs Roach soothed. 'Doctor Dunne said you were going to get the clothes to dress her in. I'll come back up in a couple of minutes and we'll pick them together, there's a good girl,' Mrs Roach said comfortingly, giving Rachel a hug.

'What am I going to do without Mam?' she whispered. 'I wish I was dead too.'

'There, there, there,' the sergeant's wife said sadly, patting her head as if she was a child. 'There, there, there.'

The next few days were a living nightmare. When she saw her mother in her coffin in the funeral parlour that evening Rachel finally realized that Theresa was gone. Forever. Ronan was in a dreadful state. At least she'd been with her mother when she died. He hadn't had a chance to say goodbye. Rachel and he cried in each other's arms as they stood at the foot of their mother's coffin. William urged them to control themselves. Such public displays were anathema to him and the more upset his children were, the further he distanced himself from their grief.

Harry called to pay his respects, shocked by the suddenness of the death. William was not pleased to see him. Harry didn't want to cause tension so he kept his visit short and told Rachel he'd see her at the removal of the remains. The neighbours were extremely kind and brought in cakes and bracks and tarts for the callers. All the coming and going to the funeral parlour, and then to the church the following evening, kept Rachel and Ronan busy. And they had to make tea for all the people who called. She didn't have time to think. She didn't want to think. It was too frightening to think. At night Rachel took the tablets the doctor had given her and fell into a drugged sleep almost immediately. And woke in the mornings feeling heavy-headed, dry-mouthed and woozy knowing that something awful had happened and trying to remember what it was. Then memory would return and reality would intrude on her drug-induced amnesia. Panic and fear would grip her and her heart would start its frantic frightened pounding.

She woke the morning of the funeral to hear the rain pelting out of the heavens. She started to cry. There was nothing worse than watching a coffin being lowered into wet sodden ground.

'You could at least have given her a fine day,' she said bitterly to the small statue of the Sacred Heart that stood on her chest of drawers. Rachel felt sick to her stomach. The sickness of dread. The thought of the ordeal ahead made her heart pound. What if she fainted in the church and had to be carried out? What if she got hysterical at the grave and made a scene?

'You can't do it. You can't make a show of yourself. Mam would be mortified and disgusted. You can't let her down,' she told her reflection in the mirror. She looked like death herself. Her eyes, red-rimmed, were sunk into her head. Big dark circles around them. She was as white as a ghost and her cheeks were sunken because she couldn't eat. Maybe if she stopped eating she too would die. It was all she wanted. To die and be placed in the grave beside her mother. Her pain and grief would be over. She'd have no more worries. She'd never have to see her father again. It seemed like a very inviting solution. If she stopped taking the tranquillisers the doctor had prescribed for her and let them pile up for a couple of days she could take an overdose of them. Going to sleep and never waking up seemed like a very gentle way of committing suicide.

There was no-one she wanted to live for. Not even Harry. Rachel felt terribly guilty about herself and Harry. If she hadn't delayed to have coffee with him in Bewley's she could have got an earlier bus home and been with her mother when she had the heart attack. Maybe if the doctor had come earlier, Theresa could have been saved. It was God's way of punishing Rachel for all those lies she'd told about going away for the weekends when she'd been curled up in Harry's big bed, doing things that were against the sixth commandment. If it wasn't for her and her wicked ways Theresa might still be alive. No wonder God hadn't listened to her prayers. Why should He when she'd been sinning away, Rachel thought miserably, racked with guilt.

'Rachel, get up, you'll be late.' William knocked on the bedroom door, jerking her back to reality.

'I'm coming,' she said flatly.

She didn't faint in the church. She didn't have hysterics in the graveyard. She just stood clutching Ronan's hand tightly as she watched the undertakers lower Theresa's shiny coffin into the dark dirty recesses of the earth. At that moment she felt more scared and alone than she'd ever felt before. Rachel knew those feelings would be with her always.

Afterwards, some girls came over to Ronan to offer condolences. A lot of his friends had come from Dublin. His girlfriend, a gentle brown-eyed girl, squeezed Rachel's hand and said she was very sorry. William curtly told Ronan that the graveside was neither the time nor the place to be chatting to girls, he was to go home with Rachel and make the tea for the mourners. Ronan was furious.

As they moved around the kitchen, buttering brack and filling cups with tea, he looked at her and said quietly, 'I've had it with him, Rach. Whether he likes it or not, I'm going to America for the summer. If you've any sense you'll go and get a job in Dublin and stay with Harry and get out of here before he ruins your life like he ruined

Mam's. If you come back here in the summer to work in the Tea Rooms, you'll never be free of him. There's nothing here for us now. Nothing to keep us. Mam's gone. She'd want you to go and be independent. She wanted you to live in college even after her heart attack last year. She was always saying it to me. She told me if anything happened to her, to make sure you left home and had a life of your own,' Ronan said grimly.

'That's what I'm going to do. And you should do it too. As far as I'm concerned *he* . . . ' he jerked a thumb in the direction of the dining-room, where William was accepting condolences, 'can get lost. If he thinks I'm working in that damned fruit farm one more summer, he's got another think coming.'

'No, son! I won't allow it.' William lowered his reading glasses and raised cold eyes to Ronan. Rachel looked on with apprehension.

'I'm going, Dad, and that's the end of it,' Ronan said firmly.

'I've just told you, Ronan. I will not permit it and I don't want to hear another word on the matter. I can't believe that you're even thinking of such a thing and your mother only days in her grave.' William's tone was frosty. He picked up his paper and continued to read, signalling that that was the end of the conversation. It was a week after their mother's funeral. Rachel was getting ready to go back to Dublin to take her exams. Ronan had just told his father that he was going to America to work for the summer holidays. The response was very much what he'd expected. He looked at Rachel and went upstairs. Rachel could hear him moving around his bedroom.

Twenty minutes later he was downstairs. He had two rucksacks full of clothes and belongings. He ignored his father.

'Goodbye, Rachel, I'll see you in Dublin before I go,' he said. He kissed her cheek. 'Think about what I said.'

He stood at the back door and turned to address his father. 'I'm going to America as soon as my exams are over, Dad, if you don't like it there's nothing I can do about it. I'll write to you. Whether you write back or not is entirely up to you.' Rachel watched him leave and envied him his courage.

'You can't go back to Rathbarry for the summer. Don't be daft, Rachel,' Harry said crossly. Rachel had just taken her last exam and Harry was waiting for her when it was all over. She couldn't even remember the questions, she thought in a daze, as she sat in a quiet corner of the Cat & Cage sipping a soda water and lime. Anyway she didn't care whether she passed or failed. She didn't care about anything any more.

'Are you listening to me, Rachel?' Harry asked.

'Yeah.'

'Look, you've got to follow Ronan's example. Rachel, you're nineteen, you can't live at home forever.'

'If I'd been at home when I should have been at home, maybe my mother might still be alive,' Rachel said.

'For Christ's sake, Rachel! Will you cut that out!' Harry exploded. 'You're not responsible for your mother's death. If I hear that once more I'll blow a fuse. Stop thinking you're being punished. You've done nothing to be punished for.'

'I told her lies. She thought I was on field trips. And I wasn't, I was in bed with you.'

'Rachel, you're still a virgin, for God's sake. All you did was tell a few white lies because your da's too unreasonable to allow you to live some sort of a life of your own. That's no reason to be punished by God. He's not much of a God if that's the way you think he behaves. Grow up, Rachel.'

'Will you leave me alone?' Rachel snapped. 'You're telling me what to do. Ronan's telling me what to do. My father's telling me what to do. I wish you'd all bloody well leave me alone.' She got up and stalked out of the pub.

Harry raced after her. 'Where are you going?' he demanded.

'I just want to be on my own for a while,' she said heatedly. 'I'm going to go and visit my mother's grave. I need to be near her.'

'I'll come with you,' Harry offered.

'No, Harry, I want to go on my own. I'll see you.'

'But are you going to come back to Dublin or what are you going to do?' Harry asked.

'I don't know. Right now I don't care,' Rachel muttered.

'What about me?' Harry demanded.

'God, you're as bad as my father.' She turned on him. 'Doesn't anyone care about me? Why are men so bloody selfish?'

Harry threw his eyes up to heaven. He didn't know how to cope with Rachel in this humour.

'I'll phone you tomorrow,' he said evenly.

'Suit yourself.' She scowled and walked off towards the bus stop leaving Harry looking after her in dismay.

Harry downed another pint. He felt like getting pissed. Rachel was a changed person and he didn't know how to deal with her. It was obvious she was still very shocked by her mother's death. But why did she have to torture herself? He'd heard that when people were grieving they weren't thinking straight at all. Rachel was the proof of that. She wouldn't kiss him any more these days. She wouldn't even let him put his arms around her to comfort her. She was in a very deep depression and he couldn't seem to help her at all. It was extremely frustrating. Now that Ronan was gone, he was all she had left. Why wouldn't she lean on him and let him help her? And why was she letting her father dictate to her still? Couldn't she see that William was the major problem in her life? Harry scowled. The very thought of that man made him angry. Until Rachel stood up to him, she would never be free.

*   *   *

William wrote out his list in his neat precise writing. It was time to get some routine back into his life. Theresa had gone to her just reward. He and Rachel would have to get on with it. There were only the two of them now. Ronan had made his choice and deserted his family. Theresa had been far too soft with their son, allowing him to go and live in Dublin had been a big mistake. Now William was suffering the consequences.

He sighed deeply. Theresa had grown so stubborn in her later years. It must have been the medication. When he'd married her, she had been a docile gentle girl, content to bow to his greater knowledge. Well he might have failed with his son, but he still had a chance to mould his daughter. She too had taken advantage of her mother's soft nature and William had not been able to prevent it, for fear of causing Theresa to collapse. Theresa was gone now. It was his responsibility to pull in the reins. He would not shirk his duty, no matter how Rachel resented it. She was seeing far too much of that Armstrong layabout. He was a bad influence. Ronan was the proof of that. Well Harry Armstrong wasn't going to ruin his daughter's life by putting notions in her head, William would make sure of that. She would thank him in the end. Someday, when she had children of her own, she would understand how hard it was to be a parent and she'd thank him. He looked forward to that day. With a self-righteous sniff, William replaced the top on his fountain pen and went to make himself a cup of tea.

Rachel knelt at her mother's grave, picking out the dead flowers and rearranging the wreaths more tidily. She felt deeply unhappy. Why had she treated Harry so badly? It almost seemed as if she was blaming him for her mother's death. It wasn't his fault. But why couldn't he just give her a little peace? He wanted her to decide what she was doing for the summer. When she couldn't even think straight. What was it about men? Ronan had taken off. He hadn't thought that she could have done with his company for a while to help her cope with the loss of their mother. Her father . . . well he was a selfish bastard anyway, she thought bitterly. Maybe Harry and Ronan were right. Maybe she should leave home.

'What should I do, Mam, what should I do?' People said going to the grave gave comfort. It only made her feel worse, she thought as she sobbed quietly. A light drizzle started. Rachel stood up, wishing that she didn't have to go home to the house that was so empty and cold without her mother. 'I'd better go,' she said. She stood very still, willing Theresa to send some miraculous message to her. They said those who were dead took care of the living, and that you could always sense the presence of someone you'd been very close to. Rachel couldn't sense anything, she thought despairingly. She didn't feel comforted or protected or reassured. She just felt completely and utterly alone.

Her father was sitting at the kitchen table when she went in. 'Ah, Rachel,' he greeted her. 'How did your exam go?'

'I think it went all right,' she said flatly.

'I'm sure the examiners will take into consideration that you've been bereaved,' he responded. 'Now,' he said, handing her a list. 'We've got to get back into a routine. Your mother wouldn't want us to fall to pieces without her. Now that you're finished for the summer, I've made out a list of the dinners we could have on a weekly basis. Roast on Sunday, cold cuts on Monday. Pork chops on Thursday and so on. I'd prefer you to grill rather than fry. We'll naturally have fish on Fridays.' Rachel studied the list silently. He took her silence for assent.

'By the way,' he said stiffly, 'that Armstrong bloke rang looking for you. I told him I'd prefer it if he didn't get in touch again. I consider him to be an extremely bad influence and not the type of person you should consort with. I don't want you to see him again.'

'You had no business—'

'That's enough, Rachel, I don't want any back cheek,' William said sternly, pointing his finger at her, his eyes like two chips of ice. 'I won't allow you to treat me with disrespect as long as you are living under my roof. If that doesn't suit you, go, like your brother.'

Rachel stared at him. Her father was giving her an ultimatum. Stay under his thumb, or leave home and stand on her own two feet. Both choices filled her with dread. Wordlessly, she left the kitchen and walked upstairs to her mother's room. She sat in the rocking-chair where Theresa had spent many hours. The room was as it had always been, with all her mother's belongings dotted around. The silver-backed brush, comb and hand-mirror lay neatly on the dressing-table. The two little candlestick holders with the painted cherubs stood on the mantelpiece guarding the statue of the Sacred Heart. The scent of Theresa's rosewater lingered. Rachel put her head in her hands and rocked backwards and forwards. She had a choice to make. Whatever choice she made was going to have a big effect on her whole future, she thought in apprehension. It looked as if she was going to have to decide between Harry and her father.

Chapter Twenty-Seven

Rachel hadn't long to wait for the showdown. Two hours later she heard the doorbell ring, she knew it was Harry. William's edict that Harry was not to contact Rachel would have been like a red rag to a bull to her boyfriend. Harry loathed her father because of the way he treated her and Ronan.

She heard her father answer the door. Heard a sharp exchange of voices.

'Rachel,' she heard Harry call, 'Rachel?' She was too weary to feel anger, or dismay, or any other strong emotion. She walked slowly downstairs to where Harry stood on the doorstep.

'Get your bags, Rachel,' Harry ordered. 'You're coming with me.'

'She's doing no such thing, you good-for-nothing pup.' William was puce with rage. 'The . . . the unmitigated cheek of you to come and stand on my doorstep and back-answer me, after I expressly told you on the phone to stay away from Rachel. I've a good mind to have the law on you.'

'Are you going to stand there and let him talk to me like that, Rachel?' Harry said furiously. 'Are you going to stand there and let this selfish ignorant bastard threaten me?'

'By God, son, you go too far.' William's voice rose an octave to a high-pitched squeak. 'Get off my doorstep and never darken my door again.'

'Are you coming, Rachel? This is your last chance to make a decent life for yourself. Come to France with me for the summer, or go over to Ronan in America. Or do you want to stay here in Rathbarry and be nothing, and do nothing except dance to your father's tune?' Harry glared at her.

She looked at them, her father purple with fury, Harry pale with anger. Rachel saw two men engaged in a mighty power struggle. And she was the pawn in their game. Much as she loved Harry, Rachel saw, with a sudden shock of recognition, that he was as much a control freak as her father. He enjoyed telling her what to do. He expected her to do what he said. They rarely argued because Harry went into a huff if he didn't get his own way and she hated to see him annoyed. Harry was a kind, caring, protective young man. From the moment he'd rescued her from Patrick McKeown all those years ago he'd been her Prince Charming. But looking at him now, head to head in battle with her father, demanding that she leave with him, Rachel knew that if she left with Harry she would end up hating him. Harry would always see her as someone to be rescued, someone to be looked after, someone to be told what to do. She'd had enough of that to last her a lifetime. If she left Rathbarry, she was going to have to do it on her own.

'Leave me alone, the two of you. Stop ordering me around. I'm sick of it,' Rachel said tiredly.

'If you don't come with me, now, it's over between us,' Harry warned.

'You're as bad as he is for issuing ultimatums,' Rachel declared angrily. 'You're as much a bully as he is.' She pointed a finger at William, whose Adam's apple was doing a marathon. 'I'm not going to be bullied any more, by anyone,' she said quietly, more to herself than to the two men standing in front of her.

She walked back upstairs to her own bedroom and closed the door behind her. She was too drained to think. Her mother's death had used up every ounce of emotion she had. She was too numb to feel anything. She undressed and got into bed, though it was still bright outside. She heard the front door close and

Harry's footsteps echo down the garden path but she felt nothing. Harry had behaved as badly as her father. When she heard her father knocking on her door and asking her if she wanted supper, she ignored him. She would finish her teacher training and get a job, and never, ever, feel dependent on any man again. She would use her father for her own purposes. Let him pay for her education and then someday, when he least expected it, she would turn around and tell him to sod off. She'd buy her own house in Dublin, she'd come and go as she pleased. And she would never set foot in her father's house again. Her independence would be her greatest victory over all of them. Independence made you invincible, she thought as her eyelids drooped. Rachel lay in a half-stupor, banishing the world and all its worries from her mind, as she planned her great future, just as she'd done as a child.

Chapter Twenty-Eight

'Well how did your first day at the new school go?' Helen ran downstairs to give her niece a hug.

'Helen, it was great. I know I'm going to love it here in Dublin.' Paula dumped her schoolbag under the stairs and followed her aunt into the bright airy modern fitted kitchen which was a far cry from the old-fashioned cramped kitchen they had at home. 'I'll make you a cup of coffee,' she offered.

'No! I'll make you one,' Helen declared. 'Sit down there and we'll have a natter. You tell me all about it and then we'll have dinner around six. How does that sound?'

Paula gave her the thumbs-up. 'Sounds good to me, Aunt!'

'Oh stop calling me Aunt, for heaven's sake!' Helen laughed. 'It makes me feel like a geriatric.'

'Thirty-five's practically geriatric,' Paula teased. It was nice to see her aunt in good humour. When Anthony left her to go and live with his secretary she had been deeply upset. Paula was stunned to hear that her uncle had left Helen and that he'd been having an affair. Helen had covered it up and kept it to herself. She gave Paula the bare outline of facts. Tears welling in her eyes as she spoke. Paula hadn't pressed her. Now that she was living with her aunt, there'd be plenty of time for Helen to talk about it, if she wanted to. Paula was trying to be as kind as she could to Helen. She knew that her company had helped to ease the loneliness of Helen's separation.

Actually, Paula didn't miss her uncle at all. It was nice that there were just the two of them in the house. She could waltz around in her nightdress in the mornings and spend as long as she liked in the bathroom. Anthony was always nice to her but he was a bit dry and pompous. Helen, once she got over him, should go and find herself a man who enjoyed a laugh and a good time. She was much too young to bury herself at home pining. Paula intended to see that she didn't.

'Did you meet anyone nice at school?' Helen interrupted her reverie. She placed a mug of milky coffee and a plate of jam doughnuts in front of her. Paula took an eager bite out of her doughnut. This would be a treat at home. Here in Helen's it was commonplace. 'I met a very nice girl called Jennifer Myles. I'm sitting beside her because her best friend, Beth, had a very serious accident and she's got to have lots of operations and things. She won't be back at school for ages,' Paula explained. 'We came home on the bus together. She lives in Wadelai.'

'That's not too far from here. If you want to invite her to the house anytime, or any friends you make, you're welcome to do that, darling.'

'I've joined the basketball team. I'm having a try-out tomorrow. Jenny introduced me to everyone. So I'll be late coming home from school,' Paula explained as she licked her fingers to get the last bit of jam and sugar.

'Here, have another one.' Helen pushed the plate towards her. Paula didn't know the meaning of the word diet, and didn't need to know it either. She took one enthusiastically.

That night she sat at the neat desk Helen had bought for her in her lovely cream and yellow bedroom. She was writing a letter to her mother and father. Paula had promised that she would write each week and let them know how she was getting on. Her parents were particularly anxious to know how she liked her new school. Paula sighed. She couldn't honestly say she was missing home, because she wasn't. But her mother would have been hurt if she knew that.

Paula loved being in Dublin and being with Helen. It was like a permanent holiday. She *did* miss her parents and her sisters and brothers. But she wasn't dreadfully homesick. Far from it. She didn't miss St Margaret's Bay one whit. She wondered if she was a bit odd. When her sister Rebecca heard that Paula was going to live with Helen and go to school in Dublin, she told Paula that she'd hate to leave home and her family and friends to go to a big city and have to start at a new school where everyone was a stranger. And Rebecca was older than she was! Paula didn't see it like that. A new school held no fears for her. It was all a great adventure.

Paula felt that it was fated that she should come to live with Helen. That night when she'd had the brainwave, when she'd suggested it to her aunt, it had felt so *right* somehow. Her parents had been surprised, and a bit dismayed. But Paula pleaded with them. Wheedled and begged as only she knew how. She grimaced as she remembered the arguments and how terrified she'd been that her parents would refuse to let her go.

'You can't just go and land in on top of Helen like that. It's not fair on her,' Maura argued.

'Don't let that stop her coming, Maura,' Helen said quickly. She thought it was a wonderful idea. 'I'd love her to come and live with me. It's very lonely up there on my own. I'd love Paula's company and I'd take good care of her. But it's a very big decision to make and I think you and she should talk it over. I'll stay down here for a few days and see what you decide,' Helen suggested.

'What happens if you and Anthony get back together? He mightn't want to have Paula living with you.' Pete frowned. Her father wasn't happy with the idea, Paula could see that.

'There's no likelihood of that. Ever!' Helen declared emphatically. 'I don't want him back, even if he leaves her. It's too late now. I never thought I'd say it, but I'm glad I have no children. All I have to think about is myself and I don't want Anthony Larkin or his goddamned mother back in my life,' Helen said bitterly.

'Yes, but Helen, what if he decides you should both sell the house?' Maura asked gently.

'He won't do that,' Helen explained. 'When we got married, he bought that house with money an uncle left him. There's no mortgage on it. He and that secretary of his bought an apartment in Ballsbridge. It's not as if he hasn't got a roof over his head. He's told me the house is mine. It's his way of salving his conscience.'

'Please, Mam, Dad. I'll work really hard at school. And anyway I'll be leaving home to get a job in a few years' time, so I'll just be going a bit earlier, that's all,' Paula interjected.

'It's a big upheaval, Paula. And you're doing your Inter Cert next year. Your mother and I will have to think about it,' her father said firmly.

'Please, Daddy, it's what I really want. It was my idea in the first place. It would make me very, very happy,' Paula begged earnestly, giving her father's arm a squeeze. His face softened.

'We'll see, Paula. It's a big step to take and we'd miss you.'

'But Dad, I'd be home some weekends and the holidays. You'll probably see just as much of me as you do now.'

'That wouldn't be hard,' her father said fondly. 'You're always gadding about.'

In the end, after much discussion, her parents agreed to allow her to go to live in Dublin with Helen, if her aunt could get Paula into a secondary school. They would see how things were going before any final decision was made. If, at Christmas, her school report was not impressive, or if Helen changed her mind about having her there, Paula would come back to St Margaret's Bay.

There was no way that was going to happen, she assured herself. She was going to work damn hard. Paula didn't mind work. She knew it was vital to get decent marks in her exams. The harder you worked the better you got on. Parents and teachers drummed it into you. If that's what it took, well so be it. Helen got her into a secondary school in Drumcondra and Paula was delighted.

She wasn't going to have much choice about hard work, anyway. That Sister Barty was a tough cookie and she'd given the Inter Cert year a stiff talking-to. Usually, the first day back at school was fairly relaxed but they'd got right down to their studies today. They hadn't even been given a half-day. Much to the dismay of her new classmates.

Paula sucked her pen thoughtfully. On the whole, she felt she was going to like them, except for a girl called Eilis McNally, who had a very superior air and who told her that she'd probably find a school in the city totally different from one in the country. The way she said 'the country' sounded extremely dismissive and sneering. As if she was suggesting that life in the country was like something from the dark ages.

'Don't mind her,' Jennifer Myles murmured. 'She's a right little bitch. She thinks she's absolutely *IT*. Just because her father's some sort of producer in RTE. She's always name-dropping. You'd think she knew Gay Byrne personally the way she goes on.'

'Thanks,' Paula said and Jennifer smiled. Paula had been relieved by this friendly overture. For the first hour or so the other girl had been very quiet, and, Paula thought, a little standoffish. But later, when they got talking between classes, Jennifer confided that her best friend Beth had had a terrible accident and was in hospital having operations on her discs. She had been advised to stay back a year. No wonder Jenny hadn't been bright and bubbly or over-friendly. But as the day progressed they'd shared a fit of the giggles, when Eilis, reciting a stanza of Keats's *Ode to a Nightingale*, declaimed, 'Thou wast not born for death, immoral Bird!'

'Tsk! Good gracious, Eilis McNally, don't you know the difference between immoral and immortal? And you've chosen to do Honours English,' Miss Walton tutted, much to the Superior One's chagrin. 'Kindly consult your dictionary tonight and write out the words immoral and immortal and their meaning. Show them to me tomorrow,' the English teacher ordered. Paula enjoyed every minute of the other girl's discomfiture. Eilis blushed to the roots of her hair, amid titters and giggles from her classmates. *That* was a mistake the girl from 'the country' wouldn't make, Paula thought with satisfaction. She was going to be extremely careful to shine at her studies. Eilis McNally was not going to get the chance to watch a teacher make a show of *her*. As soon as she'd finished her letter home, she was going to do her homework to perfection. 'Start as you mean to go on,' she murmured as she began her epistle.

Eilis McNally scowled to herself as she searched through her English dictionary for the word immoral. Miss Walton was a sarky bitch and it had been mortifying to have made a mistake like that in front of that stuck-up new girl, Paula.

Eilis knew she didn't like Paula from the minute she walked into the classroom, and had Sister Imelda making a fuss of her as if she was the Queen of Sheba. She couldn't explain it. Eilis just knew instinctively that Paula was a threat. Eilis considered herself the most popular girl in the class. People looked up to her and were impressed by her background and all the famous people her father knew. She even had a book of autographs which her father had collected for her. The girls at school would give their eye-teeth for it. When they had friendly basketball matches at lunch-time, everybody wanted to be on Eilis's team. It was considered an honour to be picked. Well one thing was for sure. She wouldn't be picking that Paula one. With her huge blue eyes and her shiny blond hair. She acted as though she was a film star. You'd think that a new girl coming into the class would be a bit shy, but she'd swanned in full of confidence as if she owned the place.

With any luck, she'd prove a dud at basketball. Maybe she was as thick as two short planks. Brains *and* beauty were a very rare combination, Eilis decided hopefully as she buckled down to the onerous task of explaining the difference between immortal and immoral.

Paula finished pressing her school uniform and laid it neatly on the back of a chair. She'd written her letter, done her homework, and was all prepared for school the following morning. It was ten-thirty and she felt tired. It had been a long and somewhat stressful day. At least now that she knew what to expect it would be easier. She was glad she was sitting beside a girl as nice as Jenny Myles. She was looking forward to her basketball try-out tomorrow. If there was one thing she was good at, it was basketball. She'd played a lot of it at school in Waterford and had gold and silver medals to prove it.

She made the hot chocolate for supper. Helen was relaxing in front of the TV. She'd spent the evening practising her shorthand, trying to get her speeds up again. She told Paula that she wanted to get herself a job. She didn't want to be supported by Anthony for a minute more than she had to. Pete and Maura sent a postal order for Paula's keep every week. Helen protested. But Pete insisted. Fair was fair, he said.

Paula sighed, leaning her elbows on the fitted kitchen counter. She'd love her aunt to be her happy, bubbly self again. It would be good for Helen to get a job. She could get out of the house and stop brooding. Paula gazed out at the back garden, noting that the lights were on in the house next door. The detectives must be in there, she mused.

Helen had told her that the house next door was let to three detectives while the owner was away in Africa. So far she'd only spotted them briefly, going from the front door to their cars. One of them was a fine thing, she decided. She looked forward to getting to know him.

The lights of the houses at the end of the long garden still fascinated her. Paula loved looking at the windows of the semi-detached houses, wondering who lived in them and what they did.

It was so different. At home their house had fields behind it and the sea in front of it. It was still strange to lie awake at night and hear the subdued continuous sound of the traffic on Griffith Avenue, instead of the roar of the sea. Sometimes she had to pinch herself to let herself know she wasn't imagining it all.

Conor lived in digs somewhere on the other side of the city. He'd begged her to get in touch with him when he'd heard she was coming to live in Dublin. He was crazy about her, he told her, and he wanted them to spend a lot of time together.

'I'll see,' Paula told him coolly. She felt differently about him since the night she'd lost her virginity. His swaggering man-about-town image had always impressed her. Until he'd had to prove it. What a chancer! He'd pretended he'd slept with his other girlfriends. Boasted about it even. And then, when it finally came to the crunch, he'd showed that the nearest he'd ever come to having sex was in his dreams. Paula would never forgive him for the disappointment of her first time. She'd been so looking forward to it, after all those months of heavy petting. She was not going to give him a second chance. But she might keep him dangling. If he was going to university, he'd be going to parties and the like. Conor might come in handy, Paula decided as she stirred the hot drink. But he needn't think for one minute that he was going to sleep with her again. The next time she slept with a man, it would be with someone who knew what he was doing. She wondered what the detective next door would be like in bed. She smiled. He looked impressive anyway. Six foot, shoulders like a barn door and lean and rangy for good measure. Her eyes sparkled with anticipation at the thought of the flirtation to come. Jauntily, she picked up the tea-tray and walked in to her aunt. 'Supper is served, Madame,' she said cheerfully.

'Paula, you're a darling! I'm so glad you're here with me,' Helen declared.

'Me too, Helen. Me too,' Paula agreed happily.

The nights were getting chilly, Helen brooded. She hated getting into a cold bed. She should have switched on the electric blanket earlier. It was something that had never bothered her when she was sharing a bed with Anthony. She'd always cuddled into him and been warm in minutes. She felt a surge of rage and resentment as she slipped in between cold sheets. Anthony was the cause of this, Anthony and his two-faced sweet-as-pie secretary was the cause of everything. Her humiliation. Her loneliness. Her fear of the future. She veered from exuberant optimism to deep depression. All this was the fault of her shit of a husband and his designing little whey-faced fancy woman.

Helen gingerly stretched out and waited for the electric blanket to warm the bed. She hated the nights now. During the day she could keep herself occupied. But alone in her room at night, all those horrible thoughts and emotions crowded in on her and she couldn't evade them. Every night she went to sleep angry.

Stephanie Larkin, her vicious, malicious mother-in-law, had opened Helen's eyes to her husband's affair. She'd phoned one evening to talk to Anthony. But he wasn't at home. When Helen told her this, her mother-in-law said sweetly, 'Oh yes, I forgot. He must be having dinner with Molly. He mentioned something to me about it. She's such a sweet girl. So *sympathetic*. She'll make some man a wonderful wife and of course she's *devoted* to Anthony. He'd be lost without her.'

'Is that so?' Helen said calmly, furious that Stephanie seemed to know exactly what her Anthony was doing. All he'd told Helen was that he was working late. Come to think of it he seemed to be working late a lot recently, she reflected as she put the phone down. You'd think that he and Molly were having a rip-roaring affair the way her mother-in-law was talking. The thought amused her. Anthony was the last person in the world who'd have an affair. He was far too strait-laced.

She asked him where he'd been when he came home late that night. 'Working! The auditors are coming next week. I want everything to be spot-on.'

'Your mother said you were having dinner with Molly,' she said lightly, as she made him a cup of tea. A dull red blush suffused his face.

'Yes . . . well yes, we did have a bite to eat,' he said hastily. 'She's worked very hard the last few weeks.'

'Where'd you go?' Helen was a bit miffed that he hadn't mentioned it. She didn't particularly like Molly. She was always very polite to Helen but she felt that it was an insincere politeness. When Helen ever heard the phrase 'still waters run deep' she thought of Molly Kelly.

'I took her to the Russell,' Anthony said stiffly. Helen was astonished. The Russell Hotel was posh and expensive. A place you'd go to splash out for a birthday or wedding anniversary if you were fairly affluent. Molly must have been doing Trojan work.

'Very nice,' she murmured. 'Some people have all the luck!' She meant it as a joke but Anthony turned on her angrily.

'Molly's an extremely hard worker, Helen. She deserved a night out. And I can tell you one thing, she's a very loyal employee.'

'What's bugging you, Anthony? I only made a simple remark,' she exclaimed.

'You can be very smart with your remarks sometimes, Helen,' Anthony said huffily as he left his tea and stalked up to bed.

'God, you're touchy,' she shouted up the stairs after him. 'What difference does it make to me whether you bring her to the Russell or Bewley's?'

Anthony ignored her. Helen marched back into the kitchen and flung the dirty crockery into the sink. She slammed the press doors as she got clean cups and saucers to set the table for breakfast. The old familiar niggle of pain in her ovaries twinged and she scowled. That was a sure sign her period was imminent. Maybe if her husband spent more time at home making love to her and less time worrying about his business affairs she might have been pregnant long ago. If only he'd go for those tests that she was always at him to have. At least she'd know then whether it was her fault they couldn't have children. There was little likelihood of her conceiving in the foreseeable future. Anthony hadn't been able to get an erection the last two times they'd tried to make love. And now, when she made a move, he made an excuse.

He wouldn't even talk about it. That was the thing that hurt most of all. She knew he blamed her. Helen just knew it. But there was nothing she could do about it. When they went to bed, her husband stayed on his side. For all the contact between them, they might as well have been separated by the Atlantic Ocean.

She tossed and turned, wondering why he'd been so touchy. He was very considerate towards his secretary. But why make such a song and dance about an innocent remark? She thought about what her mother-in-law had said. How the hell did Stephanie know that Molly was sweet and understanding unless Anthony had told her so? And why would Anthony be going around saying such things to his mother?

Two days later, Anthony arrived in from work, a grim set to his jaw.

'Helen, there's something I have to tell you. I can't put it off any longer. I'm leaving you. I'm going to live with Molly. We've been having a relationship for some time and I want to be with her all the time. I'm sorry. I can't stand this any more.'

Helen's mind reeled. Was she imagining it or had her

husband just told her that he was having an affair with his secretary? That he wanted to leave her? She was having a nightmare. She must be.

'What!'

'You heard, Helen,' Anthony muttered.

'How long has this been going on?' She was stunned.

'What difference does it make?' he said wearily. 'I can't live with you any more, Helen. I can't take the nagging. The hassle and resentment every time you get your period. Have you any idea what it's like to be expected to make love just because it's the right time of the month? I just don't want to make love to you any more. It's an ordeal, Helen. A bloody ordeal!' He glared at her and she could see that he was really angry. 'Do you know something, Helen? This obsession of yours about having a child has destroyed our marriage. I tried to give you everything. But it means nothing to you. How do you think I feel every time you come home from Maura's and you keep going on and on about what a dote Paula is? About how lucky Maura is to have six children? How the *hell* do you think that makes me feel? Have you any idea?' he raged with pent-up fury that was unleashed with all the force of a damburst.

'But Anthony—' she protested but he held up his hand to stop her.

'I don't want to hear, Helen. I've had it. There's nothing that you can say that'll make me change my mind. Molly's a loving gentle person. Like you were when I married you first. She doesn't make demands on me. She accepts me for who and what I am. I want to be with her. I find peace when I'm with her,' he said quietly. His tone of voice told her he was serious. She had lost him.

'You know something, Helen?' He jammed his hands in his pockets and stared out the kitchen window. 'My mother emasculated me and always has done. And so have you! Well I've had enough of it. Had enough of women and their emotional bullying. I'm never letting a woman do that to me again.'

263

In the darkness of her bedroom, Helen lay wide-eyed replaying that traumatic evening as she'd done every night since he left.

'I'm not a nag. I'm not a bully,' she whispered as tears trickled down the side of her cheeks and she started to sob. 'All I wanted was a baby. I had the tests done and there was nothing wrong. Why couldn't you have had them too, you bastard? Why did you let me take the blame for it?' A sliver of light sliced the darkness.

'Are you all right, Helen?' Paula whispered. And then her niece slid into bed beside her and put her arms around her. 'Don't cry, Helen. It's going to get better,' she said comfortingly.

'It's better already, having you here, darling,' Helen said gratefully, squeezing Paula's hand. 'I don't know what I'd do without you.'

Chapter Twenty-Nine

Paula lay on the bed, took a deep breath and pulled in her stomach. 'Jenny, give us a hand here, will you?' she asked her friend, who was applying eyeshadow at the pretty kidney-shaped dressing-table. Paula had bought a brand-new pair of Falmers jeans and was having difficulty with the zip. Between them they got the zip up. Paula eased herself off the bed and bent and stretched to loosen the skin-tight jeans. She was in great form. This was going to be her first night out with the girls since June.

It was wonderful to have two such good friends as Jenny and Beth. They had all really clicked. Paula had settled in very well at school. She, Jenny and Beth became firm friends. She'd been invited to their houses and she'd met their families. They had a lot in common. Paula had had to share a bedroom with her sisters, just like Jenny and Beth. They all had to do plenty of housework, although compared to what it was like at home, and what her two friends had to do, Paula got off very lightly at Helen's.

They both thought she was really lucky to have a lovely room to herself, where she could play her records, study and relax and entertain her friends. That was the height of luxury to them. It was so much more peaceful in Helen's house. They'd both slipped into the habit of coming down to Paula's, rather than her going to their houses. Helen was delighted that Paula had made nice friends and always made the girls more than welcome.

It felt like having two extra sisters, Paula thought happily as she watched the girls getting ready to go out. Beth wasn't long out of hospital after another operation and she was raring to go. They were going to Mick's, the local disco, and then Sandra O'Reilly was having a party because she had a free house, so they were going to go on to that.

It was great to be back in Dublin, Paula mused as she brushed her shiny blond hair. It was hard to believe that she'd been here a year now. Everything had worked out very well. She'd gone home to St Margaret's Bay for the summer holidays and worked in the hotel. She would have preferred to spend some of the summer in Dublin. But Helen had pointed out that her parents would expect her to spend her holidays with them. They wanted her to be at home, it would be hurtful if Paula insisted on staying in the city.

It had been nice to be at home. Everyone had made a fuss of her. All her old friends had been dying to hear about life in the big smoke. Apart from Monica Boyle, of course, who had made sneering sarcastic remarks about the city not being all it was cracked up to be. Paula'd had no difficulty getting her job back in the hotel. But Monica hadn't been taken back.

Paula met Conor at home too. He'd been dying to start dating her again and had reproached her vigorously for not keeping in touch, especially when she too was living in Dublin. They could have seen each other often, *especially* when they'd slept together once. Conor had never understood why Paula had dropped him like a hot potato. It had been a huge shock to him. Why? he asked her again and again. All Paula ever said was, 'I think it's for the best, that's all, Conor.'

Paula had one big fault, she knew it herself. She could never forgive someone who let her down. It was a flaw in her character, but that's the way she was. She always held a grudge. Conor had let her down badly. It had changed things, and she no longer respected him. Besides, she was meeting loads of fellas at the discos she went to with Jenny and Beth. If you were going with someone you couldn't play the field and flirt and have fun with other blokes when you were out, she reasoned. Paula didn't want to start going steady again. It had been different when she lived at home. Going with someone was of the utmost importance in the village. And the fact that Conor had often been allowed to borrow his father's car was a huge bonus if you wanted to go into Waterford to the pictures or for a meal. But in Dublin you didn't need a fella with a car. You could just hop on a bus and go into town any time you felt like it. It was a real liberation.

Not that she was gadding about all the time. Paula knew she had to work hard. If her school reports slipped, she'd be back home to St Margaret's Bay in the wink of an eye. Paula had no illusions about that. That had been the agreement and she intended to keep it. Where her education was concerned, her parents would stand for no nonsense. Pete and Maura were very pleased with her school work so far. Her Christmas report had been excellent and Paula felt confident about her Inter Cert exam, she'd assured them.

Her confidence had been justified. Her results came last week and she'd got eight honours.

That was another reason why she was looking forward to the night out. Jennifer had done well also and both of them were going to really let off steam and relax now that the long wait for the results was over.

'Quick, look,' Beth exclaimed. 'Green Car is hanging out his shirts.' She was standing at the bedroom window having a gawk out.

Paula and Jennifer rushed over to join her. 'His name is Brendan, I think,' Paula murmured as the three of them ogled the fine thing in the adjoining back garden. 'But wait until I tell you the bad news. They'll all be leaving at the end of the month because the landlord is coming back from abroad to live there. The nice one told Helen.'

There was a chorus of dismay as Jennifer and Beth digested this piece of information. Observing the talent next door had occupied many pleasant hours over the months since they'd all become friends. They had christened the three detectives Green Car, Blue Car and Grey Car, for the colours of the cars they owned. In spite of Paula's best efforts, she knew no more about her three neighbours than what Helen had told her when she'd first come to live there. All she ever got out of them was a 'Hello,' or a 'Howya' as they went in and out of the house. They didn't have nine to five hours so it was hard to keep track of them. Nevertheless, through constant observation, they had ascertained that Grey Car was dating a nurse. This was not considered a great tragedy, however, as he wasn't that good-looking. Blue Car was into hurling and was the friendliest of the trio. He might say 'How's it going?' or 'Great day today,' rather than the more monosyllabic greetings of his colleagues.

It was Green Car who aroused the most intense interest and curiosity in the trio. He was extremely good-looking in a tall dark and handsome way, and he had a brooding taciturn air that was immensely challenging. Jennifer maintained he would have made a great Heathcliff. They didn't know if he was dating anyone, but he went out every Friday and Saturday night, looking spruce in casual clothes. Paula had never seen him bring home a girlfriend as the other pair did and so she nursed a secret hope that there was no-one steady on the scene.

'He's got great muscles, hasn't he?' Beth said approvingly. The detective was wearing a white T-shirt that showed off his fit and lean physique. 'He looks a bit like Robert De Niro.'

'Hmmm,' agreed Paula. 'I wouldn't mind spending a night in his bed, I can tell you.'

'Do you believe Eilis McNally has slept with her boyfriend or would you say she's only spoofing?' Jennifer asked, craning her neck to get a better look at the Adonis below.

'Don't mind her,' Beth expostulated. 'She's the biggest spoofer going. She just likes everyone to think she's a woman of the world, mixing with the glitterati in RTE.'

'I wouldn't think anyone in our class has done it? Would you?' Jenny turned to Paula. Paula looked at her friend quizzically. There was something endearingly innocent about Jenny. She wondered if she'd be shocked if she told her she'd slept with Conor.

'I wouldn't say Eilis has—'

'Who'd want to sleep with her with her frizzy red hair and her big bug-eyes? It's a wonder her fella ever gets a chance to kiss her. She never stops bragging and pontificating,' interjected Beth, who detested Eilis McNally. Eilis never lost the opportunity to make a sly dig at Beth because she'd had to stay back a year.

'What are you doing in a fourth year classroom?' Eilis would say, pretending to joke. 'Go back down to third year where you belong.' The trouble with Eilis was that she was mad jealous of the three of them because they'd become such friends.

'Don't be so pass-remarkable, Beth,' giggled Jennifer. 'She's not *that* bad-looking. Why do you think Eilis hasn't done it, Paula?'

'Because her boyfriend's not that pushed about her. Just watch them when they're together. She's real possessive. She wraps herself around him and he just doesn't like it, he's always wriggling away. If you ask me, I think he's more interested in his career prospects. He's got his eyes set on RTE, where her da works.'

'How do you know?' Jennifer was mystified.

'He told me,' Paula said airily.

'When?'

'Do you remember that disco we went to in Belvedere at Easter? Most of the class were there and so was Eilis. She was off in the loo doing a job on her make-up and Anne Gleeson introduced me to him. He told me he was interested in being a sound engineer and he was hoping Mr McNally might be able to help him get a job in RTE when he's finished studying. Eilis wasn't too pleased when she came back. I think she thought I was trying to chat him up.' Paula laughed.

'As if you'd want to chat him up, and you with fellas falling all over you.' Beth snorted. 'I wonder has Jane Daly done it?'

'I'd say she has,' Jennifer said. 'She's crazy about Frank, they've been going together since first year. I wouldn't have the nerve to sleep with a fella, would you?'

'Naw!' Beth said glumly. 'Look at my sister getting pregnant when she was only sixteen. The hassle it caused at home. I'd be petrified I'd get preggers.' She turned to Paula. 'Would you do it?'

Paula gave a little smile. 'Actually I've done it,' she admitted. Beth and Jennifer stared at her wide-eyed.

'Have you? What was it like?'

'Weren't you scared of getting pregnant?'

Paula laughed at the faces of them. They looked somewhat shocked.

'I'll tell you one thing, girls, it isn't all it's cracked up to be, that's for sure.'

'Isn't it?' Beth was disappointed.

'Well of course, I only did it the once,' Paula admitted. 'I was so unimpressed I didn't go for a repeat performance.'

'Did it hurt?' Jennifer was curious. Paula wrinkled her nose as she tried to remember.

'I can't really remember, it all happened so fast, to be honest.'

'They say once you've had it, you can't live without it,' Beth remarked. 'Do you find you're always thinking about it?'

'Oh Beth.' Paula had to laugh. 'Mind, when you see the likes of him down there you can't help but . . . '

'I wish I had your nerve,' Beth said admiringly. 'Did you use a johnny?'

Paula shook her head. 'No, I made sure it was the safe

time of the month. I was very careful, there's no point in taking risks.'

'Well it looks as if I'll die wondering unless a fella asks me to marry him,' Beth said glumly. 'The way things are at home with my sister and the baby, Ma doesn't even like me going to discos.'

'Would you say Brenda ever did it with that guy she was going with?' Paula cast an inquisitive eye at Jenny.

Jennifer shrugged her shoulders. 'She never let on to me. But I heard her once saying to Eddie that "it" hadn't arrived yet and she went around looking awfully worried. I didn't dare ask her though, you know Brenda, she'd take the nose off you.'

'Hmmm,' Paula agreed. Although she wouldn't say it to Jenny in a million years, she just couldn't take to Brenda at all. Brenda treated Jenny like a little slave. She expected her to run around after her. Jenny had to go to the shops for Brenda's goodies when she was on a binge. Brenda had Jenny doing her ironing. There'd be a mega-huff if Jenny refused. Paula had seen it happen. If Brenda was her sister, there'd be ructions. Paula wouldn't take that crap from anyone. She had a feeling too that Brenda didn't particularly like her. Whenever Paula was in Jenny's house, Brenda treated her very offhandedly. It didn't particularly bother Paula, the less she had to do with Brenda the better it suited her.

'We'd want to hurry on,' Jennifer declared.

'I'm all ready.' Paula made a final check in the mirror. The jeans looked terrific, and the cerise silky shirt looked casually elegant. Her long blond hair fell over her shoulders like a curtain of gold. Her eyes were bright and clear, her face lightly tanned and glowing after a summer spent in St Margaret's Bay. It was great being able to buy her own clothes. That summer job was a godsend. She'd made a lot of extra money in tips. Since Helen's separation, her aunt wasn't able to treat her as lavishly as she'd done when Paula was a child. Not that Paula minded, she liked being independent. It was a thrill buying stuff with money she'd earned herself.

'Have a good time, girls.' Helen smiled at them as they all trooped down the stairs. 'Don't be too late coming in. I'll leave some ham sandwiches out for you.'

'We won't, Helen.' Paula gave her aunt an affectionate hug. 'And thanks for the sangers.'

'Thanks for having us stay, Mrs Larkin,' Jennifer said politely.

'Yes thanks,' echoed Beth.

'You're welcome. I won't be expecting you up before lunch-time.' Helen held the door open for them.

'You're dead lucky with your aunt, Paula,' Jennifer said enviously as the girls walked down the garden path. 'There's no way I'd be allowed stay in bed until lunchtime at home on a Saturday morning.'

'Me neither.' Beth sighed.

'Helen's the best in the world,' Paula said happily. 'She really understands what it's like to be our age. I wouldn't get away with half the things I get away with here if I was at home. I wouldn't be allowed lie in until twelve either. Saturday's mad at home. All the hoovering and dusting and polishing has to be done.'

'Same here,' echoed the girls.

'Howya, girls. Off for a night on the tiles?' Blue Car was walking up the road, a tennis racquet in his hand.

'Hi,' Paula said cheerfully. Blue Car smiled back. 'Are ye off into town?'

'Yeah, we're off to a party,' Paula said hastily, feeling it would be unsophisticated to admit that they were going to the local disco. Prudently Beth and Jennifer said nothing, letting their leader do all the talking.

'Talking of parties,' Blue Car announced. 'We're having a party next Saturday week. Some of the nurses from the house up the road and some of the blokes from the station are coming. If you want to bring a bottle and call in, feel free,' he invited.

'Sure, yeah, we've nothing planned so far for next Saturday,' Paula said lightly.

'Great stuff, see ye Saturday.' Blue Car waved and carried on up the road.

'Yes! Yes! Yes!' Paula exulted. 'And about time too.'

'He's got a real Cork accent, hasn't he?' Beth giggled. ' "Off for a night on the tiles?" '

'He must think we're much older than we are. What will we bring for a bottle?' Jennifer wondered.

'A bottle of wine will do fine,' Paula said.

'I think I'll just say I'm going to Mick's, at home,' Beth decided.

'Good thinking,' Jennifer agreed. 'I'll do the same. Will you tell your aunt or will she mind?'

'Not at all, she thinks the three of them are very nice. They've never caused her any hassle since they came. I know she was a bit worried when she heard the house was going to be let. I don't think Helen will mind at all,' Paula said confidently. 'This is the chance we've been waiting for, girls. I can't wait.'

Thrilled with themselves, the trio swanned down the street all ready to boogie.

Helen watched the three girls through the hall window. They all looked lovely. Paula especially. She loved the bubbly anticipation of their night at the disco. It only seemed like yesterday that Helen had been off out with her friend Breda. All dressed to kill and made up to the nines, on the hunt for a man. She'd been happy then. Happy and carefree. Never in a million years would she have seen herself as a separated wife, alone and lonely.

'Oh stop whingeing,' she chided herself crossly. 'You're not doing too badly.'

She'd come a long way since last year. Then she'd wallowed in her misery, been scared of the future and blamed her husband for everything. Now she had a job. She was secretary to the managing director of a large travel agency and she loved it. She was earning her own money and she'd told Anthony that she was able to keep herself.

He had wanted to keep paying her a monthly sum, but Helen was adamant. She didn't want his money. She could stand on her own two feet. Anthony protested but she'd cut him off and told him to give it to Molly as she was quite content to be a kept woman. It was a bitchy remark, she knew, but it had just burst out of her in spite of her best intentions.

'There's no need for that,' Anthony said furiously. 'It's beneath you.'

'Oh don't annoy me, Anthony. I know why you want to go on giving me money. It's to salve your conscience, and make you feel better,' she'd accused.

'Look, I still feel responsible for you. I want to look after you financially,' Anthony argued.

'Well I don't want you to look after me financially. I don't *need* you to look after me financially. I can do it myself, thank you,' Helen retorted, ignoring his look of displeasure.

Did he think she was going to be the dependent little wife, grateful for his largesse, forever? Huh! snorted Helen as she left him sitting in the Shelbourne, where they'd arranged to meet. She'd gone in to Brown Thomas and treated herself to a bottle of Chanel No. 5, to celebrate her financial independence.

The job had given her back confidence and self-esteem. It was good to have to get up in the morning and go to a job that challenged and excited her. Paula had commented on how much perkier and more zestful she'd become. Helen's face softened into a smile as she thought of her precious niece. Having Paula come to live with her had been the best thing she could have done. She was such good company, they enjoyed living together. It was fun to go into town on Saturday, window-shopping and occasionally having a little spree. They went to the pictures, the theatre, art galleries and museums. They dined out every now and again. Sometimes they drove to the coast in Helen's Ford Capri.

Paula had made her get out of the house and start

living. She had been sympathetic up to a point and then she'd more or less told her aunt to get on with it. Helen admired her niece greatly. She worked very hard at school, because she was ambitious and because she didn't want to give Maura and Pete any excuse to bring her back to Waterford. She didn't abuse Helen's trust by staying out later than she should. In fact she caused Helen no worry at all. For someone so young she was very mature, Helen reflected. It must have been because she grew up with older siblings and was much in the company of adults. Her niece's self-confidence never ceased to amaze her. Paula had an air of real assurance. But then, she always had. The result, no doubt, of all the praise and attention that had been lavished on her as a child.

She was talking of doing some language courses when she finished school. She'd confided to Helen that she was going to look for a part-time job this term, and the money from that, plus her summer earnings, would be put aside for the fees. Paula was an inspiration to her, Helen thought, feeling a bit ashamed of her own self-pity. It would do her good to go and broaden her mind. Maybe she'd join a night class or something. She'd go down to Drumcondra library first thing in the morning, while the sleeping beauties were still oblivious, and see what evening courses were on offer. Paula'd be delighted when she heard. She always encouraged Helen to get out a bit more. Well so she would, she decided happily. And what was more, her boss had offered her a late season holiday at a ridiculously low price. Helen resolved she would phone Maura right this minute and insist she come to Spain with her. It would be a way of saying thank you for allowing Paula to live with her. Maura deserved a holiday more than anyone. They'd have great fun together. It would be lovely to have her sister all to herself for two weeks. Helen was sure that Pete wouldn't object in the slightest. He was very good like that where his wife was concerned. In fact he'd probably be all for it. It wouldn't cost Maura anything expect for her spending money. The thought of going abroad again delighted her. There'd been no skiing holiday this year, no trip to the sun. All the things she'd taken for granted when she'd been with Anthony. What the hell, who needed a husband when she could organize these luxuries herself, she thought proudly. She could arrange for her friend Miriam to come and spend the nights with Paula. Miriam was great fun and very obliging, Paula got on well with her.

No longer down in the dumps, Helen went to phone Maura.

Eilis McNally glowered across the dance floor at Paula Matthews, who was dancing and thoroughly enjoying herself. The girl was surrounded by fellas who were all trying their best to impress her. It was always the same at the disco. La Matthews swanned in and instantly became the centre of attention. It was very galling indeed. Who was she, only a blow-in from some scutty little village in the back of beyonds? And yet, wherever she went, people danced attendance on her. It was the same in class. After only a few weeks, she'd become extremely popular. The teachers thought the sun shone out of her arse. She was always to the forefront at lessons and at sport. She was a blooming good basketball player too. The basketball coach couldn't keep his eyes off her shapely tanned legs. Eilis often caught him ogling Paula, who always looked radiantly healthy, vibrant and athletic in her short navy sports skirt and crisp white T-shirt. You'd think she'd been away in Spain or somewhere with that tan she'd got in the summer. Eilis always felt like a frumpy pasty-skinned dumpling beside Paula. Even tonight her classmate looked like a model in those impossibly tight jeans, she thought enviously. Eilis, though not fat, was a good size fourteen. Never in a million years would she ever look as well as Paula Matthews did in her jeans.

The only thing Miss Matthews was no good at was maths. She hadn't much of a clue and generally only managed a D in her grades. It always gave Eilis enormous satisfaction when the maths teacher read out their grades after their weekly test. Paula's name was called directly after hers. Eilis frequently got a B and sometimes an A grade. The D sounded very poor in comparison. Eilis made a point of smiling at Paula when the marks were read out, hoping that the other girl would feel discomfited. Paula was usually engrossed in whispering to Jennifer Myles and didn't even notice. Her poor maths mark didn't seem to bother her at all, which made Eilis as mad as hell. Paula acted as though she didn't exist. If there was one thing that did not suit Eilis, it was being ignored. Until Paula Matthews arrived, Eilis was the Queen Bee in the class. Her crown had passed to the supremely confident, impossible-to-ignore country miss. Eilis didn't like it one little bit.

'What a pathetic party,' Paula said in disgust as Sandra O'Reilly's boyfriend threw up half-way up the stairs on his way to the loo. 'We should've stayed at the disco!'

'I don't know about you, but I'm ravenous,' Beth moaned. 'There's nothing here only popcorn and crisps. You'd think from the way Sandra went on today, there was going to be a banquet.'

Paula took a sip of her cider. 'We could always split and go back home and have the ham sandwiches Helen left out for us,' she suggested. Sandra's party was heading for disaster. The next-door neighbours had knocked already to complain about the loud music. A crowd of fellas who none of them knew had gatecrashed, two of them were out in the back garden puking and the other three were drinking as much cider as they could lay their hands on. Sandra herself was pissed, conked out on the sofa, and Eilis McNally was giggling away to herself.

'Where's Jenny?' Paula asked.

'I think she's a bit pissed, actually,' Beth confided. 'She's in the kitchen drinking black coffee to try and sober herself up. She doesn't want to make a show of herself in your aunt's house.'

'For God's sake, she only had two cans of cider.' Paula scoffed.

'Yeah, but she's not used to drinking, like you are,' Beth explained.

'You make me sound like a hardened drinker.' Paula grimaced. 'Come on, let's collect Jenny and go.'

'Party-poopers,' Eilis tittered. 'Can't stay the pace.'

'We're going clubbing in Leeson Street actually, Eilis,' Paula drawled. The other girl's jaw dropped open. Much to Paula's satisfaction.

'You just think you're the bee's fuckin' knees, don't you, Miss Paula Matthews?' Eilis snorted. 'Well let me tell you something. You're not. They might be impressed by your airs and graces down in the back of beyonds where you come from. You country bumpkin. Up here, we're not.' Paula was astonished at her classmate's outburst. She knew that Eilis didn't particularly like her. The feeling was mutual. Paula sometimes felt that Eilis was a little jealous of the fun she and Jenny and Beth had. That wasn't Paula's problem. She had as little to do with the other girl as possible and left her to her own devices. Now here she was being venomously abusive for no apparent reason.

'Grow up and get lost, Eilis,' Paula said, disgusted.

'Don't you talk to me like that, ya snobby little wagon.' Eilis staggered to her feet. It was obvious she was well jarred. 'I don't like you, Paula Matthews. You just get up my nose as well as giving me a major pain in the arse! So what do you think about that then?' she challenged aggressively, hands on her hips. Paula gave her a long cold look.

'I'm devastated.' Her tone dripped with sarcasm. She turned her back on her raging classmate and walked out of the room, leaving Eilis almost in tears of frustration.

'That shut her up,' she murmured to Beth as they made their way to the kitchen to collect Jenny.

'She's really pissed, isn't she?' Beth was horrified. 'She shouldn't have spoken to you like that. How ignorant.' Paula laughed at her friend's indignation.

'Listen, Beth, don't worry about the likes of Eilis McNally. I knew a girl like her in St Margaret's Bay called Monica Boyle and she was a prize bitch. I'm well used to handling the likes of that one in there,' she said calmly. Eilis's outburst had been a surprise, but it didn't particularly bother Paula. People either liked her or they didn't, and obviously Eilis didn't like her. Paula didn't intend to lose any sleep over it.

'I think I'm drunk,' Jennifer moaned when they found her. 'I'm slurring my words.'

'Don't be daft, Jen, you couldn't get drunk on two cans of cider. It's only your imagination,' Paula said briskly.

'Oh!' Jennifer sounded vaguely disappointed to hear that she wasn't as inebriated as she thought she was.

'Come on, we're going to split. Let's go home and have some hot chocolate and ham sandwiches.'

'Great idea,' Jennifer enthused.

An hour later, they sat in Helen's kitchen and tucked into a tasty supper. They were in their nightdresses, and looking forward to tumbling into bed and sleeping their brains out.

'Did you see the get-up of McNally? Did you ever see anything like the hot pants?' Beth sniggered. 'Who did she think she looked like? Raquel Welch!'

'Some hope,' chuckled Paula. 'Sandra looked lovely though. She's very pretty.'

'She was pretty pissed too,' Jennifer said. 'I think she was crazy to have a party like that in her house. I bet the neighbours will be doing their nut. I'd say they'll complain when her parents come back from their holidays. Just as well Grandpa Myles didn't live next door, he'd have caused a riot. He's always moaning at Brenda and me for playing the stereo too loud,' she confided.

'I wouldn't like to have to clean up all that puke.' Paula shuddered. 'Imagine the smell in the house tomorrow.'

'Urgg! Paula, stop!' Jennifer made a face.

Paula laughed and yawned. 'I'm looking forward to my lie-in. I hope it's raining in the morning. I love having a lie-in when it's lashing rain.'

'Me too,' Jennifer agreed. 'And we've got the party to look forward to next Saturday.'

'I'd say it will be a great party compared to tonight,' Beth said.

'You can say that again,' Paula declared, eyes sparkling with expectation.

Chapter Thirty

'I don't think so, darling,' Helen said. Paula's heart sank.

'But Helen, it's next door. They're detectives. They won't make a racket or anything. They're much too responsible. We'll only stay for an hour,' she pleaded.

'No, Paula. I'm sorry, love. They've had parties before that have been very noisy. The neighbours complained. People were very drunk at them. I just don't think you and the girls are old enough to go to a party like that,' Helen said firmly.

You should have been at Sandra O'Reilly's party last weekend, Paula thought sulkily. She wasn't used to her aunt refusing her anything. In fact it was the first time in her life that she could remember it ever happening. And she didn't like it.

'But Helen, it's not as if it's miles away or that we're going to be out until all hours. Couldn't we just pop in and make an appearance to be polite and then come back here after an hour or so?' Paula tried a last desperate appeal.

'Paula, please don't ask me again. My mind's made up. Obviously that chap who asked you doesn't realize how young you are. That's not surprising, you all look much older than sixteen. But I'm responsible for you while you're living here in Dublin, and you know as well as I do, love, that your mam and dad wouldn't allow you to go either. Be fair now.'

'It would have only been for an hour.' Paula pouted.

'No, Paula, I'm sorry. Now that's the end of it. Invite the girls over by all means but the party is out, I'm afraid. Besides, I'm sure Mrs Myles and Mrs Cleary wouldn't let Jenny and Beth go.'

Paula knew her aunt was right there. Mr and Mrs Myles were quite strict, as was Mrs Cleary, but still Paula knew that Beth wouldn't be allowed to go to that party if she asked. The plan had been to say that they were going to a disco as usual.

Paula had never even considered that Helen would not allow her to go. It was a tremendous shock.

'We'd want to hurry on if we're going to get to a matinée,' Helen said cheerfully, beginning to clear away the dinner plates. 'I love going to the pictures on a wet Sunday afternoon.'

'I don't feel like going. I'm going to my room,' Paula said huffily.

'Suit yourself.' Helen's tone was very cool.

Paula stalked out of the kitchen. She felt humiliated and angry. She wasn't a *child*, for heaven's sake. But Helen had just treated her like one. What on earth was she going to tell the girls? It was going to be very embarrassing indeed, especially when she'd so confidently told them that Helen wouldn't mind them going to the party at all. If Helen thought she was going to go to the pictures after that rebuff, she had another think coming. She would be as frosty as anything with her aunt until she changed her mind, Paula thought angrily as she flung herself down on her bed and picked up the Mary Stewart novel she was reading. The sound of press doors being slammed and crockery being handled none too gently as the washing-up was done told Paula that her aunt was equally annoyed.

Let her be, she thought furiously, jumping off the bed to close her bedroom door. If Helen was mad, well, she certainly wasn't as mad as her niece.

'The trouble with that girl is she gets away with too much,' Helen muttered as she cleared the table and flung the knives and forks into the wash basin.

'The first time I ever refused to let her do anything and

282

look at the carry-on.' She felt wretched. There had never been bad feeling between them before. She would have liked to let Paula go to the party. She wasn't very strict with her, but this time she had to put her foot down. Helen knew that Maura and Pete would not approve. They had been so good to allow Paula to come and live with her in Dublin. They trusted her to bring up their daughter responsibly. She couldn't allow her to go to a party where there would be plenty of drink. It just wasn't on. That would be to fail in her duty to Maura and Pete. Helen could not do that. No matter how annoyed Paula was.

Helen sighed. She felt very down in the dumps. She could have done without having a tiff with Paula today of all days. She'd been trying her best to stay upbeat, to pretend that today was just another day, and she'd almost succeeded. An afternoon at the pictures would have helped to keep her mind occupied for another couple of hours. She'd planned to take Paula for a meal as a treat afterwards. Now it looked as if that plan was scrapped, she thought dejectedly. Whether she liked it or not she was on her own this afternoon. On her own with the thoughts she'd been trying to avoid this past week. In another life, in happier times, Helen had always greatly looked forward to her wedding anniversary. Anthony always brought her out for a champagne dinner and made a big fuss of her. Once, he'd given her the surprise of her life and whisked her off to Paris for the weekend. That had been a really happy time. Helen smiled at the memory and sat down at the kitchen table and poured herself another cup of coffee. There had been many happy times, especially at the beginning. It hadn't all been bad. Now that she'd got over that first intense hurt, Helen realized that, unpalatable as it was, she had to take some responsibility for the break-up of their marriage. Those horrible words when her husband had accused her of nagging him and emasculating him had struck deep. Over and over she'd remembered how he'd said it was an ordeal to make love to her. God, that had killed her. No wonder he'd become impotent with her. She had been so selfish in her desire to have a child. She'd pressurized Anthony until, without her being aware of it, she'd destroyed her marriage and sent him into the arms of another woman. She didn't condone it, but now, much as it still distressed her, Helen could understand how her husband had turned to Molly for comfort.

Anthony and she had little contact now but at least when they did meet they were civil towards each other. The last time they'd met was at the funeral of a mutual friend. They'd gone for a drink after the funeral. Their grief had united them and they'd shared memories and talked of old times. Swallowing her pride, Helen had apologized for treating Anthony the way she had during their marriage.

'I didn't realize what I was doing to you . . . to us,' she said huskily. 'I'm as much to blame as you are.' It had been hard to say that, but once she'd said it, she'd felt much less angry, less self-pitying. She could see that her husband was much happier and more relaxed than when they'd been together. Life with Molly obviously suited him. He'd never come back to her.

Sometimes anyway, she knew she wouldn't want him back. Helen enjoyed single living. Doing what she liked when she liked. It was nice not having to cook if she didn't feel in the humour. It was wonderful to have a lie-in on a wet Saturday, with magazines spread all over the bed. She loved her job too. Going back to work had been the making of her. She had to make decisions. Pay her own bills. All this helped to give her back the confidence that had been so badly dented by Anthony's affair. There were times, now, when she felt quite resigned to her lot, and could even look to the future with equanimity. But today wasn't one of them. Today she felt she had failed Anthony and failed herself. Would she ever have another relationship? Would that be a disaster too? It would be nice to love someone and have them love her. She felt very much alone.

*   *   *

'Sorry, girls, the party's off,' Paula told her friends the following day at school. 'Helen's doing her responsible aunt bit. What a drag!'

'You can't really blame her,' Jenny said. 'If my parents thought I was going to a party like that, they'd freak.'

'Oh for heaven's sake, Jenny, we're not children!' Paula scoffed. 'It's not an orgy we were going to.'

'I know that, Paula!' Jenny retorted. 'But all the same.'

'Do you think you could persuade her to change her mind?' Beth queried.

'No,' Paula said glumly. 'But when she goes on holidays with Mam in a few weeks' time, I just might have a party myself and invite them.'

'You wouldn't dare.' Beth was deeply impressed.

'I would, too,' Paula declared defiantly.

'What about the woman who's going to be staying with you at night?' Jenny asked.

'Oh I don't know.' Paula's defiance wilted. 'Imagine having a baby-sitter at my age. It's humiliating.'

'You wouldn't stay on your own in a house at night, would you?' Beth demanded.

'Of course I would,' Paula exclaimed. 'That wouldn't bother me at all. Would you not?'

'You're dead right I wouldn't.' Beth shuddered.

'Beth, I despair of you,' Paula said loftily. 'Have you no sense of adventure?'

'None whatsoever!' Her friend giggled.

'Are you coming to the disco then?' Jenny asked.

Paula shook her head. 'Naw. I'll just have a night in for a change.'

'You mean you're just going to sulk in your room and make your aunt feel bad,' Jenny said tartly.

'So what!' Paula growled. Jenny could be very astute sometimes. The bell went just then and the conversation was forgotten.

Paula lay in bed listening to the sound of the Dubliners singing *The Rocky Road to Dublin*. The party next door was in full swing and she was feeling totally fed up. She would have given anything, *anything,* to be in there flirting and dancing. So near and yet so far, it was unbelievable. She and the girls had spent so much time admiring Green Car and tonight could have been the night when she got to know him. She could have been dancing with him at this very moment if Helen hadn't been such a spoilsport. Paula had tried once more to persuade Helen to relent this morning, but she was adamant. Paula gave her the cold treatment all day and spent most of it in her room. She'd gone to bed at nine. It was now one am.

There seemed to be a huge crowd next door. People had been arriving since the pubs closed and the sound of car doors banging was constant. The windows were open and the noise of the party vibrated through the normally peaceful close. Helen had been right about the noise. It was loud, and getting louder by the minute.

By five am that morning, Paula ruefully admitted that her aunt had known exactly what she was talking about. There were ructions going on next door. There had been two rows already. Neighbours knocked on the door and demanded that the music be turned down. A squad car arrived at one stage, but it didn't stay long. There was a lot of laughter and cheers from the revellers when the guards knocked on the door and were welcomed to the party.

Paula lay in bed feeling a bit of a heel. She hadn't been very nice to Helen. In fact she'd behaved childishly. As the Wolfe Tones belted out *The One Road* Paula slid out of bed and walked out to the landing. In the darkness she could see a glimmer of light under Helen's door.

She knocked softly and entered. Helen was reading.

'I'm sorry, Helen.' Paula was contrite.

'That's OK, Paula, I know you were disappointed, but you can see now why I wouldn't let you go,' Helen said wryly.

'I acted really childishly, sorry about that.' Paula was abashed.

'Ah forget it,' Helen grinned. 'Isn't it some carry-on

though? The neighbours are crazy to bother ringing the police. They're not going to do anything because half of them in there are policemen or detectives. I'm afraid grinning and bearing it is the only solution. It shouldn't go on for much longer. It will be daybreak in another hour or so.'

'I bet the house will be in some state,' Paula commented as someone started singing *It's a Long Way to Tipperary* and the rest of them joined in with gusto.

'Poor Nick,' Helen frowned. 'I hope they straighten the place up before he comes home.'

'What's this Nick like then?' Paula yawned and hopped into bed beside her aunt.

'He's a nice man,' Helen said. 'He's a structural engineer, he owns his own company. He oversees projects abroad sometimes. That's why he's in Africa. His marriage broke up too. That was one of the reasons he went away the last time.'

'What happened?' Paula asked.

Helen sighed. 'He found his wife in bed with his best friend. It was dreadful. He was terribly cut up and bitter about it. I never felt so sorry for anybody in my life. At least Molly Kelly wasn't my best friend. It's bad enough finding out your husband or wife is having an affair. But imagine finding out the affair was with your best friend? Imagine catching them in the act? How horrible!'

'Does he know about you and Anthony?'

Helen shook her head. 'I wouldn't imagine so. He'll get a bit of a surprise when he comes home.'

'You can say that again.' Paula grimaced as the unmistakable sound of breaking glass came from next door. A man cursed vehemently and loudly.

I think I'll skip the party when Helen's away, Paula thought drowsily a half an hour later as the last car door banged and shouted goodbyes were said. A horn beeped loudly before blessed silence descended on the road.

* * *

287

It was amazing how quiet the house was without Helen, Paula reflected as she dusted and polished one Saturday several weeks later. Her aunt and her mother had phoned that morning from Marbella, giggling and laughing like schoolgirls. They were having a ball abroad. Paula was delighted for them. Especially for her mother. Maura really deserved the break.

Since she left home Paula had begun to realize that her mother had a hard enough life. Constantly in the kitchen, cooking meals for her brood. She washed and ironed and managed to look after them all on a not very substantial budget. And she was rarely in a bad humour. Paula smiled as she thought of her mother's laughter on the phone when Paula warned her not to go having any affair with one of those hunky Spanish waiters. Maura had come up to Helen's for a few days before the holiday proper. Paula made a great fuss of her. She brought her breakfast in bed. Took her into town. Went for walks down to the Botanic Gardens. Maura enjoyed every minute of it and Paula had been glad to have the time with her mother and make her feel very special. Sometimes she felt she'd been a little bit selfish taking off out of St Margaret's Bay the way she had. Her eagerness to leave must have been a bit hurtful to her parents, although they'd never said anything. When she'd finished tidying up, she'd write a nice long letter to her dad, she decided. He was so proud of how well she was doing at school. He'd been very chuffed by her Inter Cert results. He always made a fuss of her when she went home. Her dad was the best in the world, Paula thought fondly as the phone rang.

It was Miriam, Helen's friend, to say she'd be in a bit late tonight, and not to worry. Paula assured her that it was fine. Jenny and Beth were coming over to stay for the rest of the weekend so she wouldn't be on her own. Miriam was a very nice woman and great fun, but Paula quite enjoyed the few hours on her own and would have been perfectly happy to spend the entire fortnight by herself. She was cooking dinner for the girls tonight and as a special treat she'd bought a bottle of wine. They weren't going to go to a disco. They were going to have a nice meal and flop in front of the fire and watch TV. It was going to be A Girls' Night In sort of a night. She'd want to get her skates on though, Paula decided, catching sight of the time. She still had a lot to do and she wanted to make a cheesecake for dessert.

An hour and a half later she was like a demented lunatic in the kitchen. 'Why, when you want something to turn out right, does it always turn out a disaster? And when you don't give a damn, you toss something up in five minutes and it's bloody perfect?' she muttered as she gazed in dismay at the cheese sauce, which had gone terribly lumpy. A brainwave struck. She'd let it cool a little and blend it, and it would be fine. The cauliflower florets were all ready to be lightly steamed. Roast stuffed pork steaks were giving off the most mouth-watering odours from the oven. The roast potatoes were crisping nicely. As soon as she'd blended the cheese sauce she'd run upstairs and change her sweatshirt and brush her hair. She washed up the dirty crockery and set three trays. The plan was to eat in front of the fire.

The sauce had cooled sufficiently so she poured it into the blender and stuck the plug into the socket. The blender roared unexpectedly to life and she, the wallpaper and the ceiling were splattered liberally in creamy, lumpy, yellow sauce. Frantically, Paula pulled out the plug and the noisy whirring stopped. She must have touched the on/off switch when she was bringing the blender over to the socket and not realized. 'You idiot! You great bloody pillock,' she cursed herself. There was cheese sauce everywhere. In her hair, on her face, on her top. Horrified, she clambered up on a chair and on to the counter top and started to wipe the ceiling with a damp dishcloth. Would it stain? she fretted. Or would the marks go away when it was dry? She needed this like a hole in the head. She didn't want the girls to come and see this chaos. Or Helen to come home to find the ceiling destroyed. A glance at the kitchen clock told her she had half an hour to go before Beth and Jenny were due to arrive.

The doorbell rang. 'Oh shit,' she muttered, wiping herself off with the dishcloth. 'Oh piss off and go away,' she fumed as it ding-donged again. A third ring told her the caller was going nowhere. It was too early for the girls. Definitely. Beth Cleary couldn't be on time to save her life, let alone half an hour early. Jenny was always giving out stink about being kept waiting when they were going anywhere. But if it wasn't the girls, who was it? Miriam had a key, and Paula wasn't expecting anyone to call.

Crossly she flung open the front door and saw a man standing on the steps. He looked somewhat taken aback to see her. 'Hello,' he said politely. 'Is Anthony in, please?'

'No, sorry.' Paula shook her head.

'Oh! Do you know when he'll be back?'

'I've no idea.'

'Would Helen be there, then?' he asked courteously.

'Sorry, no,' Paula said curtly.

'And you must be one of the nieces?' the man remarked.

What's it to you? she wanted to retort rudely. 'Yes, that's right.' Her tone was unfriendly. The man looked at her curiously.

'Look, I'm sorry to disturb you. My name is Nick Russell, I'm Anthony and Helen's next-door neighbour. I've been away and I just came in to apologize. I believe the lads gave a very noisy party recently. It won't happen again.'

'Right, I'll tell Helen, thanks,' Paula said agitatedly, aware that time was running out. She had to clean up the mess in the kitchen, as well as herself. Chit-chatting with a neighbour was not on her agenda right now.

'Fine, just tell your aunt and uncle I called, I'll see them around,' the man said casually. Before he had even taken two steps down the garden path, Paula had closed the door and was racing back into the kitchen, Nick Russell and his apologies the last thing on her mind.

Chapter Thirty-One

'You should have seen the state of me, Helen. I looked like the Wreck of the Hesperus standing there with cheese sauce all over me.' Paula giggled as she and her aunt drove home from the station after putting a tanned and glowing Maura on the Waterford train.

'Poor Nick.' Helen laughed. 'Have you seen him since?'

'No,' Paula answered. 'I don't think he's staying there at the moment. He seems to have decorators in. He got new windows and doors put in last week.'

'I saw that,' Helen remarked. 'The house looks very well. It had got a bit run-down.'

'Hmm,' murmured Paula, who had more on her mind than Nick Russell and the state of his house. Yesterday, during basketball practice, Barry Keating, the school's part-time games coach and PE instructor had massaged her calf when she'd got a bad cramp. Their eyes met. It was the most wonderful feeling. It was as if there was no-one else in the school yard. Paula knew Barry liked her. They always had good fun in a teasing sort of way. He was a very popular member of staff and he got on well with all the girls. He encouraged them, pushed them, and motivated them to win their matches. Lots of the girls fancied Barry and were always trying to show off in front of him.

Paula played it cool. She treated him in an offhand sort of way and concentrated on perfecting her game. Barry went out of his way to pass a few comments to her, usually inconsequential remarks about the match or the training or whatever. It made Paula feel good when she was discreetly singled out for that special bit of attention. But it was no more than she expected.

When the match was finished, Barry went over to her, ostensibly to find out how her leg was. But after asking her if she was OK, he very quietly asked if she'd like to go for a drink with him.

'That would be nice,' she murmured back.

'How about Saturday?'

'That doesn't suit me,' Paula said. 'Sunday's better.'

'Sure, where would you like to go?'

'Somewhere in town might be the best.'

'Upstairs in the Oval is nice and private.' Barry smiled. 'We don't want to run into any of this gang.'

'Eight then,' Paula said before striding off into the changing rooms.

You handled that very well, she thought approvingly as she stood under the powerful jets of water, letting the heat and steam soothe her aching muscles. It had been a good move to say Saturday didn't suit. She certainly didn't want to give him the impression that she was over-eager. That was always fatal. Anyway Saturday didn't suit her. That was the day her mother and Helen were due back from their holidays. She couldn't take off on a date and leave Helen on her own, on her first night home.

'I've some news for you.' Paula grinned at Helen as they drove into the driveway.

'Let me guess, you're taking lessons in Cordon Bleu,' Helen joked.

'Rotter,' retorted Paula. 'It isn't quite as exotic as that. I've got a date tomorrow night.'

'Tell me all!' her aunt exclaimed as they let themselves into the house.

'He's my PE and games teacher, he's good-looking, very athletic, and great gas.' Paula summed up her date succinctly.

'What age is he?' Helen couldn't disguise her surprise.

'About twenty-two. He's not a full-time teacher. Miss Doherty is our full-time teacher. Barry works part-time with different schools,' Paula explained. 'You'll like him, Helen, honest. If we start dating or anything I'll bring him home to meet you.'

'Don't you think he's a little bit old for you?' Helen arched an eyebrow.

'He's only six years older,' Paula said lightly, hoping against hope that her aunt wasn't going to make a song and dance about her date with Barry.

'Wouldn't you be better off going with a boy nearer your own age?' Helen asked.

'Oh Helen, all the ones I've met are nice, but they're so *boring*!' Paula couldn't hide the exasperation in her tone.

Helen laughed. 'Paula Matthews, I've never met anyone like you! Boring indeed. Just be careful then. Don't neglect your studies or that will be the end of it,' Helen cautioned. 'Where are you going with this Barry?'

'Just for a drink first and then probably the pictures.'

'No more than a glass of wine for you, Miss, and I want you to be home by midnight at the latest. OK? You've to be up for school the next morning,' Helen warned.

'No problem, Helen . . . and thanks.' Paula gave her aunt a hug, which was warmly returned.

The following evening, Paula sat in a snug little corner of the Oval, sipping a glass of white wine as she waited for Barry to arrive. He was late, she noted disapprovingly. If he asked her out again he could collect her. Now that Helen had given the OK, there was no reason for him not to call to the house. 'I wouldn't dare sit in a pub on my own. Be a bit late so you won't have to,' Jenny had warned when Paula told her about the date. Jenny and Beth had been agog when Paula informed them who her date was to be.

'I don't want it to get around though,' Paula warned. 'Barry thinks it might not go down too well with the nuns. You know, him being a teacher and everything.'

The girls assured her that no-one would hear it from their lips. Paula knew that they were deeply impressed that Barry had asked her out. They were also impressed that she was meeting him in a pub. It surprised her that two city girls like Beth and Jenny should be so naive. When Paula came to Dublin first, she'd expected that most of the girls in her class would be sophisticated city slickers. This wasn't the case at all. It was no problem for Paula to wait on her own in a pub, but she knew that plenty of the girls at school wouldn't be seen dead alone in a pub. In many ways she felt much more grown-up than her classmates. But then she'd always felt much older than she was, even as a child.

'Hi Paula, sorry I'm late,' Barry apologized. 'I was trying to get parking, sorry about that.'

'That's OK,' Paula said lightly. A first mistake could be forgiven. He looked very well in his grey cords, red and grey jumper and black leather jacket. He smelt of aftershave. She was impressed. She had always seen him in a track suit and trainers.

'What would Barty say if she could see us now?' Barry laughed. Paula joined in. One of the things she liked about Barry was his sense of humour. He ordered a pint and another glass of wine for her and they sat chatting away, enjoying each other's company. They were so engrossed in their conversation they didn't notice the time. It was too late to go to the pictures so Barry suggested they go for a meal. He took her to a small intimate restaurant off Dame Street. Paula thoroughly enjoyed herself.

'I've got to be home by twelve,' she said regretfully as they lingered over coffee.

'Pity,' Barry said, taking her hand. 'There's a full moon out. I was going to take you up to Howth so we could watch it shining over Dublin Bay.'

'Beneath that tough athletic exterior lurks a romantic heart,' Paula teased. A trip to moonlit Howth sounded very enticing. But she'd promised to be in by twelve and she didn't want to blot her copybook with Helen on her first date with Barry.

· 'Howth sounds lovely,' she murmured, running her

thumb along his forefinger. 'But tonight I'm Cinderella.'

'Maybe next weekend?' Barry inquired.

'Why not?' smiled Paula, happy that there was going to be another date.

She didn't ask him in when they got home at five to midnight. Paula had to be up for school the following morning and she was sure her aunt would be less than pleased to know that she was downstairs having coffee with her PE teacher.

'See you at school on Wednesday then,' Barry said as they sat in the car. 'But we'll be just casual about things, no point in stirring up gossip.' He leaned over and kissed her very lightly on the lips. Paula kissed him back, and was sorry that they didn't have more time. She wouldn't have minded a good snog. She found Barry extremely attractive. She was fairly certain that Barry Keating was no novice when it came to lovemaking.

'Did you have a nice time?' Helen called out as Paula walked quietly past her aunt's bedroom.

'I'd a lovely time, Helen.' Paula went into Helen's bedroom. 'He's asked me out next weekend as well.'

'I've a proposition to put to you.' Helen's eyes twinkled.

'I'm all ears.' Paula sat down on the side of the bed.

'I saw Nick going into his house so I asked him in for a cup of coffee.' Helen laughed. Paula thought the holiday had done her so much good. She was lovely and tanned and healthy-looking. She seemed much more on top of things.

'Did you tell him about you and Anthony?' Paula asked gently.

'Yes I did, love. He was very shocked and most sympathetic. He knows what it's like. He's been through it too.'

'What's this proposition then?' Paula yawned.

'You were saying you were thinking of getting a part-time job. Well I know of a job that wouldn't be very hard, and would pay good money. A job which you are more than capable of doing—'

'What is it, Helen? I'm dying to know!' Paula exclaimed. Helen laughed at her niece's impatience.

'Calm down, it's nothing dramatic but it will suit you down to the ground with your hotel experience and everything. Nick asked me if I knew of anyone around who'd be interested in a part-time cleaning and house-keeping job. All he wants is someone to keep the house hoovered and dusted, and to shop for groceries and so on. I suggested you,' Helen announced.

Paula was nonplussed. 'But I was kind of rude to him.' She grimaced. 'He surely wouldn't want me to work for him.'

'When I told Nick about you working in the hotel for the summer, he said if you can keep a hotel clean, his house will be no trouble to you. I think he'd be glad of someone who's not a complete stranger. You never know who you can trust these days,' Helen remarked. 'Anyway it's up to you. If you're interested you've to call in to him tomorrow evening. He's going to be there until seven. If you don't want it just let him know.'

'How much is he going to pay?' Paula queried. Her aunt mentioned a sum that made her eyes widen. Five pounds a week for part-time work was a *fortune*. This guy must be loaded! It would be ideal really. She wouldn't have to travel anywhere, so she'd save on bus fares and hassle. And one man on his own could hardly make much of a mess. If she could clean fifteen hotel bedrooms, she could certainly handle one house.

'Sounds good to me,' she informed her aunt as she gave her a goodnight kiss.

'That's what I hoped you'd say, Paula. I think it's ideal for you and it won't interfere too much with your studies. Now hop it to bed, or neither of us will be able to get up in the morning.'

'It's great to have you home. 'Night,' Paula said fondly.

' 'Night, love.' Helen snuggled down in her bed and switched off the lamp.

It had been an eventful day, Paula decided as she

undressed and got into bed. A date, and an offer of a job. Life could only get better, she decided with satisfaction. She was asleep in minutes.

At five-thirty the following day Paula stood on her next-door neighbour's doorstep. She wasn't quite sure what to expect. He might be very cool – after all, she'd been a bit tetchy with him, to say the least. She shivered in the cold breeze and rang the doorbell again. She heard the sound of someone running down the stairs, then the door opened and Nick Russell stood there looking harassed.

'Ah, Paula, come in. I'm on a call to Kenya. Can you excuse me a minute? Go into the sitting-room, I'll be down shortly,' he said and ran upstairs again. There was the smell of fresh paint everywhere. A decorator's trestle-table lay alongside a half-papered wall in the hall. If the house was being redecorated, then it would be clean from the start, Paula reflected. To think she was standing in Green Car's old abode. She missed the detectives and wondered where they'd moved to.

'Sorry about that, Paula.' Nick reappeared. 'It's nice to meet you again, thank you for calling.' He shook hands with her, a good firm shake that she liked. If there was one thing that Paula found to be a complete and utter turn-off, it was a limp handshake. There was nothing limp about Nick Russell's handshake. Paula studied the man in front of her. He was in his late thirties, or early forties, she guessed. He was of medium height, lean and fit-looking with a deep tan. His eyes were an unusual very dark blue, almost indigo. He had a piercing stare. Deep laughter lines around his eyes suggested good humour. Although they could have been caused by squinting in the sun. He had a straight nicely shaped nose, a firm mouth, strong jawline and a chin with an attractive dimple. He had thick fair hair that was bleached from being in the sun although she could see some grey at his temples. He wore a well-cut navy business suit and a crisp white shirt. Not bad for a middle-aged man, reckoned Paula approvingly. His wife's lover must have been a

297

real dish if she had left Nick for him, she thought.

'So, Paula. Helen tells me you've worked summers as a chambermaid in a hotel and that keeping a house relatively spick and span would pose no difficulties to you?' he said briskly.

'No problem at all,' Paula said confidently.

'And you'd shop for me and send out laundry and let me have one untidy room, i.e. my office?' He smiled. And she liked him. He had a faint west of Ireland accent that was most attractive.

'Certainly,' she agreed, smiling.

'I won't ask you to make cheese sauce,' Nick teased and Paula's mouth dropped open. What a blabbermouth Helen was, she thought, mortified.

'It will cost you more if you do,' she said coolly and Nick laughed.

'I'll bear that in mind. So do we have a deal?'

'Sure,' she agreed. 'When do you want me to start?'

Nick rubbed his jaw reflectively. 'I'm hoping the workmen will be finished by the weekend. I'm staying in the Skylon at the moment. Let's say this day week. How about if you come in Monday and Friday? I'll leave out a list of shopping on Friday for you. I hate shopping.'

'I'll do that for you, Mr Russell,' Paula said politely.

'Good Lord,' he exclaimed in horror. 'For heaven's sake don't call me mister or I'll sack you. It makes me feel ancient.'

'OK, Nick, see you Monday week.' Paula laughed.

'I'll get a key cut and drop it in. Tell Helen thanks for her help. It's a great relief to have got myself organized.' He grinned boyishly and Paula realized that he wasn't old at all. When he smiled like that he looked much younger.

At least he wasn't some crusty old codger. And he seemed good-humoured enough. It could be a very pleasant way of earning money. Roll on Monday week, Paula reflected. But roll on Wednesday first, Paula was looking forward to seeing Barry again.

Chapter Thirty-Two

'I wish you didn't have to go home for Christmas. It was the same last year,' Barry murmured into Paula's hair as he brushed it aside to kiss her neck and earlobe. They were sitting in his car in the lay-by at Griffith Park. Barry was giving her a lift home from a basketball match she'd just played against Eccles Street. They'd lost. It was dark and wet. Paula knew she had to get home to give Nick's house a hoover and polish.

'I'd better get home, Barry,' she said regretfully.

'Couldn't you even come back for New Year's Eve? We're going to have a party. It's going to be great.'

'Look, Barry, I've told you,' Paula said crossly. 'I've got to go home for Christmas whether I like it or not. Helen's coming as well and I can't go rushing back to Dublin. My parents would be hurt.'

'All right then,' he growled. 'I was just asking. That's what I get for going with a schoolgirl, I suppose,' he added sarcastically.

'Well then, the simple answer to that is stop going with a schoolgirl. Isn't it?' Paula snapped. 'I'll walk the rest of the way from here.'

'Oh give over, it's lashing rain,' Barry retorted, starting up the engine. They drove to Paula's house in icy silence. When they got there, he got out, opened the car boot and handed her her sports bag and coat. She turned to go.

'Wait a minute! What about Saturday night?' he asked.

'What about it?' Paula drawled. 'I'm only a school-girl. What are you asking me for? Go and ask someone *grown-up*.'

'Suit yourself,' Barry declared and got into his car, slammed the door and revved the engine. The car sped off down the road.

'I will, don't worry,' Paula responded sharply. Oh sod this for a lark, she scowled, retracing her footsteps down Helen's garden path. She wasn't going to bother changing out of her games gear. She'd just go straight in to Nick's as she was. The job had worked out very well, she reflected as she let herself into the empty house. She got on fine with her employer. He was a fairly tidy man and it wasn't hard to keep his house clean and neat, and do his shopping. Nick had told her several times that he was very pleased with the way she kept his house. He was a generous man and bought her a bottle of perfume or handmade chocolates on his occasional business trips abroad.

She had just changed Nick's bed and was polishing his bedside unit when she heard him racing up the stairs. She glanced at her watch. It had just gone six. Nick was never home before seven on a Monday evening. She always had the hoovering and polishing finished before he came home.

'Hi Paula,' he greeted her briskly. 'You couldn't do me a huge favour, could you?' he asked, shrugging out of his jacket, loosening his tie, and unbuttoning his shirt.

'Sure. What's up?' It was obvious he was in a rush. She couldn't help noticing how tanned he was against the whiteness of his open shirt. He'd a nice hairy chest too, she thought approvingly.

'I've got to go to London unexpectedly and I've managed to get a seat on an eight o'clock flight. Do you think you could make me a cheese sandwich or something, with a cup of coffee? I didn't have time for lunch today and I'm starving. And would you ring a taxi for me for seven?'

'Nick, you'll give yourself ulcers,' Paula scolded.

'And you'll get a cold in your kidneys in that get-up,' Nick declared in amusement.

'I came straight from basketball,' she explained, catching sight of herself in the mirror. Her little navy skirt

300

just barely covered the tops of her thighs, leaving a bare expanse of leg.

'It looks much better than an apron,' he teased. He was shirtless now and his deep blue eyes were smiling at her. She smiled back. It suddenly dawned on Paula that Nick Russell was a bit of all right. She'd been working for him for over a year now, but she hadn't really taken much notice of him, *that* way. She'd been too taken up with Barry. And now here he was, with those blue, blue eyes smiling at her. He'd a rather sexy bod too, from what she could see. It was vaguely unsettling. She'd never thought of Nick like that.

'I'll go and make you something to eat,' she said firmly.

'Thanks, Paula. You're a gem,' Nick said gratefully as he strode into the bathroom.

So are you, she thought glumly to herself as she hurried downstairs to the kitchen. What on earth was wrong with her? It was Barry she fancied and Barry who turned her on. Why on earth was she suddenly finding her employer quite fanciable? Up until now, she'd just been interested in the five pound note Nick gave her every Friday, not in him. Was it because she'd had a row with Barry? That was most probably it, Paula decided as she grilled some bacon and scrambled some eggs. Forget about Nick Russell, you daft pillock, she told herself sternly. He was about twenty years older than she was. Old enough to be her father. A crush on Nick was something she needed like a hole in the head. 'Cop on to yourself, Matthews,' she muttered as she made toast for the scrambled eggs.

Upstairs, she could hear the shower running. He was always rushing about. Nick was consumed by his business. Although he'd told Helen that he'd come back to live in Dublin because he was 'cutting down.' That must be why his marriage failed, Paula suggested. But Helen said that he'd only started to work like that when his wife had left him, to blot out the misery he'd felt at finding her in bed with his best friend. Helen seemed to think he'd been a pretty good husband. From what Paula had seen of him, Nick was a considerate, kind person. She often felt sorry for him, coming in from work with no-one to share the good and bad points of his day.

Helen sometimes asked him in to share their evening meal. He always said how nice it was to taste home cooking as he usually ate in hotels or restaurants. Helen and he got on very well. But then of course, they had a lot in common.

'That smells good.' Nick appeared at the kitchen door. She caught a whiff of his aftershave. His hair was still damp. She had a mad urge to dry it for him. Stop it! she thought furiously. This was crazy.

'A sandwich would have done fine. I didn't mean you to go to so much trouble.' He lifted a rasher off the grill and scoffed it.

'Sit down and eat it properly,' Paula instructed shortly. 'You shouldn't eat standing up.'

Nick eyed her quizzically. 'You're not in very good humour today,' he remarked as she put his meal on the table in front of him. 'Is there a reason?'

Paula sighed. 'Sorry,' she apologized. 'I didn't mean to be rude.'

'Why don't you sit down and have a cup of coffee with me and tell me what's wrong,' he suggested as he devoured his meal. 'You didn't have a row with Helen or anything, did you?'

'No, not with Helen. I had one with my boyfriend.' Paula sighed again as she poured herself a cup of coffee.

'What's wrong with him? Or am I being nosy?' Nick's blue eyes stared into hers.

'He wants me to stay in Dublin for Christmas,' Paula said irritably. 'And he knows I can't. Then he had the nerve to say that's what he got for going with a schoolgirl,' she exclaimed indignantly. She didn't see the glint of amusement in Nick's eyes, or notice the brief upward curve of his mouth in a smile he hastily banished.

'I suppose he's just going to miss you, that's all,' he said soothingly.

302

'Huh!' snorted Paula.

'And what did you say to him?' Nick struggled to keep his amusement under control.

'I told him to go and find himself a grown-up girlfriend,' Paula declared.

'How much older is he?' Nick took a gulp of his coffee.

'He's only six years older, for God's sake. Who does he think he is? Methuselah?'

'I suppose six years makes more of a difference because he's working and you're not,' Nick murmured diplomatically.

That's rich, thought Paula in wry amusement. Considering I've just discovered that I fancy *you* all of a sudden. Imagine Nick's reaction if she told him *that*. What was his type of woman? Paula hadn't a clue. Since she'd come to work for him, he'd never brought a woman home as far as she knew. But then, she hadn't been interested enough to care. He could very well have and she just hadn't seen any signs of it. Perhaps he was going to London to see a woman. The thought depressed her.

'Are you doing anything for Christmas?' she asked, changing the subject.

'I don't really like Christmas any more. My marriage broke up at Christmas, I try and ignore it these days,' Nick said quietly.

'I'm very sorry, Nick, I didn't mean to pry or anything,' Paula said hastily.

'Of course you didn't, Paula,' he said briskly. 'It was a simple straightforward question. I'll miss you and Helen. It must be hard on her as well?'

'Yeah,' Paula agreed. 'It's times like this that bring back memories.'

'Well she's lucky she's got you. And I'm lucky I've got you.' Nick smiled. 'Can I really take advantage, and leave the washing-up?'

'Course you can. Go and do your packing. When will you be back?'

'Thursday, I hope.' Nick got up from the table and carried his dishes over to the sink.

'Leave them, go on,' Paula ordered. She could see by the clock on the cooker that he hadn't much time left.

'Right, thanks.' Nick headed back upstairs to pack. By the time she had the kitchen cleaned up the taxi had arrived.

'Paula, I'm off. Listen, give yourself a treat.' Nick came into the kitchen and pressed a five pound note into her hand. 'Thanks for the grub, it was a lifesaver.'

'I can't take that, Nick. It was no trouble at all,' she protested, trying to give it back to him. His hand curled around hers and he folded her fingers around the note.

'Please, Paula,' he insisted. She couldn't refuse his generosity.

'See you next Friday, then.'

'Bye, Nick. Mind yourself, and thanks.' Paula followed him out to the hall and stood at the door waving until the taxi was out of sight. She walked slowly upstairs to finish the polishing.

'Now, Paula Matthews, I'm having none of your non-sense. Get this house tidied up, go home and stop acting the maggot,' she ordered herself. She threw her eyes up to heaven when she caught sight of herself in the mirror, talking to herself.

Helen had kept Paula's dinner hot for her. 'You're late,' she remarked. Paula explained the reason.

'Poor Nick, he's always on the go. So much for cutting back,' Helen reflected. 'But then, he hasn't much to come home to, has he? Oh, by the way, Barry phoned for you. He asked me to ask you to phone him tonight.'

'OK, thanks,' Paula said, pretending a cheerfulness she did not feel.

'I'm off to have a drink with some of the crowd from work. It's the birthday of one of the reps,' Helen announced. Paula smiled. Helen had become much more outgoing in the last year.

'Don't come in tanked,' Paula teased. 'Have fun.'

'I will.' Her aunt laughed. Paula looked at her admiringly. She was wearing an elegant beige trouser-suit and a black polo-neck jumper. Her make-up was flawless. Her hair, styled in a well-cut bob, gleamed healthily. Although she was in her thirties, she looked ten years younger.

When she'd gone, Paula took her coffee into the sitting-room and plonked herself down by the fire. She would have left Barry to stew but she was unsettled by the episode at Nick's house. She wanted to talk to Barry and hear him apologize for his behaviour.

'I'm sorry, Paula, I didn't mean what I said.' Barry was contrite.

'It's OK, Barry. I have the house to myself. Helen's gone for a drink. Do you want to come over?'

'Yeah, sure,' her boyfriend said eagerly.

'Barry,' she said softly, 'bring a few Frenchies.' There was a stunned silence.

'Are you sure? It's not because I called you a schoolgirl, is it?' Barry asked, incredulously. He'd been trying to get her to sleep with him for months.

'No, Barry, it's not,' Paula said firmly. 'I want to, that's why.'

'See you as quick as I can,' Barry said, laughing.

Paula flew upstairs and had a quick shower. She slathered herself in body lotion, and applied some perfume to her pulse spots. Then she slipped on a silky negligee that she'd bought with such an occasion in mind. Why had she decided that tonight was the night for herself and Barry? The image of a pair of dark blue eyes, and the memory of a strong hand curled around her own, came unbidden to her mind. Was it because of what she'd felt this evening? Paula sat in front of her dressing-table and brushed her hair. It had been *her* decision to date Conor and sleep with him. *She* decided to date Barry. Now it was her choice to become his lover. *She* was in control. Nick Russell was most definitely not on her agenda. That could be very dangerous ground indeed. The doorbell rang. Calmly, she drew her negligee around her and walked downstairs.

Barry was no Conor Harrison. This time Paula was not disappointed. Barry was an experienced lover. They'd had many steamy passionate encounters on their dates but this time there was no frustrating, unsatisfactory ending to their lovemaking. They kissed and caressed each other with mounting excitement and need. Barry teased her to the peak of desire before he finally entered her and, slowly and sensually, brought her to a long shuddering climax.

That night, in bed, in the dark, Paula was pleased with herself. It had been so different from her first time. *Now* she knew what all the mystery was about. It had been the most pleasurable experience of her life. There'd be many more of them, she knew. Barry was crazy about her. While he was making love to her he'd told her over and over again that she was sensational. He wanted them to go away for a weekend together so that he could have her all to himself. They'd spend the whole time in bed, he promised. Paula stretched like a cat in the warm cocoon of her bed. The idea certainly appealed to her. She wanted more. She could tell Helen she was going away with the girls on a school trip. Or say she was going on a residential retreat. Or even to an inter-county basketball event that would take up a whole weekend. There were plenty of excuses to go away for a weekend. Helen had no reason to doubt her. Paula didn't want to deceive her aunt. Of course not. But the less Helen had to worry about the better. Paula had to lead her own life. She wasn't a child any more. Everyone had to grow up sometime, Paula assured herself. Helen had had to. Maybe she might not have slept with Anthony, but she'd defied her father to be with him. Paula was defying no-one. Times had changed, that was all. If that meant telling a few fibs to prevent Helen from worrying, it couldn't be helped.

Chapter Thirty-Three

'Paula Matthews has to report to Mother Andrew at the end of class,' a breathless first year student told Miss McGrath at the door of the classroom.

'You heard that, Paula?' Miss McGrath, the history teacher, turned to Paula, who was sitting in the first seat of the row nearest the door.

'Yes, Miss McGrath,' Paula said politely, wondering what the hell was going on. Mother Andrew, or Andy as she was irreverently referred to behind her back, was the headmistress of St Theresa's. A summons to her office was extremely rare and usually serious. If it had been urgent, she would have been summoned immediately. But she'd been instructed to wait until the end of class, it obviously wasn't drastically serious.

What could Andy want her for? A thought struck her. When the Leaving Cert exam was over, St Theresa's usually held an open day for the new pupils coming the following September. Parents came too, and afternoon tea was served in the big refectory. Before tea, speeches were made, one of them by a sixth year student. The sixth year student selected for this important task was usually the girl the nuns were most proud of. It was considered a great honour. Paula smiled. Obviously she was being chosen this year. That wasn't a great surprise to her. She knew she was a good all rounder. Diligent at her studies, good at games, and very popular with staff and students alike. Just the type of pupil needed to make an excellent impression on new students and their parents.

Paula sat up straight and flicked back her hair. It was flattering to be selected all the same. After all, she'd only arrived at the school in her Inter Cert year. She was looking forward to her interview with the headmistress. She would do the school proud as the sixth year representative.

Eilis McNally felt a little tingle of excitement as she heard the message being relayed to Paula Matthews. Ms-Mega-Confident-Smarty-Pants was about to come tumbling down off her throne. About time too. Paula had been a thorn in her side these past few years. Not any more, ha, ha. Eilis smirked. Not after Mother Andrew had finished with her. How she'd love to be a fly on the wall at *that* interview.

It was so near the Leaving too, only a couple of weeks to go. Perhaps Paula would be expelled. That would be glorious! Even if she wasn't, the trauma of what she was about to endure would throw her off her stroke. Hopefully, she'd do really badly in her exams. Eilis cast a furtive glance in Paula's direction.

It was incredible, Eilis scowled. Her classmate didn't look the slightest bit concerned about her forthcoming interview with the headmistress.

'What do you have to say about this, Paula?' Mother Andrew said icily. She handed Paula a photograph. Paula took it, looked at it, and was stunned.

It was a colour photograph of her in her games gear being kissed by Barry beside his car. The idiot! she thought furiously. She remembered that day. It was after a basketball match at St Maria's. He'd given her a lift home so she hadn't bothered to change. Usually Jennifer and some of the others were with them. Barry often gave the girls a lift after a match. But Jennifer was off with the flu that day and he hadn't said anything to any of the others. He'd parked down a lane by the school. And as she'd been putting her gear in the boot, he'd leaned in and kissed her and stroked the inside of her thigh at the same time. Paula laughed and enjoyed it, and they'd gone back to his flat and made love.

They were usually very careful and discreet. Only Jennifer and Beth knew of the affair. Or so Paula had thought. Obviously someone else had copped it. But who and why this? She looked at the photo again and handed it back to Mother Andrew. Stay calm, she warned herself.

'Well!' demanded the headmistress. 'What do you have to say about this? You don't deny that it's you?'

'Of course not, Mother,' Paula said coolly.

'Kissing Mr Keating!'

'Yes, he gave me a lift after the match,' Paula stated matter-of-factly. 'He was glad I scored the winning point.'

'And so he *kissed* you? And *groped* you?' Mother Andrew said incredulously.

'Barry is my boyfriend, Mother. He has never . . . groped . . . me. And I object to having to stand here discussing this. My private life is just that . . . private,' Paula said firmly but politely. Mother Andrew's jaw dropped gratifyingly. She was momentarily speechless. She stared at Paula, horrified.

'Are you telling me that a member of my staff is dating one of my pupils? This is outrageous! Wait until your aunt hears of this, Miss.' She was purple with anger.

'My aunt is very fond of Barry, Mother, he's often at our house,' said Paula, the wide-eyed innocent. As if to say, so what's the big deal?

'Mrs Larkin knows you are seeing one of your teachers? A man very much older than you, and she condones it?' Mother Andrew said in disbelief.

'Six years is hardly anything, Mother. My aunt has no objections at all. She's a very sensible woman. As I said, she's very fond of him.' Her tone was calm. She was perfectly composed. Her implication was that Mother Andrew was wildly over-reacting. Let Andy phone Helen. Paula had nothing to fear. She almost hoped that the headmistress would do so. It was all totally ridiculous really. Paula could see that Mother Andrew was completely taken aback by her attitude. She'd probably expected her to start stuttering and stammering and so on. No chance, Paula thought. She certainly wasn't going to be invited to make the open day speech now.

'Is there anything else, Mother?' Paula asked briskly. 'I've got to go to work this evening.' It was Friday. She had shopping to do for Nick, and she had to collect his laundry.

'You work as well?' Mother Andrew said disapprovingly, staring at the self-confident young woman in front of her.

'Oh certainly, Mother, but it doesn't interfere with my studies. I don't let anything interfere with my studies,' Paula said pointedly. 'I want to better the five honours I got in the mock exams.'

There was no answer to that. 'You may go,' Mother Andrew said coldly.

'Thank you, Mother,' Paula said politely.

She walked down the great wooden stairs to where Jenny and Beth were waiting for her.

'Well! What's up?' Jenny asked.

'Andy knows about me and Barry. Someone sent a photo of us kissing after a match. I'd love to know who did it,' Paula said furiously. 'Whoever it was thought I was going to get into trouble. Well they can think again because Andy nearly wet herself when she heard that Helen knows all about him and is very fond of him. What could she say?'

'I'd love to have seen her face.' Beth giggled.

'She went all purple and blotchy. You know the way she does when she's mad. I should have told her Barry's a fantastic lover as well. That would really give her something to get upset about,' Paula said wickedly and they all guffawed as they ran down the steps of the school, nearly bumping into Eilis McNally in their haste to get to the bus stop.

'What's so funny?' the other girl asked curiously, staring intently at Paula.

'Nothing that you'd be interested in, Eilis,' Paula retorted. She wasn't going to say anything to Eilis McNally about what had gone on with Andy.

'You had to go and see Andy after last class, didn't you? What was the royal summons for?' Eilis asked chummily. Paula looked at her. Why on earth was Big-Mouth McNally being so friendly? They'd hardly talked since the row at Sandra O'Reilly's party. Eilis McNally's curiosity was obviously getting the better of her. Why was she loitering around the entrance when all her cronies were long gone? Could it have been Eilis who took that photo? Paula wouldn't put it past her.

'What do you think, Eilis?' Paula asked pleasantly.

'Oh! . . . Oh . . . I don't know. A summons to Andy is usually something serious. I remember before your time, Marion Lyons was called to the office and told that her aunt was dead. But it couldn't be anything like that. Because you were laughing coming down the steps,' Eilis said, flustered. Her face had gone scarlet. Paula *knew* she had sent the anonymous photo to Andy.

Eilis was editor of the school magazine and she always took photos of the teams when they won their matches. She must have seen Barry kissing her and taken a photo of them. The spiteful little wagon, Paula thought furiously. She was sorely tempted to let her classmate have it. But instinctively she knew that that was precisely what Eilis wanted. No, Paula decided. She wouldn't give Eilis that satisfaction. Much better to play it cool. That would drive the spiteful little cat up the walls.

'You're absolutely right, Eilis,' Paula said airily. 'It was nothing serious at all. Mother Andrew was just giving me a reference I'd asked her for some time ago. And a glowing reference it is too, bless her.' Paula smiled sweetly and brushed past her flabbergasted classmate.

'I'm finished, Paula. That fucking little cow sent that photo to the other three girls' schools I work in. You know I'm only part-time in all of them. Andrew told me the budget for next year didn't cover the services of a part-time PE teacher. She's given me two weeks' notice. That's the line the others have taken as well. Budget cuts my arse! I bet the phones have been hopping all morning. Sanctimonious bitches. They'll blacklist me in every girls' school in the city.' Barry sank his head in his hands. They were having a drink in the Addison Lodge. Barry was shattered. 'I should have known better. I should have known something like this would happen. Wait until I get my hands on Eilis McNally,' he gritted.

'Surely they won't go that far,' Paula soothed.

'Of course they bloody well will,' Barry snarled. 'Why did you have to go and have a row with that cow McNally? Look at the trouble you've got me into.'

'You got yourself into it, Barry. I told you to be discreet but of course you couldn't keep your hands to yourself. So don't blame me,' Paula flared.

'Well it's true, McNally's got at you by getting at me. Except I've much more to lose. She must have thought you'd be expelled. But I'm the fall guy here,' Barry said bitterly. 'Come on, I'll drop you home, I've had enough.'

'I'll walk, thanks,' Paula said coldly.

'Suit yourself.' Barry glared. He grabbed his jacket and turned on his heel. Paula stared after him in fury as he barged through the door.

Barry didn't care. He was fuming. Why had Paula got up Eilis McNally's nose so much that the bitch had done such a malicious thing? He was just going to have to change his plans, he thought angrily. He'd arranged to take a holiday in Australia during the school holidays. His brother lived there. He was always asking him to go out and join him. Fuck it, he just might do that, Barry decided as he slammed the car door and sped out of the car park. There'd be no bloody nuns in Australia breathing down his neck. Australia was a man's world. Just what he needed. He'd had it with women.

*　　*　　*

How dare Barry walk out on her, Paula raged. No man walked away from her the way Barry just had. It was totally unfair of him to blame her for what had happened. It was all Eilis McNally's fault. And Barry's for being so careless. She walked briskly along towards Mobhi Road. If Barry was going to behave like a shit, he could piss off. She didn't need him. There were plenty more men in the world. And some of them were a lot more interesting than Barry Bloody Keating.

An image of deep blue eyes, a straight nose and a firm mouth teased her memory. A recollection of a tanned body against a crisp white shirt made her sigh. Barry had a smooth, bare chest. Boyish really. Nick Russell's dark tangle of chest hair was much more masculine. Nick was a man . . . The longer she worked for him the more he intrigued her. Even though she'd been sleeping with Barry, she'd been very much aware of Nick. And the task of running his house created an intimacy between them. Nick had never made a pass or anything like it. His behaviour was above reproach . . . unfortunately. She wondered what it would be like to make love to him. Paula gave a shiver of pleasure at the thought. That was a private little dream she would keep to herself. Let Barry get down on his knees and beg her to come back. She'd consider it. But things had changed. His attitude had disgusted her. In a couple of weeks she would finish school. She was eighteen years old. An experienced young woman. Paula smiled in the dark as she walked home and felt invigorated by the thought of a new love affair. She would let Nick know that she and Barry were no longer together. When he saw that the field was clear and she was interested in him, he might respond. What did she mean he might respond. He *would* respond. Her confidence was supreme. The seduction of Nick would be her greatest challenge.

Chapter Thirty-Four

'Please, Paula, stop being childish.' Barry stood blocking her path as she made to enter the games room.

'I'm not being childish and I'm not discussing it here,' she snapped. It was a week after their row and Barry wanted to make it up. Paula was not so inclined. Barry had said some very hurtful things and blamed her for the whole mess he was in. She couldn't help Eilis McNally's spite. And it was Barry's own fault anyway. If he'd kept his hands to himself he wouldn't have got into trouble. She knew why he wanted to make up too. He wanted to have as much sex as he could with her before school finished and he headed off to Australia. Barry loved making love to her. And she'd enjoyed it. But dating Barry, and having sex with him, had lost its attraction. She knew it was crazy but now it was Nick who filled her thoughts.

'Come on, Paula. I've said I'm sorry, let's go for a drink tonight,' Barry pleaded.

'OK then.' She relented. She was being a bitch, she knew. Barry had been good to her. He deserved more than a rude brush-off. But it was over whether he liked it or not. He was going to Australia and she had to look to her future and she wanted Nick to be her future.

'Look, Barry, I'm in a hurry. I've to get home to clean Nick's house. Call for me at eight and we'll have a drink. Just one, mind. I've got to get some swotting done for the exams.' Her tone was brisk. Barry threw his eyes up to heaven.

'I was hoping to have a bit more time than that. We haven't been together in over a week.'

'And whose fault is that? One drink, that's all, Barry,

I'll see you later,' Paula retorted and stepped around him and went in to join the rest of the team in the games room.

An hour later she was at Nick's. Paula hoovered and polished with vigour. She took great pride in keeping Nick's house spotless. He was extremely appreciative. She glanced at her watch, it was almost seven. He should be home soon. He generally worked late on the evenings she cleaned so as not to get under her feet. Paula always had fresh coffee percolating and cream cakes or doughnuts waiting for him when he got home. Nick had a very sweet tooth.

The time ticked away. She had done all her chores. Where the hell was Nick? She was dying to see him. In a few more weeks she'd have to go home to St Margaret's Bay for the summer and she wouldn't see him for ten weeks. Although she was looking forward to seeing her family, the thought of spending ten weeks in St Margaret's Bay did not exactly fill her with delight. She would be working in the hotel as usual. Paula smiled wryly. Once, working in reception had been all she aspired to. She'd got her wish and now it bored her. But then that was her all over, she thought glumly. When she got what she wanted, she got bored and moved on to something else. It was the same with men. First Conor, now Barry. She was a fickle woman for sure.

But with Nick it would be different, she thought happily as she heard the crunch of the car up the drive. Nick would satisfy every want and need. She would never ever be bored by Nick.

He looked tired when he came through the front door. But his face creased into a smile when he saw her and her heart lifted gloriously.

'Hi, Mrs Mops, still here!' he joked, shrugging out of his jacket and loosening the knot on his tie.

You are the most gorgeous man, Nick Russell, Paula thought to herself. Not even Paul Newman had eyes as blue as Nick's.

'I didn't get in until late,' she fibbed. 'I've fresh coffee on, do you want a cup?'

'You spoil me,' Nick said affectionately.

'Someone should, you work too hard,' Paula said lightly.

'Hard work never killed anyone, but I'll tell you one thing, Paula, I'm dreading the summer.' Nick followed her in to the kitchen and stood next to her as she poured the coffee. She loved having him so close to her.

'Why are you dreading the summer?'

'Because you'll be gone, and I'll have to do my own shopping and I won't have treats like this to look forward to.'

'You could always get someone else in,' Paula suggested.

'I couldn't be bothered just for the summer. I suppose I'll have to consider that when you spread your wings.' He made a face.

'That won't be for another year anyway, I've to go to college first,' Paula said soothingly.

Nick looked at her quizzically. 'Maybe you want to spread your wings now. You won't have time to come in when you're at college. Do you want me to get someone else in?'

'Of course I don't!' Paula was horrified. 'I wouldn't go home this summer only that my parents like to see me. And college won't be that different to secondary school. The money's very handy,' she added although she knew if Nick was only paying her a pittance she'd still want to work for him.

'Well that's a relief to know. I'll tell you, Paula, you'll be a hard act to follow.'

'And flattery will get you everywhere,' Paula teased. 'Here's your cream cake.'

'Aren't you going to have a cup of coffee with me?' Nick asked.

She glanced at her watch. It was getting late and Barry

was picking her up at eight. 'I'll have a quick one.' She poured herself a coffee.

'I suppose you've a few hours' swotting ahead of you. At least the end is in sight,' he said encouragingly as he handed her the plate of cakes.

'No thanks, you have them. Barry's taking me for a drink at eight.' Paula was unenthusiastic. She really didn't want to go out. She knew Barry was not going to take too kindly to being told it was over. Even if he was going to Australia in a few weeks' time. His ego would be hurt. She'd have broken it off with him even if he wasn't going to emigrate. Their affair was over. A clean break was the best.

'And how's the great romance?' Nick smiled.

'It's over.' Paula looked him straight in the eye.

'What!'

'It's over,' she repeated. 'Barry's emigrating to Australia.' She didn't want to go into the ins and outs of what had happened. Nick put his mug down and put his arm around her.

'I'm sorry about that, Paula. Are you heartbroken?' His eyes were full of sympathy as he looked down at her. Paula savoured the feel of his arm around her and the solid reassuring feel of his shoulder against her cheek. This was absolutely unexpected and utterly blissful. She was so tempted to kiss him. His mouth was only inches from hers. She wanted to kiss the steady beating pulse at his throat and run her fingers through the dark tangle of hair where he had opened his shirt at the neck. Paula swallowed hard.

Nick mistook her silence. 'Don't be upset,' he said gently. 'It probably seems like a terrible thing now, but I can guarantee you one thing. You'll come back to me after the holidays and there'll be a new romance. A new man. You're young, you should be having lots of fun. Don't tie yourself down. Believe me, it's a big mistake to rush into anything.' His eyes darkened at

317

some private pain. He'd married young, Helen had told her. Maybe he was referring to that.

'I'm not upset, really,' she murmured. She wanted to say, I won't have a new man. I don't want a new man. I just want *you*. The phone rang, its shrill intrusive ringing shattering her precious moment. Paula cursed it from the bottom of her heart.

'Who's this?' Nick threw his eyes up to heaven. He went to the hall to answer the call. Paula sipped her coffee. If Nick was going to fall for her, he was going to have to see her as more than an immature eighteen-year-old. Maybe when she went to college he might realize that she was finally grown-up. In a way it was a drawback him knowing her since she was a schoolgirl. It was an obstacle that would have to be overcome.

'That was Killian Scott.' Nick ran his hand over his shadowed jaw. 'He wants me to go and play a game of squash.' He sat at the table and tried but failed to suppress a yawn. Paula's heart went out to him. How she longed to put her arms around him and tell him to forget about going to play squash and come upstairs to bed with her and she would make him forget his tiredness.

'Don't go if you're tired, Nick.' She refilled his coffee cup.

'Ah, I might as well. Once I start playing, I'll be fine. I need to keep fit anyway.' Nick shrugged. 'I won't be here for the next three weeks. I'm off to Africa, so don't worry about shopping. And I'll be thinking of you when the exams start.' He smiled at her, his eyes crinkling up at the sides, and she felt like crying. She'd hardly see him again before going home, if he was going to Africa for three weeks.

'Mind yourself in Africa,' Paula admonished.

'And you mind yourself. And good luck tonight,' Nick responded. He walked out to the front door with her.

'See you,' she said glumly.

'Cheer up, Paula. The exams will be over soon, and

there's lots of other fish in the sea. The men of Waterford will be queuing up to date you,' he said encouragingly. Impulsively she turned and leaned up and kissed him on the cheek.

'Thanks, Nick, you're the best.'

'You're welcome, Mrs Mops,' Nick said affectionately and then the damned phone rang again and he waved at her before he went to answer it.

He'd said she'd get over Barry, Paula mused as she ran a comb through her hair and put on some lipstick ten minutes later. If only he knew. Having Nick's arm around her had been exquisite. She'd felt utterly cherished. It was the nicest feeling she'd ever had in her life. She wanted more.

'I've said I'm sorry, Paula. I was up the walls. I'll only be here for another few weeks. Don't be mean,' Barry said angrily. She had just told him that this was their last date and he couldn't believe his ears.

'Barry, even if you weren't going to Australia I'd still be breaking it off,' Paula said coolly.

'But why? We've had rows before.' Barry couldn't figure it out.

'It's nothing to do with rows, although you were pretty nasty.' Paula's tone was tart.

'Well, what's it got to do with?' he demanded.

'Let's just leave it, Barry,' Paula said wearily.

'There's someone else, isn't there?'

Paula said nothing.

'Isn't there?' he said angrily.

'Barry, we had an affair. It was nice while it lasted, we had fun. Let's go our separate ways and have happy memories to look back on. Don't ruin it by arguing,' Paula said quietly.

'But I still want you,' he protested. 'Paula, please, come on, let's go back to the flat and make love. I miss you,' he said huskily.

'No, Barry. Even if it wasn't over, I've got to go home

and study. I've got the Leaving coming up. You know that.'

'Oh for God's sake! You'll walk the Leaving.' Barry glowered.

'I'm going, Barry.' Paula stood up and looked down at him. 'I wish you all the best in Australia. I'm sorry Eilis McNally was such a cow. Take care.' She leaned down, kissed him lightly on the cheek and turned and walked out of the pub.

Barry watched her go. He knew there was no point in going after her. Once Paula made up her mind about something that was it. Nothing would sway her. There was someone else involved. There must be. Why else would she go cold on him? Sex had always been great between them. But earlier, when he'd tried to kiss her, she'd been unresponsive and unloving.

Barry was most put out. No girl had ever broken it off with him before. He'd always done the ditching. But that was Paula. He scowled. He wouldn't have minded a lusty couple of hours with her. He'd been counting on it. He was as horny as hell and when he'd seen her in her tight jeans and skimpy T-shirt he could have jumped on her there and then. Paula had the sexiest body he'd ever seen. He loved watching her play basketball in her tiny navy skirt and white top. It always turned him on. Paula had no inhibitions. She enjoyed lovemaking. Whoever she was interested in now was a lucky bastard, he thought sourly as he went to the bar and ordered another pint. Drowning his sorrows was his only option tonight.

Nick drove home from the fitness centre where he'd played a vigorous game of squash with his friend. He was glad he'd gone. He felt invigorated. And once he'd got on the court he'd enjoyed it. It cleared his mind. God knows he'd need a sharp mind for his trip to Africa. One of his engineers had made a mighty cock-up of one of their projects. He was going out to sort it out. Whatever Jeffrey Dean had had his mind on, it hadn't been his job.

320

A woman was involved, according to Larry Andrews, Nick's manager. Seemingly Jeffrey was involved with a married woman and there'd been high drama when the cuckolded husband had found out. Nick's mouth tightened into a grim line. He'd been a cuckolded husband once himself. He wouldn't wish it on his worst enemy. Even now the memory of walking in on Eleanor, his wife, and Neil, his best mate, and finding them in bed together caused pain. If it had been anyone but Neil, he might have forgiven her. But he couldn't cope with it being Neil.

They'd been childhood friends. They'd grown up together and sown their wild oats together. Neil was closer to him than a brother. Neil had been best man at his wedding. Nick gave a wry smile. What a wedding that had been. A party to beat all parties. He'd married too young. He'd fallen hard for Eleanor with her dark sultry looks and come-to-bed eyes. The more she kept him at a distance the more he wanted her. He'd been besotted. And he'd wooed her like no woman had ever been wooed before.

The first few years of their marriage had been happy, but gradually she got bored. She needed new challenges and adventures and he was too busy trying to get the business up and running to see it. Neil had been a challenge. Neil with his sense of fun and spontaneity. He had always been the extrovert one, Nick the calmer, quieter one of the two.

Eleanor had dropped Neil soon after Nick had discovered their affair. She'd begged him to take her back, but he was too gutted. Every time he looked at her, he saw Neil. She had destroyed their marriage and a friendship he'd valued more than anything. There was no future for them. He'd gone to Africa and worked like a man possessed trying to get the poison out of his system. Nick sighed. It was gone, more or less, he supposed. He'd got over the worst of it. But it was lonely going into an empty house at night, he reflected as he turned up the drive. He could see Paula's light still on in her bedroom. Poor Paula, he thought affectionately. Young love seemed such a serious thing at the time. If she had any sense she'd steer away from steady relationships for a few years and have some fun for herself. She was a great girl. He smiled as he switched off the engine. He'd been a bit worried about taking her on to clean for him. Most teenagers were far more interested in blokes and make-up and giggly chats with their friends than polishing and hoovering and keeping a house clean. But she had surprised him. She kept the place like a new pin and was so dependable. There was always food in the fridge, and she went to some trouble to buy the things he liked. He enjoyed coming home the nights she cleaned. It was nice to see the lights on in the house and to know that there was fresh coffee waiting for him. He'd miss her this summer. And after she was finished in college next year, she'd be gone for good, and he'd have to get someone else. He'd miss his bouncy little Mrs Mops. He'd buy her something really special in Africa this time, Nick decided. A nice piece of jewellery. Just to show that he really appreciated her.

'Oh Nick, it's beautiful! Oh Nick, thank you.' Paula flung her arms around him and kissed him on the jaw. He hugged her back, pleased with her reaction.

'I thought you were a bit down in the dumps when I was leaving and I just wanted to say thank you for the way you've looked after me. You're the best Mrs Mops in the world,' Nick teased.

Paula fingered the delicate filigree gold bracelet with its exquisite mother-of-pearl stones and felt indescribably happy. I love you, I love you, I love you, she wanted to shout. She looked into his smiling blue eyes, still bluer against the deep tan he'd acquired in Africa, and wished the moment would go on for ever.

'You're easy to look after, Nick,' was all she could say, she was so moved by his gift.

That night, Paula sat in her bedroom gazing at her bracelet. To think that Nick had bought her such a personal gift. Not the perfume and chocolates he usually bought. It gave her immense hope. What she felt for Nick was totally different to anything she'd ever experienced before. Normally, she was extremely confident in her dealings with men. She knew she was intelligent and attractive. She knew men were drawn to her. When she was interested in someone, she let them know. But it wasn't like that with Nick. She wanted him to make the first move. It was important to her that he did. What she wanted from Nick was something far more precious than a flirty affair. Buying the bracelet for her was a big step, Paula thought happily. Things could only get better. Maybe when she came back to Dublin after the summer their relationship would develop. It was her dearest wish.

It had been the longest summer of her life. St Margaret's Bay had been deadly dull. In desperation she'd even gone out with the assistant manager of the hotel. But it had been a very half-hearted affair. She'd hardly let him kiss her. All Paula could think about was Nick. She couldn't wait to get back to Dublin.

When she arrived back in Dublin she was deeply shocked to hear from Helen that he'd had to go to Africa again. This time he'd be away for six months. He wouldn't be home until the end of January. He'd asked Helen to ask Paula to carry on looking after the house and, thoughtfully, he'd arranged for a standing order to be paid into her bank account.

He arrived home smothering with the flu, which he'd got in London on his way back from Africa.

'For God's sake, Nick, go to bed, this minute,' Paula urged as she put her hand against his forehead and felt him burning with fever. She'd been waiting for him to arrive home and had a fire lighting and a meal prepared.

'Paula, I'm sorry I can't eat the lovely meal you went to so much trouble to cook. This thing just hit me out of the blue and it's knocked me out,' he apologized. She could hear the hoarseness in his voice.

'Just go to bed, I'll make you a hot whiskey,' she said, taking his coat from him.

'It's good to be home, Mrs Mops.' He smiled at her. But he looked grey and exhausted beneath his tan.

'Bed!' Paula ordered.

She heard him moving around upstairs as she boiled the kettle for the hot drink. 'I'm just going into Helen to get some cloves,' she called.

'Poor Nick,' Helen exclaimed when she heard the news. 'I suppose coming from such a hot climate to London, in the middle of winter, didn't help. Have you got a lemon?'

'Yep.' Paula was anxious to get back in to her darling Nick.

'Hold on until I see if I have anything in the medicine box that might help,' Helen instructed. Paula tried to quell her impatience as her aunt rummaged around in the bathroom. What rotten luck for Nick to arrive home with the flu.

'Here's some Asprin, they're good for a flu.' Helen handed her the packet. 'I thought I had some Lemsips but I couldn't find them.'

'I'll make him a hot whiskey,' Paula assured her. 'We can call a doctor tomorrow if he's no better.' She hurried back next door and put a clove into the glass, sliced a lemon, added a good measure of whiskey and a spoon of brown sugar and topped it up with the boiled water.

There wasn't a sound from Nick's room when she knocked on the half-open door. She peered in and saw in dismay that he was already asleep. Paula put the hot whiskey and a glass of water on his bedside table and stood gazing down at him. He lay with just a sheet flung over him. Against its pristine whiteness he was deeply tanned. Paula devoured the sight of him. How fit he was, the lean flat plane of his stomach hadn't a hint of weight. She longed to trace her fingers through the dark hair on his chest that tapered tantalizingly down to a thin dark line along his abdomen and disappeared under the sheet. She wondered if he was naked. Paula felt the heat of desire and bit her lip hard. She'd missed him so much. She'd dreamed of making love to him many times in the warm humid nights of the summer when she'd lain in bed frustrated and aroused by her erotic fantasies. She wanted to kiss and caress and arouse him and make him desire her the way she desired him.

Very gently she reached out and shook him softly, her fingers lingering against the hardness of his shoulder, the palm of her hand resting against the rough hair on his chest.

'Nick, I've brought you a hot drink and some Asprin.'

His eyes flickered open. He looked at her feverishly.

'Sit up, Nick, and take these.' Paula held out the tablets. Nick hauled himself up against the pillows and swallowed them obediently. She handed him the glass of water and he took a gulp of it.

'Here's your hot whiskey.'

'Mrs Mops turns into Florence Nightingale,' Nick said hoarsely and she laughed.

'Thanks, Paula, I'd be lost without you.' He took a few sips of the drink and handed it back to her. He could hardly keep his eyes open.

'Is there anything I can get you? Is there anything I can do for you?' she asked as he lay back against the pillows.

'No, I'll be fine thanks, Paula. You've done more than enough already.'

'Go to sleep, Nick.' Paula drew the sheet up over him. 'You should have the duvet over you as well.'

'I'm too hot.'

'That's only because you have a temperature,' she said. 'You're not in Africa now.'

'No, I'm home, and Mrs Mops is ordering me around as usual. Some things never change.'

'If you feel bad during the night, phone me,' she urged.

'I will,' he promised.

'I'm glad you're home, Nick,' she whispered as she

leaned down and gave him the lightest butterfly kiss on his forehead.

'Me too,' he murmured and she knew he was almost asleep.

Please God . . . please please please let Nick fall in love with me, she prayed as she froze the uneaten meal and cleaned up. She wasn't normally one for prayer but this was so important Paula felt that divine intervention was necessary. She wanted so badly to take care of Nick, to love and cherish him and share his life. She felt very close to him. They had a great relationship, all it needed was for him to realize that he loved her. Then they would be the two happiest people in the world.

She looked in on him before she left. He was asleep, limbs sprawled to the four corners of the bed, the sheet pushed half off him. Gently she drew it up over him, her fingers brushing his chest lightly as she did so. Some day she would cover that gorgeous sexy chest in kisses. Paula shivered at the thought of all she would do to Nick and all he would do to her.

Once he fell in love with her, it would be perfect.

Nick didn't fall in love with her that winter, that spring, or even that early summer. Paula was at her wits' end. He treated her as he always had, in the teasing affectionate manner that meant a lot to her but that just wasn't enough.

She could make the first move, she knew. Indicate in some way that she was attracted to him, but she wasn't sure how he would react. It could ruin everything if he took it the wrong way.

It had to come from him. Only that way would she be truly sure that he loved her and wanted her. Maybe the thing to do was to spend some time away from home after her college exams. And when she came home, he would see her in a different light and realize how much he missed her and needed her.

Paula knuckled down to her language studies with grim

determination. She couldn't afford not to do well in her exams. Whatever career she decided upon would most certainly be influenced by her results. And she wanted to get the best. It was hard to concentrate sometimes though, her thoughts would stray and she'd fantasize about the moment Nick would take her in his arms and tell her he loved her.

It would happen, she assured herself over and over. Perhaps going away was the best thing. Maybe she was just suffering from a massive case of infatuation. Paula doubted it. Nevertheless, she decided that once her exams were finished she was going abroad. She needed a break. She'd worked like a Trojan all year. She needed to sort out her head . . . and her heart.

Chapter Thirty-Five

Brenda pulled a towel over her head and held her face over a basin of water. She was giving her skin a steam treatment to try and help it recover from the excesses of Christmas. She hadn't stopped eating junk the whole time. Of course it didn't help working part-time in a newsagents. There was chocolate everywhere for the taking and her skin was suffering as a result. The sooner she was called for the Corporation or the Eastern Health Board or the County Council, the better. Her name was on a panel and it was just a matter of time. Brenda wished it was immediately, she was getting a bit browned off waiting.

Kathy had got into the bank and was earning good money. Brenda longed to have a full-time job. She was doing a commercial course as well which was a bit of a pain in the neck. It was just like being at school. She patted her skin dry, slipped out of her towel and stepped into the bath. It was a pleasure to ease down in to the hot water and she took two slices of cucumber from a saucer on the corner of the bath and placed them on her eyelids. It was cool and refreshing. Brenda settled back to enjoy a good soak.

She wanted to look good tonight. There was a party on and she'd been looking forward to it for weeks. She and Eddie were going and, of course, Kathy and Kenny. They'd had such fun this Christmas. It was nice being part of a foursome, and even nicer being part of a twosome. She really loved Eddie. To think they'd been going with one another all this time. Four years. It was hard to believe. Brenda smiled to herself as she stretched out her hand, turned on the hot tap and topped up the bath water.

She and Kathy had been double-dating Eddie and Kenny ever since that Saturday so long ago when they had gone to the Dandelion Market and she'd had to bring Jenny along as well. It had looked like being such a disaster instead of the start of the most wonderful thing in her life.

Eddie was the best. He made her feel so special. He was always buying little treats for her. He'd bought her a gold bangle for Christmas and she'd been so happy when he'd placed it on her wrist and kissed her under the mistletoe. Of course he could afford to buy expensive presents now that he was working in Post and Telegraphs as a trainee installer. She bought him a camera. Eddie loved taking photographs. He was always experimenting. Looking for the perfect shot. No doubt he'd be prancing around with his camera doing his Lord Snowdon act tonight, she thought fondly.

A sharp ta ra on the door jerked her out of her reverie.

'Are you going to be in there all night, Miss?' Her grandfather's irascible tones penetrated her steamy haven.

'I'll be out in a minute,' she hissed.

'Well don't be long. Some of us have weak bladders.' She heard him stomp down the stairs. No doubt he'd be moaning to her father about her hogging the bathroom. Brenda hated her grandfather's guts. Ever since he'd come to live with them four years ago, he'd done nothing but cause trouble. He was always moaning and whingeing, telling her parents that they were much too soft in the rearing of their children. It drove her mother mad and she'd start giving out to her father-in-law and then her father would tell Kit to be quiet and there'd be a row. Since her grandfather had come to live with them, there wasn't a bit of peace in the Myles household.

Brenda felt very sorry for her mother. She had no choice in the matter. She was lumbered with Grandpa Myles whether she liked it or not. They'd all been at school, her father was out all day working, but her unfortunate mother got very little respite from Grumps.

Fortunately, she got on well with Eddie's parents, she mused as she reluctantly pulled the plug in the bath. If she and Eddie ever got married, as was her dearest wish, and it so happened that she ended up having to take care of one of his parents, Brenda felt she'd find it much easier than her mother had.

Mrs Eddie Fagan, it just sounded so *right*. To be Eddie's wife was all she wanted. She was crazy about him, she thought happily, as she cleaned out the bath and tidied up her beauty accoutrements. How wonderful it would be to get married and have a house of their own, away from the squabbling that went on here.

'I'm finished,' she yelled down the stairs.

'It's about time too,' her grandfather growled as he walked slowly up the stairs, limping on his lame leg. Brenda didn't deign to answer and slammed her bedroom door.

'Cranky old git,' she muttered as she sat down at the dressing-table and started to apply her make-up.

'You can say that again,' Jennifer said glumly. She was sprawled on her bed reading one of Brenda's Mills & Boon romances. 'Angela Reilly invited me over to her house to see in the New Year and HE had to put his oar in. He said I should be with my own family to see in the New Year and midnight was much too late for me to be out. And now I've to be home at half ten. It's going to be just so embarrassing saying I'm not allowed stay. I wish he'd just mind his own bloomin' business. I'm sick of him. He's a pig!'

'Why don't you just say these things to Ma on the quiet and don't let him know anything?' Brenda queried as she smoothed on her foundation.

'He's always stickin' his big nose in,' Jennifer fumed. 'You're lucky you can do what you like 'cos you've left school. And you have a fella. I think I'm going to be left on the shelf. Who'd want to go with me after meeting Grumps?'

Brenda smiled at her sister's mournful tone. 'You won't be left on the shelf, you idiot,' she retorted. 'You're much too pretty.' This was true, she thought privately. Jenny was lovely-looking with her silky black hair and luscious black-lashed brown eyes. Compared to her, Brenda felt quite plain. She studied her reflection in the mirror. Brown hair, which fell straight to her shoulders, framed an oval face. Her eyes, grey with flecks of hazel, were her best feature. Her nose, in her own opinion, was a bit too sharp, her lips on the thin side. Her figure was OK. Nothing spectacular. She'd put on a bit of weight over Christmas, she could see it in the thickening of her waist. She'd have to watch it. Playing basketball and swimming would help. Fortunately they were her favourite sports and she looked forward to resuming them after the holidays.

No, Jenny was definitely prettier than she was. But tonight Brenda didn't care. She felt like a million dollars and she had a gorgeous pair of black bell bottoms and a red skinny rib jumper that she'd treated herself to. With her gold bangle and her nice cameo choker that she'd got in the Dandelion ages ago, she'd look quite glam.

'If you want to put on a bit of my make-up you can, only do it now because I'll be taking it with me,' she offered her younger sister in a rare burst of generosity.

'Yeah, thanks.' Jennifer shot off the bed with alacrity, unable to believe her luck.

'Don't let Da see you wearing it or there'll be a row,' Brenda warned as she coated her lips with *Coral Frost*, her current favourite lipstick.

'You look gorgeous,' Jennifer breathed as she applied foundation with a rather too heavy hand.

'Go easy, you don't want to end up looking like a tart,' Brenda admonished, grabbing the tube from her.

Ten minutes later both of them were made up to their satisfaction and ready to go out for their respective celebrations.

'You go on and just call out "see you later," and I'll go in and say goodnight. Make sure you wipe off that make-up before you come in tonight,' Brenda instructed.

'Thanks a mill, Bren,' Jennifer said gratefully. 'Happy New Year and give Eddie a big kiss from me at midnight.' She giggled.

'You bet.' Brenda grinned as she headed towards the sitting-room.

''Night, folks. Happy New Year,' she said, utterly relieved that she didn't have to spend the rest of the evening at home. Sean and Gerard were playing chess under the Christmas Tree. Her father was snoring in the armchair. Her mother was knitting an Aran jumper and watching the TV at the same time. Her grandfather was doing his crossword.

'Happy New Year, Brenda, don't be too late,' her mother smiled.

'I won't,' Brenda assured her.

'That's a very tight jumper and it's too revealing. Surely you've something to say about your daughter going out dressed to make a cheap exhibition of herself.' Grandpa Myles drew his bushy eyebrows together in a stern frown and glared at his daughter-in-law.

Kit's mouth tightened into a thin line. 'I'll ask you to keep your unwelcome remarks to yourself, please,' she snapped.

Brenda scowled ferociously at her grandfather.

'The trouble with women today is they have no respect for themselves. And that's why men have no respect for them either. If you had any respect for yourself you wouldn't go out dressed like a floozie,' her grandfather lectured.

Brenda was strongly tempted to tell him to shut up and mind his own business. But that would only start a row and so with great difficulty she ignored him, kissed her mother on the cheek, and left.

'Some day I'll let him have it, the old bastard,' she muttered furiously to herself as she walked the short distance to Kathy's. The lads were collecting them from there.

'What's wrong?' Kathy asked in concern when she saw her friend's glower.

'That old ratbag and his interference.' Brenda grimaced.

'Ah forget him, Bren, we're going to have a great night tonight.' Kathy was as bubbly as champagne. 'You're going to get a surprise tonight,' she smiled happily.

'Oh! What?' Brenda snapped out of her bad humour, intrigued.

'Wait and see,' her best friend teased.

'Ah go on. Tell me,' wheedled Brenda. Whatever it was, she had never seen Kathy looking so radiant. Working in the bank had made such a difference to her friend. She was now always perfectly made up and she was able to afford to buy lovely clothes. Brenda couldn't help feeling a little bit envious at times. 'What is it?'

'Oh Bren, I can't keep it to myself a minute longer. But don't say a word to anyone. Now promise.'

'I promise, I promise, now quick, tell me.' Brenda was mad with curiosity.

Her friend took a deep breath. 'Kenny's asked me to marry him. We're going to announce our engagement tonight at the party. Isn't it brilliant?'

Brenda couldn't believe her ears. Kathy and Kenny were going to get married. She stood rooted to the step in shock.

'Well! Say something, instead of standing there with your mouth open,' she heard Kathy exclaim as if through a fog.

'It's . . . it's great. I'm thrilled for you.' She flung her arms around the ecstatic Kathy.

Liar! said a little voice in her head. In truth she felt deeply, disgustingly jealous of her best friend. Kathy'll never have to worry about being left on the shelf was the first thought that flashed through her brain as she hugged her. It was funny, she had always secretly felt a bit superior to Kathy. She'd always felt that her and Eddie's relationship was much more romantic and passionate than the rather tomboyish friendship that Kathy and Kenny shared. And now here they were announcing their engagement.

'When are you getting married?' Thank God her voice sounded normal.

'Oh not for ages yet. We want to start saving for a house first. Oh, but Brenda, I'm just so happy. I really love Kenny and he really loves me. It's just wonderful. This is the best New Year of my whole life.'

'Lucky you.' Brenda couldn't help but smile at her friend's excitement.

'Maybe when Eddie hears, he might get the same idea and pop the question!' Kathy exclaimed.

A ray of hope illuminated her gloom. That's exactly what might happen. The thought of Kathy being Mrs Kenny Lyons while she was still Miss Brenda Myles . . . spinster was terribly depressing. Oh God, please let Eddie ask me to marry him, she sent up a heartfelt prayer.

'We could have a double wedding,' she said lightly, pretending not to take the suggestion seriously.

'Mmm . . .' agreed Kathy enthusiastically as she caught sight of her beloved walking down the street and waved happily to him.

Her best friend's unexpected news had completely taken the wind out of Brenda's sails and, although the party was lively and good-humoured, she didn't enjoy it as much as she'd anticipated. She found herself putting on a show of gaiety that she did not feel. She hated her own disloyal jealousy. It wasn't a very nice trait. But it was what she felt right now.

There was jubilation when Kenny made the announcement at midnight and slipped an elegant solitaire onto his fiancée's finger.

'It's gorgeous, I hope you'll be very very happy.' Brenda hugged Kathy warmly but the sight of the ring sparkling on the third finger of her friend's left hand left her feeling even more miserable and envious. It wasn't that she didn't want Kathy to be engaged and happy. She did. It was just she wanted that for herself as well.

'Well what do you think of that?' Eddie asked her as they danced to a slow set.

'It's great. I hope they'll be really happy. It was a bit of a surprise, though. What do you think?' Brenda nestled her head against his shoulder and felt an answering tightening of his arms around her.

'I think they're mad,' Eddie declared. Brenda was chilled by his words.

'Why? I think it's very romantic.'

'You would,' her boyfriend teased. 'Imagine all the saving they're going to have to do. Now that they have a bit of money for the first time in their lives they should be enjoying themselves, going places, doing things. Just like us.' He nibbled the lobe of her ear.

'Yeah, but they've just got engaged. They won't be getting married for ages.'

'Well I still think they're mad,' reiterated Eddie as the music livened up and he twirled her around and started jiving.

It wasn't too hopeful, Brenda thought despondently as she lay in bed that night. Eddie sounded as if he wasn't going to get married until he was forty. She kept picturing Kathy's radiant face as she looked at Kenny when he slipped the ring on her finger. Will that ever be me? she wondered dispiritedly. What a way to start the New Year, down in the dumps and full of gloom. This is ridiculous, she told herself sternly. She'd work on Eddie. Think positive, she resolved as her eyelids began to droop.

The following week she was called to the County Council. Thrilled, she rang Eddie to tell him the good news.

'Let's celebrate, I'll get a bottle of wine on the way home from work. Why don't you come over to my house? You know the parents had to go down the country for a funeral, so we'll have the place to ourselves.'

'Yeah, Eddie, I'd love that,' Brenda agreed enthusiastically. What a stroke of luck, getting called for her new job so early in the New Year. It was a great start. She'd be earning good money. She'd be able to give up that boring old commercial course. It was a perfect way to begin the New Year. Well almost perfect, she amended, thinking of Kathy and her engagement ring.

'Look, why don't you come into town to meet me and we can go for a meal and go home together,' her boyfriend suggested.

'You're on,' she agreed happily.

A couple of hours later she was standing, all dolled up, waiting for him under Clerys clock. It was a freezing, bitterly cold night and sleet stung her face. Brenda shivered. She was looking forward to going back to Eddie's and curling up in front of the fire with a glass of wine. She watched a photographer take a picture of a couple who, arms entwined, told him they were on honeymoon. They looked blissfully happy, she thought enviously.

'Hiya.' She turned around to find Eddie smiling at her. 'Come on, let's get out of here, it's bloody freezing.' He linked her arm in his. They crossed the width of O'Connell Street, dodging the traffic, and ten minutes later were sitting at a window table in the Sunflower Chinese restaurant, gazing out at the night scene below them. They talked companionably of the events of the day and Brenda thought, as she tucked into her meal with relish, how happy she was just to be with Eddie. To know she would be with him for the rest of her life would make her the happiest girl in the world.

Later, in front of the blazing fire, she returned his kisses passionately. It was a rare treat to be on their own in such comfort. When he started removing her clothes, she made no protest. Both of them were still virgins. They'd had many intimate moments in their four years together. She'd had to tell in Confession that she'd indulged in heavy petting. She'd endured many a priestly lecture, but she'd never allowed Eddie to go the whole way.

336

He moaned a bit sometimes but he understood. Going the whole way was a big step.

'This is lovely,' he murmured as he slipped her bra off and started to kiss her breasts, the tip of his tongue flicking across her nipples. Brenda gave a little shiver of pleasure and slid her hands down along his torso and inside his underpants. Eddie groaned and raised his head to look at her. 'I've French letters upstairs, Bren, please, let's do it,' he entreated. Brenda was tempted. Maybe if she did, he would finally realize that they should be together always. Maybe it would be a step towards a proposal.

'All right,' she whispered.

'Oh Brenda, I love you.' Eddie kissed her passionately. 'I've been wanting us to do this for so long.'

'I love you too, Eddie,' she whispered back, happy and petrified at the same time.

'I won't hurt you,' he said gently.

'I know you won't.' She caressed his cheek softly. It wasn't that that she was worried about. All she was afraid of was getting pregnant. Kathy's sister had got pregnant when she was sixteen and it had been a huge disgrace. There was no way Kathy and Kenny were going to sleep together until they were married, her friend confided when Brenda jokingly told her not to dare do IT before her. Well she might not be engaged but she'd be a woman of the world before Kathy was, Brenda thought with a sense of wry satisfaction while Eddie went upstairs to get the French letter.

He didn't hurt her, he was very gentle and there were times she thought it was very nice even. But most of the time she just kept thinking, please God, don't let me get pregnant.

For the next three weeks she was terrified that her period wouldn't arrive on time. As the day drew near she got extremely tense and spent her nights imagining how she would tell her parents if she was pregnant. Maybe the shock would give Grumps a fatal heart attack, she thought cruelly. She began to feel a bit off in the mornings.

Was it the beginning of morning sickness and was she imagining it or were her breasts slightly tender? It was nerve-racking. Brenda greeted her period's painful arrival with a huge sense of relief. The pain was almost welcome, she decided as she lay in bed with a hot-water bottle on her stomach, bathed in contentment. It fascinated her how women could quite cheerfully have sex outside marriage and not be the least bit concerned about getting pregnant. She had no faith in condoms, or any other method of contraception. It wouldn't have mattered what she used. The fear of getting pregnant and the guilt she was feeling about committing sin were robbing her of any enjoyment whatsoever.

Although they were now sleeping together as regularly as circumstances would permit, Eddie had so far not mentioned anything about getting engaged. Brenda, feeling resentful, started nagging and dropping broad hints. Why should she be undergoing all this suffering and worry each month waiting for her period? If she was married, she wouldn't give a hoot. It wouldn't bother her in the slightest if she got pregnant. The more she thought about it, and compared her situation to Kathy's, the more she wanted to be married.

She would stop at jewellers' windows and go on about the gorgeous rings in them, pointing out the kind of one she'd like if she *ever* got engaged. Eddie did not like being pressured one little bit. She knew she was pushing it and she knew it annoyed him, but somehow she couldn't stop herself once she got started.

Then, several months later, her period was late and she really freaked. 'If I'm pregnant, we'll have to get married,' she'd told her ashen-faced boyfriend.

'I know . . . I know,' he growled, not a bit sympathetic. Brenda had been up the wall. Yet when her period finally did arrive, she was vaguely disappointed. Eddie would have married her if she'd been pregnant.

A week later, Eddie phoned her at work and told her he wanted to meet her in town for a chat. He sounded strained and Brenda couldn't dispel an ominous feeling of unease.

They went into The Fleet and ensconced themselves in a quiet little nook. Eddie went to the bar to get their drinks and Brenda wondered why he'd been so insistent on seeing her tonight. She'd been due to play a basketball match and the captain was not pleased when Brenda phoned to say she couldn't make it. 'Well! What's so important?' she inquired with forced cheeriness as he placed the drinks on the table and sat down beside her. Whatever was wrong, Eddie looked awfully serious.

'Brenda, I love you. I always will. But things have got too serious between us and I never meant for that to happen. You want to get married. I know you do. But I don't. I want to have a life before I get married.' He looked at her in desperation. 'Brenda, I want to break it off,' he blurted out.

Chapter Thirty-Six

This isn't happening! It can't be true. He can't want to finish with me. Her thoughts whirled around her head like dervishes spinning madly out of control. She wanted to scream Stop! Stop! And put her hands to her temples to try and squeeze out these horrible thoughts. But she couldn't do that sitting in the back of a taxi. The driver would think she was a loony. Brenda gave a little shiver as she clenched her hands together tightly. It was a lovely summer's evening, but after the shock she'd just had, she felt icy cold.

Eddie wanted to finish with her after four years together. After sleeping together, after all they'd shared together, he wanted to end it. An hour ago, she'd had a boyfriend. She'd had a future planned as his wife. She'd been so sure they'd end up married. Not as quickly as Kathy and Kenny obviously, but some time in the years to come she'd imagined herself walking down the aisle arm in arm with Eddie. An hour ago life had been worth living. Now, it was a disaster.

She sat in the back of the taxi replaying the scene in The Fleet.

'I want to break it off.' That's what Eddie had said. She'd sat staring at him, uncomprehending. Hearing the words, yet not taking them in.

'Brenda, I hate to do this but I feel trapped, I don't want to make commitments. I want to do things, go places and I don't want to be unfair to you.'

'We don't have to get married,' she said in desperation. 'Can't we just go on as we are?'

Eddie shook his head.

'It won't work.'

'But I love you,' she pleaded.

'I know,' Eddie said miserably. 'I'm sorry but I can't help the way I feel. It's over, Bren. Don't make it hard on yourself. I won't change my mind.'

When she'd heard this, Brenda knew there was no point in arguing. She knew Eddie. Once he'd made up his mind about something, that was it. Nothing would change it. If she'd thought that begging would change his mind, she would have thrown her pride to the four winds and pleaded with him to reconsider. She would have humiliated herself, cast all dignity aside, done anything. But she knew it would make no difference. Eddie wanted out and there was nothing that she could do or say that would make him change his mind. There and then, her whole world collapsed around her ears. Numb, she'd sipped her drink to try to ease her constricted throat. Then he offered to walk her to the taxi rank in O'Connell Street. He planned to stay in town, he told her flatly.

They walked the few hundred yards to the taxi rank. Eddie kissed her on the cheek, handed her the money for her fare and then he was gone, striding back towards O'Connell Bridge, and she was alone in the back of the cab wondering if she was having a dreadful nightmare.

It was no nightmare, this was for real, she told herself as the taxi passed the Rotunda and turned right into Parnell Square. Eddie had blown her out and she was on her own. The pain of it was intensely physical. It was as if her heart was immersed in boiling oil. She felt scalded inside. She wanted to cry with abandon. If she'd been told at that minute that she was dying, she couldn't have cared less. She loved Eddie, he was all she wanted. Nothing else mattered. Brenda sat in the back of the taxi, as rigid as a board. She made automatic responses to the driver's chatty conversation. Seeing that he was getting nowhere and that his passenger obviously had other concerns on her mind, he stopped talking and left her to her thoughts.

It's over, it's over, the hateful refrain danced around her head as she stared unseeingly out the window. What am I going to do now? she asked herself in panic.

She felt the utmost relief when the driver pulled up outside her own front door. She paid him and flew in the front door, wanting only to reach the sanctuary of her room where she could cry her heart out. Please don't let Jenny be there, she thought frantically. Brenda just wanted to be very much alone.

'You're home early,' her mother observed, on her way to the kitchen.

'I've bad period pains. I'm going to bed,' Brenda lied.

'Do you want me to bring you up a cup of hot milk or anything?' Kit asked solicitously.

'No, Ma, I'll be fine. I just want to get into bed and have an early night,' Brenda murmured.

'Go on, lovie, you look a bit pale,' her mother replied and Brenda hurried upstairs and closed her bedroom door. Jenny wasn't there, to her great relief, and flinging herself on her bed, she buried her head in her pillow and sobbed.

'Oh Eddie, Eddie, Eddie, I love you,' she cried. 'How could you do this to me? How could you treat me like dirt? Haven't you any feelings for me at all?' Anger, bitterness, even hate, consumed her. One minute she was going to show him that she'd manage perfectly fine without him. She'd have a boyfriend in no time. Wasn't Shay Hanley at work always flirting with her and suggesting they go for a drink? Let Mister Eddie put that in his pipe and smoke it. He'd go mad when he saw them together. But it would be too late then. Because she was finished with him. For good.

The next minute she was desperately trying to think of ways to get Eddie back. Maybe if she had an accident, he'd come rushing into the hospital full of remorse, begging her to take him back.

A while later, she undressed and got into bed properly, snuggling down in the comforting hollow of her bed.

Brenda heard her mother open the door and ask if she was OK, but she kept her head under the sheets and pretended she was asleep. When Jennifer came to bed, she very kindly did not put on the light and Brenda lay in the darkness, silently weeping, her heart aching with pain and grief for the future that was lost to her.

Eddie Fagan crossed O'Connell Bridge feeling as if a huge weight had suddenly been lifted from his shoulders. The ordeal he'd been dreading so much was finally over. It hadn't been half as bad as he'd expected. He knew Brenda was shocked and hurt and he pitied her but she hadn't made the fuss he'd expected her to. She'd just sat there with that awful stunned look on her face. Eddie felt a twinge of guilt.

It's better this way, he told himself firmly, heading for Mulligan's of Poolbeg Street. After the fright he'd got when her last period was late, and Brenda said they'd have to get married if she was pregnant, he knew that was the end of it between them. Getting married was the last thing Eddie wanted to do. He thought Kenny and Kathy were nuts and had told his mate that very emphatically. But Kenny said Kathy was the girl for him, he wanted no other and the thought of marriage held no fear for him. Well it wasn't for Eddie, and once Brenda started putting on the pressure he started feeling extremely trapped. His feelings for Brenda began to be coloured by resentment. They seemed to be fighting all the time. The pregnancy scare had been the straw that broke the camel's back. A wife, kids and a mortgage had loomed terrifyingly. It was like a nightmare come true. He was only in his teens, for God's sake, and so was Brenda. Why did she want to be smothering herself in marriage? Why did she take it all so seriously? There was so much living to be done. Women! These things meant so much to them. Eddie sighed.

Never again, he vowed, as he ordered himself a pint of Guinness. No more serious relationships. From now on it was strictly love 'em and leave 'em. Brenda had taught

343

him a serious lesson. She was a great girl, they'd had fun and if Kathy and Kenny hadn't decided to make eejits of themselves they might still be dating. Brenda would get over their split. In time, like him, she'd enjoy her freedom and see that getting hitched so young would have been a terrible mistake. Maybe she was even thinking like that this minute. Feeling much more cheerful, Eddie ordered another pint, and one for his friend Noel, who had just arrived. This was his first night of freedom and he was going to enjoy it.

Chapter Thirty-Seven

'I'm going to fail maths. I just know it,' Paula moaned as she struggled to remember the theorem she'd learned off by heart twenty minutes ago.

'Whoever invented the Leaving Cert should be strung up by the goolies,' Jennifer muttered as she fretted over a balance sheet that would not tally.

'How do you know it was a man?' Paula leaned back in her chair and stretched and yawned. Jennifer gave her a pitying look. 'Don't be daft. You don't think a woman would be that stupid?'

'You've a point there,' Paula conceded, reluctantly getting back to the task at hand. The girls were up to their eyes in revision. It was the Saturday before the start of the Leaving Certificate exams. Intense swotting was the order of the day. They were studying in Paula's bedroom. All that disturbed them was a blackbird singing in a deep pink cherry blossom tree that flowered in exuberant profusion outside Paula's bedroom window. Jennifer gave a deep sigh. She felt restless. It was a lovely day outside, there was a real hint of summer in the air, heat in the sun, and the breeze was balmy. And she was sitting inside, with her head stuck in a balance sheet.

Brenda had gone on a hike for the weekend. Her mother was on a flower-arranging course. Beth had taken her niece to the Zoo. Practically everyone Jennifer knew was having an interesting and exciting weekend. It would be such a relief to have this blooming Leaving Certificate over. The way adults went on about it, you'd think it was the be-all and end-all of life itself. Jennifer frowned, sucking the top of her pen. What was she going to do when she left school in June? She didn't have a clue. So much depended on her results. She didn't particularly want a job in the bank, like Kathy, Beth's sister. She *certainly* didn't want to be a punch card operator like Brenda. Her sister was always moaning about how boring her job was and what a bitch Bugs Bunny Powers was, it didn't sound at all appealing to Jennifer.

Paula, who was good at languages, was going to do courses in Spanish, French and German. She wanted to work as an interpreter in the EEC or the UN. So she maintained. *She* certainly wouldn't consider anything as mundane as a career in the civil service. Jennifer smiled. Paula's self-confidence was breathtaking. She oozed it, and always had, from that first eventful day two and a half years ago, when Sister Imelda had put her sitting beside Jennifer at school.

Everything about Paula was colourful and vibrant. She was by far the most sophisticated girl in the class. She had a well-paying part-time job. Her aunt had just started to teach her to drive. Most daring of all, she'd just had a rip-roaring affair with the PE teacher. Paula had done an awful lot for someone who had just turned eighteen. Jennifer, who'd be eighteen in August, often felt that her life was deadly dull in comparison.

The ink started leaking from the top of Jennifer's pen. That was the last thing she needed. 'God, I'm really browned-off,' she muttered grumpily as she wrapped the ink-stained pen in a sheet from her jotter.

'Join the club.' Paula sighed.

'I don't know what you've got to be browned-off about.' Jennifer snorted. 'Do you fancy going to the disco tonight? You haven't been out with me and Beth for ages.'

Paula shook her head. 'I'm not in the mood.'

'Oh,' Jennifer murmured. Paula hadn't been to the disco because she'd been dating Barry.

'Are you and Beth going?' Paula asked brightly.

346

'Dunno.' Jennifer was unenthusiastic. She didn't feel like going to the disco. She wasn't in the humour for doing anything.

'I think it's time we had our lunch,' Paula said briskly. 'Then I'm going to get you to ask me my French verbs, and that's me finished. I'll go down and make lunch and we'll have it sitting out on the patio.'

Jennifer stood up abruptly and gathered her books. 'Actually Paula, I'm not hungry. I don't feel great. I think I'll go home.'

'Are you sure, Jenny? What's wrong?' Paula was concerned.

'Oh, just my period. I'll see you in school on Monday,' Jennifer said hastily. She left Paula's bedroom and hurried down the stairs with Paula in close pursuit.

'Do you want me to walk home with you?' Paula asked anxiously.

'No, no, I'll be fine, see you,' Jennifer muttered as she opened the door and let herself out, leaving her friend standing mystified behind her. She walked rapidly, feeling agitated and unhappy. Her own behaviour had surprised her, let alone Paula. But she'd felt terribly resentful. Paula hadn't been to the disco for ages. You'd think she'd make an effort once in a blue moon to go out with her friends on a Saturday night. If *she* was going with a fella, she wouldn't drop her friends like hot potatoes, Jennifer thought dourly.

She slowed her pace. It was warm and she was beginning to feel hot and bothered. She'd treat herself to a Coke in the Winkel. Jennifer exhaled a deep breath. She felt very down in the dumps. Everything seemed uncertain lately. What was she going to do when she left school? How was she going to do in her exams? Would she ever have the nerve to do the things Paula did? She crossed the Ballymun Road and went into the shop. She was parched with the thirst. A nice cold Coke would do the trick.

Jennifer treated herself to a packet of Tayto and a bar of fruit-and-nut. Her period was due. She hadn't told Paula

347

a fib. She always craved sugar and salt coming up to it. The chocolate and crisps would assuage the craving, that was her excuse for a little binge, she thought wryly. There was a good magazine selection too, so she browsed for a while and finally bought *Photoplay*, a film magazine.

'Oh, and could I have a straw as well for the Coke?' she asked the pleasant woman behind the counter.

'Certainly, dear, it's a lovely day, isn't it?' She handed Jennifer the straw.

'Yes,' Jennifer agreed, 'it is.' In fact it was so nice, she just couldn't face the idea of going home to spend the rest of the afternoon indoors studying. She saw a 13 bus coming down the road. On impulse she ran across the road and raced to the bus stop. Panting, she got on and sat on the long seat near the door. She wasn't going far. Only to the Botanic Gardens.

She wanted to be on her own for a while. She couldn't face going home to listen to Grandpa Myles giving out about 'The Youth of Today.' His current favourite gripe. He was always on at Sean and Gerard, her younger brothers, telling them constantly that their hair was too long and asking them were they men or monkeys. No, today she needed peace and quiet. She might even get a bit of swotting done in the sun. Paula would just have to ask someone else to hear her French verbs today. It wouldn't kill her to come out with Beth and me on Saturday night, would it? Jennifer asked herself crossly.

Brenda maintained that Paula had dropped the girls like bricks when Barry came along. Well he was off the scene now. Paula could make an effort. According to Brenda, Paula only used Jennifer when it suited her. Of course Brenda would say things like that. Brenda and Paula didn't get along very well. They always tried to score points off each other. The other day Brenda had, all in fun, or so she'd pretended, remarked that one of the reasons young girls went with older men was that they were looking for a father figure. 'Is that true, Paula? You'd know. You were dating a teacher,' she'd asked innocently.

'A six-year age gap hardly makes Barry a father figure, Brenda,' Paula drawled. 'Barry and I had a very adult relationship. I suppose that's a bit difficult for you to understand as you haven't had one yet,' she added with a sweet smile. Brenda was fit to be tied. She rarely got the better of Paula. There was a pair of them in it, Jennifer thought, and invariably, she got caught in the crossfire. It could be wearing at times.

The great grey high wall that encircled the Botanic Gardens was fringed spectacularly by magnificent flowering cherry blossom trees. The branches, laden down with voluptuous pink and white flowers, dipped over the walls scattering petals on the footpath. It was lovely to see all the colour and vibrancy, after the stark bleakness of winter. As she passed through the tall green entrance gates, Jennifer could see neat beds of tulips and crocuses and snowdrops. Under the trees clumps of rippling daffodils and jonquils were a glorious yellow and white contrast to the emerald grass. Jennifer's spirits lifted at the sight. Summer was here and that always cheered her up, no matter how down she was. When the hassle at home got too much or Brenda was in one of her moods, a walk on her own in a park or tree-lined street always helped restore her equilibrium. She quickened her step past giddy children playing at the drinking fountains. There was a lovely tranquil spot down near the Rose Garden and the river. She'd have her little picnic and then settle down to study.

Other students had had the same idea, she saw as she walked along the curving riverbank path, and enjoyed the gurgling bubbling melody of the river as it meandered towards the small waterfall that was edged by weeping willows.

Jennifer found herself a spot in the sunlight on a mound of grass near the river. Two other girls sat together studying. Two fellas sat further away. One of them, a brown-haired cheery-faced bloke, lifted his head and smiled at her. Jennifer smiled back. He must be a student too, she deduced. He had a satchel overflowing with thick tomes and he was sitting on an old army jacket. He looked a bit older than a Leaving Cert student.

She laid her jacket on the grass, opened her crisps and Coke and took a long satisfying draught of the chilled drink. She raised her face to the sun and enjoyed the feel of its warmth and brightness. Contentedly, she licked the last traces of salty crisps from her fingers and took out her *Exploring English* poetry book and began to read Tennyson.

The afternoon passed pleasantly. Several hours later Jennifer was pleased with what she'd achieved. Geography had followed English poetry, and then business organization, and Spanish. Her efforts helped banish her previous bad humour. Jennifer stretched and rooted in her bag for the bar of chocolate.

'Did you get much done?' she heard a voice ask, and looking up she realized that only she and the affable student remained.

'Yeah, loads. Much more than I thought. Did you?' She responded to his friendliness.

'I'm pleased enough. Are you doing the Leaving Cert?'

'Yeah, unfortunately,' grimaced Jennifer, unwrapping the bar of chocolate. 'Would you like a piece?'

'Oh, yes please.' His eyes lit up as he sat down beside her. 'I'm starving now. Fresh air gives you an appetite.' He accepted half the bar gratefully and wolfed it down. Jennifer smiled. He reminded her of her brothers.

'What exams are you studying for?' she asked, munching her own portion of chocolate rather more sedately.

'I'm doing electronics in Bolton Street Tech,' he said. I knew he wasn't a Leaving Cert, Jennifer thought triumphantly. 'I was studying in the library but it was so fine I couldn't concentrate. I decided to come up here instead. It doesn't feel as much like work here.' He grinned and Jennifer smiled back. He had an open sort of face. His eyes, a lovely hazel, were wide and clear. His skin was a ruddy weather-beaten colour. He looked like someone who spent a lot of time outdoors. Jennifer couldn't quite make out his accent. It was not a Dublin one, or Cork or west of Ireland. Her curiosity got the better of her.

'You're not from Dublin, are you?' she asked.

He shook his head. 'No, I'm from a place called Rathbarry. It's a village in Wicklow, not far from Bray.'

'I knew you weren't from Dublin,' Jennifer declared. 'Where do you stay? In a flat?'

'Naw, I wish I did. I'm in digs in Phibsboro, and the landlady can't cook for buttons.' He threw his expressive eyes up to heaven. 'If it wasn't for the chippers I'd starve. You should see her version of Irish Stew!' He made a horrible face and she laughed.

'Why don't you move into a flat and do your own cooking?'

'My da doesn't approve of flats and as I can't afford to put myself through college, I don't have any choice in the matter,' he said glumly. Jennifer's maternal heart melted. It must be awful to have to eat horrible food. If he was anything like her brothers, his grub would be of immense importance. Fellas were always scoffing.

Impulsively she turned to him. 'Would you like to come back and have some tea in my house? We usually have a fry-up on Saturday and my mother's a very good cook, she does lovely homemade bread and scones and tarts and things.'

'Thanks very much but I couldn't really barge in on top of your family like that. I'm a stranger. I'm sure she wouldn't be too impressed.'

'Oh she wouldn't mind at all and besides, she's at a flower-arranging course. My dad's working overtime until late tonight. My sister's away so if you could put up with two noisy brothers and a cranky grandad, it's no problem. I'll be cooking the tea anyway and I won't poison you, I promise. My name's Jennifer Myles, by the way.' She held out her hand.

'Thanks very much, Jennifer, that's very nice of you, I love a fry.' He smiled broadly and shook her hand in a good hearty handclasp. 'My name's Ronan Stapleton.'

Chapter Thirty-Eight

'That was lovely, Jennifer,' Ronan said with heartfelt pleasure, as he mopped up the last of his fried egg and red sauce with a crispy piece of fried bread.

'She's not a bad cook is our Jennifer,' Grandpa Myles noted. 'You must be someone special. She's never brought a lad home before. I was beginning to think that she was going to turn into an old maid like that sister of hers.' Grandpa Myles belched and patted his stomach. Sean and Gerard guffawed. Jennifer was mortified. She didn't know where to look. Trust him, just trust him to make a show of her. She was furious.

Ronan glanced at her and gave the tiniest wink. 'Jennifer could teach my landlady a lot about cooking,' he remarked politely to the old man. 'Yesterday the woman cooked cabbage. You could have poured it out of the saucepan.'

'Let me tell you one thing, son. No woman knows how to cook cabbage. I'm always at me daughter-in-law to cook it in the bacon water, but she'll have none of it. Cooking cabbage is an art, son, an art,' Grandpa Myles proclaimed. 'Some day I'll cook you a feed of cabbage and you'll see what I mean. Excuse me now, I want to watch the news. Why don't you come in and watch it with me while Jennifer's doing the washing-up?' he invited.

'I couldn't leave her to do it on her own after a lovely feed like that,' Ronan said firmly. 'I'll give her a hand here.'

'Suit yourself so.' Grandpa Myles marched out of the kitchen. Followed hastily by Sean and Gerard, who were eager to escape the washing-up.

'Sorry about that,' Jennifer apologized, pink-cheeked.

'Aw, don't worry, I know what it's like. My dad's the headmaster at the local primary school. Sometimes he'd embarrass you with the things he comes out with. I don't mind so much now, but sometimes my sister Rachel gets really annoyed. He asked a friend of mine, who was bringing her to her Debs Ball, if his intentions were honourable.'

'That's *awful*! It's exactly the kind of thing Grumps would do. She must have been very embarrassed,' Jennifer exclaimed.

'Oh she was. She's very shy at the best of times too,' Ronan said as he began to clear the dishes. 'She's training to be a teacher in St Pat's in Drumcondra.'

'Oh!' Jennifer was surprised. 'Is she in digs with you?'

'Oh God, no!' Ronan declared. 'My dad wouldn't allow that. He's very old-fashioned, you know. He thinks she couldn't manage on her own in Dublin. So he collects her off the bus in Bray. I feel sorry for her. She has to traipse into town to get the bus and she misses all the social life at college.'

'How come you're allowed to stay in digs then?' Jennifer asked as she ran the hot water into the sink. Mr Stapleton sounded like a bit of a dictator – in the Grandpa Myles mould.

'I'm doing a computer studies course at night. I want to get a job in computers eventually,' Ronan explained. 'My father wanted me to go to university and get my degree but the course in Bolton Street was right for me. I really had to stick to my guns.'

'I don't know what I'm going to do. I suppose it depends how I get on in the Leaving.' Jennifer sighed.

'Listen, there's a party on in the college next weekend if you'd like to come to it. Bring some of your friends if you want. It should be a bit of gas. It'll be a good excuse for you to get away from your studies. What do you think?' he asked diffidently as he neatly stacked the dishes he'd dried.

353

Jennifer smiled shyly. 'That would be nice,' she agreed. She liked Ronan Stapleton. He was easy to talk to. Jennifer had never bothered much with fellas. Beth and Paula were much more extrovert than she was. The only fella she'd gone with was Gary O'Shea and that had only been for a couple of months last year. Gary had taken her to the pictures once. In the darkness of the cinema she'd spent half an hour trying to fend off his sweaty-handed gropes. Disgusted, she'd stood up and left him protesting that she was a prude and everybody came to the pictures to have a snog in the back seats. What made her so different? The next Saturday at the disco she heard him tell a crowd of his friends that she was a stuck-up bitch who wouldn't part her legs. They'd guffawed and she'd been horrified.

'Shut your mouth, you pathetic little creep, the nearest you'll ever get to a girl is in your dreams. Because any girl with an ounce of sense, like Jennifer here, wouldn't let you touch her with a ten-foot barge pole,' Paula'd said coldly.

Gary reddened. 'Shut up you, ya culchie. Can't she fight her own battles?'

'Certainly, I can.' Jennifer recovered her composure. 'But I wouldn't waste my breath on the likes of you.' She'd turned and walked away and left him blustering to his friends that she and the Culchie from Waterford were just a pair of lezzers.

Jennifer looked at Ronan's honest open friendly face, and knew instinctively that he'd never treat her like that. 'I'd love to come to the party,' she said happily. 'And I'm sure Beth, my friend, would too.'

Ronan Stapleton walked briskly across Cross Gun's Bridge, towards Phibsboro. He felt very pleased with himself. He had just fallen head over heels in love, and he was as full as an egg as well. That had been some feed Jennifer had given him. Jennifer Myles, Jennifer Myles. What a pretty name, and what a pretty girl. He smiled. Jenny was lovely-looking with her silky black hair and

354

gorgeous black-lashed gentle brown eyes. The minute she'd sat down on the grass in the Botanics, he'd been very taken with her. There was a serenity about her that was unusual. After she'd had her little snack, she studied very methodically, oblivious to all around her. When she responded to his first overture and started chatting, Ronan had been delighted. When she asked him to tea, he'd been stunned. But when he walked home with her, they'd talked away and he'd started to feel as if he'd known her all his life. He'd never felt like that with a girl before. It was a shock, falling for someone as suddenly as that. Certainly, he'd been out with girls. Especially since he'd come to Dublin. Some of them were nice too. It was far easier to go out with a girl in Dublin without having his father annoying him. But this girl had really knocked him for six. And he'd met her parents, as well as the hilarious old grandfather. Her parents had been very nice and didn't seem to find it strange that she'd asked him to tea on the spur of the moment. They'd even invited him to call again.

Whistling, Ronan walked on. He'd bought her an ice cream on the way home from the Botanics and left himself short for his bus fare. The allowance his father gave him didn't go very far. The money he'd earned working on the fruit farm during the summer had gone on his books and clothes.

He was going to have to think about getting some kind of a part-time job to supplement his income. Dating girls had not been on his agenda. Ronan's main aim was to free himself from his father's financial grip. He'd had enough of authoritarian parental control. He wanted his independence. The sooner the better. Now that he'd found the girl of his dreams, totally unexpectedly, even if it was sooner than he'd planned, he wanted to do as well as he could at college and get a decent job. Invigorated, he entered the dingy hall of his landlady's house, raced upstairs to the damp shabby room and sat at his desk and studied until well past midnight.

'What do you think of the lad Jenny brought home?'
Jim Myles lay with his hands behind his head watching
his wife perform her nightly ritual. Kit smoothed in her
night-cream and then rubbed some into the palms of her
hands and massaged each elbow. It was a routine she
never failed to follow. Jim liked it. Its familiarity was
vaguely comforting. Everything was all right in their little
world when Kit sat down at her dressing-table at night
and he had a little chat with her before going to sleep.

'I thought he was a very nice chap. To tell you the truth,
I was very pleased. I hope she starts going out with him.
It would be good for her. She never brought that O'Shea
lad home. Not that they were going together for long.'
Kit started to brush her hair.

'He's made a hit with Dad.' Jim chuckled. 'He told me
he was going to cook him a feed of cabbage the "proper"
way.'

'Hmmm,' murmured Kit dryly. 'Imagine the poor
unfortunate, though. He's not getting fed properly
in those digs. I hate to think of a young lad like
him not getting a bit of decent grub. Could you
imagine if it was our pair? Jenny's got a soft heart,
hasn't she?' Kit smiled. She could understand why her
daughter had asked Ronan back for tea. She would
have done the same herself once.

'She's got a soft heart like her mother.' Jim held back
the covers for Kit and put his arms around her as she
snuggled in against him.

'He has nice manners. There's a bit of breeding there,'
Kit said with satisfaction and then gave a prodigious
yawn, echoed by her husband.

'I think I'll ask him to dinner some Sunday. If Jenny
keeps in touch with him. What do you think?'

'It's fine by me,' Jim said drowsily.

I'll cook roast beef and mushy peas, Kit decided before
she too fell asleep.

*   *   *

Her period had come with a vengeance. Jennifer lay curled up in bed with a hot-water bottle on her stomach. The cramps were awful but she didn't really care. At least she would be OK for the start of the exams and even more importantly for the party next week in Bolton Street Tech. She smiled to herself. It was hard to believe that a day when she'd been so down in the dumps could have turned out so well.

Meeting Ronan had been the nicest thing. She still couldn't believe that she'd invited him home for tea. It had been an impulsive thing to do. Most unlike her. But it had all gone well except for that dreadful moment when Grumps opened his big mouth. It had been nice of Ronan to laugh about it and give her that little wink. He seemed very understanding. He said his father sometimes embarrassed him. It created a little bond between them. Mr Stapleton sounded like a right dictator. Jennifer was glad she wasn't his daughter. She was really looking forward to the party. Beth was thrilled with the invitation, needless to say.

'It's much more sophisticated than going to Mick's. Is Paula coming too?'

'I have to ask her first.'

'Well, we'll go ourselves,' Beth said briskly.

Jennifer laughed at Beth's no-nonsense attitude. Paula would probably be mad with her for taking off the way she had earlier. Finally, Jennifer phoned. She apologized for rushing off the way she had done. 'I just felt harassed, I needed to be by myself,' she explained.

'I thought you were annoyed with me for not going to the disco,' Paula said frostily.

'Well I was a bit miffed. It was just the humour I was in.'

'That's OK,' Paula said magnanimously.

'I went to the Botanics for a walk and I met a nice guy called Ronan Stapleton. He's a student in Bolton Street. There's a party there next Saturday, Beth and I are going if you want to come.'

357

'OK,' Paula agreed.

'Great,' Jennifer said happily.

She burrowed down in the bed and cuddled her hot-water bottle. It had been a lovely day, she decided, period pain and hurt feelings notwithstanding. Next Saturday would be even better.

Chapter Thirty-Nine

'He's very nice, Jenny,' Paula approved. They were in the students' restaurant in the Tech. The party was in full swing around them. Ronan had gone to get them some beers and the three girls were sitting taking in the scene. Paula had come and they were all ready to enjoy themselves. Orange and red seemed to be the predominant colours, the music throbbed loudly, a fug of smoke enveloped the place and the dim lights gave a night-clubbish atmosphere. Jennifer felt on top of the world. She felt confident about her exams. She'd been able to answer most of the questions. The heat was off and she was going to enjoy herself.

Ronan had been waiting for them at the side entrance. He'd led them down the wide stairs to the party and squeezed her hand and said how glad he was that she'd come. He'd smiled that wide boyish smile. Jennifer smiled back, oblivious to Beth and Paula grinning at each other.

'It's love!' Beth clutched her heart dramatically. Jennifer never heard her, she was too busy looking at Ronan wending his way through the throng to get their refreshments. He's very nice, she thought happily, thinking that it must have been fate that made her go to the Botanic Gardens that day.

'I've never seen so many pint glasses in my life,' Paula remarked and Jennifer emerged from her daydream. It was closing time and there was a steady stream of new arrivals from the Bolton Horse pub across the street. The girls were all staying at Paula's. They could stay out a bit later than they would if they were at home. Helen was not quite as strict as their parents.

Ronan arrived back with a tray containing their drinks, a plate of ham sandwiches and a bowl of peanuts. 'I grabbed these while the going was good,' he laughed. 'There won't be much left when this horde of savages gets loose.' He indicated a group of students who were leaning against a pillar chatting. Before the girls knew it, about ten of them arrived over, pulled up chairs and demanded to know how 'Stapo' had managed to surround himself with the three most gorgeous women in the room.

The ratio was about ten fellas to every girl. Jennifer, Beth and Paula were in constant demand for dancing. The girls were having an absolute ball.

'This is great fun,' Jennifer murmured as she and Ronan smooched to a slow set.

'I wasn't too sure if you'd really enjoy it. Your friends are having a good time. I like them,' he said.

'They like you too,' Jennifer smiled. 'But I'll have to go home with them when they're going. I'm staying at Paula's aunt's house, you see.'

'Don't worry, it's no problem,' he assured her. 'But I was wondering if you'd like to go to the pictures some night next week. I'd ask you tomorrow but I always go home on Sunday and come back on the bus on Monday morning.'

'I'd like that,' Jennifer said. 'But I'll have to OK it at home. I'm only allowed out at weekends. You know, with the exams. My parents are a bit strict.'

'I bet they're not as strict as mine,' he teased. 'All I want to do is to make sure you'll see me again. You just tell me when it suits.'

'Sure.' She gave him a spontaneous little hug and he hugged her back.

'You have my number. I'll just casually mention it tomorrow and see how it goes down with Ma and Da. We can fix something up,' Jennifer said as the dance ended and they went to rejoin the girls.

'He's asked me to go to the pictures.' Jennifer confided to Beth and Paula much later. They were in the loo, prior to going home. It was two am and they knew they'd want to get going. Time was pushing on.

'Are you going to go?' Beth asked. 'You'd be mad not to. He's nice. Just your sort.'

'I know.' Jennifer beamed at her friends. 'Ronan's the nicest fella I ever met.'

'Look at the colour of your woman,' Beth hissed, giving Jennifer a nudge in the ribs as a bespectacled girl with red curly hair weaved her way across to one of the cubicles. She was green in the face.

'I'm going to be sick,' she slurred as she staggered into a cubicle and threw up.

'I suppose we'd better wait and see if she's all right,' Jennifer murmured as Beth and Paula made faces at the retching sounds. Five minutes later, the girl re-emerged. Her glasses were perched on top of her head and, whereas she'd been a ghastly green before, now she was pure white.

'Are you OK, do you need any help?' Jennifer asked kindly as the girl rinsed out her mouth and washed her hands.

'I'm fine, it must have been those bloody ham sandwiches.' She tried, but failed, to focus on Jennifer. 'Stay cool,' she waved a limp hand and then she disappeared out the door.

'God, I hope those sandwiches were OK,' Jennifer declared. Was it her imagination or was she starting to feel queasy?

'There was nothing wrong with those sandwiches,' Paula snorted. 'Didn't you see her? She's stoned out of her skull. She was smoking pot!'

'How do you know?' Jennifer couldn't believe her ears.

'You can smell it down there.' Paula laughed. 'You pair, you haven't a clue.'

'If my mother knew I was at a party where people smoked pot, I'd be murdered.' Beth was half dismayed, half thrilled.

'Imagine if it was raided.' Jennifer was an avid watcher

of American detective series on TV and there were always drug busts on them.

'Somehow I don't think that's going to happen. Anyway go and say goodbye to Ronan. We'd better leave this den of iniquity pronto and get a taxi. I don't fancy walking to Griffith Avenue,' Paula ordered.

Ronan, being a gentleman, walked up towards the Plaza cinema with them and along to the taxi rank in Parnell Square.

'I'll phone you tomorrow.' He smiled.

'I'll be waiting,' Jennifer assured him as he held the door of the taxi open for them.

'Of course you can go to the pictures with Ronan once the exams are over,' Kit said after she'd consulted Jim.

'Thanks, Mam, thanks a million.' Jennifer was ecstatic.

'You'd better say thank you to your father as well,' Kit reminded her.

'I will, of course I will.' Jennifer went off in search of her father.

Kit smiled, remembering how she'd had to ask her parents' permission to go to the pictures with Jim. Her palms had been wet with perspiration. She didn't mind Jennifer going out with Ronan, and, to give him his due, Jim hadn't minded either.

Kit was glad Jennifer was going out with a chap. It would do her good. Not that she'd want her daughter to be as sophisticated as Paula. No, Kit thought. Paula was a nice girl and everything, but she was far too grown-up for her age. She'd often wondered if Jenny felt a bit left out of things as both Paula and Beth were dating. But her daughter never let on if that was how she felt. Nonetheless, Kit was glad Jenny had met a nice chap. She wouldn't feel left out of things now. The way you worry when you're a mother, Kit thought wryly as she went downstairs to make the tea.

* * *

'He's a student! Dead loss,' Brenda declared as she shoved her rucksack into the bottom of her wardrobe and then started to dry her hair.

'Why?' Jennifer demanded.

'No money!' Brenda said succinctly.

'I don't care,' she declared. 'I don't care at all.' Nor did she. When he phoned she'd been sitting by the phone waiting for it to ring.

'I can go,' she said almost before he'd finished his hellos. Ronan laughed. And she'd had to laugh too. If Brenda'd heard her she'd have killed her for being so eager. Brenda maintained you should never let a fella know how much you fancied him because it put you at a disadvantage. As far as she could see, Brenda had not taken her own advice and had put too much pressure on Eddie. He'd chickened out. It was all very confusing. Well she wasn't going to start worrying her head about things like that. No doubt Paula'd have advice for her too. They could all keep their advice. Jennifer felt very much at ease with Ronan. She wasn't going to start using any subterfuges to get him to fall for her. That just wasn't her way.

Chapter Forty

'What do you think of this one?' Kathy pointed to a length of flowered chiffon material. Brenda eyed it dubiously.

'It's a bit fussy for a bridesmaid's dress.' She frowned. Her friend's face fell.

'Isn't there anything you like?' Kathy asked with a faint hint of exasperation.

No there isn't, Brenda wanted to say. I hate all these materials. I don't want to be bridesmaid at your blooming wedding. I just wish you'd go off and elope so I won't have to see Kenny putting the ring on your finger. And what's worse, have to walk down the aisle with Eddie because he's your bloody best man. With difficulty, she kept her mouth shut. Don't be such a bitch, she remonstrated with herself. Kathy's your best friend. Try and show some enthusiasm.

Brenda sighed. It was hard to muster enthusiasm for Kathy's wedding. Her pal was in a tizzy of excitement. They'd spent the entire morning looking at fabrics for the wedding and bridesmaids' dresses. Traipsing from one end of town to the other. Kathy had agonized over the vast arrays of silks and satins before finally selecting a luxurious duchess satin, although the wild silk was equally enticing and she spent ages making her decision, much to Brenda's irritation. The previous weeks had been spent studying huge books of patterns with hundreds of beautiful styles of wedding dresses. In the end, with Brenda's help, Kathy had chosen a Butterick design with a fitted bodice and wide princess-style flowing skirt. It looked sensational.

Although she was trying her best to be as sensitive and

364

supportive as a best friend and chief bridesmaid should be, Brenda was finding it all a terrible trial.

It was now more than six months since Eddie had broken it off and she was still devastated. Not that she was letting on, of course. She was out every night of the week with her new friends from work. She even went drinking in the Autobahn with Kathy and Kenny, knowing that Eddie was occasionally there. He never brought a girl with him and as far as she knew, he wasn't seeing anyone else. So Kenny told Kathy, who always kept Brenda informed of developments.

When he was there, she was ever so bright and bubbly. She went on about her new job and her weekends away with An Óige. Brenda behaved as if she hadn't a care in the world. At night though, in the darkness, listening to Jenny sleeping peacefully, she would lie enveloped in despair, wondering if the pain and heartache would ever go away. Wondering if she would ever stop loving Eddie. Wondering if she was going to end up an old maid languishing on the shelf.

Everybody thought she'd got over the break-up very well, even Kathy was fooled. But then she was so immersed in her approaching wedding she wasn't really seeing much further than the end of her nose. And besides, Brenda felt she couldn't always be a wet rag, it wasn't fair to her friend. Kathy confided once that she felt a bit guilty. Everything had worked out so well for her and Kenny and she was so happy while Brenda was so miserable. So Brenda disguised her misery as best she could and tried to be as normal as possible. But it wasn't easy, Brenda thought wryly, her bright bubbly performance should earn her an Oscar.

If only they knew. Her mother hadn't seemed that surprised when Brenda told her of the split. 'He's young, you're young, you've got all your lives to lead. Eddie's right, Brenda, go and enjoy life. There's lots of other fish in the sea.' That was Kit's sympathetic but bracing advice. Her mother couldn't see what there was to be so upset about. Even Kathy, who knew her so well, had no inkling of how deep the hurt was. And so Brenda's defence was to let on that everything was fine. Eddie was relegated to her past and life was going smoothly on. Only in the privacy of her room could she let the façade drop and be as miserable as she felt. Jenny was sympathetic up to a point but she really didn't understand. Brenda knew her sister thought she was mad to be mooning over her ex-boyfriend, hoping against hope that he might come to his senses and realize the mistake he'd made.

Brenda dreaded the wedding. How ironic that she would indeed be coming down the aisle arm in arm with Eddie. Sometimes she fantasized that, when Eddie saw her in her bridesmaid's dress, and saw Kathy and Kenny exchanging vows, he'd have a complete change of heart and ask her to marry him as they danced around the floor during the reception. It was a slender thread of hope that carried her through the worst nights.

'Brenda. Are you listening to me?' Kathy gave her a poke in the ribs. 'Is there anything here that you like?'

'Ah . . . mm.' Brenda came to with a start and stared at the bewildering array of fabrics in front of her. A turquoise chiffon caught her eye. 'This one looks nice,' she murmured, fingering the soft material.

'Oh Brenda! It's gorgeous!' Kathy enthused, pulling out the bolt and holding it up against her friend. 'It does wonders for your eyes. Here hold it, and have a look in the mirror there and see what you think.' Brenda surveyed herself with the chiffon held against her. It *did* look good. Kathy fussed around, arranging the material this way and that. 'Oh what do you think, Bren? Will we get it?' she bubbled.

'Shouldn't we see what Beth thinks first?' Brenda asked. Beth, who was in hospital recovering from yet another operation on her back, was Kathy's second bridesmaid.

'Oh, yeah, Brenda, I just wasn't thinking for a minute,' Kathy responded. She fingered the material. 'Why don't we get a sample of it and pop in to see Beth on the way home? And I'll get it on Monday at lunch-time if Beth likes it. What do you think?'

'Great idea,' Brenda agreed, beginning to feel more cheerful. It certainly was beautiful material, very soft and sensuous. And it did bring out the colour of her eyes. Maybe when Eddie saw her in it, he'd be bowled over. Her spirits rose buoyantly. There *was* light at the end of the tunnel. She was going to get Eddie back. She just knew it. Kathy's wedding was going to be the happiest day of her life. Every single second of misery that she'd endured was going to be worth it for the moment Eddie took her in his arms and asked her to be his girlfriend again.

'Wait until Eddie sees me in the dress,' she said to Kathy, a hopeful glint in her eyes. Her friend looked at her in amazement and caught the drift of Brenda's thoughts. Her eyes lit up.

'Yeah, Bren. Wait until he sees you. He won't be able to take his eyes off you. The pair of you have to follow me and Kenny on the dance floor. It could be the moment when it's all on again. Oh Brenda, I'd love if that happened,' Kathy said and Brenda knew she really meant it.

'Me too. Oh me too, Kathy, 'cos I still love that guy,' she whispered.

'Ah Brenda,' Kathy hugged her close, full of sympathy. 'Don't worry, you're going to look like a million dollars. Eddie won't know what's hit him. You'll see,' Kathy declared happily, pleased that Brenda was beginning to look forward to the wedding at last. It was extremely awkward having Eddie for best man but he was Kenny's best friend. All the same it was difficult not to take sides and, being fiercely loyal to her friend, Kathy rather felt that Eddie had behaved like a cad.

'You know what I was thinking?' Brenda smiled. 'I might get highlights in my hair. After all, if my mother can do it, I can.' She laughed. 'That's what I'll do. I'll get my hair highlighted. I'll go on a diet, I've been pigging out so much I've put on a stone. It will be a new me,' she said excitedly. 'Eddie Fagan, look out for dynamite.'

Happy for the first time since that dreadful evening when Eddie had broken it off with her, Brenda felt a surge of energy. 'Let's pick out your veil, and then we can go look at shoes,' she suggested effervescently.

'God Bren, I'm whacked,' Kathy grimaced. 'Let's go and have something to eat first.'

'Oh yes! Good thinking. I'm starving,' Brenda agreed happily.

Chapter Forty-One

'Brenda, can you meet me after work? I need to talk to you.' Kathy sounded a bit tense.

'What's wrong?' Brenda queried, keeping a wary eye on the supervisor. Miss Powers lived up to her name. She was power mad and a right old cow with it.

'Can't talk now. I should be back at my desk,' Kathy said hastily. 'Meet me in the Abbey Mooney at five-fifteen.'

'OK,' Brenda said cheerfully. 'Is everything all right? Kenny isn't chickening out, is he?'

'Naw!' she heard her friend chuckle.

Brenda watched Bugs Bunny Powers stalk towards her. Oh shit, she thought furiously. Now she was in for an ear-bashing. Brenda hated Miss Powers's guts and the feeling was mutual.

It was the view of all twelve punch card operators whom Hilda Powers supervised from nine until five, Monday to Friday, that she was a frustrated, malicious old spinster. She was in her early forties, and lived with her ageing mother in Terenure. She drove a black Morris Minor of which she was inordinately proud.

Miss Hilda Powers lived for her work. The County Council was the be-all and end-all of her existence. It was an honour to be employed by them and complete loyalty was the very least she could offer. Hilda Powers's life was dedicated to running her small kingdom in an office block at the back of Parnell Square. She was a very conscientious worker. She expected nothing less from her minions. Hilda was a tall gangly string of a woman with lank thin black hair that fell untidily over her face. She had a long sharp nose and two slightly protruding front teeth. Her nickname, Bugs Bunny Powers, actually suited her. Like the cartoon character, Hilda spoke in a fast twittering high-pitched tone and sarcasm was second nature to her.

'Miss Myles,' she said in her nasal twang. 'It would match you better, Miss Myles, if you attended to your duties with the same fervour you devote to arranging your social life. You have been told before, Miss Myles, that phone calls are not to be encouraged unless it is something of the utmost importance. This is your second phone call this afternoon. It is a phone call too many. Now kindly get back to your machine and get on with your work immediately. You may deduct five minutes from your afternoon tea-break, to make up for lost time.'

For God's sake! Brenda fumed. What a prize bitch. Imagine having to work in this office with that bossy old bat for the next heaven knows how many years. It was an unbearable thought. She didn't even like the job, she thought glumly as she walked reluctantly back to her machine. It was dead boring!

She sat at her big bulky machine and stacked her cards in position and switched it on. The clickety-clack of it was enough to drive anyone mad, she thought sourly as the cards fed through automatically. She was dealing with water rates and if it wasn't for the rest of the girls and the laughs they had, Brenda would have died from boredom.

Last month she'd made a bad mistake. She and another girl had been sending out the bills. The other girl had punched in the wrong code. Brenda hadn't noticed and had verified it and all the bills had gone out with the wrong information. There were ructions, when angry rate-payers phoned to query the mistakes. Miss Powers was nearly apoplectic. Her face went red, then purple, then white as she laced into them and told them what she thought of them and their work. How *dared* they make a show of her and her section? After that, she kept a very strict eye on them and Brenda was finding it very hard to keep a civil tongue in her head and not let the sarky bitch have it. She hated being made a show of in front of the other girls, but they assured her that Miss Powers was always like that. She'd start picking on someone else, one of these days.

Brenda sighed deeply. How she had longed to get this job. She'd thought it would change her life dramatically. Well maybe it had, she thought ruefully. She was now a slave of the County Council, at the mercy of Hitler Powers. If some man didn't come and rescue her and marry her, a slave she was likely to stay. It was a thought that depressed her hugely at times. But then there were other times, when she was out dancing on Saturday night, or away hostelling, or on a spending spree, when she decided that it was great having her own money. She could spend it on what she liked. Maybe if she left the County Council and got another job, she'd feel happier, Brenda mused as her cards jammed in the machine and her supervisor gave a squawk of displeasure.

By five pm Brenda was ready for the loony bin. She'd made a mistake with her codes and had to redo the work and, what was even worse, hand-punch it in. Miss Powers was not pleased and called her an incompetent, careless worker. Only the sympathetic grins of her co-workers kept her going.

At least she had her date with Kathy in the Abbey Mooney to look forward to. Maybe they would go for a meal before going home. She'd have to ring her mother to say she was going to be late. Kit always insisted on knowing if she was going home for dinner or not. She went mad if Brenda didn't let her know and a dinner was wasted.

'That's fine, Brenda,' her mother said when Brenda phoned her. 'I'll leave the dinner in the pot. It's stew, so you can heat it up.' Glad that it had been no big deal, Brenda went to the ladies, retouched her make-up, brushed her hair and set off jauntily down towards O'Connell Street.

It was a beautiful spring evening. Birdsong filled the

air, even over the noise of the cars and buses. Passing the Gresham Hotel, Brenda could see the decorative flower boxes bursting with pansies and crocuses and lovely cheerful yellow daffodils. It had been a long dark cold winter. Now that summer was in the air, she felt light-hearted and optimistic. Only two months to the wedding. Two months to having Eddie's arms around her. Two months to being his girl again. If all went well.

And it will go well, she vowed as she passed the Savoy Cinema, scene of many a happy outing with Eddie. She quickened her footsteps. Kathy worked five minutes away from the Abbey Mooney and Brenda didn't want to keep her waiting in a pub by herself for long. Last week, when she was in the Parnell Mooney waiting to meet her cousin Pamela, a man sat down beside her and started chatting her up and making really personal remarks about what a sexy figure she had. She'd nearly died when he'd told her that she'd a great pair of knockers. Mortified, she'd stood up and walked outside. She would have loved to have the nerve to pour his pint all over him. Why did he feel he had the right to sit down beside her and start harassing her like that? She'd given him no encouragement. In fact, she'd tried to be as inconspicuous as possible behind her magazine because she wasn't too comfortable sitting in a pub on her own.

When you were going with a fella, you never had to worry about things like that, she reflected as she passed Clerys and paused for a quick look in the window at the spring fashions. A delightful floral sundress caught her eye. It would look lovely with a tan, Brenda thought. Maybe on pay-day she'd treat herself.

She found Kathy at a table near the door and plonked herself down beside her.

'Hiya,' Brenda greeted her best friend cheerfully. 'What are you having to drink?'

'I'm fine,' Kathy assured her. 'I'll get it. A Bacardi and Coke as usual?' She arched a neatly shaped eyebrow.

'Lovely.' Brenda settled into her chair, all ready to

enjoy a good chat. The afternoon at work with all its difficulties seemed very far away.

'Well? What's happening?' She smiled at Kathy when her friend returned and handed her the drink. Kathy sat down opposite her. She didn't look very happy, Brenda noticed.

'Is something wrong, Kathy?' she asked, concerned. The other girl gave a heavy sigh.

'Brenda, this is very awkward . . . ' she started. Brenda felt a little jolt of dismay.

'It's OK,' she said hastily, 'if Evelyn wants to be your matron-of-honour after all. I know you can't afford three bridesmaids.' Evelyn was Kathy's married sister, she had a right to expect to be with her sister on the altar, Brenda thought glumly. But she did feel disappointed. She'd been looking forward like mad to wearing her fabulous chiffon dress. She'd had a first fitting already and it looked as if it was going to be gorgeous.

'No, no, no,' Kathy assured her quickly. 'It's nothing like that at all. Of course you're going to be my bridesmaid. Evelyn doesn't mind at all. Actually she's quite relieved. She doesn't like churches, she'd panic up at the altar. Or faint!'

'What's wrong then?'

'Oh Brenda, it's that Eddie.' Kathy frowned.

'What's wrong with him. Doesn't he want to be best man?' Brenda asked dismayed.

'No, it's not that.' Kathy paused and took a deep breath. 'The truth is, Brenda, he asked Kenny last night if he could invite someone to the wedding with him. He's started going with someone else.'

Brenda stared at her friend. 'Eddie's going with someone else!' she repeated, utterly shocked.

'I'm sorry, Bren,' Kathy said gently, leaning over to give her hand a squeeze. 'If it was up to me I'd tell Eddie where to get off and not bother his arse coming to the wedding, but I can't. He's Kenny's best friend, just like you're mine.'

Brenda sat numb as all her great plans for the *rapprochement* crumbled to dust.

Eddie was seeing another girl. She couldn't take it in. It was unbelievable.

'Who is she?' she asked unhappily.

'Someone from work,' Kathy answered. 'Look, Bren, what you've got to do is pretend you don't give a shit at the wedding. Don't let him see that you care. Why don't you go and ask someone yourself? Two can play at his game, you know.'

'Who could I ask? I don't know anyone,' she replied dully.

'Oh come on, Bren, there must be someone. What about that fella Shay you were telling me about, that you think fancies you?' Kathy urged.

'Oh Kathy.' Brenda burst into tears. 'I don't want to go with anyone else. I just want to go with Eddie. Why is this happening? How can he go with someone else? Don't I mean anything to him? Maybe I shouldn't have given in and slept with him. Maybe he doesn't respect me.' She wept, oblivious to the stares of the other customers.

'Sshh, of course it isn't that. Maybe you're better off without him,' Kathy murmured, pink-cheeked.

'How would you like it if I said you'd be better off without Kenny?' Brenda sobbed.

'I . . . I didn't mean it like that. I'm sorry, Brenda,' Kathy said, flustered. 'Come on, stop crying. People are looking.'

'Let them look, I don't care,' Brenda hiccuped. This was almost as bad as the night Eddie had broken it off with her.

'Come on, Bren, let's go home,' Kathy suggested.

'I think I'll get pissed,' Brenda announced.

'You will not! Eddie Fagan's not worth a hangover three days before pay-day,' her friend said firmly. 'If you want another drink I'll get you one and then we're going home.'

'Let's go home now.' Brenda stood up. 'I've had enough for one day to last me a lifetime.'

An hour later she was at home sitting in front of a plate of stew. As soon as her mother left the kitchen she chucked it all into the fire.

'What's wrong?' Jennifer inquired from the other end of the table.

'Eddie's going with someone else. He wants to bring her to the wedding.' Brenda's voice wobbled.

'Ah Bren, will you forget about him? I saw him the other day with a girl and I can tell you one thing. He's not moping around wasting his life thinking about you,' her sister said crossly.

'You saw her! When? Why didn't you tell me?' Brenda was horrified.

'What was the point?' Jennifer said in exasperation. 'Will you get it into your head that it's over and you're not doing yourself any favours by pining over him.'

'How would you know what it's like, you've never even gone out with a fella,' Brenda retorted cruelly.

'Watching you was enough to put me off,' Jennifer riposted.

'Bitch.' Brenda scowled.

'Sorry, Brenda.' Her sister was instantly contrite. 'I didn't want to tell you because I knew you'd be hurt.'

'Thanks. What did she look like?'

'Pretty ordinary.'

'Yeah but was she fat or thin? What colour was her hair?' Brenda had to torture herself with the gory details.

'Brenda,' Jennifer said patiently. 'I didn't stare, it would have been rude, but as far as I can remember she had fair hair, she had a nice figure and that's all I can tell you.'

Brenda digested this information as her heart sank like lead.

'I suppose you wouldn't go to the shop for me and get me some chocolate?'

'It's too late. They'll be closed.'

'The chipper won't.'

'Brenda, you're after losing weight, don't go and start stuffing yourself with chocolate. You'll put it all back on again.'

'Who cares? I'll go myself,' she said in her best martyr voice.

'Oh all right, give me the money,' Jennifer said with bad grace.

'And get something for yourself,' Brenda ordered.

Twenty minutes later she was chomping her way through a packet of crisps, a large chocolate bar and a packet of biscuits. She ate them without tasting them and afterwards she was disgusted with herself for being such a pig. Brenda hardly slept that night. Her greatest fear had come true.

The following morning, while she was on her tea-break, she noticed Shay Hanley come into the canteen. Brenda smiled and waved at him. She watched him in the queue. Shay was nice enough, she supposed. If she wasn't in love with Eddie, she would probably be interested. He was of medium height, with fair hair and nice brown eyes. He was a bit shy and he made her feel a most vivacious and amusing person. When Brenda was at one of the office dos she was very much the life and soul of the party. It made her feel good when people laughed at her jokes and she liked being popular. Shay was an electrician. He always bought her a drink when they were in the pub and he often stopped to have a chat with her. Brenda knew he liked her. In her eyes though, Shay had one big drawback. He wasn't Eddie.

Nevertheless, she needed a man for Kathy's wedding. She was damned if she was going to be a wallflower and watch her ex prancing around with his new girlfriend. Saving face was the name of the game. 'Hi Shay.' She smiled flirtily as he walked towards her table. 'Sit down until I tell you Bugs Bunny's latest.'

Chapter Forty-Two

'You look lovely, Brenda,' her mother assured her as she stood in her bridesmaid's dress the night before the wedding.

'I've put on so much weight,' she moaned. It was soul-destroying. The dress, which had been made six weeks ago, had to be let out because she'd put on half a stone.

'Well you would stuff yourself with chocolate,' Jennifer murmured. Brenda glared at her. As did Kit.

'Well it's fine now, lovie, I only had to let it out an inch. It really suits you,' her mother encouraged. 'Come on upstairs and have a look at it in the mirror and see for yourself.'

'Be the hokey, it's Salami and the Seven Veils!' Grandpa remarked cheerily as he encountered them at the foot of the stairs. Jennifer giggled.

'Salome and the Seven Veils actually,' Brenda retorted coldly. You daft old idiot, she would have liked to say but her mother was there so she restrained herself.

'Salami, Salome, it don't matter. You look nice,' her grandfather grunted.

'Oh!' Brenda was taken aback. It wasn't often she got a compliment from her grandfather. In fact as far as she could remember, this was the first time. 'Thanks,' she murmured.

'In that rig-out, you should have no trouble getting another fella seeing as that Eddie yoke blew you out. That might put a smile on your face, it's so long these days it's a wonder you don't trip over it. You should go out there and get a lad and go and get married like your friend there. You don't want to be an old spinster now, do you?' He eyed Brenda sternly.

'For God's sake!' Kit exclaimed. 'Would you go and sit down and read your paper and not be annoying the girl.'

'I'm only giving her a bit of advice. And good advice at that. But if that's your attitude, I'll keep my good advice to myself, thank you very much.' He stomped off in a huff.

'Come on, Salami,' grinned Jenny. 'And don't trip over your veils.'

Brenda eyed herself in the long mirror in the wardrobe. The dress was very pretty, she had to admit. The vivid turquoise brought out the colour of her eyes and the soft flowing style disguised her weight gain. She'd had her hair highlighted, and the rich chestnut glints were very flattering. All in all she was quite pleased with her appearance, she decided.

The following morning, Brenda awoke to the sound of thunder and rain. Poor Kathy, she thought in dismay. What a disaster of a day. Putting the Child of Prague statue in the garden overnight obviously hadn't worked. So much for superstitions. She turned over and snuggled down. It was a treat not to have to get up for work. Not having to put up with Bugs Bunny gave her enormous pleasure. It was, Brenda reflected, a bit like mitching school.

'See you at the hotel tonight, Paula and I'll be there around seven,' Jenny said, rooting for her umbrella in the wardrobe.

'Paula Matthews is coming?' Brenda was surprised.

'Yeah, Beth asked Kathy if she could and she said yes. It's only for the afters anyway. See you later,' she said jauntily.

That Paula one had a hard neck, Brenda thought crossly. Imagine wangling an invitation to the evening part of Kathy's reception. Miss Paula Matthews was far too big for her boots. Such confidence. Such style. And she from some little village in the back of beyonds.

She acted as if she was someone. Paula's perfect figure, big blue eyes and fabulous blond hair always made Brenda feel ungainly in comparison.

Brenda had overheard Paula telling Jenny that she was mad to allow her elder sister to order her around. 'I wouldn't run after my sisters like you do,' Paula'd scoffed. '*They* run after *me*.'

Brenda was furious. The little biddy, just who did she think she was? She was giving Jenny ideas about herself. Brenda noticed that Jenny wasn't half as obliging as she used to be. Between Brenda and Paula, there was no love lost. Not that anything was ever said, of course. Brenda always more or less ignored her. She pretended that she had far more important things on her mind than her sister's country friend. The news that Paula was coming to the hotel later did not put her in a very good humour. She was going to have enough on her plate today coping with being with Eddie, without having Her Highness Matthews observing everything with her sharp blue eyes.

Brenda gave a soft groan. She almost wished she was going in to work after all. The thought of seeing Eddie and his girlfriend was giving her butterflies in her stomach. Please God, don't let me make a disgrace of myself, she prayed silently under the bedclothes as a particularly loud crack of thunder sounded overhead. What would it be like when she looked into his eyes? How would she keep her voice normal when Eddie introduced his girlfriend? How would she be able to sit and watch as he danced around the floor with her? He who had told her she was the best jiver in Ireland. Eddie and she had always enjoyed dancing. They'd danced very well. Dancing was not Shay's forte. Whenever the gang from work went to a disco, he sat nursing a pint unless Brenda dragged him onto the floor. Then he wiggled about stiffly with none of Eddie's panache. It wasn't fair to make comparisons. Shay was a nice bloke. He treated her like a lady and she never had to put her hand in her pocket when she was out with him. And he had accepted her invitation to the wedding.

It was a huge relief to her that she wouldn't be manless at the wedding. She would be on an equal footing with Eddie. That was very important to her. Pride and face-saving was all. By acquiring a new girlfriend, he had shown very clearly that Brenda was past history. So today she was going to look her absolute best. Eddie's new woman wasn't going to outshine her, she told herself firmly. She treated herself to another ten minutes in bed and then she showered and dressed and went down to Kathy's.

The Cleary household was in a state of pandemonium. Kathy was still in her dressing-gown in a state of near hysteria.

'What's wrong?' Brenda asked.

'Oh it's Granny! She forgot to turn off the hot water tap in the sink in the bathroom and now all the bloody hot water's gone and it will take ages to heat and I haven't even had a shower. I can't *wait* to start living in my own house.' She burst into tears.

'Oh come on now, Kathy, it's only pre-wedding nerves,' Brenda soothed her. 'Look, come and have a shower in my house, then we'll go to the hairdressers as planned and after that it's all plain sailing.'

'Thanks Bren, you're a great old buddy,' sniffled the bride-to-be.

'Don't worry, I'll get my own back.' Kathy's great old buddy smiled, giving her friend a comforting hug.

In the relative peace of the Myles household, Kathy had her shower, ate some toast and drank a cup of coffee and very soon regained her composure. By the time she'd had her hair styled, she was back in command and it was a composed and very pretty bride who arrived at the church only five minutes late.

Brenda and Beth were waiting to help her out of the car. Fortunately the rain had stopped, although it was a rather blustery day and Kathy's veil and flowing dress swirled

380

around her. 'Is Kenny here?' Kathy asked breathlessly, trying to unwrap the veil from around her neck.

'Yes he is,' Brenda assured her, as she ushered her friend into the porch and fussed around making her presentable.

'Is Eddie here?' Kathy murmured.

'He's here.'

'Were you talking to him?'

Brenda shook her head. 'They were here before Beth and I came. Beth went up to them. I didn't bother.'

'Are you OK?' Kathy gave her arm a squeeze.

'I'm fine so let's get going,' Brenda said with feigned cheeriness. To tell the truth, she was dreading the moment of seeing Eddie. Her insides were quivering with nerves. Her mouth was dry. She felt a bit sick. Imagine if she did something awful like fainting.

'I suppose we'd better get this blasted photograph taken,' Kathy said, quite unaware of her friend's angst. The photographer fiddled around with his lens, arranged Kathy and her father in a pose and clicked away. Then it was time for the walk up the aisle. As the notes of the wedding march filled the church, Kathy and Mr Cleary walked slowly up the aisle with Brenda and Beth in step behind them. As Brenda followed her best friend up the long aisle of Our Mother of Divine Grace Church, she was beset with conflicting emotions. She was happy for Kathy. She was envious of her. The pain in her heart was unbearable at the thought of Eddie waiting at the altar rails with Kenny. This should have been their dream too. They too should have been standing at the foot of the altar waiting to be married by the parish priest. Instead, Eddie was parted from her, and among the throng who were gazing at the bridal procession was his new girlfriend.

They passed the half-way mark, where the aisle extended to the two side doors, and for one brief panic-stricken moment Brenda had the crazy urge to race out the side door to her left and run past the prefabs and across The Green to the safety of home and her bed. She swallowed hard. Then it was too late. They were in the top half of the church. Kenny and Eddie turned to greet them.

When they reached the altar, Brenda took a deep breath and helped Kathy arrange her veil before taking her bouquet from her. Only then did she permit herself to look in Eddie's direction. He smiled at her, that old familiar much-loved smile, and she saw him give a tiny wink. Brenda's heart lifted, soared to the heavens. There was still something between them. She just knew it. It was as if there wasn't another soul in the universe, let alone the church, when she met his eyes. She went through the ceremony of her friend's wedding holding tightly to the tiny sliver of happiness which his wink and smile had given her. When Kenny put the plain gold band on Kathy's finger, the pang of jealousy that stabbed her made Brenda feel ashamed. She hated herself, but she couldn't help it. Please, please God let that be me and Eddie sometime, she silently implored as she stood at the foot of the altar beside her best friend and the fella she loved more than anyone else in the world.

Brenda raised her eyes to see if he was looking at her, but Eddie's gaze was firmly on the bridal pair as they made their marriage vows and he refused to glance in her direction. Her little sliver of happiness shattered. If he'd met her eyes at the moment when their best friends became man and wife, Brenda would have felt his thoughts were the same as hers. But he'd distanced himself by keeping his eyes averted from her during that part of the ceremony. All these thoughts raced round her brain and, although she tried hard to concentrate on the Mass booklet in her hand, it was impossible.

Walking down the aisle with Eddie at her side, behind the new Mrs Lyons and her husband, was the most bittersweet experience of Brenda's life.

Kit watched her daughter walk out of the sacristy behind the bride and groom with her arm in Eddie Fagan's and pitied her from the bottom of her heart. She knew this wedding was an ordeal for her. Brenda still had her heart set on marrying Eddie. She'd watched Brenda mope around the house in the months following their split and hoped that the hurt would wear off and Brenda would see that life could be fun if she gave it a chance.

Why was her daughter so intent on getting married when she had a good job and a chance to live an independent life? It mystified Kit.

She had gone from her parents' house to living with her husband. She envied young girls today who set up home for themselves in flats. They had fun and freedom. Her niece Pamela was living in a flat in Ranelagh with two other girls and they were having a whale of a time. Why couldn't Brenda go and do something like that? She was earning good money and Kit wouldn't stand in her way if she announced one day that she was leaving home to share a flat with some of the girls from work. It would be good for her daughter to get out there and stand on her own two feet. There was no doubt about it, getting married and having children meant that you never had time to do what you wanted until they were reared. Much and all as she loved her brood, Kit decided she wouldn't be one bit sorry when the days of cooking dinners day in, day out, washing and ironing clothes, and all the rest of it, were finished.

It amazed her that Brenda, who'd seen what her mother had to put up with, was still totally in love with the idea of getting married to Eddie. Oh sure, Kit mused as she watched Kathy gliding radiantly down the aisle, it all looked very romantic and desirable. The white dress, the ring, the red carpet and all the palaver. A honeymoon in Benidorm. That was all Brenda could see. But that wasn't marriage, Kit thought crossly as she glanced at her husband, who was stifling a yawn. She had, over the past few months, tried gently to point all this out to Brenda. Marriage consisted of disappointments and suppressed anger and bills and mortgages and a thousand

and one slings and arrows. Of course there had been moments of happiness and fun, especially when she and Jim were newly-weds. But if anyone thought that such bliss lasted, they were living in a fool's paradise. Her daughter could not be told. Even though she was seeing this nice lad, Shay, Kit knew she was still hankering after Eddie and her rose-tinted dream.

Kit thought Kathy and Kenny were ridiculously young to marry. Not of course that she'd been much older herself, but neither she nor her husband had ever had the opportunities that were available to today's young people. Kathy's mother was ecstatic to have a daughter getting married. She'd given Kit a sly dig about things not working out between Brenda and Eddie.

'You must have been looking forward to a wedding yourself,' she'd said with an air of smug superiority. As if to say my daughter's made it. Yours hasn't!

Kit had wanted to tell her not to be so bloody stupid. Marriage wasn't the be-all or end-all these days. For God's sake, Lizzie Cleary was in even worse circumstances than Kit, with sons and daughters and a grandmother and an illegitimate grandchild and a husband who was as lazy as sin, all living in the same house. And this she considered better than being single.

If I'd had my time over again I might have done it all differently. If I'd known what was in store for me, Kit thought a trifle glumly. There's worse things than being free and single.

'That was a nice wedding,' Jim murmured. 'Do you remember ours?' Kit's eyes softened as she looked at her husband. His hair was quite grey now, the lean trim figure of his youth had gone soft and a bit paunchy. He looked very middle-aged. She sighed and slipped her hand in his. It wasn't a bed of roses for him either. No doubt marriage wasn't the idyll he'd anticipated either. He couldn't have foretold that his father would end up living with them.

The last year or so hadn't been as bad as before, Kit conceded. Grandpa Myles was a bit more in awe of her since she'd drowned him with milk several years ago. And then she'd gone out and made herself join clubs and the like in an effort to have some interests outside the home. She had trained herself to ignore her father-in-law's diatribes. Most of the time now it went in one ear and out the other. And she didn't lose her temper or get hot under the collar as much as she had before. Kit had learned that the only person she was really upsetting when she did that was herself. It was a pointless exercise.

She felt Jim give her hand a squeeze. Compared to many, the marriages of her dead mother-in-law and Lizzie Cleary being the two examples that sprang readily to mind, Kit supposed she and Jim weren't doing too badly.

'Of course I remember.' She smiled. 'And just look at us now.'

'You're a fine-looking woman, Kit. I was a lucky man.' Jim smiled down at her and for a brief moment all the sorrows and disappointments disappeared and it was as if they were young again. Her spirits lifted. Today was a rare day out for herself and Jim. No Grandpa Myles for an entire day. She was looking forward immensely to sitting down to a dinner she didn't have to prepare or wash up after.

'I didn't do too badly myself,' she said fondly, much to Jim's pleasure. Was it a lie, or did she really mean it? Kit wasn't too sure. She pushed the thought to the back of her head, unwilling to confront it, and concentrated on keeping her spirits high. She was going to enjoy the day. And if her daughter had any sense she'd do likewise.

'Would you fix this blasted flower thing, it's wilted?' Eddie grinned at Brenda as they stood outside the church waiting for the photographs to be taken. Silently, Brenda repinned her ex-boyfriend's carnation on his lapel. She could smell his aftershave and the clean familiar scent of him. She had to fight the urge to put her arms around him and rest her head on his shoulder.

'There you go,' she murmured. 'It's fine now.'

'Great stuff. Now the fun starts and we can enjoy ourselves. How is it going anyway?'

'Great, great,' she said airily. Not for anything would she let him know how she felt. As they walked down the aisle, she vowed to herself that if anyone was going to do the running it was going to be him. Pride was all she had left now that he had this new woman. Pride would have to get her through the day. He had deliberately not looked at her during the exchange of rings and that hurt. Well to hell with him. He'd had his chance. If he thought she was going to dance attendance on him all day he had another think coming. Fix his wilted flower indeed, she thought indignantly.

'You look very well, your hair suits you like that,' he remarked chattily.

Is that right? she was tempted to drawl sarcastically. She just couldn't understand how he could stand there chatting as if she was just some close *acquaintance*. She'd been to bed with him, for God's sake.

'Thanks, I got it done for the wedding,' Brenda said. Not wanting Eddie to get the impression that she'd got it done to impress *him*. 'Look, excuse me for a minute, Eddie, I just want to go over and talk to Shay for a minute. He doesn't know anyone here.'

'Oh, yeah, yeah, sure,' he shrugged. 'I'll just go and have a chat with Anna, she's in the same boat.'

Brenda knew she was being petty but she was glad she'd got Shay's name in first. Let Mister Eddie Fagan see that he wasn't the only one who could go and get a new partner.

'Hi Shay.' She slipped her hand into his and hoped Eddie was looking. 'Once the meal is over I'll be able to come and join you.'

'Don't worry about me, everybody is being very nice,' he assured her. 'Your ma and da are lovely.'

'I know.' Brenda smiled. 'I just wanted to see if you were OK, it can be a bit of a drag when you don't know people.'

'I'm fine.' He smiled at her, his brown eyes warm and friendly. 'Did I tell you, you look gorgeous in that dress. And I like what you've done to your hair. I'll be lucky to get a dance, I suppose.'

'Go on with you, Shay Hanley, *I'll* probably have to drag *you* onto the dance floor.' Brenda snorted.

'You'd better go, the photographer looks as if he's about to have a nervous breakdown,' Shay remarked. 'It's tough being a bridesmaid.'

'You can say that again.' Brenda laughed as she turned away and began walking towards Kathy and Kenny. Out of the corner of her eye, she was aware of Eddie looking in her direction. Let him look, she thought triumphantly, gazing straight ahead of her. I hope he's eaten alive with jealousy. Was there a chance of that, she wondered, or was it all just one-sided? He obviously knew about Shay, no doubt Kenny had told him that she was bringing someone to the wedding. She was dying to have a good look at the girl he'd been talking to. But she didn't want to be caught in the act, so to speak. She'd have to choose her moment.

She got her chance while Kenny and Eddie and Kenny's brothers were being photographed. The girl was making jokey comments to Eddie about his monkey suit. Brenda, who was standing to the side out of Eddie's line of vision, was able to have a good look without being noticed.

Her first reaction was one of slight shock. This Anna wasn't much to look at. Brenda had been expecting someone stunning, for some reason. But this fair-haired girl with the pear-shaped figure was rather ordinary-looking. Brenda felt somewhat miffed. What did this creature possess that she didn't? Brenda was taller, and in spite of her recently acquired half-stone, thinner. She had better hair. She didn't have freckles either, which Anna possessed in abundance.

What did Eddie see in her? A heart-stopping thought struck her. Maybe Anna was better in bed.

Would you just stop it, Brenda Myles! she ordered crossly. She was her own worst enemy.

'Everything OK?' Kathy slipped an arm through hers.

'Of course.' Brenda smiled.

'What do you think of her?' Kathy inclined her head in Anna's direction.

'I thought she'd be a bit more glamorous, to be honest,' Brenda confided.

'Hmm . . . Farrah Fawcett she ain't.' Kathy grinned. 'And you look great today. Did Eddie say anything?'

'He said he liked my hair,' Brenda said glumly.

'Cheer up, wait until you're dancing around the floor with him. You never know what might happen,' the bride declared as her husband came over and announced that he was posing for no more photographs.

'But we've got to get the ones of the in-laws together,' Kathy protested.

'Sorry, I've had it,' Kenny growled. '"Right foot pointed, elbows tucked in, eyes on me." We'll be here all day listening to that crap. People are getting hungry. And I could do with a pint.'

'Kenny Lyons, don't you dare spoil my wedding day.' Kathy glowered. Brenda discreetly moved away and left the newly-weds to their first marital row.

Several hours later, having been wined and dined, everybody was in great humour again. The meal was delicious, the speeches funny, but now it was time for the dancing and Brenda could feel her insides knotting up. She watched Kenny take Kathy in his arms and, as the band played the old Nat King Cole hit *When I Fall in Love*, she got a lump in her throat that nearly choked her. Her best friend looked radiantly happy as they waltzed around the floor.

Will it ever be me, waltzing around the dance floor with my new husband, Brenda wondered forlornly.

'Come on, Brenda, we're next. Let's show them how to do it.' Eddie took her by the arm as the band started to play *Shake Rattle and Roll*. She was laughing and breathless when they finished jiving and when the band started to play *It's Now or Never* and Eddie's arms were around her like in the old days. As they waltzed around the floor, now crowded with other dancers, Brenda rested her cheek against Eddie's and savoured their closeness.

'It's like old times,' he murmured.

'Yeah,' she agreed wistfully and then, before she could help it, the words popped out. 'I miss you like crazy, Eddie,'

His arms tightened around her. 'I miss you too, Bren, we had good times. But we can't go back.'

She finished the dance with him and excused herself. She headed towards the ladies' toilet and, having made sure she was quite alone in the safety of the cubicle, Brenda sat on the lid of the loo and cried her eyes out. She was just beginning to compose herself when she heard the outer doors open. Brenda heard a voice she recognized. It was Denise Boyle, a girl she and Kathy had been to secondary school with.

'Kathy looks terrific, doesn't she?' Brenda heard her say.

'Gorgeous, the dress is out of this world.' The other voice was that of Jilly Clarke, also an ex-classmate.

'Brenda's put on a bit of weight though, hasn't she?' Brenda nearly fell off the loo seat in horror when she heard this. She could hear the sound of hair being brushed and perfume being sprayed. Jilly's voice drifted into the cubicle.

'You know I think she still fancies Eddie. Did you see the way she was looking at him when they were dancing? Talk about wearing your heart on your sleeve.'

'But sure she's going with that other bloke and Eddie's going with Anna Saunders,' Denise retorted.

'That doesn't mean anything,' Jilly scoffed. 'Eddie dumped her. I bet she'd have him back at the drop of a hat.'

'I always thought Brenda and Eddie would be the first of the gang to marry. You could have knocked me down with a feather when I heard they'd split,' Jilly declared.

'Hmm . . . I bet you could have knocked poor old Brenda down with a feather too, and to think Kathy and Kenny, of all people, made it first.'

'Wouldn't really fancy Kenny Lyons myself, to be honest.' Denise giggled. 'I wouldn't like him all over me in bed.'

'Well you won't have to worry about that, will you? He'll be all over Kathy tonight. Come on, let's see if there's any talent out there. If Brenda and Kathy can get fellas so can we!' Tittering raucously they exited the ladies leaving Brenda shocked and outraged.

'Fucking bitches,' she swore, her cheeks burning against the palms of her hands. She took a couple of deep breaths. Had she been so obvious? What had Jilly said – 'wearing her heart on her sleeve?' Brenda sank her head in her hands. Why in the name of God had she blurted out to Eddie that she missed him like crazy? Talk about making a doormat of herself. Where was her pride? She would have gone home there and then except she knew that Kathy would never forgive her. Brenda took another deep breath. She was going to make that catty pair eat their words, she thought grimly. And she was going to salvage something of the disaster with Eddie. She marched out the door of the cubicle and splashed cold water onto her blotched face. Then she took out her make-up bag. Thank God she'd had the presence of mind to bring it in to the loo with her.

Slowly, and with great care, Brenda redid her make-up. No-one must know that she was having anything but a ball. The first people she encountered when she walked back to the reception were Jennifer and Paula.

'You look brilliant.' Jennifer smiled.

'Very nice,' added the blonde bombshell, who was dressed in a figure-hugging black dress that clung in all the right places. Although she was the same age as Jenny, Paula was light years ahead in terms of sophistication, Brenda thought sourly, unimpressed by the lukewarm 'very nice.' Well at least Jenny hadn't noticed anything so she must look OK, she thought with relief. Now to go and put on the act of her life. 'I'm just going to dance with Shay, I haven't had a chance to be with him all day. See you later. Have fun,' she told the younger girls.

With her head up and her shoulders back, Brenda walked over to where Shay was sitting. 'Come on, Shay Hanley,' she said briskly. 'You've been getting away with murder . . . now you're going to dance.'

For the next three hours Brenda danced, sang, and gave the impression that she was having the night of her life. Even Kathy was fooled. When they went upstairs so that Kathy could change into her going-away outfit, she said warmly, 'I'm so glad you enjoyed my wedding, Bren. I was very worried you wouldn't, with Eddie and everything.'

'I'd a lovely day, Kathy,' she assured her. Not for a minute would she spoil her friend's illusion. Kathy's mother arrived with Beth and the rest of her sisters and they had no more time to talk. It was only when she tossed her bouquet at Brenda and left the hotel in a flurry of hugs and kisses that Brenda's composure started to slip.

'Are you OK?' Shay asked as tears glittered in her eyes. Brenda shook her head, unable to speak.

'Come on. Let's take a walk in the grounds,' he murmured, leading her out through a side door. The breeze was cool against her hot cheeks, and in the dark Brenda bowed her head and let the tears fall. Shay stood protectively in front of her with his arms around her.

'She'll be back from her honeymoon in two weeks,' he tried to soothe her. 'I suppose it's a bit like a sister getting married. Is it?'

Brenda nodded, silently. At least Shay thought it was because of Kathy that she was crying. He hadn't connected her tears to Eddie.

'Don't cry,' he said kindly and she leaned her head on his shoulder. Any shoulder was better than none, even if it wasn't Eddie Fagan's.

'I think I'd like to go home,' she said shakily.

'Right then, we'll go so,' Shay said briskly. He was mightily relieved that she wasn't going to take him dancing in Leeson Street as she'd suggested earlier. He wasn't much of a dancer, discos weren't his scene but Brenda really liked to boogie. A few hours on his own with her suited him down to the ground. He'd had enough socializing for one day.

'I'll get your bag and stuff and tell your ma and da I'm taking you home, why don't you sit in the car?' Brenda nodded. They walked over to the car park and Shay opened the door of his Ford Cortina. Wearily Brenda sat in and rested her head on the head rest. Her head was throbbing, but at least the ordeal was over. Brenda knew without a doubt that Kathy's wedding was one of the worst days of her life. All she wanted to do was to go to bed and blot it out of her mind forever.

Chapter Forty-Three

'You take your first tablet on the first day of your next period and continue taking them for twenty-one days. Then you take a break for seven days and after that you start your next pack. Keep an eye on your weight and don't smoke,' the lady doctor in the Well Woman Centre instructed. Brenda nodded and slid the slim pack into her handbag.

'If you've any problems come back to us. You've got to come back every six months to renew your prescription and to have a check-up. OK?'

'Right, thanks,' Brenda murmured. She was glad the ordeal of examination was over. It was the first time she'd had an internal examination and smear test. At least it had been done by a lady doctor, she'd have died if it had been a man, she thought as she left the clinic. She ran up the steps onto Leeson Street and avoided the eyes of passers-by. Brenda was feeling uncomfortable. She'd gone to the clinic to get on the contraceptive pill. The worry she'd endured when she'd been sleeping with Eddie was unforgettable. Never again would she put herself through that trauma.

She saw a 13 bus heading across Leeson Street Bridge and raced across the street towards the bus stop. What a stroke of luck, at least she wouldn't be hanging around for hours waiting for a bus. She headed upstairs. There weren't many other passengers on the bus, it was late evening, between the rush hour and the time when people started going into town. Settling back in her seat she drew out the pill packet and studied the literature that accompanied it. She was a bit apprehensive about going on the pill. According to the contra-indications she could suffer headaches, and perhaps a blood clot. Brenda was also feeling rather guilty. Pre-marital sex was a sin, according to the Church, and here she was, taking steps to prevent pregnancy and lead a life of debauchery.

Well not a life exactly, she thought wryly. A fortnight would be a more accurate description. In two months' time she was going on her first foreign holiday and if the chance to have a foreign affair came her way, she was going to grab it. She'd listened to girls at work who had indulged in two weeks of passion with hunky sexy Spaniards. Being manless and almost twenty-four was bad. Being celibate was a disaster. Sometimes it seemed to Brenda that everyone in the country except her was having a relationship.

The last time she'd had sex was with Eddie. She and Shay had never got that far. She'd broken it off with him three months after Kathy's wedding. Much to his dismay. Shay was a nice bloke, but she just wasn't interested and that was the truth. If she couldn't have Eddie, she didn't want anyone, she'd decided. There had been a few casual dates with other fellas but nothing that lasted. Now, she was almost twenty-four. Practically middle-aged. She was constantly thinking about sex. Brenda remembered her nights of passion with Eddie. If some sexy Latin male in Puerto Carlos decided to seduce her, and she really fancied him, she had made up her mind to enjoy every minute of it. Hence the visit to the Well Woman Centre. Of course she hadn't told them she was going to have a foreign affair. They might think she was a slut. She'd fibbed and said she was getting engaged soon and wanted to be protected in case she and her fiancé decided to sleep together. The doctor told her she was very sensible.

If only she knew, Brenda sighed as the bus conductor appeared at the top of the stairs and she shoved her bits and pieces back in her bag guiltily. Sensible wasn't the word to describe her. Horny was much more appropriate.

*   *   *

'I think I'm going to be sick,' moaned Joan Regan from the seat behind Brenda as the coach careered along a winding stretch of the Costa del Sol.

'Here's a sick bag,' Brenda offered. She had taken the precaution of swiping a few from the plane. She felt a bit queasy herself. It was all that drinking. They'd spent an hour in the bar at Dublin Airport lowering shorts and then they'd ordered drinks throughout the two and a half hour star flight. She wasn't used to drinking that much and the twisting and turning of the coach wasn't helping.

'Be careful in the sun with those pale skins,' the courier was saying from the top of the bus. 'Use plenty of suntan lotion and don't do too much sunbathing for the first few days or you'll end up like lobsters. Drink is very cheap here. San Miguel is the most popular beer. But be careful, you'll get drunk a lot quicker on it because of the heat and dehydration,' the glamorous blonde cautioned. Brenda looked at her admiringly. Her skin was golden, her hair had lovely highlights that shone even in the subdued lighting of the coach. She looked very healthy and athletic and had a terrific figure.

Brenda looked at her pale milky-white limbs. Having a tan invariably made you look better and she was going to take it easy and not get sunburned on her first few days. She settled back in her seat and peered out the window. It was pitch-dark. All she could see was a swift blur of whitewashed or terracotta houses, their shutters closed against the night. She was dying to see what it was like in daylight.

It had been incredibly exciting getting off the plane and feeling the cloying heat of a midsummer Spanish night. The sound of the crickets fascinated her. It was all so different . . . so *foreign*.

Brenda felt giddy and happy. The further the plane flew south, the giddier and happier she'd got. It seemed that all her mundane little problems fell far behind her. *This* was living. Sipping drinks in airport lounges. Browsing through the duty-free. Treating yourself to perfumes and make-up. Brenda treated herself to a bottle of *Laughter* and some *Charlie* lipstick and matching nail varnish. She felt a bit like a film star, in her glamorous sunglasses and her white jeans and black T-shirt. She'd been nervous when the plane took off but none of the others seemed to take much heed of it so she took her cue from them and relaxed.

She had been looking forward to this holiday for such a long time. Ever since the brochures had come out in January and four of them at work decided to take off together. They invited Brenda and she invited her cousin Pamela. The excitement was mighty as they made their plans.

Three of them had been away on holidays before, but for Brenda and two of the others it was a totally new experience. She could hear Joan snoring behind her. Joan had never been abroad before either and was even less used to drinking than Brenda was. She was pissed out of her skull.

'Look at the sleeping beauty,' giggled Tara across the aisle. Tara had been away several times and was a seasoned traveller and could hold her drink. Tara was one of the most self-confident people Brenda had ever met. Even Bugs Bunny held no fears for Tara, who could put the pernickety supervisor down with ease.

'As long as she doesn't puke all over the place,' grimaced Julia, who was sitting beside the comatose Joan.

Pamela nudged Brenda in the ribs. 'That pair don't get on the best, do they?' she whispered.

'Don't mind them, they're always arguing. At least we won't have to put up with them. We've got our own studio apartment,' she murmured. Because there were six of them on the holiday, they had to split up. The other four were sharing a four-bed apartment, and Brenda and Pamela were to have an adjoining studio. Brenda was a bit disappointed that they weren't all together.

She and Pamela were given a tiny studio at the rear of the apartment block. The others were given an apartment in a completely separate complex because of overbooking. They were all furious. Joan even roused herself from her stupor to mumble that if they weren't put together she was going to sue. Then she sat on her suitcase and fell asleep again.

'Look, I'll fix you up all together tomorrow,' the harassed courier assured Brenda and Pamela. 'Just for tonight will you take the accommodation here and I'll be around first thing to get you moved.' With bad grace, they agreed. It was three am and they were too tired to argue.

'This is a real pain in the ass,' grumbled Brenda as she stared around the poky little studio. It had a sofa which doubled as a bed, underneath which was a small pull-out bed. Two easy chairs, a small dining table and chairs, a kitchenette with a two-ring cooker, a fridge and a sink, comprised the rest of the contents. A tiled bathroom completed the accommodation. The Ritz it most definitely was not!

'Well what a dive,' complained Pamela as she surveyed their abode.

'Sorry about this,' Brenda apologized, feeling dreadful. After all, she'd asked Pamela to come on holidays and this was what she'd found.

'It's not your fault, Bren. It was that smarmy little shit in the travel agency. Boy, is he going to get an earful from me when I get back home,' Pamela fumed. 'Come on, let's go to bed and tomorrow we'll kick up a fuss until we're put with the others,' she declared, disappearing into the bathroom to wash her teeth. Two minutes later a blood-curdling shriek nearly gave Brenda a heart attack. Pamela flew out of the bathroom, babbling.

'Brenda, there's something *horrible* in the bath. It's got huge eyes and a swivelly head and hundreds of legs. I . . . I'm not going in there again.' Brenda swallowed hard and patted her distraught cousin on the shoulder.

'I'll handle it, just let me find something to kill it with,' she said dry-mouthed, her heart palpitating. This was not part of the plan. Holidays were meant to be enjoyed. They weren't supposed to be dread-inducing ordeals. There was a mop beside the sink and, taking a deep breath, Brenda prepared to do battle.

Peering around the shower curtain, she could see the grotesque insect eyeing her balefully. She whacked the mop in the direction of its head and ran shrieking out of the bathroom when it flew up into the air and started buzzing around. Frantically, Brenda slammed the bathroom door. 'Oh God, I'm not going in there again,' she jabbered hysterically. 'It's huge!'

'I'm bursting to go to the loo,' wailed Pamela. Brenda groaned. Come to think of it so was she. She had a sudden brainwave.

'There's toilets down by the swimming-pool, I noticed them when the courier was bringing us here. We can go there.'

'This is ridiculous!' stormed Pamela as they walked along in the dark, towards the swimming-pool. The lighting was very poor when they eventually did reach the pool area. And the toilets were in complete darkness.

Two very disgruntled young ladies finally lay down to go to sleep. They'd been asleep ten minutes or less when the occupants of the apartment above them arrived back home from a night out and proceeded to have a party. This went on for about an hour and when silence at last descended, Brenda checked her watch and saw that it was five-thirty am. Fuming, she shoved her head under the pillow and tried to go back to sleep.

They woke several hours later, heavy-headed and grumpy. 'Let's see what the place is like in daylight,' Brenda suggested, trying to inject some holiday spirit into the strained atmosphere. She felt a spark of excitement. She was looking forward to seeing the famous blue skies and sea of the Mediterranean. She flung open the dark green shutters. It was pouring rain!

Brenda couldn't believe her eyes. Great sheets of rain from low-hanging lead-grey clouds pounded the roads and buildings. The sea, across the road, was as grey as the skies. The beach was a dirty pallid brownish colour. To the west, behind low hills, deep rumbling peals of thunder accompanied spectacular sheets of purple-hued lightning. To think she'd spent a fortune to come to Spain and escape from the rain at home. Life surely was a bitch, she sighed in disgust.

'I think I'll go back to bed,' she told an equally crest-fallen Pamela. 'I'm knackered.'

'No don't,' Pamela said, tousle-haired and bleary-eyed from her bed on the floor. 'Let's be waiting for the courier in reception. We'll take our luggage with us. I'm not spending another minute in this hole.'

At this stage Brenda was too fed up to care. She dressed in the clothes she'd worn the previous day and, desperate for a pee, ventured gingerly into the bathroom. It was still there on the wall by the ventilator, its swivel eyes gazing malevolently at her. She went to the loo and shot out the door. She'd wash her teeth and have a shower in their new apartment.

The girls sat at a table in a small bar facing reception so that they could pounce on the courier the minute she arrived. They were hungry and the waiter assured them that 'The Big English Breakfast' was their speciality.

Twenty minutes later he triumphantly placed a platter each in front of them. Two stringy fatty rashers, a scut of a sausage, a watery fried egg and a spoonful of beans on a slice of toast comprised 'The Big English Breakfast.'

Pamela met Brenda's disgusted gaze. '*Bon appétit*,' she said dryly as the waiter reappeared with two cups, from each of which dangled the string of a teabag.

By the time the courier eventually arrived, around half eleven, the pair of them were in such a temper they were ready to take the next flight home.

'If you could just spend one more day here, there'll be a studio available in Santa Lucia Apartments tomorrow.' She smiled pleasantly.

'No way!' Brenda exploded. 'We didn't book to stay here. These apartments are much cheaper than the ones in Santa Lucia,' she glared. 'Which, I might remind you, is what we paid for. You get us out of this kip or we're suing for our money back.'

'We've taken photographs of this place. We couldn't even use the bathroom because it was infested with dreadful insects and we'll use them as proof in the court case,' Pamela said coldly. The courier paled slightly.

'OK, OK, leave it with me. I'll make a phone call to Santa Lucia and see what they can do,' she said placatingly.

'Do that!' Brenda retorted. If that smarmy little git of a travel agent thought he was going to get away with ripping them off he had another think coming. He'd picked the wrong pair to tangle with. Brenda and Pamela weren't going to meekly accept what was dished out to them.

'That told her,' Brenda whispered to her cousin as they listened to the courier blathering away in Spanish. Five minutes later she came back to them.

'I've sorted it out,' she said briskly. 'They didn't have a studio available so they've put you in a four-bed apartment. You'll be beside your friends. I'll order a taxi for you and I'll follow behind on my scooter.'

'Thank you,' Brenda said politely. But when the courier went back to the phone she winked at Pamela and said gleefully, 'A four-bed apartment for just the two of us. It was worth a night in this hole. Don't let her see that we're pleased though, in case she decides to put us back in a studio if one becomes available during the week.'

The Santa Lucia Apartments were about a mile away and it was a far superior apartment block. The apartment was clean, if simply decorated, and it was much nicer having a separate bedroom. The bathroom housed no grotesque insects, and there were plenty of fluffy white towels and lots of loo paper. The other place had boasted no such luxuries.

'We may ask you to move tomorrow, when a studio becomes available.' The courier smiled ingratiatingly.

'We're not moving anywhere. Here we are and here we'll stay,' Brenda said firmly. 'I'm not spending my holidays packing and unpacking. We're not the tribes of Israel, you know. It's not our fault that your company overbooked. That's your problem, I'm afraid.'

'Fine, fine,' the courier said hastily. 'I'll leave you to your unpacking.'

'God, Brenda, I didn't realize you could be such a tough cookie,' giggled Pamela as they began to unpack their clothes.

'Me neither,' Brenda said ruefully. 'It was just I felt so mad. What with the rain and everything. Well we might as well be miserable in a bit of comfort. At least the girls are next door. It doesn't sound like they're up yet, the shutters aren't even open.'

'We'll just unpack, have a shower, and a cup of tea. They should be up by then,' Pamela suggested.

'I'm dying for a shower, I'm ponging,' Brenda remarked as she filled one of the drawers in the wardrobe with bikinis and T-shirts and hoped against hope that she'd get the opportunity to wear them.

That night, the six of them went out on the razzle. It was still raining, but they didn't care. They were going to have a good night and see what talent was about. After all, getting a tan wasn't the only reason one went on a foreign holiday, they assured each other, laughing as they climbed out of the taxi. If they couldn't have sun, they were definitely going to have fun.

Sitting at the bar, consuming Piña Coladas, they laughed and chatted and passed remarks on the talent. Predictably, Tara was the first to be asked to dance. She looked stunning in a pair of tight white jeans and a red boob-tube.

Eve, with her cascading auburn locks and striking green eyes, was next to go. Pamela soon followed. Brenda, Julia and Joan sat at the table sipping their drinks watching the others dance around the dance floor. I hope someone asks me, Brenda thought anxiously. It would be mortifying if all the others were asked to dance and she wasn't. Maybe going on holidays with three glamour pusses like Tara, Eve and Pamela wasn't such a good idea after all. She cast a glance at Julia. She was sipping her drink morosely. She was wearing a sundress which didn't really suit her. It squashed her breasts up and made her look dumpy and all that white freckled bare skin was not appealing. At least I look a bit better than that, Brenda comforted herself. She was wearing pale green Bermuda shorts and a loose white cotton top. If she'd had a tan, they would have looked much better on her. Mind, the teabag job she had done on her legs looked almost as good as a tan. Joan didn't look particularly happy either as she scanned the floor hoping she too would be asked to dance.

'Dance pleezze.' Brenda heard a foreign accent in the region of her left ear. Happily she turned to accept, but her smile faltered a little when she saw a small weedy man with a scraggy moustache in front of her. Just her luck, she thought glumly. Still, a dance was a dance was a dance. Better than being left a wallflower. She walked out with him on to the dance floor.

'*Sprechen Sie Deutsch?*' he asked her and she knew from the guttural sounds that it wasn't Spanish he was speaking.

'*Deutsch, Deutsch*,' he repeated.

'*Non comprende*,' Brenda answered, not sure whether she was speaking in French or Spanish.

'Irlande,' she added for good measure.

'Aha! Aha!' Her companion nodded knowledgeably. 'British.'

'No, no, Irlande, Irlande,' Brenda repeated. What did he mean British when she'd just told him she was from Ireland? Did he need a geography lesson as well?

'*Ich bin ein Deutscher.*' He beamed and she noted that the state of his teeth left a lot to be desired. Something clicked. *Deutsch*. Wasn't that German?

'German?' she asked brightly.

He nodded so enthusiastically she thought his head was going to fall off.

'*Ich bin ein Deutscher. Ich bin ein Deutscher.*'

Bully for you, she thought dejectedly. So much for meeting a Spanish hunk. He gabbled away as they danced. And then he pulled her closer and ran his hands over her hips.

'Stop that!' Brenda said crossly, removing his hands. Two minutes later he was trying the same trick. She gave him an elbow in the ribs and pulled away from him. 'Piss off, you dirty little man, don't think you're going to maul me,' she said angrily as the dance ended and she stalked back to their table.

'What a little skunk,' she growled to Julia and Joan. 'Talk about Russian fingers and Roman hands.' The music changed and the sound of Abba pulsated. 'Come on,' she ordered the other pair. 'Let's boogie.'

Brenda loved dancing. Once the music inspired her she was completely uninhibited and danced to enjoy herself. It had been one of the greatest bonds she'd had with Eddie. She danced under the swirling lights enjoying the beat and the atmosphere. When the next slow set came, reluctantly she left the floor. She could have danced for hours.

Tara was still dancing with her original partner. Pamela was dancing with someone different. Eve was at the table with Joan and Julia. 'Enjoying yourself?' She grinned at Brenda.

'Yeah, are you?' Brenda took a thirsty gulp of her San Miguel.

'It's a good disco, the talent's not great though. The Copa down the road is supposed to be good too, we could go down there later,' she suggested.

'Sure. Let's try everywhere,' Brenda agreed. The next minute the amorous German was beside her.

'Dance?'

'Piss off, you.' Brenda glowered. He got the message and turned to Julia.

'Dance?'

'No thank you,' Julia said primly. He cast a hopeful eye in Joan's direction.

'Get lost, Romeo,' Joan snorted. He slouched away to try his luck elsewhere.

'Come on, girls, let's try our luck in the Copa,' Eve laughed. Tara and Pamela said they were happy enough where they were. The rest of them headed off to sample the delights of the Copa.

They didn't get home until the early hours. Tara and Pamela were still out, so Brenda left the light on in the hallway and fell into bed. She was fairly squiffy, although not as smashed as Joan and Julia, who had had cocktail after cocktail. Brenda was glad she wasn't sharing a bedroom with the two of them. Julia had already puked and it was a sure thing that Joan would too. It had been a good night though, she thought drowsily, even if the weather was a disaster.

Brenda surfaced around half ten next morning. Pamela's bed hadn't been slept in. Where was she, Brenda wondered anxiously. Yawning, she strolled into the lounge and kitchenette area and flung back the curtains. Sunshine streamed in through the windows. The sky was the bluest she had ever seen. The azure waters of the Mediterranean glittered like crystal. Brenda's heart lifted as she gazed on the scene. This was more like it, she thought with satisfaction. How bright the sunlight was, it dazzled the eye. And the colours! She'd never seen a sky that blue. She wasn't going to hang around, she decided, she was going to get out there fast. But where the hell was Pamela?

A muffled groan caused her to spin around in the direction of the sofa. Who the hell was that? Brenda's eyes widened at the sight before her.

Chapter Forty-Four

'Oooh,' Brenda heard Pamela sigh. Mortified, she saw that her cousin was wrapped in the passionate embrace of a very tanned and very naked Spaniard. Brenda retreated hastily to the bedroom.

She was stunned, and, she had to admit to herself, more than a bit shocked. Pamela was doing a very steady line at home. News of an engagement would not have come as a surprise to the families. And here she was having a passionate fling with someone she'd met on her first night abroad.

Don't be such a hypocrite, she argued with herself. You've gone on the pill in case the same thing happens to you. What are you feeling so offended about? Yeah but Pam's almost engaged to Sean. If she was still going with Eddie there was no way she'd consider having a foreign fling. In fact she probably wouldn't even be on this holiday. It was a bit much that she couldn't even go into the kitchenette to make herself a cup of tea. Did Pamela expect her to just ignore the fact that they were having sex on the sofa and go about making her breakfast as if they weren't there? It was infuriating, to say the least. The sun was shining, the sea was begging her to swim in it, but her suntan lotions were in the small sideboard in the lounge and because of Don Juan out on the sofa, she was trapped in the bloody bedroom! Was anything going to go right on this holiday?

'I'm going out there,' she muttered furiously after twenty minutes. The unmistakable sound of creaks and grunts and sighs had died down. From behind her bedroom door she could hear the murmur of voices and then she heard the toilet door close. Maybe it was him. Maybe he'd leave after he'd been to the loo. He'd better!

Brenda heard the shower being turned on. The man, in heavily accented but good English, invited Pamela to join him. The bloody nerve of him. The unmitigated cheek, she sizzled indignantly. Did he think he owned the apartment? It wasn't fair! Brenda had paid the exact same amount as Pamela to share the apartment and now she couldn't even have a shower because some gigolo was in there. In high dudgeon, she pulled out drawers and slammed wardrobe doors shut as she gathered together her bikini and towel. By God she'd have it out with Miss Pamela later on. She collected her lotions and Harold Robbins novel from the lounge, walked out onto the balcony, and slammed the French doors behind her.

Julia was sitting on the adjoining balcony having a cup of tea. She was wearing dark sunglasses and was still in her nightdress. 'Morning, Bren. God, have I a hell of a hangover,' she groaned. I'm not surprised, you little plonker, Brenda thought crossly. She hadn't come on holidays to listen to Julia whingeing about her hangovers or to watch Pamela behaving like a tart.

'Do you think I could have a quick shower in your apartment? Ours is engaged.'

Julia arched an eyebrow. 'But there's only two of you, there's four of us,' she said, puzzled.

'Look, Julia, Pamela's in ours with some fella, they could be there for hours. The sun is shining and I want to go and sunbathe and I need a shower after being out on the town last night. It will only take five minutes,' she snapped.

'Oh! Sure!' Julia's eyes were out on stalks. 'Tara never came home at all, she phoned twenty minutes ago to say she'd met this hunk and stayed in his villa and he's taking her out in his speedboat today.'

'Lucky her,' Brenda said dryly. Pamela obviously wasn't the only one who'd scored last night. 'Eve's up at the pool already,' Julia volunteered.

'How's Joan?' Brenda inquired.

'Dead to the world. She puked all over the hall when we got in last night, at least I made it to the loo.' Julia rested her aching head on her palm. 'I'm never drinking again,' she proclaimed. 'If I came home like that after a night out Ma'd kick me out of the house, so I don't drink much at home. Last night was the first time I ever really got locked,' she confessed. 'I think I'll go back to bed for a while. I feel awful.'

'Some of those cocktails pack a mighty wallop, so go easy on them. And you shouldn't mix your drinks. You should try and drink lots of water before you go to bed, it helps prevent a hangover,' Brenda advised kindly. She wasn't going to make a pig of herself drinking. You could have hangovers at home, but you'd never get weather like this. Getting a great tan was high on Brenda's agenda.

Twenty minutes later, feeling much more refreshed, she was sipping strong coffee and eating soft crispy bread rolls and honey at an umbrella-shaded table by the pool. Her bad humour was somewhat soothed by the heat of the sun, the sapphire sea, and the rich purple-pink hues of the tumbling bougainvillaea. This was another world, and she wasn't going to let Pamela and her Don Juan upset her for another second. She finished her breakfast with relish and then walked over to the lounger beside Eve's. She gazed at her colleague in admiration. She looked every bit the sun-worshipper, stretched out on the lounger, with her limbs oiled and gleaming. She already had a light golden colour because she'd sunbathed every chance she got at home. Her emerald bikini displayed her slender figure to perfection.

Brenda pulled her stomach in. She was not in as good a shape as Eve, she thought enviously. The pill had added a few pounds and her waist, hips and thighs were not as firm as she'd like them to be. But she didn't look too bad in her black bikini, she assured herself, catching sight of a dumpling-shaped middle-aged woman who didn't seem to mind letting it all hang out. Briskly Brenda oiled the lily-white limbs that marked her out as a newcomer. By this time next week, all going well, she'd be lying back, tanned, watching the next batch of pale new arrivals.

It was a relaxing morning. She and Eve chatted or read or just lay with eyes closed enjoying the heat of the sun. By noon though, the sun became intense. And after a swim in the warm waters of the Mediterranean, both girls decided caution was the best policy. There was no point in getting scorched on the first day. They'd come out again later in the afternoon.

Brenda let herself into the apartment wondering if the lovers were still at it. The sofa had been tidied up, the sheets and pillows put away. She could see through the half-open bedroom door that Pamela was in bed and the room was in semi-darkness. Of Don Juan, there was no sign. Well that was something, she thought with satisfaction as she put on the kettle and peered in to the fridge to see what she could have for lunch. They had bought some provisions with them so she settled on cream crackers and cheese.

She was sitting in a shaded corner of the balcony reading her book and sipping a beer when Pamela made a sheepish appearance through the French doors.

'Hi,' she murmured. 'I suppose you think I'm a bit of a slut.'

You can say that again, Brenda gave a mental sniff. But the wrath she'd felt earlier had dissipated somewhat. She didn't want to get into a row with her cousin.

'It's none of my business, Pamela. You're on your holidays, you can do what you like. But I would like to be able to make myself a cup of tea in the mornings or go to the loo if I need to. I've paid my share for the apartment too,' she pointed out mildly.

'Well you didn't have to go haring off like you did, slamming doors and things. Antonio is not King Kong, you know,' Pamela said huffily.

'Look, Pamela, it was embarrassing for me to walk in on the two of you having it off. What did you expect me to do, prance around and ignore the pair of you huffing and puffing while I made myself a cup of tea? I was stuck in my room and then when I went to go and have a shower, he was in it. So I don't know what you're being so snippy about,' Brenda retorted.

'Oh come on, Brenda, I know what's wrong with you. You expect me to be ashamed and to behave as if I was in the wrong. Well I'm not bloody well going to. You're not my mother, and you're right, it is my business, so get lost.'

'Pamela!' Brenda was very taken aback by her cousin's defensive outburst. The last thing she wanted to do was to have a row on holidays.

'Well you just sound so bloody self-righteous and you make it sound so sleazy,' Pamela retorted hotly.

'Well I don't mean to. It was just a bit awkward, that's all,' Brenda muttered.

Pamela said nothing and walked back into the apartment. Brenda got up and followed her. 'Come on, let's have a cup of coffee out on the balcony. It's a humdinger of a day. I've been for a swim, it's gorgeous.' Pamela took the proffered olive branch eagerly.

'I'd love a cup of coffee, Bren, and I'm dying to go for a swim. I'll just slip into my bikini.'

Brenda made the coffee and carried it out to the table on the balcony, where she was joined a few minutes later by her cousin.

'Isn't this the life?' Pamela stretched contentedly. 'This time last week I was stuck in the office organizing a trip to Brussels for my boss, and after all my efforts, when I'd booked the flight, hotel and the rest of it, he turns around and cancels it. Well he can go to Timbuktu this week for all I care. I'm on my holidays for two whole weeks and I'm going to enjoy every second of it.' She cast a glance at Brenda. 'Do you think I'm awful for sleeping with Antonio last night?' There was a pleading in her tone that struck Brenda. Usually, her cousin was very self-assured.

'I thought you and Sean were on the verge of getting engaged. So I *was* a bit surprised,' Brenda murmured.

Pamela gave a sigh that came from her toes. 'We are, I mean we've talked about it.' She took a sip of her coffee and grimaced. 'I'm going to marry Sean, we're getting engaged when I go back home. That's why I came on this holiday. It's my last chance to have a bit of fun before all the saving and settling down. I love Sean, I do, Brenda, honest. But you know something?' She gazed earnestly at her cousin. 'I just wanted to do it with someone else. Just to see what it was like. Is that such a crime? I know girls who have slept with loads of blokes. Look at all the people who have affairs? I felt that while I was still un-engaged, so to speak, I could do it and no harm done. It was my little treat to myself before I become the perfect wife and mother. Sean will never know unless you tell him.'

'Of course I won't,' Brenda exclaimed.

'Thanks.' Pamela smiled. 'You're a pal.'

'What was it like then, this night of passion?' Brenda asked, intrigued.

'Oh, Bren, it was something else,' her cousin enthused, and then blushed.

Brenda laughed. 'Tell me about it. Is it true then that Latin men make great lovers?'

'Well I only have Sean to compare him to, but Antonio had a really sensual quality about him, if you know what I mean.' Brenda nodded.

'Last night, I decided for once in my life to give in to lust and forget about feeling guilty and just be guided by the needs and desires of my body. We've been brought up to think sex is something good girls don't enjoy. Well last night was an absolute pleasure for me and I'll never forget it. I think every woman should do what I've done at least once in her life as long as she takes care not to get pregnant,' Pamela declared. 'It was a celebration of my body and my femininity. I feel very sexy and sensual and desirable. I don't consider that I did something so terrible that God is going to punish me.'

'Of course you don't,' Brenda agreed. She could quite understand now Pamela's reasons for having her affair. It sounded like a very fulfilling and satisfying episode. To be honest, after listening to her cousin, she wouldn't mind having one herself, Brenda thought wryly.

The opportunity came several nights later. They all went dancing in one of the plush night-clubs on the glitzy mile of discos, clubs and hotels that made up Puerto Carlos. As usual, Brenda was boogying away, enjoying herself. As soon as the slow set started she made her way back to the table and was just about to sit down, when a dark-haired, good-looking man came up to her.

'Will you dance with me, Señorita?' He smiled at her, showing even white teeth. His voice was deep, accented and ultra-sexy. She could see Julia and Joan looking at her enviously. So far, they weren't having much luck with men.

'Thank you,' she smiled. He led her on to the dance floor. 'My name is Raul Suarez, and you?' He smiled into her eyes and she had to admit he was just gorgeous.

'Brenda Myles.'

'May I say, Miss Brenda Myles, you are a very very good dancer. I have been watching you, and now let us enjoy this dance, because I, too, love to dance.' He took her in his arms and expertly led her around the floor. He had a natural grace and rhythm. Brenda relaxed into the dance and began to enjoy it. Raul held her lightly against him and she could smell the warm masculine scent of him. He didn't maul or try to grope her, much to her relief. It seemed as though so many of the men she'd danced with these past few nights were just out for a cheap thrill. He was in his early thirties, she judged, and was well dressed and very well groomed. His ebony eyes were fringed by long jet-black lashes which matched the colour of his hair. His skin had an attractive olive tinge that gave him a faintly swarthy air. His mouth was firm and good-humoured. And, as her gaze rested on his lips, she wondered what it would be like to be kissed by him. For the first time since Eddie, she felt physically turned on by a man. It was a delicious sensation. She hadn't believed that she would ever want another man. In the last few years, there hadn't been one man who she'd have wanted to kiss, let alone sleep with. Except for those film stars of her fantasies that kept her company in the dark lonely nights. Now she knew *exactly* what Pamela was talking about when she'd described why she'd slept with, and was still sleeping with, Antonio.

No-one at home, not even Eddie, had ever looked at her the way Raul Suarez was looking at her this minute. His eyes, dark and desiring, made her feel deliciously wanton.

With difficulty she dragged her gaze away from his and turned her cheek slightly. He responded by resting his cheek against hers and murmuring in that heavenly voice, 'Dancing is one of the greatest pleasures on earth, don't you agree, Brenda?' He rolled the r in her name, making it sound exotic.

'Mmmm,' she sighed against his jawline and moved a little closer. His arms tightened around her and they smooched together, enjoying the carnality of the rhythm of their bodies and the soft music and the dim lights. Brenda could have danced close against this gorgeous sexy man all night. They danced to two more slow sets until the music changed and the sound of funky disco music broke their idyll. Reluctantly they drew away from each other.

'We must have champagne,' Raul decreed, clicking his fingers at a waiter. Wow! thought Brenda to herself, deeply impressed. If he could order champagne he must be loaded. 'Come, there are some nice seats further to the back, it is more private, we can talk.' He took her by the arm and led her to a small alcove which had several two-seater sofas. They sat on one and he turned to face her. 'So,' he smiled. 'Your name is Brenda, you dance divinely. That is all I know, tell me more.'

Brenda laughed and took the glass of bubbling champagne the waiter handed her. 'What do you want to know?'

'Everything.' He waved his hand expansively. She told him she was Irish and on two weeks' holidays. Brenda didn't mention that it was her first time abroad, she didn't want to appear gauche. She promoted herself to Bugs Bunny Powers's job, feeling that a punch card operator was not quite impressive enough. She told him that she shared an apartment with her cousin. Another little fib. But to say that she lived at home with her parents still would make her feel immature and girlish, and did not go with the woman-of-the-world impression she was trying to give him. He seemed impressed, listening attentively to her as she spoke.

Raul told Brenda that he owned a travel agency and lived alone in a villa further down the coast. He had travelled all over the world, but had never visited Ireland. 'Maybe,' he said, eyes twinkling devilishly, 'that is something I will rectify very soon.' Although she suspected that was the kind of line he used with every foreign female he chatted up, Brenda didn't care. He had charm, buckets of it, even if she knew that he was out for nothing more than a good time. Just as she was. He oozed charisma. No-one had ever bought her champagne before, no-one had ever danced with her like that before. Enjoy it, she told herself firmly as he refilled her glass.

'Would you like to go for a drive?' he asked, caressing the inside of her wrist lightly with his thumb.

'That would be nice,' she murmured, thinking of other places she'd like to have his thumb caress. Brenda knew the evening would end in much more than a drive. Raul was very obviously interested in her and she was flattered. That was why she'd gone on the pill. In case something like this happened. To hell with it, she thought, throwing caution to the winds. If Pamela could do it so could she. It had been so long since she'd had a man's arms around her and Raul was a fine thing.

'I'll just tell the girls I'm leaving,' she said, and liked the way he stood up politely as she left the table. Good manners were such a turn-on, she thought happily. Brenda hoped she was as much a feminist as anyone, but she could say truthfully that she loved it when a man walked on the outside, gave up his seat, or held a door open for her. It made her feel feminine and protected and special and if that was supposed to make her feel any less equal, well it just didn't.

Tara and Julia were at the table, Pamela was dancing with Antonio and Joan was dancing with a red-headed Corkman. 'That's a fine thing you got off with,' Tara approved. 'I wouldn't say no to him myself.'

'He bought me champagne. He owns a travel agency and he lives in a villa down the coast.' Brenda couldn't resist boasting. For all her fabulous looks and sophistication, Tara had only landed a bank clerk, albeit a very handsome bank clerk. He was up at the bar buying a round of drinks.

'Hot stuff,' Tara exclaimed with a hint of envy.

'He's only after one thing. You know that, Brenda,' Julia interjected disapprovingly.

'So am I,' Brenda drawled, irritated by the other girl's prim attitude. Julia was getting on all their nerves. It was clear that she wasn't really enjoying her holiday. She spent her time moaning about the heat, the food, the mosquitoes and anything else she could moan about. She never lost a chance to make a snide remark to Tara and Pamela about Spanish gigolos. No doubt after tonight Brenda would be included in her barbs.

Brenda knew that the other girl was feeling left out because she hadn't been asked to dance much, or hadn't got a date yet, so she tried to be extra nice to her. She always made sure to tell her she looked very well when they were going out at night, and shared make-up and perfume with her. She even lent her the baggy white cotton top that was the only thing she had that would fit the other girl. Julia latched on to her like a limpet and confided that she was disgusted with Joan, who'd turned out to be a right plonkie. Brenda tried to explain that Joan was on holidays and having a bit of fun and a good time, but Julia was having none of it. Joan had dropped even more in her estimation, Julia declared. At least Joan was making an effort to enjoy herself, Brenda was tempted to retort, but she restrained herself. There was no point in adding fuel to the fire. Julia was determined to be a wet blanket and disapprove of everything the others did. She was now looking at Brenda coldly. No doubt Brenda too had dropped in her colleague's estimation.

Tough, she thought as she saw Raul heading in her direction. 'See you later,' she said hastily. She didn't want Raul to get too near the stunning Tara.

'Have fun.' Tara grinned.

Julia ignored her.

'I will. 'Night, Julia,' she saluted the other girl.

''Night,' came the curt response.

She's only pea-green with jealousy, Brenda thought crossly. Why did she have to try and ruin everything with her prim and proper ways? Just because she couldn't get a man.

'Ready?' Raul inquired.

'Sure,' Brenda said brightly, putting all thoughts of censorious Julia out of her head.

'Good! There is a beautiful full moon tonight, I will bring you to a very romantic place. You will like it. I promise.' He smiled warmly at her. His expression sent a little shiver of excitement through her. He took her by the elbow and the light pressure of his firm fingers on her tanned skin was delightful. Her eyes widened when he opened the passenger door of a metallic grey BMW.

'This is gorgeous,' she breathed, sinking into the luxurious front seat.

'Yes, I think so too.' He laughed.

They drove through the gaudy, neon-lit, bustling town, with its rowdy happy revellers, down along the coast, past peaceful, slumbering villages, until they came to a small headland overlooking a moonlit bay. A primrose yellow moon cast dancing rippling reflections on the white-tipped indigo waters below. A thousand stars twinkled in ebony skies. The scent of jasmine was heavy on the warm night air. The sound of the crickets, and the surging beat of foaming waters breaking against the rocks, were all that broke the stillness of the night. It was the nearest to paradise Brenda had ever been.

A small track led to the beach. Expertly, Raul manoeuvred the car down along its narrow length. I bet he's done this a few times, Brenda thought. He brought the car to a stop, leaned across and opened the dashboard and took out a tape. 'We have our very own night-club under the firmament.' He smiled as the melodious seductive tones of Andy Williams singing *Moon River* wafted out of the stereo system. Raul got out and held open her door for her. 'Let's dance,' he suggested.

'Let's.' She smiled back happily, as she kicked off her shoes and took his outstretched hand.

He held her close, his body hard and lean against hers. It was wonderful having a man's arms around her. It was a delight to feel the firm plane of his jaw against hers as they danced cheek to cheek in the moonlight. When his hands slid down over her hips to mould her closer against him, Brenda did not protest. When he turned his head and lowered his mouth to hers, she raised hers eagerly for his kiss. It was a long, slow, languorous kiss, that went on and on. His hands caressed her, sliding sensuously over her body, slipping inside the material of her sundress to cup and fondle her breasts. Brenda arched herself against him as her body responded to his touch. With impatient fingers she unbuttoned his shirt and ran her fingers over the soft tangle of black hair which covered his chest and snaked down to a narrow line that disappeared inside the band of his trousers. Raul murmured husky endearments to her in Spanish. Gently he eased the material of her dress up her thighs and slid down her panties. Brenda didn't care, she wanted him to make love to her there and then. Feelings and desires that had lain dormant flamed into need and longing. To be needed and wanted and to need and want in return was all that she wished for at that moment. The joy of desiring someone other than Eddie was such a liberation for her. After all these years she was finally free of him. Ardently, Brenda returned Raul's kisses, all inhibitions swept away as she sought to arouse him as much as he was arousing her. His quickened breathing and the sensual movement of his body against her told her she was succeeding. She was just unbuckling his belt when the sound of a car's engine gave them pause. A moment later the headlights of a car lit up the track as it slowly made its descent to the beach. Raul cursed harshly in his own language as he drew away from Brenda.

'This place is getting too crowded. Let's go.' He scowled, took her hand and led her back to the car. Brenda gave a deep disappointed sigh. Raul tenderly kissed her on the lips. 'Soon,' he whispered huskily. 'Soon.' He reversed the car and headed back up the track and out onto the narrow road that led to the main road.

'Are we going to your villa?' Brenda asked, stroking his tanned forearm as he drove the powerful car at speed along the highway.

'Aah . . . no,' he said quickly. 'My mother is staying for a few days, and you know what mothers are?' He smiled. 'They think you have never grown up.' Brenda nodded, although she was rather disappointed. She'd been hoping to spend the night with him at his villa. It was probably very luxurious and most likely had a pool as well. But she could understand why he wouldn't bring her home if his mother was there. Spanish mothers went in for chaperons and the likes for their daughters, so Señora Suarez might not look too kindly on a strange young woman spending the night with her son.

'Where are we going?'

Raul turned to look at her and let his hand slide up along her inner thigh.

'I thought we might go back to my office. It is quiet and private and I have a room there where I relax when we close for siesta.'

'Sounds nice,' she breathed. His touch was sending quivers of pleasure through her and she wished they were at the office already.

'Will I put in another tape?' Brenda suggested.

'There's a Julio Iglesias one in the dash there, you might like it.' Raul flicked open the compartment for her and switched on the light. There were several tapes and she picked one out and studied it. It wasn't the Spanish crooner's cassette so she replaced it and selected another one. That wasn't the one either. She was reaching in towards the back when something glinting in the light caught her eye. Her heart sank and a wave of dismay washed over her as she pulled out a gold wedding ring and turned to confront the man at her side.

'You're married, Raul, aren't you?' she said quietly. 'All that rubbish about your mother staying at your villa is just a cock-and-bull story.'

'Come on, Brenda,' he said lightly. 'What difference does it make? You'll be gone in a week or so, it's not as if we're going to have a long committed relationship. We are ships that pass in the night, as they say. There is no harm in having one night of pleasure and it will be very pleasurable, believe me,' he urged persuasively, his hand sliding even further up her thigh.

For a moment she was tempted to think as he did. After her holidays she'd never see him again. She might never in her life again meet a man as sexy and hand-some as Raul. An image of Julia's disapproving face popped into her mind. Bad enough that Brenda was going to spend the night with a man she'd only met that evening, but a *married* man. Julia'd look down her aquiline nose at her for ever and a day if she knew about this. Not that she'd ever know. Not that anyone need ever know, Brenda argued with herself. You'd know! she thought glumly. Why the hell had she suggested putting on another cassette? She could still be sitting in blissful ignorance of Raul's marital status. Brenda gave a huge sigh and slumped back in her seat. The evening was ruined. Even if she did go with Raul and make love with him, she'd feel as guilty as anything.

'Take me home, Raul,' she said dispiritedly. He turned a seductive gaze upon her.

'You don't mean that,' he said huskily, pulling in and cutting the engine. He gave her a deep sensual kiss. She tried to enjoy it as she had before, but she couldn't.

'Just bring me home,' she said quietly, pushing him away.

'What a pity,' Raul drawled. 'It would have been a great night.'

'Maybe, maybe not.' She smiled ruefully. 'We'll never know.'

It could have been such a great night, Brenda thought as the Aer Lingus 737 lifted off the runway at Malaga Airport and soared into the sky. She peered down at the lights twinkling beneath them. Somewhere down there was the little bay where she'd spent the most hot, sensual moments of her life. It had never even been like that with Eddie. She'd been too scared of getting pregnant. Too desperate for him to marry her. With Raul, there'd been none of that. It had just been lusty pleasure with no commitment or responsibilities, until she'd discovered he was married. If only she'd been able to ignore that. But she couldn't. She wasn't that sophisticated, she thought regretfully. Would she ever experience moments like that again? God I hope so, Brenda thought fervently as the plane banked and headed north.

'Kathy, he was the most gorgeous hunk. I'm telling you.' Brenda sighed.

'He sounds it.' Her friend grinned. They were sitting in the Autobahn pub having a drink and Brenda was telling Kathy all about her holidays.

'Brenda, you look a million dollars,' Kathy declared. 'I feel such a frump beside you.' She patted the large bump that meant she could no longer even see her toes. Kathy was eight months pregnant and wished it was all over.

'Imagine me in a bikini.' She giggled. 'You wouldn't have stood a chance with your Raul if he'd seen me first.'

Brenda laughed. 'It was great for my ego I can tell you, especially since Tara and Eve were on the scene. I really enjoyed that holiday. I feel I'm ready for anything.'

'Great stuff,' Kathy approved. 'Who knows, you might meet a Raul out in Tamango's some night.'

'Let's hope he's not bloody well married,' Brenda snorted.

'Speaking of being married,' Kathy murmured. 'Guess who got engaged last week?'

'Who?' Brenda was agog. There hadn't been any engagements in the offing that she knew of. Kathy was looking at her a little strangely.

'Um . . . well.'

'Who, Kathy?' Brenda said sharply. She was beginning to feel a little disquiet.

Kathy took a deep breath. 'It's Eddie . . . He and Anna announced their engagement last Saturday on her birthday. They're getting married next June.'

Chapter Forty-Five

'The goddamn fucker!' Brenda burst out. 'He's getting *married*! I don't believe it. What about all that crap he gave me about wanting his freedom to do things? To go places, for God's sake!' She was furious. She felt like thumping the daylights out of Eddie Fagan. She wanted to kick him in the balls, poke his eyes out, pull his hair out in great big chunks and just tell him exactly what she thought of him. And to think she'd thought she was over him. What a laugh.

'I know, I know, but that was over four years ago,' Kathy said placatingly.

'Yeah. But what's he done? Where's he gone? Shag all. Shag anywhere. The bastard.' A thought struck her. 'She's not pregnant, is she?' Her tone was faintly hopeful. Maybe they *had* to get married.

'No, no, nothing like that.' Kathy shook her head.

'So he's doing it because he's madly in love with her and he wants to. Huh!' snorted Brenda. 'Well I hope he and Miss Fat-Arse live unhappily ever after for the rest of their miserable lives.'

'Brenda!' Kathy tried to look disapproving but she couldn't help laughing.

'Well she is a fat arse.' Brenda grimaced. 'And now I'm dead sorry I didn't sleep with Raul. I can tell you one thing, he'd have wiped the floor as a lover with that shithead Fagan!'

'Come on, Brenda, stop that now,' Kathy said firmly. 'You're not still in love with Eddie. You only think you are. And you're just annoyed that Eddie's getting married. If this Raul guy hadn't been married and he'd decided you were the woman for him, I bet you would have fallen for him. Am I right?' Kathy demanded.

'Don't be ridiculous.' Brenda scowled. Although privately she conceded that Kathy had a point.

'I'm not being ridiculous. I'm being objective,' Kathy retorted.

'Oh is that what it is?' Brenda said sarcastically. 'How do you know whether I'm over Eddie Fagan or not?'

'Well if you're not, you should be. You're a fool if you're still carrying a torch for him. He's not carrying one for you, Brenda. Why are you wasting your life? You should be out there having a ball.'

'I don't want to have a ball,' Brenda said forlornly. 'You're married. Pamela's going to get married. Eddie and Anna are getting married. I just want to be married like everybody else.'

Chapter Forty-Six

'I don't want you to go, Ronan,' Jennifer sobbed, burying her head against her boyfriend's shoulder.

'I have to go, Jennifer, it's the only way I'm going to earn good money. And I want to have my own money. Especially now that Mam's gone. I'll be home in September. I don't want to leave you either. I just have to go, that's all,' he said miserably. They held each other tightly as passengers flocked around them to pass through the boarding gate for the transatlantic flight to New York. Once more, his flight number was called.

'I'd better go, Jen, I'll phone, and I'll write as soon as I've settled,' Ronan pulled away from her. And then he pulled her back into his arms and kissed her and Jennifer could taste the salt of a tear on his lips. His shoulders were thin and bony under her touch. He'd lost weight since his mother died. The thought of him going off to America alone and knowing no-one there nearly broke her heart.

She watched him go. He turned once, to wave, and then he disappeared around the curve of the duty-free and she burst into tears. Gulping and hiccuping into her hanky, she struggled for control. Making a show of herself wasn't going to help anyone, especially Ronan. She blew her nose and headed in the direction of the coffee bar. She didn't feel like going home just yet. When Jennifer was feeling miserable she liked to be on her own. Unlike Brenda, who loved to share her woes with the world.

She bought herself a cup of coffee and sat at a table overlooking the apron. Planes taxied to and fro. She could see the enormous jumbo jet Ronan would soon be flying across the Atlantic in, fuelling up. She felt so sorry for him. He'd gone through a very rough time in the last couple of months. His mother's sudden death had been a terrible shock. She, Paula and Beth had gone to the funeral. It had been desperately sad. His poor sister Rachel had been hysterical. Ronan introduced Jennifer to her, but the poor girl was far too shocked to make much of a response. She'd met the father too. She hadn't liked him. He was very curt. Jennifer knew he was probably in shock and that was understandable, but the cold angry look he'd directed at Ronan when he'd introduced Jennifer to him chilled her. She said how sorry she was for his trouble and made to shake hands but Mr Stapleton ignored her. He told Ronan in a very sharp voice that this wasn't the time or place to be standing chatting to girls and to kindly get on home to greet the callers to the house. Poor Ronan was disgusted but Jennifer told him not to worry. She understood that his father was upset, she assured him, and anyway, she whispered, she and the girls had just come to the funeral to offer their sympathies.

'But you can't go home without a cup of tea. It's a horrible day and you got drenched at the graveside,' he protested.

'Don't worry about us, Ronan, we'll be fine.' Jennifer wanted to put her arms around him and hug him but, of course, she couldn't do a thing like that with his father only a few yards away.

A week later Ronan met her in Emma's restaurant, their favourite haunt. Over coffee and a pizza, he told her that he was going to America despite his father's overwhelming opposition. William Stapleton was furious with his son.

'If I let him dictate to me over this I'll never be free of him. I've got to make my stand sometime. It might as well be now,' Ronan told her, and his voice was very firm.

Mr Stapleton had allowed his only son to fly off to America and he wouldn't even bring him to the airport. That shocked Jennifer. How could a father do that to a son? His sister Rachel should have defied her father and come to see him off. Family life could turn out to be the fiercest battlefield, Jennifer thought glumly as she drained her coffee. Ronan and his father were estranged. Look at Grandpa Myles and her aunt. They hadn't spoken to each other for years. He'd never seen his two granddaughters from that side of the family. And it looked as if he never would. All through bitterness and pride.

She'd never meet Ronan's mother now, she thought sadly. She'd sounded like a very nice gentle woman from the way Ronan spoke of her. It was hard to know how she could have married someone like his stern dominating father.

The big 747 started moving very slowly away from the terminal. Jennifer felt a lump come to her throat. Poor Ronan, she could imagine what he was feeling. Jennifer made a hasty exit. She couldn't bear to stay and watch the take-off. The airport was crammed, the holiday charter flights were taking off every ten minutes. Everybody seemed full of cheer and good spirits. But the airport seemed the saddest, loneliest place in the world to her at that moment.

An hour and a half later, Jennifer let herself in through the front door. She'd been waiting ages for buses.

'Jenny! Is that you?' she heard her mother call over the banisters.

'Yeah, it's me,' she called back. Kit came down the stairs.

'How did it go? Your father wouldn't have minded giving Ronan a lift, you know that, don't you?' her mother said gently, putting an arm around her shoulders.

'I know that, Mam.' Jennifer was very grateful. Her parents had been more than kind. They'd allowed Ronan to stay with them the night before. Her dad had offered to give him a lift to the airport but Ronan had politely refused the offer. He wanted to go away with as little fuss as possible. Jennifer felt that her father's presence at the airport would only have underlined the contemptible behaviour of Mr Stapleton.

'There was a phone call for you while you were out,' Kit said, her eyes twinkling. 'I think it might cheer you up.'

'Who was it?' Jennifer didn't feel anything would cheer her up. Unless it was a call from Ronan to say he'd changed his mind and had got off the plane before it took off.

'Sister Bartholomew.'

'Barty!' Jennifer was horrified. She was finished with St Theresa's. She'd never heard of Barty phoning anyone at home before.

'What did she want?'

'Mother Andrew wants to see you this afternoon.' Kit smiled at her daughter's dismay.

'What!!' she shrieked. 'Holy Divinity, what have I done to deserve this? What does she want to see me for? Did she tell you?'

'Look, Jennifer, go and see the woman. Listen to what she has to say and come home and tell me,' her mother insisted firmly.

'Couldn't you have said that I was away or something?' Jennifer moaned.

'Jennifer, go!' Kit ordered.

The school looked very empty as she ran up the steps and rang the doorbell. It was strange not to see hordes of girls chatting and laughing and bustling to and fro. The last time she'd been here was to do her Leaving Certificate exam a few weeks ago. She hadn't expected to be back so soon, she thought wryly as she pressed the doorbell again. A young maid answered the door. Having ascertained Jennifer's business, she ushered her into a small side parlour.

Waiting in the quiet, old-fashioned room, Jennifer inhaled the familiar scent of wax polish. It was a smell she always associated with school. The parquet floor shone, polished to within an inch of its life. The antique sideboard and bookcases hadn't a speck of dust. Jennifer started to feel nervous. This is ridiculous, she told herself. But she just couldn't help it. The urge to run was getting stronger by the second. The eerie stillness of the school was broken only by the muffled sound of a bell ringing in the convent.

As silently as she had left, the young girl reappeared. 'Mother Andrew will see you now,' she said softly. Jennifer followed her down St Anthony's corridor until they came to a big oak door. Jennifer's eyes widened. That was the door that led to the convent. None of the pupils had been allowed to enter it. Once, Miriam Brennan had gone through it for a dare, while the rest of them waited, giddy with excitement, to find out all about what it was like in the Holy of Holies. Unfortunately Miriam had managed to penetrate only a few feet into the citadel before she was rumbled. The escapade had caused uproar and been the talk of the school. Miriam was suspended from school for a week and the entire school were warned at Friday assembly that any other girl caught repeating the act would be expelled.

In spite of herself, Jennifer felt a spark of excitement as she walked through the door that the maid held open for her. She found herself in a long hallway painted in a warm shade of peach. Arched windows overlooked the nuns' rose-filled garden. Vases of flowers stood on the windowsills, their fragrances intermingling with the whiff of polish. A huge statue of St Theresa, the Little Flower, for whom the school was named, rested on a white lace-covered altar. A votive lamp burned steadily beneath it. Exuberant sprays of gladioli made a dramatic display. Somewhere, Jennifer could hear the sound of laughter. The calmness and serenity about the place was very soothing. It was not at all what she'd expected. It was lovely. White doors lined one side of the corridor. The maid paused outside one of them and gave a gentle knock. Jennifer heard Mother Andrew bid them enter.

She was standing facing the door in a pretty primrose-coloured sitting-room. Sun streamed through the window. The furniture was simple and modern. Two chintz-covered armchairs were separated by a small coffee table which was set with a tray containing delicate china, a pot of tea, a plate of paper-thin ham and cucumber sandwiches, a plate of fresh scones lavishly topped with jam and cream and a plate of rich fruitcake.

'Jennifer, dear, thank you for coming. Please, sit down and have tea with me.'

'Thank you, Mother,' Jennifer murmured as the head-mistress poured a cup of tea and handed it to her.

'Now dear, eat up. So I won't feel guilty at tucking in myself. Watching one's weight is such a scourge, isn't it?' Mother Andrew's eyes sparkled. Jennifer laughed. Funny how she'd never noticed the laughter lines around Mother Andrew's eyes. Today, in the pretty sitting-room, she seemed so . . . so human. Not the austere, humourless figure known as 'The Head.' The pupils had had little communication with their head nun, unless, as in Paula's case, they were in trouble. She was a distant fear-inducing figure, far removed from their orbit. It was strange to think of her as an affable, slightly plump middle-aged woman who liked scones dripping with jam and cream. It was a most pleasant surprise.

'Did your mother tell you what I wanted to talk to you about?' Mother Andrew inquired, holding out the plate of sandwiches. Jennifer took one and shook her head.

'Take a few, dear, they're very small, one bite and they're gone,' the nun urged. They were delicious, Jennifer decided. She was rather hungry, come to think of it. She hadn't eaten much breakfast and she'd missed lunch. She ate another sandwich with relish.

'I have a proposition to put to you, Jennifer,' Mother Andrew declared, patting the side of her mouth with a linen napkin. 'I've thought long and hard about who would be most suitable for my requirements. And you, my dear, are the perfect candidate. I do hope you'll agree to what I have in mind.'

Jennifer sat with sandwich poised in mid-air.

'Jennifer,' she heard Mother Andrew ask. 'How would you like to travel?'

Chapter Forty-Seven

'Pardon, Mother?' Jennifer wasn't sure if she'd heard right.

'I said, how would you like to travel?' Mother Andrew smiled. 'Let me explain. My niece is married to a wealthy businessman. She has two young children. They have the loan of a villa in Spain for two months. She is looking for an au pair. Someone who can speak Spanish, and someone who would be good with children. Her own girl has left her in the lurch, and she needs someone in two weeks' time. She asked me if I could recommend someone.' Mother Andrew paused and looked Jennifer straight in the eye. 'She wants someone reliable and trustworthy and with a sense of responsibility. I think you fit the bill in every way.'

'Oh!' Jennifer was stunned. 'Paula can speak better Spanish than I can,' she blurted out, saying the first thing that came to mind.

Mother Andrew's eyes grew cold. 'Perhaps, but Miss Matthews is a bit too fond of the boys. I couldn't possibly recommend her.'

You idiot! Jennifer cursed herself. What was wrong with her? Here she was, being offered the chance of a lifetime and she'd just recommended Paula for the job. She needed her head examined.

'Am I to take it you wouldn't be interested in the position?' Mother Andrew raised an eyebrow and studied Jennifer intently.

'Oh, I would. Certainly I would,' Jennifer said hastily. This was one time in her life when she couldn't dither. If she didn't take the job there'd be plenty more who would.

Paula would jump at it. Being an au pair in Spain for the summer was a far more exotic prospect than working in a hotel in Waterford. Mother Andrew relaxed. 'Splendid,' she beamed, taking a bite out of a scone with relish. 'It will give you an excellent opportunity to improve your Spanish as well as broadening your horizons. It's very interesting to study another culture. We can be a little bit insular on this small island of ours. There's a whole big world out there, Jennifer. Before I became headmistress of St Theresa's I worked in our convents in Africa and Latin America. They were the best times of my life.' Mother Andrew's deep-set blue eyes had a faraway look in them before she remembered herself.

'Now,' she said briskly. 'Your mother has no objections, nor does she think your father will have any. So I can tell my niece I've found the perfect au pair and give her your phone number? You can make your own arrangements with her from there.'

'Thank you, Mother,' Jennifer said. 'And thank you very much for recommending me for the job. I'm very grateful.'

'Just do a good job, dear. Enjoy yourself. And always remember you're a St Theresa's girl!' the headmistress replied.

Twenty minutes later, Jennifer was walking down the steps of the school, still in a daze. In two weeks' time, if Mrs Curtis approved of her, she was going to be on her way to the Balearic island of Majorca, to spend the summer in a luxury villa. It was like a dream.

This had been a day of such contrast, she mused. Misery at the airport this morning. Huge excitement and anticipation this afternoon. She'd been due to start holiday work in the jam factory the week after next. It was a relief not to have to do that for the rest of the summer. Going to Majorca and spending the rest of the summer in the sun would be a great way to pass the time until she got her exam results and could start looking for a job.

Jennifer remembered something. She had arranged to

430

spend a week in St Margaret's Bay with Paula. That would have to go by the wayside. Maybe she'd go for a weekend, but she'd never fit in a week. She'd have a lot to do. She'd need a passport and pesetas and some suitable clothes. She'd need suntan creams and moisturizers. Excitement bubbled. Calm down, she told herself. She had to do her interview first to see if Mrs Curtis liked her. Jennifer very much hoped she would.

'Aunt Josie tells me you have good Spanish and are most reliable.' Gillian Curtis ran long fingers through her highlighted ash blond hair and took a long drag on a slim white menthol cigarette.

'Aunt Josie?' For a moment Jennifer was thrown. 'Oh, you mean Mother Andrew.' She laughed. It was strange to think of her headmistress as 'Aunt Josie.' 'Well, I took honours Spanish in my exam. It's my favourite subject,' Jennifer explained.

'I haven't a clue about Spanish, so you'd have to do all the talking. Do you think you'd be able for it? The villa has its own housekeeper, but I don't think her English is great.' Mrs Curtis looked at Jennifer with big limpid blue eyes. She gave Jennifer the impression of being a dumb blonde type. She was in her mid-thirties, Jennifer judged, and exceedingly glamorous and sophisticated.

They were in her sitting-room, in a huge house over-looking the sea in Sandycove. Two children, a boy of six and a girl of three, were squabbling on the seat of the bay window.

'Gavin! Emma! Please! Stop it now, Mummy's getting very annoyed.' Gillian gave an exasperated sigh and threw her eyes up to heaven. 'They usually aren't this naughty.'

'I want to colour Winnie the Pooh, Mummy, an' he's taking my crayons,' whined the little girl, a dainty replica of her mother.

'Shut your gob, they're *my* crayons,' the little boy retorted crossly.

'*Gavin*!' Mrs Curtis was horrified. 'Darling, how can you be so naughty in front of Miss Myles? She won't want to come and work for us.'

'Don't want her to come an' work for us. I want Liz to come back an' mind us,' he said sulkily.

'Darling.' Mrs Curtis gave another of her dramatic sighs. 'Liz left us to go and work for Angie Baldwin.' She turned to Jennifer. 'I thought Angie was a good friend of mine, and what did the bitch do only pinch my au pair. I was devastated. *Devastated*. I'd expect your complete loyalty,' she declared.

'Of course, Mrs Curtis,' Jennifer murmured.

'Oh my gawd, don't call me Mrs, it makes me feel so *old*. You must call me Gillian.' The other woman gave a little shriek and a giggle.

'Gillian,' Jennifer amended.

'Mummy, he's doing it again,' Emma bawled. Gillian looked helplessly at Jennifer.

'What would you do with them? It was outrageous of Angie filching Liz like that.'

Jennifer took a deep breath. It was obvious action was required. Gillian didn't seem to have much control over her children.

'Can I have a look at your crayons?' Jennifer stood up and walked over to the window seat, where the children were pushing and shoving each other. She sat on the seat between them and picked up the huge box of crayons.

'There's millions of crayons here,' she said lightly. 'Why don't we divide them up exactly so that you both have the same?'

Gavin eyed her warily. 'Don't want to,' he muttered.

'Oh come on, you're a big boy and big boys always share with their little sisters,' she wheedled. 'Can you swim?' she asked, diverting his attention as she began to divide up the crayons.

'No,' he said sulkily.

'Your mammy. Your mummy,' she corrected herself, 'tells me there's a swimming-pool in the villa. If you're a good boy and I come to work for Mummy, I'll teach you to swim,' she promised.

'Will you teach me to snorkel?' he asked excitedly.

'If you're good.' Jennifer smiled.

'Here, she can have 'em all. I'm going to play with my train set,' Gavin announced. 'As soon as we get there, will you teach me?' he demanded.

'It depends on how good you've been. Mummy will tell me, but I'm sure a big boy like you is going to be very good.'

'I like you. What's your name?' He came and stood in front of her, his brown eyes studying her intently.

'My name's Jennifer, Gavin. How do you do?' She held out her hand.

He looked at his mother, who was sitting looking at the three of them in amazement. 'Shake hands, darling,' she murmured. He placed a small hand in Jennifer's and gave a little shake.

'I'm going to play with my train set now,' he said and marched out the door.

'Will you teach me to swim too?' Emma demanded petulantly.

'If you're a good girl,' Jennifer said firmly. It was clear to see that both children were extremely spoilt and in need of some firm but kind discipline. If she took on this job she certainly wasn't going to stand for any nonsense from them, she decided.

'Jennifer, sweetheart, could you start immediately?' Gillian gushed.

'You lucky sucker, I can't believe it. God, I'd give my eye-teeth for a job like that,' Paula exclaimed when she heard about Jennifer's new job.

'The only trouble is, I won't be able to stay with you for a week,' Jennifer apologized.

'Ah Jen,' Paula shrieked down the line. 'You've got to come down. It's the only thing that's keeping me going. This place is as dead as a dodo. I arranged to have this week's two days off added on to next week's so I'd have four days to entertain you. You can't let me down.'

'Sorry, Paula, I've got to arrange to get my passport and some currency and clothes and the rest of my bits and pieces. I'll come for the weekend,' Jennifer said firmly. She knew Paula of old. Her friend would wheedle and badger until she got her own way. It just wasn't possible unfortunately.

'I'll be on the six pm train, Friday night. See you then.' Jennifer's tone was crisp.

'Oh! OK then,' Paula said and hung up with bad grace.

'You have all the luck,' Brenda declared when she heard Jennifer's news. 'Two months doing nothing in Spain. You know you get away with murder! If I'd been asked to be an au pair when I left school there's no way Ma and Da would have allowed me to go,' she said enviously.

'I won't be doing *nothing*, Brenda,' Jennifer said in exasperation. 'I'll be looking after two spoilt little brats. And I'm sure if you'd been given the chance Mam and Dad wouldn't have stood in your way,' Jennifer declared huffily.

'Are you kidding?' Brenda snorted. 'Dad would have had a fit if he'd known I was going to the Dandelion. Never mind Spain.'

'Oh you're always the same, Brenda. You're such a begrudger. Couldn't you be pleased something nice has happened to me? Just for once?' Jennifer snapped. Her bubble of excitement was beginning to dissolve. Paula and Brenda had been less than enthusiastic for her. Maybe she was making a mistake. Maybe going to Spain as an au pair was not a good idea. The kids, on first acquaintance, were certainly not endearing. Gillian, although she was pleasant in a scatterbrained sort of a way, seemed to run a household that bordered on the chaotic. Maybe she should ring her up and say she'd changed her mind.

* * *

434

'You'll do no such thing, Jennifer Myles. You get your ass out to Spain if I have to kick it every step of the way!' Beth exclaimed when Jennifer confided her doubts that evening, as they sat waiting for a free tennis-court in Johnstown Park. Jennifer laughed.

'Thanks, Beth. You're a pal.'

'You should know Brenda by now, you're mad to let her get under your skin. And as for Paula . . . ' Beth shook her head. 'I'd say she's disappointed you're not going down for the week. She might be thinking that if it wasn't for slyboots McNally taking that photo of her and Barry, it might have been she who was asked.' Beth bounced the ball up and down on her racket. 'That could be the way she's thinking. I don't know. She's a great friend and all. But you know Paula, she likes to be number one.'

'Yeah, I know that.' Jennifer sighed. 'That was an awful thing Eilis did. Imagine being that jealous of someone? Imagine being so vindictive? Still, Paula could have pretended to be pleased for me. I would have, if it was the other way around.'

'I'm sure she'll be delighted for you when you go down there Friday night,' Beth said reassuringly. 'Come on, there's our court. Let's pretend the ball is fish-face McNally and whack the daylights out of it.'

'I can't believe I won't see you for two whole months.' Paula sighed. 'I really envy you, Jenny. I'm delighted for you. Honest. But I envy you too. And that's the truth.' They were undressing for bed in Paula's bedroom in St Margaret's Bay. Jennifer was sleeping in Rebecca's bed. Rebecca was spending the night with a friend.

'Maybe you could come out for a week and stay in a bed and breakfast place or something,' Jennifer suggested.

Paula's eyes lit up. 'I never thought of that. Maybe Helen could get me a cheap flight over. It would give me something to look forward to. This place is driving me mad.'

'I think you've a lovely home and your parents are

435

dotes.' Jennifer unhooked her bra and slipped her nightdress over her head. She was dying to get into the quilt-covered bed. She'd slept in it a few times before. It was the most comfortable bed she had ever slept in. It had an old-fashioned bolster topped by big soft duck-down pillows and getting into it was like snuggling into a cocoon. It was lashing rain. The train had broken down and been delayed for over an hour and a half. It had been freezing cold, despite the fact that it was supposed to be summer. Paula insisted they go for a drink when Jennifer finally reached St Margaret's Bay. They'd got drenched on the short walk home from the pub and all Jennifer wanted to do was to sleep. But Paula wanted to have her moan.

'No, I don't mean Mum and Dad are driving me mad. Of course not,' Paula said hastily. 'Or even home. I just mean the thought of spending the summer holidays working in the hotel is a bit of a drag. I know I'm in reception now and, believe me, it's a thousand times better than doing the rooms. I just feel terribly restless. I'd love to get away from everyone and everything for a while, like you.'

'I'll probably be mad homesick,' Jennifer retorted as she slipped in between the fresh crisp sheets and sank into bliss. She could hear the sea pounding the pier, the rain battered the small square windowpanes. It might be midsummer but it sounded like the middle of winter. This bedroom was made for weather like this, she thought approvingly as she gazed around at the old-fashioned pink floral wallpaper and the faded dusky-pink pelmeted curtains. The ceiling sloped down in the shape of the roof. Two small lamps cast a warm glow in the snug little room. She yawned, hoping against hope that Paula wasn't in the humour for a great long chat.

Paula echoed her yawn. 'I'm whacked,' she moaned. 'Thank God I don't have to get up in the morning. You'd better make the most of your lie-in. It might be the last one you'll get for a while. Those kids will probably be up at daybreak.'

'Mmmm,' Jennifer murmured. She was feeling much better in herself. Paula had been genuinely pleased to see her and, despite her declarations of envy, Jennifer knew she wished her well. It was a pity she couldn't come as well. That would have been the icing on the cake.

'Mind yourself, lass. Don't come back telling us you've a bun in the oven from some Spanish Casanova.' Grandpa Myles bestowed a final benediction on Jennifer just before she left for the airport. She didn't know whether to feel amused, exasperated or indignant at his remark. 'Goodbye, Grandpa, and mind yourself.' She bent and kissed his lined cheek.

'I'll miss you, lass, you're the only one who has any time for me,' he muttered and she was shocked to see a suspiciously bright glitter in his eyes.

'I'll write to you,' she promised. 'Every week.' He'd got old-looking. There were times when she could murder him but there were times when she couldn't help but be fond of him. She leaned down and hugged him tightly. *God bless and protect him, keep him in Your tender loving care, free from all harm and danger. Amen.* She blessed him silently with the old familiar prayer of her childhood.

'See ya,' she whispered and tried to swallow the apple-sized lump that had lodged in her throat. Mother of God, you'd think you were going to Australia for years. She chastised herself for her silliness as she hugged her younger brothers and followed her parents out to the car.

Kit kept up a stream of chat as they drove along the back road to the airport. They passed St Pappin's School and Church, now dwarfed by the high-rise towers of Ballymun. The farms of long ago swallowed up by flats and houses. The narrow winding country road now a wide dual carriageway.

Excitement entwined with loneliness as the control tower and terminal buildings of the airport came into sight. Jennifer smoothed out the telegram she had received from Ronan that morning and smiled at the message.

Have a ball! it said. Jennifer took a deep breath and sat up straight. That was precisely what she was going to do. 'Majorca here I come,' she announced, smiling at her mother.

Chapter Forty-Eight

'This is a nightmare.' Gillian lit up a cigarette and inhaled deeply.

'Mummy, I want to wee,' Emma whinged. Gillian looked helplessly at Jennifer.

'Could you?' she asked. 'And then could you see if you can get some trolleys?' They'd been waiting for their luggage for the past twenty minutes. Palma Airport was chaotic.

'Come on, Emma,' Jennifer said.

'Don't want you, want Mummy,' Emma pouted.

Come on, you little brat, Jennifer thought to herself. 'Mummy has to wait until the cases come out. Come on, let's go or we'll miss it. It's great fun when they all go around the black belt there. It's like a merry-go-round.'

That did the trick. The little girl took her hand and Jennifer battled her way through hordes of people standing around the various luggage carousels. She did her best to avoid the lucky ones who had luggage trolleys, which in some hands were lethal weapons as she found to her cost twice as her shins became victims of the mêlée.

'I like Liz better than you,' her young charge informed her as she presented Jennifer with a bare bum for her to wipe. Tough, Jennifer felt like saying as she did the necessary, I don't like you at all! But she restrained herself, admirably. She knew she was going to have to make the best of it, after what she'd had to put up with on the flight. 'We have to get to know each other,' she smiled as she pulled up the little girl's panties and straightened her dress. 'Now let's go and see if the luggage is arriving.'

By the time they'd pushed their way down to their

carousel, the luggage had indeed started to move and Gavin was sitting in the middle of the belt, much to his mother's consternation.

'Darling, get off, get off, quickly!'

'This is fun, Mummy,' her son shouted as he evaded her grasp. That woman is ridiculous, fumed Jennifer as she raced around the other side. A good slap on the arse or the threat of the wooden spoon would work wonders on that pair. Gillian didn't believe in corporal punishment. She liked to see children 'expressing' themselves. Reasoning was the best way to correct a child, she'd informed Jennifer during one of their chats when she explained what duties being her au pair entailed. It was clear that reasoning had no impact on Gavin as he pranced along the conveyor.

Jennifer plucked him off the carousel, much to his disgust. He immediately started a tantrum. 'You'd better stop that at once, Gavin,' Jennifer said sternly. 'Do you see that policeman over there with the gun in his holster, he'll drag you off and throw you in jail,' she added cruelly. It worked. Gavin was a coward at heart.

'Oh dear, I hope that won't give him nightmares,' Gillian murmured distractedly. 'I can't see any sign of our cases.'

'I'll go and get a trolley,' Jennifer suggested.

'I want to go too,' Gavin insisted.

'An' me,' Emma piped up. Gillian fluttered her limpid-eyed gaze at Jennifer.

'Would you be a darling and take them?'

'Certainly,' Jennifer said politely, feeling very tempted to sneak off into the middle of the crowds, and book herself a flight out of this hell as fast as she could. Two months as an au pair in Spain had sounded so glamorous. She hadn't even been on Spanish soil for an hour and it was beginning to feel like a nightmare.

She gripped the two children tightly by the hand, and battled her way through the charter flight crowds out to the exit of the arrivals hall. Dozens of couriers stood in the foyer, clipboards in hands, greeting their clients. The heat made her clothes stick to her. It would be nice to be a courier, she thought wistfully, as Emma fidgeted. It was a cloudy oppressive day, the humidity was very high. Jennifer felt as if she was breathing steam. She stood, pausing to review the situation. There hadn't been one free trolley in the terminal. Her best bet, she decided, was to follow someone who had one. She noted the taxis outside the building. They should have no trouble getting one when they finally collected their baggage. An elderly couple pushing a trolley began walking in the direction of a fleet of coaches to the far right of the terminal building. Perfect, thought Jennifer, I'll nab theirs when they're finished. They walked on . . . and on . . . and on, right down to the last coach. She breathed a sigh of relief when they finally drew to a halt.

'Come on. Quick!' she said to the children, who were dragging their footsteps.

She was almost there when a skinny little man wearing white shorts and a striped T-shirt stepped over to the couple and spoke to them, pointing at the trolley. They smiled and nodded and, much to Jennifer's frustration, handed over the precious trolley to him as soon as they'd unloaded their luggage onto the coach. Jennifer felt like crying. This was worse than the quest for the Holy Grail.

It was another fifteen minutes before she eventually laid hands on a luggage trolley. Gavin wanted to push it. Emma screamed and insisted she wanted to push it too. Jennifer solved the contretemps by plonking Emma in the front basket and making Gavin stand on the bars. She was perspiring as she pushed them back to the terminal. Gillian, surrounded by luggage, was gazing around anxiously, looking for them.

'Thank goodness, Jennifer. I was beginning to worry,' she said in her breathless little-girl voice. 'I wish Bryan was here to organize things, it's a bit much leaving me to bring two children to a foreign country.' Her tone was petulant, it reminded Jennifer of Emma.

'It took ages to get a trolley, but at least there's plenty of taxis outside so we shouldn't be here for much longer,' Jennifer assured her. She grabbed her own luggage, which was still revolving on the carousel, and then organized Gillian's on the trolley. She had to carry her own because there wasn't enough room. Ten minutes later, Jennifer had her charges settled in a taxi and they were on their way.

They were driving past the enormous yacht-filled marina of Palma when the clouds opened and a flash of lightning seared the sky. 'Oh my God!' shrieked Gillian. 'I'm absolutely petrified of thunder and lightning.'

You would be, Jennifer thought unsympathetically as Gillian gave dramatic little shrieks with each crash of thunder. Jennifer was beginning to realize that her employer was a very silly woman. She'd asked Jennifer three times if she was sure she'd given the taxi driver the right address. Then she wanted to stop to get some bottled water just in case there wasn't any in the villa. It was vital to get bottled water, she explained. She told Jennifer she must be absolutely scrupulous about making sure that the children didn't drink tap water.

Jennifer asked the taxi man to stop at the nearest supermarket while Gillian looked on in awe at her au pair's fluency. Jennifer was sure there'd be bottled water at the villa, but the way Gillian was going on she decided that the best thing to do was to humour her. No wonder Bryan, the husband, had skedaddled off to Brussels on business. He probably knew exactly what he was missing.

Half an hour later, looking out the car window through a torrent of water that the windscreen wipers were hardly able to cope with, Jennifer got her first blurry view of the villa as the taxi passed through black wrought-iron gates. They drove up a curved driveway to a whitewashed single-storey terracotta-roofed sprawling villa. Moments later the great oak front door opened and a small plump dark-haired woman dressed in a black dress and white apron stood smiling at them.

442

In a flurry of excitement Gillian and the children rushed out of the taxi into the villa, leaving Jennifer to deal with the luggage. She and the taxi man carried the bags in to the hall and Jennifer paid him from the wad of notes Gillian had given her.

'*Bienvenida, Señorita,*' the housekeeper greeted her, tutting and throwing her eyes up to heaven and gesticulating at the weather. '*Me llamo Conchita Fernandez.*'

'*Encantado de encontrarle. Me llamo Jennifer,*' Jennifer smiled.

'*¡Usted habla Español!*' the housekeeper exclaimed in delight and began to gabble away. Jennifer laughed.

'*Lentamente, lentamente.* Slowly, slowly,' she urged.

'Jennifer, Jennifer, isn't this superb?' Gillian appeared from the lounge, beaming.

'It looks nice,' Jennifer agreed, gazing around her at the huge parquet-floored hall decorated with old chests and an antique sideboard on which stood a glorious array of flowers.

'Nice! It's *gorgeous!*' Gillian enthused. 'Come on, let's explore.' The housekeeper led them on a tour of the rooms and Jennifer was deeply impressed. She had never seen such luxury in her life.

'Oh Conchita!' she exclaimed when she saw her own room with its *en suite* tiled bathroom. It was a beautiful room. White walls were offset by a selection of watercolour landscapes. Green shutters covered the window. The bed had a luxurious white candlewick bedspread dotted with peach and green cushions. A small desk, a bedside table and lamp, a wicker chair and a large oak wardrobe completed the furnishings. Beautiful rugs lay on the polished wood floors. This would be her haven, Jennifer thought happily as the peace was shattered by the sound of the children squabbling.

Time for bed, she decided as she reluctantly left her lovely room to see what the argument was about.

Two hours later Gavin and Emma were tucked up in bed sound asleep. Jennifer had given them their tea, read them a story and promised, if it was fine in the morning, that she would teach them to swim in the pool outside, which now rippled under the onslaught of wind and rain. Maybe it was wishful thinking, she mused as the thunder rumbled away. Gillian, exhausted by the traumas of the day and terrified by the thunderstorm, retired to her room, unable to eat the delicious supper that Conchita had prepared for them.

'I'm going to take a sleeper,' she told Jennifer. 'Be a darling and keep an ear out for the kids in case they wake up,' she murmured tremulously as another crash of thunder sent her scurrying to her bedroom.

Jennifer was delighted to be rid of the lot of them. She sat at the exquisitely set table with its sparkling glassware and cutlery and ate her chicken salad with relish. She could see a horseshoe of lights curving around the bay. Pine trees swayed outside the window, and small lanterns illuminated the grounds of the villa, revealing an immaculately manicured lawn and tubs of exotic coloured flowering shrubs.

Conchita's daughter, Estella, cleared away the dishes and Jennifer sat in happy solitude. She was pleased that she'd coped so well today. It was nice, she thought, to know that people depended on her. Gillian clearly expected her to take charge, and she had. Her Spanish had been more than sufficient for their requirements. Jennifer made up her mind to spend as much time as possible speaking Spanish with Conchita and Estella.

It was good to stand on her own two feet, she decided. At home, she had Brenda telling her what to do and Jennifer was inclined to let Paula make the decisions and be the leader. She was going to have to make decisions here. It was about time she grew up, she thought. After all, she was almost eighteen. It was time to start acting her age. Here, she was not the daughter, or granddaughter, not the younger sister or friend. Here, she was Jennifer Myles, Spanish-speaking au pair. In charge!

Invigorated, she began to write a long letter to Ronan.

Fifty dollars in tips. Not bad, thought Ronan, as he changed out of his green and gold bell boy's uniform and stood under the cold shower. It was sweltering in New York. He'd been working since six am in the Manhattan Tower Hotel. It was now almost seven-thirty and he had to be at work in the Dixie Southern Style restaurant by eight. He was earning good money. He was living in a small one-roomed bedsit in the Bronx with plenty of cockroaches for company, compared to which the digs in Phibsboro were a paradise.

Ronan didn't care, he was hardly ever there anyway. He was working all the hours God sent and when he did get home at night he went straight to bed and slept like a log. There was no point in spending money on a palace when he was never there and besides he was saving hard. He glanced at his watch. He wasn't sure what time it was in Spain, they were six or seven hours ahead of the US. Jennifer would be there by now. Probably fast asleep. He missed her very much. There was something about Jennifer that made him feel he had known her all his life. There was something kind and serene about her. Paula might be more sophisticated and glamorous, Beth more jolly and extrovert, but Jennifer touched a chord in him.

They had both agreed to go out on dates if they wanted to while they were parted for the summer. Ronan had taken a friendly Scots girl called Maggie to the pictures on a rare night off. But it was Jennifer he thought of last thing at night.

He had a five-page letter to her on the locker beside his bed. He would finish it tonight after work and post it in the hotel in the morning, Ronan decided as he dressed rapidly and headed off to catch the subway to work.

It had turned into a ten-page letter to Ronan. She told him about all that had happened on their journey to Majorca.

She'd told him about Gillian and her theatricals. About Emma and Gavin and how spoilt and badly behaved they were. She described her room. The view from her window, the sound of the crickets, the storm, it was as if he was sitting in the room beside her and she was telling him all about it.

When she was finished, she peeped in at the children. They were fast asleep. As was their mother, snoring resonantly, helped by the brandy and sleeping tablet she'd consumed. Satisfied that all her care had no need of her Jennifer had a quick bath before slipping beneath cool white sheets. She was asleep in minutes.

It rained solidly for five days. Gavin and Emma outdid themselves in boldness. Gillian left them completely in Jennifer's charge while she spent most of her time in bed or in the bath quaffing brandy, and reading Jackie Collins novels and *Cosmo*.

On the sixth day, Jennifer woke to sapphire skies and sun-drenched seas. It felt like being reborn, she thought with pleasure as she gazed at the colourful vista from her window. Gavin appeared in her bedroom, closely followed by Emma. Both were in their swimsuits.

'Can we go swimming now?' Gavin demanded. Jennifer felt sweet power surge through her.

'As soon as you've had breakfast and tidied your bedrooms,' she insisted. Usually, breakfast-time was a battleground. And getting them to tidy their bedrooms was a Herculean task.

'But I want to go swimming. NOW,' Gavin screeched.

'There'll be no swimming at all,' Jennifer scowled, 'until breakfast is over and beds are made.'

'Mummy will let us go swimming if we want to,' Emma scoffed.

'Your mummy doesn't know how to swim so she won't be able to teach you,' Jennifer said smugly, playing her trump card. 'And I won't teach bad children to swim, or,' she glared at Gavin, who was kicking the end of her bed in temper, 'snorkel . . .'

It was two very well-behaved children who finally sat down to breakfast, having tidied their rooms under Jennifer's gimlet eye.

'It's a miracle,' murmured Conchita.

Jennifer explained the reason for the personality changes.

'I'll pray for good weather every day,' laughed the housekeeper as she prepared a tray for Gillian, or the 'Sleeping Beauty' as she privately called her. Jennifer liked Conchita and Estella. They were good-natured and good-humoured. Kindly correcting her when she made mistakes in her Spanish.

'Can we go now?' Gavin asked, shovelling the last of his cornflakes down his throat.

'Remember I told you, you have to wait for an hour after eating before you go swimming. It's very dangerous to go swimming immediately, you could get cramp and drown,' Jennifer explained. Gavin looked crestfallen. Sometimes she felt sorry for the children in spite of herself. It wasn't their fault that they were spoilt rotten because Gillian always gave in to them. 'Let's go for a walk down town, and if you're good you can buy something with your pocket money, and then we can swim when we get back,' she proposed.

Squeals of delight followed this suggestion. Twenty minutes later the trio were heading down the circular drive towards the small town of Santa Juan. It was incredible how different the place was when the sun was shining, Jennifer thought, gazing around in delight at the glorious vibrant Mediterranean colours. In the near distance, just below them, Santa Juan curved in a U-shape to embrace the glittering blue waters flowing between the two wide verdant headlands. Villas and small blocks of residential apartments dotted the landscape, perched amidst the pines. There were also several modern apartment buildings and evidence of new building sites. The tourist trail was catching up with Santa Juan, Jennifer reflected.

Gavin and Emma skipped ahead of her. They were

walking down a gentle hill, passing terracotta-roofed whitewashed villas nestling among exotic flowering shrubs. It was all so different from the ordinary street she lived on at home. It seemed idyllic and unreal, and the light was so bright, the colours far more vivid than at home. It was very hot too. Even though they'd protested, she'd insisted the children wear sun hats.

'Look, look, Jennifer,' Gavin yelled excitedly and Emma dashed back to hold her hand as a tiny green lizard scooted across the footpath.

Urrg! thought Jennifer, disgusted, but she didn't let on, and oohed and aahed with forced enthusiasm. They reached the bottom of the hill and followed the curve of the road until it joined the bustling main street. Supermarkets, cafés, perfume shops, pharmacies, book and newspaper shops, clothes and souvenir shops beckoned. Jennifer couldn't wait to explore. But not today. Sunday was her day off, that was the agreement. On Sunday she would come down town by herself and browse to her heart's content.

Sundays became the days that Jennifer lived for. Looking after two boisterous easily bored children was no picnic. She needed that one day to replenish her energies. Usually she got up early and went to Mass in the small church at the far end of town. Then she went to one of the bookshops, or Librarias, as they were called. Jennifer loved to pass an hour or so flicking through glossy magazines like *Der Spiegel* and *Paris Match*, reading about the jet set of Europe. There was usually an article about Princess Caroline, who fascinated Jennifer. They were of an age, but their lifestyles were totally different. Previously, when she'd read about the young princess from Monaco, and her life of parties and pleasure, Jennifer felt vaguely dissatisfied with her own humdrum existence. She was determined to break out of her own boring little rut. Jennifer had certainly taken a major step in that direction by coming to Majorca. After her perusal of the magazines, she usually bought one of the English newspapers, even though they were a day behind. Then she would go to one of the open air restaurants, order croissants and coffee and sit munching and reading.

After that, she might go shopping, spending several hours browsing. Sometimes she took the bus into Palma to go sightseeing. Gillian hired a car and they travelled around the island. They visited the Caves of Drach, a pearl factory in Manacor, and went to several huge open air markets. But Jennifer loved taking off by herself with no children hanging out of her. Sundays were real treat days.

Usually around four in the afternoon, after lunch in a café, she would head for the beach and toast her limbs and swim and read until after seven. Then she'd go back to the villa, shower and change and go to meet her friend Charlotte at the El Alhambra night-club.

Charlotte was an au pair also. Jennifer had met her at the beach one day. Emma came screeching over to Jennifer, who was trying to read the novel *Hotel*, claiming that a boy had pushed her in the sand. She was whingeing and whining as only she knew how and Jennifer felt like picking her up and dunking her, head-first, into the sea. Admirably, she restrained herself and soothed the little girl with promises of an ice cream on the way home.

'Sorry about that,' she heard a pleasant voice say. 'My brats think they own the beach.' Jennifer looked up to find a smiling fair-haired girl holding a toddler by one hand and a squirming little boy by the other.

'Say sorry to the little girl,' she insisted, and Jennifer knew by her accent that she was from the north of England.

'Get lost an' leave me alone.' The little boy struggled against her hold.

'Say sorry or I'm going to spank you, Oliver,' the girl insisted. 'And I won't let you have a ride on the donkey in the square.'

'Sorry,' the boy said sulkily.

449

'Right then, off you go and play. I don't want to hear another word,' the girl said crossly.

'Isn't it awful the way you have to bribe them to be good? I'm telling you, if he was mine, I'd sort him out. My name's Charlotte. I'm these darlings' au pair.'

'I'm Jennifer, I'm an au pair too, and I know exactly how you feel.' Jennifer laughed, delighted to meet someone in the same boat as herself.

'Will I come over and join you, or do you just want to be left in peace?' Charlotte asked.

'Oh, come on,' Jennifer said eagerly, pleased by the idea of getting to know someone. She got up and helped the other girl bring over buckets and spades and towels to the spot where she'd been sitting.

'Why don't you and Gavin go and build a big castle with a moat?' Jennifer suggested to Oliver, who was scuffling sand in their direction. The two boys eyed each other warily.

'Go on,' insisted Charlotte. Five minutes later they were busily engaged in building a castle and they were the best of friends.

'Thank heavens for that. You know they get lonely for kids of their own age.' Charlotte sighed. Emma was playing with the toddler, a two-year-old called Sally. They both seemed contented enough too.

Charlotte's employers were a British couple who owned a large clothing factory in the midlands. They owned a villa, not far from where Jennifer was staying. They came to Majorca for three months each summer. Charlotte was expected to wash and iron clothes and make breakfast and tea and wash up after it, as well as looking after the children. Jennifer's job was much less onerous. After all, there was a housekeeper and a maid at the villa.

Charlotte had been working with the Reeves for over a year, she explained, but she was getting fed up. As soon as the holidays were over she was going to leave her job and travel.

They got into the habit of meeting at the beach daily

and often arranged little outings together for the four children. Gillian was perfectly happy with this arrangement.
All she wanted to do was loll around the pool sipping
Bacardi. The less she saw of the children, the more it
suited her. She needed to relax and re-energize, she told
Jennifer. She had so much entertaining to do when she
was at home, she was completely exhausted.

Charlotte's day off was Sunday also, so she and Jennifer
started going out together on Sunday nights. They enjoyed each other's company, they shared moans about
their employers and their brats of children, and they
enjoyed being chatted up at the disco. Sunday nights
made the rest of the week worth while.

The days slipped lazily by. Gillian, who had met several
other couples, was spending a lot of time at a posh golf
and leisure club just outside of town. Several times, a tall
blond man called to pick her up at the villa. He was a
tennis pro, she explained to Jennifer. His name was Sven
and he was helping her to improve her game. She sparkled
vivaciously whenever he was around. Once, when Jennifer
was bathing the children, she'd looked out the window
and seen Gillian and Sven embracing by the pool. She
was deeply shocked. Gillian was married. Her husband
phoned regularly to see how she and the children were
and to explain that business was keeping him from joining
them. It was quite obvious, after several weeks, that Sven
was doing far more than coaching Gillian at her tennis.
They were spending a lot of time together. According to
Conchita they were having an affair. Jennifer thought the
housekeeper was exaggerating.

One afternoon Jennifer had to bring the children home
early from the beach because Emma was feverish. As
she walked towards Emma's bedroom, she realized that
the tennis pro and Gillian were making passionate love
in the master bedroom.

Later, when he'd gone, Gillian breezed into the lounge
and poured herself a drink. 'I suppose you must know
by now that Sven and I are more than good friends,' she

451

said, giving a breathless little giggle. She was wearing a designer swimsuit and a vibrantly patterned sarong. She was glowing.

'It's none of my business,' Jennifer murmured, embarrassed.

'Sweetheart, the reason my dearly beloved husband hasn't found the time to grace us with his presence is because he's screwing the ass off that prize bitch Angie Baldwin. Not only did the slut pinch my au pair, she also pinched my husband.' Gillian scowled. 'The loan of this villa was a heaven-sent opportunity for them to get me out of the way so they could spend the summer fucking each other's brains out. Not,' she drawled, 'that Angie Baldwin has any brains. She's the proverbial dumb blonde. I mean, she can't even throw a dinner party without cocking it up. She thinks Châteaubriand is wine, for God's sake!' Jennifer hid a smile. She wasn't too sure what Châteaubriand was, but it was a bit rich for Gillian to be calling Angie a dumb blonde. Gillian took a thirsty sip of her Bacardi, lit a menthol cigarette and sat down gracefully on one of the sofas.

'You wouldn't believe how kind I was to her when she joined our bridge club, she hadn't a clue. They'd just come into money and had bought a house in Killiney, not far from us. I introduced her to our friends. I took her shopping. I treated her to lunch in the best restaurants. Invited her to our parties. I bent over backwards to introduce her to our set, even though she was obviously out of her depth,' Gillian said viciously. Jennifer was fascinated. It was the first time Gillian had spoken about herself or her background.

'Her husband owns a chain of bookies and snooker halls!' Gillian turned up her dainty little button nose scornfully. 'They're very *nouveau riche*. You should see the house, sweetheart. Ghastly! Pink frills and flounces everywhere. It's like a bordello.'

'Really,' murmured Jennifer, not sure what else to say.

'She's got this huge conservatory with artificial plants, my dear. It's so dreadfully common.' Gillian grimaced. 'Common or not, Bryan fell for her hook, line and sinker. She was always wearing these really skin-tight dresses that barely covered her boobs or her ass. She was forever asking him stupid questions about work and telling him how interesting it all sounded and how she admired him. Of course he fell for it, the pathetic idiot. He's been unfaithful to me all our married life and I've turned a blind eye to it, but to take up with that tart was the final insult. Sauce for the goose is sauce for the gander, Jennifer. So I'm going to enjoy Sven. Every glorious inch of him,' she declared.

'Would you never think of leaving your husband?' Jennifer ventured, wondering how Gillian could bear to stay married to such a philanderer.

'God no!' Gillian was horrified. 'Give up my lovely house, my foreign holidays, my parties. Bryan lets me spend what I like, it's an unspoken agreement between us. As long as I don't hassle him about his women, he doesn't hassle me about what I spend. I'd be far too much of a coward to start out on my own. I like the security of marriage. I like my luxuries. I like being Mrs Bryan Curtis. That's one thing Angie Baldwin will never be, however much she thinks she will. Bryan will never leave me. He has it too easy.' Gillian gazed at Jennifer with her limpid blue eyes. 'Let me tell you something, sweetheart. There's no such thing as the perfect marriage. I can promise you that. Now that you know, you won't mind if I spend the night with Sven, will you? Bad and all as you might think I am, I would never let the children see me with another man. Thank you for being so discreet earlier.'

'Sure, it's no problem,' Jennifer said.

'You're a real pet, Jennifer, and I'm very pleased with your work. You're much better with the kids than Liz was. I like the way you can be firm but kind. She let them away with murder. Angie Baldwin, you did me a favour.' Gillian laughed. 'I'm going to give you a tenner

453

extra a week from now on, you deserve it.' Gillian drifted out through the French doors to catch the last rays of the sun. Jennifer watched her go and felt sorry for her. It was an empty life that she led, for all her money and style. And her husband sounded like a right creep. More power to Gillian for having her own affair.

Towards the beginning of August, Gillian announced glumly that Bryan was coming to spend the month. It was clear that she wasn't looking forward to her husband's arrival. Neither was Jennifer, particularly. They had all got into a nice little routine. Gillian was happy having her affair. She stayed with Sven several nights a week. Emma and Gavin were not as whiney as at the beginning. They knew now that when Jennifer said something she meant it. When they'd arrived in Majorca they would go and wheedle and pester Gillian if Jennifer said no to something. But now Gillian backed her up, much to Jennifer's relief. It had been a hard-fought battle at first, but it was working out well and all of them were quite enjoying themselves. Gavin and Emma were happy with their playmates. Charlotte had been over to the villa several times and Gillian liked her. And the two of them were teaching the children to swim in the pool.

Now Bryan Curtis was coming to stay, and Jennifer had the feeling that once their father arrived, the children might start acting up again. Gillian was disgusted. She wouldn't be able to see Sven for a while. Conchita and Estella were dying to see 'the husband.' It would be very interesting indeed to see what went on in the next few weeks, Jennifer wrote in her daily letter to Ronan.

Chapter Forty-Nine

'Good to meet you.' Bryan Curtis held her hand for much longer than was necessary. Jennifer disliked him on sight. He certainly wasn't what she expected. For some reason, she'd expected Gillian's husband to be tall, handsome, rather suave. Bryan was none of these. He was medium height, stocky, with a thickening waistline and the beginning of a paunch. She guessed he was in his early forties. He had the look of a man who'd enjoyed too many long boozy business lunches. His eyes were a watery blue, and he had thick wet lips. Angie Baldwin's taste left a lot to be desired, Jennifer felt.

'Gill tells me you're working miracles on the monsters,' he said, his eyes roving up and down her tanned leggy figure. Jennifer felt uncomfortable. 'She didn't tell me how pretty you were,' he added, giving her what she could only describe as a lecherous smile. Jennifer's heart sank. Imagine having to put up with him for a month.

'They're no trouble, Mr Curtis,' she murmured. It was ten-thirty, the children were in bed and Gillian had just collected him from Palma Airport.

'*Mr Curtis!* Good heavens. The name is Bryan,' he said expansively.

'Bryan,' she echoed politely. Gillian reappeared, much to her relief.

'Come and join us for supper,' she invited.

'I have a bit of a headache. I think I'll have an early night,' Jennifer fibbed.

'Oh, you poor thing,' Gillian exclaimed.

'That's usually the kind of thing my wife says,' Bryan joked. Gillian glared at him.

'Goodnight then,' Jennifer said hastily and made a quick retreat to the safety of her room. Flinging herself on the bed, she shook out Ronan's latest letter to reread it and savour it in peace and quiet. There were letters from Paula and her mother as well. They'd all arrived that morning but she'd only had the chance to skim through them. Gillian had been up to ninety. The children, aware that their father was coming, were excitable. It had been a long day. It was nice to be alone with her mail.

Ronan was working like a demon. He'd saved a lot of money. He'd gone to Atlantic City for the weekend and won twenty dollars on the gambling machines. His boss in the restaurant had told him if he wanted to stay in America he could become manager of the restaurant because he was the best worker he'd ever employed, Ronan wrote proudly. He had phoned home but William wouldn't speak to him, and Rachel was too intimidated to say more than a few words. Jennifer felt terribly sad for him. She'd love to be with him, to put her arms around him and tell him not to take any notice of his bastard of a father. He'd told her that he missed her and that the highlight of his day was when one of her letters arrived. She felt the same, she'd assure him.

Paula's letter was much shorter. She was fed up in St Margaret's Bay. She missed Dublin and Helen, and working for Nick. Jennifer's job sounded a thousand times more interesting, Paula moaned. She wished she was living the life of Reilly in a luxury villa in Majorca. Barry had pissed off to Australia, and though she was dating the assistant manager of the hotel, it was only a summer romance, while she was at home. Helen had told her she wouldn't be able to get her a cheap flight until later in the season so it looked as if she wouldn't be able to meet up with Jennifer. She seemed totally fed up, Jennifer thought. Which wasn't like Paula. Somehow or other, Jennifer couldn't imagine Paula putting up with Emma and Gavin. She chuckled at the thought. Being an au pair was not half as glamorous as Paula imagined it was.

Her mother's letter was cheerful and newsy. All about the boys and Brenda and what Grandpa Myles's latest was. Reading it, Jennifer felt suddenly homesick. Soon she'd be home, she comforted herself. And then what? No job, waiting for her exam results. All at once going home didn't sound that appealing.

The following day, she was swimming with the children in the pool when Bryan appeared through the French doors.

'Daddy, Daddy,' Emma shrieked, galloping up the steps at the shallow end.

'Look at me, Dad, Dad, look at me I can belly-flop!' Gavin shouted, clambering out of the side of the pool and falling in dramatically.

'I told you not to do that, Gavin,' Jennifer said sternly as he came up gasping and spluttering.

'My daddy lets me,' Gavin said cheekily, repeating the exercise. Great, thought Jennifer in disgust. All my hard work down the drain. Before she knew what was happening, Bryan had slipped out of his robe and belly-flopped into the pool himself.

'Dad, that was brill!' his son exclaimed, casting a triumphant look at Jennifer.

Prat! she thought as Bryan surfaced and swam towards her.

'Morning, Jennifer, you're a sight for sore eyes,' he greeted her chummily.

'Morning,' she said coolly. She wouldn't give him the satisfaction of calling him Bryan.

'You've a lovely colour.' He ran a finger down her arm. Jennifer froze. He was deliberately standing very close to her, ogling her.

'I think I'll get out now.' She swam sideways around him down to the far end of the pool. She was furious. The cheek of him, touching her like that. And looking at her like that. Who did he think he was? Paula would have cut him down to size with a few well-chosen words, but

457

Jennifer wasn't one bit sure how to handle the obnoxious Mr Curtis.

The next week was a nightmare. He constantly sought excuses to touch her and make lewd joking remarks to her. Jennifer was very uncomfortable. Gillian ignored him. The kids were as bold as brass.

'I'm sick of him,' she complained to Charlotte as they sat sipping San Miguel beer at a café overlooking the bay. 'He's revolting. He thinks he's God's gift. No matter how rude I am he still keeps harassing me. Even in front of Gillian.'

'He sounds like a right moron,' Charlotte observed. 'Do you know what my beauties did? They had a party last night and Stella told me if I cleaned up this morning, she'd pay me extra seeing as today's my day off. Well I cleaned up, it took me two and a half hours, the place was in a shambles. And in the end, I had to give the kids their breakfast because the other pair had such hangovers, so I might as well not have had a day off. Do you know how much extra the mean slag gave me? Five bloody quid. I've a good mind to pack my bags and split.'

'Would you go home?' Jennifer asked.

'Naw,' Charlotte said vehemently. 'I'd go to the Costa on the mainland. I know a couple of girls who did that, they made great money working in bars and restaurants. It would be a hell of a lot better than what I'm doing. Talk about slave labour!'

'It sounds good,' Jennifer remarked.

Charlotte's eyes lit up. 'Let's do a bunk! We'd have a great time. It's high season, I bet we'd have no trouble getting a job. We could stay with one of my friends until we got a place,' she said excitedly.

Jennifer laughed. 'Are you mad? We couldn't just take off.'

'I could,' Charlotte said glumly.

Lying in bed that night, having endured Bryan's smutty remarks, Jennifer was sorely tempted to phone Charlotte and tell her she would join her in the flight to the Costa del Sol.

Two days later, she had just put the children to bed. Gillian was lying down with a headache. Bryan was pacing around in a bad humour. He'd been drinking.

'Do you fancy going for a drink?' he asked. 'It's high time I took you out for a meal. You deserve a treat for working so hard.'

'No thank you. I'm only doing the job I'm paid to do. There's no need for you to feel you have to treat me,' she said politely. A meal with Bryan Curtis was not Jennifer's idea of a treat.

'Come on, Jennifer.' He slipped an arm around her waist, his fingers sweaty against her skin. 'Let's get to know one another a bit better.'

'Look, do you mind?' Jennifer struggled to evade his embrace. 'I don't go for meals with married men.'

'Oh for goodness sake, Jennifer, don't let that stop you. Gillian won't mind, we have an open marriage.'

'Well I suggest you close it,' Jennifer snapped, trying to pull away.

'Oh come on, stop playing hard to get. You're beautiful, I want to touch you,' he said hoarsely, trying to kiss her.

Jennifer nearly died of fright and shock and revulsion. 'Let go of me!' She fought against him trying to push him away. His hands mauled her, touching her breasts and thighs. A lamp crashed to the ground in their skirmish. It didn't stop Bryan, his breath was hot against her cheeks, she could feel him trying to force his leg between hers.

'What the hell is going on here?' Gillian stood at the door. Jennifer felt Bryan's hold loosen. Panting she pushed him away.

'You're despicable. You're a dirty revolting slob. How dare you treat me like that! How dare you lay your slimy hands on me! You make me want to vomit,' Jennifer sobbed, rushing out of the room. She felt dirty. Bile rose in her throat and she just made the bathroom in time. She retched miserably. Afterwards, she sat on the edge of the bath, shaking. She could hear Gillian and Bryan shouting at each other.

'You're pathetic,' she could hear Gillian yelling. 'Thinking a lovely young girl like that would be interested in you, you vain bastard. Go back to that slut Baldwin, she's just as vulgar as you are. Her taste is where you should be, in the gutter.'

'Shut the fuck up, you,' Bryan yelled back. 'You're no fucking angel.'

Listening to them shouting obscenities at each other, Jennifer knew she wasn't going to spend another minute under their roof. Adrenalin coursed through her. She packed her case swiftly, throwing her clothes in any old way. She got her passport out of the drawer, and her pesetas. Then she slipped out of her room quietly and walked towards the kitchen. At least she didn't have to pass the lounge, where she could hear Gillian and Bryan still arguing bitterly. She let herself out the back door. It was dark out, and there was a small side gate she could use which meant she wouldn't have to walk down the illuminated drive.

As soon as she was out of the grounds, she half ran down the hill towards town. She knew where Conchita lived, she was sure the kindly housekeeper would put her up for the night until she decided what she was going to do.

Conchita was horrified to see her standing outside her apartment with her case. In a great flurry, she ushered her into the living-room.

'You must have a brandy,' she insisted, pouring Jennifer a stiff drink. 'Tell me what happened.'

As best she could, in Spanish, Jennifer told her about Bryan and his shocking behaviour. Conchita let out a string of curses, gesticulating wildly.

'You must stay here, of course.' She hugged Jennifer tightly. Conchita was nothing if not motherly, Jennifer thought gratefully.

The following morning, Conchita left for work, having promised that neither she nor Estella would divulge Jennifer's whereabouts. Jennifer lay in bed. It was strange not to have to get up and feed the children and plan their day. She stretched luxuriously.

No way was she going back to that villa. She'd had enough of Bryan Curtis and his sleazy behaviour. Let him look after his children for the rest of the month. Since he'd arrived they'd been as bold as ever in their pathetic search for attention. She couldn't face another minute with that family.

'They're going crazy,' Conchita reported gleefully that evening. She was enjoying the intrigue immensely. 'They asked me if I knew where you were. I said no. They rang Charlotte and of course she didn't know. The kids were running wild. *He* . . . ' Conchita said it with disdain, 'was shouting at her to do something with them. She tells him to fuck off, it is his own fault you left. I tell you, Jennifer, they are not happy people.'

Jennifer sighed. She didn't feel too good about leaving Gillian in the lurch, but she couldn't go back if Bryan was there. 'I'd better ring Charlotte, she might be worried,' she said to Conchita.

'Congratulations. I'd have slapped the dirty bugger in the chops if I'd had the chance,' Charlotte said vehemently on hearing the news. 'What are you going to do?'

'I don't know yet,' Jennifer said. 'Conchita said I can stay as long as I like but I don't like putting her out. Maybe I should get a flight home.'

'Don't do anything hasty,' Charlotte instructed. 'I'll talk to you tomorrow.'

Jennifer put the phone down and went out and sat on Conchita's small balcony. The sun was setting, tinting the sky with great swathes of pink and purple and gold. It was breathtaking. The waters of the bay were glassy, mirroring the colours of the sky. Crickets chirruped. The air was heavy with the scent of jasmine. Jennifer knew she didn't want to go home.

461

The following afternoon, Charlotte phoned.

'Meet me in Manolo's Bar in half an hour,' she instructed. Jennifer did as she was told. She found Charlotte sitting at a table under the awning. At her feet lay her suitcase. 'Here.' She held out an envelope to Jennifer.

Mystified, Jennifer took it and opened it. It contained an airline ticket to Malaga Airport.

'Costa del Sol, here we come,' Charlotte grinned.

'What?' Jennifer couldn't believe her ears, or her eyes.

'We're going. The flight is at nine tonight. I've spoken to a friend of mine there, we can stay in her apartment until we get a place of our own. Are you coming or not?'

'What about Stella and the kids?'

'What about them?' Charlotte snorted. 'I've had enough of being treated like dirt. I'm going, Jennifer, even if you're not.'

Jennifer felt a *frisson* of excitement. She wasn't usually a very impulsive person but there was something exciting about the idea of heading off to a new city. She had more than enough money to keep her going. She might as well have adventures like this now, before she ended up like Brenda, desk-bound and in a rut in the County Council.

'I'm coming too,' she announced. 'How much do I owe you for the ticket?'

'We can fix that up later. Do you think I could come and spend what's left of the afternoon in Conchita's? In case they send out a posse.'

'Of course, come on,' Jennifer said hastily. 'Conchita won't mind, I'm sure.'

'You must stay with my cousin Raphael. He owns apartments near Fuengirola. I will give you a letter to give to him. And then I won't have to worry. I will know you are in safe hands,' Conchita declared when she heard of the plan.

'Thanks for everything, Conchita.' Jennifer hugged the plump, kind-hearted woman. She'd grown fond of her.

There was much kissing and gesticulating and blessings bestowed when the taxi came to collect them and Jennifer waved until they were out of sight. She felt sad leaving Santa Juan, it was a lovely little town.

She phoned Gillian from the airport. She felt it was the least she could do.

'Please come back. Bryan was drunk. It won't happen again,' Gillian pleaded. Jennifer felt torn. She knew that the other woman had genuinely depended on her. It had been fine when they were there on their own. But the thought of seeing Bryan Curtis again made her feel nauseous.

'I'm sorry, Gillian, I can't,' she said contritely.

'Please, Jennifer.' The familiar breathless voice floated down the line. In the background, a harsh loud voice slurred.

'Tell that stuck-up little virgin to go to hell. She's not setting foot under my roof again.' It was Bryan, obviously drunk.

'Goodbye, Gillian,' Jennifer said gently and hung up. She felt sorry for the woman. The decision had been made for her. Bryan evidently had no desire to see her again. The feeling was mutual, Jennifer scowled. She was well out of it.

'Come on, our flight's been called.' Charlotte rushed over to her.

Twenty-five minutes later they were heading north towards Malaga, and the lights of Majorca were disappearing into the inky night.

The first thing she was going to do when she got settled was to call Ronan in New York to give him her new address. After that, she'd call her family. Jennifer peered out into the pitch-black sky. It was only a short flight to the mainland. Would they get a job easily? Would Conchita's cousin have an apartment free? Edificio Rosa sounded like a nice name for the building. They had barely levelled out after fifteen minutes of flight when Jennifer felt the plane begin its descent towards Malaga

463

Airport. Excitement and apprehension created little knots in her stomach as the plane lost height steadily.

Charlotte winked at her. 'Free at last,' she laughed. 'Things can only get better.'

'Absolutely,' Jennifer agreed. If she didn't like the Costa del Sol, she didn't have to stay there. She could always go home. But if she liked it, she might stay a month, or six months. She was as free as a bird, she thought happily, she might as well make the most of it. Beneath her she could see the long curve of Spain's southern coast, its lights twinkling in the darkness. Excitement overtook her. She was dying to see what was in store for them.

Chapter Fifty

Jennifer was almost sick with excitement as she saw the bus from Madrid, dusty and grimy, pull into the terminus. It was nearly a year since she'd seen Ronan and she couldn't wait to fling herself into his arms and hug the daylights out of him. She'd been living for this moment since last November when he'd phoned her and told her he'd come and spend two weeks in Spain with her.

If anyone had told her that she would spend a year away from home working on the Costa del Sol, she'd have said they were mad. But that was exactly what she'd done, Jennifer thought happily, watching the bus manoeuvre into position. After the flight out of Majorca, as she and Charlotte called it, they had got jobs in an English-owned restaurant and bar called the Cock & Bull. Jennifer loved it. It was hectically busy, but the tips were good and she was having the time of her life. She enjoyed dealing with the customers, mostly English and Irish tourists. Her social life was frantic. She'd really come out of her shell and was enjoying the feeling of being completely independent for the first time in her life.

Ronan had written to her a month after she'd arrived on the mainland, to tell her that he was dropping out of Bolton Street Tech and was staying in America to study computers. Jennifer decided there and then that she was going to stay in Spain for a year. She'd got her exam results, three honours and passes in the rest of her subjects. Nothing spectacular like Paula's five honours. She didn't want to go home and join the civil service or the Corporation. Jennifer just didn't want to go home if Ronan wasn't going to be there.

Naturally, her parents were not pleased by her decision. Stern phone calls were made by Jim and Kit, who told her to come home and get a proper job. Or go and study for another year, like Paula was going to. She wasn't to be acting like some sort of hippie, Jim declared. It was much easier for Jennifer to be firm from a distance. She told her mother that she was now fluent in Spanish, and that a French waiter was teaching her French. She'd be as fluent as Paula would ever be after her language courses.

'I'll just stay a year,' she promised. 'And then we'll see.'

'We'll see nothing,' growled her father. 'You just get yourself home before Christmas, Miss, and settle down. I've a good mind to go down to that head nun of yours and eat the face off her for putting ideas in your head.'

Her father's disapproval only increased her resolve to stay. She couldn't be bothered going home to a load of hassle about getting a job. She was making good money in Spain, her languages were improving a hundred-fold. She had no-one telling her what to do. Go home! Not on your life! Jennifer told Ronan in one of her letters.

You stick to your guns and I'll stick to mine, he'd written encouragingly. They wrote to each other twice a week and phoned each other once a month. When he'd suggested coming for a holiday the following summer, Jennifer was delighted. No way now was she going home. Not even for Christmas. If she went home for Christmas, she knew her father would not be in favour of her going back to Spain. If she insisted on going there'd be a huge row. Jennifer didn't want that. So, when December came, she phoned home to say that the restaurant and bar would be open Christmas Day, for all their British customers who wintered on the Costa. She couldn't get time off.

Her father wouldn't speak to her on the phone for a month after that. Kit was more understanding. Brenda told her she was being selfish. Paula called her a lucky sucker and Beth told her on no account was she to come home, the weather was terrible and everyone had colds and flu.

The winter months had been pleasant enough on the south coast of Spain. The intense heat of the summer gave way to balmy warmth although at times it lashed rain. There were some ferocious storms with fork and sheet lightning, the likes of which Jennifer had never seen before. Mostly though, the weather was fine and, because they didn't have to work the long hours they'd had to during high season, Charlotte and Jennifer were able to spend some time travelling the three hundred mile coast that stretched from Almeria down to Gibraltar. They sampled the sophisticated elegance of Marbella and Puerto Banus, gazing with unadulterated envy at the huge yachts in the marinas. They window-shopped in the expensive boutiques which sold only the most exclusive labels. Jennifer enjoyed sightseeing in the jet-setter's paradise but she really loved the pretty, unspoilt Andalusian villages with their whitewashed haciendas and villas set amidst beautiful orange groves.

She wrote and described every excursion to Ronan. Soon she'd be able to bring him to those places herself, Jennifer thought happily as the bus finally drew to a halt. Discreetly she sprayed some *Apple Blossom* on her neck and wrists. She felt a little shy now that it was time to see Ronan. It had been a scorcher of a day, but as the sun started to dip in the sky a light breeze had blown up. Jennifer was relieved. The last thing she wanted was for Ronan to see her all hot and bothered and sweaty.

She saw Ronan before he saw her. Jennifer stared at him. He had changed so much. He'd been gaunt and lanky and skinny that last day when she held him close in Dublin Airport. The Ronan who got off the bus was broad and muscular, and very tanned and fit-looking. His wide hazel eyes hadn't changed though. He looked at her, smiled that old familiar lopsided smile, and his eyes crinkled up in that much-loved way.

'Ronan, Ronan,' she said joyfully and threw her arms

around him, laughing with happiness as he lifted her up in the air.

'Ah Jenny! You look beautiful. I've missed you so much. I thought I'd never get here.' They kissed eagerly.

'I can't believe you're here,' Jennifer said breathlessly, as she drew away from him and stroked a finger down the side of his cheek.

'Me neither.' Ronan hugged her again.

'You've changed so much.' She smiled. 'You look . . . so . . . so healthy.'

'Well fed, you mean.' Ronan laughed. 'The food's so good over there I had to join a gym to work out or else I'd be a right pudding.'

'I hope you'll like Spanish food,' Jennifer said.

'You know me, Jenny, I'd eat anything. And right now I'd even eat one of my ex-landlady's Irish Stews. I'm starving.'

'Come on,' Jennifer grinned. 'I know this gorgeous little seafood restaurant, even you won't be able to finish what's on your plate.'

'Want to bet?' Ronan scoffed.

They lingered over the delicious meal, delighted to be together again. It was wonderful to be able to tell each other all their news instead of having to put it in a letter. It was nearing midnight before they eventually got back to Edificio Rosa, Jennifer's apartment block.

'Are you sure your friend doesn't mind me staying?' Ronan asked.

'Charlotte! Are you joking?' Jennifer retorted. 'She's always having visitors. You're my first one. And anyway,' she added shyly, 'if it's OK with you, you'll be sharing my room. I've made up a camp bed.'

'Look, Jenny, I'll sleep out in the lounge on a couch, I don't want to put you out or make you feel uncomfortable,' Ronan said earnestly.

'You won't. You'd never get a wink of sleep in the lounge, Charlotte keeps very late hours, and anyway I'd like you to share my room.' Jennifer blushed.

'I'd like that too, very much.' Ronan drew her into his arms and kissed her lightly.

'Well that's settled then,' Jennifer said briskly. If her parents knew she was sleeping in the same room as a fella they'd go spare, she thought a little guiltily. But she didn't want Ronan sleeping on the sofa, it was far too short for his long frame. And besides, she wanted to be with him, she wanted them to become closer, more intimate. Through their letters to each other they had come to know each other's innermost thoughts. Their letters were written from the heart. They hid nothing from each other. They shared their ups and downs. And now that he was here with her, she didn't want to be shy and silly. She wanted to be as comfortable with him in the flesh as she felt when she wrote to him.

'This is very nice.' Ronan looked around approvingly as she led him into their second-floor apartment.

'I like it,' she agreed. 'I like its simplicity.'

The lounge dining-area was an L-shape. Painted white, in the Mediterranean tradition. It was a cool haven from the scorching heat of summer. The furniture was pine. A pine bookcase and sideboard lined one wall. A long tweedy sort of sofa, covered in gay rugs and cushions, was placed along the other. Two old armchairs that had seen better days were placed one on each side of the huge French windows that led to a small balcony. Because they were on the second floor and on an incline, they were able to see the sea in the distance, over the rooftops of the apartment blocks across the street. It certainly didn't compare with the magnificence of the view in Santa Juan but Jennifer didn't mind. She was far happier here on the Costa than she'd been with the Curtises.

The alcove at the other end of the room contained a pine dining table and four chairs. These were supplemented with the white chairs from the balcony when there were more than four for dinner. The floor throughout the apartment was tiled and very easy to keep clean. There was no clutter. And much to Jennifer's joy, dusting and polishing were kept to a minimum. Often, she thought back to Saturday mornings at home and all that dusting and polishing of her mother's brasses and ornaments which took a whole morning's attention. The only ornament she and Charlotte had was a faintly lopsided candelabra with white candles in it, for use on the frequent occasions when the electricity went off due to thunderstorms.

While she had no time for ornaments, Jennifer was a sucker for paintings. Landscapes and seascapes mostly. She'd bought paintings of little Andalusian villages. Paintings of purple-pink bougainvillaea tumbling over the wrought-iron balconies of green shuttered windows. Paintings of whitewashed village chapels. Of boats fishing in the pearly mists of dawn and the flaming seas of sunset. Her favourite was of an old fisherman mending his nets in a small fishing village with the splendour of the Sierra Nevada behind him. This was the real Spain, not the gaudy neon-lit high-rise tourist town where she lived and worked. Charlotte teased her when she arrived home with a new painting, but Jennifer knew that when the time did come for her to leave the Costa, her paintings would always have the power to bring back the happiest memories of her life in Spain.

'You've quite an art gallery, now,' Ronan commented as he studied her collection. He, of course, knew all about them. Jennifer had written and described every one of her acquisitions.

'There's more in the bedroom.' She laughed leading him down the hall, past the small kitchen, to the bedroom. The pretty room was a study in simplicity. Her small divan, with its colourful spread which matched the curtains, was under the window so that she could see the sea on waking. A white chest of drawers and wardrobe unit was the only other piece of furniture. A vase of wild roses on the windowsill, a vivid splash of colour against the white. The camp bed, neatly made up, was placed beside her own bed.

'No wonder you don't want to go home. Who'd want to face our wild winters and draughty houses after this?'

'I'll have to go sometime.' She sighed. 'I'll be nineteen in another couple of weeks. I suppose I'll have to go and get a "proper job," as my dad calls it. I can't be a waitress in Spain all my life.'

'I've been checking out the situation at home.' Ronan put his arms around her. 'I'm not going to have any trouble getting a job there. Everyone is looking for experienced computer people. Dropping out of Bolton Street and going into computers in America was the best thing I could ever have done. Another year there and I'll be able to pick and choose,' he said confidently.

'That's brilliant, Ronan. You deserve everything you get, you've worked so hard for it.'

'So have you,' he said stoutly. Their eyes met. He put his arms around her and kissed her. Gently at first but then with an increasing urgency. She wanted to respond but couldn't. A feeling of agitation and panic overtook her and Ronan, sensing her tension, drew away from her.

'What's wrong?' he asked. 'Don't you want to kiss me?'

Jennifer buried her face in his shoulder. 'Yes Ro, of course I do,' she said miserably.

'But . . . ?' he probed.

'Ronan, I don't want to go all the way. I'd be dead scared of getting pregnant, and I'd feel a bit guilty . . . you know . . . about having sex before marriage and all that,' she blurted out.

'Jenny, hey Jen, it's all right. Whatever you want is fine with me,' Ronan assured her. Jennifer burst into tears.

'I'm sorry, Ronan, I know everyone's doing it these days and that I'm just old-fashioned. I'd love to be like everyone else and have the nerve to do it. And now I feel a real failure. I'm nearly nineteen and I'm still a virgin. Charlotte's slept with loads of fellas. Paula's slept with two. I'm sure Brenda slept with Eddie. There's just me

471

and Beth left. The last of the red-hot virgins,' she said shamefaced.

'Well there's me as well,' she heard Ronan say. 'And I'm older than you.' Jennifer stared at him.

'You've never done it? After all this time living in America, with all those liberated women I'm always reading about in *Cosmo*?' She was astonished.

Ronan laughed and sat down on her bed drawing her down beside him. 'Girls aren't the only ones who feel scared and guilty, you know. Of course I get as horny as hell. Sure, I've had the opportunity. My father once told me if I defiled a woman before marriage I was responsible for consigning her soul to eternal damnation as well as my own.' Ronan scowled. 'Jenny, I'm an adult. I've put myself through college and looked after myself in America but I sometimes still have to try and convince myself that my father's word is not law any more and I can do as I please.' He gave a rueful smile. 'I could cope with consigning my own soul to eternal damnation, but I sure couldn't cope with sending yours.'

'Oh, Ronan, that's horrible!' Jennifer protested. 'Isn't it awful that we've been brought up to feel such guilt about sex? I wish I could be different. I wish I could be like Paula.'

'I'm glad you're not like Paula. You're perfect just the way you are.' Ronan gave her a hug.

'What a pair we are,' she said wryly.

'We're a perfect pair,' Ronan declared, and this time Jennifer kissed him. She felt safe within the circle of his arms, the relief of being able to explain to him exactly how she felt had eased all her agitation and tension.

They spent fourteen carefree happy days together. Because it was not yet high season, her boss kindly allowed her to take time off and they hired a car and went exploring Andalucia and Granada. They stayed in little guest houses and enjoyed very much being a couple again. Tentatively at first, and then with growing confidence and delight, they learned ways of giving each other pleasure without

472

taking that final step. Both of them longed to but couldn't because it would have been ruined by guilt. Because they understood each other, it made it easier and in some ways it strengthened their relationship.

The day before Ronan was due to leave, Paula phoned Jennifer to announce that she was coming to Spain the minute her exams were over. 'I've wonderful news for you,' she bubbled across the crackling telephone lines. 'There's a chance of a great job for the two of us next year. It will suit us down to the ground and we'll be together. I'll tell you all when I get there. Oh Jenny, I can't wait.' Paula sounded terribly excited.

'What is it? Tell me,' Jennifer demanded.

'I'm going to be cut off, Jenny. I'll be there soon. You'll find out all then. Bye.' Jennifer heard the click and then the line went dead.

'What's up?' Ronan asked from the sofa, where he was sprawled reading the massive novel *Exodus*. A mighty thunderstorm raged outside and rain was bucketing down in sheets. They hadn't been saying much to each other. Both of them dreaded the moment of parting.

'That was Paula,' Jennifer said excitedly. 'She's coming here after her exams. She says she's got two jobs lined up for us that will suit us down to the ground. Then she was cut off.'

'Ring her back,' he suggested.

Jennifer shook her head. 'You know Paula, always the mystery woman. It will keep, whatever it is. She won't tell me anyway over the phone. So there's no point in me trying to worm it out of her. I wonder what it is though,' she pondered. 'Maybe it's something to do with the hotel in St Margaret's Bay. I don't know if I want to work in a hotel.' She made a face.

'Don't let Paula talk you into doing anything you don't want to do,' Ronan warned.

'As if I would,' Jennifer exclaimed indignantly.

'Paula's a very determined girl when she gets an idea into her head,' Ronan said.

'So am I.'

'I know that, Jenny, it's just you're very soft-hearted and she winds you around her little finger sometimes,' Ronan said firmly.

'She's a good friend,' Jennifer was defensive, not sure if Ronan was implying some sort of criticism of Paula.

'I know, and so is Beth.' Ronan closed his book and stood up to put his arms around her. 'You're going to be faced with a bit of a dilemma because of them sometime in the future,' he said seriously.

'Why?' Jennifer was mystified.

'Actually,' he teased, 'you're going to be in a very tough situation. Brenda's got to be considered as well, after all she is your only sister.'

'What are you wittering on about, Ronan?' She gave him a dig in the ribs.

'Bridesmaids,' he said airily. 'Which of them are you going to choose to be your chief bridesmaid? Or do you want to elope?'

Jennifer stared at her boyfriend, gobsmacked.

'Well?' Ronan smiled at her and took her hand in his. 'If there's going to be a bridesmaid, there's got to be a bride. Jenny, will you marry me?'

Chapter Fifty-One

'Oh, Ronan.' Jennifer could hardly speak.

'Jenny, please!' Ronan's air of confidence disappeared. 'Don't keep me in suspense. Will you marry me? I love you. I knew the minute I saw you that day in the Botanic Gardens that you were special. I couldn't imagine being with any other girl for the rest of my life. I can't face going back to America until I know. I've been trying to pluck up courage all day to ask you.'

'Yes, yes, yessss.' Jennifer was ecstatic. 'Oh Ronan, I'm so excited.'

'Me too.' Her new fiancé grinned boyishly as he swept her off her feet and kissed her soundly.

Later, when their ardour and excitement had cooled a little and it had stopped thundering and raining, they walked along the damp beach and made plans. They decided they would wait until Jennifer's twenty-first birthday to announce the engagement. Ronan would be home from America by then and would hopefully have a job. He would speak to her father then. Until then, their engagement would remain a secret. Their special secret. They spent the night talking, making plans for their wonderful future.

They were both exhausted and bleary-eyed when they got up at the crack of dawn to get a taxi to the bus terminus. Ronan was flying home to Dublin via London. He wanted to see his sister Rachel before he flew back to America. His father wanted nothing to do with him so there was no point in going to Rathbarry. Rachel and he had arranged to meet in Dublin.

They were very subdued on the journey. Saying nothing, just holding hands tightly.

'At least you've got Paula and her news to look forward to,' Ronan comforted her as the terminus came into sight.

'I'm going to miss you so much. I wish we could get married today.' Jennifer's voice wobbled.

'Come on now, Jenny. I need a job so I can provide for you when we get married and I won't be in a position to do that for a few years,' Ronan said earnestly.

'And I thought I was old-fashioned,' she teased, squeezing his hand as the taxi drew to a halt.

'I love you,' she whispered.

'I love you too,' he echoed, holding her tightly.

'Keep writing,' he said, as he pulled away from her reluctantly.

Jennifer nodded, unable to speak. This was the second time they'd had to say goodbye. This time was infinitely harder. She felt as if her heart was being stung by a million nettles as she watched Ronan walk away from her. How could she wait until she was twenty-one before they were engaged? She wanted to be with him now. She'd suggested going to America with him, but he said no. It wasn't that he didn't want her, he explained. But her parents would not be happy about it and he didn't want their marriage to be blighted by bad feeling. Jennifer knew he was right. Both their parents were very traditional. But it didn't stop her from wishing that she could go and be with him. He gave a final wave and was gone from sight. She cried the whole way home.

That night was lonely without his reassuring presence on the camp bed beside her and she tossed and turned trying to sleep. She relived his proposal and smiled. Going on about bridesmaids like that. He was right too, she was going to have a dilemma about her bridesmaids. Brenda would definitely want to be chief bridesmaid, feeling it was her right because she was sister of the bride. Paula wouldn't want to play second fiddle. Beth, bless her heart, wouldn't give a toss. The thought of being Ronan's wife made her exquisitely happy. She'd known exactly what he meant when he'd told her she was special and that he'd known from the first moment. So had she. Even though she'd met some nice blokes here in Spain, none of them compared with Ronan. Paula would probably think she was dull and boring but one man was more than enough for Jennifer as long as that man was Ronan.

She was in for some exciting times ahead, she reflected, burrowing down under the flimsy sheet. What with choosing a chief bridesmaid and waiting to hear how her parents would react to news of her engagement. Not to talk of Ronan's father and his sister. Imagine having William Stapleton for a father-in-law? She grimaced in the dark.

Well if she was inheriting Mr Stapleton, Ronan would be inheriting Grandpa Myles. On the whole, she felt Ronan was getting the better bargain. Grandpa Myles liked Ronan. No doubt he'd be pleased for her when he heard her news. Her mother had written once that the old man lived in constant fear of Jennifer coming home with a 'giggleeo' as he called it. Jennifer chuckled. No fear of that. She caressed the gold cross and chain that hung around her neck. Ronan had bought it for her as an engagement present. It made her feel close to him. She yawned. She was dead tired. It had been an exciting forty-eight hours. Paula's phone call and a proposal within minutes of each other. What was this new job going to entail? Would she be interested? Ronan's words came back to her.

'Don't let Paula talk you into anything.' She wouldn't be, she decided sleepily. She'd hear what Paula had to say and she'd make up her own mind. Then she'd write to Ronan and tell him all about it. Whatever Paula's news was, it couldn't be half as exciting as hers. Imagine being almost engaged to Ronan Stapleton. In a few years' time her name would be Jennifer Stapleton. She said it aloud a few times just to test it out. It sounded nice. She was sure her parents would be glad for her. They liked Ronan very much. He'd be in Dublin with his sister Rachel by now. Lucky Rachel, Jennifer thought enviously. Not, she thought tiredly, that Rachel really was that lucky. From what Ronan had said about her, she had a dreadful time with that old tyrant of a father of hers. When Jennifer and Ronan had a house of their own, Rachel could come and live with them for a while if she wanted. It would get her away from her father and help her stand on her own two feet.

She'd write to Ronan and suggest it. It would please him, Jennifer thought as her eyelids drooped.

Chapter Fifty-Two

It was scorching, Paula's flight was delayed and Jennifer sat flicking through a magazine in the arrivals hall in Malaga Airport. She was dying to see her friend. She couldn't wait to tell Paula about Ronan's proposal. It was very hard keeping it to herself. She was so happy she longed to tell everyone. She'd only tell Paula, Jennifer promised herself. The family would find out on her twenty-first.

Paula, when she finally emerged through customs, looked stunning. She was wearing white jeans, a white T-shirt and dark glasses. She carried a large black holdall type bag on her shoulder that was emblazoned with the words *Saint Tropez*. She looked like a film star. Jennifer grinned, some things never changed.

Paula had to look twice before she recognized Jennifer. 'My God,' she breathed. 'Look at you! Look at the tan. You're glowing, Jenny. You look *fantastic*.'

Jennifer laughed. 'I've loads to tell you.'

'Me too. Oh, Jenny, it's great to see you. I've loads to tell you, too,' Paula enthused. They hugged delightedly.

'Come on, let's get out of here, I've taken the day off.' Jennifer led the way out of the airport and hailed a taxi.

Paula gazed out the window in delight. 'The skies are so blue. It's lashing at home. Can we go to the beach?' she asked eagerly.

'Don't you want something to eat first?' Jennifer asked.

'No, no, I'm too excited. I just want to feel that sun scorching me. I'm so white and you're so brown,' she added enviously. 'I can't believe I'm here. I can't believe I'm not going to work in St Margaret's Bay for the summer. I can't believe I'm finished studying. I can't believe I'm *free*,' she exclaimed exuberantly. 'It's a pity I missed Ronan, did you have a great time?'

Jennifer nodded. 'Guess what, Paula? He's asked me to marry him. We're getting engaged on my twenty-first. You're the only one I'm telling,' she burst out.

'I don't believe it!' Paula exclaimed. 'I'm shocked.'

'I know,' Jennifer smiled. 'I'm a bit shocked myself. But Ronan's the one for me.'

'I can't let you out of my sight before you're up to something,' Paula teased. 'I always knew you and Ronan would make a go of it. He was the only fella you were ever really interested in. You're perfect for each other. I know you'll be really happy.'

'Ronan's staying in America for a good year or two until he's got all the experience and qualifications he needs. He's gone into computers, so he doesn't think he'll have any trouble getting a job when he comes home. I suppose I'd better start thinking about getting a "proper" job after the summer.' She made a face. 'I love it here, though. I love the freedom of being away.'

'Here comes your fairy godmother, your wish is my command. If you want a "proper" job that gives you the freedom of being away, I've got just the one for you,' Paula declared. 'Wait until I tell you *my* news.' She sat back against the leather seat of the taxi that was now speeding along the coast road and turned to Jennifer, her eyes sparkling.

'How would you like to be a courier?' she asked.

'What?' Jennifer was stunned.

'How would you like to be a courier?' Paula repeated, grinning. 'You know Helen works for this travel agency guy. Well he's expanding his operations and he needs more couriers. Helen told him that I'd just finished a course in languages and that you've been working out here for a year and he immediately set up an interview for me. Which I passed with flying colours.' She giggled. 'He wants to interview you, but it's only a formality really after what he's heard about you from me and Helen. He wants us to do a training course and spend some time working in the office next winter and then be ready to take up work either on the Costa or Majorca next Easter. We get paid in Irish money, we have our accommodation paid for and we each have a car. That's far better than most couriers, who are usually paid in local currency, only have scooters and some of them even have to pay for their own accommodation. What do you think?'

'I don't know what to think.' Jennifer was flabbergasted.

'Come on, Jenny. It's a great chance. Kieran does Greece, Portugal, Italy, Malta . . . everywhere. We'll get to see the world. Helen says he's doing really well. He's a dead nice guy. He's very informal. He doesn't act a bit like a businessman but he's got a great business going. It's the chance of a lifetime. Especially as Ronan's not even at home. You might as well be working abroad as in Dublin for all you'll see of him,' Paula urged. 'It's ideal for us with our languages. And you know the Costa like the back of your hand by now. Kieran was very impressed by the fact that you've lived here. It's perfect. You don't want to end up stuck behind a typewriter in the Corpo or the civil service. Look at Brenda, for God's sake! If that's not enough to put you off, nothing will. Beth's thinking of doing my language course and being a courier too. She decided after hearing about our job offer. The three of us could have an absolute BALL!' Paula wheedled.

'My parents would have a fit,' Jennifer declared.

'No, no they won't. That's the great thing,' Paula beamed. 'I called up to collect a parcel for you from your mother. There's rashers and sausages and pudding and a tea brack and a Madeira cake in it for you. I was telling her about the job and she was pleased, because you'd be working for an Irish company rather than doing casual work. She thinks it would be a great way to see the world. I told her to talk to Helen and she said she would. And she's going to talk to your da. Brenda was drooling at the mouth with envy.'

Jennifer laughed. 'Poor Brenda, I asked her to come out but when she heard you were coming . . . I mean she didn't think she could afford it,' Jennifer amended hastily.

'It's all right, Jenny, I know what you mean,' Paula said dryly. 'Brenda and I just rub each other up the wrong way, that's all. Now forget about Brenda. What do you think? Are you going to take the job and have a life of travel and excitement or are you going to die of boredom in a nine to five office job? I know what I'm doing, but it's up to you.'

Chapter Fifty-Three

'I wish it was over.' Jennifer followed Paula off the bus and straightened her skirt. She was feeling a tad nervous. Her interview with Kieran Donnelly, managing director of TransContinental Travel, was at eleven and although Paula had told her that he was very nice, Jennifer couldn't help feeling apprehensive. It was her first serious job interview. The interview with Gillian Curtis and her spoilt offspring was nothing in comparison.

'Maybe he won't think I'm suitable for the job,' Jennifer fretted as they walked towards the travel agency.

Paula gave a tsk of impatience. 'Will you stop it, Jenny! You're getting yourself into a tizzy over nothing. Why wouldn't you be suitable for the job? You speak fluent Spanish. You speak French. You've lived in Majorca and the Costa and you're much more qualified for a courier's job than I was when I went for my interview. Kieran's not a bit intimidating. He's dead cool, it won't be like an interview. Believe me.'

'I just get nervous, that's all.'

'I'm telling you, it will be a doddle and then we've got lunch with Helen to look forward to,' Paula reminded her.

'You're right,' Jennifer said, fingering the gold cross and chain Ronan had given her. 'I must give the appearance of confidence. First impressions are everything. Is my jacket creased?'

'Your jacket is fine. Everything's fine. You look *très chic*,' Paula assured her. 'I love it when you wear your hair in a French plait.' A motorcyclist in a leather jacket and a black helmet roared past them, braked, and slowed to a halt a little further on. He turned and waved.

'Do you know him?' Jennifer asked.

Paula had a big grin on her face. 'Yeah, I know him.' She quickened her pace. '*That*, Jenny, is Kieran Donnelly.'

'You're joking!' Jennifer couldn't believe that the tall figure astride the Harley-Davidson was the managing director of TransCon and Helen's boss. She'd been expecting a suave sharp-suited yuppie type. They came abreast of him as he removed his shiny black helmet.

'Morning, ladies,' he greeted them.

'Hi Kieran, this is Jenny Myles. Jenny, Kieran Donnelly.' Paula made the introductions.

'Hi Jenny. Pleased to meet you.' He held out his hand.

'Hello.' Jennifer smiled as they shook hands. He had lovely dark smiling eyes. He didn't seem the slightest bit intimidating or stand-offish. Jennifer decided she liked him immediately. He was young to be so successful, she mused, observing the tall well-built man sitting astride the powerful bike. Paula had told her that he was in his late twenties. His thick chestnut hair was mussed from his helmet. It gave him an endearing boyish air. He had a strong tanned face and an aura of confidence and self-assurance that belied his casual laid-back appearance.

'I bet you're wishing you were in Spain today,' Kieran said as the cold wind lifted dried dead leaves and swirled them along the street. A spit of rain gave a foretaste of showers to come. 'I'll see you inside, Jenny. Don't get wet.' Kieran pulled on his leather gauntlets and refastened his helmet. The drops of rain got heavier and she and Paula ran for the shelter of the agency while Kieran zoomed down a side alley to get to the car park.

'I told you he was nice, didn't I?' Paula said triumphantly as she led Jennifer through a carpeted foyer and along a wide corridor lined with offices. There was a great air of hustle and bustle about the place. A buzz of activity that made Jennifer's adrenalin flow. She wouldn't mind being part of this at all, she thought happily.

'Hi Jenny.' Helen came out of one of the offices and smiled broadly as she saw the girls. 'Kieran's not in the office yet. But he's arrived. I heard him down in the car park,' she said dryly. Helen did not approve of the Harley-Davidson.

'Who's taking my name in vain?' Kieran rounded the corner and strode towards them. 'Hi Helen, sorry I'm late. That meeting with the car hire firm went on longer than I thought. Am I in your bad books?'

'Go away, you chancer! You knew very well Miss Johnson was scheduled to have a meeting with you before you both interview Jenny. I've rescheduled it for two this afternoon, because you have a meeting with Matthew Lynch from the insurance company in forty-five minutes.'

'That was kind of you, Helen,' Kieran said dryly. 'Come on, Jenny, let's go into my office before I'm overwhelmed by my secretary's kindness.'

He led her into an airy bright office dominated by an enormous mahogany desk and worn leather chair. 'The desk and chair were my dad's. I took over the company when he died,' Kieran said when he saw Jennifer looking at them.

'It's a fine desk. Mahogany really stands the test of time, doesn't it?' Jennifer stroked a finger along the smooth polished grain. 'When I lived in Spain I saw beautiful antique furniture. I'd love to have brought some home,' she said wistfully.

'Maybe you'll get your chance yet.' Kieran smiled. To her surprise he motioned to a sofa in the corner of the room. She'd expected him to sit behind his desk. 'I much prefer informal interviews,' he explained. 'Will you have a cup of coffee?'

'I'd love one, thanks,' replied Jennifer feeling much more relaxed. 'Black, no sugar.'

He poured four cups of coffee from a percolator on a small side table in the corner of the room. 'I always bring Helen out a cup around this time if I'm here. It's really to try and keep in her good books so she won't arrange a plethora of meetings for me to go to. But it doesn't work.' He laughed. 'What does Paula take in hers?'

'She takes it black too,' Jennifer said, deeply impressed that the managing director of TransCon did not expect his secretary to make his coffee and that *he* made *hers*.

'Tell me about Spain while we're waiting for Miss Johnson to join us,' Kieran said a few minutes later as he sat down beside her on the well-worn sofa.

'I loved it,' Jennifer enthused and, as if she was chatting to a friend, she told him about Majorca and the Costa and how beautiful they were outside the tourist haunts. 'Andalucia is beautiful. The mountains, the orange groves, the scenery. If I was a courier I'd try and get people to spend some time in the real Spain, even if they only left the resorts for one day. Just to see that there's more to Spain than sangria and paella and pubs and cheap cafés,' she was saying vehemently when a tall well-groomed woman knocked and entered the room. She was elegantly dressed in a tailored suit. Her make-up was flawless. She was in her thirties, Paula had said. But her stern-faced appearance belied her age.

Kieran stood up. 'This is Miss Johnson, our personnel manager.'

'How do you do, Miss Myles. If Mr Donnelly is agreeable, we will start the interview immediately. I have a meeting shortly and I like to be on time for my meetings,' she said frostily, with a cold glance in her boss's direction. 'I've brought your file with me. May we start?' She arched a perfectly shaped eyebrow in Kieran's direction.

'Certainly. If you care to go through Jennifer's CV, please. Would you like some coffee before we start?' Kieran asked politely.

'Thank you, no.' Miss Johnson was not to be bribed with coffee, even if it was Bewley's freshly ground and roasted.

She sat on a high-backed chair, her spine ramrod straight, and scanned the CV in front of her. Soon the questions were coming thick and fast. Jennifer answered to the best of her ability, aware that Kieran was listening intently.

'You worked in Majorca as an au pair. How is it you did not furnish references from your employer there? I know we have one from the owner of the bar you worked in, and one from your headmistress. I would have expected you to include one from the woman who employed you last year,' Miss Johnson said.

Oh hell! thought Jennifer in dismay. 'I thought two references would be sufficient, it generally is. So I got one from my most recent employer, after all, I worked for him far longer than I did for Mrs Curtis.' If she had to get a reference from Gillian, she could forget the job. Gillian would most certainly tell her to take a running jump. It was just as well she'd got a reference from Mother Andrew prior to the débâcle in Majorca.

'Two references are perfectly adequate,' Kieran interjected firmly. 'And I think from what I've heard that Jennifer is very much the type of person we are looking for.' He eyeballed Miss Johnson. She held his gaze.

'It is a very responsible position. We need someone who is willing to work hard and shoulder responsibility. The customer is always right no matter how wrong he or she is. Our couriers must have tact, diplomacy and a great deal of patience—'

'As well as warmth and enthusiasm,' Kieran interrupted with a smile. 'I think we're very lucky to find a candidate with all of these traits. I'm very impressed with your languages and experience of Spain. To have someone who knows both Majorca and the Costa is an added bonus. Don't you think so, Miss Johnson?'

'Indeed,' the personnel manager said tightly.

'Great then. I won't delay you any longer, I don't want you to be late for your meeting.' Kieran uncoiled his long legs and stood up.

'And we have one this afternoon. I hope you'll make *this* one.' Her sarcasm was unmistakable.

'Oh rest assured I will, Miss Johnson. I wouldn't miss it,' Kieran said coldly, and for the first time Jennifer saw the steel in him. He might seem laid-back and casual but there was no doubting his authority when he spoke in that tone of voice.

'Very well.' Miss Johnson closed her file. 'Shall I tell Miss Myles of her pay and conditions or will I leave that to you?'

'I'll attend to that.'

'I'll see you on the training course, Miss Myles,' Miss Johnson said stiffly.

'Yes, thank you,' Jennifer murmured as the other woman stalked out of the room.

'I inherited Miss Johnson. I think she thinks my interviewing methods are unorthodox, to say the least. But I prefer informality if possible. I think when people are relaxed you get a better sense of them,' Kieran said calmly. 'And my sense of you, Jennifer, is that you'll make a great addition to the team I'm building up. So if you care to join us in TransCon, the job is yours. What do you say?'

'I say I can't wait, Mr Donnelly.'

'The name's Kieran. My door is always open if you have any problems or suggestions or just feel like a chat.' Her new boss smiled broadly. 'Welcome to TransCon.'

Chapter Fifty-Four

'Modulate your voice, Jennifer. Pitch it to the people at the end of the bus. Stop gabbling, please. You want your clients to be able to hear and understand the information you are giving them. Do you understand?' Jennifer nodded.

'Yes, Miss Johnson,' she murmured.

'Good, now begin again.' Jennifer could see Paula eyeing her sympathetically as she began once more to give her introductory speech to the rest of her colleagues, who were pretending to be tourists on a foreign holiday.

It was six months since her fateful conversation with Paula on the sunny south coast of Spain. She'd been home two weeks, it was bitterly cold. Brenda and Grandpa Myles were getting on her nerves. She missed Ronan badly and, as she listened to Miss Johnson rabbiting on, she wondered if she had made a terrible mistake.

'I should have stayed where I was,' she grumbled to Paula at break-time.

'Don't talk nonsense,' her friend said briskly. 'The training course only lasts three weeks, then it's practically Christmas. We have a couple of months of office work and after that you'll be back in Spain before you know it. Easter won't be long coming.'

'She's a real wagon, isn't she?' Jennifer remarked as she watched the personnel officer engage the office supervisor in animated conversation.

'She's as hard as nails, that one,' Paula said. 'You should hear the things Helen has to say about her. I'd love her job though. She can put the likes of us through hell. She even gets to fly out to the resorts to check up on things, I've heard. Although someone usually sneaks a warning phone call from the office if they get the chance.'

'I hope she's never on a bus when I'm making a speech. I'd get stage fright. It's very intimidating having her sitting there when you're trying to be poised and self-confident. At least we're starting the make-up and grooming course this afternoon, that should be interesting,' Jennifer said. 'And I do like the uniform.'

'Yeah, it's very smart, isn't it,' Paula agreed. 'Royal blue is such a fresh colour. It's gorgeous with the tan and I love the culottes. I can't wait to get back to Spain and really start on the job properly.'

'I hope none of my clients ever dies. Did you hear Miss Johnson telling us the procedure? One of the girls had someone drown on her last year,' Jennifer said anxiously.

'Don't be worrying, Jenny, the agency will be there to help. It's not as if we've no back-up. And our Spanish is fluent, some of the girls can only barely get by. We'll be fine,' Paula declared. 'Kieran is very impressed with us, Helen told me. We're going to do well here, Jenny,' she said confidently.

'I like Kieran.' Jennifer smiled. 'He's not a rip-off artist. He runs a good agency.'

'I suppose it pays to,' Paula mused. 'People will come back again and again if they're happy with their holidays. One of the reps was telling me about this travel company she worked for, who used the cheapest of cheap accommodation, and she often had to go in after the maids had been and clean up after them, on hand-over day. The aggravation she had to put up with from clients nearly gave her a nervous breakdown, although she sympathized with them. At least we won't have that to put up with.'

'I hope we get to Greece sometime. Since we speak Spanish, we might only be sent to Spain or the Canaries.' Jennifer sipped her coffee and took a bite out of a chocolate éclair.

'Don't worry, I have that under control,' Paula assured

her. 'I've arranged for us to do Greek lessons starting from next week. A Greek woman, who's married to an Irish man, gives them in her own home. Her name is Elena, she's lovely. I got her name from the college I was at,' Paula announced.

'Good thinking.' Jennifer was impressed.

'Are you coming out for a drink tonight?' Paula asked as they finished their coffee.

'I might join you later. I've arranged to meet Rachel Stapleton, Ronan's sister. He asked me would I organize something. He worries about her. The father is a real shit, he keeps interfering when she tries to live her own life. She finds it hard to stand up to him,' Jennifer explained.

'Where are you going?' Paula asked.

'We're going to meet at Clerys, after that I don't know. We'll probably go for something to eat. I'll have to see what she wants to do.'

'Beth and I are going to the Addison for a chat and a drink. Why don't you bring Rachel?' Paula invited.

'I'll see, Paula. She's very shy. She might not want to. If you see me you see me. If you don't you don't. OK?' Jennifer responded.

'OK,' Paula agreed.

As she stood shivering under Clerys clock, Jennifer thought nostalgically of the balmy breezes of the Costa, so different from foggy, damp, freezing cold Dublin. It was the middle of the evening rush hour. Hundreds of people hurried along O'Connell Street. Bumper-to-bumper traffic spewed out vile polluted fumes. Jennifer buried her face in her thick woollen scarf. Of Rachel, there was no sign.

She shuffled from one foot to the other to try and keep warm. No doubt the other girl had got caught in the atrocious traffic. Jennifer thought longingly of the blazing fire that her mother would have in the kitchen at home. She'd far prefer to be sitting down to a plate of corned beef, cabbage, creamed potatoes and parsley sauce at home, than be standing here waiting for Ronan's shy sister to arrive. But what could she do? Ronan wanted her to be friends with his sister. He'd given Jennifer the home phone number and, when she'd phoned one Friday night, a man's voice had answered. Jennifer assumed it was the father. She'd asked to speak to Rachel.

'Who is calling?' His cold imperious tone chilled her at the other end of the phone. She felt like saying, 'None of your business,' but just said politely, 'Jennifer Myles.' Jennifer felt he didn't recognize the name. Of course it was more than two and a half years since his wife's funeral. He'd hardly acknowledged her condolences. Rachel came to the phone.

'Hello,' she said shyly.

'Hi, Rachel, this is Jennifer, Ronan's girlfriend. I'm home from Spain for a few months. I thought maybe we could meet for coffee or a drink or something,' Jennifer suggested cheerfully. There was a silence at the other end. 'Of course, if you're up to your eyes or anything, I understand,' she said hastily, not wanting the other girl to feel she had to do something she'd rather not do.

'I'd like that,' Jennifer heard Rachel say in a low voice. 'Ronan's told me a lot about you in his letters.' She probably had to keep her voice down because Mr Stapleton was earwigging. They arranged to meet under Clery's clock and then Rachel said a quick goodbye and hung up.

Maybe she'd changed her mind, Jennifer thought glumly as she watched a 19A bus disgorge its passengers. If it had been going in the opposite direction she'd have been very tempted to get on it and go home.

'Hello, is it Jennifer?' she heard a shy voice ask. She turned to see a thin girl with fair curly hair and big blue eyes, hidden behind thick-lensed glasses. She gave a vulnerable waif-like impression and had none of Ronan's ruddy vitality. Jennifer, soft-hearted to the core, felt like putting her arms around her and giving her a great big hug.

'Hi,' she said warmly. 'I'm very glad you came. I was

492

hoping you would. Ronan will be delighted we've met at last. I know I met you at the funeral,' she said gently, 'but you were in no state to talk to anyone.'

'No,' Rachel said sadly. 'I wasn't.'

'Are you hungry? Will we go for something to eat? Or would you just like to go for a drink?'

'I don't mind,' Rachel said shyly. 'Whatever you want.'

'I'm starving,' Jennifer laughed. 'I'm doing this training course and all the concentration has me ravenous. I could murder bacon, egg and chips. There's a little café further up, we could go there.'

'OK,' Rachel agreed. Jennifer gave a little inward sigh. Rachel was a woman of few words, she certainly didn't take after her more exuberant brother.

Gradually, as the other girl started to relax in Jennifer's company, she became more talkative. She asked Jennifer about being a courier and what the job entailed. She seemed fascinated by Jennifer's tales of her life in Spain, and said enviously, 'You've done so much with your life. You've seen so much. Mine is so dull and boring in comparison.'

'Why don't you do something about it? Why don't you go over to Ronan when you're qualified?' Jennifer asked gently.

Rachel gave a mirthless laugh. 'You're looking at the greatest coward going, Jennifer. I keep telling myself I'm going to do something drastic with my life. But I never do anything.'

'The longer you leave it, the harder it gets,' Jennifer said.

'I know, it's . . . it's just . . . well after Mam died, and then Ronan had the row with my father and left for America . . . I lost all my confidence. I felt very much alone. Home in Rathbarry is the only place I don't feel scared. Isn't that daft?' A bright pink suffused her cheeks and she looked away, as if embarrassed at having revealed so much of herself in her little outburst.

'That's very understandable, Rachel,' Jennifer said,

493

feeling very sorry for the young woman in front of her. 'Someday the time will be right for you to get out there and do whatever you want.'

'I'd like to have my own place in Dublin, someday,' Rachel confided.

'You will too,' Jennifer said supportively.

They chatted away for ages, but Rachel refused Jennifer's invitation to go for a drink, saying she had an essay to finish. They promised to meet again.

'You didn't bring Rachel with you?' Paula asked, several hours later when Jennifer joined her and Beth for a drink in the Addison.

'She wouldn't come. I tried to persuade her, but she said she had to get home. It's awful. That father of hers should be shot. He rules her like a dictator,' Jennifer exclaimed. 'Ronan is right to be worried about her. She's only young like us and she's like a middle-aged woman. She was wearing a sort of calf-length woollen skirt and a cardigan fastened up to the neck like an ould wan. And you should see the glasses! And you know,' Jennifer paused to have a sip of her gin and tonic, 'she has the most beautiful eyes. They're very blue. I'd love to get my hands on her and get her hair styled and put her in fashionable clothes, and get her to wear contact lenses.'

'She sounds a pretty miserable sort,' Beth remarked.

'She is!' Jennifer agreed. 'And I don't think she's in any fit state to do anything about it. She's still in bits over her mother, God help her. I'll just have to see what I can do about her. I'm going to meet her next week as well. Maybe I could get her to come out of her shell a bit. It's a pity I'm not in Spain, she could have come over for a holiday. It would do her all the good in the world to get away from that old yoke of a father of hers.' Now that she'd really met her future sister-in-law at last, Jennifer decided she wasn't going to let Rachel Stapleton bury herself away in Rathbarry for ever.

'Did you hear about Eilis McNally?' Beth interjected, grinning broadly.

'No . . . What?' the other pair queried in unison.

'She's given up the job in the Department of Social Welfare and joined the Hare Krishnas.'

'I don't believe it!' giggled Jennifer.

'God help them! She should have taken a job as a photographer for the gutter press. She has enough experience after her carry-on with me and Barry,' snorted Paula, who had never forgiven Eilis for her dastardly deed. The other two guffawed.

'And wait until you hear about Cynthia Jones . . . ' Jennifer and Paula settled down to hear Beth's news and enjoy a good juicy gossip.

'The wandrin' minstrel returns. What hour of the night is this for ya to be coming in?' Grandpa Myles declared, several hours later, as Jennifer closed the front door behind her. 'You should hear the giving out of yer woman upstairs.' He jerked his thumb upwards in the direction of Brenda's room. Jennifer sighed.

'What's the matter with her?'

'Ah, she was givin' out that you didn't ask her to go for a drink with ye. Ye know the way she carries on. Come on and I'll make ye a cup of cocoa and we'll have a chat in the kitchen an' she'll be asleep before you go to bed,' he suggested. 'Your ma an' da are already gone. I was waiting up for ya,' he said, leading the way to the kitchen. Jennifer stifled a yawn. All she wanted to do was to go to bed. But her grandfather was dying for a chat. He was so pleased that she was home. It was touching. The only thing was, he'd keep her up until all hours. Still, it was probably better to sit listening to him for a half an hour than go up and get an ear-bashing from Brenda.

She made her way upstairs an hour later. She was banjaxed. Grandpa Myles would talk the hind legs off a donkey, she thought tiredly. All she wanted to do was to get into bed and sleep her brains out. The light was out, she noted with relief. Brenda was asleep. She'd undress in the dark so as not to disturb her. She stole quietly into the bedroom and began to undress.

'Where were you?' Brenda demanded, switching on the light. Jennifer's heart sank at the sulky tone in her sister's voice.

'I went for a drink with the girls,' she said lightly.

'Lucky girls,' Brenda said sarcastically. 'They see more of you than I do. I was really looking forward to you coming home. I was looking forward to having a few nights on the town with you,' she moaned.

'We will have a few nights out. I'm only back a wet week.' Jennifer tried to keep the irritation out of her voice. Brenda could be so childish sometimes.

'You think more of that pair than you do of your own sister,' Brenda sulked.

'How about if we go out tomorrow night for a drink?' Jennifer said placatingly.

'We could go to Tamango's.' Brenda perked up and sat up in bed all ready for a chat.

'Sure,' Jennifer agreed glumly. She didn't want to traipse off to a nightclub tomorrow night. All she wanted to do was to come home, relax, have a bath and a chat with her mother and flop. But if she said that to Brenda, her sister would go into a mega-huff.

'Don't sound too enthusiastic. I bet if it was that Paula one who wanted to go out, you'd go flying.' Brenda sniffed.

'Look, I said I'd go out with you tomorrow, Bren. I'm a bit tired, that's all.' Jennifer pulled her nightdress down over her head and got into bed and pulled the soft plump eiderdown up under her chin.

'It's just that I'm glad to see you home,' Brenda said plaintively. 'I want to hear all your news. You're really lucky, you know. Getting a job in Spain, and now training to be a courier. It's such a glamorous job compared to my boring old slog. I'd love to have had the chance to skedaddle off to Spain like you did.'

Jennifer gritted her teeth and counted to ten. 'Why don't you do it now, then? It's not as if you're Methuselah or anything.'

'It's not that easy,' Brenda sighed. 'You were lucky.'

'Brenda, luck had nothing to do with it. I just got up off my ass and did something with my life. You can do the same if you want to. You're as bad as Rachel Stapleton.'

'Who?'

'Oh no-one,' Jennifer muttered. It was typical of Brenda, she fumed. Just because she was in a rut, she was annoyed that Jennifer was making a go of things. Jennifer wouldn't have minded looking for a flat, except that her mother would be hurt. Coming home to live after having your own place was extremely difficult, especially when you were sharing a room with a sister like Brenda. Roll on Easter, she thought, stretching her legs gingerly between the cold sheets.

Chapter Fifty-Five

'What do you think of that Brenda one?' Jennifer viciously swatted a fly that was buzzing around her, with her clipboard. She and Paula were waiting with dozens of other couriers for the arrival of their star flights at Palma Airport.

'She's a gas woman all right,' Paula remarked as she straightened the elegant black Spanish-style bow that was keeping her blond hair back from her face.

'Imagine, we're here working in Majorca, and she could have booked her holiday with us in TransCon, and instead she takes off to the Costa. I mean, I ask you.' Jennifer was most put out.

'Maybe she felt we'd cramp her style or something.' Paula yawned. 'No doubt if we'd been assigned to the Costa, she'd have come to Majorca.'

'I suppose you're right. You know Brenda, she's as odd as they come.' Jennifer peered into arrivals. 'No sign yet, I hate it when the flights are delayed.'

'At least we got our return flight checked in smoothly. Did you hear your woman asking to be put in first class on a charter flight? She caused a right rumpus.' Paula grinned.

'She was pissed out of her skull,' Jennifer snorted. 'I wouldn't like to be her tomorrow morning. She's going to have a hell of a hangover.'

'She puked on the bus.' Paula scowled.

'Yuck!' Jennifer grimaced. 'My lot were fairly OK. Apart from Mr and Mrs Burke, who were having the mother and father of a row. You should have heard them. She called him a pathetic old Casanova, and he called her a dried-up old prune. It was hilarious really. Mind you, he was an awful old lecher.'

'And people think being a courier is glamorous.'

'It's fun though, isn't it?' Jennifer grinned.

'Oh yeah,' Paula agreed. 'This time last year I was doing exams. Would you believe it? That year just flew. Are you sorry we weren't sent to the Costa?'

Jennifer shook her head. 'Not really. Majorca's gorgeous, especially at this time of the year. The start of the season is always the nicest time. It's going to get fairly hectic during July and August though.'

'I wonder will Gillian and Bryan be coming to Santa Juan?' Paula teased.

'Wash your mouth out with soap, Paula Matthews,' Jennifer exclaimed, giving a shudder as she remembered her former employer's assault on her.

'Here's our gang.' Paula nodded in the direction of a horde of pale-skinned new arrivals pouring through the arrivals in their direction, when they saw the TransCon logo. The two of them were rapidly surrounded by clients.

'See you later,' Paula said, when they had sorted out the new arrivals. She was doing the north of the island. Jennifer took care of the southern end.

Half an hour later, Jennifer stood at the front of the luxury coach, pointing out the marina on their left and the massive illuminated Palma Cathedral towering above them to the right. The cathedral was one of the island's most beautiful tourist attractions. The first time she gave her speech, she'd been nervous and her voice was a little shaky as fifty pairs of eyes focused on her. But it was no trouble to her now, she actually enjoyed it. It was nice bonding with a new group. She liked the sense of exhilaration and anticipation among new arrivals. And because she genuinely loved the verdant picturesque island, Jennifer took great pleasure in telling her clients that there was far more to Majorca than beaches and sangria.

She had built up a good working relationship with the

agency, the coach drivers and the apartment owners, whose apartments TransContinental Travel block-booked for the season. Arrival and departure days were very hectic. She looked after two flights a week and had clients in ten apartment blocks between Palma and Paguera, including stops in Santa Ponsa and Magalluf. By the time she did her visits and dealt with the paperwork back at the office the day was gone. Some nights she took clients on organized excursions to barbecues and fancy dress nights and the like.

The commission she made from selling the trips went into a special savings fund for her future with Ronan. He was saving like mad, he told her. If both of them saved really hard they might be able to get married sooner than they had planned. It would mean they needn't have a long engagement. But she'd have to give up being a courier. She couldn't very well work on the continent and leave her husband at home. Still, that was a long time away. She wouldn't be twenty-one until August twelve months so that gave her another season away, at least. Maybe then Kieran would give her a job in the TransCon office. She liked the travel business. She could always work at the front desk if her boss was willing and there was a vacancy. In the meantime she and Paula were having a ball in Majorca.

One night, while waiting for a flight, Jennifer and Paula were joking and laughing with one of the couriers from another agency. His name was Rick. He was a real ladies' man. Tall, blond, blue-eyed and sexy, he fancied Paula like mad and was always trying to make a date with her. She wasn't interested but, Paula being Paula, flirted nevertheless. Rick was down on bended knee, begging her to go for a meal with him, and she was laughingly refusing, much to Jennifer's amusement, when a polite cough caused them to turn around. Miss Johnson from head office stood looking at them. Jennifer and Paula nearly died.

They were half-way through the season and Jennifer

and Paula were expecting such a visit but they thought that she would visit their colleagues on the Costa first. And they would have warned Jennifer and Paula of the impending visit. Miss Johnson was not known as a sneaky cow for nothing.

'The other passengers will be through shortly, I only have hand luggage.' She indicated a Samsonite shoulder bag. 'It's just as well, perhaps,' she said coldly. 'I sincerely hope that this is not your usual carry-on. You are wearing the company uniform. You are the company's representatives abroad. What sort of an image are you giving the company? If other couriers . . . ' she gave Rick a supercilious glare, 'want to act in an undignified manner, that's their business. I won't have *my* couriers acting like silly teenagers. Is that clear?' Rick moved discreetly away and made hilarious faces behind the supervisor's back.

'Is that clear, Miss Myles? Miss Matthews?' Miss Johnson demanded.

Jennifer was on the verge of a fit of the giggles. All she could see was Rick mimicking the supervisor behind her back.

'Yes, Miss Johnson,' she heard Paula say. Jennifer knew Paula was furious to have been caught in such a ridiculous situation. Paula prided herself on being the epitome of sophistication.

'Yes, Miss Johnson,' Jennifer managed to say. She hoped her boss wouldn't notice that the nail varnish on her thumbnail was slightly chipped. Miss Johnson was a stickler for good grooming. Chipped nail varnish was a big no-no.

'Good. Please greet your clients. They're coming through,' Miss Johnson said haughtily, making a note in her folder. She watched like a hawk as they went through the arrivals procedures.

'I bet she'll come on my bus, the old bitch,' Paula muttered as they walked towards their buses. 'She never liked me because I got the job through Helen. Now she's really got something on me. I bet she can't wait to get back to Kieran. I hope someone pukes all over her on the bus.' Jennifer felt sorry for Paula, but she was relieved that Miss Johnson would not be coming on her bus. Paula was probably right. After the episode in the airport, she'd most likely want to see how Paula performed. If there was one thing Miss Johnson enjoyed, it was getting people rattled.

'I'll go with Miss Myles,' Miss Johnson declared. Oh shit! thought Jennifer in dismay. She thought she'd got away with it. Out of the corner of her eye she saw Paula grinning.

'See you later,' her friend said sweetly as they parted to board their respective buses.

Miss Johnson sat in the front seat right under her nose. Briskly, Jennifer walked down the aisle of the coach checking off names. One couple was missing. She got off the bus to search for them and saw Paula bringing them over. 'They were on my bus. They took one look at Jolly Johnson and decided they'd prefer to come with me.' She giggled. 'Can you believe the way she walked in on us just when that idiot was down on his knees? Wait until I get him,' she whispered.

'I'd better go,' Jennifer said hastily. 'She's sitting on the bus like she's got a poker stuck up her ass. I'll see you at home if I haven't drowned myself somewhere.'

'Good luck,' Paula murmured.

Jennifer explained the situation to her driver, Carlos, in rapid Spanish. 'Don't drive too fast,' she warned. 'I want to keep my balance.'

'I'll catch her eye in the mirror and seduce her with lusty glances, she looks as if she could do with a man,' Carlos, ever the chauvinist, suggested with a grin.

'Stop it, Carlos, and behave yourself,' Jennifer begged. 'Come on, let's get going.' She was beginning to feel very hot under the collar indeed. She took a deep breath, smiled and began her speech.

'Good evening, ladies and gentlemen. My name is Jennifer Myles. I'll be your rep for the next two weeks and on behalf of TransContinental Travel, may I welcome you to Majorca.'

'The island of tits, bums, booze and nookey,' a voice called from the back of the bus. Why are you doing this to me, God? Jennifer asked the Almighty in despair as she ignored the interruption. Trust her to have three pissed lads on the bus tonight. Miss Johnson wrote furiously in her precious folder.

'Stop the bus, we're three thirsty Cork men, we want to go and get a drink.'

'Boys, you'll be able to drink all you want to when I leave you off at your apartment, there's a disco bar nearby that stays open late,' Jennifer said pleasantly.

'Yo.'

'Great stuff.'

'Good on ya.'

The three of them roared from the back of the bus.

'But if you just listen to me for a few minutes now, I'll tell you how to make sure you don't ruin your holiday before you've even started it,' Jennifer said firmly.

'Sound girl ye are,' one of them shouted. Jennifer felt like going down and giving him a box in the jaw. His friend told him to shut up. Jennifer's heart sank. Don't let them start a fight, she thought in dismay. That's all I need. She glared at the trio.

'Right,' she said briskly, as they drove out of the airport. 'First of all I'll just tell you a little about the island and what to expect. And what to eat and drink. Bank and shopping times and so on. Then tomorrow, when I come to visit you at your apartments, you can have your questions ready and we'll have a get-to-know-one-another session.' Fifty faces gazed at her, expectantly. The fifty-first sat stony-faced in the front seat. Jennifer smiled confidently, giving no sign of the nervousness she was feeling, and began her spiel.

'Could you stop the bus, Jennifer, I have to go for a slash?' came a slurred voice from the rear of the bus. It was one of those nights, she decided. To hell with it. She might as well go with the flow and forget about Miss Johnson.

'Come on,' she said with pretended cheeriness. 'And then I don't want to hear another word out of you.'

'You'd think it was for spite,' she told Paula later as they sat sipping a beer on their small balcony. It was almost four am. The pair of them had to be up early in the morning for their client meetings. But they needed to wind down after the stress of Miss Johnson's arrival. 'One of the fellas saw her sitting on her own when he was getting off and said if she was lonely, she knew where they were staying. You should have seen the face of her,' Jennifer giggled, utterly relieved that the ordeal was over. Once she'd got rid of her merry men, everything else had gone smoothly enough. 'She has a list of our apartments and the times of the meetings. God knows where she'll strike tomorrow.' Jennifer yawned.

'She's incredible though, isn't she?' Paula mused. 'Not a hair out of place. Make-up flawless. Grooming immaculate. I've never seen her look less than perfect. She's only about thirty-five, you know. But she's a real dry pain in the ass. I wonder has she a man in her life?'

'If she hasn't, she could have. Carlos offered to seduce her,' Jennifer laughed.

'He's a great character.' Paula was amused. 'But not even Carlos would put a smile on Jolly Johnson's mush. Come on, let's get to bed. We've a long day tomorrow. We'd better phone the office in Malaga and let them know she's on her rounds.'

'Hmm,' agreed Jennifer. 'Forewarned is forearmed.'

'You handled that situation last night very well, Miss Myles. And I'm glad to see that you've redone your nail varnish. You're inclined to speak a little too quickly sometimes. Guard against that,' Miss Johnson said crisply. The supervisor had come to one of Jennifer's meetings. She held out her hand. 'I won't see you again after I've checked up on Miss Matthews. I'll be sending in a good report on you. Just remember that when you are in uniform you must behave with dignity.' She gave Jennifer a limp handshake.

'Thank you, Miss Johnson,' Jennifer said, very pleased with herself. She'd worried that Miss Johnson would not be at all impressed after the disaster last night. But obviously the supervisor thought Jennifer had handled it well. It was great for her self-confidence. She hoped Paula would be as lucky.

'She never said anything like that to me, the poker-faced wagon,' Paula exclaimed. 'She just sat there scribbling in her folder and then gave me the lecture about behaving with dignity while wearing the uniform. She never said *anything* about a good report. She's probably going to tell Kieran that I'm totally unsuitable to be a courier.'

'He knows you're good enough,' Jennifer said.

'But she could say anything when she goes home. She doesn't like me,' Paula argued glumly.

'Forget about her. Anyway I don't think she's malicious. She's gone to torment the poor souls on the Costa. We can relax.' Jennifer was light-hearted. They were back in the office making up their reports. There was a ton of paperwork to get through and they were tired after their late night and client meetings all day. The phone rang. It was the hospital in Palma. Jennifer listened and scowled.

'What's up?' Paula asked.

'It's one of those idiots from Cork. He's broken his leg and his wrist. I'd better go over. It's a pity he didn't break his neck while he was at it,' she said crossly. 'Where the hell are my car keys?'

'The joy of being a courier.' Paula smiled as she bent her head to fill in a report on a customer complaint.

'If this is joy, I can't wait to get to paradise!' Jennifer snorted as she rummaged through her bag in search of the elusive keys. 'Hasta la vista!'

Chapter Fifty-Six

Rachel arranged the strips of grilled bacon, sausage, pudding and tomato neatly on a warm plate and brought it to the table. Her father sniffed appreciatively. 'That smells very nice,' he approved. 'Where's yours?'

'I'm not hungry,' she answered quietly. She felt extremely tense. She'd been putting off this moment for ages.

'I hope you're not on one of these silly diets. It's very important to eat properly. You're far too thin, Rachel,' William said sternly as he cut his bacon into neat pieces. He was such a prissy eater, she thought. Not like Ronan and Harry, who loved their grub and ate with relish. William was a dietician's dream. He slowly chewed each mouthful and took ages to eat a meal. Rachel once read that you were supposed to chew your food thirty times. William came close to that. She scowled watching his jaws working over a small piece of bacon.

She poured tea, buttered a slice of bread for herself and smeared it with blackberry jam. It was all she wanted. Even that made her feel nauseous. Tell him! Tell him! she urged herself, trying to screw up her courage.

'I've made arrangements for my TP,' she murmured.

'Pardon?' William stopped chewing and put down his knife and fork. 'I didn't catch that, Rachel, speak up.'

She took a deep breath. 'I said I've made arrangements for my teaching practice in September.'

Her father looked perplexed. 'What arrangements? You don't have to arrange anything. You'll be doing it in my class.'

'No, Dad. I decided not to. I thought it would be

506

better to do it in an outside school. I think it's more professional. I want the examiner to judge me on my own merits,' Rachel said hastily.

'Nonsense. Of course he'll judge you on your own merits, my being headmaster won't affect you at all. And you'll be much more confident in familiar surroundings,' William said dismissively.

Confident! In front of you. You must be joking, Rachel thought scornfully. She tried again. 'I just feel—'

'Whatever arrangements you've made, cancel them. I have it all worked out,' William interrupted, forking a sliver of grilled tomato into his mouth. As usual, it was obvious that he was not the slightest bit interested in what she felt. 'You can take sixth class for maths and Irish. I'll work on it beforehand with you.'

'Dad, I'm doing my teaching practice in St Catherine's Primary School, I've fixed it up with Sister James.' Rachel pushed her bread and jam away from her.

'Why didn't you consult me about this?' William glared at her. 'Sister James must think that I'm a most negligent father if I wouldn't organize my own daughter's teaching practice. You've made a show of me!' he declared.

Rachel fumed silently. The ego of him. He only cared about what his peers thought of him. He wanted to control every part of her life. How she longed to pick up his grill and dump it over his bald head, and watch the runny yellow egg yolk dribble down his aquiline nose as she told him with great venom to get lost and leave her alone and not be annoying her. Why couldn't he have died of a heart attack, and not her mother? How idyllic life would have been then. There was something else she had to tell him too, she might as well get it over and done with. There was no good time to tell William anything. He didn't like being told things. *He* liked doing the telling.

'When I've finished my TP and when I go back to St Pat's in October, I've decided to spend my last year living in. Commuting is just too time-consuming. I don't want anything to interfere with my studies,' she said in a rush.

'Indeed and you won't be living in. If there's anything guaranteed to interfere with your studies, it's living in a hall of residence with other students who just want to party and have a good time and aren't the slightest bit interested in their studies. No, Rachel. I won't permit it. You're managing perfectly well here.'

'I'm going to live in,' she argued.

'As long as I pay your fees, Miss, you'll do as I say!' William roared, pointing his finger in her face. He was very taken aback by Rachel's defiance. It was something to be nipped rapidly in the bud. 'Now, I don't want to hear another word.'

Rachel stood up. Her knees were shaking. She knew this was her moment. If she flunked it she might just as well give up the idea of having any sort of a normal life.

'If you don't like it, you don't have to pay my fees,' she quavered. 'I have enough money to pay my own. I'm doing my teaching practice in St Catherine's and I'm living in, and I'm going to Clonmel for a few days' holidays with my friend Pauline this evening.' She didn't wait for her father's response. She walked quickly out of the room, hurried upstairs and grabbed her pre-packed bag. 'Don't falter now, Rachel Stapleton,' she muttered as she heard her father's footsteps on the stairs.

'Now just a minute, young lady—'

'Sorry, Dad, I'm in a bit of a rush, I'll be late for Pauline if I don't hurry. See you in a few days.' She brushed past him and ran downstairs.

'You haven't told me anything about this!' he blustered. 'I don't know what kind of a girl this Pauline is.'

'She's very nice. Bye.' Rachel flew out the door. She hadn't exaggerated when she said she was in a hurry. She was meeting Pauline opposite Heuston Station at six and she had to get the bus from Bray. She'd taken the precaution of ordering Danny Allen's taxi to take her to Bray and she saw with relief that he was parked at the church, where she'd asked him to pick her up. Rachel hurried along the street without a backward glance. Danny got out of the cab and took her bag from her. 'I'm in an awful hurry to get to Bray, Danny,' she said hastily, afraid her father would come up the road and cause a scene.

'No problem,' Danny assured her. Rachel turned in the seat and looked out the back window. She could see her father in his slippers, arms akimbo, standing at the front gate. Safe in the taxi, a sense of triumph made her feel uncharacteristically brave. She leaned forward. 'Danny, could you drive down the street and go the tenacre field's route, I just want to wave to my dad, I left in a bit of a hurry.'

'Sure, Rachel,' the taxi driver said obligingly as he did a quick reverse and headed down the street. The expression on William's face was more of amazement than anything else. Up yours! Rachel thought exultantly as she gave him a demure wave. The face of him, when she'd told him she had her own money for her fees. The *power* having her own money gave her. It had been worth saving every penny she'd earned in the Tea Rooms for this moment. Harry and Ronan had been right when they'd said she should leave her father and stand on her own two feet. She'd taken her first step today and it felt marvellous.

Rachel settled back into the seat as Danny drove along the winding country road towards Bray. Her face grew sad. Harry and she had never got back together after the night of his ultimatum. Each had let the other down. Harry, because he'd tried to bully her as her father had. Rachel, because, as Harry saw it, she'd chosen her father over him. Harry had gone grape-picking in France that summer, less than two weeks after their contretemps, and she hadn't seen him until the following October. They'd bumped into each other one weekend. They'd hugged and said 'hello.' But the old intimacy was gone and there had been a sort of strain between them as they stood outside the chipper making polite small talk. It had been a relief to each of them when a sudden shower started and they'd said hasty goodbyes and run for the shelter of their respective houses.

Harry had a car now and he was working in a big law firm in Dublin. He also had a new girlfriend. A long-legged brunette who looked extremely glamorous. Rachel had seen her in Rathbarry with him, the odd weekend he came home to visit. She'd known that Harry wouldn't be on his own for long. It didn't bother her as much as she'd thought it would. Men were just a load of hassle, she told herself. She was better off without them. Being manless wasn't so bad. It would have been different if she'd never had a boyfriend. She'd experienced the boyfriend bit, done the dating bit, and even the heavy petting bit. These all brought their own problems and the fewer problems she had to deal with the better.

Once she passed her finals and had a job she'd start to live again, Rachel promised herself. In the meantime, she was looking forward to spending a few days with Pauline in Clonmel. Rachel couldn't help smiling at the thought of Pauline Hegarty. Pauline was the complete opposite to her. A zany, bubbly flibbertigibbet, Pauline lived life to the full and only studied when she absolutely had to. She would never have passed an exam without Rachel's help. Rachel envied her friend her sunny optimistic nature. But Pauline also had a kind heart. When Theresa died, Pauline had sat for many hours listening to Rachel talk about her mother. It helped Rachel greatly. Most people didn't want to talk to her about her mother for fear of upsetting her. Neighbours often crossed to the other side of the street when they saw her coming. Unsure of what to say. William was the last person she could talk to about her mother and Ronan had left home.

Pauline instinctively knew that Rachel wanted to talk, and with a sensitivity that belied her effervescent personality, she handed out tissues, made tea and let Rachel cry her eyes out as she talked of Theresa. It had been a relief for Rachel to be able to talk about her mother. Pauline had given her no advice. She hadn't expressed an opinion one way or the other as to whether Rachel should stay at home or go to France with Harry. She just kindly said that Rachel shouldn't make any hasty decisions. Making decisions when one was recently bereaved was not wise. Her kindness was a balm to Rachel's troubled soul. If it hadn't been for Pauline, she would never have got through her exams, or through the misery that followed her row with Harry.

Pauline had often invited her to visit her home but Rachel always put it off. But she needed some respite after the stresses and strains of the exams. And Rachel had planned the confrontation with her father in the knowledge that she could go and stay with her friend for a few days.

Pauline was sick of her summer job in a biscuit factory. She'd phoned Rachel and said she was leaving it and going home and invited Rachel to come with her for a few days. Rachel impulsively decided to take her up on her offer. The Misses Healy had been understanding about her need for a few days off so Rachel made her plans to drop her bombshells and be ready to escape the flak.

As Danny drove into Bray, Rachel felt pleased enough with herself. She hadn't chickened out. She'd got the better of her father. She had her own money and she damn well deserved a holiday.

'I didn't think you'd be here,' Pauline said with a broad grin, as she pulled in opposite Heuston at six-thirty. Punctuality was not one of her virtues so Rachel hadn't quite got to the panicky stage. She got into her friend's Volkswagen and they chugged along the Naas Road.

'Jemima's not in the best of form.' Pauline grimaced as the car began to vibrate as she accelerated to fifty. 'I think I've to get the wheels balanced or something, she's going a bit peculiar once I hit fifty.' Pauline knew nothing about the mechanics of her car nor did she wish to know anything about what went on under the bonnet. She knew it needed petrol to go, which she bought when the needle was well past the empty mark. She occasionally put water in the battery and in the radiator, when she thought of it. She couldn't figure out the air gauges and rarely, if ever, put air in her tyres. Oil was a rare treat for Jemima. Rachel was fascinated by this. Her father had a specific routine for looking after his car which never varied. Everything was checked on a weekly basis. His car was washed and polished every Saturday. It was immaculate. Pauline never washed her car. It was always littered with empty crisp bags. She cheerfully called it a tip-heap on wheels but nevertheless it was a much-loved car. Her father had given it to her as an early twenty-first birthday present to make life easier for her while she was in St Pat's.

'Did you bring your bikini?' Pauline asked out of the blue.

'Oohh, no,' Rachel said. 'I didn't know I'd need one.'

'Well you will. Look at the weather. It's glorious! We'll go to the beach in Waterford. You can get one in Dunnes tomorrow.'

Rachel wasn't sure if she wanted a bikini. She'd never worn one, she'd feel far too self-conscious. She'd buy a swimsuit instead.

They had a most pleasant journey to Clonmel. Rachel enjoyed looking at the countryside and the fine houses as she listened to Pauline's non-stop chatter. They stopped in Kilkenny for a meal. Rachel thought it was a beautiful city. The huge castle looked very dramatic in the evening sun and Pauline promised that they would spend a day shopping in the town during her few days' break. Rachel began to feel almost exhilarated. This was just what she needed. She should have done it ages ago. Theresa would be very pleased if she was looking down on her now, Rachel thought sadly.

They were scorching through Callan, a village built on a narrow street, when disaster struck. A plume of steam erupted from under the bonnet, causing Pauline to curse volubly. 'Balls on it, I think the radiator's run dry. For God's sake don't tell my father.' A young lad stood watching as Pauline waited for the steam to cool and then tried to twist off the radiator cap. She couldn't manage it. Her language was vicious and Rachel listened in admiration to the way her friend expressed her anger. She could imagine her father's face if he ever heard her cursing the way Pauline was.

The youth could take no more. He sidled over, took a dirty handkerchief out of his pocket, gave the cap a twist and off it came. 'Stay there and I'll get some water,' he instructed.

'I'm hardly going anywhere,' Pauline muttered a dry aside to Rachel. 'Steve McQueen he ain't.' The two of them looked at each other and started to giggle. Twenty minutes later they were on the road again with a full radiator and a bottle of water just in case.

'I'm a disgrace to the feminist cause,' Pauline declared. 'I must do a course in car maintenance. Imagine breaking down in Callan of all places.' They drove on, the countryside getting more beautiful by the mile, until Pauline pulled in at a gorgeous spot that overlooked a spectacular valley. 'This is called the V, I always feel I'm home when I get here. You should see it in the autumn, the colours are breathtaking.' Rachel could imagine it as she stared out at the stunning views.

Soon after that they reached the perimeter of the town. Pauline lived in a big detached bungalow on the outskirts. Her parents greeted them warmly and Rachel was shown to a pretty guest room and invited to make herself at home. Pauline was an only child and it was clear that her parents doted upon her.

Around eleven, she dragged Rachel to her feet and told her they were going to a disco. Mr and Mrs Hegarty never batted an eyelid. Obviously this was par for the course. Rachel marvelled at it all. If she arrived home and then said she was going to a disco at eleven, William would have a fit.

'I'll need a holiday after this,' Rachel declared the following Monday. It was eight-thirty, and Pauline was calling her to get up. She'd been to discos and parties. She'd gone on pub crawls and sung in ballad sessions. She'd played tennis and badminton and gone to a barndance on the Sunday night. That was great fun. At first she'd been shy, and couldn't make head nor tail of the steps, but everyone else was in the same boat and half the fun was turning left when you should be turning right as the MC bellowed the instructions from the stage.

'Today we're going to flop,' Pauline announced. 'The sun is splitting the trees, there's clear blue skies. Let's hit the beach.' Mrs Hegarty made them a sumptuous picnic and they set off for Waterford in trusty old Jemima. Rachel had her new bikini on under her new shorts and T-shirt. Pauline had insisted she go on a little spending spree and advised that you got a much better suntan in a bikini.

Pauline was an avid sun-worshipper. Rachel watched in amazement as she spread her towel on the beach and laid out an array of creams and lotions beside her. 'Come on. Strip,' she instructed, 'I'm going to teach you how to get a suntan.' Rachel felt embarrassed as she slipped out of her shorts and T-shirt to expose an expanse of milky-white limbs. 'Now cover yourself with that.' Pauline handed her a big yellow bottle of suntan milk, called Delial. Rachel sniffed it. It had a gorgeous smell. She did as she was told.

'Now make your bag into a pillow, put it on your towel, lie down with your book, listen to the sea and the birds and if you don't feel relaxed after today, I'll eat my hat,' Pauline declared. Twenty minutes later she was snoring her head off.

Rachel lay on the warm sand, feeling the heat of the sun soaking into her skin. It was a lovely sensation. The sound of the sea was like a lullaby. The sky was blue above her. A warm breeze rippled across her stomach like a caress. She felt a wonderful lethargy spread through her. Rachel emptied her mind and lay, thinking of nothing in particular, just listening to the sea and the birdsong and the gentle shushing of the balmy breeze. Her eyelids grew heavy. She slipped into a dreamless snooze.

There was no need for Pauline to eat her hat. Rachel

went home energized and refreshed after her few days away. And she had her first proper tan. As she sat on the coach to Dublin, she decided two things. She would save for a car. And from now on, whenever she had the chance, she would try and do some sunbathing. It was a marvellous way to relax, she'd discovered.

William was very cool with her when she got home. Curtly, he told her that there was some post for her. Letters from Ronan. He asked her nothing about her little holiday. Rachel didn't care. She just wanted to have a bath and unpack.

She was back at work the following day. The Tea Rooms were busy and the day passed quickly. At five o'clock she couldn't wait to get home. She made up two ham and salad rolls. One for William, one for herself. If her father thought she was going to turn around and cook a dinner on a lovely sunny evening, he could think again. She couldn't wait to get out to top up her tan. She raced home. She could see her father over in the newsagents, buying his evening paper and chatting to Mrs Morrissey. Perfect, Rachel thought, as she threw his roll on a plate and put a cup beside it. She ran upstairs, got into her bikini and grabbed her towel and book and suntan cream. She peered out the window to see if he was coming yet and was pleased to see he was still chatting. William loved the sound of his own voice. She poured herself a glass of milk from the fridge. Two pork chops reproached her. Thursday was pork chop day. She didn't care, the sun was shining and the top left-hand corner of the small patio was a sun trap.

Five minutes later, she was sitting against the wall, face up to the sun, welcoming its delightful bright heat. She heard her father's footsteps come around the side of the house. She kept her eyes tightly closed. William stopped short. 'Good grief!' she heard him say. Rachel ignored him. She heard him open the back door.

'Where's the dinner?' he growled.

'On the table,' she said airily. There was silence. Then

the sound of pots clashing and muttered imprecations. Rachel stayed firmly put. She wasn't his servant. He'd been at home all day. He was on holidays now. Why hadn't he cooked the dinner himself? The sun poured its heat down on her and delicious lethargy once again spread through her limbs. A smile crossed her face as she heard the sizzle of meat on the pan. William could cook his own dinner from now on. As far as Rachel was concerned, the worm had turned, and not before its time.

Chapter Fifty-Seven

Rachel gently placed her mother's photograph on her desk and smiled down at it. 'Well Mam, here I am at last. Living in. I wish you were at home so I could tell you all about it. Dad's going mad, of course. But he didn't try to stop me because he knows I have some money of my own saved. You'd be proud of me,' she said sadly.

'Don't get into the dumps on your first day here,' she told herself. 'Be positive. Start as you mean to go on.' Rachel stood in the middle of the room that was to be her home for the next eight months. It was a nice room. The walls were painted pink. To her right was a wardrobe and bed and there were bookshelves along the wall. To her left was a sink and mirror, more shelves and a desk and chair and noticeboard. The window was at right angles to the desk and had a view across the campus to the college buildings. It was clean, bright and airy but best of all it was thirty-five miles from her father's house. He had no say here. He couldn't interfere in her life.

There was a knock on the door. Rachel jumped. Idiot! she thought to herself as she went to see who it was.

'Hi, welcome to the Glen.' Pauline's cheery greeting made Rachel smile immediately. The Glen was the name of the hall of residence she was now living in.

'Can you believe it! I'm here.' Rachel laughed.

'And about time too. Now we're all going over to the Cat & Cage for a jar. Are you coming?'

'I haven't finished my unpacking,' Rachel said hastily.

'Get your purse and stop your nonsense. This isn't Rathbarry!' Pauline ordered.

'OK,' Rachel agreed. To hell with the unpacking, she'd a whole eight months to unpack. Now was the time to start living. She spent a most enjoyable evening in the pub, much to her surprise. Her classmates were trying to outdo each other with horror stories about their teaching practice. Rachel found herself telling them how one child in her class was so hyperactive that a strategy had been prepared in advance to deal with his disruptive presence.

'So all the time I was being assessed, Billy Shields was going around from classroom to classroom with a "note for the teacher," which said *Examiner in school hang on to Billy for a while* . . . He had a wonderful time, everyone had little jobs for him to do and they kept him occupied until I was finished.' Rachel grinned.

'That was nice of them,' Keith Nolan exclaimed. 'Two little gurriers started a fight in my class and the rest of the little savages yelled, "Give 'im a puck in the snot, Doyler, an' kick the goolies off 'im." How I longed for the days of corporal punishment. There's a lot to be said for it.'

'Huh,' snorted Lillian Byrne. 'I had a mother in to complain that her daughter was being picked on by the teacher and she wanted to know where the teacher was. So I tried to explain that I was doing my teaching practice, and the other teacher was up in the staff room. She was furious and said no unqualified teacher was going to *practise* on her Charlene. She was going to phone the department immediately. According to her, her husband didn't pay his taxes so their Charlene would be taught by amateurs. I wouldn't mind but Charlene's as thick as two short planks and isn't a bit interested in learning anything.' There was a chorus of guffaws. Rachel started to relax. This was good fun. She was going to enjoy this last year to the full.

The following Friday, she was walking through the grounds after lectures, on her way to the Glen, when she spied a familiar grey Cortina. Anger suffused her. What the hell was he doing here? Making sure that she came home for the weekend no doubt. Would her father ever let her live her own life? she fumed. She remembered that Pauline was going to visit an aunt in St Vincent's Hospital. Jemima was still parked outside the college so she hadn't left yet. A reckless gleam came into Rachel's eyes. She backtracked and took a different route so she didn't have to pass the car park. She was breathless when she got to her room. Hastily shoving her dirty laundry into her knapsack, she gathered her books together and put her coat on. She locked her door and went downstairs to Pauline's floor and knocked on her friend's door. Pauline opened the door. Rachel was pleased to see that she had her duffel coat on, ready to go.

'Hiya,' she greeted Rachel.

'Hi, listen, you're going in to St Vincent's, aren't you? Could you drop me off as near to town as you're going? I can get the bus on the quays.'

'Sure,' Pauline agreed. 'I'm almost ready to go. I have to write the Get Well card, that's all.'

'I just want to pop over to the shop to get the paper to read on the bus. If I stand at the traffic lights can you pick me up?'

'Fine,' Pauline agreed. 'See you at the lights.'

Rachel felt a glow of triumph. Ha! she thought scornfully, William would sit watching the main gate for her and she'd be gone through the side gate. Her father could sit stewing for as long as he wanted.

She hurried downstairs and made her way across the lawns to the side gate of the grounds, looking neither to the left nor right. There was a gap in the traffic and she raced across the road to the newsagents. There was a queue. Rachel sizzled with impatience as she waited to pay for her evening paper. She decided to treat herself to *U* magazine as well. She'd just paid for her purchases when she saw Jemima's purple bonnet edge out the main gate. Rachel waved away the offer of a paper bag, grabbed her change and ran. She was waiting at the traffic lights when Pauline pulled up. The traffic was free-flowing but heavy. Another half an hour and it would be the usual Friday evening snarl-up. And William would be well caught in the middle. She was going to enjoy her few hours of peace and quiet at home. She'd have a nice tea without having to listen to William pontificating.

She caught the bus by the skin of her teeth, and was lucky to get a seat upstairs. A few stops further on and the bus would be jam-packed. Rachel flicked through her magazine in a desultory manner but she couldn't concentrate. She sat back and peered out the window. It was raining heavily. The rain hopped off the surface of the Liffey causing little ripples. The tide was high. One of the Guinness boats down on City Quay gave a mournful hoot. Rachel turned and watched as the ship steamed slowly down river on her journey to Liverpool. She'd like to go on a ship sometime. A cruise would be exotic. She wished she was brave like Ronan's girlfriend, Jennifer. She lived in Spain on her own. Ronan was mad about her. It was just as well Rachel liked Jennifer. Imagine if Ronan got married to someone she didn't like. That would be a disaster. Harry had a brother-in-law he couldn't stand and he rarely saw his sister because of it. He'd told Rachel that it put an awful strain on the family. His mother was very upset by it all.

Ronan was all she had. William didn't count. Jennifer would be well able for William Stapleton. Jennifer was an independent young woman with a mind of her own. Rachel admired her enormously. William would not bully Jennifer.

Rachel wondered if he was still sitting in the car waiting for her.

She and Pauline were off early because one of their lecturers was sick. William didn't know that, of course. He'd wait patiently until five-thirty when she should have been finished. Good enough for him, Rachel gave a little smile. She hadn't asked him to come and collect her.

She decided to treat herself to a taxi from Bray. She'd be home in no time then. She looked at her watch. It was just gone five. The traffic was still moving well. By the time William left, it would be bumper to bumper. That would teach him to pull a fast one on her again, Rachel thought grimly. She'd be on the look-out for him in future on Friday evenings.

An hour and a half later, she put a match to the fire in the parlour. William had set it. While she waited for it to light up, she went out to the kitchen and made herself a pile of hot buttered toast, and opened a tin of pilchards. She made a mug of milky coffee, put everything on a tray and went in and sat in front of the fire and switched on the TV. She had a thoroughly enjoyable tea in front of the blazing fire. It was lashing rain and knowing that her father was sitting in a traffic jam somewhere, and knowing that she'd got the better of him, was very satisfying. She washed up, made herself another cup of coffee and sat contentedly munching a packet of chocolate biscuits as she watched the weather forecast and saw that it was going to be a wet weekend.

'What are you doing home?' Rachel started out of her doze to find her father glaring at her.

'Pardon?' She pretended innocence.

'Do you realize I went all the way to Dublin to collect you, out of the goodness of my heart? I had to sit in a traffic jam three miles long at Shankill,' William fumed. His hair was wet, where he'd got drenched coming from the car to the house. His glasses were dripping. He took them off and peered at her as he wiped them.

'What way did you come out of college?' he demanded.

'The usual way,' Rachel said offhandedly.

'Well how come I didn't see you?' he snapped.

Rachel shrugged. 'We were off early and I got a lift to town. I didn't know you were coming to collect me.' There was no answer to that.

'I've got some eggs for the tea. You can boil them or poach them,' he said coldly.

'Oh, I've had my tea, thanks. I'm just heading upstairs to work on an essay,' she fibbed. She knew very well he expected her to cook his tea for him. Well he had another

521

think coming. She was in a reckless mood having got the better of him. Rachel marched upstairs.

She hadn't the slightest notion of doing an essay. She rooted in her rucksack and pulled out the Georgette Heyer romance that she'd started reading the day before. Rachel closed the door of her little haven behind her. It was a horrible night out. The branches of the oak tree flicked against the windowpane. The rain was coming down in torrents and the wind whistled down the chimney. Rachel kicked off her shoes, slid under her quilt, switched on the bedside lamp and settled down to a quiet read. It had been a good week, she mused. She loved living in the Glen. She'd outwitted her father, who wouldn't be so quick to take her for granted again, and she'd had a nice few hours of peace and quiet to enjoy her tea. Up yours, Dad. She mentally gave William the two fingers as she found her page and started to read.

Rachel found life much easier as a residential student. She'd been extremely lucky to get a room. Second and third year students sometimes had to get flats off the campus depending on the number of first year students arriving. Fortunately for her, there'd been no such problems this year. She'd got a room with no trouble and she was spared the ordeal of having to put up with her father on top of the stress of taking her finals.

Rachel liked the freedom of living to suit herself. It was nice not to have to traipse into town to get the bus home after lectures. It was wonderful not having to get up at six-thirty in the morning. It was a treat to turn over on cold dark wintry mornings, knowing that she could lie in until quarter to nine if she wanted. It only took five minutes to walk across to the college.

In college, there was no such thing as 'Thursday is pork chop day' either. Rachel developed a taste for Kentucky fried chicken. She frequented the fast food restaurant across the street with great regularity. She took to pizzas and curries with gusto and soon had almost forgotten what pork chops tasted like. She enjoyed the chats and gossips in the kitchen over coffee. It was interesting to watch the various romantic entanglements on campus. Hearts were broken. Tiffs and rows occurred. Rachel was fascinated by it all. It was like being part of a big family. A unique experience for someone as lonely as she'd been for most of her life. How she would have loved to share it with her mother.

She wasn't as outgoing and gregarious as Pauline but Rachel went to discos and parties. Her life was positively hectic compared to the one she'd lived at home. Rachel kept herself occupied because it stopped her thinking about her mother. Time had dulled the shock and trauma Rachel had gone through over her mother's death but grief and loneliness were very near the surface. It wasn't as bad when she was in Dublin. But it hit her afresh every time she walked in the door at weekends, how empty and lonely the house was without her mother.

William took care of himself perfectly well the weekdays she was in Dublin. But the minute she arrived home, he expected her to cook his meals for him. He also expected his weekly laundry to be washed, dried and ironed for him. Rachel resented it greatly. Sometimes she tried to make a stand, saying she had too much study to do, but the hassle she got was not worth it, so she gritted her teeth and got on with it.

Her father had been very cool with her since she'd made her stand about living in college. He never asked about her life on campus and she never told him. There wasn't much conversation between them. It didn't bother Rachel. She had no feelings of affection for her father. She endured his sarcasm, his put-downs and his constant undermining of her self-confidence with silent passivity, but inwardly she raged. She still could not engage her father in a row. His aura of authority had not diminished. If anything it had increased. As soon as she stepped in the front door on Friday evenings, her father let her know that no matter how independent she thought she was during the week, he was in charge once she was home. It was easier to say nothing. It always had been. She comforted herself with the thought that the time would come when she could pack her bags, leave home and never come back.

Her last year at St Pat's flew by. As she packed her case Rachel didn't feel one bit excited or exhilarated to know that her three years of study were finally at an end. She wrapped the photograph of her mother in tissue paper and gently laid it on the towels in her case. It was hard to believe that her year in the Glen was over. The exams had been tough, but Rachel was confident of passing. She sighed as she zipped her case shut. It had been very easy to live at college. It was a protected sort of environment. She could make her forays into the big bad world. She could dip in and out of college social life as it suited her. She would have to make her own social life from now on. The thought intimidated her. She wouldn't have Pauline to lean on any more. Pauline had decided she was going to work abroad and had got a teaching job in Singapore through a business contact of her father's. She couldn't wait to start. Rachel admired her. And envied her. Pauline wasn't the slightest bit nervous. She was eagerly anticipating her great adventure. If Rachel was in her shoes she'd be a nervous wreck.

Rachel knew that, for the time being, she was going to have to continue living at home. She had accepted a job as sub in St Catherine's for a teacher who was going on maternity leave. In the meantime she'd applied for several advertised permanent positions. Getting the sub's job in Bray made life easy for her. It was a safe job. She wouldn't be testing herself like Pauline would. Apart from teaching a class of her own, she wouldn't be experiencing anything new. She knew, even as she accepted the job, that she was being chicken.

Rachel was disappointed with herself. She could have refused the job. She'd have got one somewhere else. But no, she'd grabbed it like a safety net. It gave her a great excuse not to go out and confront the world. After all her brave talk and plans she'd gone scuttling back home like a little crab seeking shelter. Where was her courage when she needed it most? Why was she so scared of depending on her own resources to see her through? Was she scared that she wouldn't make it on her own? If she didn't try she'd never know the truth of it, Rachel told herself sternly.

The job in St Catherine's was a stop-gap, she promised herself over and over to try and erase the sense of failure she was already feeling. She'd save the money she made there and buy herself a car. That would be her first step on the road to independence. *Then*, she'd take a job away from home. It was the only way she'd get out from under her father's thumb. The sub's job would give her a breathing space. But Rachel knew if she stayed at home she'd slip back into all her old introverted ways and all the little battles she'd won would be worth nothing.

Chapter Fifty-Eight

Rachel stood in Room 4 of St Catherine's and stared out the window. She could see children racing towards the entrance to the primary school. Some ran, others dawdled. Little ones held on to parents' hands, some confident, some crying already. She was prepared for the day ahead. At least she wouldn't have another teacher in the room with her. Or an examiner, assessing her performance. She'd have the examiner several times during the year as she had to get her diploma, but today she'd be on her own, trying to cope with twenty-five four-year-olds.

She was glad to be at work. The summer had been long and boring. The weather hadn't been great although she'd made the most of whatever sun was there, trying to top up her tan.

She'd worked in the Tea Rooms as usual and it had been a good season for the Misses Healy, but Rachel had felt stultifyingly bored. If this was a foretaste of her life in Rathbarry, it wasn't much to look forward to. But there was nothing in the world to stop her leaving home once she had a few bob saved. Her first priority was to buy herself a car.

A woman and her little girl came into the classroom. Her first pupil, Rachel thought with pride.

'Hello.' Rachel knelt down and gave the little girl a smile. 'What's your name?' The little girl stuck out her tongue.

Oh God! Rachel thought crossly, although her smile never faltered. She hoped the rest of her charges weren't going to be as surly. She gave the brat, whose name was

Orla, a name badge and told her mortified mother not to worry.

It was a sorely trying first hour. There were tears and arguments as well as two puddles of wee on the floor. Eventually Rachel got the infants seated around the round tables. Much better than the old two-scater desks, set in rows. The classroom was a much friendlier environment than she'd known as a child in her father's school.

Rachel had put bright posters and pictures on the walls and, once the last parent left and the tears subsided, she began to relax and take charge. To take their minds off their traumatic separations, she suggested a game of 'I Spy.' This proposal was received with delight and a riotous, noisy game ensued. Rachel observed her new charges. Already she could see who were the lively extrovert characters and those who were shy and timid. She would take a special interest in the shy ones. No-one knew better than she what it was like to be shy and timid at school.

She'd seen one potential little bully hit another little boy who'd promptly started to howl.

'That's very naughty, Robert,' Rachel said sternly. 'Say sorry to Francis.'

'Get lost,' the little boy said truculently. Rachel marvelled at his insolence. Not even Patrick McKeown, the bully of her childhood years, would have told a teacher to get lost. It's a good job you're not in any class my father teaches, Rachel thought wryly.

She turned to the rest of the class. 'Robert will not be allowed to play any more games until he says sorry. No-one is to hit anybody else or teacher will get very cross.' There was silence as twenty-five pairs of eyes stared solemnly at her. Her pupils were impressed by the note of authority in her tone, Rachel noted with satisfaction.

'Is everyone going to be good?'

'Yesssss, teacher,' came the chorus.

'Right,' Rachel said cheerfully. 'Let's have a game of musical alphabet. Mary, go up to my desk and bring me the big bag of letters, please,' Rachel instructed a shy little girl who wasn't joining in. The child hesitated. 'They're on my desk, pet, will you get them for me?' Rachel said encouragingly. The small fair-haired child reminded her of her young self. The little girl went up to Rachel's desk and brought her the letters.

'Very good.' Rachel smiled. 'You're such a good girl I'm going to make you the A girl.' Rachel took the large cut-out A and pinned it to Mary's uniform. The little girl was as proud as punch and smiled shyly. You won't be shy when I'm finished with you, Rachel thought firmly. She was determined to imbue her shy pupils with as much confidence as she possibly could.

Brazen as could be, Robert arrived up to her for his letter. 'You haven't said sorry to Francis yet, Robert. You can't play any games until you've said sorry.' They stared at each other.

''S not fair, I did nuttin'.' He sulked.

'No games until you say sorry to Francis,' Rachel said resolutely.

'Sorry,' came the muttered grudging response. Rachel felt a surge of triumph. She knew it was vital to let her pupils know from the beginning that she was in charge.

'I didn't hear that, Robert. And it's not me you have to say sorry to, it's Francis,' she insisted.

'Sorry, Francis,' Robert muttered. It was enough for her.

'Here's your letter, Robert,' she said briskly. 'No more hitting. Now everybody, let's play musical alphabet.' She took out her tin whistle and prepared for the learning game.

A happy bunch of children greeted their parents at noon. Rachel was exhausted but very satisfied by her first day as a teacher. Most of her class would look forward to coming to school the next day. She had already promised them a game of musical numbers, since the musical alphabet had been such a success. They were all dying to hear another story from the huge book of Bible stories she had. Rachel was looking forward to it herself. The day had flown. She'd surmounted all its challenges. There'd been a good sense of cohesion in the class and already little bondings were taking place as her pupils began to make new friends. She would keep a sharp look-out for her shy children. Rachel was determined that her pupils would remember their schooldays as a happy positive time. Light years away from her own. She collected her coat from the staff room and had a chat with the other teachers, who were friendly and encouraging. She felt very pleased with herself as she cycled along the dual carriageway. It was a great boost to her confidence.

Her father was sitting at the kitchen table reading his paper. There was no sign of any lunch preparations. In future, Rachel decided, she was going to eat in Bray and just have a light tea when she got home. She wasn't going to be a slave for her father. He was only five minutes from work. He didn't have to face a long cycle after school. William's curiosity got the better of him. 'How did it go?' he asked. Rachel was on such a high, she bubbled enthusiastically about her new pupils and the games of I Spy and musical alphabet. William eyed her coldly.

'No wonder children are going into second-level education unable to read or write. This new-fangled method of teaching is totally unsuitable. Children need discipline and order. Running around classrooms playing musical chairs is arrant nonsense.'

Rachel was furious. How typical of him to disparage her work. He couldn't let her have her little moment of triumph. Not even once. How she loathed him. Vicious anger surged through her. He wasn't going to get away with ruining her first day at work. She glared at her father. 'Let me tell you one thing. My pupils are not going to be cowed by the bullying you call discipline. When I started school I felt sick every morning. I wet the bed. Well I can tell you, not one of those children is going to come into my class in the morning feeling as I felt. I can guarantee that. Today was fun for them, and they learned something. Those children aren't afraid of me the way the poor unfortunates in your class are afraid of you. I'll be a hell of a better teacher than you ever were.'

'How dare you talk to me like that!' William said with icy fury. 'You think you're an expert after one day's teaching. I've been teaching for more than forty years. I know what I'm talking about.'

Rachel took a deep breath. She felt sick, her father's domineering ways still intimidated her but she had to make her stand. She'd worked damn hard during her training. He couldn't take that away from her.

'No,' she said. 'You don't. You're a dinosaur. Your teaching methods are crude and out of date. You should have retired at sixty instead of clinging on to your little bit of power. You're pathetic—'

Her father, his eyes two slits of fury, raised his hand and gave her a swift hard slap across the face. Rachel paled in shock.

'Enough,' William raged. 'You have respect when you speak to me, my lady. Or you can get out of this house. Now get out of my sight.'

Rachel walked slowly upstairs. She was shocked. But in a strange way she felt triumphant. William was normally very restrained and reserved, even in his anger. He had hit her and that proved that she'd really provoked him. Her hurtful words had hit home. She was glad. The day would come when she would leave this house. But she would make the decision, not William. She would leave home when it suited her. She wasn't going to waste good money paying rent. Not when she had a car to save for first, and then a mortgage. She would live frugally. She would save hard. And then she would go and never come back.

William would be retiring in another few years. The time would come when he would need her. Age was no respecter of people whether they be headmasters in village schools or not. But she would not be there when he needed her. And he would only have himself to blame.

Chapter Fifty-Nine

Heathrow Airport was jam-packed. Huge snake-like queues formed at check-in desks. Paula's heart sank. She left Jennifer to stand guard over their trolleys, filled to the brim with luggage, and sprinted along the concourse to the nearest monitor. Head thrown back, she searched for their flight number and check-in desk. All she could see were flights delayed or, even worse . . . cancelled. 'Oh God, come on, now, don't let me down. Please let our departure be on time,' she muttered as she anxiously scanned the board. She recognized the flight number and gave a great sigh of relief. It was on time. She noted the number of the check-in desk. Now that they were on the last lap home, Paula couldn't wait to get there.

She was dying to see Helen and her family. But most of all she wanted to get home to see Nick. Would all that time away have made any difference to his feelings towards her? When he saw her, would he finally realize that she was a woman now? Not just the teenager from next door who had cleaned his house for a bit of pocket money. Well more than pocket money, she chided herself. Nick had been extremely generous.

Jennifer was amazed at her excitement about going home. But Jennifer didn't realize why Paula was so looking forward to it. The longing to see Nick was almost physical. She longed to have those incredibly blue eyes smile into hers. Longed to feel his mouth against her cheek and his arms around her in the hug he would surely give her when he welcomed her home. It would be so nice to savour the clean manly essence of him. And to hear his voice with that gorgeous soft sexy western accent

. . . oh bliss, oh joy. Listening to Nick Russell speaking was a turn-on in itself. Although she had kissed quite a few men, and would no doubt kiss a few more, no kiss in her entire life would ever be as cherished as the kiss Nick had given her on the cheek that day he had said goodbye to her and wished her well on her last trip abroad. It had been months and months ago, but it was as though it had been yesterday. She had played it out in her head over and over again, all the time she was away.

Paula smiled happily as she made her way back to a patiently waiting Jennifer. If all went as planned she would have far more than kisses and daydreams. Nick Russell was going to fall head over heels in love with her if she had anything to do with it. And by God she was going to make sure of it. Once she had kissed him properly she'd blow his mind, she just knew it. And then she'd take him on that trip of ultimate pleasure and there would be no going back. Nick would be hers and she would be his and she would make him so happy and satisfied he would never *ever* want to look at another woman.

Juan Carlos had taught her much and for that she was very grateful. Her inexperience would not be a problem for her and Nick. She knew how to please a man and thanks to Juan Carlos, who had been an experienced lover, she knew how to please herself.

Jennifer couldn't understand why Paula wasn't devastated about leaving her Spanish Romeo. Paula had met him soon after they first arrived in Majorca. He owned an estate agent's firm and he was very much the suave sophisticated man-about-town. He was drop-dead gorgeous-looking, with dark intense eyes and jet-black hair. They clicked immediately and he had wooed her determinedly. When Paula had come back for a second tour of duty on the island, Juan Carlos was ecstatic. Then they became lovers. Paula had decided to sleep with him to see if it would make any difference to her feelings for Nick. In case it was just some silly teenage crush she had on him. It hadn't made the slightest difference. Nick was still the man for her. Nevertheless, Paula enjoyed her affair with Juan Carlos. He was so crazy about her, he'd even flown out to the Canaries twice during the six weeks she and Jennifer were working there.

Juan Carlos proposed marriage more times than Paula'd had hot dinners, she remembered fondly. She'd miss him, of course. He'd been great fun and they'd had many happy times. But she didn't ache for Juan, or crave being near him, or want to send him wild with passion and desire the way she did with Nick. As the time got nearer to their return to Ireland, whenever Juan Carlos made love to her, she'd closed her eyes and pretended it was Nick. Once, as she reached orgasm, she had actually breathed Nick's name. Fortunately her lover had been making so much noise himself he hadn't heard.

No, she would feel no enormous sadness at leaving Juan Carlos. She would miss him, but she wasn't the least bit heartbroken. Actually, she was relieved to have ended the affair. Juan Carlos had become very demanding, sulking, because she wouldn't accept his proposal. But he had never been part of her long-term plans. Only one man mattered to her. Nick was at home. Nick would be hers. It was meant to be. She just knew it.

'Where do we go?' Jennifer interrupted her reverie.

'That one over there. Come on, let's get going.' Paula grabbed her trolley and strode towards their queue. 'Can I have the window seat?' she asked over her shoulder.

'Sure,' Jennifer agreed.

The wait seemed interminable before their luggage was finally disposed of and they had their boarding cards and were heading to the departure lounge and duty-free. Although she had a bottle of Chanel No. 5 in her luggage, Paula decided that she might as well treat herself to another one and on impulse she put another bottle of Hennessy brandy into the basket. That was for Nick. She had already bought him a bottle in one of the duty-free shops on the island, but what the hell, she'd buy him the moon if she could. She'd just flutter her eyelashes and pretend innocence if she was stopped at customs.

They were still queuing to pay for their last-minute goodies when they heard their final boarding call and had to stand, steaming with impatience, as the person in front fumbled with dollars and Deutschmarks, confusing a thoroughly irritated cashier. Then they had to run, panting, with their clanking bottles and hand luggage, the length of the departure lounge to their boarding gate and, eventually when they boarded and were settled into their seats, had to endure another thirty-minute wait on the tarmac.

'If we get home it will be a blooming miracle,' Paula fretted. Jennifer wiped perspiration off her forehead and gave a mighty yawn.

'I'm knackered, I don't want anything to drink when they come around. If we ever get into the air and they deign to come around at all. Wake me up when we get to Dublin.' With that Jennifer gave another huge yawn, tucked her head down on her shoulder and within seconds was asleep. Paula grinned. Jennifer had absolutely no staying power. Even though they had partied until dawn that morning, she felt full of beans and wide awake. But then she had a reason. A reason for happy anticipation. Today, hopefully, she would see Nick.

Paula settled back to while away the flight with her favourite fantasy. The fantasy in which Nick, eyes hot with passion and desire, mouth hungry and sensual, hands seeking and caressing, moulded her eager body to his. She would caress and fondle and stroke and kiss him, taking him to the edge, bringing him back, sending him wild with desire until he came inside her, shuddering with a powerful uncontrollable need that only she could satisfy. As the jet thundered along the runway and lifted itself into the air, Paula leaned back in her seat and gave a voluptuous stretch as delicious tingles of desire rippled through her. If she felt like this now, heaven only knew what she'd feel when she saw Nick for the

534

first time in so long. She'd probably have an orgasm on the spot, she thought in amusement.

Never in her life had she felt such lust for a man. It frightened her a little. It meant she wasn't in control. But that was the attraction Nick held for her. Not being in control in a relationship with a man was unique for Paula. She wanted much more than lust from a relationship with Nick. Everything about him fascinated and attracted her. His manliness, his kindness, his sense of humour, all drew her to him. He had the most beautiful manners too. Paula smiled, remembering how once when she had been about to lug the hoover down the stairs, he had taken it from her and walked downstairs ahead of her.

'A gentleman always walks down the stairs in front of a lady in case she slips, so he will be there to catch her.' Paula could remember the cultured voice of Sister Catherine teaching them etiquette. She'd thought it sounded so gallant. When Nick had gone out of his way to carry the hoover downstairs *and* walked in front of her, she had felt a warm glow inside. Sometimes when he'd been on his way to work and she'd been on her way to college, he'd given her a lift to the bus stop. He always opened the car door for her. Good manners were such an attractive trait in a man, she mused, glancing out the window and seeing cotton wool clouds beneath them. She had no time for feminists who scorned a man for giving a woman his seat in a crowded bus or train, and scorned the woman for taking it. Men were men, women were women and *vive la différence*, Paula maintained. Being equal did not mean being any less feminine. She was *anyone's* equal and better than a lot. Some men, of course, overdid it. Juan Carlos would have prostrated himself at her feet and let her walk all over him, he was so smitten by her. It had been very irritating at times. If they had a row, he was the first to apologize. He was very appeasing. If she said black was white, he'd agree with her. Barry had been a bit like that too. She'd always got her own way with Barry. She'd always been in control. He'd been a bit of a doormat really, Paula reflected. There was no way she'd get her own way with Nick. Nick Russell was no doormat. Nick was the type of man who would never in a million years be impressed by one of her famous pouts or sulks. She could never see herself behaving with him the way she behaved with Juan Carlos or Barry or Conor. Badly!

Paula gave a wry smile, she knew she could be a snooty bitch if she didn't get her own way. Nick wouldn't take that from her and that was what made her want him so much. Nick would never succumb to her flirting and coquetry. She'd tried that already and it hadn't worked. Much to her dismay. Nick had just treated her like a silly teenager. Teasing her about her boyfriends, and the length of time she spent on Helen's phone to her girlfriends. And all the time she had badly wanted him to treat her like an adult. The way he treated Helen.

Paula envied her aunt those long conversations with Nick in the garden or over coffee. She envied their relaxed easy way with each other and the bond they shared because of being betrayed by their respective spouses. She loved the way Nick kept an eye out for Helen. He was great for fixing her drains or cleaning gutters or starting her car when the battery was flat. He was a kind neighbour, that was for sure, and her aunt was lucky to have him. Lots of men just wouldn't bother.

A horrific thought struck her. What if she discovered that he had acquired a girlfriend during the time she was away? That would be her worst nightmare. And had been all the time she had lived next door to him. He was such an attractive man, she couldn't understand why women weren't throwing themselves at him in droves. She'd never seen him bring a woman home to the house while she'd worked for him. He'd never said that he was seeing someone or going to dinner or the pictures or the theatre with a date. But then he was consumed by that damned job of his. And, she reasoned, after finding his wife in bed with his best friend he probably wanted nothing to do with women. Time healed all wounds, or so they said.

Maybe when she was away, he'd met a woman who would make him forget the hurt and pain he'd suffered.

Paula gave a deep sigh, her previous high evaporating rapidly. She wanted to make him forget his hurt and pain. She wanted to make him happier than he had ever been in his life. If only he would give her the chance. She wouldn't badger him about his working hours the way his wife had. Paula understood his commitment to his job. It was a very responsible job, it was part and parcel of what he was, she could understand that. A nagging partner she would not be.

She'd have to give up being a courier though, if she and Nick got together. She couldn't be off gallivanting on the continent. She wanted to be with him. When she got home she was going to have a meeting with Kieran. She had suggestions to make. She'd kept her eyes open all the while she'd been working. There were policies TransCon could implement that would increase their business. She'd seen some interesting concepts that she thought her boss should seriously consider. It was exciting. She was dying to get Kieran on his own and have a good talk about her ideas. Miss Johnson insisted on calling him Mister Donnelly. It drove Kieran mad, none of the rest of the staff called him that. He always had time for a chat when he met staff and he listened to comments and suggestions. Well she had plenty of comments and suggestions for him, she thought happily as the plane began its final descent into Dublin.

Bubbles of excitement fizzed through her as she peered eagerly out the window. She could see the coastline of Ireland on her left with its patchwork of green and earthy brown fields. After the parched volcanic landscape of Tenerife, it was a delight to look at. Dun Laoghaire appeared and Paula could see a ferry sailing serenely towards the harbour. Then the twin red and white tipped ESB chimneys in Dublin Port came into view, and she knew she really was home. Excitement mounted. 'Wake up, Jenny, we're home. Look, look, there's Howth. Look

at the sea, Jenny. Oh, look, there's the airport . . . ooohhh
I can't wait to see them all.' The words tumbled out as she
craned her neck to see everything. The plane was swaying
gently from side to side, the flaps were down, her ears were
popping, but she didn't care. Nick, Nick, here I come, her
heart sang. A brainwave struck her. Helen was collecting
her. They'd be home by two. Nick was never home early
on a Friday. So after she'd had lunch with her aunt and
a good long chat, she could nip into Nick's with the
brandy and the gorgeous cashmere jumper she'd bought
him and leave it on the table for him and then he'd have
to call into Helen's to see her.

The edge of the runway appeared and then they were
skimming over it, then a bump and they were down. The
green perimeter whizzed past, then the jet began to slow
and the terminal appeared. Paula was so excited that she
had her seat belt unfastened and her and Jennifer's hand
luggage and duty-free all ready before the plane drew to
a halt. She was in a frenzy of impatience as she waited for
their luggage to appear. 'Would you calm down?' Jennifer
grinned.

'I can't help it,' Paula said happily. 'It's just great to
be home.'

'Do I look all right?' Jennifer asked anxiously. 'I
hope Ronan was able to get time off, I'll be terribly
disappointed if he's not here.'

'Come on, let's go freshen up. This place is a mad
house,' Paula suggested.

'Well it is Christmas. It's cold, isn't it?' Jennifer
shivered. Their blood was thinned from months in the
sun and, despite the stuffy air in the arrivals hall, she was
freezing.

'It's gorgeous,' Paula declared over her shoulder as
they made their way through the crowds to the loo. They
brushed their hair, retouched their make-up, assured each
other that their tans hadn't faded and headed back out
to the carousel. The baggage had come through and
they loaded their trolleys and headed for customs. Paula

swanned along, head up, pushing her trolley, her hand protectively on her bag of brandy bottles lying at the front so they wouldn't clank. Jennifer, who looked as guilty as hell, careered along beside her, her trolley all over the place.

'Smile, for God's sake,' Paula hissed. Jennifer smiled, and almost collided with a pushchair.

'Blasted yoke,' she scowled. They emerged through customs, unscathed.

'Ronan's here!' Jennifer squealed, pointing through the brown-tinted doors to the thronged barriers. Her face wreathed in smiles, she half ran towards the doors. Lucky you, Paula thought enviously at the expression of pure happiness that shone in Jennifer's face. Imagine having Nick waiting for her and to be able to run into his arms. She scanned the smiling faces along the barrier and her breath caught in her throat. He was there! Nick was there! She couldn't believe it. Nick was there standing beside Helen, smiling at her with that crinkly much-loved smile which made her want to fling herself into his arms and say 'I love you' over and over again. He must have taken a half-day to come and meet her. He must have been looking forward to seeing her as much as she was looking forward to seeing him. He must love her too, she thought, deliriously happy. Abandoning her trolley, Paula raced over and hugged the daylights out of Helen. Then, with happiness sparkling in her eyes, she threw herself into Nick's arms and felt his tighten around her. She buried her face in his neck and cheek and heard him say, 'Welcome home, Paula. It's great to see you.' The joy of hearing his voice, of having his arms around her, of feeling the reassuring bulk of his body against her was indescribable. She knew this was the happiest moment of her life.

'Paula, you look stunning,' she heard Helen say. 'Look at the colour of you!' She was so glad she'd worn the peach cotton sweatshirt over her white jeans. It showed off her tan. She drew away from Nick, who was smiling at her with those unforgettable deep blue eyes. She had to fight the urge to kiss him passionately. Being held in his embrace was the most exquisite feeling. Paula felt utterly cherished.

'I can't believe I'm home,' she murmured.

'Thank God you are! This woman has been in a mega-tizzy. She's hoovered the house umpteen times.'

'Don't mind him,' Helen laughed, kissing Paula again. Paula put her arms around her and then looked at her aunt in surprise. Helen had put on weight. Paula could feel it as she hugged her. Her face, which was usually on the thin side, was more rounded. Her skin was peaches and cream and she was glowing.

'You look pretty stunning yourself, Helen. I'm glad to see you've put on a few pounds, it suits you.'

Helen blushed, and looked at Nick.

'What are you up to, Helen?' Paula laughed. 'Have the pair of you been pigging out on Chinese takeaways?' They both had a weakness for Chinese food.

'It's not Chinese food that's put my weight on, darling. You won't believe this. I can hardly believe it myself.' Her aunt blushed again. 'I'm pregnant, Paula.'

Paula couldn't believe her ears. 'You're . . . but I mean . . . I thought you couldn't . . . Anthony . . . ' she stuttered.

Helen shook her head. 'I didn't think I could either . . . after all this time . . . It's not Anthony, darling . . . '

Nick put his arm around Helen and smiled ruefully at Paula. 'Your aunt and I are going to have a baby, Paula, and I know you'll be very happy for us. As happy as we are ourselves.'

Chapter Sixty

Paula stood, stunned. The noise of the airport dimmed around her. All she could hear was the sound of her own heart beating. A crushing grief enveloped her. She wanted to cry. She wanted to run away by herself and curl up like a child and cry and scream the shock and grief out of her. Nick and Helen. Helen and Nick, the refrain ran through her mind. She felt as though huge nails were being hammered into her heart. She wanted to die.

'There! I knew she'd be shocked,' Paula heard her aunt say as if from some great distance.

'Paula, I love Helen. I'll take great care of her, don't worry,' Nick said gently, mistaking the reason for her horror.

'I love Helen,' he'd said. The nails went in deeper, harder. She swallowed, tried to say something, and couldn't.

'Are you disgusted, Paula?' Helen asked, distressed. Paula shook her head and with an immense effort of will managed to say, 'Of course I'm not disgusted. It's just the . . . the . . . ' She nearly said 'shock of it,' but she said 'surprise of it' instead. 'I didn't think you could ever have children.'

'Well I didn't think so either,' Helen said wryly. 'So when Nick and I . . . well let's just say at my age, I didn't think . . . We weren't very careful . . . and here we are.' Her voice trailed away.

'We were as shocked as you are, believe me,' Nick declared, smiling down at Helen. 'But we're very happy.'

'You're the first to know,' Helen said, and there was pleading in her tone. 'I didn't want to write to you or

541

tell you over the phone. I wanted to tell you myself. I thought you'd be happy for me.'

'Oh, Helen. I am. I am! Honestly.' Paula threw her arms around Helen and hugged her close. She knew how much this meant to her aunt. All the years she had longed for a child. If it had been anyone but Nick's she would have been thrilled for Helen. Over the moon. Ecstatic. But how could she feel like that, knowing that the man who meant everything to her was her aunt's lover and father of her child? 'Is everything all right? How far are you gone?' Paula asked, striving to sound normal. After all, Helen was forty-one. A bit old to be having her first child.

'Everything's fine. I'm as healthy as an ox. And Nick's treating me like a queen.' Helen laughed.

'She is a queen, isn't she?' Nick said lovingly, giving Paula a hug.

'Yes, yes she is, Nick.' Paula smiled but the pain in her heart nearly took her breath away.

'I'll just pop over and say hello to Jennifer, and we'll go. Nick's going to treat us to lunch,' Helen said hesitantly. She walked over to where Jennifer was being greeted by her mother and Ronan and Grandpa Myles.

Paula fussed at her trolley, unable to look Nick in the eye. The last thing she wanted to do was to go for a meal. She'd choke if she tried to eat anything. Her throat felt so constricted it was actually painful.

'Paula, you're not happy about this, are you?' she heard his deep voice above her.

No! she wanted to shout. No, I'm not happy. You can't love Helen. You love me. It's *me* that should be having your babies. *I* love you.

'I love Helen very much, Paula,' Nick continued. 'I honour and respect her. I'll always look after her and the baby. We're trying to get divorced so that we can get married eventually. We both have another chance at happiness. Be glad for us. Don't upset Helen by showing your disapproval. Is it such an awful thing to have happened?' he asked gently.

Paula's lip wobbled. Don't disgrace yourself, she told herself fiercely.

'I am glad, Nick. Honest. Helen deserves every bit of happiness and love she gets. And so do you. I know you'll be very good to her. How could I not be happy when she's found someone as nice as you?'

Nick put his arm around her and hugged her. 'You're a great girl, Paula. The best. Thanks for that,' he said.

'You're welcome. It's true,' she whispered. She knew she was going to start bawling in a minute. 'I'm bursting to go to the loo. Will you mind my trolley? I'll be back in a jiffy,' she said hastily.

'Sure.' He smiled. 'I'll tell Helen.'

Paula walked towards the toilets as calmly as she could. Was this all real, or was she having a nightmare? She bit her lip, hard. It hurt. She wasn't in a dream. Her world had just come crashing around her and she didn't know what to do. There was a queue. She stood behind a woman with a screaming toddler. At least he could give vent to his feelings, she thought. She badly wanted to scream herself. She caught sight of her reflection in the long wide wall mirror. She looked very normal. Tanned, healthy, glamorous. She couldn't see any evidence of the turmoil that was raging inside. Nobody could point a finger at her and say, that girl's life has just been ruined.

A cubicle became vacant. With the utmost relief Paula entered the tiny haven of privacy and shut out the world. She pulled down the top of the seat and sat with her head in her hands. She took great deep breaths, trying to compose herself. If she started to cry she'd never stop. It was a luxury she could not afford.

Nick was lost to her, now. Paula knew that. If it had been any other woman she would have gone to battle. All was fair in love and war. She would have done everything in her power to get him to fall in love with her. She should have taken her chance when she was at college. But it hadn't seemed right then. He still saw her as a student. She'd gone abroad a girl and come home a woman and now it was too late. Far far too late. Helen was in love with Nick. It was unmistakable. It shone from her eyes when she looked at him. There was no doubt. Paula was an authority on loving Nick.

And Nick was in love with Helen. His tenderness and protective gestures spoke volumes. His proud gaze said more than words. His happiness was evident. He looked years younger. Happiness did that to people. He was only forty-two anyway. But the strain seemed to have gone from his face. He looked carefree.

'Oh God, oh God. Why? Why did You let me fall in love with him when You had him planned for Helen?' she muttered. Her resolve not to cry was weakening. She wanted to give in to herself and bawl and run away. She couldn't. Helen would know something was up. She couldn't ruin Helen's happiness. No mother could have given Paula the love Helen had. She owed it to her aunt to pretend to be happy for her. She owed it to her aunt to forget Nick and all the feelings she harboured for him. For once in her life, Paula was going to have to behave in a most unselfish manner. Was she capable of it?

She sat in the tiny cubicle, composing herself. She took a deep breath and opened the door. She sprayed a little perfume behind her ears and retouched her lipstick. Nothing like war paint for hiding behind, she thought ruefully, inspecting her reflection. She looked fine. Normal. Drawing on every resource she possessed, Paula walked out to where Helen and Nick were standing.

'Come on, folks,' she said briskly, patting Helen's unmistakable bump and smiling at her aunt. 'If that child is as hungry as I am, she's in trouble. I'm starving. Let's go and have this lunch you've been talking about. I want to hear all the news.'

'We want to hear all yours.' Helen slipped an arm through her niece's.

'My news is dead boring compared to yours.' Paula laughed with false gaiety. 'I want to hear all about the baby. What are you going to call it? Do you want a boy or a girl? Whose house are you living in, or are you being ultra-modern and having separate residences?'

'We're making it up as we go along.' Nick laughed, taking the trolley from her and pushing it with ease.

'Wait until your mother hears!' Helen made a wry face.

'She'll be delighted,' Paula said firmly, knowing it was the truth. 'Have you told Anthony yet?'

Helen's face darkened. 'No,' she said. 'When I think of all the years of misery I went through thinking it was my fault I couldn't have a baby. I . . . no . . . I haven't told him yet. I don't think he's entitled to know. Nick and I are thinking of putting the two houses up for sale and buying one together. I'll tell him then.'

Paula felt her heartache almost choke her. Buying a house together sounded so intimate. It indicated long-term commitment. How was she going to cope with this for the rest of her life? One thing was sure, she'd have to get a place of her own now. A masochist she was not. Watching Nick and Helen together in an intimate relationship would send her over the edge.

Lunch was a nightmare for her. In an effort to pretend that she was delighted for the two people she held so dear, Paula kept up a stream of gay, witty conversation. She told them of the ups and downs of being a courier and about her and Jennifer's life abroad. By the time they finally got home to Helen's house she was mentally and physically exhausted. Pleading great fatigue as a result of an all-night party followed by two flights, Paula insisted she had to go and lie down. Much to Helen's disappointment.

'But we've so much to talk about, and Nick's got to get back to work. I was really looking forward to having you to myself.'

'I'll just lie down for an hour,' Paula promised. She was dizzy from the strain of it all. And she hadn't fibbed about being tired. She was dead on her feet. Ten minutes later, she was lying in her much-loved familiar bedroom. It had started to rain outside. The blue skies of her homecoming had turned leaden and grey and much more wintry. Rain lashed hard against the window, the steady drumming made her feel cosy and snug in her comfortable bed. Too tired and numb to dwell on what had happened, Paula's eyes closed and sleep cloaked her misery for a while.

'She's upset, Nick.' Helen sighed. 'I know she's making a big effort. She hardly ate any lunch. She just picked at it.'

'Helen, the girl's exhausted. She didn't get to bed at all last night. She had two flights, she didn't know whether she was on her head or her heels. She'll be fine when she wakes up.' Nick put a comforting arm around her and gave her a kiss.

She snuggled in against him. 'I'm going to phone Maura this afternoon. Now that Paula knows, I don't mind telling anyone.'

'Just one thing struck me,' Nick said reflectively. 'When we sell the houses, Paula might feel she's got to get a flat or something. As far as I'm concerned she'll always have a home with us.'

'Oh, Nick. That is kind,' Helen said gratefully. 'Paula's been so good to me, I'd hate her to feel left out.'

'Well she won't be, so stop worrying. Now I'd better get back to work, I believe it's very expensive rearing children,' he added, patting her bump. 'Daddy's going to work, baby, be good for your mother.' He held his hand over her stomach and was rewarded a few minutes later by a faint rippling movement. 'Isn't that something else?' he said in wonder. 'I never thought this would happen to me.'

'Me neither, Nick. I can't believe it. I've never been so happy in my life.' Helen put her arms around him and kissed him ardently. 'Do you have to go back to work?' she murmured, nuzzling his earlobe.

'I could delay it.' Nick traced his lips along the side of her neck, down to the tiny pulse that beat at the base of her throat.

'Will we go into your house?' Helen sighed with pleasure.

'Why?' Nick raised his head and looked at her in surprise.

'Well . . . Paula . . . you know?' She made a little face.

'Paula'll have to get used to it because we're going to be doing a lot of it.' Nick laughed. 'Anyway I'd say she's dead to the world by now, but if you really want to go to my house, we'll go. It's a shame to waste that lovely fire though.'

'I suppose it is a bit daft.' Helen began to undo his shirt buttons. 'Paula would laugh at me for being so old-fashioned.'

'Yes she would,' Nick agreed. 'Now forget about Paula and start doing wild, wanton, wicked things to me, like you did last night.'

'You're an insatiable beast, Nick Russell,' Helen teased, and giggled as he growled and gave her a lovebite.

An hour later, she lay stretched on the sofa in front of the fire. Nick had added more coal and logs to it before he left and it blazed up the chimney, the logs hissed and crackled and sent out a lovely scent of pine. Helen felt utterly relaxed and content and sensual after their lovemaking. It was still raining outside. She didn't care. It was luxury to lie in the comfort of her sitting-room, listening to the elements outside, knowing that she didn't have to go out in it. It was a treat to have the day off work. Making love in front of the fire in the middle of a working afternoon seemed so decadent. Helen grinned. She'd never made love on the sofa in the afternoon with Anthony. He'd been strictly a bedroom man.

How her life had changed in the last year. When Paula went off on her second tour of duty, she'd felt even worse than the first time. The house had seemed so empty. Nick knew she was depressed. He took to calling in much more often than before. He would invite her into his house for coffee. Nick was very easy to talk to. She didn't need to put on a façade with him. And he didn't need to with her. One gorgeous sunny Sunday afternoon, he'd suggested going to Howth for a walk. It had been delightful. And they'd had fun. They started going out at the weekends and usually ended up having a Chinese meal. They were extremely relaxed in each other's company. One night, it had just seemed the most natural thing in the world for her to kiss him and thank him for a wonderful evening. The kiss had turned into a night of passion she would never forget.

Helen smiled at the memory. Sex with Nick was incredible. It made her feel young and vibrant again. As young and vibrant as Paula was. She'd looked like a model at the airport, in her peach and white with the lovely tan. Helen sighed. Maybe Nick was right, maybe Paula was just tired. Once she had time to get over the shock, she'd be thrilled for her and Nick. If ever they were lucky enough to get married, she'd ask Paula to be her bridesmaid. It would be a lovely way of sharing the happiest day of her life, Helen smiled as a shower of sparks flew up the chimney. She wished her niece would wake up, they had so much to talk about.

Paula stretched, yawned, and stretched again. It took her a minute to remember where she was. It was dark and rain was pelting against the window. Home, she was home. Happiness flickered and then she remembered. Nick was in love with Helen. They were going to have a baby. Tears brimmed in her eyes as misery engulfed her. She felt a great tightness around her chest. How ironic that she had been worried that Nick might be seeing someone. In her wildest dreams, she'd never considered Nick and Helen as a couple. And they were going to have a baby. It was worse than her worst nightmare. Burying her face in her pillow, Paula sobbed her heart out.

Chapter Sixty-One

'*Should old acquaintance be forgot . . .*' the Matthews family chorused on the stroke of midnight as they all stood in a circle holding hands, singing in the New Year. On one side of Paula stood Helen, on the other, Nick. She was holding both their hands, pretending to be as happy as a lark, as she sang the rousing chorus. But she was intensely aware of Nick's hand in hers. He and Helen had arrived that afternoon to spend the New Year in St Margaret's Bay. They were staying in the hotel despite Maura and Pete's protestations. They had wanted them to have their room and they would have slept on the couch. Helen wouldn't hear of it. Paula was relieved that they were staying at the hotel. Being with Helen and Nick was very difficult to endure.

'Happy New Year, Paula.' Nick enfolded her in an embrace and kissed her cheek lightly.

'The same to you,' she murmured, returning his kiss. Paula savoured the brief precious moment. Then Helen kissed her, and hugged her tightly, her rounded bump an irrefutable reminder to Paula that Nick could never be hers.

Would this night never end, she thought unhappily as they all trooped to the front door to let out the old year and bring in the new. Usually Paula revelled in the New Year celebrations. Bells were ringing, car horns tooted, there were great sounds of revelry from the hotel. She wanted to clamp her hands over her ears and shut the din out. She wanted to hide up in her bedroom, but there was no privacy there either. Rebecca, her sister, had come home from Cork for a few days and was full of chat and gossip.

She had nowhere of her own to go to. Now that Nick was more or less living with Helen she felt uncomfortable in the house in Dublin. It was time to think of the future. She'd been putting it off ever since she'd come down home. Paula shivered in the cold night air and slipped back inside to the now empty sitting-room. She poured herself a brandy and went into the kitchen and sat down at the table. A fire still blazed in the grate, its embers red and glowing in the half-light. This kitchen had hardly changed since she was a child. The scrubbed pine dresser full of shining crockery. The pretty gingham curtains which her mother made every other year matched the cloth on the table, which was laden with sandwiches and cakes and buns and bracks. The old chiming clock that had been chipped years ago, when Rebecca had knocked it off the mantelpiece, was still going strong. The small pantry off the kitchen, where her mother kept her homemade jams and marmalades and chutneys and her soda breads and scones, gave forth mouth-watering aromas that evoked memories of her childhood. When she'd been a little girl, her mother would go into the pantry and cut a slice of freshly baked brown bread, butter it and sprinkle sugar on it. Paula would stand beside her, watching her every move. Then she'd take her precious slice of brown bread and sugar and sit on the back doorstep and eat it slowly to make it last as long as possible.

Paula sighed at the memory. She wished she was a child again, free of all her troubles and heartache. It had been good to come home. Her parents' joy at seeing her was balm to her bruised soul. She visited her married sisters and brothers and played with her nieces and nephews. Their lives were so different to hers. Louise, her eldest sister, had three children. Her life and conversation revolved around them. Thomas worked on the fishing boats with their father and had one baby. Her other two brothers were in England. Rebecca worked in an insurance company in Cork.

It gave Paula a little jolt to realize that she was far closer and had more in common with Jennifer and Beth than she did with her own siblings. She was a bit like an outsider in her own family. And it was her own fault. She'd been so interested in making a life for herself in Dublin that she'd neglected to look after her relationships at home, especially with her sisters. True, they always made a fuss of her when she came home and they loved hearing about her exciting life abroad but she couldn't confide her woes to them as she could to Jenny and Beth. She had told Jenny all about Nick. Paula knew that her sisters had an image of her as a glamorous sophisticate who had a glitzy high-flying lifestyle. It was an image she had fostered. Paula liked the way they looked up to her. They thought she was successful. They were impressed by the way men flocked around her. How could she turn around now and tell them that she'd made a complete and utter fool of herself by falling in love with a man who had not the slightest interest in her, because he was in love with their aunt. Glitzy sophisticates on pedestals did *not* make disastrous mistakes like that.

So she put on a brave face and tried to get into the Christmas spirit. The old traditions of her childhood still existed. Her father was still on the quest for the perfect Christmas Tree. The crib and candle ceremony were still her mother's pride and joy, only this time it was the grandchildren who placed the statues in the crib and watched with awe as the Christmas candle was lit.

Why couldn't she have been more like her mother and her sister Louise? Paula thought miserably as she saw the expressions of pride and pleasure on their faces as they watched the children's excitement. They were content with their lot. If she'd stayed at home and got a job in the hotel she'd probably be married and a mother herself by now. She might have been happy.

All over the Christmas, she had tried not to think about New Year. Maura and Pete had persuaded Helen and Nick to come and spend it with them. They had met Nick several times over the years when they visited Helen in Dublin. Both of them were delighted that Helen had found happiness. Maura was overjoyed that Helen was pregnant. She knew more than anyone how much being pregnant meant to her sister. All those years of yearning for a child of her own and now the miracle had happened. Maura kept telling Paula that she was thrilled about it and that Nick was a lovely man until Paula felt like screaming her head off.

Once, she did scream her head off. She went for a walk on the beach. It was lashing rain. And there was a howling gale. Paula didn't care. The wilder, wetter, windier it was, the better. There wasn't a soul around. The sea was an angry leaden cauldron, bubbling and boiling as it smashed against the rocks spraying great jets of spume in the air. The surging turbulent sea matched her mood. She felt so churned up inside. She had so many decisions to make. She'd been putting it off and putting it off. But Paula knew she couldn't go on living with Helen and Nick. The three days she'd spent with them before coming home had almost torn her apart. Yet she didn't want to seem to be leaving Helen in the lurch either. If she said she was moving out Helen was going to be dreadfully upset. She said over and over that she and Nick wanted Paula to live with them. Paula would just have to be diplomatic about it and say that the time had come for her to get her own place.

She could say she wanted to buy her own place as an investment. Although it would be a terrible waste of money to buy a place right now. She'd only be living in it for a few months of the year. That was another thing that troubled her. Paula wasn't sure if she wanted to continue being a courier. She'd done it for two years. She'd enjoyed it. But it was time to move on. Especially as Jenny was planning to stay in the office. She and Jenny made a good team. It wouldn't be half the fun without her. But what was she going to do? What did she want to do? Paula thought in desperation. She wanted to scream. She climbed up into the dunes, opened her mouth and yelled and screamed until she was hoarse. The shrieking of the wind and the roar of the sea drowned out the noise she made but she didn't care. It was a great way of letting the frustration and anger out of her system. After her outburst, she went back down to the water's edge and walked for miles along the curving beach. The wind was in her face, the spray from the sea and the rain soaked her, but she couldn't care less. It was beginning to get dark as she turned towards home. In the distance she could see the lights in the windows in the village. How welcoming they looked against the lowering sky. She was lucky, she mused. She had a family waiting at home who loved her. Maura and Pete were making the greatest fuss of her. Paula had always taken it for granted. She shouldn't. After what had happened with Nick, Paula was never going to take anything for granted again.

She saw the rich amber glow of the lamp in the sitting-room and focused on it as the light dimmed and darkness rolled in over the horizon and the shrieking of the gale intensified. For the first time in her life, Paula felt a deep sense of appreciation for her parents and her home. Usually she couldn't wait to get back to Dublin and her hectic social life. Not this time. She wanted to stay in Maggie's Bay and hide and lick her wounds. And pretend her problems didn't exist.

But they did exist, Paula thought, sipping her brandy.

'What are you doing hiding in here?' Nick poked his head around the door. 'Is everything OK, Paula? You're not your usual exuberant self,' he said. She looked into his blue eyes and saw his concern. He came around and put his hand on her shoulder. 'Is it me and Helen? Is it because of the baby? Talk to me, Paula. We've always been able to talk. Don't shut me out.'

How she longed to tell him she was miserable because she loved him. How she wanted to have him hold her in his arms and soothe her and kiss her and tell her everything would be all right. She wanted to blurt out her longing for him and to hell with the consequences. Paula struggled to quell the powerful urge to be selfish.

'Tell me,' he urged. 'What's wrong?'

Paula took a deep breath. 'It's nothing really, Nick. I'm missing Juan Carlos. And I always think New Year's a bit lonely without someone you love at your side,' she lied magnificently. She had to admire herself even in her despair.

'You love this guy?'

Paula couldn't look Nick in the eye. 'You know me,' she said wryly. 'I fall in love at the drop of a hat.'

'Paula, you'll really fall in love one day and believe me you'll know it.' Nick squeezed her shoulder. His voice was full of sympathy. She fought the urge to press her lips against the back of his hand.

'Yeah,' she murmured. 'I suppose I will.'

Chapter Sixty-Two

'I'm giving you a month's notice, Kieran. Here's my letter of resignation,' Paula said quietly. Her boss took the letter she handed him, scanned the contents, and looked at her quizzically.

'Sit down, Paula,' he invited.

'My mind is made up. I don't want to talk about it,' she declared.

'Paula, act like a grown-up. You don't just come in, give me a letter of resignation and swan out as if that was the end of it. You're going to be leaving me in the lurch. I'd at least like to know why. I think you owe me that courtesy. After all, I took you on in the job. Trained you, and gave you your chance. I invested time and money in you. And, apart from business considerations, I'd like to know as a friend or mentor, which I consider myself to be, why you're leaving so abruptly. Is there anything wrong? If so, can I do anything about it? Are you dissatisfied with your job? Are you going to another travel company? Don't just come in to me and say, "I'm resigning and I don't want to talk about it." I expect much more from you than that, Paula, so sit down. I'll get us some fresh coffee and we can talk,' Kieran said calmly.

Slightly ashamed, Paula sat down. Kieran was right. It was high-handed and bad-mannered of her to waltz in and hand him her letter of resignation and say that was the end of it. He was entitled to an explanation, at least. She was, after all, leaving him stranded. Letting him down.

Paula sighed. It wasn't what she wanted to do. But, when she came back up to Dublin with Helen and Nick, she decided she'd had enough. She couldn't face the situation any more. She wanted out. Paula made up her mind that she was going to go to London. She'd get a job somewhere. Her multilingual skills would guarantee her that. Helen was at the maternity clinic this morning so she wasn't at work. Which was why Paula had chosen today to resign. She'd have felt a bit awkward knowing that Helen was in the outer office, unaware that she was resigning.

Kieran came back into the office with a percolator of fresh coffee and two mugs. 'You take black, don't you, Paula?' he asked.

'Yes.'

He handed her a mug of coffee and, instead of going behind his desk, he sat down in the chair next to her. 'I know I could be wrong, but I feel this has got to do with Helen and the baby,' he said gently. Paula looked at the tall good-looking man beside her and was surprised by his perceptiveness. Kieran was always on the go, organizing this, that and the other. He was young to be so successful. Only in his early thirties. He was ambitious, hard-working, and demanded a lot from his staff. Yet he was a very considerate employer. He didn't miss much, Paula thought wryly.

'Partly,' she said. 'Helen's having a baby and she and Nick will be setting up home together. I think it's time I got a place of my own. To be honest, Kieran, I want to move on. Being a courier was great. I enjoyed it. I did a good job. But I want to start building a career for myself.'

'You're absolutely right, Paula. This is the time to start thinking about your future. I can understand that. Before we continue. Have you got a job lined up?'

'No . . . I was thinking of going to London,' Paula confessed.

'Phew, what a relief.' He smiled. 'I thought you were going to one of the opposition. You might have heard me talking about Lorna Dunne? She worked for me a couple of years back. I taught her everything she knows about the travel business. She left me and went to another agency for a while. Now she's set up on her own and she's trying to poach my couriers. She's a tough, hard-working woman but she doesn't know the meaning of loyalty or integrity and she doesn't have an ethical bone in her body. When you started waving that letter around and wouldn't talk about it, I thought you might be going to her.'

'I wouldn't do that, Kieran. This Lorna might not have any integrity but I do. I wouldn't play dirty like that,' Paula exclaimed indignantly.

'I know, I'm sorry,' Kieran apologized. 'It's just, once bitten, twice shy. Now, let's get down to business here. I've plans for you, my girl.'

'Have you?' She was curious now.

'You know I want to expand. I took on board your suggestion about doing more up-market holidays for clients who don't want run-of-the-mill charter holidays, but who aren't in the Concorde and stretch-limo bracket either. I've been thinking about this for a while. I want to get into the villa holidays business. We can do from fairly basic to luxury. I want someone in with me on this from the beginning. I want this to be your baby.'

Paula looked at him in amazement. This was totally unexpected.

'Don't look so surprised, Paula. I wanted you to be a courier to get experience. But I never intended for you to keep on as a courier. I want to put your talents to much better use. You're very intelligent. You're multilingual, you're interested in the company. Your suggestions are spot-on. I'm not going to waste good material like that. I've always had a long-term plan for you. I've other plans for Jennifer. I can honestly say that each of you has a big future within this company, if you want it. I'm going to give you your chance. I want you to organize our new venture into luxury villa holidays. I want you to check out the locations and the accommodation on offer. It's something we can do in conjunction with the charter flights. The year after next, I want our Holiday Villa brochure out there with the rest of them. Maybe I hadn't planned it quite this soon, but hell,' he waved her letter of resignation at her, 'I can't let you slip through my fingers, so let's go for it. I'll give you an expense account, a raise in salary and commission on holidays sold. What do you say?'

Paula stared at him. What a chance he was offering her. It would be something to get her teeth into. What a challenge. She could feel her adrenalin going. She could do it too, she thought confidently. It would mean a lot of hard work. But she thrived on that. Plenty of people wanted to go on holidays that were different. But which were organized for them. Villa holidays were getting popular. It was time for TransCon to branch out. They were successful in what they did but that was no reason to rest on their laurels. This could be a whole new success story, Paula thought excitedly.

There'd be lots of travel involved. Spain, Greece, France, Portugal. They could have villas everywhere they had holiday locations. She remembered some of the beautiful villas she'd seen for rent in Majorca and on the Costa. All her ennui lifted. She would throw herself into this project. Put her heart and soul into it. She'd be so busy she wouldn't have time to think about Nick. And she'd definitely move out and get a place of her own.

'Let's go for it,' Paula said enthusiastically. 'Let's get the show on the road.'

Chapter Sixty-Three

'For they are jolly good fellows,
For they are jolly good fellows,
For they are jolly good fe . . . ell . . . ows,
And so say all of us.'

Jennifer laughed with pleasure as she and Ronan were toasted by family and friends. It was the first Sunday of the New Year and Kit was throwing a little party to celebrate their engagement, which they'd announced on Christmas Day. They had decided to wait until Christmas to make the announcement because Jennifer was working abroad on her twenty-first birthday. Ronan was in America. Now, he was home for good and Jennifer had asked Kieran to put her name down for a full-time office job when one came up.

'Well! Well! Well! Ya beat your sister to it. She'd want to get her skates on,' Grandpa Myles cackled as he shook hands with Ronan. Brenda shot him a daggers look from where she was standing by the Christmas Tree.

'Stop that, Grandpa,' Jennifer murmured. 'It's not nice.'

'Well she's not nice. She called me a cantankerous old crab the other day. No wonder she's going to end up an old spinster. Who'd have her?' Grandpa snorted. Brenda turned purple and advanced on her grandfather.

'Do you remember once you told me the right way to cook cabbage?' Ronan remarked casually, stepping in between the old man and his enraged granddaughter. 'I was trying to remember *exactly* how to do it.'

'Ah now, son, there's a knack, d'ya see.' Grandpa

Myles was delighted to have a captive audience for a subject dear to his heart.

'I'll ram that little Antichrist's false teeth down his scrawny little neck,' Brenda fumed.

'Ignore him, Bren,' Jennifer soothed.

'Ignore him! You couldn't ignore that loudmouth, no matter how hard you tried. The cheek of him making remarks like that in front of *her*!' She glared at Paula, who was chatting to Beth and Rachel on the sofa. Fortunately, Paula didn't see the glare. Jennifer sighed. Family occasions were always fraught with danger when Brenda and Grandpa Myles were in the same room.

'I suppose *she'll* be announcing her engagement one of these days,' Brenda sneered.

'No, Brenda, she won't be,' Jennifer said gently. She wasn't going to tell Brenda that Paula was in bits over Nick Russell. This was supposed to be the happiest time of Jennifer's life. Brenda could have made some effort to be gracious and pretended she was pleased for her. Why was she always so jealous?

'Is Kathy coming later on?' Jennifer tried to change the subject. Brenda threw her eyes up to heaven. 'The baby is sick, and she wouldn't leave her with a baby-sitter. That's all you get these days with Kathy. Kids! It's so *boring*!'

'Look, I'd better go over and say a few words to Rachel, I haven't had much of a chance since she arrived,' Jennifer murmured.

'She's not a bit like Ronan,' Brenda observed. 'She's not the world's greatest conversationalist.'

'She's had a hard life,' Jennifer said.

'Haven't we all? Anyone who's had to live with that little Napoleon,' Brenda glared at her grandfather, 'knows what a hard life's all about.'

'Why don't you move out and get a flat if you find it so difficult?' Jennifer tried to keep the irritation out of her voice.

'We can't all take off like you did, Jenny,' Brenda said

loftily. 'I didn't like to leave Ma to put up with him all by herself.'

Bitch! Jennifer was furious. Brenda could be a right cow. Trying to make her feel guilty for going to Spain. It was all an excuse. She wouldn't have the nerve to get off her fat ass and go and do something with her life instead of wallowing in her rut and moaning about it. 'I'm going to talk to Rachel,' Jennifer said coldly. Brenda was taking all the good out of her engagement party.

'What's up?' Ronan asked as she walked past him to talk to Rachel. 'You look as if you could murder someone.'

'I could. Brenda!' Jennifer scowled. Ronan put his arm around her waist and drew her out into the hall.

'What did she say?' he asked.

'Oh she was just having a dig at me for going off to Spain. She says she couldn't do it, because she wouldn't go and leave Ma to put up with Grumps all by herself. She's trying to make me feel bad.'

'Ignore her,' Ronan said firmly. 'You're too soft with her. One of these days you should let her have it and that would settle her hash for her.'

'Yeah, well I don't want to cause a row here. It would be the height of bad manners. Let's forget it and *pretend* we're having fun.' Jennifer sighed.

'Look on the bright side, it could be worse. My dad could be here.' Ronan laughed.

'Ronan Stapleton!' exclaimed Jennifer. But she had to laugh. William and Ronan had had a *rapprochement* of sorts. When Ronan came back from America, he went to Rathbarry, told William he was home for good and intended to get married. He bluntly asked his father whether he was going to keep the row going for ever. William sulked for a while before holding out the olive branch. He invited his son to bring his bride-to-be to tea some Sunday.

Jennifer was delighted with the news. It had always worried her that Ronan and his father were estranged.

561

At least father and son were talking again even if they would never be close. She couldn't say she was thrilled at the prospect of having tea with Mr Stapleton but she would put up a good front for Ronan.

'What plans are you two hatching?' Kit appeared from the kitchen with a plateful of sandwiches.

'We think we might elope,' grinned Jennifer.

'Ah don't do that! You'll do me out of the chance to wear a big hat.' Kit laughed. 'Now bring in these sandwiches and mix with your guests and stop trying to have a sneaky snog.'

'Some chance in this house,' Jennifer retorted. She took the plate from her mother and went to rejoin her guests.

Kit dried the last glass and put it in the press, switched off the light in the kitchen and went in to the sitting-room. There wasn't a sound in the house. Jim was in bed, as was Grandpa Myles. Everyone else had gone to a night-club in town. The embers in the grate glowed. Kit threw a log on them and watched the flames lick around the base of it. Only the soft glow of the Christmas Tree illuminated the room. It was nice sitting in the half-light. She decided not to switch on the lamp. The party had gone very well, she mused. Jennifer and Ronan were as happy as could be.

Kit sighed. They were setting out on the rocky road of marriage with such optimism. She hoped nothing would spoil it for them. From what she'd heard, Ronan's father was a tough nut. That poor girl Rachel had an awful time of it. Kit hoped he'd never have to go and live with Jennifer and Ronan the way her father-in-law had come to live with her. Grandpa Myles caused more rows in the house. He and Brenda didn't get on at all and it could be very wearing listening to them sniping at each other. Brenda was in terribly bad form ever since she'd heard about Jennifer's engagement.

Kit absentmindedly popped a chocolate into her mouth. Brenda had no get-up-and-go in her, unlike Jennifer. She moaned about Bugs Bunny Powers and the hard time she gave her at work and yet when Kit suggested she change her job, Brenda shrugged her shoulders and said she'd think about it. If only she could meet someone and settle down. That was all she wanted. It was funny the way life went. Jennifer had never really been pushed about going with fellas, had never expressed a desire to marry and now she was engaged to the love of her life. Brenda had always wanted to be out on dates or going with someone. She'd dated quite a few lads since the break-up with Eddie, but none of the romances seemed to last. Kit sometimes thought that her eldest daughter's desperation to get a husband frightened men off. It was all a worry. Even when they were grown-up, you worried about them. In fact, Kit decided, as she finished off the few remaining chocolates, you worried about them even more.

'This time next year, we should be in our own house,' Ronan murmured against Jennifer's ear as the taxi drew up outside her house.

'Are you going to come in?' She snuggled in close against him.

'No, I'd better not. It's hard to get taxis this time of year, I'll hang on to this one,' Ronan said regretfully.

'Would you not stay the night on the sofa?' Jennifer asked. 'I hate the thought of you going back to that old flat.'

'No I won't,' Ronan replied. 'Your parents were very good to put me up until I got a place of my own. I don't want to take advantage. We'll start looking for a place of our own soon.'

'I can't wait. The sooner the better,' Jennifer said. She didn't relish the thought of sharing with Brenda for much longer.

'We'll go to tea with Dad next Sunday. There's a few new estates being built in Dean's Grange and Shankill, on the way to Rathbarry. We can start having a look at the show houses and get a few ideas. What do you think?'

'Brilliant,' Jennifer agreed happily. 'That's a great idea. Ronan, you're a genius.'

'I know,' agreed her intended modestly. 'You're a very lucky woman.'

'What can I say to that?' laughed Jennifer. She gave him a loving kiss and stood waving after the taxi until it disappeared around the corner of St Pappin's Road.

Chapter Sixty-Four

Brenda shivered and yawned as she dressed for work, and cursed as she looked out the window and saw a lone magpie sitting on the telephone line. Just her luck, she thought glumly. A lone magpie was the first thing she'd seen on New Year's morning a few days before. What an omen. What a way to start the New Year. It was bad enough starting a new year knowing that your younger sister had just got engaged and you were still on the shelf, without single magpies to add to your misery.

It was the morning after Jenny's engagement party and she was whacked. She'd a hell of a hangover too. And she was utterly depressed. The thought of facing yet another year working under Bugs Bunny Powers was enough to make her weep. She was sorely tempted to get her mother to phone in and say she was sick. But she'd already taken five sick days and only had two left. And they had to last her until April. How she envied Kathy, able to stay at home all day with her children. She was her own boss, she could get up when she liked. Do what she liked, when she liked. It couldn't be *that* hard to mind two children, even if they were only babies. Poor Kathy had got caught very soon after the birth of her first baby and found herself unexpectedly pregnant, much to her dismay. Brenda couldn't understand what the fuss was about. At least Kathy was married, she had her own house, and a very nice one at that, she had a husband who was nuts about her and she didn't have to go out to work.

'See you later,' she said to Jennifer, who was struggling to wake up. Her sister gave a grunt. Brenda wasn't sure if it was a friendly grunt or not. She'd been a bit mean to poor old Jenny at the party last night, she thought guiltily. Implying that Jenny had waltzed off to Spain without a thought for their mother. Jenny had been hurt. It was her special night, after all, even if Brenda envied her from the bottom of her heart.

'Do you want me to bring you up a cup of tea before I go?' Brenda feigned a cheeriness she did not feel. She wanted to try and make amends.

'Naw. Thanks.' Jenny yawned.

'Don't go back to sleep or you'll be late for work,' Brenda warned.

'Kieran gave me the morning off, he knew about the party,' Jennifer said drowsily and then turned over and burrowed down under her quilt and went fast asleep again.

Brenda looked at her. Why didn't things like that happen to *her*? Why couldn't Bugs Bunny tell her to take a morning off? Snowballs would roast in hell before that happened, Brenda thought glumly as she brushed her hair and slapped on a bit of make-up.

A few minutes later she cursed frantically as she saw the 13 bus disappearing down the road. The last thing she needed was to get a late. Bugs Bunny loved giving lates. It was her ultimate power-trip. Brenda started to run, she might get a 19A on the Ballymun Road if she was lucky. It was raining and it was hard to run with an umbrella whipping around in the wind. Brenda felt like crying. The year was turning out to be a disaster and it was only a few days old. She made the 19A by the skin of her teeth and stood in the aisle panting. She wouldn't have minded a seat but the bus was packed so she resigned herself to standing all the way into town.

The bus broke down at Hart's Corner. Brenda was ready to explode as she got off the bus with the rest of the grumbling passengers. She couldn't decide whether to start walking or wait for another bus. There wasn't a bus in sight anyway so she decided to walk. She'd just stuck up her umbrella when she heard a car horn toot.

She turned and saw a small van pull in. On the outside in big black letters was the writing HANLEY ALARMS.

The passenger door opened and she heard her ex-boyfriend Shay say, 'Hi Bren, do you want a lift?'

'Shay! How are you?' she said, closing her brolly and easing herself into the van. 'Isn't it a horrible morning? The blasted bus broke down and I'm heading for a late. Bugs Bunny's day will be made.' Brenda smiled at Shay.

'Is old Bugsy still going strong?' Shay laughed.

'She sure is.' Brenda sighed as they moved into the stream of traffic. 'Aren't you lucky you're your own boss? It must be great. When did you start up your own business?'

'A couple of years ago. I was doing a lot of nixers, putting in alarms and I just decided to go for it.'

'Well congratulations, Shay, I hope it works out well for you,' Brenda said.

'It's going OK, thanks.' He smiled. Shay had nice eyes. He wasn't wearing a wedding ring either, she noted. Although that didn't mean anything these days. Lots of men didn't wear wedding rings.

'How's all your family?' Shay inquired as he negotiated his way into the outer lane.

'Fine. Jenny got engaged at Christmas,' Brenda said brightly.

'That's great news. Have you got anything on the burner yourself?' he asked casually.

'Not me.' Brenda laughed in what she hoped was an offhand manner. 'You know me, Shay, I like to be footloose and fancy-free.'

'I thought you'd be well married by now,' Shay remarked.

'And how about yourself?' Brenda did not care to get into a discussion about her single state.

'Me? I'm like yourself, Bren. No-one special.'

'I suppose you've been too busy building up your business,' Brenda murmured.

'Yeah, something like that,' Shay agreed.

'I hope I'm not putting you out,' Brenda remarked as they passed Berkeley Road Church. 'Just let me out wherever it suits you.'

'Listen, I'm going to get you into work on time. Bugs Bunny can do without her thrills for today,' Shay declared.

'Thanks very much, Shay.' Brenda was touched. Shay had always been extremely nice and good to her. Only she'd been so in love with Eddie and it had meant nothing.

Minutes later Shay pulled up outside the office. It was a minute and a half to nine.

'Thanks a million, Shay,' she said hastily. 'I'd better fly in case the lift is out of order.'

'You're welcome.' He leaned over to help her open the door.

Brenda smiled at him. 'See you,' she said.

'Mmm . . . would you fancy going for a drink sometime?' he asked diffidently. Brenda paused. Did she want to see Shay again? A vision of Jenny's sparkling solitaire came to mind. She saw Patsy Kelly, a spinster in her late fifties, puffing up the steps to the doors. She'd be like that unless she did something drastic, Brenda fretted. Years of misery until she collected her pension beckoned. Brenda turned back to Shay.

'I'd love to go for a drink, Shay. It would be nice to catch up on all the news.'

'When suits you?'

'I'm free tonight,' Brenda replied. Years ago she would have played hard to get and suggested Friday night and let him wait for a week. But times had changed and so had circumstances. She was twenty-five. No spring chicken. Jennifer, four years younger than her, was engaged. Her best friend was married and the mother of two children. Eddie, the love of her life, was married. And she was rapidly approaching her sell-by date. Desperate measures were called for.

Chapter Sixty-Five

'Do you intend giving up work once you're married?' Mr Stapleton queried, as he passed Jennifer a plate of scones.

'No, I don't think so. I like my job, and two salaries will help pay the mortgage,' Jennifer said. Talk about the Spanish inquisition, she thought to herself. Her father-in-law to be hadn't stopped quizzing her since she sat down to tea. Ronan was in the kitchen making another pot of tea. Rachel sat silently at the other end of the table.

'I wouldn't have liked my poor dear departed wife to have had to work, once we married. Call me old-fashioned, if you will, but I like the idea of a man providing for his wife.' William gave a tight little smile.

'I like the idea of being able to contribute to buying our house and to sharing in its upkeep. I like the idea of being Ronan's partner. Whatever we do, it will be a partnership. And, as I say, I like my job,' Jennifer said firmly.

'Oh, you're one of these feminist independent career types we hear so much about.' William pretended to be amused. 'Ronan told me you lived in Spain. Didn't your parents mind you being in a foreign country by yourself?' His comment and tone implied that Kit and Jim were negligent parents. I've had enough of you, Buster! Jennifer decided.

'Not at all,' she said lightly. 'My parents felt it was a great opportunity for me to travel and learn about other cultures. They were always very anxious for us to stand on our own two feet and be independent. They're not the clingy sort, thank goodness.' She smiled sweetly. 'They want us all to live our own lives. They don't expect us to dance attendance on them. You know, like some parents who never let their children grow up,' she added pointedly.

William pursed his lips. 'I see,' he said curtly. Rachel smiled at Jennifer.

'Your parents seem to be very sensible people,' she said demurely.

'Oh, they are,' Jennifer said. 'My mother said you must come to dinner some Friday and stay the night, and not go rushing back to Rathbarry. You could come house-hunting with Ronan and me some Saturday. It will give you an idea if you ever look for a place of your own.'

'I'd like that,' Rachel agreed enthusiastically, ignoring her father's cold stare.

'You'd like what?' Ronan arrived in with the teapot.

'I've asked Rachel to stay some Friday night. She can come house-hunting with us. It will be good experience for her if she ever decides to buy her own house.' Jennifer knew Mr Stapleton was seething but she didn't care. He was a horrible man and he needn't think he was going to get away with trying to slag off her parents.

'Great idea,' Ronan approved, giving Jennifer a tiny wink. He knew exactly what she was up to.

William couldn't take any more. 'There'll be no need for Rachel ever to get a house of her own. She'll always have a home here.'

'Oh yes, I know that,' Jennifer gushed. 'But you know us career women these days. We love our independence.'

'Mmmm . . . That's all very well,' William said disdainfully. 'But I see the result of this sort of thinking and how it affects children I teach. Children whose mothers aren't content and want to go out working and be . . . ' he paused and gave Jennifer a supercilious look, ' "independent." As a result we have these so-called "latchkey kids." I think society will suffer because of it.'

'Maybe, economically, these women have no choice,' Jennifer argued politely.

'Nonsense.' William made his favourite retort.

'Jennifer has a very good point there,' Ronan said sternly. 'We were looking at houses today and if she wasn't working, we wouldn't be able to get a mortgage. And when we do get one we won't be able to manage unless she works. That's not nonsense, Dad. That's a fact of life, unfortunately.'

'Well I suppose if you're going to live in a palace . . .' William sniffed. 'There are some nice cottages down by tenacres that you'd be able to afford.'

'We have to work in town, Dad. Commuting isn't on. Apart from the inconvenience, it's expensive.'

So stick that in your pipe and smoke it, Jennifer thought. If she never saw Mr Stapleton again she wouldn't care. When you married someone you took on their family as well. The thought of having Mr Stapleton as her father-in-law did not make her ecstatically happy. Having met him for the first time she found him cold, superior, arrogant and narrow-minded. Grandpa Myles was saintly in comparison. For Ronan's sake, of course, she would tolerate his father. But she didn't have to like him and she wouldn't let him treat her in the dismissive rude way he treated Rachel. And she certainly wouldn't let William Stapleton interfere in her marriage. If he tried it, he'd soon realize his mistake, Jennifer resolved as she lay in bed that night thinking over the events of the day.

Chapter Sixty-Six

'Paula, I'm ringing from the hospital. Helen's started the baby.' Nick sounded agitated.

'I'm on my way,' she said, coming instantly awake. A glance at her alarm clock showed her that it was just gone three-thirty am. She dressed quickly and let herself out of the flat. She'd moved in over two months ago, but she'd been so busy that half her stuff was still in boxes. Soon, she promised herself. Soon, she and Beth and Jenny would organize it. It was a nice roomy flat on the first floor in a double-fronted redbrick house on Griffith Avenue. It was self-contained, and she was pleased enough with it. Not that she spent much time there, she thought wryly as she unlocked her newly acquired Corolla and sped off down Griffith Avenue. The roads were deserted and the traffic lights at the junction opposite the Garda Station were green. Minutes later, she was passing the Skylon, and the Bishop's Palace.

'Let me see, Holles Street,' she muttered to herself, planning her route in her head. The best plan was to go via the Five Lamps, down along the quays and turn right at the road before the road for the gasometer. As far as she could remember that road led directly to the hospital. It took her about five minutes to get to the quays. The moon shone on the glassy river. On the opposite quay the Isle of Man ferry, *The Lady of Man*, floated serenely at anchor in her berth. TransCon did an Isle of Man package holiday brochure, maybe she should look into the villa holiday idea there, Paula reflected. 'Forget work,' she muttered as the huge bulk of the gasometer loomed into view. She peered anxiously to her right looking for Lime Street. She almost overshot and had to jam on the brakes.

Was this the right road? It was eerily quiet, she thought as she drove past silent dark blocks of flats. In the distance she saw the façade of the hospital. Spot-on, Paula thought with satisfaction. She saw Nick's Volvo, and parked behind it. The porter rang upstairs to tell Nick she had arrived and minutes later he walked through the swing doors, looking tired and worried.

'Paula, thanks for coming,' he hugged her. 'She's having a very difficult time. They're concerned. They might have to do a Caesarean. If anything happens to Helen I'll never forgive myself. She's too old to have a first baby.' He rubbed his hand along his jaw.

'Stop it, Nick. She'll be fine. She's in the best place. There's expert care and all the equipment. Stop worrying,' Paula said sternly. 'Go back up to her. I'll be down here.'

'You're the best in the world, Paula, you should have seen Helen's face when I told her you were downstairs.' Nick smiled.

'Tell her we're all in this together and to hurry on, the suspense is killing me,' Paula ordered. 'If you hear anything let me know.'

'I'll be up and down,' Nick promised. 'I'm not allowed to stay while they're examining her.'

It was a long night. Nick looked more haggard and worried each time he came down to her. If he looked this bad, God help Helen, Paula thought in dismay. She could hardly imagine what her aunt was going through. The wait seemed interminable. Every time the doors swung open her heart leapt, as she hoped it was Nick with good news. Each time he made an appearance she knew by the expression on his face that the ordeal was not over. He urged her to go home and go to bed. She refused.

The dark night gave way to a golden sunrise. Paula watched the pink-tinted sky through the window and heard the sound of a milkman's lorry with its clattering jangle of bottles. At seven-thirty, Nick appeared briefly to tell her that Helen was having a Caesarean. At least something was being done, Paula reassured him. Helen's ordeal would soon be over. An hour later he appeared again, his face wreathed in smiles.

'It's a little girl,' he exclaimed. 'We've got a little girl. She's beautiful. The two of them are fine, now.' Paula burst into tears.

'It's all right, Paula. It's over.' Nick hugged her tightly.

'I'm so happy for Helen.' She sobbed against his shoulder. 'I'm really glad it's a little girl. I know she was dying for one.'

'Me too,' Nick murmured against her hair. 'Me too. I can't believe it. I can't believe I'm a father.'

'You'll be a great father.' Paula wiped her cheeks, and rooted for a handkerchief.

'Here,' he said, offering his. 'I begged the nurses to let you come up and see them and they said you could come for a minute. Helen's a bit groggy.'

'Oh Nick.' She started to blubber again.

'Stop it or I'll be crying too,' he said, taking her by the hand. Holding his hand gave her a moment of happiness.

'Only for a minute, mind,' the nurse said.

Helen lay propped against her pillows. Her face was grey, her eyes were bloodshot but she smiled radiantly when she saw Nick and Paula.

'Look, darling,' she murmured as Paula bent to kiss her. 'Isn't she beautiful? I'm the happiest person alive.' Paula's eyes brimmed again as she saw the tiny baby nestled in Helen's arms. She stared in awe at the perfect little face with the rosebud mouth and the little nose. Her skin wasn't red and wrinkled because she hadn't had a normal birth. She'd just been lifted out of the womb. She had a little head of black hair but when she opened her eyes and stared up, Paula knew she would have eyes like her father's.

'She's exquisite, Helen. She's beautiful. Congratulations.'

'Darling, you've been so good to me. I'll never be able to repay you,' Helen said gratefully, her own eyes sparkling with tears. 'We're going to call her Nicola Paula. Will you be her godmother?'

'Of course I will, Helen. Now get your rest and I'll see you later,' Paula urged, as the nurse appeared, ready to evict her. 'I'll phone Mam and let her know the news.'

'Thanks, pet.' Helen squeezed her hand.

'I'll see you later, Nick,' Paula said. 'If you need anything doing, let me know.'

'Sure, thanks.' Nick hugged her again, but his eyes were on Helen and their baby. Paula slipped away to let them share their joyful intimate moments.

She was right into the rush hour traffic so she decided not to go back home. She could have a shower and breakfast at the office. There was no point in going back to bed, she just wouldn't sleep. Her mind was racing. Her emotions in turmoil. Helen, Nick and the baby were a family now. She felt such a mixture of emotions when she saw the baby. Happiness for Helen, sadness for herself. The pride and love in Nick's eyes as he looked at Helen were painful for her to watch. She hated herself for feeling as she did. She felt mean. She wanted to be happy for Helen. If only she'd fallen in love with another man.

Paula sighed as she swung on to Pearse Street. Life was full of 'if only's.' There was nothing she could do except grit her teeth and get on with it. At least she had her job to keep her going. She'd been out to Majorca and the Costa viewing villas. She was going out again the following week to make a final selection and to get them photographed. After that, Portugal. Life was hectic and that was just what she needed.

Six weeks later, Paula stood in church holding her precious goddaughter. Her tiny little fingers curled tightly around Paula's thumb. She was fast asleep. She hadn't made a sound all through her christening ceremony. Paula gazed in wonder at her perfect little features. Her eyelashes were so long. Her little nose was adorable. Her mouth, the prettiest one Paula had ever seen.

'My little precious,' she crooned.

Helen came and stood beside her and gazed proudly at her daughter. 'Isn't she the best baby?'

'Yeah.' Paula smiled, bending her lips to Nicola's cheek. 'She's the best baby in the world.'

'And you're the best niece.' Helen slipped an arm around Paula's waist and hugged her.

Don't say that, Paula wanted to cry. She'd spent the morning trying not to think of how attractive Nick looked. And how blue his eyes were and how kind he was being to Helen. She'd watched them together cooing to the baby and hated them for their happiness. Then she'd hated herself for that and spent the rest of the morning telling herself that she was a disloyal bitch for having these thoughts.

Forget him, she told herself over and over again. But how could she forget him when her life was so closely entwined with his? She couldn't stop visiting Helen and the baby or being part of their lives. Helen would be devastated if she did. She wouldn't understand at all. And why should she? Helen had no idea that her beloved niece loved and lusted after her partner and father of her child. Nick didn't even know it. The only person who knew was Jenny. She had to tell someone. And she was closer to Jenny than anyone.

Jenny offered to come and spend the christening night with her. She knew today would be an ordeal. She knew Paula wanted to get it off her chest. Tonight, Paula promised herself, was the last night she would talk or think about Nick. That was the end of it now, she decided as she stood watching him chatting and laughing with Maura and Pete. The best way of forgetting Nick was to find another man to fall in love with. Instead of staying in, moping. She'd ask Jenny to go out on the town with her. The city was full of eligible bachelors, she'd have no trouble finding a man.

But I don't want a man. I only want Nick, her inner voice said.

Well you can't have him, so tough bloody luck, she argued back. Get off your ass and cop on to yourself, Paula Matthews, or you're going to be miserable for the rest of your life. It's entirely up to you.

Chapter Sixty-Seven

Relief, that was what she felt most, Brenda decided, as Shay slid the wedding ring on to the third finger of her left hand. Not happiness, not excitement, just a deep, deep sense of relief that she was finally married. Rescued from the lonely isolation of her spinster's shelf. Even if Shay were to drop down dead beside her she'd have the comfort of being a Mrs now that the ring was finally on her finger. Now she was just like Kathy, and all her married friends. She was part of that special club. A married woman and not some waif peering longingly through the windows, like the beggar at the banquet. Brenda rejoiced. Now she no longer felt threatened by Jenny's engagement. Another thought struck her as she knelt for the priest's blessing. She was a Mrs, and Paula Matthews, for all her sophisticated glamour, was still only a Miss. Brenda felt exhilarated, invincible. She could face anything. Her fear of being left on the shelf could never haunt her now. She had achieved her greatest ambition.

Brenda could live with the fact that Shay was only second best. It was far preferable to be married to Shay than never to be married at all. When Eddie had got married her dreams had crumbled into dust. Wallowing in heartbreak was not what she wanted to spend her life doing. Brenda was nothing if not pragmatic. Eddie was her past, Shay was her future. He loved her. He wanted to provide for her. She was perfectly happy to let him do so. Shay was a nice man. She was lucky.

Brenda smiled at her new husband. He looked very nice in his suit. And the new moustache he sported made him look a little like Tom Selleck. It was a pity he didn't possess Tom Selleck's build. Shay barely topped her. He didn't tower over her like Eddie had.

Stop that! she ordered herself crossly. Here she was only minutes married and she was making comparisons. She was not going to live her life like that. She was very grateful to Shay for proposing. He had no idea of the huge favour he'd done her by saving her from spinsterhood. From now on, she would never allow the memory of Eddie to enter her mind again. If she did, she'd only be unhappy. Brenda had no intention of being unhappy. She intended to savour every moment of this new life. Shay and herself had agreed that she would leave her job whenever she got pregnant. She'd be getting a nice big gratuity.

There'd been a marriage bar when she'd started working. Married women had to leave work. That was all changed and women no longer had to resign on marriage. Brenda had the option of forgoing her gratuity and staying on at work. An option she hadn't considered for a second. She couldn't wait to escape. The idea of not having to suffer Bugs Bunny's sarcastic barbs for much longer was another great source of joy. Brenda looked down at her wedding ring. She'd picked a wide one. She didn't like those wishy-washy thin ones that were all the rage now. A good wide wedding band made her feel nice and married. A warm contented glow enfolded her. Brenda knelt for the remainder of her wedding ceremony, admiring her wedding ring, and feeling utterly contented.

Shay surreptitiously loosened the knot in his tie, as he sat in his chair watching the rest of the guests receive Holy Communion. It was hard to believe he was a married man. He felt slightly dazed by it all. Everything had happened so fast in the last few months. The engagement, buying the house, planning the wedding. It was all a blur. To tell the truth he felt a bit of an onlooker in all of it. Brenda had done most of the organizing and he had merely followed instructions. She was a great organizer, was his Bren, Shay thought admiringly. From the minute he'd impulsively asked her to marry him, Brenda had arranged everything.

He'd had a few pints on him the night he proposed, he thought wryly. He'd surprised himself as much as Brenda. And now here he was, sitting beside his wife at their wedding. It was a nice feeling. He was looking forward to their honeymoon and then to coming home to live in their own house. It was going to be very pleasant to come home to a wife after work. Much nicer than going home to an empty flat with fish and chips for his dinner. Brenda was a good cook. She was good at everything. She was very outgoing and loved socializing. What she saw in an old stick-in-the-mud like him, he didn't know. But she'd been delighted when he'd asked her to marry him and had hugged him ecstatically. Shay had felt very proud at that moment.

The day after he'd proposed she'd booked the church and hotel and made him take the day off work to go and buy an engagement ring. The speed of it all took him by surprise, and he hadn't time to draw breath since. He was certainly going to flop on his honeymoon, he decided. Brenda could wind down and relax, now that all the fuss was over. And then they could come home to their new house and start enjoying married life. He rubbed his thumb against his wedding ring. It felt strange. Slightly irritating actually, Shay mused. No doubt he would get used to it.

Kit slipped her left foot out of her shoe. Her bunion was killing her and the shoes she'd got to match her outfit, although very decorative and fashionable, were much too narrow for her. Still, it was all in a good cause. As mother of the bride she had to look her best.

Kit smiled fondly at the sight of her two daughters up at the altar. One engaged, one married. People often said that when one went the rest would soon follow. To say she'd been surprised when Brenda had arrived in that evening last July to announce that she was engaged, was an understatement. You could have knocked her down with a feather. When she declared that she was getting married the following February, there was a stunned silence. Although they hadn't named the exact date, it was generally understood that Jenny and Ronan were getting married that year. It had been a bit hard on Jenny, who felt she had to postpone her wedding so that Kit and Jim wouldn't have the expense of two weddings in the one year.

Still, Kit hadn't seen Brenda as excited and full of anticipation in a long time. It was a joy to watch her making plans and decorating her house. Kit was very happy for her daughter. It was a great relief to know that Brenda had got what she had so long desired. And Shay was a very nice lad. As was Ronan. She was a lucky woman to be getting two fine sons-in-law.

Jennifer tried to quell the surge of resentment she felt as she followed Brenda and Shay down the aisle. It wasn't that she wasn't glad for her sister. She was, of course. But because of Brenda's surprise naming of the wedding day, she and Ronan, who'd planned to marry in May, felt they had to put it off. Even though they were going to pay for their own reception, Jennifer didn't think it was fair on her mother to have to plan two weddings so soon after each other. Kit had suggested a double wedding but Jennifer and Ronan decided against it. Brenda would want her own way too much and they could foresee mighty rows. Besides, they wanted their own day to be very special and personal.

Brenda had apologized for upsetting her plans, but had made no suggestion of rearranging her own. She was intent on getting down the aisle as fast as she could and nothing and no-one was going to stand in her way.

Jennifer caught sight of Ronan as she passed his pew. He looked rightly pissed off, she thought glumly. She couldn't blame him. She felt exactly the same. Forcing herself to smile, Jennifer followed her sister out the door of the church to where the photographer was waiting to record the happy day.

Brenda stood in front of the mirror in the hotel bedroom and delayed the moment when she would have to take off her bridal gown to change into her going-away outfit. It was such a beautiful dress. White taffeta, that rustled every time she moved, was fashioned into a full-skirted creation that would have graced any princess. Her white veil fell in pristine folds over her recently body-waved hair. Brenda knew, looking at her radiant image in the mirror, that she had never looked so well. She hated to take off the dress that meant so much to her. She hated to leave her reception, which was great fun. She would have liked for the day never to end.

It had been a wonderful success. Even Grandpa Myles had enjoyed himself and sung his party-piece, *Red Sails in the Sunset*. Then, for an encore, he sang *The Red River Valley*. She'd been a bit worried that he wouldn't shut up, but Jim bought him a double brandy and he was quite happy to sit in at the table for the rest of the evening commenting on everything. He'd given them a hideous barometer with a clock in it as a wedding present. Brenda was certainly not going to put it anywhere it could be seen. You'd think it was the eighth wonder of the world, he was so proud of it. It had cost a tidy sum but it was still hideous and Brenda would have far preferred money.

Kit and she had been very worried about what would happen if Ellen, his estranged daughter, accepted her invitation to the wedding. Kit had agonized over whether to invite the family or not but Brenda wanted her cousins there. Tough luck if Grandpa Myles was uncomfortable about it. Ellen decided not to go. She would not let bygones be bygones even at this stage of her life. Pamela, her husband and Susan came, but kept well out of their grandfather's way and the occasion passed off without incident. It was a wonderful wedding. It was an awful shame that it was almost over.

'Come on, you'd better get out of your dress and into your going-away outfit before the band decide to finish up. Everybody wants to do an arch for you.' Jennifer interrupted her reverie.

'I hate taking the dress off,' Brenda said, smoothing the lovely shiny material.

'I know, it's a lovely dress.' Jennifer eased the veil off Brenda's hair.

'I know you're probably a bit upset that I got in before you, Jenny,' Brenda said hesitantly. 'I didn't do it on purpose or out of malice. It was just . . . it was because I didn't want any delays in case anything went wrong. I'd have died if Shay had changed his mind and got cold feet. You probably think I'm mad, but I really wanted to be married more than anything else. It's all right for you, you're four years younger than me. I'll be twenty-seven this August. Practically thirty you might as well say, I couldn't delay things . . . ' Her tone was supplicating. Brenda felt she owed her sister some sort of explanation. Jenny and Ronan didn't exactly dance up and down when they heard her wedding plans. She saw Jennifer take a deep breath. Then, to Brenda's delight and relief, her sister put her arms around her and hugged her warmly.

'I hope you'll be very happy, Bren. I'm glad you've got what you wanted. Shay's a lovely fella.'

'I know,' Brenda felt a lump in her throat as she hugged her younger sister back. Jenny was a real old softie and always had been. 'Thanks for everything, Jenny. This has been the best day of my life.'

'Come on. Don't get maudlin!' Jenny said crisply. 'If you don't get a move on the band will be gone and so will the guests.'

'Right,' Brenda agreed, stepping out of her beloved dress. She was wearing a silken white slip, and her skin gleamed golden in contrast. 'The sunbeds did a good job, didn't they?' She admired her colour approvingly.

'Yeah,' Jennifer sighed enviously. 'I wish I was off to the Canaries for two weeks.'

583

'I can't wait,' Brenda said excitedly. 'Two weeks in the sun is just what I need. Life can only get better.' She gave a happy laugh and slipped into her posh new suit. She caught sight of her suitcase, packed with summer clothes. What bliss it would be to leave February's wet cold dreary weather behind. Her glance alighted on the neatly handwritten labels. Mrs Brenda Hanley . . . She smiled. Brenda Myles no longer existed. She was not sorry to see the back of her.

Chapter Sixty-Eight

Brenda gloried in the warmth of the sun as she lay on a lounger beside a glittering pool, under skies so blue and bright she had to wear sunglasses. She could see Shay sitting in the shade of the building on the balcony of their whitewashed apartment across the terrace. He wore a big hat on his head and socks on his feet. He was reading a thriller. Shay was not one for the sun or the heat, Brenda thought regretfully. She *loved* it. Jennifer, Kathy and Beth had given them the honeymoon as a wedding present. Two glorious weeks in Tenerife. Jennifer arranged it all and got it at a good price with TransCon. A huge basket of fruit and a bottle of champagne were waiting for them when they arrived. And the couriers were making a terrific fuss of them. It was great having a contact in the travel world, Brenda thought happily, stretching out like a cat.

It was late in the afternoon, her favourite time for sunbathing. They were into the second week of their honeymoon and her tan was coming along nicely. Today, she decided, she would risk using oil. She'd been extremely careful, and used high protection factors at the beginning. But the end of the holiday was in sight and she wanted to go home with a fantastic tan. If she started to use oil instead of sun milk, that would really bring it up. She sat up and rooted into her beach bag and pulled out a bottle of Ambre Solaire. Brenda uncapped it and inhaled its scent appreciatively. She adored the smell of suntan oil, it was so evocative of sunny climes. It always reminded her of that first exciting holiday abroad and her *almost* foreign affair with the sexy Raul. That first holiday had been special. She'd been on holidays since, of course. Holidays arranged by Jennifer. After all, it was a bit daft to cut off her nose to spite her face just because of Paula Matthews.

Brenda scowled as she slathered oil on her limbs. That was another reason she wanted a super-duper tan. It got up her nose that Paula always sported a tan. She invariably had an aura of glowing vitality that was immensely attractive. Brenda wanted to emulate her for as long as the tan lasted. She might even treat herself to a few sunbeds when she got home.

She hadn't invited Paula to the wedding. After all, she was Jenny's friend, not hers. Kit wanted to invite her. She considered her a friend of the family and was quite happy for her to come to the main event. Brenda said an emphatic no. There were other people she'd much prefer to invite. She'd sent her an invitation to the afters. After all, she did want Paula to see her in all her finery, looking her very best. She wanted to feel smug and superior in her married state. Brenda felt she was one up on her old adversary. She wanted to rub it in. Paula left it to the last minute to say she wouldn't be making an appearance at the evening do. She had some trade reception to attend. Brenda was quite miffed at her non-appearance. Paula, as usual, had done her out of her small victory.

Brenda lay back on her lounger and let the slanting rays of the evening sun brown her oiled limbs. She spent a very pleasant hour imagining herself with a fantastic tan, arm in arm with Shay, bumping into Paula, whose jaw would drop at the stunning sight in front of her and whose eyes would glitter with ill-concealed envy at the sight of the wide gold wedding ring on Brenda's left hand. It was a nice little fantasy. It made her feel good, she thought drowsily before she fell into a light doze.

A shriek from the balcony jerked her to wakefulness. Shay was frantically waving his book at some insect that was attacking him. Brenda felt a stab of irritation. Could she not even relax on her lounger for half an hour without some drama to disturb her?

'It's the last time I'm coming on a sun holiday, Bren,' he scowled as she went to his assistance. 'This place is full of wild animals. And the heat is killing me.'

'Go and sit in a cold bath for a while,' she said unsympathetically. She'd been listening to his moans for the last eleven days. It was taking all the good out of the honeymoon. 'And don't forget it's the Mr & Mrs competition tonight. I've entered our names.'

'Oh, Brenda! Do we have to? I hate things like that,' Shay protested.

'Ah come on, Shay, stop being such a party-pooper. It will be great fun.' She tried to keep the irritation out of her tone. Honestly, Shay was such a stick-in-the-mud sometimes.

'It's not my scene, Bren, you know that,' Shay muttered.

'Is *anything* your scene?' she asked sarcastically.

'It was your idea to come here, not mine,' Shay argued. 'It was all arranged before I knew anything about it.'

Brenda could not deny the fact. She had arranged the honeymoon to suit herself and had assumed that Shay would be delighted with her plans. She didn't want to fight with him. It would spoil things. It was hard to keep civil though because he was very tetchy. The heat was really getting to him.

'Ah, poor Shay.' Brenda leaned over and kissed the tip of his sunburned nose. 'Next year we'll go to Siberia, that should suit you perfectly. No sun and no people.'

He laughed. 'I'm not that bad,' he retorted. 'We'll go to your Mr & Mrs thing if it makes you happy.'

'You make me happy,' Brenda murmured sexily, putting her arms around him and nuzzling his ear.

'This is much nicer than turning to a cinder in the sun and taking part in daft competitions.' Shay stroked his hands along the smoothness of her bronzed back and started to kiss her. The evening shadows deepened and the light turned to dusk bathing the room in an amber glow as Brenda and Shay made passionate love on the sofa.

Later in the bathroom, as Brenda prepared for her night on the town, she opened her toilet bag to get out her deodorant. A full packet of the pill lay at the bottom of the bag, untouched. Shay would have a fit if he knew she wasn't taking them. Brenda felt no guilt at her deception. She wouldn't be taking them again for a while. The sooner she got pregnant the better, as far as she was concerned. The agreement was that she would leave work after her maternity leave. Shay presumed that she wouldn't want to get pregnant immediately. He didn't know that Brenda had no desire to be bossed around by Bugs Bunny Powers one minute more than she had to.

She smiled at her reflection in the mirror. Her eyes were bright, her hair was getting nice tints, because she sat on the balcony in the evenings with lemon juice in it. She had the best tan ever. And maybe, right now, she was pregnant already. Bubbles of anticipation fizzled through her. It would be wonderful having a baby. Kathy and she could have coffee mornings and watch their toddlers play happily. It would be nice strolling down to the shops or around Johnstown Park pushing her pram. All the neighbours would peer in and congratulate her on her son or daughter. It was marvellous that she'd got a house so near home too. Maybe she should have looked at a few more, as Shay had advised, but the one up near the terminus had come on the market and she'd jumped at it and persuaded him to buy it.

It had a good back garden for children to play in. That was one of the arguments she'd used.

'We won't be having children for a while. We don't have to rush anything. I think we should see the new ones out in Swords,' he'd suggested.

'Swords is miles out,' Brenda protested. The trouble with Shay was that he kept putting things on the long finger. If it wasn't for her they'd never have had a house, and if it wasn't for her, they'd probably be forty before she got pregnant. Just as well that she was able to persuade him to her way of thinking most times. She'd got her house with the big back garden. And if things went to plan maybe a child would be playing in it sooner than he thought, Brenda reflected happily as she applied some grey eyeliner to her lower eyelid. If all went as she hoped there'd be a baby in the house for Christmas.

Chapter Sixty-Nine

'Oh hell!' Jennifer cursed.

'What's up?' Ronan poked his head around the sitting-room door.

'They've painted over the wallpaper underneath the first layer. It's going to be almost impossible to strip. I'm sick of this.'

'Well if you will insist on buying an old house with character,' Ronan said in an 'I told you so' tone of voice.

Jennifer threw her damp sponge at him. He picked it up, dipped it in the bucket of water and waved it menacingly as he advanced towards her. Jennifer shrieked and took to her heels.

'Don't you dare,' she warned.

'Too late,' Ronan taunted as he chased her upstairs.

'Ronan. Stop. Stop,' Jennifer screeched as he caught her and gently began to squeeze the sponge.

'What's it worth?' he demanded.

'I might give you a kiss,' she giggled.

'Not enough.' Ronan squeezed again and a trickle of water ran down the side of her face.

'It's all you're going to get,' she teased.

'I don't want your kisses, woman. I want half that Crunchie you have in your jacket pocket.'

'That's not fair! You ate yours. You couldn't wait until we were having a cup of tea. You're always the same,' Jennifer protested.

'I offered you a bite.' Ronan shook the sponge threateningly.

'Big deal!' snorted Jennifer. 'You're looking for *half* of mine.'

'This is the woman who's going to share all my worldly goods, and she won't even give me half a measly Crunchie.'

'I'll give you a bite when we have our tea if you behave yourself,' Jennifer said.

'I don't want to behave myself.' Ronan dropped the sponge and started to kiss her. Jennifer wrapped her arms around him and kissed him back passionately. They kissed and caressed, lying on the bare floorboards of the back bedroom. Since they'd had to postpone their wedding, because of Brenda's nuptials, they'd discussed sleeping together. Although she wanted very much to sleep with Ronan, Jennifer knew all the good would be taken out of it afterwards because she'd feel guilty. Ronan knew and understood this and he never put pressure on her. He wanted their first time to be a happy momentous occasion for them. He didn't want it to be ruined for Jennifer. But it was difficult. They were young and healthy and in love and now they had to wait far longer than they'd planned.

A knock on the front door interrupted their passion.

'Who the hell is this?' Ronan muttered, fixing his clothes. Jennifer fastened the buttons on the old shirt she was wearing and pulled up the zip of her jeans.

'Want to buy a line, Mista?' A young lad of about ten stood at the door with a card and pen.

'No!' growled Ronan.

'What's it for?' Jennifer asked, noting the boy's crest-fallen look.

'It's for the school, Missus. De furst prize is five hundred pounds. Second, a TV. An' third's a bottle of whiskey,' he said hopefully.

'How much?' she asked.

'Fifty pence, Missus.'

'All right, we'll have two then,' Jennifer said, ignoring Ronan's deep sighs. She filled out their names on the sheet and rooted in her bag for a pound.

'Here.' Ronan took one from the pocket of his jeans

and handed it to the young collector. 'We'd better win,' he said.

'I hope ya do, Mista,' he said cheerfully, pocketing the money. 'Thanks.'

'You're as soft, Jenny Myles. I can see we're going to end up in *Stubbs Gazette* the way you're going on,' Ronan declared.

'Ah, did you see the little face of him, Ronan? He was thrilled with himself when he sold two lines. And we might win,' she smiled, hugging her boyfriend. 'Come on, we'll have a cup of tea and I'll share my Crunchie and then we'll get back to work.'

They sat on two upturned boxes in the kitchen, drinking tea and eating chocolate. It was a small kitchen. The house itself was small, a two-up, two-down, redbrick house in Drumcondra. They'd decided, after much discussion, to go for a small house first. They had also decided not to have children in the first few years of their marriage, until Ronan got himself established in his career. He was working in a computer firm, developing programs for software. It would lead to greater things, he assured Jennifer.

She was now Kieran Donnelly's secretary. Helen had gone on maternity leave and decided she wasn't going to continue working after the birth of the baby so Kieran paid for Jennifer to do an intensive word-processing course and then a short secretarial course before Helen left. Jennifer had worked in the office with Helen for a few weeks before Helen left and now she enjoyed organizing Kieran and his office.

He was good to work for. He let her make decisions and use her initiative. He wasn't always breathing down her neck. She missed being abroad sometimes. But she was far happier to be at home with Ronan than gadding about the continent like Paula. Jennifer knew she was lucky to get the office job. It suited her, just as Paula's challenging new career suited her. If it wasn't for Brenda and her wedding everything would have been perfect.

She'd been shocked when Brenda had breezed in and announced she was engaged and that she was getting married early the following year. Jennifer and Ronan had tentatively decided to wed that May but hadn't said anything much about it until they were sure their plans would work out. Jennifer had mentioned it casually in conversation with Brenda. That was why she felt terribly hurt that her sister had made her own arrangements with a callous disregard for her and Ronan's plans. Brenda hadn't even the decency to discuss it with her. Even if she'd said do you mind, Jennifer wouldn't have felt as bad. But Brenda just steamrolled ahead. She was getting married in February and that was that.

Kit wouldn't object to another wedding that same year, she assured Jennifer. But Jennifer demurred. She knew it was an expensive time, even if she and Ronan paid for their own wedding. A wedding was a hectic time, especially for the bride's mother, and Kit would have been exhausted after two weddings in quick succession. There was nothing to do but grin and bear it. But it was hard, especially when Brenda waltzed in after her honeymoon, tanned and glowing and full of the joys of spring, and said Tenerife was OK, but she preferred Spain. After all the trouble Jennifer had gone to. She'd made sure that there was a basket of fruit and a bottle of champagne in the apartment when they arrived. And she'd booked the best apartment for them. Brenda might have preferred Spain, but she could have kept it to herself.

Talk about gratitude! Ronan went red in the face when he heard this and there'd have been a row, except that Jennifer kicked him in the shins. Ronan often said that Brenda took Jennifer for granted and it annoyed him very much. There were times when she'd say or do something and he'd be dying to have a go at her. He would have let Brenda have a piece of his mind except that he knew it would upset Jennifer, who hated rows of any sort.

Ronan was furious when he heard about Brenda's wedding plans. Jennifer had a terrible job persuading him not to say something that would cause a row. She couldn't blame him. She was mad herself. But if a quarrel started who knew where it would end and things that were said in the heat of anger could never be unsaid.

Ronan was always cool towards Brenda now. They'd been invited to dinner in Brenda and Shay's new house a week ago. Brenda made a spaghetti bolognese and served a side salad and garlic bread. It was very tasty and they all enjoyed it. But then she'd turned around after dinner and told Jennifer to make the coffee because she'd been killing herself all afternoon preparing and cooking the meal.

'Sure,' Jennifer agreed. 'Go in and sit down, I'll bring it in to you.' Shay had gone into the sitting-room to relax as well, leaving Jennifer and Ronan staring at each other over a table full of dirty dishes.

'We're going home,' Ronan said furiously. 'You don't ask someone to dinner and then turn around and tell them to make the coffee. That girl is pig-ignorant and dead lazy and he's not much better. She obviously expects us to do the washing-up too. By God I'm going to tell her where to get off. She's not going to treat you like that, Jenny! Big deal, so she made a dinner. What did she invite us for if it was going to be such a hardship?' He stood up, a ferocious scowl replacing his normally cheerful expression.

'Please, Ronan, don't say anything. Please don't start a row,' Jennifer pleaded.

'Jennifer, she treats you like a bloody little servant. Do this, Jenny. Do that, Jenny. Make the coffee, Jenny. It's not on. She's not going to treat you like that when I'm around. I won't have it.'

'You sound exactly like your father,' Jennifer hissed furiously. 'Don't say, "I won't have it," to me.'

'That's a nice thing to say, I don't think.' Ronan was furious. 'I'm only thinking of you.'

'Sshh! Keep your voice down, Ronan,' Jennifer muttered.

'Why? Are you afraid the Prima Donna might get upset? Fuck the Prima Donna!'

594

'*Ronan!*' Jennifer remonstrated. 'Don't use language like that.'

'Well she'd drive anyone to bad language.'

'Your family's not perfect either. Your father could do with a lesson in manners,' she snapped.

'There's no need for that. You're being childish,' Ronan retorted.

'Well if you're going to criticize my family, I'll feel free to do the same with yours.'

'That *is* childish.'

'Oh, shut up!'

They glared at each other.

'Are we going or staying?' Jennifer asked miserably, furious with her sister for behaving in such a rude fashion and putting her in this position.

'We're going,' Ronan declared. She followed him to the kitchen door. He stopped short and turned around. 'I didn't think you'd come,' he said.

Jennifer shrugged. 'We were invited as a couple, we'll leave as a couple. Just because she's my sister doesn't mean I have to approve of her behaviour,' she said despondently.

Ronan put his arms around her. 'Come on.' He gave a wry smile. 'We'll do the washing-up and make the bloody coffee and we'll know better than to accept an invitation to dinner the next time.'

'I love you, Ronan Stapleton.' Jennifer rested her head against his shoulder.

'I love you too.' He hugged her. 'It's not your fault you've got her nibs as a sister.'

Jennifer frowned at the memory of the disastrous dinner party as she washed up the cups and set the boxes neatly under the sink.

Keeping Ronan and Brenda from having a humdinger of a row was not going to be easy.

Chapter Seventy

'Aaah! Oh God. Oh God! GOODDDD!' Brenda yelled.

'I don't feel too good,' Shay mumbled, ashen-faced. His knees gave way and he fell in a dead faint.

'For heaven's sake,' the midwife said irritably. 'Get him out of here. Mrs Hanley, breathe like you were taught at your classes.'

'I'm dying,' moaned Brenda. 'And he faints! I'm the one in agony and he passes out. Ooooohhhh. Please. Please give me something.'

'Push, Mrs Hanley.'

'I *am* pushing,' she groaned and burst into tears. This was the worst moment of her entire life. If she'd had the slightest notion that childbirth was going to be this bad, she'd have made Shay wear a dozen condoms and she'd have taken double the amount of contraceptive pills. This was a nightmare beyond her worst dreams. It was bad enough being sick morning, noon and night for the first three months. It was mega-awful putting on three stone and not being able to see her feet. But it all paled into insignificance compared to this torture.

'Push harder, Mrs Hanley. The head's almost through,' the detested voice of her tormentor instructed. I hate you. I hate you, you inhuman sadist. Bugs Bunny Powers is a saint compared to you, Brenda thought savagely as she gritted her teeth and pushed as hard as she could.

'Once more, there's a good girl,' the midwife approved. Brenda gave a loud yell, pushed as hard as she could and sagged back against the pillows covered in perspiration as she heard a whimper and then a lusty cry.

'Congratulations, Mrs Hanley. You've a lovely baby girl,' she heard the midwife say.

'Never again, never ever again,' Brenda muttered to herself as she fought down waves of nausea. The nurse placed the baby in her arms. Brenda looked at the scrunched-up wizened little red face. She's not very pretty, she thought despondently, trying desperately to summon up some maternal feelings.

You're a disaster as a mother already, she reproached herself. She started to cry. Why couldn't Shay be here with her? Kenny had been with Kathy for her two births and they both said it was an incredibly moving experience. That was what most people said about childbirth. But she hadn't felt that it was a wonderful moving experience. How could anyone say that lying with your legs parted and your feet in stirrups as you pushed and panted was *wonderful*? Childbirth had been the most horrible, painful, humiliating experience of her life. And now she couldn't even bond with her baby. She was obviously a most abnormal mother. The thought made Brenda cry harder. The nurse took the baby from her. 'It's all right, Mrs Hanley, it's just reaction and you're exhausted. We'll stitch you up and send you back to the ward. You can have a sleep and you'll be fine.'

Stitches! Brenda thought in horror. God, would the nightmare never end?

The nurse was right, Brenda thought with relief the following morning. She'd slept the rest of the night through and she was dying to see her baby when she woke up. Relief flooded through her. She wasn't abnormal at all. It had been a fearful thought. Brenda cuddled the baby to her. She didn't look as red and puckered as she'd been before and when she opened her blue eyes Brenda thought she was the most beautiful baby in the world. Adrenalin surged through her. The ordeal was over. The family would be arriving to offer congratulations later. And she'd never have to set foot in that depressing office again once she'd worked her notice. She was practically free at last, she thought with delight. Maybe it had all been worth it after all. Now was the start of the rest of her life. Even the pain and discomfort of her stitches could not dent Brenda's mood of exhilaration and optimism.

'Would you be able for some breakfast, Mrs Hanley?' The nurse plumped up her pillows and straightened her sheets.

'Would I what? I'd eat a horse this minute.' Brenda laughed. 'I'm ravenous!'

That afternoon Brenda sat in happy anticipation of her visitors. She had successfully managed to breastfeed the baby and she felt very superior to the lady in the next bed who hadn't managed it at all and had to resort to the bottle. She was very sore, even sitting was an agony, but she didn't care. The ordeal was over and soon she'd be a lady of leisure.

She put her make-up on with pleasure. She'd felt like a terrible frump in the last six weeks especially. She hadn't bothered to put make-up on or get her hair done or anything. She'd just waddled around looking like a slob. It was definitely diet time, Brenda assured herself as she brushed blusher on to her cheeks. She wanted to be thin for Jenny's wedding. She was matron-of-honour and Paula Matthews was a bridesmaid. There was no way she was going up the aisle looking like a dumpling, beside La Matthews, Brenda vowed.

Shay arrived with flowers and chocolates. 'Sorry I fainted, Bren,' he apologized yet again. Brenda was in a mood to be magnanimous. 'You were lucky. I'd have given anything to faint. Let's not tell the others,' she said.

'Right,' he agreed with relief.

'What do you think of her?' Brenda asked proudly.

'She's lovely.' Shay smiled, peering into the little cot beside Brenda's bed. 'What are we going to call her?'

'I like the name Savannah,' Brenda declared. She'd been reading a romantic novel during her pregnancy and was very taken with the heroine's name.

'Savannah Hanley!' Shay said doubtfully. 'It's a bit . . . unusual . . . '

'How about Natalie, then?' Natalie Wood was one of Brenda's favourite actresses. Shay's jaw dropped. Natalie Hanley sounded even worse than the first one.

'Oh for God's sake,' Brenda said irritably. 'You come up with something then. I want to have a name picked before everyone comes in to see her.'

They hadn't got down to a discussion of names before because Brenda had been nervous in case anything happened to the baby. She'd thought it was tempting fate to pick a name before it was born.

'I like the name Joan. Or Joanne, ' Shay suggested.

'Shay, how *boring*!' Brenda didn't want her child to have a boring run-of-the-mill name. Natalie and Savannah sounded exotic, very Hollywood. 'Look, we said if it was a boy you could name him. And if it was a girl I could name her. Didn't we?'

'Well Natalie and Savannah are out,' Shay declared, in an uncharacteristically firm tone of voice.

Brenda pouted. 'You didn't have to go through the agony of having her. Stop sitting there like a dictator telling me what to do and go down to the shop and get me a couple of magazines and a can of Coke. I might as well make the most of my few days here,' she said huffily.

Shay sighed as he waited in the queue to pay for the magazines and Coke. Brenda was very volatile lately. No doubt it was her hormones. He'd be glad when they were back to normal again. It was hard to believe he was a father. He'd got an awful shock when Brenda told him she was pregnant shortly after they'd returned from their honeymoon.

It wasn't what they'd planned. He would have preferred to wait for a few years before having children. He thought she was on the pill, but she told him she must have forgotten to take it a couple of times when they were on their honeymoon. He would have liked Brenda to continue working for another year or two. It was expensive buying a house. His business needed to expand if it was to support the three of them. The only thing was, Brenda would be getting her gratuity so that would help.

The baby was a lovely little thing. He'd been captivated by her once he'd seen her. He was dying to have a hold of her. She was so tiny. And he loved her little mop of black hair. Poor old Brenda, she'd had a hard time of it all the same. He wouldn't say anything else about the names. He'd be able to name his son, whenever that happy day arrived. Shay paid for the Coke and magazines and threw in a packet of chocolate biscuits and a bunch of grapes as well. It would be nice to have her and the baby home. It was lonely in the house on his own. It reminded him of when he'd lived in a flat. It was much nicer being married than being on your own, he thought as he walked back to the ward.

'Here you go, love.' He smiled at Brenda.

'Sorry for snapping,' she apologized.

'It's all right, Bren.' Shay leaned over and gave his wife a kiss. 'Can I have a hold of the baby?'

'Just lift her out of the cot,' Brenda said, taking a long draught of her Coke.

Gently, Shay leaned into the cot and picked up his daughter. She made a little face, opened her eyes briefly and looked at him and fell asleep again. He cuddled her in against his shoulder and felt as proud as punch.

'This is great, Bren.' He beamed.

'Wait until you're faced with your first dirty nappy,' she teased.

'I don't care,' Shay said. 'I'm the luckiest man in the world, I've got two lovely women in my life.'

'Brenda, she's absolutely gorgeous.' Jennifer picked up her new niece and gazed at her admiringly.

'Give me a go,' Kit said.

'Yes, give Gran a go,' Brenda ordered.

'Don't you dare call me Gran,' Kit exclaimed in horror, taking her granddaughter from Jennifer and studying her intently. 'She's got Shay's nose and chin.'

'I think she looks like Brenda,' Jennifer argued.

'Not at all,' Gerard teased. 'She looks like Grumps.'

'Wash your mouth out with soap, you,' Brenda remonstrated with her younger brother.

'Only kidding, Bren,' he joked. Brenda grinned. She was in top form and thoroughly enjoying herself. It was delightful being the centre of attention. Kathy and Beth were due in later and the girls from work had promised to visit. She felt like a queen holding court.

'What are you going to call her?' Kit asked. Brenda looked at Shay.

'It's up to you,' he said.

'Well I was thinking of Savannah or Natalie, but Shay doesn't like those names so I'm going to call her Claudia,' Brenda declared. 'Claudia Emma Hanley.'

Chapter Seventy-One

Brenda sat with her feet up on her desk. It was her last day at work. She'd had to come back to the office to work out her notice, otherwise her maternity leave wouldn't have been paid. She was getting a nice fat gratuity. Half of it was going towards paying off the mortgage and getting the central heating installed. The other half, she would keep for herself to buy a car. She already had it picked out. A nifty little Citroën. She'd paid the deposit on it. By the weekend she would be the proud owner of a car. She'd be able to go where she pleased and be a woman of leisure.

Well not leisure exactly. Taking care of Claudia was much more demanding than she'd thought it would be. It wasn't as bad now as it had been the first few weeks when she'd been having four-hourly feeds. Kit had been a lifesaver during those dreadful days after she'd come out of the hospital and been in such a panic, thinking she was doing everything wrong.

Kit was taking care of Claudia while Brenda worked her notice. From next Monday morning Brenda would not have to get up at the crack of dawn and stand at a bus stop getting drenched. She'd have to get up and feed Claudia, but she could go back to bed for a little snooze afterwards. She'd got into that habit when she was on her maternity leave. It was most enjoyable.

Bugs Bunny marched into the office. She saw Brenda sitting with her feet up on the desk. Brenda waited for the remonstration that she was sure was coming. The supervisor gave her a cold look . . . and said nothing. Brenda was disgusted. She'd been all prepared to tell Bugs to get lost. She'd been planning this day for so long. What she wasn't going to say to Bugs Bunny. She was going to really let her have it and tell her what a sly, gawky skinny bag of bones she was. She was going to tell her she was a frustrated old spinster who shouldn't be taking her frustrations out on the girls who worked for her. Everybody in the office was waiting for the confrontation with huge anticipation.

Hilda Powers sat at her desk at the top of the room facing her minions. She looked at her wristwatch, and the clock on the wall. It was fifty-nine seconds to nine. She waited for the second.

'Begin,' she ordered.

Brenda leaned down and drew a magazine out of her bag. She ignored her humming machine, a computer which was far more advanced than the huge old yoke she'd hammered on years ago. The girls cast surreptitious glances in the supervisor's direction. Bugs Bunny stared straight ahead as if Brenda did not exist. There was a palpable air of disappointment. Bugs was obviously not going to rise to the bait. Brenda took an apple out of her bag and started to chew on it. Hilda Powers never flinched.

Wagon, thought Brenda disappointedly. She began to read an article about how to please your man. Dress up in sexy underwear, it advised. Ha! She gave a mental snort. She'd tried on a silky camisole top and the French knickers she wore on her honeymoon recently and had recoiled in horror at the image in the mirror. The top didn't meet the pants any more and a big spare tyre of white flesh bulged out between the gap. She'd have to go on a diet before she could try seducing Shay in sexy underwear. She remembered once wearing suspenders and stockings and high heels for Eddie. He'd got really turned on. Brenda sighed. It wasn't quite the same with Shay. But she didn't mind so much now. She'd seen Eddie and his wife recently. They looked very happy. He'd given her that old attractive grin of his and congratulated her on the baby and then he was gone. To her surprise the old ache seemed to have dulled and she wasn't even upset. Now that she had Shay and Claudia and her own house and the prospect of giving up work, she was as content as she'd ever been. It was good to let the past go.

After she finished the magazine she picked up her library book. It was called *Decade* by Jacqueline Briskin and it was brilliant! Engrossed, she didn't notice the envious looks of her colleagues or the tight-lipped stare of Miss Powers.

They all went to the pub at lunch-time. Brenda got quite tiddly from all the drinks the girls bought her. She read her book for the rest of the afternoon and at four-thirty stood up and told the girls that she had some shopping to do and would see them later in the pub for her booze-up. She waited for Bugs Bunny to forbid her to leave. The supervisor ignored her. Brenda toyed with the idea of saying 'Goodbye, Bugs Bunny, knowing I'll never have to see you again is worth even more to me than my gratuity.' But in the face of the supervisor's silence, she thought it might be undignified. Besides, she'd know then that she'd really got to Brenda.

Brenda took a leaf out of her supervisor's book. She ignored Hilda. Slowly she emptied her belongings out of her drawer. She took one final look around and walked out of the hated office for the last time. She'd expected to feel exultant, but instead she felt a sense of anticlimax. She walked down to Roches Stores and treated herself to some make-up and a new angora jumper. Then she strolled back up to the Parnell Mooney, bought herself a gin and tonic, and sat waiting for the girls to arrive.

It was a great booze-up. They stayed in the pub until closing time and then went off to Leeson Street, where they boogied until the early hours. Brenda let her hair down and thoroughly enjoyed herself. It was ages since she'd danced. Shay didn't like dancing and when she'd been pregnant she couldn't go dancing anyway. Tonight she was making up for lost time. In the taxi going home, she fingered the elegant gold bangle the girls had given her as a going-away present. They were a good bunch and they'd promised to keep in touch. She must have them all out to the house for a meal sometime.

Brenda loosened the button of her jeans. She'd have to do something about her weight. She was going to be matron-of-honour at Jenny's wedding soon and she didn't want Madame Matthews looking like a sylph beside her.

She'd start tomorrow, she thought woozily. To get back to the weight she was when she got married would be her goal for Jenny's wedding. Now that she was going to be at home all day she could eat sensibly and take plenty of exercise. In no time at all she'd be slim, trim and brimful of energy, Brenda thought with enormous optimism.

Chapter Seventy-Two

'I look like a big horse beside her,' Brenda moaned as she sat in the hairdressers beside Jennifer, waiting for Paula and Beth to come down from the beauty salon, where they were having a professional make-up job. The bride and matron-of-honour had had theirs done first.

'Oh, for God's sake, Brenda, will you give it a rest?' Jennifer was up to ninety. She was getting married in two hours' time. Grandpa Myles and her mother had had a row. He said he wasn't coming to the wedding so there were mega-huffs at home. Poor Ronan had a septic throat and all Brenda cared about was that Paula looked thinner than she did.

'There's no need to snap the nose off me,' Brenda said huffily.

'You're my matron-of-honour, Brenda. You're supposed to support and help me, not whinge about how fat you think you are. I wish this blooming wedding was over.'

'That's a nice way to talk about your wedding day.' Brenda sniffed. 'And God knows it's costing you an arm and a leg. Why you couldn't have been satisfied with just me as your matron-of-honour, I don't know.'

'I wanted Paula and Beth to be my bridesmaids because they're my best friends,' Jennifer gritted.

'Oh well, it's your money,' Brenda said snootily.

'Yes,' Jennifer said coldly. 'It is.'

'Only some people have more money than sense.' Brenda stuck her head in a magazine, leaving Jennifer sizzling with temper. Brenda had done nothing but make comparisons between her wedding and Jennifer's. She was the same about their houses. Why couldn't she be happy with what she had?

'Cheer up.' Paula arrived and sat down beside Jennifer. 'This is the happiest day of your life,' she added wryly.

Jennifer laughed. Paula was a great support to her, jollying her along when family tensions got unbearable.

'I've been telling her that.' Brenda gave Paula a frosty look.

Paula gave an equally frosty look back. 'Well let's start *making* it the happiest day of her life then.' She dipped into her expensive soft leather holdall and produced a bottle of champagne. This was followed by four slender champagne flutes.

'Let's drink to the happy bride,' she said fondly, popping the cork.

'Thanks, Paula, that was very thoughtful.' Jennifer was delighted.

'Champers! Oh great,' declared Beth, who had joined them.

Brenda said nothing, furious that she hadn't thought of it herself.

They sipped the bubbly and Jennifer began to relax. There was nothing she could do about Grandpa Myles and her mother. They'd have to sort it out between themselves. Ronan was on antibiotics. There was nothing she could do about his septic throat. If Brenda wanted to act the martyr, let her. Jennifer decided she was just going to go with the flow. Getting herself into a tizzy was not going to help anyone and it would only ruin her day.

'Have another glass,' Paula urged.

'I don't mind if I do,' giggled Jennifer, getting into the party mood.

Thanks to Paula she was in much better form when they arrived home. Kit met them at the door. She'd been to the hairdressers first and she looked very smart, Jennifer thought. Her mother had gone on a diet for the wedding and she'd lost almost a stone. It suited her.

'Girls, the dresses are pressed and laid out on my

bed. Use my bedroom to change in. Jim and the boys have showered and shaved and they're in the sitting-room out of the way. Himself,' she threw her eyes up to heaven, 'is in his room sulking.'

'Is he coming to the wedding?' Jennifer grimaced.

'Don't ask me.' Kit scowled. 'If he's not careful, he'll be going to his funeral.'

They all laughed. And Kit started to laugh herself. 'Imagine him asking me to phone the hotel to ask the chef to do him a few potatoes in their jackets because he doesn't like croquette potatoes. And could he have a dish of boiled rice instead of Pavlova. He's an awful character. I'm more to be pitied than laughed at,' she declared good-humouredly. Jennifer was relieved. Because good-humoured was not how she would have described her mother earlier.

'You let him sulk if he wants to. He's not going to ruin our day,' Jennifer said firmly.

'Right,' agreed Kit.

The four trooped upstairs to Kit's bedroom and began to change into their gowns. The bridesmaids' dresses were ice-pink off-the-shoulder taffeta. They were lovely on Brenda and Beth but Jennifer had to admit that Paula, with her golden tan and blond bob, looked stunning.

She stepped into her hoop and tied it around her waist. Paula eased the white raw silk wedding dress with the scalloped neckline over her head and shoulders and draped its rustling folds over the wide petticoats and hoop.

'Jennifer, it's fabulous on,' she exclaimed. She hadn't seen the finished wedding dress because she'd been in Greece for the past week. Brenda stood with the veil in her hands and lowered it onto Jennifer's upswept hair.

'You look beautiful, Jenny,' she declared.

'Thanks, Bren,' Jenny said gratefully, all bickering for-gotten. 'So do you.'

'Girls, we'd want to get a move on,' Beth suggested, looking at her watch. 'The car will be here any minute, and I think I heard the photographer arrive.'

608

Just then Kit popped her head around the door. 'Oh, Jenny,' she exclaimed, looking at her daughter. Her eyes brimmed with tears.

'For God's sake, Ma! Don't start me off,' Jennifer warned, feeling a lump in her throat.

'Sorry, pet,' Kit sniffed. 'I know I promised. It's just . . . God it only seems like yesterday I was bringing you to Pappin's for your first day at school.' She burst into tears.

'Come on now, Mrs Myles,' Beth soothed. 'You'll ruin your make-up and if Jenny starts crying she'll ruin hers and the photographer won't be very pleased.'

'You didn't cry at my wedding,' Brenda observed.

'For God's sake, *Brenda*!' Paula was disgusted.

'You mind your own business.' Brenda turned on her and glared at her.

'The photographer wants to know if you're ready yet.' Jim bellowed up the stairs. 'And am I to let the neighbours in, Kit?'

Kit wiped her eyes. 'I'd better get into my dress.'

'Here, let me help,' Beth offered.

'We'll be down in a minute,' Jennifer called, furious with Brenda for being so childish. If her sister started any shenanigans and ruined the wedding, she'd never forgive her.

They fussed around Kit, helping her into her mauve dress and black jacket. It was a lovely outfit and she looked very smart. Paula retouched her make-up for her and five minutes later they all descended the stairs behind Jennifer. Jim stood at the bottom of the stairs looking at them in admiration.

'You're all a sight for sore eyes,' he exclaimed. Gerard and Sean wolf-whistled. Grandpa Myles, unable to contain his curiosity, opened his door and observed them all with a penetrating stare.

'All this fuss and faddle over a wedding. In my day, there wasn't any of this carry-on. Be that as it may, you look very nice, Jennifer,' he said testily, stepping out into the hall to have a closer inspection. 'Who's bringing me to the church?'

Kit gave Jennifer a discreet nudge in the ribs. Jennifer nudged her back.

'You'll be going with the boys in the wedding car as soon as the photos are taken,' Jennifer said cheerfully.

'Another waste of money,' Grandpa grumbled. 'Call me when it's time to go.' With that he marched back into his room and shut the door firmly behind him.

'So put that in your pipe and smoke it,' grinned Jennifer. At least he was coming to the wedding, she thought. Between himself and Brenda no doubt one of them would start a row but she wasn't going to worry about it now.

They spent the next twenty-five minutes posing for photos and accepting congratulations from the neighbours. But at twenty minutes to two, Jennifer announced that it was time for her brothers and Grandpa Myles to leave. 'I don't want to be late for Ronan and the car's to collect the girls before coming back for me and Dad, so let's get a move on.' She'd promised Ronan faithfully that she wouldn't be late.

Neither was she. At two o'clock precisely, she walked with her father up the aisle of Our Mother of Divine Grace Church as the music of the wedding march floated over her head. A little over a year ago she'd walked up this aisle behind Brenda, now she was walking up it as a bride. It was hard to believe her wedding day was here at last. It had seemed so long in coming. Especially when they'd had to postpone it. Poor old Ronan, she thought lovingly as she saw him turn to watch her progress up the aisle. It was bad enough getting a septic throat but getting it on his wedding day was rotten luck.

'Hi.' She slid her hand in his when she reached his side.

Ronan leaned over and kissed her on the cheek.

'You look beautiful,' he said.

Jennifer felt perfectly calm now that she was beside

him. All her nervousness disappeared. This was what she wanted. To be with Ronan for the rest of her life. She said her vows clearly and distinctly, looking into Ronan's eyes. Jennifer felt very serene as he placed the ring on her finger. She was surrounded by warmth and love as her family and friends looked on and wished them well. The priest invited them to pray that God would always bless their marriage.

Dear God, please let me never fail Ronan. Let me always be there to love and support him and let him be there to love and support me. I place our marriage in Your tender loving care to keep it free from all harm and danger. Amen, Jennifer prayed earnestly. Brenda had told her that she couldn't wait for her wedding Mass to be over so she could get to the hotel and start enjoying herself. Jennifer didn't feel like that at all. She and Ronan had carefully picked out the Gospels and readings that moved them. They'd picked their hymns with care. As she listened to the young soprano singing the *Ave Maria*, Jennifer was very glad they'd both put such an effort into making their wedding Mass as beautiful and spiritual as it was. She felt it was a most special moment in her life. A moment that could never be repeated. She'd remember it for the rest of her life.

She was sorry when the priest said, 'Now go in peace to love and serve the Lord,' and then gave his final blessing. The three-quarters of an hour had gone by in what seemed like five minutes.

'Come on, Mrs Stapleton.' Ronan took her hand. 'Let's go and sign the register.'

It was strange to write Jennifer Myles for the last time. It would take a while to get used to her new surname, she reflected as she signed her name and handed the pen to Ronan. He added his signature with a flourish and then they walked back out to where their guests were waiting to follow them down the aisle.

Outside the church they were immediately surrounded. Jennifer enjoyed being hugged and kissed by the family and friends who were happy for her and Ronan. Even Mr Stapleton gave her a prim peck on the cheek. Rachel hugged her warmly. 'I'm really glad we're sisters now,' she beamed.

'So am I.' Jennifer hugged her back. 'And I hope we'll be seeing a lot of you. The guest room's all ready and waiting.'

'You will,' Rachel assured her. She was wearing a drab olive green suit which made her look about forty. Jennifer promised herself that she was going to take Rachel in hand and go shopping to buy young fashionable clothes for her.

Jennifer was ravenous by the time they finally sat down to their meal. But when she took the first mouthful of her spring lamb she was dismayed.

'If that was a lamb, he'd had a lot of exercise,' she heard Grandpa Myles say quite audibly. Jennifer was mortified. But her grandfather was quite right. The lamb was tough and muttony.

'God, Ronan, this is awful,' she muttered. 'Talk about being ripped off. Wait until I get that creep of a manager.'

'Will I go and tell them to take it back and serve something else?' Ronan whispered.

'They probably haven't got anything else. It would be embarrassing to ask everyone to hand back their dinner. This is terrible.' Jennifer was distressed.

'It's too late to do anything about it now, Jenny, we'll just have to put up with it for the time being.' Ronan sighed. He couldn't eat anyway but the manager of the hotel was going to get a roasting from him, and he was going to demand some of their money back. Having to pay in advance left you with little comeback when you were ripped off like this. You were at the mercy of the hotel.

Jennifer fretted about the meal. It ruined the rest of her wedding day, despite everyone's protestations that the meal had been fine. When Grandpa Myles saw how upset she was he went and gave the manager a ferocious ear-bashing.

'You should be ashamed of yourself, ruining a girl's wedding like that and embarrassing her in front of her friends and family. If that was spring lamb I'll eat my hat. I can tell you one thing, young fella, it would be a lot more tender than your so-called lamb! So what are you going to do about it then, matey?'

In vain the harassed manager tried to pacify Grandpa Myles by saying that it had been a long wet winter and the lamb wasn't as tender as in previous years.

'Cut out your spoofing, lad. What are you going to do to make amends?' Grandpa Myles was not to be put off. Much to Jennifer's delight. Good enough for you! she thought unsympathetically. Give him hell.

In the end, unable to take any more, the manager offered a free bar for an hour. By the time the dancing started everyone was in great form and the meal was forgotten as the guests boogied the night away.

Jennifer was so annoyed about the meal that she told Ronan she wasn't going to stay in the hotel as planned. She informed the manager that they weren't spending the night in the hotel and he could go whistle if he thought she would pay for the room. She didn't give him time to bluster an answer as she swept upstairs to change into her going-away outfit.

'Where would you like to stay, Ro?' she asked as they divested themselves of their finery.

Ronan swallowed and she could see that it hurt. He looked at her. 'It's up to you, Jenny, wherever you want to go, we'll go.' She knew he was putting on a cheerful act for her.

'You know where I'd like to go?' she said softly. 'I'd like to go home to our own house.'

Ronan smiled at her. 'That's exactly what I was thinking but I didn't want to do you out of a night in a plush hotel.'

'Oh, I've got plans for you,' Jennifer teased.

'What?' grinned Ronan.

'Wait and see.'

An hour later they drew up outside their little redbrick house. Ronan paid the taxi man, carried their luggage into the house and came back for Jennifer. 'Now, are you ready for this?' he asked, sweeping her into his arms.

'My hero,' Jennifer laughed as her husband carried her over the threshold of their home.

'What have you got planned for me?' he asked as he dropped her gently on to the couch.

'Go upstairs and get into bed,' she ordered. 'I'll be up in a minute.'

'I'll be waiting.'

Jennifer had swiped three oranges from the complimentary fruit basket in the hotel room. While she waited for the kettle to boil, she squeezed the oranges and poured the juice into a long glass, she added sugar, and a spoonful of honey. Then she poured a measure of whiskey and filled the glass with hot water.

'Be a good boy and take your medicine,' she instructed Ronan, who had lost no time in getting into bed. She stood over him as he sipped his hot drink. Jennifer kissed her husband on his forehead when he handed her the empty glass. He was very hot. 'I'll be up in a minute. I'll just lock up downstairs.' She pulled the sheet up under his chin.

'You're a wonderful wife,' Ronan teased.

'I know,' she agreed smugly.

She pottered around downstairs, enjoying the feeling of being in her own house at last. Ten minutes later, she switched out the lights, locked the front door and walked upstairs yawning. She was jaded tired. She could hear Ronan's low rumbling snores from half-way up the stairs. So much for a night of sex and passion, she thought grinning. Well they'd waited this long. Another night wouldn't kill them. And hopefully by morning Ronan would be feeling better.

Chapter Seventy-Three

'You made a holy show of me!' Brenda fumed. 'Just because there was a free bar for an hour didn't mean you had to try and drink the place dry.'

'Aw shut up, Brenda,' Shay groaned from beneath his pillow. 'I've a terrible headache.'

'Good enough for you,' Brenda retorted. 'I've no sympathy for you.'

'Would you give it a rest?' Shay growled.

'No, I won't give it a rest,' Brenda snapped. She had no intention of letting her husband away with it. She'd been mortified at the wedding when he'd insisted on singing some dreadfully gloomy Leonard Cohen song that he'd forgotten half the words of. She'd seen Paula Matthews sniggering with that boss of hers and Jenny's. Kieran somebody or other. He was a fine thing too. He arrived at Jenny's wedding on a huge black Harley-Davidson. He fancied Paula too. Brenda knew it by the way he looked at her and danced with her and listened attentively to what she said. Paula didn't seem to be very interested in him. She hadn't been flirty or seductive.

Brenda frowned. No wonder Paula had men falling all over her. She'd looked stunning in the ice-pink bridesmaid's dress. Her figure was perfect, her tan golden, her hair a shining silky blond bob. Brenda felt like an elephant beside her. She'd tried so hard to lose the weight she'd gained since Claudia was born. But it clung stubbornly. Her waist was thick, her stomach and thighs flabby and her bum was a disaster. It was her own fault, of course. Since she'd left work she was inclined to sit around a lot. And eat . . . Any excuse and she was nibbling, or having coffee and biscuits. Not to talk about bowls of Cornflakes and Weetabix together. She'd developed a real passion for them. Her good intention to lose weight after she left work had failed dismally. Being matron-of-honour had not been a strong enough incentive either. Brenda pinched her waist. She could definitely pinch an inch, she thought despondently. Now that the weather was starting to improve and the summer was coming, she'd start bringing Claudia out for walks in her buggy. She might join an aerobics class. Maybe she could persuade Kathy to come with her. She had to do something. She was turning into a flabby frump.

Brenda stared down at her now sleeping husband. She'd a good mind to wake him up and tell him she was going into town and that he was to look after Claudia for the day. That would fix him. Looking after a demanding one-year-old toddler was no joke.

Suddenly a dizzy faintness came over her. Brenda leaned back against the pillows waiting for it to pass. What the hell had caused that, she wondered in dismay. Holy God Almighty! Brenda had a terrifying thought. She'd felt like that once early in her pregnancy with Claudia. She couldn't be! She couldn't possibly be pregnant again so soon. She hadn't gone back on the pill because she'd kept hoping she'd lose weight and she didn't want the added half-stone that the pill always put on her. Shay had been using condoms because she hated using a diaphragm. Brenda groaned as another wave of dizziness assaulted her. Her period was a week late but she hadn't given it any thought. Her cycle was still a bit irregular. Why had she been so stupid? She should have gone straight back on the pill and to hell with vanity. She hadn't lost an ounce of weight and now, if her suspicions were correct, she'd be putting on a hell of a lot more.

Gingerly she got out of bed and walked into the bathroom. The toilet seat was up. Fury engulfed her. She slammed it down, hard, and didn't care if it cracked.

She was always telling Shay to put the toilet seat down after him. It irritated the hell out of her, as did his habit of squeezing the toothpaste from the middle. Brenda poured herself a glass of water and sipped it slowly.

Claudia was a handful. Adorable, but a handful nevertheless. How would she manage two of them? So much for her idea of a life of rest and relaxation.

She heard Shay's rumbling snores. Her lips tightened in a thin line. He needn't think he was going to sleep blissfully for the rest of the morning. She wasn't going to suffer on her own.

'Shay! Shay! Wake up. I have to talk to you.' Brenda shook him vigorously.

'Wha . . . what's the matter?' He sat up bleary-eyed.

'I'll tell you what's the matter, Shay Hanley. I think I'm pregnant!'

'Oh crikey!' Shay turned a whiter shade of pale. 'Are you sure?'

'No, but I feel like I did when I started with Claudia.' Brenda burst into tears.

'Don't cry, Bren. Maybe you're imagining it.' Shay got out of bed and put his arms around her.

'My English teacher told me I had no imagination.' Brenda wept.

'Let's hope she was wrong,' Shay said fervently.

Brenda spent a tense weekend and was up at the doctor's surgery first thing the following Monday morning.

'Congratulations, Mrs Hanley,' Brenda heard him say, as Claudia started to howl. She felt like howling herself.

'I can't believe it, Kathy,' she cried on her best friend's shoulder, later that morning.

'It's not as bad as you think,' Kathy soothed. 'It happened to me. But look at it like this, they'll all be reared together and it will make life much easier when they go to school.'

'I suppose you're right,' she sniffed. 'But that's it. Two's enough.'

'Famous last words,' laughed Kathy. 'Look, why don't I take Claudia for the afternoon and you go and put your feet up, or go into town and treat yourself.'

'Thanks, Kathy. You're a pal.' Brenda gave a watery smile. 'I'll tell you one thing. This time I'm telling them to knock me out. I'm taking anything that's going.'

'You'll be fine,' Kathy assured her. 'It's never as bad the second time.'

'Don't tell fibs, you told me Andrew's birth was ten times harder than Anita's.'

'No I didn't. I'm sure I didn't.'

'Yes you did,' Brenda said glumly. There was no point in fooling herself.

She had resigned herself to her pregnancy and was finding it much easier the second time round when she went for her first scan. She lay trying to make out the black and white images on the monitor showing her baby. The doctor took her hand and smiled down at her. 'Is everything all right? Is the baby OK?' Brenda asked anxiously.

'Everything's fine,' he assured her. 'Only it's not one baby, Mrs Hanley,' she heard him say. 'Congratulations, you're expecting twins.'

Chapter Seventy-Four

'This time last week Grandpa Myles was giving that poor manager hell,' Ronan reflected as he swung lazily in a hammock by their private villa.

'Poor manager my foot!' Jennifer scoffed from the hammock she was lying in sipping Malibu and pineapple. 'He deserved everything he got, the little rat. He ruined my wedding day.'

'Ah, it wasn't that bad,' Ronan soothed. 'The free bar was all everyone could talk about. Poor Shay was well on.'

'I know, I could hear Brenda telling him not to make a show of her and him telling her to stop bossing him around. They weren't exactly whispering.' Jennifer grimaced.

'And did you hear Dad getting on to Rachel about how she was too fond of the booze. She'd only had two glasses of white wine!'

'You know Rachel should get her own place. She should never have taken that job in Bray,' Jennifer reflected. 'She'll never do anything as long as she's living at home.'

'Jenny, you're preaching to the converted.' Ronan took a slug of ice-cold Coke.

'Let's go for a walk on the beach before dinner,' she suggested.

'A walk!' Ronan exclaimed in mock horror. 'I couldn't possibly do anything that energetic. I'm on my honeymoon in the Cayman Islands. And she wants me to go *walking*! What kind of a wife did I get?'

Jennifer eased herself out of her hammock and stood looking down at him.

'Get up, you lazy lump,' she laughed, tipping him out.

Ronan laughed. 'Be on your guard for that!' he warned.

Jennifer tied her sarong around her waist and placed a big white hat on her head. It was late afternoon and the intense heat of the day had eased but she wore her hat anyway. She walked down the tiled steps of the terrace where they had been relaxing. Ronan watched her admiringly. She was golden brown. Her long dark hair was plaited and entwined with flowers and it followed the curve of her slender sexy back. He was the luckiest man in the world, he thought happily as he sprinted down the steps to join her.

'This is really a paradise, isn't it?' Jennifer took his hand as they walked down the winding flower-edged path to the magnificent swathe of white-gold beach. The sand was like silk beneath their feet. The sea was a clear aquamarine. They walked to the water's edge and paddled along in the rippling surf.

'It's handy having a wife in the travel business.'

'Yeah, it's going to be a real perk when we're taking our holidays. It was a great brainwave of Paula's to get us to check out the scene here.'

'Oh they can use us as guinea pigs anytime.' Ronan laughed.

'She's started to make a go of that new project, I can tell you,' Jennifer said admiringly.

'Knowing Paula, I wouldn't doubt it. What will your report say?'

'Oh . . . it will say that it's the ideal honeymoon spot, and if you've got the right husband . . . heaven on earth!' Jennifer turned to Ronan and kissed him long and lingeringly. They drew apart and smiled at each other.

'I think we should call and say that two weeks isn't half long enough to make such important decisions as to whether TransCon would find Grand Cayman a suitable location for its holiday programme. I'd suggest six months on expenses.'

'Absolutely,' Jennifer agreed.

They walked slowly, utterly content in each other's company. The sun was beginning to set when they turned to walk back to their villa. Great slashes of pink and purple and gold streaked the sky. The sun was a molten red orb suspended over the horizon. Slowly it began to dip, turning the waters to flame. Ronan and Jennifer stood watching as it sank lower and lower until just the tiniest arc remained, then it too disappeared. High in the sky, a pale crescent moon, almost transparent, waited for darkness and its hour of glory.

'That was beautiful,' Jennifer breathed. Watching the sunset was one of the highlights of their day. As was watching the moonrise and the sunrise. They'd gone shopping and explored the island, of course. They spent a day in George Town, the capital. But mostly they were content to be in each other's company, relaxing and making love and enjoying their new togetherness. It more than made up for the hassles of the wedding day. Ronan's throat was fine again and there was nothing to mar their pleasure.

Ronan had his arm around her waist as they walked back up the steps onto the terrace. They walked past the rippling turquoise pool and suddenly he gave her a little push and she went flying in.

'You swine!' she protested, gasping for breath when she surfaced.

'I told you to be on your guard,' Ronan said smugly as she swam over to the edge where he was standing laughing his head off. Jennifer reached up and made to grab him by the ankles but he was too quick for her and stepped back.

'I'm no fool,' he joked.

'It's lovely anyway,' Jennifer declared as she began to swim around lazily.

Ronan dived in. 'So are you, or have I told you that already today?'

'A thousand times,' Jennifer giggled as she swam over

to him. They kissed, softly at first and then with a passion that left them breathless. Ronan reached down beneath the water and eased her bikini bottom off. She helped him remove his shorts. They stood entwined in the undulating waters and slowly began to make love, kissing and caressing and giving each other uninhibited pleasure as the skies darkened around them and the stars twinkled in the firmament.

Chapter Seventy-Five

If she'd been exhausted during her pregnancy – it was nothing to what she felt now. Brenda yawned.

'Claudia, I'm trying to feed John, please be a good girl,' she said crossly as she tried to prevent her daughter from swiping the baby's bottle. Poor Claudia's nose was terribly out of joint with the arrival of two little strangers who were taking up so much of her mother's attention.

Claudia started to scream. Her screeches added to the cacophony of wails. Lauren was yelling in her cot, waiting to be fed. John was red in the face, seeking the teat of his bottle. Claudia stamped her feet and slapped Brenda.

'Into the playpen with you, you bold girl,' Brenda snapped, laying John on the sofa, where he rent the air with his wails, his little fists flailing the air. She lifted a kicking, struggling Claudia in her arms and put her in the playpen. Claudia howled in fury. Brenda felt like howling herself. She knew she should reassure her eldest daughter and lavish attention on her but it was impossible with two small babies to look after.

She picked up John, settled him in her arms and put the bottle back in his mouth. He stopped crying and sucked greedily. Brenda looked at the downy little head nestled in the crook of her arm. He was a placid little fellow except when he was hungry. His twin, Lauren, was much more lively and demanding.

She'd known having twins was going to be hectic but nothing had prepared her for the constant feeding, changing, bathing and dressing that was her lot these days. So much for the life of leisure she'd envisaged on leaving work. She'd never worked so hard in her life and she was always exhausted.

It wouldn't be so bad if she got a decent night's sleep, Brenda thought dispiritedly, giving a huge yawn. But Claudia was teething and having a hard time of it. Lauren never slept through the night and John always woke at six for his happy hour of gooing and gaaing. Brenda couldn't remember the last time she'd had a full night's sleep. She craved sleep more than anything. Brenda was always promising herself little naps in the day but it never worked out. She could rarely get her three children to sleep at the same time during the day.

The house was a shambles. There were toys all over the floor. Wads of nappies, tubs of Sudocrem and Vaseline spilled out of a baby bag that was stuck behind one of the armchairs. Baby clothes covered the radiator. Brenda glanced out the window. There was a good breeze out today, although it was cloudy. As soon as she'd bathed the babies and Claudia, she'd hang out the wash-load that was in the washing-machine. Or maybe she should do it before she gave them their baths. Rain was forecast for the early afternoon and she was running low on clean vests.

John's eyes drooped and he stopped sucking. Brenda gave him a little nudge. John liked to linger over his bottle. He'd go for a little snooze if she let him but Lauren was yelling for hers and Claudia hadn't had her breakfast yet.

She took the bottle from him and sat him on her knee and winded him. He gave a loud burp. 'Good boy,' Brenda said, pleased. John was a topper for getting his wind up. Lauren had difficulties and was inclined towards colic.

She fed her son the rest of his bottle, winded him again, and placed him in his carrycot. He smiled contentedly at her, and she bent and kissed him on the forehead. It was a pity her other two children couldn't be as placid as their brother. John definitely had Shay's temperament.

She went out to the kitchen and got Lauren's bottle

and scowled when she saw the state of the kitchen table. Shay could have washed up after his breakfast. A sticky marmalade knife was thrown in the sink with his plate and cup. That was Shay's idea of clearing up. She knew he was busy these days and she should be grateful for all the extra business, but he left the house at the crack of dawn and often wasn't home until late in the evening. It was sometimes after nine when he got home, so he wasn't around to help out. Not like Kathy's husband, Kenny, who was a dab hand at changing nappies, hanging out clothes, hoovering and the rest of it. Kathy had it far easier than she did, Brenda thought, self-pityingly.

They *all* had it far easier than she did. Jennifer and Ronan were just back from yet another foreign holiday. One of the perks of her job. Jennifer's house was immaculate. You could walk in at any time of the night or day and there was never so much as a cushion out of place. She didn't have to dry clothes on radiators, she could afford a dryer.

And as for Paula Matthews, *her* life was a permanent holiday. She swanned around in designer clothes looking like a model out of *Vogue*, with her permanent suntan. If a baby puked on her she'd probably faint, Brenda scowled as she tested Lauren's bottle.

Life had not turned out as Brenda had planned. The twins' arrival had changed her life completely. After Claudia was born she'd been able to get out and about, have coffee mornings with Kathy and go into town and window-shop occasionally. But the twins had put a halt to her gallop. Brenda couldn't ever imagine herself having a life of her own again. She fed Lauren and put her back in her cot and took Claudia out of the playpen. She gave the little girl a kiss. Claudia was having none of it. She pouted and sulked and turned her head away. Brenda sighed. Claudia reminded her of herself sometimes.

'Come on, and I'll get you some lovely Liga for breakfast,' Brenda entreated.

'No.' Claudia glowered. No was her favourite word.

'Come on, you have your breakfast with me because you're a big girl, you're not a baby any more. You're my best helper.'

'Want my bawbaw.'

'I'll give you a bottle,' Brenda said patiently. Claudia kept insisting on having bottles now, because of the twins. Brenda had successfully weaned her off them before the twins' arrival. She crumbled up the Liga fine, heated the milk and poured it all into the bottle. She went to lift Claudia into her high chair.

'Feeg me,' Claudia demanded.

Brenda swallowed her irritation. At this rate she'd be here all day. She lifted the little girl into her arms and Claudia cuddled in close and popped her bottle into her mouth. Content now that she was the centre of her mother's attention the toddler sucked on the bottle with gusto.

Half an hour later, Brenda stood at the line hanging out the clothes. She hadn't even had her breakfast yet and she was starving. But she wanted to get the clothes out first.

The garden was like a wilderness, she noted. Shay must do a job on it at the weekend. If she had time she'd give him a hand. She felt a certain satisfaction as she saw her line of clothes fluttering in the breeze. She wasn't too far behind schedule. It was just gone nine. Maybe after the baths, when she put the babies down for a sleep, she might get the house tidied up and the clothes on the radiator sorted. If she was lucky she might get forty winks herself after the lunch-time feeds when the twins were sleeping and Claudia was dozing in her playpen. The sky was very grey. A good hour would get the clothes dry and it could rain then for the afternoon for all she cared. She'd light a fire and pull the sofa over in front of it and have a lazy afternoon. She wouldn't bother cooking a dinner today, she decided. She'd get Shay to go for burgers and chips.

Brenda's mood lifted at the thought of a lazy afternoon. She'd work like hell for the rest of the morning and then flop. Energized, she walked up the garden path to the back door. A howl from Claudia sent her sprinting along the last few yards. Brenda raced in to find Claudia with a trickle of blood dribbling down her nose. There were marrowfat peas all over the floor. An open packet lay on its side in one of her fitted presses.

'Jesus, Mary and Joseph!' she exclaimed. 'I don't know how many times I've asked Shay to put childproof catches on those bloody doors.' She lifted Claudia up and tried to peer up her nostrils.

'Did you put a pea up your nose, Claudia?' she demanded. Claudia was a holy terror for stuffing things up her nose. They'd been to Temple Street Hospital twice about it before.

'Did you put a pea up your nose? Tell Mammy.' Brenda tried to keep her voice normal. She didn't want to scare Claudia or make her feel she was annoyed with her.

Her daughter, still yelling, nodded.

Oh shit, thought Brenda. Her heart sank at the thought of another trip to Temple Street. Who the hell was she going to get to look after the twins? Kit was working part-time in a café in town. Grandpa Myles was too old to be left with such young babies. God only knew where Shay was. She'd have to ask her next-door neighbour, Mandy.

Brenda ran out the front gate in her dressing-gown with a howling Claudia under her arm. Mandy's curtains weren't pulled. She had to knock several times before she got a response. It was obvious she'd woken her neighbour out of her sleep. Mandy stood, bleary-eyed, gazing at her.

'I'm terribly sorry, Mandy, Claudia's stuffed a pea up her nose. I'll have to bring her to Temple Street. Would you be able to look after the twins for me for an hour or so?' Mandy hesitated. 'I'm really stuck, Mandy,' Brenda pleaded.

'OK, bring them in, and bring some of that Cow & Gate so I can make up a bottle for them. You'll probably be stuck there for ages,' Mandy said in resignation.

'I'll pay you back some way,' Brenda promised. 'I swear to God, they'll think I'm doing it on purpose, this will be my third time to bring Claudia in with something up her nose.'

'I know,' Mandy said dryly. This was not the first time she'd had to mind the twins because of Claudia's penchant for inserting foreign bodies up her nostrils. Brenda was too harassed to notice the tone of her neighbour's voice. 'I'll be in with them in a minute,' she said hastily, as she took off down the path with Claudia still yelling blue murder.

'I can't wait,' Mandy thought irritably as she watched Brenda's dramatic exit. Brenda Hanley and her children were becoming right pains in the ass. Brenda kept landing her kids in on top of Mandy. She always had some great drama or excuse. When Brenda moved in first, Mandy was glad that someone young and lively had moved in next door. The old lady who had lived there had been a cantankerous old soul. Giving out if the boys kicked the ball into her precious garden. 'There's a green down the road, let them play on that,' she'd grumble, making a big drama out of picking up the flowers the ball had damaged. Mandy was always nagging the kids to go and play on The Green. When the old lady decided to sell up and go to a nursing home, Mandy had been on tenterhooks to see what the new neighbours would be like. She was delighted when Brenda and Shay arrived and introduced themselves.

Everything had gone very well at the beginning, although Brenda could be a bit of a nuisance, looking for milk and sugar and the like, when she ran out. But compared to Mrs Long's shenanigans it was paradise . . . until Claudia was born. From the time the baby was only a few weeks old, Brenda had started asking Mandy to keep an eye on her while she popped down to the shops. That always took an age despite the fact that the shops were only five minutes away and Brenda drove there. Brenda got more blatant and asked would Mandy mind Claudia so she could go into town. Mandy found it very hard to say no to people. She'd say 'It's no bother' even though the last thing she wanted to do was mind a baby. She'd reared three of her own without inflicting them on her neighbours. Her nine-year-old daughter Lisa was mad about Claudia so if she was at home, it wasn't too bad.

But Lisa wasn't at home today, she thought crossly. She was at school and Mandy was going to have to endure the twins by herself.

It was great having good neighbours, Brenda thought as she turned right onto the Ballymun Road and headed south towards town. Mandy was crazy about the kids, she loved babies. She never minded looking after them for Brenda. Claudia whimpered in the baby chair in the back. What had possessed her to push a marrowfat up her nose? You'd want eyes at the back of your head trying to keep an eye on her. Brenda sighed. She should have put her in her playpen while she went out to hang out the clothes but that would have started another tantrum.

The traffic wasn't heavy and she dithered as to whether to park on Eccles Street or drive down past the hospital and risk not finding a space there. She parked as near to Dorset Street as she could and walked the rest of the way towards the hospital. She turned left down the little lane to Casualty and hoped it wouldn't be packed. Wishful thinking. The place was crammed. Brenda resigned herself to a long wait.

It was almost noon before Claudia, minus her pea, was ready to leave. Brenda was starving. She'd made up a bottle of milk and Liga for Claudia before she left home. On the spur of the moment, she decided to pop into town. It was so near the hospital. She was sure Mandy wouldn't mind keeping the twins for another hour or so.

She parked behind Bolton Street Tech and cut up to Henry Street along Moore Street. Five minutes later she was tucking into a ham sandwich and a coffee slice in the Kylemore while Claudia guzzled her bottle, sitting in a highchair and staring around with interest. This was a rare little treat, Brenda thought to herself, and at least Claudia had suffered no ill effects, although her yelling could have been heard in Howth when they'd been extracting the pea.

Now that she was in town she might have a look around for a new pair of jeans. Paula was wearing a gorgeous pair of 501s the last day she'd seen her. Maybe she would treat herself.

She tried on several pairs of jeans, getting more despondent all the while. Paula's had clung to her like a glove but Brenda was unable to fasten the first two pairs and ended up trying on a size sixteen for the first time in her life. She was horrified, especially when she turned sideways in the mirror and saw her fat bottom and the tree-trunk thickness of the top of her thighs.

'Oh my God!' she muttered in horror. That's it, I'm going on a strict diet, she vowed, regretting the huge coffee slice she'd just eaten and the large dollop of cream that she'd spooned into her coffee. Imagine being a size *sixteen*! That was the pits. There'd been a time when she was a size twelve. Feeling like weeping, Brenda left the shop, minus the jeans. Soon it would be summer and she wasn't going to wallow around in her flab. It was so easy to forget about her weight and hide her bulk under layers of cover-up clothes in winter. It would soon be time to get into summer clothes. She was going to get down to a size fourteen at least, she promised herself. She would go on a brown rice diet. It was very healthy. Shay could go on one too. He was putting on weight around his middle, she decided as she took a detour into Nature's Way and spent a fortune on health food.

She was half-way up Mobhi Road when the heavens opened. Blast it! she fumed. If she'd been home ten minutes earlier she'd have got her clothes dry.

'So sorry I'm late, the hospital was jam-packed,' she exaggerated to Mandy when she got home.

'No problem,' Mandy said in a brittle tone. 'The twins are fed and changed.'

'You're a pet,' Brenda said gratefully. 'If I can ever do you a favour.'

'Well now that you mention it.' Mandy smiled. 'It's our wedding anniversary on Friday, maybe you could baby-sit. Tom's going to take me out for a meal.'

'Oh, Mand, I'm sorry. It's Grandpa Myles's birthday on Friday and we're all going home for a party. We'll probably be staying the night.' This wasn't strictly true. They might stay a bit late but they'd definitely be coming back home. It was too much hassle uprooting three infants for a night, lugging nappies and bottle feed and the like. But she wasn't going to say that to Mandy. She didn't feel like baby-sitting on Friday night. Mandy and Tom never came home until well past midnight on their nights out.

'How about Saturday, then?' Mandy was not giving up hope.

'Aw,' Brenda said in insincere dismay. 'I think Shay's doing a nixer.'

'Sunday'll do then.' Mandy was determined. She was damned if she was going to let Brenda get away with taking advantage.

'OK,' Brenda said unenthusiastically. She knew she couldn't make any more excuses. It would be too obvious.

'We won't be *too* late,' Mandy added pointedly.

Even Brenda couldn't miss the sarcasm in that last remark. There was no need for Mandy to get huffy. She'd only nipped into town for an hour or two. It wasn't as if she'd absconded for twenty-four hours or anything.

Brenda never got the chance to lie on the sofa in front

of the fire. Lauren had colic and was very cranky and she spent the rest of the afternoon trying to pacify her. Then it was time to give Claudia her dinner, feed the twins, change them and put them to bed.

She cooked up a pot of brown rice, added a tin of tuna and some peppers and sat down to dinner. At least she'd started her diet. She was going to stick to it without fail. She'd bought some Ryvita as well. Bread was definitely out from now on.

'What's for dinner, I'm ravenous?' Shay leaned over and kissed her when he arrived in from work.

'There's a pot of brown rice and tuna,' Brenda informed him. She was engrossed in *Brookside*.

Shay made a face. Brown rice and tuna didn't sound the slightest bit appetizing. Don't say Brenda was on one of her faddy diets. When Brenda went on a diet, he had to go on one too whether he liked it or not. He lifted the lid of the pot and looked at the contents. 'Sod this,' he muttered.

'I'm going to the chipper,' he called. 'Do you want anything?' There was a long silence as Brenda struggled with her conscience.

'Get me an onion ring,' she said finally.

Shay arrived back twenty minutes later. 'I got you a single as well so you wouldn't eat half of mine.'

Brenda's mouth watered. She tore open the white paper and demolished the onion ring in three bites. It was scrumptious. Brenda knew she was a disgrace. No wonder she bulged out of size sixteen jeans. Well today had been a traumatic day. She needed a little treat, she comforted herself as she took a slice of buttered batch bread from Shay and made a chip butty. She would start her diet tomorrow, definitely, she assured herself. She'd get down to a size twelve and Paula Matthews wouldn't be the only one who could wear skin-tight jeans and look a million dollars.

She went to bed around eleven, and was asleep within minutes. At half past twelve Lauren started to cry.

'Oh no,' Brenda groaned. She gave Shay an elbow in the ribs. He snored on. Brenda dragged herself out of bed. She paced the floor with her daughter as the rest of the household slept. This was the pits, she told herself as Lauren yelled in pain, her little face contorted. This was definitely the end of her family, she told herself viciously. If she ever found out she was pregnant again, she'd shoot herself . . . and Shay with her.

Book Three

Chapter Seventy-Six

Paula held up the little sundress, hat and cardigan and couldn't make up her mind between them and the scarlet jumpsuit. In the end she bought all of them despite the fact that they cost a fortune. Shopping in exclusive boutiques on the French Riviera was not for the faint-hearted. Paula didn't mind. She could well afford to buy her precious goddaughter expensive gifts. She earned a hefty salary. But she worked for it.

Since she'd started up the Holiday Villa scheme with Kieran four years ago, she'd travelled thousands of miles. They worked night after night until the early hours with Kieran's accountants, costing and projecting. And now, finally, it was starting to pay off. The Holiday Villa scheme was established.

It hadn't been easy though. There'd been problems with accommodation. Even though she personally checked out every villa they selected for use in the brochure, the problems only started to come to light once the villas were in use. They'd made no profit at all in the first year of business, and spent a considerable amount of money relocating dissatisfied customers to luxury hotels when villas turned out to be unsuitable.

Kieran never wavered in his support of her and told her they had to expect teething problems. They had couriers in place because of the main charter holiday business so many of the problems were sorted out fairly easily. But that first year Paula criss-crossed the sun spots of Europe ironing out problems her couriers couldn't handle.

Now things looked much better. Their existing villas

were booked out for the current season. Satisfied customers were coming back, demand had outstripped supply and she was now scouring the south of France for new locations. It was her third visit this year and so far she'd inspected several villas that looked promising. She'd also met a rather dishy Frenchman called Pierre Dupré.

Paula glanced at her watch and saw that she was running late. She would have liked to sit and watch the world go by and sip coffee in one of the cafés in the Zone Pietonne and then walk along the palm-lined coast road to her sea-front hotel. Nice was not for rushing around. Nice was to be savoured at an easy-going pace. She shouldn't have dawdled so long in the boutiques.

Regretfully, Paula hailed a taxi to get her back to her hotel. Pierre was taking her to dinner tonight. She liked him, he was good company as well as possessing any amount of Gallic charm. She'd had dinner dates and lunches with lots of men in the past four years. All business affairs. Pierre was partly business too. He was the owner of several luxury villas she was thinking of using. He had property all along the French Riviera that he rented out to holiday companies. She'd made her mind up on the properties she was going to select. Tonight they would finalize the details over dinner. She would sign the papers the following morning in his office.

'*Merci*.' She thanked the taxi driver, tipped him and ran up the marble steps of the hotel and checked at reception for messages. There were several.

One from Jennifer asking her to call Kieran. One from a courier in Palma asking her to call back and one from Pierre advising her that he'd be half an hour late and had changed their dinner booking accordingly.

Paula took her key and ran up the stairs. She never took lifts unless she had to. That extra half-hour's breathing space was just what she needed. She'd return her calls, have her shower and get ready without feeling she was in a terrible rush.

638

She rang Palma first. Couriers' calls always got priority. Paula now had two staff working exclusively for Holiday Villa in the office, but she always left strict instructions that she was to be contacted if there were problems. No matter where she was.

'What's up, Trish?' she asked briskly as soon as she heard the courier on the other end of the phone.

'Hi, Paula. It's the Scullys. Last night was their final night and they had a big party and trashed the place. It's a shambles. Señor Diega is hopping mad and he's not going to allow us to have the villa any more. And the Madigans are flying out today.'

'Oh hell!' Paula scowled. The Scullys were a wealthy high-profile Dublin couple. He was a high-flying business-man, with an eye on politics. She was a 'Lady who Lunched' although her lunches were more of the liquid sort. Well they weren't going to get away with trashing a mega-luxurious villa. Peter Scully was an arrogant shit. A fat blob of a man in his mid-forties. He adored being the centre of attention.

She had met him when Kieran asked her to accompany him to a business dinner and Peter was there, lording it over the rest of the company. He made a beeline for Kieran when he saw Paula and immediately asked to be introduced. He took her hand in his hot sweaty one, his little beady eyes roved over her lasciviously. Paula looked at his fat wet lips and felt revolted.

'I'm Peter Scully,' he announced. From the way he said it, Paula knew he practically expected her to genuflect.

'How do you do,' she said coolly, withdrawing her hand. 'I'm Paula Matthews.'

'Kieran, you sly old fox you. Where have you been keeping this gorgeous bird hidden?'

'Miss Matthews is a business associate,' Kieran said coldly.

'What do you do?' Peter asked with an arched eyebrow. As far as he was concerned women were for decoration and sexual purposes only.

639

'I run the Holiday Villa Company for TransCon,' Paula said briskly.

'Tell me all about it,' he invited, giving her a leer.

Paula gave him a short concise run-down of her operation and was surprised to hear him say, 'I could do with a place like that for a week or so some time in April. I'm cooking up some deals with a few guys who live in Marbella. You say these places have live-in staff and their own pools?'

'Yes,' Paula said curtly. She didn't want Peter Scully and his entourage as clients.

'Fine, I'll get my secretary to make the arrangements. You will give me a good discount?' He smirked at Kieran. Kieran glanced at Paula and smiled.

'Sorry, Peter, it's not up to me. I never interfere in Holiday Villa's business. Paula is the boss there.'

Peter's beady little eyes gleamed. 'I'm sure the beautiful Paula will oblige,' he said confidently.

'Sorry,' Paula smiled sweetly. 'We don't do discount holidays. Try our charters if that's what you require. You will excuse me, I have to call the office.'

Arrogant bastard, she thought as she walked across the plush carpet of the function room and made for the foyer. After that put-down, she hadn't expected Peter Scully to book a holiday with Holiday Villa, but he had. Much to her disgust. Now he'd gone and trashed the place and assumed, no doubt, that he was going to get away with it. Over Paula's dead body.

'Trish, I'll get on to Legal about it. I'll get the office to phone the Madigans and offer them a refund or a suite in a luxury hotel. And if you give me Señor Diega's number I'll call him and see if I can pacify him. OK?'

'OK,' Trish agreed, calling out the number.

'I'll get the office to give you an update,' Paula said. 'Take care, bye.'

She phoned Kieran immediately. Jenny took the call. 'Hi, Jenny, how about you and Beth coming to dinner Friday night?' she asked.

640

'It's awkward. I have Rachel with me for Easter. It's a bit rude to take off and leave her at home,' Jennifer said regretfully.

'Bring her,' Paula said immediately.

'Are you sure?'

'Of course, we'll have a bit of a laugh. A friend's flying in from New York and she's promised to bring me some Häagen-Dazs.'

'We're coming,' Jennifer said instantly. She was a sucker for the rich creamy American ice cream. 'Is it chocolate chip?'

Paula laughed. 'I hope so, that's what I asked for. See you Friday.'

'OK, I'm putting you through to Kieran.'

'Hi, Paula,' she heard her boss say cheerfully.

'What's wrong with you?' she demanded. 'It had better be good or I'm charging this call to your account.'

'That's lovely, I must compliment you on your telephone manner,' Kieran retorted. 'You're a tyrant, Paula Matthews, you should hear what your staff say about you behind your back,' he teased. 'The reason I phoned is because Jolly Johnson's handed in her notice. She's going to live in Bolivia with a horse-breeder—'

'You're not serious?' Paula guffawed.

'I am serious,' Kieran insisted, laughing himself.

'Well she won't be sorry to know she'll never have to see me again,' Paula said dryly. Miss Johnson had been speechless when Kieran had told her he was giving Paula the responsibility of getting Holiday Villa up and running. She thought Paula was a lightweight who was only interested in men. It had been hard for the personnel manager to accept that Paula had actually made a success of the enterprise, and even harder to swallow that she had to have dealings with her couriers. Paula and Jolly Johnson had some mighty battles. Paula was not a bit sorry to hear she was leaving. She was dying to get home and have the dinner party on Friday. Jenny would have all the news.

'When will you be free to hold the interviews with me?' Kieran asked.

'You want me to sit in on the interviews?' Paula was surprised.

'Of course, Paula. You have to deal with whoever is taking over. I want to make sure you get on with them. I couldn't take another four years of the Jolly-versus-Paula feud. I'm nearly addicted to valium as it is!'

'Hold on until I check my diary.' Paula grinned. 'Is it an open competition?'

'Yeah, but I hope there'll be in-house applicants. I think I'd prefer someone we know. I like to be able to promote my staff. It keeps me on my toes. If I'm not careful, your operation will be making a bigger profit than mine. And you'll be looking for a bigger salary than me.'

'A Harley will do fine,' Paula retorted.

Kieran laughed. 'I have a proposition for you when you get back.'

'What?' she demanded.

'I'm not telling you. I'll let you treat me to dinner and then I'll tell you all about it.'

'Swine.' She knew Kieran of old. There was no point in asking because he wouldn't tell her. 'Before you go, Kieran. Did you hear about the Scullys?' Paula asked.

'Yeah, I did. What do you want to do about it?'

'I want to get Legal on to it. That's if it's OK with you. Or would you prefer not to? I know he's got a lot of friends in town, it might affect us. But I would like to get damages from the bastard.'

'You go right ahead, Paula. I don't think Peter has as many friends as he thinks he has. Anyway it makes no difference, he's not getting away with it. I'll back you up totally.'

'Thanks, Kieran. I'll see you soon. Take care.' Paula hung up with a smile. Kieran was a most supportive boss. She knew she was extremely lucky.

She showered and dressed and was ready and waiting when Pierre arrived with an exquisitely scented single yellow rose. 'For a very beautiful woman.'

'Flattery will get you everywhere,' Paula said lightly.

'I hope so,' smiled the Frenchman. He was not conventionally handsome. His features were too irregular for that. But he had a rugged attractiveness and brown eyes that darkened to black sometimes. He was as different to Nick in looks and temperament as could be. That was his greatest attraction for Paula.

'I've booked us a table at a little restaurant further along the coast. It serves magnificent fish dishes. I think you'll like it, the views are spectacular.'

'Sounds good. I'm hungry,' Paula responded.

'*Et moi aussi,*' Pierre replied, giving her one of his intense looks. Paula knew he was not referring to food. She felt a little tingle of anticipation. She had not slept with a man since her affair with Juan Carlos. She hadn't wanted to. Nick was always on her mind. She had thrown herself into her work and found consolation of sorts in her success. Four years was a long time to be celibate, she thought as Pierre slid a protective arm around her as he escorted her to the car.

The drive from Nice eastwards along the coast was breathtaking. It was dusk and the lights twinkled along the curve of the coast like a diamond necklace against black velvet, growing brighter and more intense as the evening deepened into night. Pierre was a good conversationalist. Paula sat back and began to enjoy herself. Further along the coast was Monaco. Trips to the casinos of Monte Carlo would be an added bonus for clients who decided to holiday on the Riviera. Paula was confident that her new location would be a big success.

Over dinner they discussed the final details and agreed on terms. Paula was satisfied. She'd got a good deal. So had Pierre. After the signing of the contracts the next day, it would be all systems go.

She bit into a delicious scallop. It was a long time

since she had eaten scallops. Her father used to bring home a big bag of them on Friday nights and lightly fry them in butter for less than a minute so that the wild tang of the sea could still be tasted. Or he'd bring home crabs and cook them and they'd all sit at the big wooden table in the kitchen, digging the meat out of the claws and the belly with the handle of a spoon, feasting and laughing. A sudden nostalgia overcame her. Helen and Nick and Nicola were to spend Easter with Maura and Pete this year. They wouldn't be in Dublin when she returned tomorrow. She wouldn't see them until the following week. Maybe they were all sitting down to a banquet of scallops or crab meat at this very minute. She wished she was with them.

'You look sad, Paula,' she heard Pierre say.

'I was just thinking of home,' she said wistfully.

'I am losing my touch.' Pierre smote his brow theatrically. 'Here I am doing my best to impress you with scintillating conversation and you are thinking of being at home. *Mon Dieu, quel désastre!*'

Paula laughed. 'Don't be so dramatic, Pierre. I'm having a lovely time. And the meal is superb.'

'No compliments about my conversation, I shall say no more,' Pierre joked.

They lingered over coffee. By the time Pierre's car drew up outside her hotel, Paula knew she was going to spend the night with him. They took the lift. They kissed as it glided smoothly upwards. It was good to feel a man's arms around her again. Pierre kissed her lightly, exploring, tasting, reminding her of how she'd always enjoyed sex. She returned his kisses, wanting more. Wanting to be swept along in a tide of passion. Wanting to erase all memories of and longings for Nick.

Pierre undressed her. Kissed every inch of her body, stroked his fingers lightly down the curve of her spine and along the soft inner part of her thighs until she was frantic with desire. Only then did he enter her and make long slow sensual love to her. Afterwards, as she lay cradling him in her arms, a deep sense of relief flowed through her. I'm over him, she thought exultantly, I must be or I wouldn't have been able to do this. Thank God, I'm over Nick at last.

Chapter Seventy-Seven

'He's a real Frenchman, oodles of charm, witty, intelligent, warm. We had a wonderful evening.' Paula refilled the wine glasses on the table as she told her pals about her latest flame.

'Sounds divine,' Beth said enviously. She was manless at the moment and working in an insurance company, which she hated. She envied her friend in the nicest possible way. 'I knew when I came to dinner tonight I'd feel jealous.'

'Don't be. I thought you were going to do a word-processing course. You really should, Beth. Everyone is using computers. You'll get the cream of the jobs.'

'Ronan will be able to help you out there. I've told you that,' Jennifer said patiently. They'd had this conversation before.

'I know, I know. It's just the thought of studying at night.' Beth sighed.

'No pain, no gain,' Paula said briskly. 'You never did the language courses.'

'Well I had secretarial skills when you were looking for someone in the office,' Beth said resentfully.

'You didn't have word-processing. I have everything on computer. I run a high-tech office and the girls I employ are up to date with all the new technology. Besides,' Paula insisted, 'you'd hate it if I was your boss. Imagine *you* putting up with me telling you what to do? Imagine if I had to eat the face off you? It wouldn't work. I told you that at the time and I'm telling you now,' Paula said firmly.

'Yeah, I know. It's just the two of you are doing so

well. You just waltzed into TransCon and now look at you. And look at me.'

'Beth, we didn't just "waltz" in, as you put it,' Jennifer said crossly. 'We both had something to offer because we'd worked at it. Both of us could speak fluent Spanish, relatively good French, and Paula can speak German. Be fair.'

'I'm sorry,' Beth apologized. 'I'm being a bitch. It is my own fault. I got a mediocre Leaving Cert because I wouldn't swot and I used my accident as an excuse. I know I've got to do something and I keep putting it off.'

'I'd do a word-processing course with you if you like,' Rachel offered. The other three turned to look at her in amazement.

'What do you want word-processing for?' Jennifer asked. 'Teaching hasn't got that technical, has it?'

'Maybe I don't want to be a teacher all my life,' Rachel retorted. 'Beth is right. You and Paula make us ordinary mortals feel dull and boring. Teaching four-year-olds how to count is OK, and there is job satisfaction when they start to cop on, but you wouldn't meet a dishy Frenchman in Beth's insurance company or in St Catherine's Primary School.' She giggled. Rachel was slightly tipsy.

They all started to laugh. 'Have more wine,' invited Paula. She was enjoying the evening immensely. She'd served smoked salmon and sour cream, decorated with dill, on thin slices of brown bread for a starter. Followed by chilli, and baked potatoes with a side salad. Now for the *piéce de résistance*.

'I'll just go and get dessert,' she said. She walked out into her compact modern kitchen. She liked living in an apartment, she thought happily as she took a huge bowl of strawberries from the fridge. She'd moved in here about a year and a half ago. It was a bright modern two-bedroom apartment off Mobhi Road. It was ideal for work and the airport. It was near Jenny and Beth, and Helen and Nick and her goddaughter. Helen and Nick had bought a house in Cremore. A stone's throw away. It was a beautiful big house that they had decorated superbly. They were very happy.

You're over him, she thought determinedly. Pierre had proved that. Tonight she felt happy. The relief of knowing that her unrequited love was over was incredible. Paula had begun to think she'd never find another man attractive.

It was a treat having the girls for dinner. There was nothing like a good giggly ladies' night for lifting the spirits. Wait until they saw the dessert. Triumphantly, she carried in the bowl of fresh strawberries and a jug of cream. Then she re-emerged from the kitchen with four dishes of Häagen-Dazs ice cream.

'Get that into you,' she declared, placing the dishes of ice cream in front of the drooling guests.

Paula was well pleased with the reactions. She spooned some strawberries into her dish, mixed them with the luscious ice cream and allowed the sinfully delicious mixture to slide down her throat. There was plenty to go around if anyone wanted seconds.

'We'll have to get a taxi home, Rachel,' Jennifer giggled. 'You can't drive, you're tiddly.'

'Do you hear the black kettle . . . ?' Rachel tittered.

'You mean the kettle calling the pot black,' guffawed Beth.

'Stay the night, the pair of you,' Paula suggested. 'Beth was going to anyway.'

'Dead right,' snorted Beth. 'I'm no fool.'

'I'll just give Ronan a ring.'

'There's no answer,' Jennifer called from the kitchen, where she was using the extension. 'I'll try Brenda and Shay's. He was going to go for a pint with Shay.' Jennifer gave a running commentary as she dialled Brenda's number.

'Oh dear.' She threw her eyes up to heaven as she came back into the sitting-room.

'Shay and Ronan went for a pint. And Brenda's baby-sitter didn't turn up, so Brenda couldn't go to her keep-fit

648

class and she's like a demon. Especially when I told her to tell Ronan I was staying the night with you because Rachel and I are in no condition to go home.'

'Poor Bren.' Paula was uncharacteristically sympathetic. 'I'd go mad if I was stuck at home with three children.'

'It was what she wanted,' Jennifer retorted.

'Yeah, but the twins were a bit of a shock so soon after Claudia,' Beth added.

'I know,' Jennifer agreed.

'I feel my time is running out,' Beth sighed. 'I'm twenty-six and no sign of a man.'

'There's no rush,' Paula declared. 'Lots of women don't start their families until they're in their thirties. Look at Brenda, tied down with three kids. She's done nothing with her life. She might have thought it was what she wanted. But I bet if you asked her to change places with you, Jenny, she'd jump at it.'

'Well you know Brenda. She's never satisfied. The other man's grass is always greener,' Jennifer said.

'When I come up to stay with Jenny, I always say that I'm going to leave Bray and get a job in Dublin and start living as opposed to existing. I'm full of good intentions and plans but once I get home it all fizzles out,' said Rachel. 'I think the other man's grass is greener too,' she added glumly. 'I think you're terrific,' she told Paula. 'You've got everything. A high-powered career that takes you to all the sun spots. Men fall all over you. You have fabulous looks and a great figure. You've got it all, Paula. I bet there's no-one in this world that you'd rather be. No-one's grass is greener than yours.'

Paula glanced at Jenny, who knew exactly what she was thinking. 'I don't think you can ever say that about anyone,' Paula said sadly.

'Oh, who cares about green grass when you can have Häagen-Dazs?' Beth was missing all the undercurrents. 'Is there any more?'

'Sure,' laughed Paula, banishing her moment of

sadness. 'It's in the fridge, help yourself. Now who'd like an Irish coffee?'

Hollers greeted this proposal. 'I take it it's unanimous.' Paula took the bottle of whiskey from the drinks cabinet and headed out to the kitchen followed by Beth in search of more ice cream.

They were sitting laughing and chatting when the doorbell chimed. They looked at each other. It was ten to twelve. Who on earth would be ringing a doorbell at that time of night? Paula went over to the video intercom and pressed the switch.

'Good God! It's Brenda!' she exclaimed. 'Top floor, first door on the right,' she said, pressing the buzzer to open the front door. A minute later Brenda stood at the door.

'What's wrong?' Jennifer was concerned.

'Oh, nothing,' Brenda said airily. 'Shay and Ronan arrived home so I just thought I'd come over and join the fun. Seeing as you're having an all-night party, I brought a bottle.' She waved a bottle of Bacardi in the air. 'You don't mind, do you?' She turned to Paula with an air of bravado. Paula glanced at Jennifer, who was sitting with her mouth open. Paula was amused at Brenda's cheek. There were times when the other girl hardly spoke to her and yet here she was as cool as you like gatecrashing her dinner party. Paula supposed if she was stuck at home with three young toddlers she might well be tempted to do something as outrageous.

'Of course I don't mind, Brenda, come in, sit down, make yourself at home,' she said politely. 'I'll just go and get you a drink.'

'Sorry about that,' Jennifer murmured as she followed Paula into the kitchen.

'Forget it,' Paula said. 'Brenda probably heard us all shrieking laughing when you were on the phone and felt a bit out of it. She doesn't get much of a chance to do anything these days. It just goes to show how desperate she is for her to show up at *my* place.'

'But she drove over, she can't start drinking if she's got to get back home,' Jennifer said anxiously.

'We'll order a taxi for her, stop panicking,' Paula retorted, pouring Brenda a stiff Bacardi.

Brenda took the proffered drink gratefully. 'This is just what I needed, girls,' she declared. 'Tell me all your news. I need to know there's a world out there besides nappies and teething rings and potty-training and so on. What's new in the travel world? By the way . . . ' She turned to Jennifer and Beth. 'Did you hear about Cora Delahunty?'

'No . . . '

'What?'

'Cora's left her husband and she's supposed to be having an affair with her father-in-law. The husband caught them in bed together.'

'You're not serious!' Jennifer was agog.

'Who's Cora Delahunty?' chorused Paula and Rachel.

'Oh, she was this awful sly show-off I went to school with.' Brenda snorted.

'Remember I showed you her once. She was wearing about ten inches of make-up and a mini up to her eyebrows. She's real tarty-looking,' Jennifer explained.

'There's a girl living on the floor below me and she's having an affair with a well-known barrister who's about forty years older than she is. He's an awful sleazeball,' shuddered Paula. 'And one day the wife arrived and caught him there. Someone must have told her. He drives a Merc and she knew he was there. Talk about uproar!'

'But look at Jolly Johnson going off with a divorced horse-breeder twice her age, to live in Bolivia,' chuckled Jennifer. 'You should have seen Kieran's face when she handed him her resignation.'

'The age of miracles is not yet past,' Paula said wickedly and the others laughed.

It was four in the morning before Brenda left, giggling, in a taxi, and the others got to bed. Paula lay in bed feeling pleasantly weary and somewhat intoxicated. It had been a fun-filled evening. Not even Brenda's unexpected arrival had marred it. Brenda had thoroughly enjoyed herself. And for once had not made one sarcastic comment. Rachel really came out of her shell and Jenny and Beth were in top form. She must do something like this on a regular basis, Paula decided. It was nice to get together with the girls. Her lifestyle was so hectic that she didn't get the chance to do it as much as she used to.

Paula yawned and snuggled down in bed. Jenny and Rachel were in the guest room and Beth was on the couch. None of them intended getting up early in the morning. They were all looking forward to a lie-in. She was going to do absolutely nothing tomorrow, Paula decided. She was meeting Kieran for dinner on Sunday night. Her treat. He was going to collect her on the motorbike and they were going to go to Howth. She was looking forward to it. She loved discussing business with Kieran. They were always plotting new schemes. She was trying to get him interested in extending Holiday Villa to the Caribbean and the Cayman Islands. Jennifer was full of enthusiasm about the Caymans. A lot of wealthy Irish people took holidays there now, weary of the European hot spots. It could be another avenue to explore.

Paula wondered what Kieran's proposition was. What great plan had her entrepreneurial boss got now? All would be revealed on Sunday.

Chapter Seventy-Eight

'How would you like to be a director of the company?' Kieran asked.

Paula looked at him in amazement. This was unexpected.

'It's no more than you deserve, Paula.' Kieran poured her another cup of coffee and poured one for himself. 'You've worked like a Trojan to make a go of Holiday Villa. It's established now and making a profit. We're a good team. And I want you on the board of directors. I want you to have shares in the company. That way you'll think twice about leaving if someone headhunts you,' he added lightly.

'I'm not going to leave,' Paula said. 'You don't have to make me a director because you think I'm going to leave.' Her voice held a trace of irritation. She didn't want to be made a director because Kieran was afraid she'd take off to some other company. She wanted him to make her a director because he knew she was capable of being one. And because he knew it was for the overall good of TransCon.

'Haven't you been listening to me at all? You've earned your place on the board,' he insisted.

'I know,' Paula said calmly. 'It's about time you made the offer.'

Kieran laughed. 'You're a tough nut, you know.'

'You've got to be in this world,' she said.

'You're cynical for one so young,' he remarked.

'You make me sound like a teenager,' she scoffed. 'I'm twenty-six. I've been around. I know life is what you make it. And you have to work for what you want.

That's not being cynical, it's facing facts. And do you hear who's talking? You're only thirty-five. You talk as if you're Methuselah.'

'Sometimes I feel like him.' He sighed.

'What's wrong?' Paula asked. It wasn't like Kieran to make comments like that.

'Nothing, really.'

'Come off it,' Paula said quietly. 'Is it the Scully thing?'

'Oh, no, nothing like that.' Kieran shook his head.

'What, then?' she demanded.

Kieran sighed and looked Paula straight in the eye. 'Tina wants to get married. She's told me it's either marriage or it's all off. She's gone to the States for a month. She wants my decision when she gets back.'

'Oh,' Paula murmured. She'd met Tina on several occasions. She was gorgeous-looking, tall, slim, vivacious. But a bit of a clinging vine, in Paula's opinion. So now Tina was putting her foot down. It had been coming for a long time but Kieran had chosen not to see it.

'What are you going to do?' she asked.

'I don't know.'

'Do you love her?' Paula met his gaze squarely.

Kieran gave her the strangest look. 'I thought I did,' he said quietly. 'Now I don't know.'

Paula sighed. She was an expert on love. Either you loved someone or you didn't. There were no half measures.

'Have you ever been in love?' he asked suddenly.

Paula's eyes grew sad. 'Yes I have.'

'You still love him.' It was a statement rather than a question.

'I love him. I always will. But I don't think I'm *in* love with him any more.' Pierre had seen to that, Paula told herself firmly.

'How come some people fall in love and it's a joy and lasts forever? I'm thinking of Jennifer and Ronan, for example. And people like you and me don't find it easy at all.' He scowled.

654

'I don't know, Kieran. All I can say to you is do what your heart tells you is right.'

'I wish I could.' Kieran sighed enigmatically. 'I wish I could.'

She'd never thought of Kieran as being troubled in love, Paula thought that night as she pressed her blouse for work the next morning. He was usually so confident and positive. Tonight she'd seen a very human side to him. It was endearing. She and Kieran had a lot in common. That was probably why they got on so well. She hoped things would work out for him.

The following evening, Paula collected Nicola's presents from the apartment and drove up to Cremore. Nick's car wasn't outside the house. She was half relieved. Not, of course, that it mattered any more, she told herself crossly. She was over Nick. She'd slept with Pierre and enjoyed it and hoped to see him again. It had been two months since she'd seen Nick. He'd been away on business when she'd visited. Perhaps she wouldn't see him tonight either. She would be just as glad.

Helen opened the door and smiled widely at the sight of Paula. She hugged her.

'Darling, come in. Did you have a nice time in France? We had a lovely ten days in Waterford,' she exclaimed.

'France was a dream,' Paula enthused. 'Where's Nicola?'

'She's outside on her swing. Come on out. We'll have coffee on the patio. Isn't it a beautiful evening? There's a real hint of summer in the air.'

It was unseasonably warm. One of those warm fine weeks that sometimes happens in April. Through the kitchen window, Paula could see her goddaughter swinging happily on the swing. Her heart lifted at the sight of her.

'Hi Nicola,' she called as she stepped out onto the terracotta-tiled patio that was ablaze with spring flowers. A huge flowering cherry blossom, its branches heavy with blossoms, dominated the back garden. It was beautiful.

'Paula! Paula!' The little girl scrambled off her swing and ran excitedly to her, her arms outstretched.

'Oh my little precious.' Paula swung her up in her arms and covered her with kisses. Nicola was the most adorable little girl. She had Helen's dark curly hair, but her eyes were Nick's, Paula thought with a little pang.

'My nose was leaking,' Nicola informed her.

'What!' Paula pretended amazement.

'She had a cold,' Helen murmured, hiding a smile.

'An' I had a cough. Do you want to hear it?'

'Yes.' Paula nodded, smiling into the little girl's big blue eyes.

Nicola gave a bloodcurdling cough. 'Hear the whistles?' she asked, making herself wheeze.

'My poor little pet,' Paula sympathized.

'An' I had to take mesadin.'

'You had to take mesadin! You poor little mutton,' she declared, hugging the little girl tightly.

'But I'm better now,' Nicola said brightly. 'Will you give me a push?'

'Of course I will,' Paula agreed.

Later, Nicola sat engrossed in the Lego Paula had bought. Helen had been delighted with the outfits.

'You're too generous, Paula.' Helen poured the coffee. She looked well. She had a great colour in her face from walking on the beach.

'How could you be too generous to Nicola? I just keep seeing things and I want to buy them for her,' Paula said matter-of-factly.

'Tell me about the Riviera.' Helen passed her a plate of chocolate rings. 'Did you meet Pierre again?'

Paula took one and dunked it in her coffee and enjoyed the taste of melting chocolate.

'I did. And we spent the night together.'

'Is this *IT*, do you think?' Helen asked excitedly. She was dying for Paula to meet the man of her dreams and settle down.

'It might be,' Paula was non-committal.

'Well this is a treat,' she heard a much-loved voice say and her heart leapt.

'Hi Helen.' Nick bent down and kissed her aunt. And then Paula was looking into his smiling deep blue eyes as his arms came around her and she felt Nick's kiss on her cheek. Felt the hardness of his jaw momentarily against hers. Savoured the smell of his familiar aftershave and wanted to weep in despair.

What a fool she'd been to think she'd ever stopped loving or wanting Nick Russell.

Chapter Seventy-Nine

Rachel zipped along the dual carriageway. She'd been looking forward to this for weeks. It was as if she was going on holidays. Jennifer had suggested that she spend a few days in her house over Easter while she and Ronan were on holiday, and she'd jumped at the offer with alacrity. She loved Jennifer and Ronan's house in Drumcondra. She knew Drumcondra well. St Pat's was only down the road. Not that she would know anyone there, except the lecturers. It was four years since she'd left college.

Rachel sighed as she passed the big mast outside RTE. It was a terrible thing to admit but the trip to Dublin was a big event in her year. The last four years had been uneventful. She had got her diploma and was confident and relaxed as a teacher. She enjoyed it. The days slipped by like the beads on a rosary as the rhythm of school terms ruled her life. She'd saved hard. Half-way through her second year the longed-for moment came and she bought her precious Ford Escort.

It was a liberation. To be able to get behind the wheel and drive where she wanted to without having to wait for buses was wonderful. It had been a huge relief to consign her bike to the garden shed for good. Cycling in and out to school on wet windy days had been a nightmare. The car had been worth denying herself spending money that first year she'd been teaching.

She also had a respectable sum in a building society. Rachel's dream of owning her own home was slowly but surely taking shape.

This was her father's last year at work. He was dreading retirement. It frightened him. No longer would he be a person of position and authority in the village. He'd just be an ordinary OAP like the rest of his peers. Rachel did not intend to be around to share his trauma. She wouldn't be able to afford to get a mortgage yet but one of the teachers at school had bought a house and needed someone to share. She asked Rachel if she was interested and Rachel had jumped at the chance. Her rent would be as much as she gave her father for her keep and she and Noreen would share the bills. Rachel couldn't wait. Her father didn't know of her plan. She had no intention of making life difficult for herself. If he knew she was intending to leave she'd have to put up with accusations of being undutiful and selfish.

It had been bad enough when she'd bought the car. Rachel scowled as she remembered how her father had criticized her parking, her driving, the car itself, and the insurance company for insuring a learner, even though he'd never sat in the car with her. He would stand at the gate when she was leaving for work watching . . . waiting for her to make a mistake. He'd be there when she came home and in the beginning, when she'd been very nervous, his critical gaze would spook her and she'd let the clutch out too quickly and the engine would conk out. This always pleased William enormously. He'd stand with a smug superior expression on his face as his points were proved.

Although she passed her test first go, to her father's incredulity, he would not accept her offer to drive him to Dublin for Ronan's wedding. She'd been sorely tempted to get into the car and go by herself. But he would only have got into one of his cold huffs and, for Jennifer's sake, Rachel hadn't wanted any unpleasantness.

Jennifer was exceptionally kind to her, Rachel reflected as she slipped into neutral at the lights in Donnybrook. Her sister-in-law took such an interest in her. She was always encouraging Rachel to be independent. She thought the idea of leaving home and sharing a house was perfect. Jennifer took no nonsense from William. Her father-in-law thought she was a lippy disrespectful young woman. As far as he was concerned Ronan could have done far better for himself. After Jennifer came to tea for the first time, William spent the entire evening giving out about her. Rachel tried to switch off. There was no point in getting annoyed with her father. The best way to annoy him was to ignore him. She let him pontificate, although she was furious at the way he spoke about Jennifer. The more Rachel ignored him, the more virulent his diatribe got. William wanted to provoke Rachel into making a retort so that he'd have an excuse to be sarcastic and cutting. Rachel had grown wise to this ploy and rarely answered back, much to his frustration. If there was one thing her father could not abide it was being ignored.

Rachel smiled to herself as the lights turned green and she slipped smoothly into gear and headed towards the canal. She hadn't told William where she was going. She hadn't even told him she was going away until she'd walked down the stairs with her bag that morning and said she was going away for a few days. That was all she said. It was none of his business where she went or what she did. She didn't want him to know she was staying in Ronan and Jennifer's house. His nosiness would get the better of him, and she wouldn't put it past him to turn up on the doorstep.

She was going to spend her time shopping and relaxing. It was wonderful to have a house to herself. She could do exactly what she liked. She'd watch TV until late at night and switch channels to her heart's content. William had total control over the TV at home. And they didn't have the luxury of cable TV. Rachel was looking forward to nights of uninterrupted viewing. She wouldn't be the slightest bit lonely or bored.

She decided to treat herself to a Kentucky Fried Chicken snack box. It was ages since she'd had one. It reminded her of her days in college. She was starving by the time she got to Drumcondra. She'd just had sandwiches at lunch-time, she'd been so anxious to get on the road to Dublin. She was dying for a cup of tea, she'd treated herself to a packet of chocolate biscuits. She needn't have bothered. Jennifer had left packets of biscuits as well as fruit, wine and a note that said the freezer was full and to help herself. She also had left a set fire and instructions on how to use the central heating. Rachel was warmed by her sister-in-law's kindness.

She poured herself a glass of wine, put the kettle on for a cup of tea and put a match to the fire because it was chilly. Then she settled down on the sofa with her snack box. It was a delightful evening. Rachel sipped her wine, channel-hopped with abandon, read a pile of Jennifer's magazines and then enjoyed a wonderful luxurious bubble bath that left her feeling completely relaxed. She lay in the comfortable brass double bed with its old-fashioned lace bedspread which matched the curtains. Jennifer had great taste, Rachel reflected sleepily. The guest room had a Regency look about it with its striped yellow and gold wallpaper and dado rail. The gold tassel on the brass bedside lamps and the main light exactly matched the shade of the wallpaper. It was an elegant but homely room. Rachel looked forward to the time when she could decorate her own house or apartment as tastefully.

Paula had an apartment, but then Paula was the most sophisticated woman Rachel had ever encountered. At first she'd been shy with her. But Paula had a way of focusing on you that made you feel you were an interesting person. Rachel was fascinated by her. Paula had tremendous confidence and presence. Men flocked about her. She oozed sex appeal.

Rachel lay in bed, thinking about Paula and her men. Some women couldn't imagine life without a man. Rachel didn't feel like that. After Harry, she'd never felt inclined to get involved with anyone. To tell the truth, she decided as she turned over and snuggled down, she didn't particularly like men. She had no great urge to be someone's wife. It was bad enough being a daughter. Rachel knew she was extremely odd compared to most girls, but then, most girls hadn't had to put up with a lifetime of William Stapleton. If she ever got married, she would do it from a position of strength. She'd have her own house, her own car and her own job. She would never give up her job and be dependent on a man. She would never be like her unfortunate mother – entirely dependent on her husband.

Sometimes, particularly before her period, when she got horny, she thought about what she was missing by not having a sex life. But even though she'd never gone the full way with Harry, she'd always felt that he'd been in control of her. Rachel, because of her upbringing, just couldn't imagine that there was such a thing as sexual equality. Sex was just another method of domination and she was determined never to put herself in a position where any man could ever dominate or dictate to her again. She was going to live in a safe little world where she was in charge of her own life and destiny. Rachel fell asleep in an unusually contented frame of mind.

Two months later, just before the summer holidays, Noreen, her colleague, got the keys of her new house. 'When would you like to move in?' she asked Rachel. Rachel didn't hesitate. She knew it was now or never. If she didn't leave home now she never would.

'As soon as I can,' she said calmly.

'The weekend,' suggested Noreen.

'Fine,' agreed Rachel. She went home that evening and began to pack all her worldly possessions into black plastic sacks. She did it in the privacy of her room. William never entered her bedroom. The only things she wanted to take with her were the quilt her grandmother had made for her years ago, and her mother's rocking-chair. She went into Bray the following afternoon and bought sheets, pillows and a duvet and brought them to Noreen's new house.

It was a modern three-bedroom semi on a new estate. Noreen told her she could have the back bedroom, which was double the size of her small room at home. It had fitted wardrobes as well. Noreen said she could arrange it whatever way she liked. It was her room to do what she would with. Rachel was delighted with it. It had a lovely view of the Sugar Loaf in the distance and the back garden faced south and was a sun trap. Rachel felt a quiver of excitement as she made up her new bed. It looked so fresh and welcoming. She was sorry she wasn't staying the night. The green floral duvet cover went nicely with the green and cream fleck wallpaper. She'd buy some pretty lampshades and cushions to decorate her room. Once she had the rocking-chair in place by the window and her books on the shelves, the place would look homely and nice.

She could hardly concentrate at work the next few days. The morning before the move, she put her black sacks in the car while her father was shaving. She would bring them to the house that afternoon after school. Then the next morning she would put her mother's rocking-chair in the back of the car. It would fit in the hatchback. She would never set foot in Rathbarry again, except to visit her mother's grave.

When she got home that evening, her father was cooking his tea. 'You're late,' he remarked.

'Yes,' she said non-committally.

'The board of management and the parish priest and teachers are planning a do for me the night of my last day at school. I presume you'll be there. Ronan and Jennifer will also be invited as my guests,' William said proudly. He would be in his element that night.

You presume too much, she felt tempted to say. But she didn't. Only one more night at home and she didn't want the hassle of a row. No way was she going to sit and listen to laudatory speeches about her father from all the lick-arses in the parish. They didn't know what he was like to live with. Let Ronan and Jennifer go if they wished, she wasn't going. William was so certain she'd be there, he never noticed that she hadn't answered him. He sat pontificating about how everyone kept telling him the school wouldn't be the same without him. He'd been there for forty-five years. He was the cornerstone of the school. No-one could fill his footsteps, he informed his secretly scornful daughter.

She went to bed early. It was strange to lie in bed and look around the little room that had always been her haven from her father and know that she'd never sleep in it again. She felt desperately lonely, suddenly, for her mother. She'd gone into her mother's room for a last look around. It was just as it had been when she died. But it felt empty. Her mother's spirit did not linger there now. The room was cold and unwelcoming. Just the musty smell of disuse. Rachel had not been tempted to stay.

She didn't sleep much, feeling coiled and tense. When dawn broke she was utterly relieved that her ordeal was almost over. While her father was shaving she packed her last bits and pieces and then made her way slowly and quietly down the stairs carrying Theresa's rocking-chair. It was awkward. She half expected her father to make an appearance at the bathroom door to find out what the noise was, but he didn't. He'd grown somewhat hard of hearing over the past couple of years. Rachel thanked God for it. It was a bit of a struggle getting the chair into the back of the car but after much pushing and shoving she managed it. She was sitting drinking her coffee when her father arrived downstairs for his breakfast.

Rachel stood up. Her heart was thumping and she could feel a tremor in her left leg. She took her house key out of her bag and placed it on the kitchen table. 'I won't be needing this any more. I'm moving out. If there's any post for me redirect it to St Catherine's. I won't be coming to your retirement do.' She didn't say goodbye. She didn't look at her father as she spoke. She walked from the kitchen through the hall and then through the front door. Rachel didn't look back.

William Stapleton stared at the key on the kitchen table. He was stunned. Was he having a dream or had Rachel just told him she was leaving home? He walked smartly to the hall window. His eyes widened with shock as he saw Rachel get into her car. Was he seeing things or was that Theresa's rocking-chair on its side in the back seat? His heart started to palpitate. She was leaving him. He never thought she'd have the gumption. Let her leave, he raged. She'd come running back. Rachel hadn't the backbone to manage on her own. She'd come running back. He had no doubt about it.

'I did it. I did it,' Rachel muttered as she drove past tenacres as if the devil himself was after her. Sanity returned and she slowed down to a safer speed. She'd done it. She'd taken the irreversible step. She felt scared and exhilarated but she was not sorry. She had not one ounce of affection for the man she'd left behind. She never wanted to see him again.

Chapter Eighty

The house was unnaturally quiet. Brenda cleaned up the breakfast dishes and didn't know whether she felt happy or sad. She kept expecting Lauren to come rushing in to tell her something, or John to come in from the garden with a daisy he'd picked for her. Even the garden looked forlorn, the swing unmoving, the sandpit empty.

Bringing the twins for their first day at school was an ordeal. Lauren was raring to go. She wanted to wear a uniform and be exactly like her older sister. But John hung back shyly, his lower lip wobbling. And Brenda wanted to gather him up in her arms and bring him back home with her. He was only an infant. Four was awfully young to start school. But that was the age they started these days. Kathy's pair had started at four and Kathy was now working part-time for an accountant who specialized in audits. She was as happy as Larry.

She felt like a *real* person again, she'd confided to Brenda. Not someone's wife. Not someone's mother. Her own woman again. Brenda knew exactly how she felt and, to her surprise, she envied Kathy. If anyone had told her she'd want to get back into the workplace she'd have told them they were mad.

It wasn't that she didn't love her children, she did. It was just that Brenda felt her life revolved totally around them. The grinding repetition of cooking, washing and keeping the house clean bored her beyond measure. There had to be more to life than this. Kathy's return to work had brought this home to Brenda very strongly. Her friend's conversation was peppered with mentions of the various jobs she'd been on and all the people she was meeting again. Kathy always looked very well but now there was an air of extra confidence about her, a pep in her step. Brenda felt positively boring beside her. It didn't help, either, that Jenny and Paula were making huge strides in their careers. Brenda had visited Jenny's recently, and Paula arrived wearing a fabulous taupe suit, carrying a briefcase. She looked like that gorgeous blonde in *Knot's Landing*. Brenda felt like the greatest frump ever. It was very depressing.

She began to daydream about turning into a career woman who wore gorgeous tailored suits and swanned around with a briefcase. She even suggested to Shay that she should come and work in the office for a couple of hours in the mornings once the twins were settled in school.

'You could always have your secretary come in part-time, in the afternoons,' she said airily.

'No way, Brenda,' Shay was uncharacteristically firm. 'Róisín's a good secretary and besides she needs the money. She's trying to rear three children on her own. You know she's a widow.'

'It would save us money, and I'd be a good secretary too,' she said huffily.

'No, Brenda.' Shay was adamant. She sulked for a week. But Brenda made up her mind. The children were going to school for two weeks before the summer holidays. By September, they'd be in school all morning. She was going to get some sort of a little job for herself.

Brenda stood in the garden, staring around. It was a beautiful morning. It was only gone nine forty-five. The hours until twelve-thirty stretched ahead of her. It was so nice she decided she'd make the beds and then come out and cut the grass in the back. She'd put her shorts on, wear a T-shirt and make a start on her tan.

By ten-thirty she was mowing the grass with vigour. She felt energized. Brenda hummed as she mowed. Out of the corner of her eye she saw Mandy go to her line with a basket of clothes. Brenda turned her back. There was a coolness between the Hanleys and the Donovans. A very frosty coolness at that. Brenda scowled as she remembered the incident that had caused it two months ago. She'd asked Mandy to mind the kids for an afternoon so that she could go to a coffee afternoon Kathy'd organized to raise funds to send a child to hospital in America for a life-saving operation. One of the prizes was a holiday in Spain, donated by Jenny's boss. Brenda was hoping like mad that she might win it. She didn't, but she had a great time chatting to all and sundry and catching up on gossip. Kathy'd invited her to stay for tea. Brenda decided she might as well, it wasn't often she got away by herself without the children.

She'd stayed until six and then sped home to collect the children. Just as she pulled up, she saw Tom, Mandy's husband, walking in through the front door. He didn't close it so she walked in behind him a minute or so later to hear him exclaim in immense irritation, 'God Almighty, has she left that shower in on top of us again? I can't afford to be feeding them every second day of the week. Does she think I go up to Superquinn to buy groceries for her gang as well as ours? Does she think I'm a bloody millionaire? Shay earns a hell of a lot more money than I do. Why can't he feed his own kids? It's a bit bloody much, Mandy. All I want to do is come home from work and sit down in my own house and relax without her bloody gang underfoot.'

Brenda cringed. She knew she'd taken advantage once too often. She knew that it annoyed Tom that she left the kids in with Mandy so often. He was sullen and cool with her, and she pretended not to notice and chattered on gaily. Tom didn't like her, but Brenda ignored it because she needed to be able to depend on Mandy to take care of the children now and again.

She was tempted to slip back out and pretend she hadn't heard Tom's outburst but Mandy gave a little gasp of dismay when she saw her standing there. 'Be quiet, Tom,' she said hastily. 'Hi, Brenda. Don't mind Tom, his ulcer's at him.'

Tom turned around and glared at her. 'My ulcer's not at me, Mandy,' he raged. 'Brenda, if I'd wanted six children I'd have had them. I don't mind doing a neighbour a favour now and again, but I'm fed up to the back teeth rearing and feeding your kids. I want to be able to come in from work and sit down with my own family. I have nothing against your children. But I don't like my wife's good nature being taken advantage of. And in case you don't realize it, it costs money to feed children. When we do our weekly shopping we do it to last us for the week, not for the benefit of your family. It would match you better if you'd cook a decent meal for your kids now and again instead of feeding them burgers and chips from the chipper, because you're too busy gadding around the countryside to look after them.'

Brenda nearly died of mortification. She wanted to turn around and say how dare you talk to me like that? But Tom had a sharp tongue. And she knew in her heart and soul that there was a lot of truth in what he said.

'You won't be troubled with them again,' she said stiffly. 'I apologize for any inconvenience caused.'

'He doesn't mean it.' Mandy was scarlet with embarrassment.

'Yes I do, Mandy. I'm fed up with this carry-on. I'm fed up listening to you moaning about it and not saying anything about it. It had to be said and I'm saying it!'

With as much dignity as she could muster, Brenda called to her children, who were playing in the front room, and walked out the door. She was furious, she was embarrassed, and she was raging with herself for not being ten minutes earlier. She'd never be able to ask Mandy to look after the kids again after this.

From then on Tom ignored her when they met. He was an ignoramus anyway, she decided. Mandy barely said hello and wouldn't look Brenda in the eye. It was a nuisance when she wanted to go anywhere. She tried to leave the children with Kit but her mother told her in no uncertain terms that, much as she loved her grand-children, she'd reared her own and she'd no intention of rearing Brenda's. 'I had to stay at home when you were young, much and all as I'd have liked to be off out enjoying myself. You'll have to do the same.' Her mother was stern about it. School couldn't have come at a more opportune moment, Brenda decided as she started to clip the edges of the grass.

Once she was happy that John had settled in well, Brenda thoroughly enjoyed her mornings of freedom. She went to town and treated herself to a few new outfits for the summer. Sometimes she and a neighbour went swimming or played a set of tennis in Johnstown Park. Once, after she'd driven the children to school, she drove straight out to Portmarnock beach and spent two blissful hours on the beach. When it was fine she took her lounger out into the back garden when she'd finished making the beds and tidying up, and relaxed in the sun. It was the nicest two weeks she'd spent in years. Exactly as she'd imagined it would be when she'd left work. When the school holidays arrived she was sorry.

September would be wonderful, she promised herself. She'd get a part-time job two or three mornings a week and flop and enjoy her peace and quiet the rest of the days. Partial freedom was in sight. Things could only improve.

It was one of the nicest summers she'd ever spent, too. The weather was kind. Most days she would pack a picnic and take the kids to Portmarnock or Donabate or the Hole in the Wall beach, where they played on the sand and she read her library books and turned a nice golden brown. It was great now that the children were older. They were much better able to amuse themselves and, apart from the usual squabbles, life was rather relaxing.

She and Kathy started walking to try and lose weight. They walked around Johnstown Park three or four times every evening. To her delight, her thighs and bum began to tone up. She watched her eating and the pounds slowly

670

dropped off. For the first time in a long time Brenda began to feel in control again. It was a good feeling. She didn't even over-indulge when she went on holidays in a rented mobile home in Bettystown with Shay and the children for two weeks. Brenda kept the vision of herself in a tailored suit, carrying a briefcase. It helped every time she felt tempted to eat a coffee slice.

Losing a stone did wonders for her determination and confidence. At the end of August, she saw an advertisement in one of the evening papers for a part-time dentist's receptionist in Drumcondra, required to work three mornings. Brenda applied for the job. Three mornings a week would suit her down to the ground.

She was as nervous as a kitten as she sat waiting to be interviewed. She hadn't told a soul she was going for the job in case she didn't get it. It was bad enough being rejected without the world and his mother knowing about it. There wouldn't be much need for her to carry a briefcase, she supposed, nevertheless it would be a start and she could always move on to greater things.

To her joy, Brenda got the job. Doctor Marshall, the dentist, was impressed that she had computer skills. He intended transferring all his patients' data on to disc. His wife would do the afternoon shift and the remaining mornings, he informed Brenda. It suited her down to the ground. Doctor Marshall was young and enthusiastic and he'd just taken over an established practice. She'd be kept busy, he assured Brenda. She didn't care. The busier the better as far as she was concerned.

Shay was a bit doubtful when she told him she'd got a job, but his wife's humour was so much improved he decided it was a good thing and took her out for a drink and a meal to celebrate.

The first few mornings had been a bit hectic what with trying to get the children out to school and the house tidy before she left for work, but gradually Brenda got into her routine. She woke in the mornings looking forward to work. She liked wearing the crisp white coat. It made her feel like a nurse and the patients found it very reassuring, especially when she had to calm the nervous ones.

She was enjoying the challenge of transferring the data onto the computer. Mrs Marshall had no computer skills, so Brenda felt important explaining the new system to her.

It was the best thing she ever did, Brenda thought happily, when she got her first pay cheque. It was extremely satisfying working three mornings a week and earning her own money and having the other two mornings off. She felt much more content with her life. It no longer seemed aimless and filled with boring routine. She was keeping her weight off too and people commented on how well she looked. When she got her second pay cheque, she got her hair tinted auburn.

Brenda got the surprise of her life on her wedding anniversary, when Shay announced that he'd booked a weekend away for them the weekend after St Patrick's weekend. She was thrilled. He'd arranged for his younger sister to baby-sit. She was a student and always in need of money.

Brenda went into town and treated herself to the most gorgeous silk navy lingerie. And then, walking past Principles, she saw a beautiful tailored royal blue suit with a long jacket, the sort Princess Di wore. Brenda gazed at it in admiration. It was elegant and classy and just the sort of suit Paula would wear. On impulse she went in and to her delight found a size fourteen in stock. To her absolute joy, it fitted her new lighter, trimmer figure like a glove. Brenda was ecstatic as she signed the cheque. It cost an arm and a leg but it was her reward to herself for sticking to her diet and getting her job and taking charge of her life again. She was on a high after her little shopping spree. It had really sent the adrenalin rushing through her.

The weekend in Hotel Kilkenny was almost as good as being on her honeymoon. Having room service breakfast with no children making demands was glorious. She and Shay explored the historical elegant town and wandered in and out of shops and through winding arch-covered streets. They lunched in the famous Kytler's Inn, and took a tour of the ancient castle with its magnificent views of the meandering river. Brenda went on another spending spree in the Kilkenny Design Centre and had to be dragged out by a laughing Shay. Arm in arm they walked back to the hotel and went for a swim in the pool and then did a workout in the gym, which left them breathless and laughing. They kissed and cuddled in the sauna and then sat in the Jacuzzi enjoying the powerful streams of water easing the aches from their unaccustomed exercise.

'I wish we could stay for a week,' Brenda said on the Sunday morning. It had been the nicest surprise of her life.

'I wish we could too.' Shay nuzzled her ear. 'It was lovely having time on our own. We should try and do it more often.' He leaned over and kissed her. Brenda, wearing her silky revealing nightdress, felt quite sexy. They'd made love several times and the knowledge that they weren't going to be disturbed by the children relaxed her greatly. She often maintained that Lauren and Claudia were the best contraceptives going.

Brenda kissed Shay's navel, and stroked her hand along the inside of his thigh, that always drove him wild.

'Oh Bren,' he breathed. 'Keep doing it!' She felt like Paige Mathison, her heroine in *Knot's Landing*. Wearing her sexy nightgown made Brenda feel wanton and desirable. She increased the pressure of her fingers.

'Aaah, Brenda, Brenda,' Shay moaned.

'Where's the condoms?' Brenda murmured.

'There's none left.' Shay groaned. Brenda stopped her stroking.

'Ah, Brenda, don't stop,' Shay pleaded. He was wildly aroused. They hadn't had so much sex in months. It was great. He couldn't stop himself. Before she could say anything he'd entered her and was thrusting wildly.

Brenda, excited by his passion, joined in the fun.

'That was the best ever,' Shay panted, seconds later. Brenda sighed in pleasure. It reminded her of one night when Eddie jumped on her because he'd been so aroused. Paula Matthews wasn't the only *femme fatale*, she thought smugly, but a little niggle of unease troubled her. Shay hadn't been wearing a condom. Although she thought it was pretty safe, you could never be absolutely sure. She'd be on tenterhooks until her period arrived. Having a baby now, at her age, would ruin every bit of freedom she'd finally earned for herself. If she found out she was pregnant, she'd kill herself.

'What's wrong?' Shay noticed her change of humour.

'I hope I don't get caught. We took a bit of a risk.'

'You'll be fine.' Shay, relaxing in the afterglow of his performance, was untroubled.

'I hope so,' Brenda murmured, snuggling down for forty winks. Shay was right, there was nothing to worry about, she was well past her ovulating period according to her calculations.

Chapter Eighty-One

'Happy Anniversary to you,
Happy Anniversary to you,
Happy Anniveerrsaaarrry darling Jennifer . . .
Happy Anniversary to you.'

Jennifer awoke to the sound of Ronan serenading her. He stood beside the bed balancing the breakfast tray in one hand and a huge bouquet of freesias and a long slender package in the other. Tousle-headed and bleary-eyed, she grinned up at him. 'Good morning, lovie, you didn't forget this year, I see,' she joked.

Ronan laid the tray gently on her knees. 'Once bitten, twice shy.' He chuckled. He'd forgotten their anniversary the previous year and had to endure weeks of teasing. He'd circled the date in red marker in his diary at work and begged Rachel to remind him in case he forgot. She'd very kindly phoned the previous week.

'Here's your card.' Jennifer leaned over to her bedside locker and took a card from between the pages of her library book and handed it to him with a small flat package.

'Let's open them together. What is it?' he asked, starting to rip off the paper with boyish enthusiasm. Jennifer couldn't wait for him to open his present. She'd planned to be awake before him but these nights she slept like a log.

'Open yours, open yours,' he instructed and she busily began to unwrap her present, keeping an eye on him. 'What's this?' he asked, astounded, holding up a book of children's names. Two tiny pairs of booties, one pink, one

675

blue, fell on the bed. Ronan picked them up and looked at them, and then at Jennifer, and then at the book and then at Jennifer again. He couldn't speak.

'Happy Anniversary,' she said softly.

'You're not . . . Are you . . . Jenny, are you going to have a baby?'

'*We're* going to have a baby,' she corrected him, beaming.

'How do you know? I mean, have you been to the doctor?' Ronan sat on the bed, flabbergasted.

'I found out last week. I suspected it for ages and I went to the doctor and I'm eight weeks pregnant. I was dying to tell you but I thought it would make our anniversary special.'

'Oh, Jenny.' Ronan leaned over and kissed her. 'I can't believe it.'

'Me neither.' She smiled happily. 'Are you glad?'

'Glad! I'm over the moon,' Ronan declared. 'I'll tell you one thing, it will get Grandpa Myles and Dad off my back. I think they were beginning to suspect I was a eunuch!'

Jennifer giggled. 'Well I suppose they think after four years we should have something to show for it. Their generation was so different from ours. I can't wait to tell Paula and the girls.'

'How did you keep it to yourself? You of all people?' Ronan got into bed beside her and took the tray on his knees as she finished unwrapping her present.

Jennifer paused from her task and smiled at him. 'Ronan, it's the hardest thing I've ever done. But I wanted you to be the first to know. I couldn't tell anybody else before I told you. And I wanted to keep it for our anniversary.'

'Well you've outdone yourself in presents.' Ronan grinned. 'I'll never be able to outdo this.'

'Ronan!' Jennifer gave a little squeal of pleasure as she saw the exquisite gold rope chain lying on black velvet. 'It's beautiful. Thank you. I'm really happy today,' she sighed, fingering the chain. 'I can't believe we're four years married.'

'Remember the lamb?' Ronan chuckled.

'Remember Grandpa Myles eating the face off the manager.' Jennifer laughed.

'There's another little present for you in your card,' she informed him.

'I was so excited about hearing about the baby I forgot to open it.' Ronan dived down the bed, nearly upsetting the tray, as he grabbed the white envelope. He opened it, read the message and a broad grin spread across his face as he opened the gift voucher for six months of training sessions at the local gym. Ronan was a keep-fit addict and liked to work out regularly.

'Thanks. You're the best wife in the universe. Imagine you're pregnant and I never even guessed. Do you feel queasy or peculiar or anything? Brenda was always feeling dizzy at the beginning, wasn't she?' he asked.

Jennifer shook her head. 'I feel fantastic. I don't feel any different. Except I get a bit tired at night. That's why I'm sleeping my brains out. I'd planned to be up before you this morning.'

'Well after last year's fiasco I thought I'd better make a special effort. I didn't do us a fry-up because I've booked lunch for us at the Deer Park in Howth at one.'

'Oh my favourite.' Jennifer lay back on her pillows and felt very pampered and cherished. 'It's nice having our anniversary on a Sunday. We have the whole day all to ourselves.'

'Let's go for a walk along the pier afterwards, then we'll come home, light the fire and get all the papers and flop for the rest of the afternoon,' Ronan suggested.

'I wonder will it be a boy or a girl,' she mused.

'What would you prefer?' Ronan munched his toast.

'I'd like twins, a boy and a girl, the way Brenda had. That would solve all problems,' Jennifer said.

'Jeepers, I never thought about twins.' Ronan looked slightly shocked.

677

'The doctor doesn't think it's twins,' Jennifer said. 'I was just saying it would be handy. But I don't mind as long as everything's OK.'

'I'll be able to play Santa this year, and I'll have to remember Mother's Day next year.' Ronan groaned. 'What am I letting myself in for?' They stayed in bed making plans, discussing names and laughing over some of the more outrageous ones Ronan selected from his book. Then they made love and took a shower together afterwards.

It was a bright blustery day. They decided to go to eleven-thirty Mass in Ballygall and then pop in to tell Kit and Jim the news before heading off for lunch. Jennifer sat beside Ronan listening to the magnificent choir singing *Be Not Afraid* and felt very content and happy.

Kit and Jim were thrilled with her news, as was Grandpa Myles.

'It's about time,' he declared, shaking Ronan's hand. 'Ye had me worried.'

'For God's sake, Grandpa, would you give over?' Jennifer was half annoyed, half amused.

'It's all right, my girl, but you don't want to be geriatrics yourselves when your children are growing up. All this nonsense about women having careers, and putting off having babies. T'ain't natural. St Paul says—'

'Don't quote that misogynist to me,' Jennifer snorted. She had no time for St Paul or St Augustine, her grandfather's favourites, and source of all wisdom concerning women, or so he thought.

'That's a big word . . . like marmalade, Miss. What does it mean?' Grandfather Myles asked huffily.

'It means woman-hater,' Jennifer said.

'What nonsense. St Paul spoke a lot of common sense about women, as did St Augustine—'

'St Augustine was a randy old goat who blamed women because he couldn't control his urges. And then he had the cheek to start maligning women when he was past it.'

Jennifer scowled. Kit started to laugh and Jim and Ronan winked at each other.

'Wirra, wirra, that's a terrible thing to say about a saint. And you a mother-to-be—'

'And I can tell you one thing, Grandpa,' Jennifer continued. 'If it's a boy, I won't be calling him Augustine or—'

'I sincerely hope not,' interjected her grandfather. 'I hope you'll be calling him Daniel after his grandfather. Not like that Brenda one and her John.' Jennifer had to laugh. You couldn't win with Grandpa Myles or get the last word.

'Will we call him Daniel if it's a boy?' Ronan asked as they drove along the sea front towards Howth. 'It's a nice name. And Grumps would be chuffed.' Ronan had a soft spot for Jennifer's grandfather.

'But what about your father, wouldn't he mind?'

'Tough,' Ronan said grimly. 'One William Stapleton is enough in the world.'

'Daniel is a nice name.' Jennifer squeezed his hand. 'And if it's a girl we can call her Danielle,' she added excitedly. Her grandfather would be as proud as punch.

'Danielle's even more exotic than Claudia,' teased Ronan.

'Oh, stop it, you.'

'Well that's the names picked with no arguments. What a team we are,' Ronan said with satisfaction as they drove through Sutton Cross.

'I wish it was November already.' Jennifer felt impatient now that she knew she was going to have a Daniel or a Danielle. She wished she didn't have to wait seven more months to have the baby. She wanted it now!

They ate a delicious lunch in the cosy dining-room of the Deer Park. She and Ronan regularly treated themselves to Sunday lunch there. The two very pleasant waitresses knew them well and always had a laugh and a chat with them. The roast beef and Yorkshire pudding was delicious, and when she was asked if she'd like another slice, Jennifer immediately said yes. After all, she was eating for two, she made excuses for her gluttony.

'Oh Ronan, look, there's Banofi for dessert. They must have known we were coming,' Jennifer enthused as she read the menu. She just adored the toffee and bananas in the crunchy crushed biscuit base which was all topped lavishly with cream. She had made it once herself when she had the girls over for dinner. Paula had produced a carton of Häagen-Dazs and she'd spread the ice cream on top. It had been out of this world.

They lingered over coffee, gazing out at the magnificent tree-lined grounds overlooking the sea and Ireland's Eye. The waitress brought them more coffee and then Ronan and Jennifer sat, holding hands, discussing how their life was about to change.

'We'll have to go house-hunting. Our little shoe-box is too small, even though it's the nicest shoe-box in the world,' Ronan said.

'Yeah, we need a house with a big back garden. It was different when we were small. It was safe to let children out to play. I wouldn't dare let a child out of my sight now,' Jennifer said sombrely.

'We'll get a house with a big garden,' Ronan promised. 'Whereabouts would you like to live?'

'Somewhere around Mam and Dad's or Glasnevin or Ballygall,' Jennifer suggested.

'Why don't we go for our walk, and take a spin around and see if there's anything for sale on the way home?'

'I'm married to a genius.' Jennifer grinned.

They strolled along the top of the pier, holding hands, enjoying the wind as it whipped against their faces. Jennifer breathed deeply, inhaling the tangy clean salty air. It was nice to get the exercise after the superb lunch they'd just eaten. The waves crashed in on the rocks, sending up great sprays of spume, and they stood watching a little trawler gallantly ploughing towards the entrance of the harbour and didn't envy the poor fishermen one bit. A young couple pushed a sleeping baby in a buggy ahead of them.

'That will be us, this time next year,' Jennifer murmured.

'I can't wait.' Ronan put his arms around her and kissed her.

'I can't either.' Jennifer was on cloud nine. They'd decided a year ago to start trying for a baby and she'd come off the pill. She'd been a bit worried in the last few months when there'd been no sign of her conceiving. When her period hadn't arrived two months ago she wondered could she be pregnant. Jennifer put off going to the doctor, and wouldn't even try one of the home testing kits in case the result was negative. But as the weeks passed and there was no sign of her period she allowed her hope to get stronger and then she instinctively knew she was pregnant. She knew that there was life inside her, the doctor just confirmed it for her.

She was a very lucky person, Jennifer decided, several hours later, as she lay cuddled on the sofa with Ronan, reading the Sunday papers in front of a blazing fire. It had started to rain and the wind was howling down the chimney. The sitting-room, with its warm buttermilk walls and cheerful cream and blue chintz curtains, was cosy and homely. Jennifer and Ronan had put a lot of effort into their house. She'd miss it when they had to sell it. But it only had two bedrooms and a postage stamp of a garden. She wouldn't even have room to store a pram. They'd been very happy in their little home for the last four years but it was time to move on, Jennifer thought as her eyelids grew heavy and she settled herself more comfortably against Ronan's shoulder.

'This is the best anniversary ever,' she murmured drowsily.

A little rumbling snore was her husband's answer to that. Jennifer smiled in the firelight and closed her eyes.

Chapter Eighty-Two

'I'm thrilled for you, Jenny.' Paula hugged her best friend warmly. 'Is Ronan chuffed?'

'Ah he's delighted.' Jennifer beamed. They were sitting in her office having a mug of coffee.

'Are you going to give up work?' Paula asked. 'I hope you won't. I'd miss you like crazy and Kieran would have a fit. He claims he's never been so organized in his life because you're much stricter with him than Helen was.'

'You'd have to be strict with that fella,' Jennifer retorted. 'Or you'd end up on Valium. I think I hear him arriving.' The unmistakable sound of the Harley's roar penetrated the first floor window.

'Are you going to tell him yet?' Paula asked.

'I suppose I'd better. To let him get used to the idea that he's going to have to get a new secretary for a while anyway. God help her.'

Kieran strode through the door, wearing his black leather jacket and his gauntlets. He'd removed his helmet on the way up the stairs. 'Morning all,' he said cheerfully.

Jennifer smiled. Kieran's sunny nature reminded her of Ronan. 'I told you to wear a suit today.' She wagged a finger at her boss. 'You've a lunch in The Commons with that journalist who's doing a profile of the company. I'm not letting you go to lunch looking like a Hell's Angel.'

'You're worse than my mother,' Kieran groaned. 'Paula, come to my aid here. Tell this woman that clothes do not maketh the man.' He straddled a chair with his long legs and ran his fingers through his dark hair, which was all over the place.

'I'm staying on my fence.' Paula grinned. 'Far be it from me to get involved in one of your arguments.'

'Coward,' Kieran taunted.

'I've a suit in the cleaners, it might be ready today. I could wear that if you feel it's absolutely necessary.' He grimaced.

'I do,' Jennifer said firmly, winking at Paula.

'You're a little dictator,' Kieran retorted.

'I am,' Jennifer agreed. 'And you need a little dictator in your life. That's why I'm going to help you choose your replacement secretary for when I'm on my maternity leave.'

Kieran's jaw dropped. 'You're not serious?' he declared.

Jennifer nodded.

'When?'

'November.'

'Congratulations, Jenny, I'm delighted for you.' Kieran stood up and came across to her desk and hugged her. 'Well that's a bit of a fib, actually.' He sighed. 'You're not going to leave me, are you? Please, Jenny, don't leave me. I'll really get going on this crèche business. I promise. I don't think I could face getting someone to replace you.' Jennifer was secretly chuffed that her boss thought so highly of her. She liked working for Kieran and she hadn't thought about giving up her job. She wasn't sure if she'd like to stay at home all day. Even Brenda was delighted to be working part-time again.

'I haven't really thought about it, Kieran,' she said. 'But it's nice to know I'm appreciated.'

'You are, you are,' he said fervently. 'Even if you do order me around and make me wear suits.'

The phone rang. 'I've work to do even if you pair haven't.' Jennifer picked up the receiver and took the call.

Ronan phoned about four that afternoon to say the computer had gone down in the office, there was high drama and he'd probably be late. Paula happened to be in the office when the call came through and, when Jennifer hung up, she suggested they go out for a meal. They hadn't been out together for ages so they phoned up Beth and made arrangements to meet in Captain America's later that evening.

They had a lovely time, gossiping and laughing, and Beth was delighted when she heard Jennifer's news. 'I almost feel sorry for you in one way though,' she said wickedly. 'I don't know how you're going to pick a godmother for this infant.'

'Oh, stop it,' Jennifer groaned. 'I suppose it will have to be Brenda. Can you imagine the huff she'll get into if she isn't godmother to my first? After all, I'm Claudia's godmother.'

'Maybe you'll have twins,' Paula joked. 'Ask Kieran to be the godfather and they'll always get free holidays.'

'You're awful,' Jennifer scolded. 'Kieran's very generous.'

'I know he is,' Paula agreed. 'I'm just kidding.'

After their meal they strolled along to the Shelbourne and relaxed over a drink. Jennifer had soda water and lime. Now that she was pregnant she wasn't drinking alcohol, and besides she had the car and she never drove and drank. It was relaxing being with the girls and they hardly noticed the evening passing until Paula said with an exclamation of horror, 'Lord Almighty, it's gone half eleven and I'm due on the seven am flight to Heathrow in the morning. I'm off to Sardinia for a few days to scout around locations and I haven't a stitch ready.'

'Lucky you.' Beth sighed. 'Surely with all the gorgeous men you meet, there must be someone who's caught your fancy.' Paula caught Jennifer's sympathetic gaze. Only Jennifer knew that Paula was crazy about Nick.

'Men are more trouble than they're worth,' Paula said lightly, but her eyes were sad.

'I'd have that kind of trouble any day,' Beth grimaced. There was no man on her horizon and she was lonely.

'Well if I don't get home, I'll be having man trouble.' Jennifer stood up to go. 'Beth, are you going to come with me or Paula?'

'I'll drop her home,' Paula said. 'It will save you all the trouble of having to go to Wadelai and back to Drumcondra.'

'OK,' Jennifer agreed. They walked her to her car and kissed her and wished her a safe journey home. Jennifer started up the engine, glanced in her mirror and slid out into the flow of traffic around Stephen's Green. She switched on her car radio. *Late Date* was just starting and she heard Val Joyce's deep mellifluous tones introducing Dean Martin, singing *Memories Are Made of This*. Very apt, she thought happily and hummed along. The traffic was light and she reached Drumcondra in less than twelve minutes. She was driving through the Botanic Avenue junction when a car broke the red light. She saw it coming, tried to swerve, but it was too late. Jennifer felt immense terror as she felt the impact of the car and was sent skidding across the road. Her last thought before darkness enveloped her was of her baby.

Chapter Eighty-Three

'I'm here, Jennifer, you're all right.' She could hear Ronan's voice from a distance. Jennifer felt very peculiar. She opened her eyes, saw Ronan gazing down at her in concern, and closed them again. The world stopped swaying.

'The baby?' she asked dry-mouthed.

'It's OK. The two of you are OK.' Ronan didn't dare tell Jennifer that the doctors were worried about the baby. She was lucky to be alive and to have escaped relatively lightly from the crash. She had two broken ribs, bruising and concussion. More seriously, she was threatened with a miscarriage.

'Ronan?' Jennifer started to cry.

'It's all right, Jennifer,' he soothed. 'The doctors and nurses are taking care of you.' A nurse came, accompanied by a doctor. 'We have to examine Mrs Stapleton,' she said gently. 'You can come back when we're finished.'

Ronan nodded and walked through the cubicle curtains. He felt like crying. When he saw Jennifer all bruised and battered he wanted to strangle the drunken driver who'd crashed into her. Kit and Jim were in the waiting-room.

'She's awake,' he said tiredly. 'I don't know what's going to happen about the baby.'

'Oh, Ronan, I'm sorry.' Kit started to cry. Ronan put his arms around his mother-in-law. 'It could have been worse,' he said gently. 'Jennifer could have been killed.' Jim went and got them coffee and they sat silently, waiting until Ronan was allowed back into the ward.

He stayed with her as long as he was allowed and begged the nurse to let Kit and Jim say goodnight to Jennifer.

'Only for a minute,' the nurse warned. After Kit and Jim had kissed her tenderly and told her not to worry, he brought his parents-in-law home. They made him stay the night with them. He lay in Jennifer's old bed but he could not sleep. All he could think of was the moment when he opened his front door to find a policeman standing on his doorstep with the news that Jennifer had been in a car crash.

Ronan started to cry. If anything happened to Jennifer he'd never get over it. She was his rock. His life revolved around her. '*Please, God, take care of Jenny and let our baby be all right*,' he prayed earnestly, wishing the night was over so that he could be with her.

She was the most beautiful baby Jennifer had ever seen. It was Danielle lying in her arms. She had big blue eyes and long black lashes and a downy head of dark hair, a little button nose and a perfect rosebud mouth. Jennifer felt utterly serene as she held her baby. It was as if they could read each other's minds.

I'm your baby, I'm Danielle.
I know, my darling. I love you.
I love you too. Don't be sad. I'll always be with you.

Jennifer gazed into her daughter's bright blue eyes. The love she felt for her overwhelmed her. All that night she held her daughter in her arms until just before dawn when the baby closed her eyes and Jennifer felt a terrible grief. She woke with a start and knew her baby was dead. Some time later she began to miscarry.

'She was beautiful, she came to say goodbye to me. She stayed with me all night. She just lay in my arms looking at me and I knew what was in her mind and she knew what was in mine.' Jennifer sobbed against Ronan's shoulder. 'I'll never forget her eyes, Ronan. Oh my baby! My beautiful, beautiful little baby.' Jennifer clung to Ronan, who tried his best to comfort her. She had obviously been hallucinating from the drugs they'd given her. But if it comforted Jenny to think the baby had come to her, he wasn't going to say otherwise.

Jennifer leaned against Ronan and felt his strength. They'd have another baby, she knew it. But no child would ever be as precious as her little blue-eyed daughter who'd come to her in the night and said goodbye.

Chapter Eighty-Four

'Can I have a word with you, Rachel?' Noreen knocked on the bedroom door. Rachel's heart sank. Not another loan. Noreen was always the same, borrowing and conveniently forgetting to pay it back. It wasn't only money she borrowed. She constantly 'borrowed' from Rachel's wardrobe and used her make-up. It was very irritating.

Rachel felt ghastly. She wasn't in the mood for Noreen. She had laryngitis and tonsillitis. The antibiotics she was taking made her feel sick. She was out on a Cert for a week. She wouldn't be back to work until after Easter, but already she was fed up being on her own in the house every day. Still, she'd rather be on her own than have to listen to Noreen rabbiting on.

'Rachel, are you awake?' Noreen called.

'Yeah, come in,' she croaked.

Noreen peered around the door. 'I won't come right in,' she said. 'I don't want to catch anything.'

Typical, thought Rachel. Her landlady was not the most sympathetic of characters.

'What's wrong?' Rachel asked.

'Well I know you probably won't be too happy about it but I'm selling the house. I've got a visa, I'm going to the States.'

Rachel was gobsmacked. 'Oh,' she said inadequately. 'Oh . . . fine.'

'I thought I'd better let you know, so you can start looking for another place. Or maybe you could go home for a while. The sign is going up tomorrow and the auctioneer expects a quick sale,' Noreen said briskly.

'I'm off now, I'm going to Wexford for the weekend. I hope you'll be feeling better. See ya.'

'See you,' Rachel murmured. She lay back against the pillows and let the news sink in. Now that it had come to it, she wasn't dreadfully sorry to hear that Noreen was selling. It meant that she was going to have to get up off her butt and get a place of her own.

She had more than enough in her building society for a mortgage but she had made no move to get a place of her own. My trouble, Rachel thought crossly, is that I don't like hassle. She pulled the duvet up under her chin and wished Noreen had not made her disturbing announcement. She was just going to have to endure a bit of hassle and that was all there was about it. Rachel felt glum at the thought. If anyone had told her she'd still be sharing with Noreen and still be teaching in St Catherine's after four years, she wouldn't have believed it.

After she left home she'd scuttled under the nearest rock she could find and stayed there. Well her rock was gone, she was out in the open now. She was going to have to sink or swim. One thing was certain, she was not going back to Rathbarry.

Rachel got up out of bed and wrapped her dressing-gown around her. She was just as glad that she had the house to herself. At least she wouldn't have to listen to Van Morrison caterwauling all weekend. Noreen played him non-stop as loud as she dared. The neighbours had complained several times.

The sitting-room looked as if a bomb had hit it. The kitchen was even worse. Noreen was dead lazy about the house. But then, she had a lodger to run around after her, Rachel thought wryly. She was sick of it, Rachel decided as she tipped a brimming ashtray into the fireplace.

Not that she had any sympathy for herself. She needn't have stayed once she'd got to know what Noreen was like. She had every opportunity to go and get her own place. She was earning good money. There were plenty

690

of houses for sale. She was just a lazy coward, Rachel chastised herself.

She tidied up the sitting-room, set the fire, lit it and made herself a cup of tea and buttered some cream crackers. Then she picked up the evening paper that Noreen had stuffed down the side of the chair. Rachel turned to the property pages and perused them with interest. She was doing sums in her head when the phone rang. It was Ronan to tell her that Jennifer had had an accident and was in danger of losing the baby. Rachel didn't hesitate.

'I'll be up in two hours,' she promised. 'I'll just pack a bag.' She raced around the place trying to get herself organized. 'Stop panicking, Jennifer needs you,' she muttered as she let her antibiotics fall. She damped down the fire and put the fireguard up. Her cup and plate lay where she'd left them. Rachel switched off the light and closed the door. For once she was going to leave her dishes. The sitting-room was a damn sight tidier than when Noreen had left it, even with a dirty cup and saucer on the floor.

Rachel put her bag in the boot, put her foot on the accelerator and drove as fast as she could to Dublin. She had decisions to make, she knew, but right now Jennifer was her priority. Her sister-in-law had always been very good to her. Now she might be able to do something to repay that kindness. It was the least she could do. Maybe when she was in Dublin she would see a house she liked. There was nothing written in stone to say she had to live in Bray for the rest of her life.

Chapter Eighty-Five

The party was in full swing. She'd been a director of TransCon for a year now and Paula had decided it was time she bought a place of her own. She'd looked at houses, and mews and apartments. She knew what she wanted. A place with all mod cons, easy to maintain, near enough to the office and the airport.

'I suppose now that you're a director, you'll be heading for Dublin 4,' Jenny had teased her, but Paula wasn't going to spend hours stuck in traffic so that she could have a posh postal address. In the end she'd bought a two-bedroom apartment not far from her rented one. It was in a small exclusive complex off Griffith Avenue, near enough to where she'd lived with Helen all those years ago.

It was on the top floor of a three-floor block. Her sitting-room looked south to the mountains. Paula decorated the apartment in light warm pastel colours. Her kitchen was pine. She bought a pine dresser like her mother had. It made her think of home. But that was where the resemblance ended. Paula's fitted kitchen was as modern as could be. She had a small utility room off it for the washing-machine, tumble-drier and ironing board. The lounge was bright and spacious. She kept it uncluttered, with just two huge plush sofas at right angles to the fire and a low marble-topped coffee table in between them. She used apricot and cream colours. It was a warm welcoming room in winter and cool and airy in summer. French doors led to a tiled south-facing balcony that ran the length of the apartment. A small alcove off the lounge opened out into a dining area. She had shelves built on the back wall and kept all her books and records and CDs neatly stacked. In front of them was a round oak table and six chairs which matched her fitted shelves.

The master bedroom was *en suite*, and Paula decorated it tastefully in peach and green. Huge mirrored wardrobes gave an impression of space, and the deep-pile pale green carpet gave the room a rich luxurious air. Patterned peach curtains matched the colour of the bedspread. The tie-backs and pelmet were trimmed with green. Kieran asked her jokingly if she thought she was Joan Collins, when he saw the bedroom. Paula endured the teasing. She'd earned her little bit of luxury. The guest-room had two divans covered in pretty pink chintz bedspreads which matched the curtains. Nicola called it her room and had stayed on 'holidays' several times.

Paula had kept meaning to have a house-warming party. But as usual she'd been up to her eyes. Christmas came and went. The current brochure was out on time and things eased off. Just before the beginning of the new season at Easter, there'd been a lull in her pace of life and she finally decided to have a hooley.

Hooley was the right word for it, Paula smiled to herself, as she listened to the hum of conversation and laughter filling her home. Ronan was teasing Jenny about something, trying to cheer her up. Jenny was still terribly pale after the accident and miscarriage, Paula noted as she walked around with a plate of hors d'oeuvres. Paula was doing her best to try and get her friend's spirits up. But she understood her need to grieve. It was a worry, though.

Beth was chatting away to Kieran, who caught Paula's eye and smiled. He had not married Tina and was not dating anyone. Rachel was laughing at something Hugh, Paula's neighbour from across the landing, was telling her. The girls from the office were flirting with Paul, Dermot and Donald, three gorgeous detectives who shared a downstairs apartment.

'I wonder what ever happened to Green Car and Co?' Jenny grinned after Paula introduced them. Paula smiled, remembering their innocent teenage infatuation. So much had happened to herself and her best friends since then. Life had been easy when she was young. She'd had no complications to trouble her. She glanced around the crowded room looking for Helen and Nick. They were kissing in the alcove. Pain darkened her eyes. Paula bit her lip and walked back towards the kitchen, unaware that Kieran was watching her. A shocked expression on his face.

Don't think about it now, she told herself fiercely as she tossed the salad she was serving with the enormous cold buffet she'd prepared with Jenny's help.

She carried it in to the dining table and said brightly, 'Come and get it.' The hordes descended on the food and there was much laughter and oohing and aahing as the guests tucked in with delight.

'Great party,' her friend Gwen assured her. This was a compliment indeed. Gwen partied the world over, from Australia to America. It was a way of life and she lived life to the full. The air hostess was looking like a million dollars in a clinging black dress which showed off her every curve. There'd been no need for her to bring Häagen-Dazs from America this time. The ice cream was on sale in Ireland now and several large cartons of the rich creamy concoction had gone into the making of two huge baked Alaskas that Paula was serving for dessert.

It was after three in the morning before the final guests left. Helen and Nick were staying the night. Nicola was staying at a friend's house and Paula impulsively insisted they sleep in her room. She'd sleep in one of the divans. Jenny, Beth and Rachel had offered to stay and help tidy up but Kieran had told them to go home. He was washing up.

'Are you sure you don't want us to help, darling?' Helen yawned.

'Go to bed,' Paula ordered.

'I'll have this place cleared up in a jiffy,' Kieran declared, expertly stacking glasses on a tray.

He washed. She dried. It only took them half an hour.

'Sit down, I'll make us a cup of coffee and then I'll head off,' Kieran said kindly. Paula was wilted at this stage so she made no demur. They sat together at the small kitchen table sipping their coffee.

'You're in love with Nick, aren't you?' Kieran said quietly.

Paula nearly fell off her chair.

'How did you know?' She was so shocked she couldn't even deny it. Was it so obvious?

'I saw your face when he was kissing Helen. Don't worry, I'm sure no-one else noticed. It's just that I know what it's like to love someone who doesn't love you,' he said sadly.

'Oh Kieran.' She stretched out her hand and took his. No-one understood better than she what he was experiencing.

'Is it Tina? But she loves you. I'm sure if you tell her she'll welcome you back with open arms.'

Kieran looked at her. 'How can you be so blind, Paula?' he asked and there was a hint of anger in his voice.

'What? . . . I don't know what you mean. If it's not Tina who is it?' she asked, perplexed.

'Oh for God's sake, Paula!' He stood up and stared down at her.

'It's you. I love you. I can't help it. Just as you can't help the way you feel about him, I can't help the way I feel about you. I've wanted to say it for a long time but something held me back. I always knew there was someone. I didn't realize it was Nick.'

'Kieran . . . I . . . I don't know what to say. ' She was stunned.

'Don't say anything. I think I've said enough for the two of us.' Kieran frowned. He walked out into the hall and shrugged himself into his black leather jacket, pulled on his leather gauntlets and picked up his shiny black helmet.

'You look like the Knight Rider,' Paula said idiotically.

'He always gets his woman,' Kieran said dryly. They stared at each other. Paula started to cry.

'Don't! Paula, I'm sorry. Don't cry.' Kieran put his arms around her and kissed the top of her head. 'I shouldn't have said anything.'

'I wish it could be different. I'd love to be in love with you.'

'Maybe you could try,' he murmured into her hair. He raised her face to his and kissed her lightly on the lips. 'What a pair we are,' he said wryly.

Paula watched him leave. She felt unnerved. She couldn't think about this now. It was too upsetting. She went back into the sitting-room and poured herself a brandy and brought it out to the kitchen. She knew she'd had enough to drink but she wanted to make herself feel woozy so that she would fall instantly asleep and not have to think about anything.

She sipped the amber liquid, feeling it warm the inside of her stomach. Imagine Kieran being in love with her! And she'd never even suspected. Looking back, now that she knew, of course it was obvious. But Kieran had accused her of being blind and it was true. She had eyes for just one man. If only she wasn't imprisoned by her love for Nick. Things might have been different. She didn't want to be in love with Nick. She'd never asked to fall in love with him. How did you learn to *unlove* someone? Paula thought of Nick kissing Helen and started to cry. Maybe they were making love in her bed right now. She shouldn't have invited them to stay the night. What kind of a masochist was she at all? She lowered her head on her arms and let the tears flow.

'Paula? Paula, what's wrong?' Shocked, Paula raised her head and saw Nick standing in the doorway.

'Oh Nick,' she sobbed. 'Oh Nick.'

Chapter Eighty-Six

'What is it?' Nick asked, full of concern, putting his arms around her. Paula rested her cheek against his bare chest. He was barefoot and wearing only his trousers. She inhaled the male musky scent of him like a drowning woman gasping for air. She could hear the steady beat of his heart against her ear. The roughness of his chest hair against her cheek told her that this was no fantasy. After all the years of dreaming, this was real.

'Hold me, Nick.' She clung tightly to him.

'Tell me what's wrong. Is it Kieran? Did you have a row?' Nick stared down at her, worried.

Mutely, she shook her head. She just wanted to stand in the circle of his arms and never move. The same wonderful feeling of being utterly cherished that she'd felt so many years ago, when he'd comforted her because he'd thought she was upset over Barry, swept over her. Being in his arms was like coming home.

'What is it, Paula? This isn't like you at all. Tell me what's wrong. Let me help.' He kissed the top of her head. 'Tell me,' he urged. 'We've always looked out for one another. If you're in trouble I want to know about it. Come on, Mrs Mops.' His use of her nickname and the gentleness of his voice almost started her weeping again.

Paula looked at him. He hadn't changed much over the years. The lines around his mouth and eyes were more defined. His tawny hair was touched with grey. But he was still the same handsome, kind man she'd fallen in love with. Her gaze rested on his mouth. He had such an attractive mouth. She loved the firm determined jut of his jaw and the sexy cleft of his chin. More than anything in the world she wanted to be kissed by him. All the years of longing for him overwhelmed her. She couldn't sustain the effort it took to fight her attraction to him. She had to know if she could make him want her, as she wanted him. She had to know if Nick could ever love her.

Paula felt as if she was in a dream.

'Nick,' she said slowly, raising heavy eyes to his. 'Haven't you ever wondered what you and I would have been like?' She put her arms around him and kissed him with all the longing and passion that had been buried deep inside her. Her hands caressed his chest, his shoulders, the strong column of his neck. She couldn't get enough of him.

Nick drew away in shock.

'Paula! Jesus, this is madness!' He stared at her in horror.

'I love you, Nick. I always have. Don't push me away.' She was beyond caring. She took his hand and placed it in the opening of her dress on her breast and kissed him again, curving herself against him, wanting to feel his response. This time his arms tightened around her and his mouth opened against hers. She felt his tongue inside her. Felt his thumb caress her nipple until it hardened in desire. 'Oh Nick,' she breathed against his mouth as she felt his body respond. Paula felt fiercely triumphant. She'd aroused him. Just as she always knew she would. She deepened her kiss, tasting him, teasing him, desire flaming through her. He kissed her back hungrily, his tongue probing, demanding. His hands slid down over her hips, moulding her against his hard thrusting body. Paula arched against him, frantic for him, as he caressed the softness of her inner thigh, his fingers tracing paths of fire upwards towards the hot aching part of her that only he could satisfy.

'Oh Nick! Nick . . . ' She almost couldn't breathe. Her heart was pounding in her ears.

'No!' he said harshly. 'No. Paula, this is wrong. What in the name of God am I doing?' He held her away from him and stared at her, shock and anger in his eyes.

'Don't look at me like that,' she pleaded. 'I love you. I need you. Please don't stop. Please, Nick, I want you inside me.'

'Stop it! What about Helen? I won't do this to Helen. I won't let you do it. I love Helen.' He gave her an angry shake.

'You wanted me just now. You can't deny that!' Paula said desperately. 'Just once, Nick. Make love to me just once. You've ruined other men for me. Kieran loves me but all I want is you. When I'm with other men all I think of is you. It's driving me crazy. Don't leave me like this.'

'I don't want to hear any more, Paula. Forget you've said all this.'

She'd never seen him look so angry. It excited her.

'You're angry because now you'll always be wondering what it would have been like, Nick, won't you?' She slid the zip of his fly down.

'Let me,' she said huskily and heard him give a little groan of pleasure as she touched him.

'Oh, God,' he muttered, his breathing ragged and uneven.

'I want you, Nick. I want to give you pleasure like you've never had before,' Paula whispered. She caressed and stroked him and heard his quickened breathing as she aroused him even more. 'You want me as much as I want you. Nick, I'll do anything you want—'

'Stop it!' His hand snaked down and grabbed her by the wrist. 'Paula, have you lost your senses?'

'Please, Nick,' she begged. 'I've wanted you ever since I was a teenager. I can't stand it any more. I really love you.'

'No! This isn't right.' His grip tightened around her wrist, hurting her. He stared down into her eyes. 'It isn't right,' he repeated harshly.

'It is. It is.' Paula caressed his cheek and then the firm outline of his mouth.

'Oh my God!' she heard Helen exclaim. In a daze, Paula turned to see her aunt framed in the doorway.

Chapter Eighty-Seven

'Nick . . . Paula . . . What are you doing?' Helen was white with shock. Paula sobered up instantly.

'What do you mean, Helen?' she said hastily. 'Kieran and I had a row, I was crying. Nick was just giving me a cuddle.' Nick, who had his back to Helen, had zipped up his fly.

'Why were you looking at Nick like that? Why were you pleading with him? What's going on?' Helen stared from one to the other.

'It's all right, Helen, nothing's going on,' Nick said wearily. 'Paula was tipsy and upset over her row with Kieran. I said I was going to call you and she asked me not to.'

'I don't believe you. I'm not a fool,' Helen said frantically. 'You looked as if you'd just been kissing.'

'Helen, please. You're wrong.' Paula was sick with fright. 'Kieran loves me . . . and I think I love him,' she lied. 'We just had a row because I wanted him to get a taxi instead of going home on the bike. I was worried and I told Nick and then I started to cry and he put his arms around me. That's all there is to it. I can't believe you'd think otherwise.'

'I'm going to bed,' Helen said shakily. 'I was waiting for Nick to bring me in a glass of water.'

'Here, I'll get it for you,' Paula offered. She poured her aunt a glass of water and handed it to her with shaking hands. Silently, Helen took it and walked out of the kitchen.

Nick stared at her. 'I hope you're happy now,' he said in disgust.

'I'll never be happy, Nick, as long as it's my misfortune to be in love with you,' she said bitterly.

'You don't know the meaning of the word,' he snapped and walked out of the kitchen leaving her shaking.

Helen lay in bed waiting for Nick. Her heart was thumping. Had she imagined it? Had Nick and Paula been embracing? What was wrong with her? she thought in disgust. Paula and Nick loved her. Why was she feeling so unsettled these past few months? It was the change. The hot flushes, the dryness, the edgy moods. It was a horrible feeling. She felt scared and unattractive. She felt middle-aged, like a different woman. She couldn't blame Nick if he found Paula more attractive. She was young and vibrant and firm of body, not like her sagging stretch-marked aunt.

Hot tears trickled silently down her cheeks. She'd made an awful fool of herself back there in the kitchen. Maybe she should go and apologize. Helen bit her lip in the dark. She had been imagining it, hadn't she? Paula and Nick would never betray her.

She heard Nick open the door. Helen lay in the dark trying to stop crying. He took off his trousers and got into bed beside her.

'Are you all right, Helen?' he asked tiredly. She was too choked up to answer. Nick turned and leaned on his elbow and looked down at her. 'Stop crying, Helen.' He gently caressed her cheek.

'Do you love me still?' She sobbed. 'Do you find me attractive?'

'Of course I love you. I'll always love you. I'll always find you attractive,' Nick said vehemently. 'Don't ever doubt it, Helen.'

'It's just, lately I feel so peculiar. I feel tired all the time. I'm getting hot flushes. I think it's the menopause,' she wept. 'I'm going to be a dried-up old prune.'

'No you're not,' Nick soothed. 'Why didn't you tell me about this before? Don't keep things to yourself, Helen.

We'll go to the doctor on Monday and get you seen to. Maybe she will give you some of those HTR things I've read about.'

'HRT.' Helen gave a shaky laugh.

'Should I go and apologize to Paula?' she asked hesitantly.

'Paula's had too much to drink, Helen. She's probably asleep by now. Leave her be until the morning,' Nick said gently. 'Now let me put my arms around you and go to sleep, I'm not used to partying until the early hours.'

'I love you, Nick,' Helen murmured sleepily.

'And I love you,' she heard him say as his arms tightened around her. She had to believe it. Wanted desperately to believe it. Nick's lips caressed her shoulder. 'Go to sleep, Helen,' he murmured. 'We've an early start in the morning.'

Helen lay in the reassuring circle of his arms and the tension eased out of her body. Nick was right. HRT might be just the thing for her. At least it would stop her thinking like a crazy woman . . . because she was crazy to think that Nick and Paula would ever betray her.

Nick listened to Helen's deep breathing and wished he could sleep. He lay in the darkness replaying what had occurred between him and Paula, over and over.

She'd said she loved him. Said she'd always loved him. It was like a bolt from the blue. There'd always been a huge bond between them, he couldn't deny that. They had a warm affectionate teasing relationship almost from the start when she'd come to housekeep for him, that had developed over the years into a love of sorts, he supposed. Not the sort of love Paula felt. She was very special and important to him, there was no denying it, but he'd never thought of her other than as Helen's niece. He'd watched her growing up from a beautiful determined teenager to a beautiful successful young woman. He'd seen men come and go in her life. There'd been that PE teacher, and then the chap in Spain that she'd told Helen about. There'd been some mention of a Frenchman. Now Kieran was supposed to have told her he loved her. He could understand why men were attracted to Paula. She *was* beautiful.

Nick groaned softly in the dark remembering her kisses. Her mouth had tasted like honey. Her body had been so sensual against his. Her breasts soft and firm and rounded. She wanted him. It was incredible. What did she find attractive about him? It wasn't just that she'd been drunk. She meant every word she said. Her urgency, her passion had aroused him so that he'd forgotten everything except the desire to explore and caress and kiss her. No-one, not Eleanor, not Helen, or any of the women he'd been involved with, had ever kissed him with such hunger and desire as Paula had. He'd have to have been made of stone not to respond. It had been madness. At least he could comfort himself that he'd come to his senses even before Helen arrived. He wouldn't have made love to Paula, he loved Helen too much. Or would he have? He'd wanted her. She'd aroused him very easily. The feel of her young firm urgent body had turned him on. He remembered the feel of her lovely breasts and the rush of pleasure and desire he'd experienced when Paula had touched him.

She was right, Nick thought grimly. Now whenever he looked at her, he would always wonder what it would have been like. The thought aroused him even more. He wanted her now. He turned away from Helen.

Oh Paula, he thought tiredly. Why me? You could have any man you desire. Why did you choose me?

Paula undressed in the dark and got into one of the divans in the guest room. She had a blinding headache. She felt nauseous. She was still trembling after what had happened. Why had she done it? Why had she snapped after all these years of damping down her feelings and gritting her teeth and getting on with it?

If only Nick hadn't come in to the kitchen. If he hadn't

put his arms around her. Once he'd put his arms around her and she'd rested her cheek against the dark tangle of hair on his chest and felt his heartbeat beneath her, she was lost. And then when he'd responded to her kisses and she'd felt the firm pressure of his mouth on hers and felt his tongue tasting her, she'd wanted him so badly she couldn't hold back. For those brief few moments Nick wanted her too. And then sanity came rushing back and he'd looked at her in disgust and told her to stop. He loved Helen. Even then, she'd begged him to make love to her. *Begged* him. Blood rushed to her cheeks at the memory. She had no pride. Just need. A need that had overpowered her so much that she had betrayed Helen and made Nick despise her. Now both of them were lost to her forever.

Paula buried her face in the pillow, too numb to cry.

There was no sleep for her that night. She tossed and turned, frantic with grief and worry. What would she do if Helen wanted nothing to do with her? Had Helen believed her when she lied and said Nick was just comforting her? She'd never be able to look Nick in the face again. Maybe they wouldn't let her see Nicola again. Her life was crumbling around her.

Around eight-thirty the next morning Paula heard voices in the next bedroom. Helen and Nick were awake. She slipped into her dressing-gown and went down to the kitchen to put the kettle on for the tea. A movement at the door made her turn around. Her heart was thumping. It was Helen. She was already dressed.

'Good morning,' Paula said warily.

'Hello,' Helen said quietly. They looked at each other.

'About last night—'

'I'm sorry, Paula, I was tired and emotional,' Helen said, embarrassed.

Relief washed over Paula. Thank you, God, she sent up the heartfelt prayer. 'I was pretty emotional myself. I think I drowned Nick,' she said lightly. 'That will teach me to drink brandy as a nightcap.' Helen held out her arms. Paula rushed into them and hugged her aunt tightly. She was consumed with guilt. But that would be her punishment. Anything was worth Helen's peace of mind. Over Helen's shoulder Paula saw Nick stop short as he saw them embracing. His blue eyes met Paula's. There was no warmth in them. Things would never be the same between them again. She had effectively quenched the affection he'd felt for her ever since they'd known each other. Paula took a deep breath. She'd ruined everything and destroyed Nick's friendship. She had to live with the consequences.

'What would you like for breakfast?' she asked quietly.

'We won't have anything, Paula. We've to collect Nicola early, Barbara has visitors coming and I don't want to impose,' Helen said.

'Won't you even have coffee?' she asked, looking directly at Nick.

'No thanks, Paula. I'll make something when we get home. Unless Nick wants a cup?'

'No, I'll wait, thanks,' he said evenly.

'Why don't you go back to bed, you look exhausted?' Helen suggested.

'Yeah, I'll do that.' Paula sighed.

They got their coats and Paula stood at the door watching them as they walked down the carpeted landing. Helen turned to wave. Nick didn't look back.

Helen had made the bed in her bedroom. Paula slid in between the sheets and tried not to think that Nick had slept between them the night before. She was completely drained and too tired to think. She fell asleep cuddling a pillow against her.

The chimes of the doorbell woke her from a deep sleep. For a minute, she didn't know where she was. Memories returned. The burden descended on her shoulders.

It was Kieran. Paula pressed the buzzer and let him in. She knew she looked a sight, she was too dispirited to care.

'God, you look rough,' he said. Tears came to her eyes. She turned away so he wouldn't see them.

'Hey, I didn't mean to upset you, Paula. Don't mind me and my big mouth,' he apologized.

'I did something awful last night,' she blurted out. 'I told Nick I loved him, I tried to get him to make love to me. Helen nearly caught us and now he hates me.' Paula covered her face and wept bitter tears. Kieran looked at her, an expression of pain and pity in his eyes.

'Come here,' he said gently and led her to the sofa. He held her until she stopped crying. 'Tell me about it from the beginning.' Paula told him and blushed as she confessed that she'd used him as a scapegoat.

'That's OK,' he said quietly. 'I just came by to tell you that what I said last night doesn't affect our business relationship as far as I'm concerned.'

'I don't know, Kieran, I don't know. I've got to get away. I've got to take a good long look at myself and see where I'm going and what I'm doing. I don't know if I'm going to stay in Ireland.'

'Don't do anything hasty,' he advised. 'Look, why don't you think about taking off for a week or two somewhere? Take Jennifer with you. She needs a break. Use any of the company facilities and just go away and relax and put things in perspective. *Then* make your decisions,' he said firmly.

Paula nodded. The thought of running away for a week or so was just what she needed.

'I'll speak to Jenny and see if she's interested,' she agreed.

'Good.'

'You're very good to me, Kieran,' Paula murmured.

'I'm a sucker for a damsel in distress,' he said lightly. 'And I'll never give up hope.'

'Oh Kieran—'

'Don't say anything. I just want you to know it. Now go and have a look through the brochures and decide where you want to go. We'll fix something up tomorrow.' Kieran stood up, kissed her on the cheek and walked out of the sitting-room. Paula heard the front door close. He was a good man. Could she ever fall in love with him? The memory of Nick kissing her crowded her mind.

'Stop it,' she gritted. She picked up the current edition of the Holiday Villa brochure and began to flick through it. Anything to take her mind off the events of the night before. With grim determination, Paula began the task of selecting her holiday location.

The Holiday

Chapter Eighty-Eight

Paula closed the Holiday Villa file on her computer terminal and sat back in her chair with a thoughtful expression on her face. With Easter coming up, many of the villas were booked. There were two vacancies in Majorca, one in Lanzarote and one in Corfu. She didn't care where they went. Jennifer could take her pick. Kieran had planted the idea in her mind and now she was anxious to get away. She needed a holiday to try and get her thoughts together. As soon as he'd left her, Paula showered and dressed and drove over to the office to see what was available. She was running away but she didn't care. The way she felt, she wanted to get as far away as possible and never stop running.

She lifted the phone and dialled Jennifer's number. Jennifer answered and Paula knew from the tone in her friend's voice that she was making a huge effort to be cheerful. The miscarriage had hit her badly.

'Hi, it's me,' Paula said. 'I was wondering if you'll be at home for the next hour or so, I wanted to pop in and ask you something.'

'Ask me what?' Jennifer wanted to know.

'I can't talk to you here,' Paula said hastily. 'I'm in the office.'

'Paula Matthews, you'll end up a workaholic!' Jennifer remonstrated. 'Going in to the office on Saturday. Are you mad? I thought you'd be wrecked after last night.'

'I am. Jenny, something happened after you left. It was horrible. I'll tell you all about it when I see you,' Paula replied. 'I don't want to go into it on the phone. Will we be able to have a bit of privacy? I know Rachel's staying to look after you for the few days. But it's too private to talk to anyone else about it, except you.'

'I'm here on my own. An aunt of theirs is in hospital and they've gone to visit her so I'll have the kettle on for you. Hurry on,' Jennifer instructed.

'I'm on my way,' Paula promised.

What on earth was wrong with Paula, Jennifer wondered as she went out to the kitchen to put on the kettle. Everything had gone very well at the party the previous night. The only people who'd stayed were Helen, Nick and Kieran. Paula'd said something horrible had happened. Jennifer couldn't figure it out at all. She stretched up to one of the presses for a packet of biscuits, and winced at the pain in her ribs. She had a lot of bruising still, although ugly purple and black had faded to a dull yellow.

Jennifer sighed. She'd tried to get into the spirit of the party last night, not wanting to be a party-pooper with a long face. It was an effort to put on a brave front. She knew Ronan was worried about her. He watched her like a hawk. It wasn't fair to him to be always crying and down in the dumps. He was as upset as she was about losing the baby, but he tried to keep cheerful for her. The least she could do was to make the same effort for him. Kieran had been his usual kind self. She was off work for as long as she wanted, on full sick pay.

And Rachel had been a topper. She'd been on a Cert with a bad dose of tonsillitis and laryngitis but once she'd heard of Jennifer's accident, she'd arrived up to Dublin to help out while Jennifer was confined to bed for the first few days home from the hospital. Rachel couldn't do enough for her. She wouldn't let Jennifer do a tap, even though she wasn't well herself. Rachel was unsettled too, knowing that she was going to have to leave the house she was living in and get a place of her own. Everybody had their own little problems, Jennifer thought ruefully as she set out the cups. She wondered what was up with Paula. A half an hour later, Jennifer was hearing all about it.

'I can't believe I did it. I can't believe I told Nick I loved him. I begged him to make love to me, Jenny, and then Helen walked in on top of us. I still feel sick when I think about it.' Paula put her hand up to her quivering lip and tried to control herself.

'Oh, Paula.' Jennifer put her arms around her friend and pitied her from the bottom of her heart. 'Maybe Nick will blame it on the few drinks you had,' she said.

'No, I don't think so. You should have seen the way he looked at me this morning. He thinks I'm the lowest of the low. And he's right. If he'd wanted me I would have made love with him there and then. Knowing that Helen was in my bedroom.'

'You were drunk, Paula,' Jennifer said firmly.

'I wasn't *that* drunk,' Paula groaned. 'I behaved very badly. And the awful thing is I still love him, I still want him. I don't know how to get him out of my head.' She started to cry. Jennifer stroked her hair. Everyone always thought Paula was such a strong, controlled, on-top-of-things type of person. They should see her now, crying her eyes out, frantic and unsure. Jennifer knew how difficult it had been for her to discover that Nick and Helen were lovers. That Helen was pregnant. She knew Paula had battled against her attraction to Nick. Her moment of weakness had cost her much.

'Do you think you could ever feel anything for Kieran?' Jennifer asked gently.

Paula wiped her eyes. 'I wish I could, Jenny. I've never thought of him like that. Kieran's just Kieran. Someone to plan strategies with, someone to argue and fight with, someone to have laughs with—'

'You could be describing many a marriage there,' Jennifer interjected, smiling. When Paula told Jennifer that Kieran was in love with her it was as if something had clicked into place. She should have seen it straight away. It was sticking out a mile. Thinking back, Jennifer remembered how Kieran always wanted to talk about Paula and would steer the conversation in that direction.

When the Scullys had been acting up, threatening legal action, Jennifer had heard Kieran tell their legal advisor, 'We back Paula the whole way on this, I don't care what money we lose.' It hadn't gone to court. The Scullys backed down and made an out-of-court settlement. Paula was away at the time and when she'd come back from her trip, Kieran sent her a huge bouquet with a note of congratulations. When Paula was in the office, Kieran was always making excuses to go and sit on her desk and chat despite Paula's protests that she had work to do. They were very alike in some ways. Full of enthusiasm for their ventures, attractive charismatic people. Both extremely hard workers. If Paula hadn't been so besotted with Nick she might have looked at Kieran in a different light. It was ironic, thought Jennifer as she poured the coffee, Kieran was going through the same pain Paula was. He was in love with her and she wasn't in love with him. It was all very depressing.

Paula took the Holiday Villa brochure out of her bag. 'How would you fancy a week, ten days or a fortnight away?' She gave a wry grin. 'Kieran got such a shock when I said I might leave the country and go abroad that he suggested I go on holidays, have a good think and then make a decision.'

'That's a good idea,' Jennifer said firmly. 'There's no point in you haring off just because you're upset now. Kieran's a very sensible guy.'

'I know. He's very generous too, it was he who suggested you come on holidays as well. He thinks you could do with the break.'

'Did he?' Jennifer was pleased by her employer's thoughtfulness.

'We can use any of the company facilities. I've checked out the availability of villas. Majorca, Lanzarote and Corfu are available. Would you be interested?' Paula asked, hopefully.

'It sounds lovely,' Jennifer said regretfully. 'I know

714

Ronan would think it's a great idea but I have Rachel staying with me for her Easter holidays. Even though she was sick herself, she came up to Dublin to look after me when I came out of hospital. It would be very rude to turn around and say, I'm taking off on holidays with Paula. Bye, bye.'

'Ask her to come along. They're all three-bedroom luxury villas, there'll be more than enough room for three of us.'

'Are you serious?' Jennifer looked at Paula in surprise.

'Sure, why not? Rachel's easy to get on with. She might enjoy it.'

'Oh, she would,' Jennifer enthused. 'She's never been on a foreign holiday and she adores the sun. It would do her all the good in the world. Are you sure you wouldn't mind if she came along? I know you're not in good form.'

'I don't mind at all if it means you'll come away for a few days with me. It would be a bit like old times, wouldn't it?'

Jennifer grinned. 'You can say that again.'

'Right, where are we going, and for how long?' Paula opened the brochure and showed Jennifer the choices available.

They decided to take the villa in Corfu. Paula said it was a beautiful villa set in an olive grove just yards from the beach. It had its own pool, Jacuzzi and sauna. A housekeeper who came from the nearby village would live in, if required. Of their four choices it was the most luxurious and the one Paula recommended.

'Sounds gorgeous, I love the part that says "set in an olive grove and yards from a sandy tree-fringed beach."'

Paula smiled. 'Are we on then?'

'I think so.' Jennifer smiled back. 'I'll see what Ronan and Rachel have to say when they get home.'

'Let me know, and I'll make the arrangements on Monday morning. I'll give the office a call and tell them to reserve Villa Athena, for ten days, from Holy Thursday. How's that?'

'Are you sure ten days is enough? Only I'd feel a bit mean going off on two weeks' holidays without Ronan. And Rachel would have to be back at school before the fortnight was out,' Jennifer said.

'Ten days is fine,' Paula assured her. 'You know me, I'll probably start to get itchy feet after a week.'

'Paula, I'm warning you, you'd want to start taking things a bit easier or you're going to get burnt out. You never give yourself a minute. You don't know how to relax any more. I'm telling you, when we get to Corfu, you're going to flop, or I'll want to know the reason why,' Jennifer scolded.

'OK, OK,' Paula laughed. 'It's a deal.' She stood up and gave Jennifer a hug. 'Thanks for everything. Thanks for being a great pal. It really helps.'

'That's what friends are for and you've done the same for me when I needed it.' Jennifer hugged her back.

It would be nice going away with Paula for a holiday. They hadn't been on one together since Jennifer's marriage. She wouldn't have to put on an act with Paula. She wouldn't have to pretend to feel cheerful when she was feeling sad. Paula wouldn't expect her to gad about like they'd done when they'd been in Spain together. She was pretty down in the dumps herself. She wouldn't want to be out discoing and partying. Rachel certainly wasn't into the hectic social life either. It could be ten days of relaxation and coming to terms with their own problems. Maybe it would do them all the good in the world. Jennifer's spirits lifted for the first time since the accident. She was dying for Rachel to come home to see what she'd say about the idea.

'I'd love to come,' Rachel said ecstatically. 'Are you sure, though? Would you not prefer to go off with Paula on your own?'

'It was Paula's idea and I think it's great. We'd love you to come,' Jennifer said warmly.

'I've no passport,' Rachel exclaimed.

'We can organize that first thing Monday morning,' Jennifer assured her.

'I'll have to go home to get clothes and things.' Rachel frowned.

'Listen to me, Rachel Stapleton.' Jennifer seized her opportunity. 'You and I are going in to town on Monday and you're going to buy a whole new summer wardrobe. You don't need to go home. You have a case up here with you. You have your toiletries and make-up. Anything else you need, we can buy.'

'I should be saving, Jenny, especially now as I'm going to have to get a place of my own.'

'Bugger saving,' Jennifer retorted. 'You've been saving for years, you must have a small fortune saved. You never treat yourself. You never go anywhere. You never do anything. All you have to pay for is the flight, the accommodation's taken care of. You badly need some new clothes. And I'm just the woman to go on a spending spree with. Isn't that right, Ronan?' She grinned at her husband, who was delighted to see a bit of her old spark.

'Absolutely, Rach, you'll be in the hands of an expert and you won't know what's hit you. But it'll be fun,' he promised. He was very pleased that Paula had suggested Rachel go on holidays with her and Jenny. It was just what his sister needed.

'Oh, all right!' Rachel threw caution to the winds. 'Will you be up to going into town?'

'Try and stop me.' Jennifer laughed.

'Try on these culottes, I've a pair of Bermudas here as well,' Jennifer instructed. They were in adjoining changing cubicles in Marks & Spencers. Rachel didn't know whether she was on her head or her heels. She'd spent the morning shopping with Jennifer. They'd bought bags of clothes in Dunnes. Swimwear, sandals, espadrilles, shorts, T-shirts. They'd been to Roches and bought two beautiful sundresses and a gorgeous Michael H summer suit. Now they were in Marks & Spencers and she was trying on trousers and leggings, Jennifer was passing in more clothes that she'd selected and Rachel felt on an absolute high. She'd gone beyond worrying about the price of things. She was now in the exhilaration stage of a spree, when everything she saw, she wanted. Jennifer was no help in urging caution. All she'd said that morning was, 'Buy it.'

'Let's see the culottes.' Jennifer poked her head through the curtains. 'They're gorgeous,' she exclaimed, staring in admiration at the khaki culottes with matching jacket and white T-shirt. 'Buy it,' she instructed.

Rachel laughed. She'd every intention of buying it.

'You know, you've a really good figure, you should make the most of it,' Jennifer observed as they sat, an hour later, having lunch in Flanagans. 'Those lycra miniskirts look fabulous on you.'

'I hope I'll have the nerve to wear them,' Rachel said.

'You'll wear them,' Jennifer said with a glint in her eye.

'She's very bossy, isn't she?' Paula grinned. She'd met them for lunch. 'Have you got everything?'

'I think so. I think Jenny's happy now that I'm practically penniless,' Rachel teased.

'I'm getting my hair done tomorrow and I'm having a leg wax. I think you should do the same,' Jennifer retorted.

'A leg wax!' Rachel paled. 'I don't think so.'

'It makes your legs very smooth, and when you've got a tan it looks great,' Jennifer declared. 'Go on. Be a devil!' she dared.

'Oh, all right,' Rachel agreed. At this stage she was game for anything.

'I'll make an appointment for your hair with Nikki, my hairdresser, and one with Susan in the beauty salon in Kris Morton's. It's exactly what you need to finish up your spree,' Jennifer assured her.

'I can't believe the difference,' Ronan said the next evening as he saw the vision before him. Rachel had been persuaded to have her hair cropped short in an elegant sophisticated layered look. Nikki had put highlights in so that Rachel's hair shone with blond glints. She'd stopped wearing glasses soon after she started working and wore contact lenses instead. When she looked at herself in the mirror in her bedroom, wearing a tight floral lycra mini and a white T-shirt, Rachel couldn't believe it was her.

It was as if she was another person. The curly hair that had straggled to her shoulders was gone. The short sharp hairstyle made her look much younger and very contemporary. Rachel couldn't believe how slim and nicely proportioned she was in her new clothes that fitted so snugly. Usually she wore loose-fitting cardigans and skirts and blouses. Really hickey clothes. When she looked at herself now Rachel had to admit that she'd been a Mary Hick. She'd never bothered much with her appearance. She'd never tried to make herself glamorous like Paula and Jennifer. From now on she would, she decided. It was fun buying clothes. She'd never looked as good. She was not going to slip back into her lazy couldn't-care-less ways after her holidays. As Jennifer said, 'Bugger saving.' She'd more than enough for a deposit on a small house or apartment. In future she was going to look after her appearance and treat herself to new fashionable clothes every so often. Blouses and cardigans would be consigned to the bin.

'What do you think?' Rachel did a twirl for her brother as Jennifer looked on in satisfaction.

'The men of Corfu will drool at the mouth when you three beauties arrive. Maybe I should go with you after all.' Ronan pretended to scowl. Rachel giggled, she felt on top of the world. She might even have a holiday affair. She was so excited by her new looks and her new wardrobe, she might do anything.

'Wasn't it very kind of Kieran to give Jennifer a free holiday all the same?' Kit remarked to Brenda as she finished washing up after the tea. Brenda had dropped the children in for her to mind for an hour at lunch-time, but as usual, Brenda had taken advantage and didn't arrive to collect her offspring until after tea-time.

According to Brenda, there'd been some sort of protest march in town, and she'd got caught up in it and the traffic had been dire. Kit had to hand it to her daughter. Brenda never used the same excuse twice and was never stuck for one either. There was no point in getting annoyed, Brenda would never change. Kit knew, when she agreed to mind the kids, that she'd be landed with them. It was her own fault. All she had to do was say no. The next time she would.

'Jenny's going on holidays, the lucky sucker,' Brenda said enviously. What she wouldn't give to go on a holiday right now this minute. Still, after the accident and the miscarriage, Jennifer probably felt the need of a break. 'Ronan's lucky to work for a company. When Shay takes his holidays he loses two weeks' work,' Brenda grumbled, as she dried the knives and forks, a job she hated.

'Oh, Ronan's not going. It's girls only.' Kit squeezed out the dishcloth and wiped the taps and draining board.

'What girls?' Brenda asked sharply.

'Paula and Rachel. It's going to be Rachel's first holiday abroad and she's dying for it. They're going to stay in a luxury villa in Corfu that has its own swimming-pool. I'm delighted for Jenny, the poor dote. It was awful her losing the baby like that.'

Brenda stared out the window facing The Green. Jealousy, hurt and rage churned inside her. Paula and Rachel were going on holidays with Jennifer, and her sister hadn't even bothered to ask whether Brenda would like to go with them. But then Brenda had always been second best to Paula in Jennifer's eyes. And you'd think Miss Wishy-Washy Rachel was a saint the way Jennifer went on about her, just because she'd come from her sick-bed to Dublin to take care of Jennifer when she came out of hospital.

Brenda would have called in to make sure she was OK. It was no big deal, she thought grimly as she flung the knives and forks into the drawer. But Brenda didn't count, she thought, feeling immensely sorry for herself. She went to the back door and called the children.

'I don't want to come home,' whined Claudia. 'We're having races.'

'I don't want to come home either,' Lauren said, copying her sister.

Brenda was in no mood to be trifled with. 'Get out to the car, the pair of you, or I'll get the wooden spoon.' She scowled.

'But Mammy, I don't want to go.' Claudia immediately burst into tears.

'Get in the car,' yelled Brenda.

'It's all right, there's no need to cause a fuss,' Kit said crossly.

'That one is never satisfied. No matter what she gets she wants more. Well she can't have what she wants all the time and the sooner she learns that, the better,' Brenda snapped as she pulled Lauren's coat on, and handed John his jacket. Claudia pulled away from her as she went to put her coat on. Brenda gave her a slap across the legs. Claudia's put-on tears turned to howls of outrage.

'Out the door, madam,' Brenda ordered. Kit looked on in annoyance. It was rich to hear Brenda going on about Claudia never being satisfied with what she had. Because if there was one person who was never satisfied with her lot, it was Brenda. Kit knew exactly what was going on. Brenda was miffed because Jennifer was going on holiday with Paula and Rachel, and she was taking it out on the children. Did she expect Jennifer to ask her to go on holiday with them? Brenda had three children to take care of. Paula and Rachel had none. Brenda was never happy. She'd thought she'd never get married and have children and be able to give up work. Then when she had her children, she thought she'd never get back to work. She was always comparing her house to Jenny's, and what she had and what Jenny had. It infuriated Jennifer, who didn't give a fig about what anyone had.

'Stop taking your bad humour out on the children, Brenda,' Kit said quietly.

'You did it often enough when Grandpa Myles was giving you a hard time,' Brenda retorted.

Kit flushed. She couldn't think of an answer. Because the remark was true. She felt like giving Brenda a clip on the ear. She'd had a hell of a lot more to put up with than her daughter ever would.

'You've a sharp tongue, Brenda Myles,' she said coldly and walked out of the kitchen.

'It's Brenda Hanley,' Brenda muttered as she gathered up the various bits and pieces belonging to the children.

'What's all the yelling for?' Grandpa Myles stuck his head out of his room. 'How's a man expected to read his paper?'

'Mind your own business, you,' Brenda snarled.

'I can see where that young one of yours gets her impudence,' Grandpa shot back. 'God help her with the mother she's got.' He slammed his bedroom door.

'Bloody old nuisance,' Brenda fumed as she marched her offspring out the front door, without bothering to say thank you or goodbye to her mother.

'Where's the kids?' Shay asked an hour later when he arrived home from work.

'In bed, they were as bold as brass,' Brenda snapped. Shay said nothing. But his heart sank. Brenda was in very bad form these days.

'What's for dinner?'

'There's a pizza in the oven. Do you want some chips?' she said ungraciously.

'I'll make the chips,' Shay offered. 'Do you want some?'

'No thanks,' she said. 'I don't want any dinner. I'm not hungry. I'm going in to watch *EastEnders*.' Shay prudently decided to remain in the kitchen, it was obviously going to be one of those evenings.

Brenda sat scowling at Sharon and Grant. Sharon had a great tan, she must have been abroad. She was a TV star, of course, she'd be well able to afford to go abroad on holiday. Brenda couldn't concentrate on the soap, she was in such bad humour. It wouldn't have killed Jennifer to ask her to go on holiday. Shay's sister could surely be bribed to look after the kids. She was delighted with the money she'd made when they went away a couple of weeks ago for their anniversary.

Shay could bloody well fork out some money for her holiday. She'd given him half her gratuity for the mortgage and the central heating as well as paying for her own car, she thought, feeling very sorry for herself. She could just imagine the fun the three girls would have. Paula, no doubt, would be out discoing every night. She was a real party animal. It would all be new to Rachel. The first foreign holiday was always the best, she thought nostalgically, remembering her own, all those years ago. She wondered what had ever happened to Raul. One of her biggest regrets was that she hadn't slept with him. Raul would have been a hell of a lot sexier than Shay, she thought crankily as she folded a pair of her husband's Y-fronts that had a hole in the arse and put them in the clothes basket beside her.

Imagine lying in the sun, with no kids demanding attention, she thought wistfully. It was pelting rain outside. It had been a desperate winter of gales and storms. Imagine blue skies and the heat of the sun on your limbs. Imagine swimming in your own pool! Brenda could take no more. She jumped to her feet, grabbed her bag and rooted her coat out of the pile under the stairs.

'I'm going down to Jenny's,' she called out to Shay, who gave a sigh of relief. There was a football match on but the humour Brenda was in, he'd hesitated to ask if he could watch it after *EastEnders*. It would mean she'd miss *The Bill*, one of her favourite programmes.

'Tell her I was asking for her,' Shay called, emptying the chip basket onto his pizza. 'Don't rush back, I'll look after the kids, you deserve a night out!' He took a can of beer out of the fridge. The evening was turning out better than he'd hoped, he thought as he heard the front door close. He put his dinner on a tray and headed for the sitting-room. He threw a log on the fire, switched channels and stretched out on the sofa. Shay could hear the kids out of bed upstairs. They could play away, he decided, as long as they didn't disturb him or his match.

'Ya bloody idiot,' he swore happily as the Spurs goal-keeper let a goal through. Brenda and her bad humour already a distant memory.

Brenda sat tight-lipped at the traffic lights opposite St Michael's. There was no point in barging in on Jennifer and demanding to be allowed to go on holiday. That would get her sister's back up immediately. She'd have to be much more subtle than that. Impulsively she pulled into the parking space in front of the shops and got out of the car and went into the Winkel. Jennifer was mad about chocolate oranges, so she bought her one, and a couple of magazines for good measure. She paid for her purchases and sat back in the car. She'd have a quick flick through *Hello!*, she decided, before she gave it to Jenny. She sighed enviously at the sight of a suntanned Princess Caroline, and her children. And then turned the page to see Princess Diana in a backless gown attending some gala, also tanned and glowing. She was going on holidays with the girl Brenda vowed, and that was it.

'Hi, Jenny,' she beamed about fifteen minutes later as she handed her sister the magazines and chocolate orange. 'Are you feeling any better? I just told Shay I was coming down to see you, to ask if I can do any-thing for you. I know Rachel's here with you, but if there's anything at all I can do let me know,' Brenda said sweetly, stepping in to the hall.

'Thanks very much, Brenda,' Jennifer said, surprised. 'I feel better than I did. The bruising's not as bad and my ribs are healing. Physically I'm on the mend.'

'I know,' Brenda murmured, and this time she did feel sorry for her sister. 'You're young, Jenny, you'll get pregnant again. I know that doesn't seem a very helpful thing to say now but I don't know what else to say.'

'It's all right, Bren, I know what you mean. Will you have a cup of tea?' Jennifer asked.

'I'll make it,' Brenda offered. 'Where's Ronan and Rachel?'

'Ronan's at the gym and Rachel's upstairs writing a letter to a friend of hers in Singapore.' Jennifer led the way out to the kitchen. It was a beautiful kitchen, despite its small size, Brenda thought, looking at the immaculate grey and white presses and worktops. One of these days she was going to get Shay to order a fitted kitchen for her.

'When are you thinking of going back to work?' Brenda asked casually, wishing she could lead up to the subject of the holiday.

'Sometime after Easter,' Jennifer said. 'Kieran's very good, he's not putting any pressure on me at all.' It was on the tip of Brenda's tongue to say, maybe you should go on a little holiday, but it seemed a little ham-fisted. Have patience, Brenda told herself sternly. She didn't want to blow it.

Just then Rachel popped her head around the kitchen door to announce that she was going to post her letter, did Jennifer want anything from the shops? Brenda stared at her in amazement. She hardly recognized her.

'Rachel!' she exclaimed. 'Your hair is gorgeous. It's changed you completely. You look terrific,' Brenda admired, noting Rachel's slenderness in a new pair of jeans and a sweatshirt.

'It's all Jenny's fault.' Rachel beamed. 'She made me go on a spending spree to buy a whole load of new clothes and then she brought me to get my hair done and have a leg wax. So I got the hair chopped. It will be handy on holiday anyway.'

Brenda's heart raced. 'You're going on holiday?' she asked lightly. 'Lucky you. Where are you off to?'

'She's coming to Corfu with Paula and me. Kieran's offered us a villa, so we're going next Thursday,' Jennifer said over her shoulder as she made a pot of tea. That soon, thought Brenda in dismay. Well she'd have to get organized fast and that was all there was about it. She was due holidays, she'd add them on to her Easter ones. If Shay's sister wasn't free, Kit would surely look after the kids, she thought, conveniently forgetting that she'd been very narky with her mother earlier that day.

'A villa in Corfu,' Brenda breathed. 'It sounds divine.'

'It's a lovely one all right. We're taking it for ten days,' Jennifer agreed, pouring the tea. Ten days, *that* was perfect, Brenda thought excitedly. It was much less outrageous to take off for only ten days instead of the usual fourteen.

'I wish I was able to go,' she said wistfully and then paused, pretending to be thinking.

'Actually,' she remarked casually. 'I'm due holidays and with Easter added on, I'd have ten days.' She smiled at Jennifer and Rachel as if she'd just had a brilliant brainwave.

'Girls, I think I'll come with you,' Brenda announced.

Chapter Eighty-Nine

'Are you sure you don't mind, Paula? I still can't believe that she only found out about the holiday on Tuesday and she's organized to come with us tonight. I suppose I could have said there wasn't a seat. But I'd have felt really guilty then.' Jennifer sat twiddling the telephone cord. Her suitcase was packed and standing in the hall. She was all ready to go and it was only nine am.

'Look, you and I'll share the room with twin beds, Brenda can have one on her own, and Rachel the other, so stop worrying,' Paula said calmly.

'Yeah, but I know Brenda's not one of your favourite people.' Jennifer sighed. 'After all, it is your holiday too and I've already asked if I could bring Rachel. And now Brenda's tagging along. It's a bit much.'

'Forget it, will you. What could you do? She practically invited herself. Beth roared laughing when I told her, and said only that she's met the man of her dreams and is going to Kinsale with him, she'd have gatecrashed as well.'

Jennifer laughed. 'I know this is an awful thing to say about your own sister, but I'd much prefer if Beth was gatecrashing and not Brenda.'

'I'll tell you one thing,' Paula declared, 'Shay's a right softie.'

'He's probably looking forward to ten days of peace and quiet,' Jennifer said dryly.

'How's Rachel?' Paula asked.

'Jumping around like a Mexican bean.' Jennifer smiled. 'You'd think we were going on a world cruise.'

'I hope she enjoys herself,' Paula said. 'Listen, I'd

better go. I want to go in to the office for a couple of hours and then I suppose I ought to go and say goodbye to Helen.'

'Do that,' Jennifer said firmly. 'You've got to act as if everything's normal.' She heard Paula's sigh.

'I know,' her friend replied.

'And say goodbye to Kieran too,' Jennifer ordered.

'Kieran's right. You are a dictator.' Paula chuckled. 'See you later.'

Jennifer hung up and walked into the sitting-room. The day ahead seemed endless. She wished she was on the plane now, she hated hanging around. She dreaded saying goodbye to Ronan.

'It's only for ten days, you idiot,' she muttered. She'd be fine once she was there. She picked up the *Hello!* Brenda had brought a few days ago and began to flick through it. She couldn't concentrate. Brenda's surprise suggestion had taken the wind out of her sails. She had to admire her sister though. Brenda had organized her sister-in-law to mind the kids. She'd got her traveller's cheques, bought new clothes, had her hair done and her legs waxed and was raring to go. Brenda was something else.

Jennifer got up and went out to the kitchen. She'd made sure the freezer was full for Ronan. She'd prepared lasagnes and bologneses and beef casseroles and chicken chasseurs. All Ronan would have to do was to stick them in the microwave. She decided to bake him a rhubarb tart, his favourite. Maybe while she was at it, she'd make him a Banofi pie as well as a special treat. Happier now that she was doing something for Ronan, Jennifer started to sieve her flour.

Rachel parked her car in the ILAC car park and took the lift down to Dunnes Stores. She wanted to buy another bikini and a beach bag. She caught a glimpse of her reflection in a mirror. It was taking a while to get used to it but she was very pleased with her new image. She must remember to live up to it. Rachel straightened her shoulders and lifted her chin as she strode into Dunnes. When she'd bought her bits and pieces, she walked up Henry Street to one of the chemists. She wanted to buy some throat lozenges. Her throat was still a bit iffy and she didn't want to take any chances. She was standing at the counter waiting to be served when her glance alighted on a selection of packets of condoms. A madness came over her. She picked up a packet and handed it to the assistant.

'And a packet of Strepsils as well, please,' she said red-faced. The assistant went on chatting to her colleague as she rang up the purchase on the till. She took not the slightest bit of notice of Rachel or her condoms. Rachel stuffed the bag into her handbag and scurried out of the shop. What had possessed her?

'Better to be prepared just in case,' she told herself as she sat in the car. After all, she was going on her first holiday abroad. Lots of people had affairs on holidays. She might even have one herself. And unlikely though it was, at least she'd have taken responsibility for her protection. It was sensible to buy a packet of condoms if she was even thinking such thoughts.

She took the packet out and studied it. Twelve Durex Elite Condoms, she read. Ultimate sensitivity. Ultimate protection. Spermicidally lubricated. They even had a little leaflet showing you how to put it on. That was handy, Rachel thought, stuffing the packet back in her bag. She'd buy a cucumber in Corfu and practise putting one on it, she decided. She didn't want to look like a right eejit should the occasion arise.

Two hours later, she pulled into the car park of the Bon Secours Hospital in Glasnevin. Her Aunt Imelda, Theresa's elder sister, was recovering from a gall bladder operation. Rachel didn't know her aunt very well. She lived in Navan. The sisters had not been that close. Rachel could only remember her aunt visiting four or five times, and Theresa had visited Navan even less. After her mother died, Rachel lost contact except for sending Christmas cards. Ronan kept in touch, he was friendly with his cousin Mick. Because she was in Dublin during her aunt's hospitalisation, Rachel visited her. She decided to pop in for a few minutes to say goodbye to her before she went on holidays.

Her aunt was delighted to see her and was very impressed with her niece's new hairstyle. 'You must come and visit me when you get home,' Imelda invited.

'I will,' promised Rachel. She stayed for a half an hour chatting. She was running down the wide wooden hospital stairs when she saw a straight-backed, bespectacled familiar figure walking up the stairs. Oh God! Rachel thought in dismay as she recognized her father. He looked as sprightly as ever, his carriage upright. She'd seen him less than half a dozen times since she'd left home. She'd never gone home for Christmas, she'd stayed in Bray on her own rather than go back to her father. The only time they did meet was on Theresa's anniversary, when she and Ronan went home to attend Mass for their mother. Her father more or less ignored her. He'd never forgiven her for not attending his retirement do and for leaving home and not coming back. She had nothing to say to him, she felt nothing for him. His absence from her life was a blessing.

'Hello,' she said politely.

William raised his hat. 'Hello,' he said with a puzzled look on his face and carried on up the stairs. He doesn't recognize me, Rachel thought in shock. Her father turned around, and stared at her.

'Good God!' he exclaimed and stood looking down at her. 'What have you done to your hair?'

'I got it cut,' Rachel said.

'You look like a trollop with your skirt up around your buttocks,' William said in disgust. Some things never change, Rachel thought as she turned away and continued down the stairs. She had no intention of standing on the stairs of the Bon Secours Hospital, listening to her father lecturing her about the length of her skirt. She was wearing one of her new lycra minis. She wasn't going to let him make her feel self-conscious about it. She ran quickly down the stairs feeling more light-hearted with every step. Rachel never looked back. William had no power over her any more. He couldn't wound and hurt her with his sarcasm. She was free of him, she thought exuberantly. She'd a good mind to go back and wave the packet of condoms in his face. It might shut him up.

'Free, free, free,' she sang to herself as she got into her car and drove back to Jennifer's house. In another couple of hours she'd be on the plane to Corfu. She was going to have a ball.

'Carol, just make sure to give John a dry Weetabix at night. It stops him wetting the bed. You can put them to bed as early as you like. Shay'll look after himself in the evenings. The kids love chips and beans and sausages. You don't have to go to too much trouble cooking dinners. It won't kill them for ten days. I have the Easter Eggs bought, they're on top of my wardrobe. Just make sure they don't eat too much chocolate and sicken themselves.'

'No problem.' Carol laughed.

'Are you sure you don't mind looking after them for the ten days?' Brenda asked, knowing that it was too late for her sister-in-law to back out.

'The money'll come in handy,' Carol said. 'And I like looking at videos. It's a treat. We don't have a video at home.'

'Oh, I must give you my video card,' Brenda said, rooting in her bag. 'Tell Shay to pay for them. I'd better say goodbye to the kids. Shay, put my case in the car, will you?' she called. Brenda was very anxious to get going. She wouldn't relax until they were on the plane. She didn't want anything to go wrong. Shay was bringing her to the airport, where she was going to meet up with the others. She was leaving home an hour earlier than the girls. She wanted to have a drink with Shay, she told Carol.

Brenda peered around the sitting-room door. The children were glued to the video of *The Little Mermaid*. 'Bye, kids.'

John rushed over to give her a hug. Claudia and Lauren continued to be mesmerized by Ariel singing about her prince.

'Bye, Claudia.' Brenda bent down to kiss her daughter.

'Sure you won't forget my present?' Claudia said anxiously.

'No, I won't,' Brenda promised as she kissed Lauren. 'Be good for Carol and do what she tells you and as a special treat . . . ' She took three Cadbury's creme eggs out of her handbag and handed them to her delighted children.

'I'll miss you, Mammy,' John said.

'I know, pet. It's only for a few days. I'll be home soon.' Brenda felt a guilty tug at her maternal heart strings.

'I'd better go,' she said hastily, not wishing to be troubled by such feelings.

Shay had put her bag in the car. 'Come on, let's go while they're looking at the video,' she said.

A wave of relief washed over Brenda as Shay drove down Collins Avenue to the motorway that led to the airport. So far so good. Only a few hours left and she'd be on her way to ten days of bliss.

'I hope you have a lovely time.' Helen hugged Paula. 'I'll be thinking of you when we're in St Margaret's Bay on Easter Sunday.'

'Oh, you're going to go,' Paula said in surprise. She'd been under the impression that they were staying at home this year.

'Nick asked me if I'd like to go. I think the break would do us good,' Helen said quietly. 'I haven't been in very good form lately. I went to the doctor on Monday and she's put me on HRT. I'm beginning to feel better already.

I want to make it up to Nick, I've been a bit of a drip the last few months. Friday night showed just how paranoid I was getting.'

'Forget it,' Paula said hastily, cringing inside. She felt very uncomfortable and tense. She and Helen were in the kitchen. Nick and Kieran were in the sitting-room. All she wanted to do was to get away. But she knew she had to call and say goodbye to Helen. Jennifer was right. She must act as if things were normal.

Kieran called her in to his office earlier that day and told her to try to enjoy her holiday.

'Have you seen Helen and Nick since?' he asked her in his direct way.

'No,' Paula said shortly.

'Are you going to say goodbye to them?'

'God, you're worse than Jennifer,' she burst out.

'If you stay away from Helen, you're going to give her reason to think that you're avoiding her. She'll start wondering about what happened the night of the party. She'll start worrying. She'll start jumping to conclusions.' Kieran gave her a steady look. 'Don't make your aunt unhappy, Paula. I'll give you a lift to the airport and we can drop in and you can say goodbye to her.'

'Why are you doing this for me, Kieran?' Paula asked heatedly. 'You know I've nothing to give you in return. Why are you putting yourself through misery? Wouldn't it be better all round if I resigned from TransCon and went to London or New York?'

'You can't run away from it, Paula. Not if you don't want to cut yourself off from Helen and Nicola . . . and Nick.' Kieran's tone was grim.

'Why are you doing this, Kieran?' Paula repeated.

'Because you're a mate, Paula. As well as everything else. We've been through a lot together. And I don't want to lose the best director the company's got. So get your ass in gear and let's get home and get your stuff and get you to the airport. Ring Jenny and tell her I'm bringing you to the airport.'

Paula stood, uncharacteristically unsure of what to do.

'Get your skates on, woman,' Kieran ordered.

'If you say so,' she murmured.

'I do say so,' Kieran retorted firmly.

'Are you and Kieran going to be an item?' Helen interrupted her train of thought.

'I don't know, Helen,' Paula said truthfully. 'He's a very special man.'

'And you're a very special woman,' her aunt said fondly.

Guilt scorched through her. 'Can I run upstairs and give Nicola a kiss, I won't wake her?'

'Of course you can. Are you sure you won't have coffee?'

'No thanks, Helen, we're running late,' Paula said quickily. As she passed the sitting-room she could hear Nick and Kieran talking. At least there weren't any strained silences. She hadn't been able to meet Nick's eyes but he'd greeted her courteously for Helen and Kieran's benefit.

Her goddaughter was fast asleep, her long black lashes sweeping down over her cheeks and a half-smile on her face. She was beautiful. Paula stood looking at her, and had an overwhelming urge to wake her up and shower her with kisses. Oh to be that innocent and untroubled, she thought enviously. She slipped quietly from the room and closed the door gently behind her.

Nick was coming out of the sitting-room as she got to the bottom of the stairs. Their eyes met. The tension between them was palpable. He went to walk past her.

'Don't walk away from me, Nick,' Paula pleaded.

He stopped and turned to look at her. He looked tired and troubled. 'I have to, Paula. For my own peace of mind. I don't want to be alone with you.'

'For God's sake, Nick. I won't throw myself at you again,' she said angrily.

'It's not you I'm worried about . . . ' he retorted. Paula

was stunned. It was the last reaction she'd expected. The enormity of what he'd said made her realize just what she'd put Nick through. Her selfish act had caused the man she loved pain, confusion and unhappiness.

'I'm sorry, Nick,' she said quietly. 'I never meant any of this to happen. The last thing I wanted to do was to hurt you or Helen.' Paula turned away from him, afraid he'd see the tears sparkling in her eyes. She took a deep breath and another and heard him walk into the kitchen. As soon as she was composed, she walked into the sitting-room, where Helen and Kieran were laughing at some remark he'd made. Kieran took one look at her and stood up.

'We'd better get moving,' he said briskly. 'Time's running short.'

'Bye, darling.' Helen hugged her. 'Where's Nick? I'll tell him you're leaving.'

'I'm here,' Paula heard Nick say with forced cheeriness. 'Have a good holiday, Paula. See you when you get back.' He put his arms around her as he usually would and gave her a hug. Before, it would have been an affectionate bear hug. Now, it was just something done to reassure Helen that everything was normal.

They stood at the door waving as Kieran opened the car door for her. Paula's face felt like cracking at the effort it took to keep her smile in place. Before they got to the end of the road, she was in tears.

Kieran kept driving. He said nothing. He let her cry.

'I'm sorry,' she said a while later, after she'd composed herself.

'You might as well get it out of your system, there's no point in bottling things up,' he said despondently.

'Kieran, we can't go on like this either. It's not fair to you.' Paula groaned. 'I'm going to resign.'

'Who said life's fair?' Kieran retorted. 'And if you resign, I'll never speak to you again.'

'Is that a threat or a promise?' Paula gave a shaky smile.

'Just go on holidays and relax. Things won't look as bad when you get back.'

I wish I could believe that, Paula thought ruefully as the twinkling lights of the control tower and airport building came into view.

'You'd better fix your make-up,' Kieran said dryly. 'It's jolly holiday time.'

He pulled in along the hard shoulder and switched on the interior light. Paula took out her make-up and did a quick repair job.

'Even Mzzz Johnson, the Colossus of the Couriers, couldn't find fault with you if she was here,' Kieran assured her as she turned her face to him for his approval.

Paula took a deep breath. 'Drive on, Macduff,' she ordered.

Minutes later, Kieran pulled up outside the set-down area.

'Are you not coming in for a drink?' Paula asked in surprise.

'No. Long goodbyes aren't good for my arthritis,' he said flippantly. He got out of the car, got a trolley and unloaded her case on to it.

'Thanks, Kieran,' she said gratefully.

'Take care, Paula,' he said quietly.

She put her arms around him and he hugged her tightly.

'Go on,' he said. 'The girls are waiting. Tell Jenny to take things easy.'

'I will. Thanks for everything.' She waved until the car was out of sight and went to join the girls.

Brenda felt a pang of envy when she saw Paula swanning up to the check-in desk in a pair of tight-fitting 501s and a white T-shirt that showed off her tan to perfection and clung to every curve. A pink Lacoste sweater that looked as if it had cost a fortune was casually draped over her shoulders. She looked superb. Brenda pulled her stomach muscles in tight. She'd felt quite satisfied with her appearance until she saw Paula.

Brenda was wearing floral leggings and a loose white

cotton jumper. She'd thought she looked casually elegant until she saw Paula. It was a pity Paula was coming on the holiday, she thought crossly. She was a real fly in the ointment. It would have been perfect otherwise.

'Hi, Brenda,' Paula greeted her. 'Where are the others?'

'They've gone to the loo. Rachel has the runs, she's nervous about flying.'

'She'll be fine once she gets a brandy inside her.' Paula manoeuvred her trolley beside Brenda's. Shay and Ronan were standing guard beside Jennifer and Rachel's.

'Hi, Paula. You look terrific,' Ronan greeted her.

Ronan hadn't said that about her and he was her brother-in-law, Brenda thought in annoyance.

'Hiya.' Jennifer and Rachel arrived. 'Are we all set to go?'

'Sure thing.' Paula made a determined effort to get in the holiday mood.

After a few drinks up in the bar it wasn't hard to pretend she was looking forward to the holiday.

Jennifer sat holding Ronan's hand. She wished they were on their way. She felt a bit mean leaving him on his own. Paula sensed what her friend was feeling and suggested casually, 'Maybe we should go, I want to have a browse around the duty-free.'

'Good idea,' Jennifer agreed. Rachel, who had drunk two brandies, was smiling happily and amenable to anything.

Jennifer hugged Ronan at the departure gate. 'I love you,' she whispered.

'I love you too, now relax and enjoy it,' he said firmly. Then he turned and hugged Rachel. 'Have a ball.' He grinned.

'I will.' Rachel gave a little giggle.

'See you, Brenda, enjoy yourself.' Shay kissed Brenda. He was dying to get home to watch the snooker.

'Would the lot of you come on? We're only going for ten days, not ten years!' Paula mocked.

'Husbands are hard to leave,' Brenda said smugly.

Oh piss off, Brenda, you couldn't leave yours fast enough, Paula was sorely tempted to retort. But she restrained herself. They hadn't even got on the plane yet. The last thing everyone needed was a tiff.

The flight was delayed by two hours. Brenda was driving Paula mad. Rachel was pissed after another brandy and Jennifer was wondering if this holiday was such a good idea after all.

'It will all seem better in the morning,' Paula muttered wryly as Brenda moaned and Rachel snored.

'That's my friend Paula, the eternal optimist.' Jennifer smiled as the boarding crew arrived and the passengers began to embark.

Twenty minutes later they were airborne. Jennifer looked at Rachel, who was drowsy-eyed beside her.

'Are you OK?' she asked.

'Jenny, this is the most exciting moment of my life,' Rachel slurred. 'I know this is going to be the holiday of a lifetime.'

'Amen to that,' grinned Paula as Rachel passed out in a stupor. Jennifer giggled at the absurdity of it. Brenda fumed because she was sitting on her own on the edge of the opposite aisle. *She*, and not Paula, should be sitting beside her sister.

The 737 roared along the runway and lifted its bulk into the air and flew south-eastwards towards England and the continent.

'Corfu, here we come,' Paula murmured, giving a wide yawn. 'Wake me up when we get there.'

Chapter Ninety

Rachel stretched, yawned and wondered why her head felt woozy. She lay in bed listening to peculiar chirruping noises and suddenly realized she was in a strange bedroom. Memory returned. She was in Corfu. She had a vague recollection of walking down the steps of a plane and feeling a hot breeze blowing. And then queueing for luggage. After that a journey in a car along winding roads that made her feel queasy. She didn't remember going to bed. She wondered if Jennifer was annoyed with her for getting pissed. It was the third brandy that had done it. She wasn't used to brandy.

Rachel eased herself gingerly out of the bed. To her surprise, she didn't have a headache. She walked over to the French windows, which were shaded by blue shutters, and opened both of them. Her eyes widened at the sight in front of her. Just below her, a large rectangular swimming-pool, set in a terracotta-tiled terrace, glittered in the morning sun. Sun-loungers with thick luxurious cushions lay awaiting them. Great urns of exotic flowering shrubs were dotted around the terrace. A small white balustrade encircled it. Steps led down to an olive grove full of blossoming trees and beyond that was a golden sandy beach that stretched between two headlands dotted with pine and cypress trees. The sea was a sparkling turquoise, the sky the bluest Rachel had ever seen. The colours were vivid and bright, like something out of a Technicolor film. Rachel gazed about her in awe.

This was unbelievable. She turned to survey her room. It was painted all in white with simple, deep blue furniture and fittings. The double bed had a blue headboard

and great fluffy white pillows and a blue and white patterned cover that matched the curtains. The small *en
suite* bathroom was tiled in white and blue. It was a
restful room. Excitement surged through her. What time
was it? Clearly she was the first up, maybe she should
go back to bed for a while. But she was far too excited
to go back to bed. She decided to shower and dress and
then explore her new surroundings.

Fifteen minutes later, Rachel, wearing one of her new
halter-neck tops and pastel pink shorts, slipped out of her
room and walked down a tiled corridor that had doors at
each side. There wasn't a sound from behind any one of
them. The girls were still dead to the world obviously. She
walked down highly polished wooden stairs which led to
a bright tiled foyer. Huge vases of flowers stood on small
blue tables. An archway opened out onto a large lounge
which had several plush sofas arranged around the room.
Big windows opened out to the terrace.

'Good morning.' Rachel turned to find a small dark-
haired middle-aged woman smiling at her.

'Your friend is having breakfast on the terrace, would
you like to join her?'

'Yes, please.' Rachel was delighted one of the girls was
up. She stepped out into the sun and felt immensely
happy. She couldn't wait to start sunbathing.

Jennifer was sitting under a huge fringed sun umbrella
drinking coffee.

'Morning.' Rachel beamed.

'Well I certainly wasn't expecting to see you out and
about so early.' Jennifer smiled at her.

'Sorry about last night,' Rachel said ruefully.

'Don't be.' Jennifer laughed. 'I wouldn't have minded
going to sleep on that flight. It was very turbulent.'

'Was it? I'm just as glad I knew nothing about it.' She
sat down and helped herself to one of the soft white
rolls. Jennifer poured her coffee.

'Try the honey, it's out of this world, and pour some
yoghurt on your muesli, it's delicious,' she advised. Rachel

didn't need to be told twice. They ate a leisurely breakfast and then fetched their books and suntan creams and got down to the serious business of sunbathing.

Jennifer lay on her lounger, gazing at the blue sky. It was very peaceful on the terrace. The lovely scent of flowering jasmine wafted along on the breeze. The shushing of the trees in the olive grove as the leaves rustled in the wind was very soothing. In the distance, the sea lapped lazily against the shore. Jennifer wished Ronan was here to enjoy it. She knew she should be making the most of her unexpected holiday, but she missed him. She'd phoned him first thing that morning. She hadn't slept very well and had woken early. She'd dreamed about the baby again.

Jennifer gave a deep sigh, she was going to have to try and accept what had happened. There was a reason for it. She'd raged at God for taking her baby from her. It was her first real trauma. She'd gone to pieces and it frightened her. For the first time in her life, Jennifer realized that no matter what she thought, God, a higher being, fate, karma, whatever-its-name, controlled her life. If her baby could be taken from her, other awful things could happen. She wished she could erase the sense of dread and betrayal that ached inside her. More than anything, Jennifer wished she didn't feel so scared.

Brenda woke and knew something was different. She couldn't hear children playing or squabbling. Shay wasn't in bed beside her. Brenda gave a long luxurious stretch. What bliss it was to have a double bed all to herself. She turned on her stomach and spread her limbs to the four corners of the bed. Maybe the sun was shining outside, there was a pool to swim in, a Jacuzzi to relax in, a sauna to make her feel like a million dollars, but it all paled into insignificance compared to the luxury of an undisturbed lie-in. Brenda yawned, stretched and was asleep again in seconds.

*　　*　　*

'Nick, Nick,' Paula breathed, and gave a long shuddering sigh. She could almost feel him, so realistic was the fantasy. She sighed deeply. Just hours in Corfu and already she'd broken her firm resolution not to think about Nick.

But how could she not think about him, she thought wildly. When he said yesterday that it wasn't her he was worried about, should they be alone, Paula had been utterly shocked. That meant that he didn't want to be alone with her because he was afraid they'd end up making love. If he'd said that to her the night of the party it would have been her dream come true. But yesterday in the cold, sober light of day when she saw how harassed and troubled Nick was, Paula had gained no satisfaction from his words. Yet, her first waking thoughts had been of Nick and she'd found herself slipping into an erotic sexual fantasy and imagined them making passionate love. Knowing that Nick wanted her added greatly to her pleasure. It was pathetic, Paula thought in disgust. She was behaving like a schoolgirl. She sat up and scowled. Her life was a complete and utter mess. One stupid, selfish moment had ruined it. She couldn't stay in Dublin, no matter what Kieran said. She had ten days to decide what she was going to do with her life. She'd better make up her mind, she thought grimly.

Paula flung back the green and white covers of her bed, strode over to the French doors and opened the shutters. Below her, she could see Jennifer and Rachel stretched out on their loungers. Paula had to smile. They hadn't lost much time. To hell with it, she'd postpone thoughts of her future. Right now she was going to join the girls and catch a few rays.

The sound of the bouzouki floated across the beach. Rachel gazed across at the fairy lights outlining the taverna and felt a tingle of excitement. They'd all decided to dine at the taverna across the beach and the music of Mikis Theodorakis vibrated through the pine-scented night, sending her adrenalin racing. It had been the most glorious day.

They'd lazed around the pool in the morning. After lunch they went down to the beach and swam in the Ionian Sea.

Through the trees, she could see the moon shimmering on the sea. A ferry sailed down along the Albanian coast, its lights twinkling like tiny stars pinpricking the dark. Real stars, so close she felt she could reach up and touch them, sprinkled the sky. Rachel had never seen such beauty.

'It's nice, isn't it?' Paula came and stood beside her on the terrace.

'It's beautiful,' Rachel enthused.

'Come on, you guys, get a move on,' Paula yelled. 'I'm starving.'

Upstairs, Brenda scowled. 'Shut your yap,' she muttered. She stood in front of the mirror and stared at herself. The sundress definitely made her look fat, *and* her shoulders were red. Roaring red, actually. She'd have to put natural yoghurt on before she went to bed, to cool them down. She pulled off the sundress. She'd seen Paula walking along the landing wearing a simple but divinely elegant white silk sundress.

Her tan was golden, unlike Brenda's scorch marks. Brenda had an immediate rethink about her outfit. It had been hard not to compare herself to Paula down by the pool today. The other girl hadn't an ounce of flab on her. Of course she worked out in a gym three times a week, Brenda thought sourly as she stepped into a pair of red Bermudas. Brenda spent half her time trying to hold her stomach in as she lay on the lounger and the other half feeling sorry that she hadn't had the chance to take some sunbeds. She was pasty white and flabby compared to Paula and Jennifer. Even Rachel was starting to get a nice tan and she had quite a good figure for such a frump. Not that she looked much of a frump now in her new clothes and with that sharp new hairstyle. Brenda had reassured herself that Rachel was no Cindy Crawford, and that in the glamour stakes, she'd be bottom of the pile. It hadn't worked out like that. Rachel was looking very with-it and presentable. It was she who was lagging behind compared to the other three.

She looked positively obese in the red Bermudas. Brenda groaned at her reflection in the mirror, her face red from all the dressing and undressing.

'Are you ready, Brenda, Jennifer?' Paula called again.

'Oh shut fucking up, you,' Brenda gritted as she pulled off the Bermudas and hauled on the ever reliable floral leggings and a long white T-shirt. It hid a multitude, she decided. It would have to do.

'I'd better go, Ronan, we're just heading out to dinner. I'll phone you tomorrow.'

'Your phone bill is going to be enormous,' Ronan laughed.

'I don't care. It's lovely to talk to you.' Jennifer smiled.

'Are you enjoying yourself?' Ronan asked anxiously.

'Today was glorious,' Jennifer said truthfully. 'It was very relaxing.'

'Good, now go and enjoy your meal and have fun.'

'I will,' Jennifer assured him. 'I'm looking forward to it. I love you.'

'I love you, too,' Ronan echoed.

'Bye.'

'Bye.'

'You hang up.'

'No, you hang up.'

'We'll hang up together on the count of three,' Ronan instructed.

'OK,' Jennifer agreed. 'One, two—'

'Two and a half.' Ronan laughed.

'Three.' Jennifer chuckled and hung up. She felt much better after talking to Ronan. The thousands of miles separating them didn't seem so many when she could lift up the phone and dial home direct. She glanced at her reflection in the mirror, she was wearing a long flowing aquamarine skirt and a black off-the-shoulder lycra top. She looked fine. In response to Paula's impatient bellow, Jennifer made haste down the stairs.

Brenda was exhilarated, she'd just finished doing a Greek dance and she would have put Zorba himself to shame. The music was very evocative. The sound of the bouzouki sweet and haunting. Her feet itched to dance and Yiannis, the owner of the restaurant, noticed her tapping feet and clapping hands and pulled her to her feet and invited her to join the dancers. Several of the other guests joined in as well, including Rachel. They were having great fun.

'Paula hid a yawn and caught Jennifer's eye.

'I'm whacked,' she murmured. 'I just want to go and sleep my brains out.'

'Me too.' Jennifer grinned. 'It must be the sea air.' They were sitting outdoors under vine-leaved, illuminated wooden beams watching the dancing and listening to the music. A balmy breeze cooled them. The melody of the sea and trees was very soothing. Jennifer felt much more relaxed.

'Brenda looks as if she's ready for an all-night session.' Paula grinned.

'She can if she wants. To each his own.' Jennifer yawned and nearly gave herself lockjaw.

'Come on, you pair, get up and dance,' Brenda urged, waltzing over to their table.

'Yeah, come on,' Rachel appealed. 'It's great fun.'

'Sorry, girls, I've had it. I can't stay awake.' Jennifer stood up to go.

'But it's only gone midnight,' Brenda protested. 'And we've been invited to a party in the apartments across the road.'

'Off you go and have fun, Bren. I'm going to bed,' Jennifer said firmly.

'Me too,' Paula said.

'For God's sake!' Brenda exclaimed. 'You're not serious. We're on holidays.'

'Exactly,' Paula murmured.

'You're acting like two old grannies. Who wants to go to bed early on holiday?'

Paula shot her a cold look. 'You stay up all night if you want to, Brenda, that's fine with us. We want you to enjoy your holiday.' The implication was unmistakable. Brenda's lips tightened at Paula's tone. Sarcastic cow, she fumed. How she'd like to tell her exactly what she thought of her, standing there oozing self-confidence. Looking down her superior nose at Brenda just because she wanted to stay dancing. She supposed such simple pleasures were far too unsophisticated for La Matthews's taste.

'Are you going or staying, Rachel?' Brenda demanded.

Rachel looked from Brenda to Jennifer. 'If it's all right with you, Jenny, I'll stay,' she said hesitantly.

'Of course it's all right with me,' Jennifer declared in amusement. 'For heaven's sake, Rachel, if you want to dance a tango on the table and stay up until daybreak it's up to you. You're on holiday. Do what you want. That's what it's all about. Come on, Paula.' She yawned again. 'Let's leave these energetic young ones to their fun, I'm past it.'

'Party-poopers,' Brenda taunted, after their retreating backs. 'Come on, Rachel, we're going to have fun.'

Chapter Ninety-One

'Does anyone want to come to Ipsos?' Brenda asked. It was the fourth day of their holiday. It was very hot and she couldn't face lying in the sun. She wanted to be out and about.

'No thanks,' Jennifer murmured. She was deeply engrossed in Maeve Binchy's latest novel.

Paula, who was racing through Deirdre Purcell's blockbuster, didn't respond, she was far too interested in finding out how the heroine was going to resolve her complicated love life.

Rachel was reading *The Rose Tree* by Mary Walkin Keane. She didn't feel like getting up, she was far too comfortable on her lounger.

'Come on, Jenny, put that book down. That's all you've done since you came on holidays. Read and sleep,' moaned Brenda. She had got out of the habit of reading and watching the other three with their noses stuck in novels was driving her mad.

'*Brenda!*' Paula lifted her head from her book and glared at the other girl. 'Would you give Jenny a break? She's on her holidays. You haven't stopped annoying her since we arrived.'

Brenda was furious. How dare Paula Matthews talk to her like that?

'Do you mind? I'm talking to my sister. It's none of your business.'

'Bren, I'm not in the humour for shopping now. I will later on,' Jennifer said firmly.

'Such company to come on holidays with,' Brenda scowled.

'You should have thought of that when you decided you were going to come with us,' Paula retorted angrily. She was fed up to the back teeth with Brenda's whingeing and moaning. Jennifer and she had come on holidays to relax and flop and get away from it all. Brenda was raring to go and ready for anything and couldn't understand the attitude of the other pair. If she didn't quit making a fuss and annoying people, Paula was going to blow a fuse.

'I'll come to Ipsos,' Rachel offered, laying aside her book. If someone didn't get Brenda and Paula away from each other they were going to come to blows. They'd been sniping at each other all day. It was Brenda's fault, she had a way of going on and on that was very irritating. It was odd, she only did it when Paula was around, thought Rachel as she slipped her shorts on. Brenda was like a spoilt little child looking for Jennifer's attention. When she was on her own, she was fine, and great company. Rachel went dancing with Brenda until the early hours every morning and it was enormous fun. But it was obvious Paula and Brenda rubbed each other up the wrong way.

'The car keys are on the small table by the front door,' Jennifer said coolly, glaring at Brenda. Trust her to make scenes and start arguments. Paula was going to go for Brenda baldheaded if she didn't stop her carry-on. It was very annoying, especially as Brenda had gatecrashed the holiday.

'Come on, Rachel.' Brenda ignored the other two.

'See you later,' Rachel murmured. This tension wasn't conducive to a relaxing holiday. Maybe when Brenda had done some shopping, she might relax a bit. She was an awful fidget. She couldn't sit down for ten minutes. She always wanted to be up and about.

'That pair are as dull as dishwater,' Brenda said crossly as she drove the small hire car down the curving drive of the villa and turned left towards Ipsos. 'They sit there with their noses stuck in books day in, day out. They go home to bed when the fun's just starting. Career women my hat! They haven't a bit of get-up-and-go in them.'

'Maybe it's because they have to work so hard, that just to laze around is a treat for them,' Rachel said diplomatically as she opened her window to allow a cooling breeze to circulate. The seat of the car was hot beneath her legs.

'I have to work hard,' snorted Brenda. 'I have a job and I have three children to rear. And you know yourself, Rachel, being a teacher, that rearing children is not easy. But I'm damned if I'm going to visit a foreign country and sit on my ass with my nose stuck in a book all the time. It's ridiculous!'

'Yeah, well I understand that too. I like going around sightseeing. I think it's because it's something different for us. We're not used to being abroad. Paula and Jenny take it for granted. They have foreign holidays every year. Paula spends half her life abroad. But it's not like that for you and me. It's a big treat for us.'

'*Exactly,*' Brenda agreed. 'That's why they should take the trouble to make sure we enjoy ourselves.'

I didn't mean that, Rachel thought to herself. She certainly didn't feel it was up to Jenny and Paula to entertain her. But she said nothing. Let Brenda get it out of her system, she thought. There'd be less chance of arguments.

'Let's go to Corfu town,' Brenda announced. 'Imagine. We've been here four days and the only places we've been to are Ipsos and Barbati. There was feck-all in Barbati, and Ipsos was like Bray on a bad day.'

What's wrong with Bray? Rachel wanted to say. Brenda had obviously forgotten that she lived and worked there.

'Maybe you don't want to go,' Brenda said glumly, mistaking the reason for her silence.

'I'd like to see Corfu, the shopping is supposed to be good,' Rachel said brightly. The thing was not to let Brenda get to you. She spoke without thinking half the time.

'Great.' Brenda was delighted. 'It's just as well you're here too, Rachel, or I'd have no company and I'd be bored out of my mind. I don't know how anyone can lie in the sun doing nothing for hours.'

'It's very pleasant, I lie out every chance I get at home,' Rachel said.

'Oh, so do I.' Brenda scorched around a bend and Rachel gripped the edge of her seat nervously.

'Don't forget to stay on the opposite side of the road,' Rachel murmured.

'Mmm.' Brenda swerved to avoid two mopeds. 'Idiots,' she bellowed. 'Look at them. They think they own the road. As I was saying,' she continued, 'I lie out at home, and I enjoy it. But that's my point. You can do that at home anytime. When am I going to get a chance to see Corfu again if I don't do it now?'

'You've a point there,' Rachel agreed. Now that she was on her way she was looking forward to exploring the capital. She admired Brenda for having the nerve to drive in a strange country. On the opposite side of the road and everything. There was no way she'd get behind the wheel of a car here. The local drivers drove like lunatics. But they held no fear for Brenda, who tooted her horn and gesticulated with the best of them. The town was only ten miles from Ipsos. Rachel did her best to take her mind off Brenda's adventurous driving by admiring the scenery and villas that flashed by. There was something Italian about many of the terracotta-coloured homes, but then Corfu was close to the east coast of Italy. The winding roads overlooked lush green valleys and ravines and the deep indigo of the Ionian Sea.

Corfu was a shopper's paradise. The winding cobble-stoned streets housed shops to tempt the meanest miser. The jewellery shops were breathtaking but Rachel loved the pottery shops and she treated herself to a beautiful blue and white platter which, she promised herself, was going to take pride of place in the kitchen of her new home, wherever it happened to be.

Brenda treated herself to a leather bag and bought T-shirts and toys for the children. Later, weary but satisfied, they sat in a cool taverna and treated themselves to coffee and baklava.

'This is the life.' Brenda smiled, licking fingers that were sticky from the honey and nut treat. 'I've really enjoyed this afternoon.'

'Me too,' Rachel said happily. It had been fun and there'd still be time to sit out and catch the dying rays of the sun back at the villa.

'Have another Malibu?' Paula raised a quizzical eyebrow.

'Why not?' Jennifer agreed. She'd just got out of the pool after a cooling swim that had refreshed her enormously. She was going to lie on her lounger and snooze for the rest of the afternoon.

'It's peaceful here, isn't it?' Paula handed her an ice-cold glass of Malibu and pineapple.

'You mean with Brenda gone?' Jennifer said wickedly.

Paula laughed. 'Well that too. We'd better put our dancing shoes on tonight and go out on the town. I've never been called an old granny before. I suppose it's no novelty to us, but it is to her and Rachel.'

'I know.' Jennifer sipped her drink. 'It's just that I've done all that. I'm enjoying myself catching up on my reading. Ronan's like Brenda when he's on holidays. He wants to go out and about and do things. This is a treat for me. I'm a lazy slob at heart. I like flopping,' she confessed.

'Me too,' Paula agreed. 'I've been to Corfu half a dozen times. I just want to tune out.'

'Rachel's enjoying herself.' Jennifer poured some Delial into her palm and began to rub it over her body.

'She's good fun. I like the way she threw caution to the winds after the second day and went topless. And roared laughing when I took the photo of her and threatened to send it to the *News of the World*.' Paula unwrapped a bar of chocolate and took a bite out of it. 'If it wasn't for her, Brenda might very well be lying at the bottom of the swimming-pool.'

'Try and ignore her, she doesn't mean it,' Jennifer said.

Huh! Paula gave a mental snort. Brenda was thoroughly selfish no matter what Jenny said. Jenny was far too soft with Brenda and always had been. Brenda walked all over her. Paula had no intention of letting her get away with it. Kieran had offered Jennifer this holiday to help her recuperate after her accident and get over her miscarriage. Brenda wasn't one bit sensitive to what Jennifer was going through. All she cared about was herself. Paula wouldn't stand for any of her nonsense, that was for sure. Jennifer was going to relax on this holiday. Paula would see to that.

'Would you like a slice of watermelon?' she asked.

'I'll get it, you've been running around after me all day.' Jennifer made to get up.

'Stay where you are,' Paula ordered. 'You can run around after me tomorrow.'

Jennifer lay back against her cushions. Paula was very kind to her. She, more than anyone, seemed to understand what Jennifer had been through. They talked for ages at night about their troubles. It was lovely to have this time to be close again. It was like when they were young and every secret was shared. Marriage and careers had imposed on their friendship a little. It was nice to be able to pick up the threads and weave the tapestry of their friendship tight again.

She felt much better, Jennifer thought with relief. Maybe her hormones had gone awry after her miscarriage. Her fears seemed to have lessened, she didn't feel so emotionally shaky. She'd even begun to think about having another baby. The doctors had told her there was no reason why she shouldn't conceive in the future. She was still desperately sad about Danielle, but it seemed to her that the baby's spirit was near her, comforting her. She had gone for a walk to the village yesterday and slipped into the tiny cool whitewashed church to say a prayer. A beautiful icon of Our Lady and the infant Jesus hung above her head. The peaceful serenity of the little church calmed Jennifer's agitation and she sat alone for half an hour thinking of her baby and of Ronan. She felt at peace when she came out of the church. Last night, she had slept soundly for the first time since the accident.

The trees murmured in the breeze. The sound of the sea lulled her senses. By the time Paula appeared with the watermelon, Jennifer was asleep. Paula smiled in satisfaction. The more rest Jennifer got the better. She needed to sleep. Paula had heard her crying softly into her pillow the first three nights of their holiday. Last night was the first night her friend had slept well. Sleep was nature's healer. She tilted the umbrella so that Jennifer's head was shaded and then went back to her lounger and picked up her novel. She was near the end of it. If she thought her own life was complicated, it was nothing compared to the trials and tribulations of the heroine's. It was much easier to read about someone else's trauma than to have to think about her own, she thought wryly, pushing thoughts of Nick and Kieran to the deepest recesses of her mind. In the tranquillity of a sunny afternoon amidst the olive groves, Paula immersed herself in her book and forgot her troubles.

Brenda and Rachel arrived home several hours later, full of the joys after their shopping trip to Corfu. Brenda studiously ignored Paula, much to her amusement. Silly prat, she thought. If Brenda wanted to be childish that was entirely up to her. It was no skin off Paula's nose. She couldn't care less. Brenda Hanley wasn't going to ruin her holiday.

Chapter Ninety-Two

'I don't believe it.' Brenda was disgusted. She got out of bed and went over to the window and opened the shutters. It was lashing out of the heavens. Great rumbles of thunder rolled across from the Albanian coast. The sky was a dirty grey. She couldn't even make out the horizon. She watched the rain dancing up and down on the terrace as the pool rippled and shimmied beneath the onslaught. It was the sixth day of their holidays. She was in a foul mood.

The last two nights, Paula and Jennifer had come dancing at the taverna on the beach. She wished they'd stayed at home. It was her own fault, of course. Brenda scowled as she got back into bed and buried her head under the pillows. Nothing would satisfy her until she'd persuaded them to party. That turncoat Yiannis, who had been flirting with her, had been smitten by Paula and had danced attendance on her, as had half the male population of Corfu. It was galling. Brenda was so furious she felt like throwing one of the Greek vases that decorated her bedroom right out on to the terrace and smashing it into smithereens.

Brenda had ignored Paula for the last two days, after Paula had the nerve to rebuke her like a six-year-old, but that made no difference to the blonde bombshell. Paula acted as if Brenda didn't exist, and had swiped her Greek admirer from under her nose for good measure. She needn't think Brenda was going to take it lying down. And that Jennifer one was no better, Brenda fumed. You'd think Paula was her sister, not Brenda. They were always laughing and giggling over their private jokes, shutting her out. Half the time they were laughing at her. Brenda was sure of it. She wasn't even going to have Rachel to hang around with today. She'd gone and got off with some Scottish bloke last night and was off sightseeing with him. Rachel had dropped Brenda like a hot potato when her skinny Sir Galahad came along.

Brenda thumped her pillows to make them more comfortable, and tried to go back to sleep, but she was far too annoyed for sleep to come so she lay imagining smart retorts that would bring Miss-Man-Snatcher-Matthews down to size.

Rachel was in a tizzy of excitement. Not even the rain could dampen her spirits. She was going out on a date. She looked at her reflection in the mirror. A smile crossed her face. Her tan had come up wonderfully. It was the deepest most golden tan she'd ever acquired and the best thing of all was, she had no strap marks. Sunbathing topless had given her an all-over, even colour. She'd been a bit shy the first day of her holidays and worn her bikini top. The other three had no such inhibitions and bared their bosoms to the sun. Paula and Jenny were used to topless sunbathing and had all-over tans to prove it. Brenda wouldn't listen to Paula's advice to take it easy on the first day and wear a high factor cream. She'd turned lobster. But Rachel listened. The following day, she stripped off to cheers and was guided by Paula as to what factor cream to use. The results were very satisfying. She looked healthy and vibrant and utterly different from the mousy Miss of two weeks ago.

Her hair was elegantly casual. She wore the smart khaki culottes and a black halter-neck. She had applied her make-up carefully and was all ready for Ken, the Scottish man who'd invited her out with him.

He was at the party she and Brenda had gone to on the first night of their holidays. He was with a group of Scottish lads. His friends were a bit rowdy. There was a lot of drinking, but Ken was quiet. Shy like herself. They'd sat in a corner, chatting, watching Brenda dancing. Ken was a carpenter from Glasgow. It was his first time in Corfu. Rachel confessed that it was her first foreign holiday. She'd been quite relaxed talking to him. He was nicer than the cocky Greek men who asked her to dance and tried to get off with her. The Greeks were too macho for her taste. Brenda was welcome to them.

Brenda's behaviour fascinated Rachel. She openly flirted with the taverna owner, Yiannis, despite the fact that she had a husband and three children at home. It was as if she was trying to pretend that she was young, free and single again. Rachel felt sorry for her. Brenda was obviously a dissatisfied woman. The party ended and Ken smiled and thanked her for her company. Rachel had enjoyed herself and went home quite happy. She didn't expect to see him again but last night he and his friends arrived at Yiannis's taverna. Ken made a beeline for her. They had a great night. The atmosphere was wonderful. Paula and Jenny danced and sang and enjoyed themselves. She and Ken took a walk along the beach. When he asked her if she'd like to spend the next day sightseeing, Rachel eagerly agreed.

She heard the sound of a car coming up the drive. Rachel glanced at her watch. Nine am. Dead on time, she approved. There wasn't a sound from any of the others, so she walked quietly down the landing in her bare feet and stood at the front door waiting for Ken.

'A great day for ducks,' he greeted her in his attractive Scots accent.

Rachel laughed. 'Do you still want to go?'

'Sure! Why not? We might as well.'

'Would you like breakfast or anything?' she asked.

'I thought we might go to this little restaurant that I've discovered on the road to Beniteses. You should taste the coffee. It's the best. And then we could drive down south. The island is only forty miles from north to south and it's only five or six miles wide in some parts. We could see a lot of it, in spite of the rain,' he suggested.

'That would be lovely,' Rachel enthused. 'Much better than hanging around doing nothing all day. What are your friends doing?'

'Nursing massive hangovers.' Ken grinned. 'It's not really my scene.'

'Or mine.' Rachel laughed. 'I had three glasses of brandy the night we flew in and I was out of it. I've no head for alcohol.'

'I must remember that,' teased Ken as he sheltered her under an umbrella and opened the car door for her. Rachel settled herself comfortably, shaking the drops of rain from her hair.

'Would you like to come to Corfu with us, Brenda? We're going shopping,' Paula asked crisply.

'No thanks,' Brenda said huffily. It might suit Paula and Jenny to go shopping today but Madame Paula needn't think that Brenda was going to come running. They'd stuck their noses in their books and left her to her own devices when she'd asked them to go shopping the other day. Well she wasn't going to go tagging around Corfu in the rain after them. They could get lost. She'd entertain herself, thank you very much.

'Fine.' Paula was not the slightest bit put out at her refusal. 'Enjoy your day.'

Brenda ignored her. Paula sat calmly drinking her coffee, gazing out at the rain. When she was finished, she stood up, brought her breakfast dishes out to the kitchen and stacked them in the dishwasher.

Brenda heard her footsteps clattering briskly up the wooden stairs.

'Bitch!' she muttered. Never again would she go on holidays with Paula Matthews. It just wasn't worth the aggravation.

'The sun's splitting the trees in Dublin,' Jennifer announced cheerfully. She'd just been on the phone to Ronan.

'For God's sake!' Brenda exclaimed. 'Don't tell me

you phoned Ronan again. I don't know why you bothered coming on holiday.'

'Well at least I love my husband enough to phone him,' Jennifer retorted, stung by her sister's tone. 'You've only phoned home once. And that was the first morning you were here and you only stayed on for two minutes. You didn't even talk to the kids.'

'We're not all loaded like you, Jenny,' Brenda flared. 'I get a pittance for my job. I can't afford long-distance phone calls. And don't you dare imply that I don't love Shay or the kids. You've a nerve.'

'Don't start, Brenda,' Jennifer warned. She wasn't in the humour for her sister this morning. Last night's sulks had been more than enough to put up with.

'Don't *you* start!' Brenda snapped. 'I came away for a bit of peace and quiet and you expect me to ring home every day and listen to Shay moaning and the kids whingeing. Don't annoy me. Just *don't*!'

'You haven't one bit of appreciation for your husband,' Jennifer retorted. 'You don't know how lucky you are, Brenda Hanley. It makes me sick watching you let that Yiannis yoke maul you around the place. You're a married woman with three children, for God's sake!'

'I know I'm bloody married with three children. It's all right for you to talk. You can come and go as you please. You're not tied down the way I am. So mind your own business,' Brenda raged.

'Tied down! That's a joke! I never saw anyone less tied down. If you were tied down you damn well wouldn't be able to come on holiday. You offload those children on anyone and everyone. You take advantage of people's good nature. You use Mam like a servant. Don't make me laugh!'

'You watch what you're saying, Jennifer Myles,' Brenda exploded. 'How dare you say I offload my kids. Shay's sister is minding them and I'm paying her good money to look after them. She'll give them the best of care.'

'Oh yeah,' Jennifer said scornfully. 'The same Carol

who took care of them the weekend you went away with Shay. The same one you moaned about to me, about the state she left the house in and the amount of cider cans you found in the bin after her. Mam had to go and cook those kids a decent meal that weekend. In fact if it wasn't for Mam those children would never get a proper feed of vegetables and meat and potatoes. All you give them is frozen burgers and chips and beans. You should be ashamed of yourself giving your husband and children that stuff day in, day out, because you're too busy gadding about or too lazy to cook a dinner. Claudia told me she loves coming to my house for her dinner because she gets gravy and meat and mashed potatoes. You'd want to cop on to yourself, Brenda. Grow up and be thankful for what you've got,' Jennifer said furiously.

Brenda was white in the face. 'You fuck off, Jennifer. Don't take it out on me because you lost your baby. I'm sick of you.' She stood up and turned on her heel and almost bumped into Paula, who had come to see what the fuss was about.

'And I'm sick of you too,' she snarled at the astonished Paula.

'Ditto,' drawled Paula.

'Smart ass,' Brenda ranted. 'I'll never go on holiday with you pair again.'

'Well you invited yourself or you wouldn't have been on this one either,' Paula retorted. 'You've done nothing but sulk and act like a child since you came. You should be ashamed of yourself.'

'Don't you dare talk to me like that, you jumped-up little scrubber. Just who do you think you are? Miss-High-and-Mighty-Company-Director-Matthews. You've always been a thorn in my side. I can't stand your guts. You just think you're *IT*. Everybody falls all over you, including Jenny. You say jump, and she says, "How high?" It's sickening. Well some of us aren't taken in by your airs and graces. You'd drop Jenny like a hot brick if you had to. All you care about is yourself and your career. It's no wonder you're not married. Who'd have a ball-breaker like you?' She was nearly crying with rage.

'You are the most pathetic, immature, jealous, selfish creature I've ever come across in my entire life. I feel sorry for you,' Paula said coldly. 'Jennifer, I'll wait in the car for you.'

'Fucking bitch,' Brenda yelled after her. Paula ignored her. That made Brenda even more angry. She had a good mind to run after her and shove her in the pool.

'Go on.' She turned to Jennifer. 'Run after your friend. You always take her side anyway. She might as well be your sister, because you don't treat me like one. I'll never speak to you again after those things you said to me.'

'That suits me fine,' Jennifer snapped. She picked up her bag and followed Paula to the car, leaving Brenda staring after them in fury.

Chapter Ninety-Three

The cheek of them! Brenda glowered as she saw the car speed out of the driveway. The unmitigated cheek!

How dare that Paula Matthews call her pathetic and jealous and selfish? Talk about the pot calling the kettle black! And how low of her to rub it in that she'd invited herself. The nerve of Jenny going on about the way she looked after her children. Her children were perfectly well looked after.

She carried her dishes to the kitchen. Paula had told the housekeeper only to come in every second day. If Brenda had been in charge she'd have had her in every day. What was the point in staying in a luxury villa if you had to put your own dishes in the dishwasher? Obviously Paula Matthews didn't have to do too much housework, if having a housekeeper was no big deal for her.

Brenda felt very sorry for herself. Here she was, stuck in the villa all day with no-one to talk to. She couldn't even lie out in the sun. She decided to go and sit in the Jacuzzi. She switched on the sauna so that it would be nicely heated up for her, and stripped off her clothes and sat luxuriating in the bubbling waters of the Jacuzzi. It took a long time for her to relax. She replayed the row over and over in her mind and the more she thought about it, the more indignant she got.

After a while she rubbed conditioner in her hair and went and sat in the sauna. The oven blast of heat was bearable for about ten minutes before she had to retire to the cold shower. She showered and sauna'd several times and then went up to her bedroom and smoothed moisturizer all over her body. At least her sunburn had subsided. Tomorrow she'd buy a higher factor protection cream. She'd die rather than ask Jenny and Paula for any of theirs. If she was very careful in the next few days, she should get a bit of a colour. That was if the sun ever reappeared.

Brenda walked out to her balcony. At least it had stopped raining, although the sky was still leaden. She could see several people sitting at tables at Yiannis's taverna across the beach. Brenda glanced at her watch. It was twelve-thirty, lunch-time. Maybe she'd stroll across the beach and have a moussaka for lunch with a glass of red wine. To hell with the others. She didn't need them.

'I should have said no at the beginning. I should have put my foot down and told her she couldn't come,' Jennifer fretted.

'There's no point crying over spilt milk now,' Paula said glumly. 'She's here and we've got to put up with her. The ordeal will be over in four days' time.'

'Well it shouldn't be a bloody ordeal,' Jennifer said indignantly. 'We're on our damn holidays. We should be enjoying ourselves.'

Paula gave a wry smile. 'It was hardly your average holiday to begin with. You came to get over the accident and losing the baby. I came to try and decide how to sort out the shambles that's my life. At least Rachel's having fun.'

'Hmmm,' Jennifer agreed. 'I'm glad she missed this morning's episode. Brenda was like an Antichrist. What is *wrong* with that girl?'

'She's always been jealous of you and me, Jenny. And she's never liked me. Today she got it off her chest . . . and how . . . ' Paula flashed a grin at Jennifer. 'What did she call me . . . ? "Miss-High-and-Mighty-Company-Director-Matthews." *And* I'm a jumped-up little scrubber. So put that in your pipe and smoke it.'

'Oh stop it.' Jennifer gave a little giggle. 'You were very restrained in your retaliation, I must say.'

'There's no point in losing your cool in a situation like that. It only makes things worse,' Paula said.

'True. It's a pity I didn't keep my mouth shut. I suppose I did overdo it, saying it would match her better if she fed her kids properly and stopped offloading them on anyone and everyone.' Jennifer sighed.

'The truth always hurts,' Paula retorted dryly.

'It's a holiday we'll never forget,' Jennifer said wryly.

'We'll need a holiday to get over it.' Paula grinned.

'Have you decided what you're going to do?' Jennifer changed the subject.

'I don't know, Jenny. I keep putting off thinking about it. When I'm driving past all these lovely villas, I keep thinking we should expand Holiday Villa. I love my job. It's a pity Kieran's gone and complicated things.'

'He's a lovely bloke,' Jennifer said gently. 'Couldn't you ever see yourself caring for him?'

'I do care for him,' Paula said. 'I worry about him when he's under pressure with the business. He works too hard. I love going out on the bike with him. I love arguing the toss with him. I just don't feel for him what I feel for Nick.'

'Can I say something to you, Paula? And will you remember that I'm saying it as your best friend?' Jennifer glanced over at her.

'Oh dear. It sounds ominous.' Paula made a face.

'I won't say it if you don't want me to.'

Paula took a deep breath. She knew from Jennifer's tone that she wasn't going to like what was about to be said.

'Shoot,' she said crisply.

Jennifer hesitated. 'Let me see, how will I put it . . . ? When you found out Nick was in love with Helen, you were devastated. Up until then, any man you clicked your fingers at fell on his knees in front of you. If Helen hadn't been involved with Nick you would have had an affair with him. You would have been very happy . . . until the next challenge came along.'

763

'I love Nick,' Paula said quietly.

'I know you do, Paula,' Jennifer said sympathetically. 'I don't dispute that. But your love for him has lasted this long because it's denied to you. You're one of the most competitive people I know, and I'm saying that to you as a compliment. I just think, if Nick had fallen at your feet like all the others, it would have run its course and you would have moved on.'

'Are you saying I'm not capable of falling in love with someone for ever? I've been in love with Nick since my teens,' Paula protested.

'I'm just saying it's because you *can't* have Nick that you love him so deeply. That's his attraction for you. But having is not always the same as wanting. If you'd had an affair with him at the start I don't think you'd be with Nick now. There are lots of ways of loving someone. The way you spoke about Kieran is the way many partners feel about each other. It doesn't always have to be as intense as the way you feel for Nick. I just think you should stop focusing all your emotions on Nick. I know you. You're very one-track-minded.'

'Do you think I haven't tried not to think about him?' Paula asked bitterly. 'Do you think I want to be in love with him?'

'Yes, Paula, I do. Otherwise I can't see why you've wasted all those years loving him, when men like Kieran were ready to sweep you off your feet,' Jennifer said quietly.

'I had an affair with Pierre,' Paula retorted.

'I'm not talking about sex, Paula, I'm talking about love. Sometimes I think, because you're so physically attracted to Nick, you confuse desire with love.'

'That's not fair, Jenny.' Paula was hurt.

'Maybe, maybe not, Nick's a very attractive man. If he wasn't, you wouldn't have fallen for him. Just think about what I've said. Because if you take off to London or New York, you'll have to give up your job, your friends, Helen and Nicola, your gorgeous apartment, and all because you can't get your emotional act together. It sounds like quitting to me, and I've never thought of you as a quitter.'

'Oh, let's talk about something else,' Paula said wearily.

'Sure,' Jennifer said brightly. 'Have you any idea what I could bring Brenda home as a peace-offering?'

'How about a garrotte?' Paula suggested with a wry grin. 'You're as soft as anything, Jenny. It's her that should be giving you a peace-offering.'

'I hate the idea of her feeling left out and being jealous of us, but let's face it, Paula, I could never talk to Brenda the way I talk to you.'

'Maybe it's just as well after the lecture I've just endured,' Paula said affectionately. 'Come on, here's a little restaurant, let's pull in and I'll treat you to morning coffee.'

'Isn't that beautiful?' Rachel pointed out a beautifully carved wooden horse. They'd stopped to explore a small craft shop on the side of the road just outside Messonghi. It had stopped raining and the air was fresher and less humid. She was enjoying her day out immensely. They stopped for breakfast at the taverna Ken told her about and he was right about the coffee. It was the best she'd ever tasted. Gradually, as they explored the island, they relaxed in each other's company. Ken told her that he was single and unattached. He had three brothers and one sister and he lived in his own house in Glasgow. He was thirty-five.

Rachel told him about her father and how they were not on good terms, and about how she was going to have to move out of the house she was living in and get a place of her own.

'Why don't you move to Dublin, and get a job there and live near your friends? They're very nice. Last night was great fun. If you lived in Dublin you'd be able to socialize a lot more with them.' He made it sound so easy. Come to think of it, she mused, it *was* that easy.

She didn't have to stay in St Catherine's for the rest of her days. She didn't *want* to stay in St Catherine's for the rest of her days. She had a lot of catching up to do. These past few days she'd had a taste of living it up. She'd never had such fun in her life. She loved being with Jenny and Paula. And poor old Brenda wasn't too bad when she wasn't in one of her humours. They'd enjoyed themselves shopping that afternoon in Corfu.

Why was she so reluctant to leave Bray? She didn't want to be smothered by that boring predictable life any more. After this, she wanted to have adventures and face challenges. It would be lovely to buy a place of her own and decorate it. She'd got some great ideas from the villa. It was uncluttered and so elegantly simple.

She was going to look for a job in Dublin and then she was going to buy her own place. That was all she'd ever wanted. Getting married was not on her list of priorities. She wouldn't deem it a tragedy if she remained single for the rest of her life. She was quite happy with her own company. But she would be miserable if she carried on living as she had until now. There were lots of things to do, a lot of countries to visit, a lot of fun to be had. A home to buy and decorate. She'd bought a platter for her dresser already. She would definitely buy a few more bits and pieces here in Corfu, just to spur her on.

'If I do move to Dublin and get a house there you could come and visit,' she said impulsively.

'I'd like that,' Ken smiled. 'And you could come to Glasgow.'

It was that simple, Rachel thought happily. No big deal at all. 'I'd love to visit Glasgow,' she agreed.

'And they left you all by yourself. Poor, poor Brenda.' Yiannis's soulful eyes shone with sympathy. 'Here, have another glass of red wine.'

Brenda's lip began to quiver at the sympathy and understanding in his voice. She had told Yiannis about the row. Doctoring it, of course, so that she came out in the best light.

'Don't cry,' he said, as he put his arm around her. They were in the villa. Yiannis had walked her home after he'd shut the taverna for siesta. They'd drunk nearly two bottles of wine between them. Brenda rested her head against his shoulder. Yiannis was a big man, six foot two. A much bigger man than Shay. He had melting brown eyes and a gorgeous broad hairy chest. She liked the way he wore his shirt open to display the gold medallions he wore. It was sexy, Brenda decided. *He* was sexy. Much sexier than even Raul had been. Brenda sighed as she remembered her first holiday romance. Raul had been suave. Yiannis was rugged. She'd stopped short of an affair then, and she'd always regretted it. How ironic that she was the married one now. Yiannis swore that he was single although she wasn't sure if she believed him or not. Anyway she didn't care. All she knew was that she felt protected and cherished with this big man's arms around her. Brenda felt very fragile and unloved after the wounding words that had been flung at her that morning. Jennifer would never have the problems she had, she thought self-pityingly as she allowed her tears to flow.

'Don't.' Yiannis kissed her tears away. His lips moved across her wet cheeks and down to her mouth. His arms tightened around her. Brenda felt the pressure of his mouth on hers, the roughness of his skin as his fingers gently caressed the softness of her breasts beneath the flimsy material of her top.

'Let's go to my room, there's a nice big double bed there,' Brenda murmured.

'Yes, yes,' Yiannis said huskily. 'And I will kiss away your tears and bring a smile to your beautiful lips.'

The rain battered against the windows and lightning flashed across the sky. Brenda didn't care. Maybe it was fate that she was here in the villa on her own with Yiannis. She could have had a foreign affair once before but she'd said no. She knew if she didn't have one with

Yiannis she'd always regret it. She loved Shay in her own way. But the thought of years of mediocre marital sex did not send shivers of excitement down her spine. The thought of a few hot wild sexy lusty hours with Yiannis did.

Chapter Ninety-Four

'We shouldn't have stayed out so late. It's after six. It's a long time for Brenda to be on her own,' Jennifer said contritely as they drove back to the villa.

'She'll have had plenty of time to cool off. I bet she's standing there waiting patiently to apologize to the pair of us,' Paula said as she swung the car into the drive.

There was no sign of life, even though the sun had started to shine again. Paula and Jennifer intended going for a swim and a sauna after their long day shopping and sightseeing.

'We'll unpack later. Let's get into the pool while there's still a bit of heat left in the sun,' Paula suggested.

'Fine by me,' Jennifer agreed. They hurried upstairs to change. Brenda was nowhere to be seen. Paula turned left at the top of the stairs to collect her bikini from the Jacuzzi room, Jennifer walked quickly down the landing. As she passed Brenda's room, she heard a giggle and the sound of a man's voice. Jennifer stood rooted to the spot. Brenda had a man in her room. She couldn't believe it. Maybe there was some totally innocent explanation. Should she knock and see if everything was all right? There was another laugh and then silence and a little moan. Jennifer was deeply shocked. She walked to her room and sat on the bed. She couldn't believe that Brenda was having sex with someone. She felt terribly sorry for Shay. He deserved better. He was a good husband and father. He'd always done his best for his wife and family. Why was Brenda so dissatisfied and unhappy? But when, thought Jennifer crossly, had she ever been any other way?

Slowly she undressed and changed into her bikini. It wasn't any of her business, she supposed. Nevertheless, it was distasteful.

'Jenny, have you any plasters? I thought I had some . . . hey . . . what's wrong? You look upset.' Paula stood in the doorway.

Jennifer motioned her to come inside. 'Brenda's got some man in her room. I heard him talking.'

'You're not serious?' Paula looked at her to see if she was joking.

'I'm not walking down that corridor again in case he comes out of the room,' Jennifer whispered.

'Well I'm going for a swim,' Paula whispered back. 'Come on, we can go down the steps of the upstairs balcony.' They had just stepped out onto the wide tiled balcony when a man walked through Brenda's French doors and ran lightly down the steps. He smiled when he saw them and waved a hand in greeting.

'*Kalisperá*,' he said cheerfully and they recognized Yiannis. '*Yássoo*, Brenda,' he called. Brenda waved. She had a sheet wrapped around her. She looked Jennifer straight in the eye.

'Did you have a nice day?' she drawled. 'I bet it wasn't half as nice as mine.' Then she stalked back into her room leaving the pair of them stunned.

She stayed in her room for the rest of the evening. There was no sign of Rachel by eleven so Paula and Jennifer decided to have an early night. As she lay in bed, Jennifer could hear the thrum of the bouzouki from the taverna across the beach. Tonight she found it irritating. She fell into a restless sleep and was wakened by the sound of footsteps walking across the balcony. She heard Brenda's French doors open, heard a murmur of voices and soon after the sounds of passionate lovemaking. She buried her head under her pillows and tried to sleep.

Rachel and Ken walked hand in hand along a moonlit beach. The bad weather had given way to clear starry skies. The warm breeze was laden with the scents of hibiscus and jasmine.

'This was one of the nicest days of my life.' Rachel smiled.

'Mine too.' Ken turned and kissed her.

'I wish you weren't going home tomorrow night,' she murmured. 'We could have had a lot of fun.'

'I know,' Ken said regretfully. 'But that's the way it goes on holidays. Ships that pass in the night kind of thing. But you're going to come and visit me, aren't you?'

'If you come and visit me?' Rachel said.

'I'll do even better than that. When you get your new house, I'll do all your carpentry work for you. Now what better offer could you get than that?' Ken laughed.

'Are you serious?' Rachel looked at him in amazement.

'Sure. Why not? I've never been to Dublin. You could show me around.'

'I'd like to do that,' Rachel smiled.

'I suppose I'd better get you home,' Ken said. The small beach wasn't far from the villa. He put his arms around her and kissed her again. Rachel responded with pleasure. She'd almost forgotten what it was like to have a man's arms around her. The last man who'd kissed her was Harry and that had been a long time ago. Their kisses became more ardent. Ken hesitated and then put his hand on her hip. Rachel didn't stop him. She didn't want to stop him. She wanted to spend the night kissing. She wanted to make love properly. She wanted to take that final step and get it over with. She didn't want to die wondering.

'I've condoms in my bag,' she whispered.

'What?' Ken looked at her in amazement.

'I've some condoms,' she murmured, beginning to feel very embarrassed.

'Have you?' he asked in delight.

'Well it was just when I was coming on holiday . . . You have to be careful these days.'

'I know,' he said smiling.

'I'm not very experienced,' she said hastily in case he thought she was a fast woman or something and expected a spectacular performance.

'Me neither,' Ken said sheepishly. 'But we could practise. There's a rug in the car.'

'Let's get it,' Rachel said. She felt much more relaxed than she'd ever felt with Harry. Tonight she really felt in control.

Ken was very gentle. He was a bit nervous too. Rachel found that endearing. It didn't hurt half as much as she'd been led to believe. She experienced some very pleasant tingling sensations that gave her mild pleasure. She was a bit disappointed that she wasn't overwhelmed with orgasms, and sand had got up her bum, which was very irritating. Making love on a beach might look romantic in films but it had its drawbacks. At least she'd done it with someone she liked and didn't feel threatened by, she thought happily as she cuddled close to Ken. She wouldn't die wondering. And the label virgin no longer applied. The closeness afterwards had been the nicest part of it all.

Dawn was breaking when Rachel slipped quietly through the front door. She and Ken were meeting the following day for lunch in the taverna on the beach. She yawned tiredly. All she wanted to do was fall into bed, but she had to have a bath. There was sand in every orifice. She was towelling herself dry, standing by her window, when she saw a man walk out through Brenda's balcony door. Rachel's eyes nearly popped out of her head when she recognized Yiannis walking down the steps.

Obviously she wasn't the only one having a foreign affair, Rachel thought in surprise. It wasn't any of her business, anyway. She was in no position to judge. Rachel pulled on her nightshirt, closed her wooden shutters so that the room was cocooned in darkness, got into bed and promptly fell asleep.

Chapter Ninety-Five

Paula sat sipping coffee and eating fresh bread rolls and honey. It was a beautiful morning after the miserable weather of the previous day. She was alone. She'd woken around seven and gone out to sit on the balcony in her towelling robe. Only the sound of birdsong broke the silence. She gazed at the barren forbidding Albanian coastline across the narrow stretch of water that separated it from Corfu. It fascinated her. Ferries and cruise liners sailed serenely past on their way to and from the bustling ports of Brindisi and Piraeus.

Paula found it hard to believe she'd been in Corfu for a week. An eventful week at that. She smiled, remembering Brenda's tirade. In three days' time, she would be winging her way home. And what had changed? She'd made no decisions. Was Jenny right? Paula twisted the belt of her gown and frowned. If she'd had an affair with Nick years ago would they have stayed together? Had she grown more in love with him over the years, because he was forbidden fruit? Was it more lust than love? She couldn't deny she yearned for him and always had since her schooldays. But it was much more than that, whatever Jenny said. It had to be. She didn't see Nick as just a challenge. Paula sighed deeply. But it was over. Love, lust or whatever. It had to be. Jenny was right about one thing. She'd wasted a hell of a lot of years coveting a love that would never be hers. It had been selfish of her. Once she'd found out that Nick was involved with Helen, that should have been the end of it. Instead she'd wallowed in her secret misery and fantasized about something she had no right to fantasize about. She

773

had totally indulged herself, nurturing secret hopes and desires. Jenny's words rang in her ears. It was a bitter pill to swallow. Thinking about Helen and the way she'd deceived her and undermined her relationship with Nick made her feel horribly guilty. No wonder Helen had been so eager to accept her explanation of the events of that night. To have thought that Nick betrayed her would have been bad enough. To have thought that he'd betrayed her with Paula would have been utterly unbearable.

Paula had a sudden urge to phone Helen and talk to her and tell her that she missed her. After breakfast, first thing, she'd call her aunt and tell her she was thinking of her.

A few hours later, she dialled the number and hoped that Nicola would answer. She missed her goddaughter.

'Hello,' an unexpected voice answered the phone. Paula was so surprised to hear Nick's voice she remained speechless for a moment. For a brief second she was tempted to hang up, but that would be a cowardly act and Paula was no coward.

'Hello, Nick,' she said quietly. 'I wasn't expecting you to be at home.'

'Helen's gone to the dentist, she has an abscess, and Nicola's got a bit of a cold on her, so we didn't send her to playschool,' he explained.

'Oh . . . I'll catch her later then.'

'Was it anything important?' The line was so good, it was as if he was in the next room to her.

Paula sighed. 'No . . . no, I only wanted to say hello. I'll see you, Nick.'

'Paula, we should talk,' Nick said quietly.

'What is there to say, except I'm sorry?' Paula said.

'Look, the most important person we have to think about is Helen, would you agree,' Nick asked gently.

'Oh yes.' Paula agreed with him whole-heartedly.

'She's very unsettled these days. She needs lots of reassurance from me. Do you think we could try and act as if nothing happened between us? I want her to think everything is normal.'

'That's the best idea.' Paula tried to keep her voice steady. 'That was why I brought Kieran when I came to say goodbye.'

'I didn't behave very well that day, Paula. I apologize,' Nick said firmly.

'Well that's settled then.' Paula's tone was crisp.

'Paula . . . I just want to say something and then we'll never speak about it again.'

'All right,' she said quietly. Her stomach was in knots. She heard him take a deep breath. This was probably where he was going to tell her that she was the lowest most unprincipled woman he'd ever met.

'If I hadn't been involved with Helen . . . It could have been wonderful for us. You're very special. I just wanted you to know that. But it's something I can't and won't dwell on any more. If I do, it will only lead to a life of unhappiness for me and Helen. I think it's the same for you. We've got to go forward.'

'I know,' Paula said softly. 'Goodbye, Nick.'

'Goodbye, Paula,' he said and then the phone went dead.

It was as if they had both said goodbye to the past just then, Paula mused. His words had given her great joy. He had acknowledged her love. And he'd forgiven her. The dreadful feeling of heaviness and sadness that she'd experienced since the night of the party lifted. She felt strangely free. Tears prickled her eyes.

No! Paula thought firmly. No more tears. It was over. All of it. She had to get on with life. She walked into the bathroom and slipped into a swimsuit then went and stood at the pool and arched her arms. She broke the water with scarcely a ripple and began to swim. They had three days' holiday and then she was going to get her act in gear. She had a new project in mind. It would take a lot of work but it would be just what she needed. Paula sliced through the water with vigour. Her mind was racing. Later she would get pen and paper and work on an outline of her new plan. After fifteen lengths she felt ravenous so she climbed out of the pool, dried off, and settled down to coffee and another roll and honey with Jennifer, who had arrived downstairs for her breakfast.

Jennifer squinted in the sun as she cast a glance up at Brenda's and Rachel's bedrooms. It was almost eleven, and there was no sign of either of them.

'Did you hear Rachel coming in?' she asked Paula, who was lying on her front reading *Vanity Fair*.

'Nope.'

'I'm going to say something to Brenda about bringing that fella in to the villa. It's a bit much.' Jennifer scowled.

Paula sat up and pushed her Ray-Bans up on her head. 'Leave her be, Jenny. It's not as if he's around the rest of the place. He uses the balcony steps. He's not pushing it. We don't want another full-scale row.'

'I just think it's awful. She's got three children and Shay at home,' Jenny burst out. She was very troubled by Brenda's affair.

'Jenny, Brenda's got to lead her own life without any interference from you. If she's not worried about it, you're daft to be sitting there getting into a state.'

'What if she gets pregnant? What about AIDS?'

'I don't think she's that stupid,' Paula said firmly. 'Now for heaven's sake will you relax, Jenny, we're going home on Saturday.'

'I know,' Jennifer said. 'Sorry. You're right.' She lay back against her lounger and picked up her book. It was ridiculous of her to be worrying about Brenda, when her sister obviously wasn't the slightest bit concerned about herself or her marriage.

Brenda stood at her window looking out at Jennifer and Paula chatting and relaxing. No doubt they'd had a few words to say about her. Let them. They didn't have to live her life, she thought bitterly. On Saturday she'd fly home to kids, a husband, a part-time job with not much likelihood of ever having a luxury holiday like this again. For the last week she'd felt like a rich film star. As she lounged beside the pool, she'd pretended all this was hers. On Saturday she'd turn into Cinderella again. It was that thought that had tipped her over the edge into Yiannis's arms. She didn't feel particularly guilty.

If she'd slept with someone like Tom, her next-door neighbour, or Kenny, Kathy's husband, she would feel guilty. But Yiannis was part of this fantasy of the last week. She'd been able to pretend that she was someone different from boring old Brenda Hanley. She was some-one exotic and glamorous, someone like Paula.

No doubt the blonde bombshell was looking down her pert little nose at Brenda's affair. It was all right for the likes of Paula, who could travel the world and had a big car and a posh apartment and whatever man she clicked her fingers at. She wouldn't know what it was like to be trapped in a rut so deep you couldn't dig yourself out of it.

Brenda gave a deep sigh. There was no point in skulking in her room and missing a glorious day, especially when she had only three days left of her holiday. She had a quick shower, put on her bikini, wrapped her sarong around her and, with head held high, stepped out onto the balcony.

Jennifer watched her sister come down the steps and mar-velled at her nonchalance. Brenda just couldn't give a shit. She'd ruined Jennifer's holiday with her carry-on. She had a nerve bringing a stranger into the villa and spending the night with him. She was Jennifer's guest in the place. She should have behaved with some propriety.

Brenda sauntered over to the side of the pool.

'Morning,' she said airily. 'Where's Rachel? How did her date go?'

'She's not up yet,' Jennifer said curtly. Resentment surged. 'And I'd appreciate it if you and that Greek wouldn't make so much noise at night.'

777

'Did we keep you awake?' Brenda drawled.

Jennifer was furious. 'Yes you bloody well did,' she snapped.

'Dear, oh dear,' Brenda said sarcastically.

Paula rolled onto her back and sat up. Her eyes were like flints. 'Cut it out, Brenda,' she said coldly.

'You mind your own business.'

'It is my business, Brenda. I'm the one whose name is on the contract for this villa. So who comes and goes is my responsibility. And to be frank I think we'd all prefer if you went to Yiannis's place in future for your . . . trysts.'

'I suppose there'd be no problem if you wanted to bring someone back. It's just because it's me,' Brenda said angrily.

'I don't have affairs on holidays,' Paula said mildly as she lay back against her cushions and pulled her sunglasses down from the top of her head.

'Oh listen to the born-again virgin,' Brenda sneered, not believing a word of it.

'I don't know if you've ever heard of AIDS, Brenda, but I find the whole idea of it very scary if you don't,' Paula retorted.

'Aren't you even afraid you'll get pregnant?' Jennifer couldn't contain herself.

Brenda got up from the side of the pool, where she'd been dangling her feet. She stood looking down at her sister with the strangest expression on her face.

'Well aren't you?'

'Oh for God's sake, Jenny! I *am* pregnant. And I hate it. I feel so trapped and afraid. And I know you want to be pregnant and you'll probably hate me even more than you do now, but I can't pretend to be happy about it. Just when I'd got some bit of a life for myself. Now I'm back to square one. It's not fair. You want a baby. I don't want this one. But what difference does it make what we want? We just have to put up with it, don't we?' Brenda burst into tears and ran back up towards her room leaving Jennifer and Paula staring after her in dismay.

Chapter Ninety-Six

'Why, Paula? *Why?*' Jennifer paced up and down the terrace. 'I would give an arm and a leg to be still pregnant with my baby. Why couldn't I have been left with my baby? Why can't poor Brenda get on with her life?'

'I don't know.' Paula shook her head. 'I'm sorry now I let fly at Brenda. No wonder she was so moody.'

'You didn't say half the things I said to her,' Jennifer said glumly.

'Well she deserved some of them even if your timing wasn't exactly the best,' Paula said gently.

'I'd better go up to her,' Jennifer said.

Brenda was lying on her bed sobbing her eyes out. Jennifer went over and sat beside her and rubbed her back lightly. She pitied her sister from the bottom of her heart. Jennifer knew how delighted Brenda had been to get her part-time job and to have the children settled in school. She'd have to give up work now. It would be almost another five years before she'd have any sort of freedom again. It was a long time.

'I'm sorry, Jenny. I know it must be very painful for you,' Brenda wept.

'It's all right,' Jennifer soothed. 'I understand what you're going through. It must be an awful shock for you. Are you sure you're pregnant? Have you had it confirmed?'

'I know, Jenny,' Brenda hiccuped. 'I always know even before I go to the doctor. I get dizzy almost straight away. And boy, have I been dizzy!'

'Why didn't you tell us?' Jennifer asked. 'At least we'd

have known why you were . . . at least we'd have known,' she finished lamely.

'How could I tell you and you after losing your baby? I couldn't do that to you. I didn't even mean to blurt it out now.' Brenda rubbed her eyes.

'I'm glad I know,' Jennifer said firmly. 'You're my sister. I want to help. You should tell me when you're miserable.'

'That's pretty much always.' Brenda sniffed.

'It's not that bad, is it?' Jennifer said. 'Aren't you at all happy?'

Brenda sighed. 'I suppose I am. I love my kids and Shay, whatever you might think,' she added defensively. 'It's just my life seems so mundane and boring. When I look at you and Paula, especially Paula, I feel dull and uninteresting.'

'But you always wanted to get married.'

'I know. I thought it was the ultimate goal. I thought to be left on the shelf was the greatest disaster that could happen a girl. And I look at Paula and Rachel, even, and wonder how I could have been so stupid.'

'But you didn't like working. You hated Bugs Bunny.'

'I know,' Brenda agreed.

'Brenda, you've got to stop looking at other people and comparing your life to theirs . . . It doesn't work like that. You'll never be happy,' Jennifer insisted. 'You look at Paula and think she has a wonderful life. On the surface it looks like that but, believe me, Paula has suffered a great deal, especially recently, over something very personal. Her emotional life is a shambles.'

'Is it?' Brenda was astonished.

'Yes, Bren, it is. Everyone has their own private problems. Don't ever envy anyone. You don't know what they've suffered. None of the three of us knew you were in bits, did we?' Jennifer arched an eyebrow. 'You put on a brave front just as Paula does, and I do, and Rachel does. So don't compare. It only makes you dissatisfied.'

'I suppose Paula thinks I'm an out-and-out bitch,' Brenda said sheepishly.

'No, she doesn't. She's feeling very sorry for you at the moment,' Jennifer said reassuringly.

'I suppose I'd better go down and apologize.'

'We all said things in the heat of the moment. ' Jennifer grinned. 'A jumped-up little scrubber and a born-again virgin were two of your better ones, I have to say.'

Brenda laughed in spite of herself. 'Mam told me I had a sharp tongue, and she was right,' she said ruefully. 'Will Paula talk to me again, do you think?'

'Of course she will. Come on,' she urged. 'We've only three days left. Let's enjoy them, have a bit of a laugh.' They walked down the stairs together.

Paula stood up when she saw them coming. 'I'm sorry, Brenda. I didn't realize you were under pressure,' she said immediately.

'I'm sorry too,' Brenda said. Her lip trembled and her voice was wobbly.

'Aw, come on.' Paula gave her a hug. 'Let's forget it all and make the most of our last few days. Come on, lie down on the lounger and put on some high factor cream. I'll bring you out a nice cold drink and a slice of watermelon. Tonight the four of us will go and have a girls' night out in Corfu. What do you say to that?'

'It sounds great.' Brenda gave a shaky grin.

'What sounds great?' Rachel appeared, looking bright-eyed and bubbly.

'We'll tell you when you've told us all about your date,' Paula teased.

Rachel blushed.

'Did you see that?' Jennifer grinned. 'Bring us all a drink, Paula, and we'll sit down and hear all about it.'

Five minutes later Paula appeared with four frosted glasses on a tray and a packet of Club Milks.

'I just put a little drop of Malibu in yours,' she said to

781

Brenda. 'Now Madame,' she handed Rachel her glass, 'begin from the beginning.'

'I have to meet him for lunch at one-thirty,' Rachel protested. 'I'd better go and get ready.'

'You'll be ready,' Paula said.

'He's coming to visit me in Dublin if I get a place of my own. He told me he'd do all my carpentry work.' Rachel smiled.

'*When* you get a place in Dublin,' Jennifer interjected.

'I've been thinking about that.' Paula eyed Rachel as she sipped her drink. 'I'm going to be doing a lot of travelling soon. Because, although he doesn't know it yet, Kieran Donnelly is going to expand Holiday Villa to the Caribbean and the West Indies. I'll be telling him so when I get back.' She smiled at Jennifer, who gave her the thumbs-up sign. 'The thing is, my apartment will be empty for a lot of the time. So why don't you use it as a base when you get a job in Dublin, until you've found a place of your own? It will give you time to look around. You won't be under pressure to buy the first place you see,' she suggested.

Rachel stared at her. 'I don't know what to say.' She was flabbergasted.

'Say yes,' Paula said briskly.

'Yes! Yes! *Yes!*' Rachel was ecstatic. She knew beyond any doubt, now, that she was going to leave Bray and find a job in Dublin. How could she not after an offer like that?

Paula turned to Brenda. 'You worked on computers, didn't you, Brenda?' she said casually.

'Yeah.' Brenda nodded.

'Well it's just a thought,' she said airily. 'Kieran's getting a crèche organized at work and if Holiday Villa expands to the Caribbean and the West Indies, I'm going to need more staff. I could take on part-timers and job-sharers and see how it works out. If you could bear to put up with me as a boss, we might be able to work something out. You'd get travel perks too.'

Brenda was speechless.

'I wouldn't be in the office most of the time. It's very much a team thing in TransCon, isn't it, Jenny? We don't go in for bosses much nowadays. Compared to the days of Jolly Johnson.' She grinned at Jennifer.

Jennifer laughed. 'True,' she admitted. 'I end up ordering Kieran about rather than the other way around.' She could have hugged Paula for her kindness.

'But, Paula, after all the things I said to you. How can you turn around and offer me a job? We've never got on.' Brenda couldn't figure it out.

Paula laughed. 'There's a first time for everything, Brenda. Besides, your hormones are awry at the moment. Let's just say I like a challenge.' She glanced at Jennifer. 'Or so your sister tells me. What a challenge it would be for us to get on. And for you to feel you were achieving something. It could all end in tears, of course. We won't know until we try, will we? We can always do a trial period.'

'When do I start?' Brenda asked.

'It's going to take me a good while to get organized, that's if Kieran agrees to this, but I think he will,' Paula said confidently. 'We certainly won't be selling holidays until next year. You can wait until after the baby's born, if you like.'

'I'd like to be in on it from the beginning, if possible. I'd like to be involved.' Brenda sat up straight and stared at Paula. 'I'd like to help you make a go of it. I can work mornings.'

Paula stared back at the woman who had always been so prickly with her and so jealous of her friendship with Jenny. It could end in tears, but somehow she had a feeling it wouldn't. 'I'd like to help you make a go of it,' Brenda had said. That was good enough for her.

'As soon as I can get the go-ahead from Kieran I'll be knocking on your door,' Paula said firmly.

'Right,' Brenda said. 'You're on. Pass me the Club Milks, please.'

'Are you expecting a baby, Brenda?' Rachel asked in surprise.

'Yes, I am.' Brenda nodded.

'Congratulations and the best of luck,' Rachel said warmly.

'Thanks, Rachel,' Brenda said, catching Jennifer's eye.

Jennifer gave her a little smile and a wink. 'If Kieran's organizing this crèche, I'd better get Ronan on the job when I get home. It would be nice to have two little cousins in it together,' she said lightly.

'Good thinking,' Paula approved. 'Rachel, I think your lunch date has arrived.'

Rachel gave a little shriek. 'Look at the state of me, I haven't a bit of lipstick on or anything.'

'You look great,' Jennifer declared.

'Go get him.' Paula grinned.

'Enjoy yourself but don't eat too much. We're having a girls' night out tonight,' Brenda told her.

'I won't. See you later,' Rachel called back as she started to walk across the olive grove to meet Ken.

The rest of the day passed lazily by. The housekeeper gave them a delicious lunch of *Avgato*, a Greek omelette, which she served with a feta cheese salad.

Paula phoned Helen, who was delighted to hear from her, and was anxious to hear how the holiday was going and wanted to know when she would be back. Brenda phoned Yiannis to tell him that she was going out that night, and the rest of the nights, with the girls. She would not be seeing him any more, she told him regretfully. He was not pleased. Brenda wouldn't have minded seeing him again. The sex had been very satisfying. But after the events of the day, she felt it might not be the wisest thing.

They swam and read and chatted lazily by the pool. Rachel arrived home around four bearing a beautiful carved wooden horse. A gift from Ken. She was thrilled with herself and had his name and address and telephone number safely tucked away in her bag.

There was a great air of jollity around the villa that evening, as the four of them prepared for their night out. All the tensions and undercurrents were gone. Enjoyment was the order of the day. Brenda drove, as she'd decided not to drink any more, because of her pregnancy. They shopped for presents. Brenda bought Shay a beautiful leather belt and tie. Jennifer did the same for Ronan. And, after some consideration, Paula did the same for Kieran. He deserved it. Rachel bought more crockery, amid much teasing. Starving after their spending spree, they trooped into a restaurant called Mezadakia, that served the most mouth-watering array of 'mezes' dishes, which left them stuffed to the gills. They lingered over coffee and indulged in a truly satisfying gossip. Then they went to a night club and danced and flirted and had great fun.

When they got home, Jennifer made more coffee and they all sat on the terrace laughing and chatting until the early hours. A day that had started off so disastrously had ended up delightfully. The four of them went to bed feeling much happier than at any time during the past week.

'Why did you do that for Brenda?' Jennifer asked as they got undressed.

'It was a bit impulsive, to be honest.' Paula grinned. 'I don't know if it will work out. It was just that she looked so miserable when she told you she was pregnant. In spite of everything I felt sorry for her. All we can do is give it a try.'

'You always tell me I'm a softie,' scoffed Jennifer. 'Brenda was very taken with the idea, though. She's determined to see it through.'

'It could work very well,' Paula said.

'And you've sorted Rachel out.' Jennifer smiled.

'Look, Jenny, she's got to get out of Bray, it's a disaster for her. She does nothing there. At least if she moves up to Dublin she can socialize with us and have a bit of fun.' Paula got into bed and stretched languorously.

'And are *you* sorted out?' Jennifer asked softly.

'More than I was when I came here.' Paula gave a little smile. 'You were right. I have wasted a lot of time. It's time to move on and stop clinging to a dream.' She turned to look at Jennifer. 'Are you OK?'

Jennifer nodded. 'As long as I've got Ronan I'll always be OK. I can't wait to get home to him. And I want to try for another baby as soon as possible.'

'I think you're right, Jenny. I'm glad you feel like that.' She yawned. 'All in all then, you could say the holiday's been a success all round despite a very shaky start.'

'I think you're absolutely right, Paula.' Jennifer switched out the light and smiled in the dark. 'In spite of rows, affairs and a rainy day, it hasn't been a bad holiday after all and the great thing is, it's not over yet.'

Epilogue

Rachel gazed down at her tan and wondered if it had faded. The nearer she got to home, the lighter her colour seemed. When she'd been dressing in the villa that evening, she'd looked golden brown in the mirror. They'd all stayed out in the sun for as long as they could before it was time to dress and leave. She sighed happily. It had been a wonderful holiday. Especially the last few days, when everyone seemed in much better form and there was lots of laughter and good humour.

She thought of Ken and a smile came to her lips. It had been a lovely surprise when he'd presented her with the carved wooden horse at lunch. She'd been very touched to think that he'd gone to the trouble of buying it for her. She looked forward very much to his proposed visit. The minute she got home, she was going to try for a job in Dublin. Whether she got one or not, she was going to take up Paula's offer of moving into the apartment. Noreen wanted to sell the house. Well she could sell it. But Rachel wasn't going to hang around while she did it. She'd made up her mind, she was going to commute to school from Dublin. If she didn't feel like driving she could always take the DART. By next week she would be installed in Paula's apartment.

Paula had told her she could move in as soon as she liked. Not that she intended staying there forever, either, Rachel told herself sternly. She would get a place of her own and be independent. And start to have fun. Jennifer had suggested that the four of them should meet once a month and go for a meal or a drink. They all thought it was a terrific idea.

Rachel felt full of energy and anticipation. She couldn't wait to move out of Noreen's. Jennifer, Brenda and Paula had offered to help move her stuff. They were as pleased for her as she was for herself. She felt warmed by their affection. Having friends was a wonderful thing. Brenda had invited her to visit any time and she would. There was something lonely about Brenda, although she seemed very gregarious. Brenda often looked at Paula and Jennifer when they were sharing a joke or chatting together and Rachel knew Brenda felt a bit left out. Paula and Jenny never noticed. It was not deliberate. They just didn't realize it.

Rachel understood. She empathised with Brenda. How often had she felt left out of things? She remembered the loneliness of her schooldays when she'd been the outsider standing on the edge of the precious circle that all were not allowed to join. Still, Brenda was much more cheerful now. The last few days had been very healing. All the horrible tensions had gone. Brenda and Jenny seemed much closer. They'd all decided at dinner last night to go away for a weekend together, sometime before Brenda's baby was born, because they'd had such a nice time these last few days.

Rachel peered out the window of the 737 and saw the south coast of Ireland come into view. There was so much to look forward to and so much to do. She couldn't wait to get started.

Brenda sucked a barley sugar to stop her ears from popping. It wouldn't be long now, she comforted herself. Jennifer, who was sitting beside her, asked her if she was all right.

'I'm fine,' she smiled and gave her sister's hand a little squeeze. Jennifer smiled and squeezed back. Brenda sat back in her seat as the plane steadily descended. It was hard to believe the holiday was finally over. They'd had such fun the last few days. It had all turned out well in the end. She couldn't believe that she was going to work for Paula Matthews . . . and that she was looking forward to it. Paula had been a revelation to her. As long as she'd known her, Brenda had always felt the other girl was a snooty know-it-all. She'd felt jealous of her and Jenny's friendship. The holiday had changed all that, when Brenda broke down and told them she was pregnant. Paula had been extremely kind to her after that. She'd brought Brenda tea and coffee and cold drinks, whatever she wanted, as she lay by the pool, and told her she was to lie back and make the most of it. 'You'll have three kids and Shay looking for attention when you get back, so lie back there and enjoy being waited on.'

They'd all been very good to her, fussing over her. Brenda had revelled in it. She felt much better too after the talk she'd had with Jenny. At least she didn't have to pretend to be ecstatically happy about being pregnant. Jenny understood. They'd gone for a walk on the beach the previous evening, just the two of them. Brenda really enjoyed it. The new closeness was very important to her. It helped lift her spirits. She didn't feel as gloomy at all now, despite the pregnancy. Jennifer told her she'd baby-sit for her once a fortnight so she and Shay could have a night out. Brenda appreciated it. And she wouldn't take advantage, she told herself firmly.

She was a bit nervous about the job. She didn't want to make a show of herself in front of Paula. That was one of the reasons she'd asked to be involved from the very beginning. The more she knew about the whole operation the better. It would be very different from being a minion in Bugs Bunny's boring office. But it would be demanding and exciting. And she'd have much more in common with Jenny and Paula. She might even treat herself to a briefcase, she thought with a smile.

She rooted in her bag for another sweet and saw the big bottle of *White Linen* she'd bought for Kit. It was a peace-offering. She owed her mother an apology. She regretted her nasty remark. She'd bought Shay a bottle of brandy as well as his belt and tie. She'd always have her memories of Yiannis and her exotic little foreign affair, but Shay was a good old stick and she knew in her heart and soul that she was lucky to have such a tolerant husband, even if it was his fault she was pregnant.

Brenda sighed. It would be nice if the baby was a boy. It would be good for John to have a brother. But this child was definitely the last one. Perhaps she'd try and persuade Shay to have the snip. It would take the worry out of sex and make life a lot less complicated.

The plane flew along the Wicklow coast. She could make out Brittas Bay over Rachel's shoulder. Soon she'd be home. And the holiday would be like a dream. But at least she wasn't going home to her rut. She had a new job to look forward to. And a closer and warmer relationship with Jenny. That was the best thing to come out of the holiday, Brenda decided. Being close to her sister meant a lot.

Jennifer was dying to get home. She'd missed Ronan terribly. Even though she had enjoyed the last few days of the holiday enormously, she was glad to be on the plane back to Dublin. She had to admit though, she was in a much more positive frame of mind than when she'd left. Those last few days had been very therapeutic. She'd really relaxed and made the most of it. Physically she felt much more like her old self. Her bruises were practically gone. Her ribs weren't sore any more. Her appetite had come back and that empty scared hollow feeling was gone. She would never stop mourning her baby. No child to come would replace Danielle. How vividly she could conjure up the beautiful little face of the child who had visited her the night of her miscarriage. She knew Ronan felt she'd been hallucinating because of the drugs they'd given her. But Jennifer *knew* her baby had come to her to say goodbye. She would derive comfort from that thought as long as she lived. Jennifer wondered would she get pregnant easily. It would be nice to be pregnant at the same time as Brenda.

She was going to really make an effort with Brenda, Jennifer promised herself. The last few days had been lovely. It had all been very relaxed and Brenda appreciated the attention the rest of them had given her. Just because the holiday was over was no reason why it should end. Brenda was delighted when Jennifer suggested a monthly get-together. It would be nice for the four of them to keep in regular close contact. They'd had some good laughs these past few days, there was no reason they couldn't have the same at home. She knew Brenda was making an effort not to moan and whinge and feel envious. Perhaps this new job with Paula would give her a boost. Maybe she'd feel part of it all now. Jennifer hoped so. She'd been a bit neglectful of their relationship in the past. All it took was a bit of effort. She'd make that effort, she thought firmly as the plane banked and the twin red and white ESB towers came into view.

Jennifer felt a twinge of excitement. They were in Dublin, they were practically home. She couldn't wait to feel Ronan's arms around her. She was dying to snuggle up beside him in bed and tell him every single detail about the holiday. He'd roar laughing when he heard about Brenda and Paula's plans to work together. He'd be delighted to hear about Rachel. He worried about Rachel. After this holiday, he wasn't going to have to worry about his little sister any more. It had been a great idea to bring Rachel on holiday with them. Jennifer had a lot to thank Paula for, she thought fondly, smiling at her friend across the aisle.

'Nearly there, if you can last that long.' Paula grinned. She knew how much Jennifer was looking forward to seeing her husband. Coming home was the best part of a holiday, Jennifer thought happily as the plane passed the Bull Island and made its final turn towards the airport.

She couldn't exactly say she was looking forward to coming home, Paula decided as the plane began its final approach and she heard the landing gear go down with a thud. Certainly she wasn't looking forward to it with the excitement of Jennifer or the anticipation of Rachel. For once, she and Brenda were in the same boat.

Jennifer had asked if she had sorted herself out, and she'd said that she was more sorted out than when she arrived in Corfu. That much was true, Paula reflected, as the fields below came closer. She wanted to develop Holiday Villa. She'd developed it successfully thus far, so leaving TransCon was not an option. She also knew that, hard as it would be, she had to put Nick and all that had happened out of her mind. He was Helen's and there was no point in making herself miserable any more. She would not allow him to occupy any space in her mind. Only on very rare occasions, when she was far away from Ireland, might she allow herself to think about the treasured words he'd said on the phone to her. 'If I hadn't been involved with Helen . . . It could have been wonderful for us. You're very special . . . ' Enough now! Paula ordered herself. Start as you mean to go on.

And what about Kieran? Paula sighed. She was looking forward to thrashing out ideas for her new project. She didn't think he'd have any major objections. She'd made a go of Phase One, as Paula liked to call it. Phase Two was a logical extension, and the way to go. She liked Kieran very much. Could loving ever follow liking? She'd never feel for him what she felt for Nick, but as Jennifer said, there were different ways of loving. She should stop comparing. There was no point in getting in a tizzy over it. She couldn't force it. If it happened, it happened. At least their business relationship was secure. That thought gave Paula comfort. She buckled her seat belt. The holiday had left her very refreshed. It had been a long time since she'd really lazed around the place. She should do it more often. The last few days had been an absolute pleasure. Even Brenda had enjoyed herself. It was the first time Paula had ever seen Brenda really joining in and having fun. It made an enormous difference to the atmosphere.

It had been lovely too, sharing a room with Jenny.

Just like old times in Spain. They'd had some great long talks. Jenny had helped her get through the worst time of her life. No matter what happened in the future, Jenny would always be there to offer sound advice and friendship. In that respect she knew she was an extremely lucky person. The plane touched down with a bump. People clapped and cheered. Paula took a deep breath. It had been a great holiday despite a shaky start. A lot of good had come out of it. But now it was time to get back to reality and get on with things. Paula stood up and gathered her bits and pieces.

'Are you ready?' asked Jenny.

'As ready as I'll ever be,' Paula said briskly. She was first off the plane.

Brenda was first through the arrivals.

'Mammy . . . Mammy,' she heard John call. Her eyes opened wide with pleasure when she saw Shay and the three children standing with a homemade banner that said in big black letters WELCOME HOME MAMMY. A lump came to her throat. Brenda abandoned her trolley and ran to embrace her family. The kids clambered over her trying to hug her. Shay stood with a big grin on his face. 'I missed you,' he said.

'Oh Shay.' She buried her head in his shoulder. 'I'm pregnant, you know,' she blurted out.

'I know,' he said calmly.

'How? I never said anything,' she said in surprise.

'Your moods always change,' he said diplomatically. 'That's why I thought the holiday would do you all the good in the world. You look great,' he smiled at her. 'You've the best tan ever.'

'Mammy, did you get us a present?' Claudia asked, her eyes bright with anticipation.

'I sure did,' Brenda said. 'I've got presents for everyone.' There were cheers and more kisses. Brenda returned Shay's hug affectionately and thought, it's nice to be home.

Rachel followed Brenda and smiled at her reception. Brenda was luckier than she knew. Ronan stood at the barrier beaming. He pretended to shade his eyes from her tan. Rachel laughed and gave him a kiss and a hug that was warmly returned. 'You look great. You should go away more often,' her brother said.

'Don't worry, I intend to,' Rachel assured him happily. 'It was the best holiday of my life.'

Jennifer's trolley was giving her dreadful trouble. It careered around the place with a mind of its own. What was it about her and trolleys? You'd think it was for spite. She struggled to catch up with Brenda and Rachel. She could see Ronan at the barrier. Her heart lifted. She saw him hug Rachel and then he was looking at her, a great big smile wreathing his face.

'Jenny.' He held out his arms wide and she practically fell into them.

'Ronan, Ronan, Ronan,' she said his name over and over as he hugged her so tightly she almost couldn't breathe.

'I missed you,' he said fervently. 'But seeing you look so well makes it all worthwhile.' He held her away from him and looked at her.

'How are you feeling?' he asked gently and they both knew he wasn't referring to her physical wellbeing.

'Much, much better,' she said softly. They kissed, oblivious to all around them.

'Let's go home,' Jennifer murmured when they drew apart. 'So I can really show you how much I missed you.'

Paula's heart skipped a beat. She couldn't believe it. Helen, Nick and Nicola were standing behind the barrier waving at her. She hadn't expected anyone to be at the airport. To see Nick with his arm around Helen, holding his little daughter, was a very bittersweet experience. She remembered another homecoming a long time ago when she'd had such high hopes. Stop it! she ordered herself briskly.

'Hi, Helen.' She hugged her aunt tightly and was warmly hugged in return.

'This is a lovely surprise,' she said.

'It was Nick's idea.' Helen smiled.

Paula turned to Nick. 'It was a nice idea.' She smiled at him. The sight of him made her heart beat faster. Some things never changed.

He put his free arm around her shoulder and gave her a hug. 'Welcome home,' he said, 'Nicola's been dying for you to come home.'

Her goddaughter beamed and planted a sloppy wet kiss on her cheek.

'I'm not grand,' she said dramatically.

'You're not grand?' Paula took her in her arms. Her insides felt shaky. This was totally unexpected. To have an olive branch held out like this was more than she could have hoped for. She felt like crying, more with relief than anything else.

'Why are you not grand?' she asked Nicola, trying to compose herself.

'Leaking nose again.' The little girl sighed and gave an exaggerated sniffle.

'That's terrible, I've got something that might help to take your mind off a leaking nose.' She handed Nicola back to Nick and took a parcel out of her carrier bag. She watched with pleasure as Nicola squealed with delight when she saw the family of Greek dolls in the box.

'Thank you, Paula,' Helen prompted.

'Thank you, Paula,' Nicola echoed.

'Someone else has just arrived to meet you,' Nick remarked. Their eyes met. I love you, she thought sadly.

Nick pointed in the direction of the flower shop. Paula

looked and looked again. Kieran stood with a huge bouquet of flowers waiting for her.

She walked towards him. 'Hi, Kieran. What are you doing here?' Her voice was remarkably steady.

'I couldn't wait,' he said quietly. 'I had to know. Are you going to leave TransCon?'

'Not if you let me start up an operation in the Caribbean and the West Indies,' Paula said coolly.

Kieran gave a holler and lifted her off her feet.

'Put me down, you idiot,' Paula laughed. 'I take it that's a yes.'

'Yes! Yes! Yes! Whatever you want.'

'I'll just get you to repeat that in front of witnesses,' she said.

'Welcome home, Paula, I missed you.' Kieran put her down and kissed her cheek.

'You won't be saying that this time next week,' Paula teased. 'But thanks anyway. It's nice to be back.' She raised her eyes to his. 'I'm really glad you came,' she said and meant it.

'Thanks very much for a lovely holiday.' Brenda hugged Jennifer and then Rachel and then, with a laugh, Paula. They were all standing outside the arrivals hall.

Rachel gave Paula a hug. 'I'll be in touch. Are you sure about me moving in?'

'Get your ass up to Dublin, fast.' Paula laughed. 'And while we're all still here let's make a date for our first reunion. Let's say this day month, in my apartment. We can have a reunion and a Welcome-to-Dublin party for Rachel. And a Good-Luck-in-Your-New-Job bash for Brenda. All in the one night.'

'Good thinking,' Jennifer approved.

'I'm looking forward to it.' Brenda was thrilled.

'And we can have a Thank-You-for-Your-Kindness hooley for Paula,' Rachel added.

'That's arranged then,' Paula said with satisfaction. 'And you know something? The best way to end a holiday is to plan another one. So let's get our thinking caps on and decide where we'll go for our weekend away.'

A chorus of approval greeted this pronouncement and then with a final flurry of hugs and kisses they went their separate ways.

THE END